TWENTIETH CENTURY LIMITED

A NOVEL

BOOK ONE ~ AGE OF HEROES

JAN DAVID BLAIS

highpoint press

FIC
BLA

TWENTIETH CENTURY LIMITED - A NOVEL
BOOK ONE - AGE OF HEROES

Grateful acknowledgement is made for permission to reprint from the following copyrighted works. *A History of Deeds Done Beyond the Sea*, by William, Archbishop of Tyre, copyright © 1955 Columbia University Press, reprinted with permission of the publisher. *The March of Folly*, by Barbara Tuchman, copyright © 1984 by Barbara W. Tuchman, reprinted with permission of the publisher, Ballantine Books, a division of Random House/Bertelsmann. *The Great Pretender*, by Buck Ram, copyright © 1955 by Panther Music Corp., copyright renewed, used by permission.

Publisher's Cataloging-in-Publication
(Provided by Quality Books, Inc.)

Blais, Jan David.
Twentieth century limited : a novel / Jan David Blais.
v. cm.
Includes bibliographical references.
CONTENTS: bk. 1. Age of heroes -- bk. 2. Age of reckoning.
LCCN 2012910144
ISBN-13: 978-1477598375 (bk. 1)
ISBN-10: 1477598375 (bk. 1)

1. United States--History--20th century--Fiction.
2. Political fiction. 3. Suspense fiction. I. Title.

PS3552.L3468T84 2012 813'.54
QBI12-600147

Cover design by Nieshoff Design, Lexington, Massachusetts. Published by Highpoint Press, P.O. 50 Watertown, MA 02471. Produced, printed and bound in the United States of America by CreateSpace.

ALSO BY JAN DAVID BLAIS

Twentieth Century Limited – A Novel. Book Two - Age of Reckoning. Highpoint Press 2012. Available as a trade paperback and in electronic versions.

Flight Path - A Novel. Highpoint Press, 1996. Reissued as a trade paperback and in electronic versions, Highpoint Press 2012.

For Barbara, Annie and Andrew

Author's Note

A number of people were kind enough to comment on the manuscript and provide advice. Andrew Blais, Annie Blais, Ed Dence, Richard Griffin, Dennis Hanlon, Jamileh Jemison, Susan Keane, John Laschenski, Nicole Malo, Willa Marcus, Lindsay Miller, Larry Pettinger, Michael W. Settle, Peter Steiner, and Charles Tuttle. And a special thank you to John S. Corcoran for review and editing above and beyond. Also Mary Sullivan and Chris Walsh for editing and copy editing, Pat Nieshoff of Nieshoff Design for cover and book design, and Nina Johannessen of Blue Iris Webdesign for website design and construction. And Paula Blais Gorgas for her suggestions and enthusiasm throughout. To everyone, named and unnamed, who encouraged me in this enterprise, my heartiest thanks. Needless to say, the author is solely responsible for any errors the book may contain.

In writing *Twentieth Century Limited,* numerous books, articles, online and other resources were helpful. A list can be found in the Works Consulted section at the back of *Twentieth Century Limited Book Two – Age of Reckoning.* Other invaluable resources included Wikipedia, Britannica Online, the New York Times Online Archives, delanceyplace, and search services of Yahoo and Google.

Disclaimer

This is a work of fiction. It is entirely a product of the author's imagination. Except for obvious references to known individuals, existing institutions and companies, and publicly-reported events, any resemblance to actual individuals, institutions, companies, or events is entirely coincidental. Because of the nature of the story – featuring print and television journalists who report the news – of necessity it makes reference to the real people who made that news, and events they were involved in. Where such newsmakers are quoted or paraphrased, the author has attempted to report their quotations or the gist of their remarks accurately. In some instances, interviews of real people by fictional characters are depicted in the story, as well as other interactions. These interviews and interactions and the dialogues they relate are entirely fictitious; the words, quotations, thoughts and impressions related are solely the invention of the author. Even here, however, the author has attempted to ascribe positions and remarks to these real newsmakers consistent with those they were reported as making in other contexts.

Watertown, Massachusetts – June 2012

"Q. Why did God make you?

A. God made me to know Him, to love Him, to serve Him in this world, and to be happy with Him forever in the next."

The Baltimore Catechism

"No experience of the failure of his policy could shake his belief in its essential excellence."

Said of King Philip II of Spain. Quoted in Barbara Tuchman, *The March of Folly.*

"Compliance wins friends; truth, hatred."

Proverbial. Quoted by William, Archbishop of Tyre in "The Problems and Motives of the Historian," from *A History of Deeds Done Beyond the Sea.*

CONTENTS

PROLOGUE

PROLOGUE

SOMESVILLE, MT. DESERT ISLAND, MAINE. SEPTEMBER 2003. The old man replays the tape for what, the tenth time? The twentieth? Bright sky and desert plain, blue and beige, plumes of dense smoke in the distance. Pan left to a reporter holding a microphone. In khaki pants and open shirt, he is hatless in the brutal mid-day sun. As the camera closes in the viewer is drawn to the eyes, dark as the behind.

"To wrap up," he is saying, "another insurgent attack. How many fill-ups did the desert take back today? How many SUVs will run dry? Not long ago George Bush assured us a rejuvenated Iraq would pay for this trillion-dollar adventure of his, but like many of his promises, this one's fading fast and will be forgotten unless we ask the tough questions." The reporter's head and shoulders now fill the screen, a faint smile crossing the familiar face. "Rest assured, ladies and gentlemen, we will continue to ask them. Paul Bernard, ETVN News, reporting from the desert outside Basra, Iraq. So long for now."

The man jabs the remote and the VCR whirs to a stop. He slips in a second cassette and the screen fills. Vehicles at crazy angles, the smoldering carcass of a Humvee, a light truck with a red cross, an SUV, more Humvees, a med-evac helicopter. Uniformed personnel stand around. Two choppers hover above the scene, heavy with dust.

"All but one person in the Humvee were killed," a voice is saying, "airlifted out within minutes of the attack. DOA on arrival at the medical facility in the Green Zone. Paul Bernard was one of them. Unbelievable. I can't find the words. ETVN's Middle East Bureau Chief survived but is in critical condition with burns over eighty percent of his body. They say he has a remote chance of pulling through. An officer riding in the lead vehicle told ABC News the attack came from over that hill," the screen shows a rise behind the road. "Most likely a rocket-propelled grenade commonly used by the insurgents, it made a direct hit on the third Humvee in line. Military personnel spotted a vehicle taking off and gave chase. Choppers were called in but the attackers had too big a lead. At last word, there's been no contact. From the Baghdad Airport Road, Ed Barkley, ABC News."

The man tosses the remote at the sofa. It bounces off and clatters to the floor. Leave it, he says, cursing softly. He shuffles across the darkened room and bumps against the desk at the far wall. He snaps on a lamp. The study is cluttered – books, awards, diplomas, photographs, residue of a life of scholarship. He settles heavily into his chair, shiny, creased leather, impetuous purchase the day of his appointment a half a century ago to the History faculty. The desk is cluttered –

books, folders, work in progress, work abandoned. Looking around the room, his gaze settles on the television, now dark, and he begins to weep. "These next days," he whispers, "must rally, must make it through."

ST. ANN'S CEMETERY, CRANSTON, RHODE ISLAND, TWO DAYS LATER. The storm didn't rate a name, yet how the heavens opened. The second I get out of the car, up comes the wind, people wrestling with their umbrellas and now it's coming down in buckets. Invitation only. TV trucks outside the gate here, police keeping them out. But for the weather, those damned news choppers would be following us around, too. The memorial next month in New York, that'll be big, but you won't find me there.

Climbing a small rise I hear the ropes groan, the canvas flap. Inside the tent, rain drowns out the priest as he commits Paul to the earth whence he came. Dust thou art and so on and so forth – more like mud today. Cronkite is here, Peter Jennings too, Dave Carney who I greeted earlier. Next come the pallbearers – his son Peter, spitting image of his father, old friend Pat, others I don't recognize, maybe from the newspaper or the network. No sign of Hamid, or of the French woman either, a class act, that one. My eyes are full as they take hold of the tape. Hand over hand, down it goes. Now the daughter has the shovel and the wife comes forward, former wife that is. Have as little as possible to do with her. Others go up but not me. Need to know your place – all too rare, these days.

Now the group is breaking up. There's a reception at the sister's but I won't be going. Volvo's letting me know it wants to go north and I couldn't agree more. All of a sudden I feel this tap on my arm – a young man, at least under that stupid hat he looks young.

"Professor Flynn?" he says.

"None other," I reply.

He sticks out his hand. "Jonathan Bernstein."

By now, I am getting soaked trying to put my umbrella back up. He reaches for it. "Here, let me give you a hand."

I pull it back. "The day I can't put my umbrella up they'll be putting *me* in the ground." I am thinking water's gotten in the works, with the wind and all. Finally, he gets it up. The name is familiar but I'm still trying to place him.

"Jonathan Bernstein, *The New Yorker*. We're on for Thursday, your place – right?"

Well he doesn't have to belabor the point, of course I know who he is now. I wonder how he managed to get an invitation. Everyone is leaving so I cut this short.

SOMEHOW I MAKE IT THROUGH TO THURSDAY. With all that's happened, the last thing I need is a visitor, but I did agree to this. First impression, he seems all right, though I do not feature that little recorder he carries around. Never liked the damn things. Way I see it, if you can't write fast enough to get something down it isn't worth getting down, plus they sap the memory. It is mid-afternoon by the time we settle down and a bit cool on the deck, but he says he wants to start out here. Joseph, my able helper, has cleared the remains from a late lunch. "Ready to begin?" I say.

He is sitting back in the chair, looking pensive. "Everything's changed. I'm not sure how I deal with it."

"What do you mean?"

He shakes his head. "I was counting on interviewing Paul, but now..."

My face suddenly feels hot. "Don't tell me your problems! Paul did you a favor. You've got a better story than you did a week ago."

He looks kind of sheepish. "I didn't mean it that way. It's just, the job I have to do just got a lot harder."

I can't believe I'm hearing this. "Young man, that is the least of my concerns. Deal with it."

He is quiet for a moment. "You're right."

I swallow hard, trying to be civil. "I'm here to help. Ask me questions. Do something."

He opens a notebook, folds it flat and stares at it a moment. "There'll certainly be an investigation. You were in the military, you know about investigations."

"Indeed I do. And count on the Army keeping it close to the vest."

"I can't understand how that could happen, not with all that security. They're saying it was random. Do you believe that?"

"How do I know? All I know is Washington's deluding itself. There is still a war going on over there."

"Obviously somebody dropped the ball," he mutters. "All right, let's begin." He thumbs the recorder on. "When did you and Paul first meet?"

"That's better," I say, "more sequential. Sixty-three. He took a room for a year. He was starting a program in Political Science."

"Your field is History."

"You've got that right."

"Describe the scene for me."

"We kept a very sociable house, Akiko and I, somebody always coming or going, and those discussions! Many an evening we talked right through the night, no two opinions the same, and Paul always right in the middle of things. Passionate young people caught up in great events. Amazing combination. Civil War's my field, mainly the slavery aspect, but I wrote a fair amount about the Sixties too. The war, turmoil on the campuses, people at each other's throats, worst shock to the nation since the Depression. Until now, that is."

"You think we're heading for something like that again?"

"Too soon to say. Even in hindsight Vietnam is tough to read. I've been meaning to ask, if I'm not mistaken you're a New Yorker."

"Is it so obvious?"

"No offense but yes. What I'm getting at, we had plenty of students from New York but Paul was one of the few Rhode Islanders I knew, which made for a special bond, my being from Boston and all. Even after he left we stayed in touch, letters, cards, the occasional visit, and when I moved back East we really caught up."

"Is it true you two were sometimes on the outs?"

"Not at all. Paul and I were friends and friends we remained, despite anything you might have heard. At any event, one day I had this idea of organizing his papers. Someday they'll be worth something, I thought to myself."

"Tell me more about the papers."

"I have some here and there's a batch in New York I've never seen."

Jonathan brightens. "They'll help me fill in the gaps."

"That's the whole idea, plus what I can contribute. I'd advise you to take a fast run through them, get a feel for what's there. I've spent a fair amount of time organizing, indexing even. What shape the New York material's in, I have no idea."

"I'll look through them tonight."

"You'll find it pretty rough in spots, and don't expect perfect accuracy. Some of it Paul set down in a hurry – it's remarkable they're as good as they are. But back to Paul," I say. "Twenty-one he was, a serious young man, steady, reliable to a fault. I used to tell him, lighten up, take up surfing – something! Of course right away everybody noticed the eyes. Dark, almost black. Felt like they were boring right through you, as if he saw things nobody else did. Excellent quality for a journalist, though in those days he had these awful glasses. At first I thought he was Mediterranean stock, the olive complexion, black hair and all. As it turns out, the Bernard line can be traced back to southern France."

Jonathan nods. "The Nice area, possibly Marseilles. That's what I've found."

"And on the mother's side Irish, of course, but don't get me started on them! You seem restless – here, take the wicker. It's more comfortable."

"I'm fine," he says, crossing his legs. "Tell me something about yourself."

"You don't really want to talk about me."

"I need to understand how you two fit together, your influence on him."

"Well, all right – if you insist." I am starting to feel better. "For starters, let me say I surprised a lot of people when I left Berkeley, but it made perfect sense. For me this is where the world started. Not here, precisely – down past Portland and Kennebunkport, all the way to Boston. Southie to be precise." I look out across the water. "Here," I say, handing him my binoculars. "Have a look. That's where the sun comes up, over the shoulder of Cadillac mountain across there."

"Quite a hill," he says, looking through the binoculars.

"Hill! You try climbing that hill! I used to do it every week until my knees gave out. First comes the aura then the sun appears over the ridge. You can't always count on seeing it, what with the fog we have, but it'll be clear tomorrow. Five-thirty should about do it."

"Five-thirty! You're joking."

"Best part of the day, Jon. But if you walk the shore, take a flashlight – those steps can be slick. On a hook inside the back door, can't miss it."

"Actually I prefer Jonathan."

"You don't impress me as a Jonathan, but as you wish. You're doing one of those long articles, I take it, four parts?"

"Three, but we may go to four now."

"What's your deadline?"

"Everything's in flux at the moment, and as you said I've got to work around what happened. That makes you even more crucial. By the way what should I call you?"

"Professor Flynn will do, or Gus – I answer to either. By the way, we need to cut it short tonight – Pedro goes against the Yankees. They'd be your team, I take it."

"Hardly. I grew up in College Point, next to Shea."

"Ah. We have an unhappy history there as well."

"People forget there was a Game Seven. I was there with my father."

"I beg your pardon, some of us remember," I say. "But I often wonder, what would happen if we ever won it all? That delicious frustration, it's kept our brotherhood of misery warm for many winters. Well, enough. Tomorrow we begin. As I believe I mentioned, my memory is a finely tuned instrument, so when you leave here, Jonathan, you'll have Paul Bernard's story, in his words, just as he told it."

PART ONE

FAITH AND WORKS

1. PATRIOTISM: AN END, A BEGINNING

"THERE'S A LOT IN THOSE PAPERS," Jonathan says. "You did quite a job pulling it all together."

"I've only been doing it for fifty years," I say. As I lift the desk blotter several papers sail to the floor, but at least the key's where it belongs. Sliding the drawer open I pull out a folder and extract several papers from it. The first, on heavy bond, is a letter in blue ink, in a regular hand. "Here," I say, passing it over, "take a look."

LATIMER TELEVISION NETWORK
Rockefeller Plaza
New York, NY 10012

August 7, 2000

My Dear Gus,

I'm finally sorting through this pile of junk you've been nagging me for. If things continue as they are with Latimer I may soon have a lot more time for you. I admit my journal-keeping wasn't up to par so I've had to create a narrative to tie things together. If I come anywhere close to the mark you can thank my powers of recall, which for some unaccountable reason have always been exceptional.

You're right, of course, I should have been more systematic. Ironic, a man of words spending so few of them on himself, though at least I was consistent, in abandoning the written word for the wonderful world of television.

Only my regard for you leads me to undertake this effort which will take many months, with no sure outcome other than the pain it will cause me and, may I dare to hope, certain others. At any event, here's the first batch.

As always,

Paul

"Anything else?"

"Here's another one, barely a year later but a world apart."

Everyman TeleVision Network
419 West 13th Street
New York City, NY 10014

September 17, 2001

Gus,

You cannot believe what it's like here. Television can't even come close. This is not about aluminum and plastic and paper, Gus, these were human beings! Alive one minute, vaporized the next.

Grasping for straws, let me say, terrible as it is, could it be something has finally shaken up this tired, selfish old country? Perhaps we'll learn from it and come back strong, but that will all be about leadership, which I fear we sorely lack. We have plenty of leaders but they're all the wrong kind. Giuliani's the same old publicity hound. Any mayor or governor with half an ounce of humanity could do what he's doing or better. Picking up the pieces is the easy part. Putting them back together will be the trick. As for George Bush, what can I say?

Obviously our project is on hold, my part of it, but I've given you enough to get started. I'll pick it up again when I can. Susan is very good, she'll give you a hand. I'm around for now, but for a change my time is limited.

I'm embarrassed to say I haven't felt so exhilarated in years. In the morning I hit the floor running. This is one hell of a story and I am privileged to be able to report it. Yes, I said report – I'm back in the field. I'll be in the studio more than I want, but mostly I'll be out there where I belong. I hope my rusty craft is up to the task. If the American people don't get the story from the likes of us they won't get it at all. Powerful forces would like nothing better. Sad experience tells us that.

God bless you, Gus. Keep me in your prayers.

Paul

Jonathan nods. "Good," he says, giving me back the letters.

I go around to my big table and take a seat behind a stack of papers. "Strong enough for you?" I ask, raising my cup.

"Just the way I like it." He looks out the window. "Where'd all this rain come from?"

"The weatherman really failed me this summer." I hand him a stack of papers, the first of Paul's papers. "All right," I say, "let's get started. Take a look at this – it's from the first journal Paul put together for me."

****

ALL RIGHT, AUGUSTUS, WHERE TO BEGIN? It's appropriate, isn't it, my first memory is of a military scene. I had other fragments, of course, my brother's face, our front yard, but my first full recollection is that scorching Sunday, the cicadas so loud you could practically see their song in the heat rising from the pavement. The year was 1945, I learned later, and I was three going on four. Needless to say others contributed some of this detail to my memory, and I filled in some later, like with the rest of what I'll be giving you.

At the head of my block several streets met to form a broad asphalt square. The turnaround, as we called it, was next to a weedy field with a big rock at one end. When I was older my friends and I played ball and hung around when there was nothing to do which was most of the time. We'd circle the turnaround endlessly on our bikes, but this afternoon, the day of my first real memory, it was crowded with people.

A couple dozen wood folding chairs were set up in the turnaround, under the big tree in front of Omer Arsenault's house. Sawhorses marked POLICE kept cars out. Omer was my best friend. He lived on the third floor of a yellow tenement overlooking the turnaround. As if chairs in the street weren't strange enough, who was sitting in the front row but Mr. and Mrs. D'Andrea, and my other best friend Angelo and his sisters. Angelo lived the next street up and his birthday was the same month as mine, June, but a week earlier. When Angelo spotted me he started making faces until his father saw him and gave him a whack on the ear.

A number of soldiers with musical instruments stood in the street, one with a huge drum hanging from a strap around his neck. Then everybody sat down and they started to play. I was so close, my throat and chest pounded like it was me being played, not the drum. When the music stopped a soldier with shiny metal on his collar got up. He said something in Italian then the name of Angelo's brother Cosmo. The soldier was tall and serious and said how brave Cosmo was. Then he went over to Mrs. D'Andrea and placed the flag in her lap. I had never seen a flag folded. I didn't know they let you do that. She crossed herself, pulled her veil down and placed her hands on the flag. I could tell she'd been crying.

Then some man in a suit came to the microphone. My mother's hand tightened on mine and she gave my father a look. The man stood right at the microphone, so close it looked like he had it in his mouth. PUHH! PUHH! PUHH! His words exploded on me! You could even hear him breathing. He kept looking over at Mr. and Mrs. D'Andrea. The man's face was very sad, he was crying or sweating, maybe both. Councilman Napolitano, my mother told me that's who it was, he went on and on and finally he stepped across to the telephone pole next to Omer's tree. I hadn't noticed the cloth on it before. He yanked a cord and the cloth fell away and you could see a piece of dark wood with gold letters and two little crossed flags, also some flowers.

A few people started clapping but my mother grabbed my hand tighter. Now she was crying too but I figured I'd better not say anything. Then Father Maloney from St. Teresa's came forward. He was wearing a black suit and said some prayers in Latin which I came to know a lot about later, let me tell you, and finished by spraying everybody with holy water from this stick with a ball on the end but I only got a few drops which was too bad, it was so hot. He sat down, then the soldier with the trumpet started playing a slow sad song all by himself. I sneaked a look around, now everybody's crying, but soon it was over and the band marched off down the street, drumming as they went.

We went back to my house and had Sunday afternoon dinner as we always did, my brother Jim, Catherine and me. My parents were quiet, which for my mother was very unusual.

2. THE HOME FRONT

"YOU WERE TELLING ME about yourself – the early years, Berkeley."

The rain has stopped but the deck is still soaked, and with the wind leaves are everywhere. Have to get Joseph to do some picking up. "I'll keep this short," I say. "I was the first, then came nine more. It wasn't for nothing our name was Flynn, if you follow me. Stevie was killed in France, he was Ma's favorite, only nineteen, she took it very hard. Two others and I, we made it through."

"Quite a record. Didn't you feel lost in such a big family?"

"Being the oldest helped." That little machine of his is on the whole time. "Why do you need that thing?" I say.

"The recorder? What's wrong with it?"

"Just another damned gadget. I'm for cultivating the memory – otherwise where is it when you need it? There are even exercises you can do."

"I'll take that into consideration. If I remember, that is."

"Now where was I?" I say. "Oh, yes, in Berkeley I had a mountain, too. Tamalpais, it was called, in Marin across the Bay. Those days I was a night person but being eighty-four now, I celebrate the dawn. Coming back here I see as a completion of the course, maybe a preview of the next act. I have a bet with myself there is a next act. Nobody knows, of course, but every year goes by I am more interested in the question, I'll tell you. For me faith always was the problem, but my desire to believe never wavered, in fact these days it's stronger than ever, as if bit by bit hope moved in and took over the place faith once was, or was supposed to be."

"Tell me more about California."

"We bought the house in forty-nine, a rambling one-story, eucalyptus everywhere, fragrant but a very dirty tree. Looking forward, we were, we had such plans. There was a stand of redwoods, new growth. I've thought about this a lot – wouldn't you know those trees growing up and the students coming through, they turned out to be our family, our only family. Nowadays, all this technology, miracles in biology. Not so, then. Ah well, timing is everything. My friends said I lost it when Akiko passed and they were right. I was damned low, miserable – nobody you'd want to be around."

"I take it Paul was a special person for you."

"For both of us." I have to pause to collect myself. "Well, enough of this."

"Keep going. This is good!"

I put my hand up. "No, though I do appreciate the attention. Closest I'll ever come to a four-part article. After all, what do you say about a teacher? A teacher's glory is of the reflected variety – the doing's more interesting than the telling."

****

I'M NOT TELLING YOU ANYTHING NEW, GUS, but the war was all anybody ever talked about. The doorbell was an instrument of torture. That next ring could be the one telling you a brother, a son, a father wasn't coming back. My Uncle Antoine's oldest son Maurice didn't come home. I knew him from the pictures in the place of honor on the mantle above our fireplace, and from the stories. The photo on the left has Maurice in the cockpit of his RCAF Spitfire during the Battle of Britain. In the other he leans against the wing of his P-38, his cap at a jaunty angle, a big grin on his face. It was in the P-38 he made those screaming low passes over our house before zooming straight up into the sky and away. My mother told me she asked him if that wouldn't that get him in trouble. Maurice just shrugged. "Hell, what more can they do to me?" The next week he left for North Africa to fight the Nazis. Six months later he was dead.

Others from the family were also away in France and Germany and the Pacific, but Maurice was the family hero, the legend. Maurice also had a square named after him, another gold-lettered thank-you on a phone pole, this one near their home off Manton Avenue going toward North Providence. I thought about these things a lot.

Late afternoons I listened for the thud on our front step, pouncing on the smooth roll of the *Evening Bulletin* with its front-page maps and lines and arrows showing the Allies advancing across Europe, daggers aimed at the black heart of the Axis. The Pacific War was more complicated, vast areas with dots for islands, but the outcome would be the same, for bullies and murderers dumb enough to tangle with our country.

The war had theaters but nobody could tell me why they were called that. What did my sister making like she was a Christmas angel have to do with the war? Nor was the war anything like the clippings my mother kept in the folder with the green ribbon in her top drawer that she pulled out when she was feeling sad. She'd show us her original name, Fiona Kelley, under the picture of a pretty woman in some pose with men in suits smoking cigarettes. At such times she'd go on it seemed like hours, reciting from memory some play or other she'd been in before she quit to get married and have us. So, you see, to call the war a theater made no sense at all.

My real love were the comic strips. On darkearly winter afternoons, I would unfurl the *Bulletin* and sprawl over it, digging my elbows into the living room carpet. With Terry and the Pirates I flew the Hump, matching wits with the mysterious Dragon Lady and her band of wily, pinch-faced Orientals. I was Buzz Sawyer's wingman on a carrier in mid-Pacific, our Wildcats tangling with the nimble Jap Zero. After supper, it was scrapbook time. My scrapbook was big to start with, eight strips to a page, and by now it bulged impressively. On close inspection you could see some of the ack-ack pounding Buzz or Terry were dried glue spots, but never mind, I lived for my heroes' exploits against the little yellow people halfway across the world – strange, unfathomable creatures, more ominous even than the German or Italian prisoners you'd see pictures of. After all, that kind of person lived in our own neighborhood, the American kind, of course, not the enemy.

There were five of us. My father and mother, my brother Jim, four years older than me, and Catherine. Two years older, she possessed my mother's fair skin and freckles, a wide mouth and a nose turned up at the end. Her red hair was a copy of my mother's, only longer. My mother spent hours brushing it, this far-off look coming over her. "Caitlin, Caitlin," she'd go on in a sing-song voice, "my little Caitlin," putting it up one way, say in braids, then brushing it out and starting over again. To me this seemed a great waste of time, though Catherine loved it.

Most days after work my father played ball with Jim and me in our backyard. Summer was baseball, pitching and catching after supper on the long, still evenings. In the fall it was dark when he came home but we threw the football around, slipping and sliding on the leaves my mother would always say how about you people raking for a change. My father could really hum a football, he and Jim outdoing each other until somebody'd catch one wrong and jam a finger. He always took something off it for me because my hands were small but Jim would fire it so hard I had to turn sideways so when it slipped through my hands it wouldn't raise a welt on my chest. When Jim was off with his friends, it was just Dad and me. Sometimes he'd return to his shop after dinner so I went looking for Omer or Angelo and we'd end up in the lot near the turnaround where there was more room and not as many windows.

"The shop" is what everybody called my father's work, a big factory building down Manton Avenue beyond St. Teresa's, almost to Olneyville. Julien Bernard, that was his name, he and my Uncle Antoine started the business, making tools and parts they sold to the mills. One New Year's I remember them talking about how good business was during the war but Uncle Antoine's face told me it was Maurice he was really thinking of.

We lived in this nice house and I, *ti-Paul,* had my own room. Most of my friends lived in tenements and shared a room with their brothers, or in the case of one person who I better not mention, a sister. The stairwells smelled of cooking, a stew of stale aromas, mostly cabbage. Some of them had linoleum floors and not just in the kitchen either, but living rooms and bedrooms too. The long hallways were great for sliding on those little rugs they don't tack down. I didn't think about my room and house and yard were better than my friends'. They were, well, different. If they happened to be better, that's just the way things were. No big deal.

I can't remember a time I didn't love books. I remember trailing behind my mother to the library, a squat red-brick building quite far from our house, poring through the children's books while she looked at the kind with no pictures. At night she often read to me. My father didn't read much, not that he couldn't, but he read the *Bulletin* and the French paper, also *Life* that came every Thursday, but he had no patience for anything else. In fact, sometimes he'd find me reading and would snatch the book away. "Paul," he'd say, turning the book over and frowning, "such a waste of time, your nose always in a book. In life there are many useful things and none of them will you find in a book."

The exception was *Le Petit Prince,* which he brought home to even the score with my mother who had given it to me in English. This was the one book he read to me, in French, of course, and as a joke between the two of us he called the hero "*ti-Prince.*" One day he showed me the author's picture in the paper, an aviator who died like Maurice. The round face and snub nose, he looked just like me! Was this my future? When I grew up is that what I would look like?

I owned other books, mostly birthday or Christmas presents, which were a lot better than the handkerchiefs Tante Héloise always gave us. You didn't have to unwrap her long flat gift to know what was it was. At this time my particular favorite was a small book you could read the regular way if you wanted, but with your thumb you could fold the pages back then riffle them forward and watch Commander Don Winslow of the U.S. Navy sink a U-Boat, the explosion and all!

Catherine's Bobbsey Twins and Little Maidas books had small print and she always had them lined up super neat on her shelf. She brought home tests with "excellent" or "100," and gold stars my mother would *ooh* and *ah* at. Not so Jim, who my mother called a project and once in a while had to see the nuns about. Between talking back and getting into fights Jim didn't have much time left for studying. Jacques was his real name and everyone said he was big for his age. He was nearly as tall as my father and weighed a hundred pounds. One time my father bought him a set of weights which he spent a lot of time lifting in our garage. Jim made St. Teresa's baseball and basketball teams the first time he tried out. He also had to repeat fourth grade.

At night I overheard my mother and father arguing about some scrape Jim had gotten himself into. I hope we survive until he's old enough for La Salle, she would say, I can't wait to hand him over to the Brothers. They know how to handle boys even if you don't. When she talked like that my father would get mad but before long he'd break out laughing. He always took Jim's side. When my mother was giving Jim a hard time about this or that, my father would put his arm around him and wink, which drove my mother wild.

"Wait til you're on the football team at La Salle, Jacques!" he'd say. "*Then* they'll see what a Bernard's made of."

My brother just sat there grinning, lapping it up. Then my father would turn to me. "As for you, *ti-Paul,* you're never any trouble, are you?" Again he'd laugh, but it wasn't the same, not the same at all.

Sometimes after one of their arguments my mother would storm out, crying, and head for her mother's the next street over, on the bottom floor of a three-decker, she lived. I'd wait in my room, alert for her step, worried she might never come back. But she always did.

Jim was my father's prize, though his temper was actually more like my mother's when she "got her Irish up," as my father called it. As a girl, Catherine belonged more to my mother. So where did this leave me? My mother said she saw in me the finer qualities, whatever that meant. "You're destined for great things, Paul," she would say, but later I came to see I was her foil to get back at my father's coarse and grimy trade, at his roughhouse Canadian clan who cut and banged and shaped metal for a living, those that weren't still on the farms up north, that is, or working in the mills.

If Jim was hearty and big for his age, I was just the opposite – undersized and, for the most part, compliant and unobtrusive. Even my face was a compromise, an average of my father's swarthy round face and my mother's sharp features, though my slender frame was clearly the Kelley side of the family. Each morning in the mirror I observed those large dark eyes staring back as I fought with my cowlicks, the only unruly part of me. At least I wasn't frail or sickly, though once a year I'd come down with something and be forced to bed, staring out the window through coldsodden eyes. Later, though, when I was in school and this happened, after the fever wore off I enjoyed pleasant days reading and listening to the radio. I was a sociable boy with many friends, but also enjoyed being alone. Winter afternoons, stretched out on the smooth hardwood floor of my bedroom, meant Jack Armstrong, All-American Boy, the Lone Ranger and Tonto, Captain Midnight's secret messages which when they were longest and most crucial, you knew the call for supper was sure to interrupt your decoding. Before bedtime it was the Green Hornet and the Shadow. As darkness fell I listened, entranced and terrified, compacting myself into the space between my bureau and the closet door, hoping somehow to escape the forces of evil.

It was on this floor I heard a solemn voice announce that a great man, FDR, had died, and some time later, heard the crowds cheering the end of the war. What a night *that* was! My parents took me downtown to see the jubilant throngs. Parades welcomed our men back, but wonderful as this was, I was troubled. What would become of Buzz and Terry? The war won, what would they do now? Fortunately, events would overtake my fears, as I awaited my own first great adventure – school.

3. FIRST IMPRESSIONS COUNT

JONATHAN SLIDES OPEN THE DOOR to the deck. It has dried out enough to work outside. "I just got off the phone with my editor," he says. "Peter Jennings has a segment on Paul tomorrow night. Six-thirty."

"I like Jennings but I always watched Paul. Though I switched channels as soon as he was finished."

"Couldn't take all that right-wing talk?"

"What got to me was the arrogance and ignorance – no, not ignorance, distortion. Those people aren't dumb, they know exactly what they're doing."

"'All Points of View, Fairly Presented.'"

"Horseshit."

"Agreed. Let's push ahead."

Later in the day Jonathan is poking around the study, which is fine, I am happy to share my library with him. "That your wife?" He points to a picture on the credenza.

I pick up the picture. Akiko and I on the deck, house in the background. "That was about seventy-five. The campus had pretty well settled down by then."

He moves to a series of pictures hanging nearby. "Your boarders?"

"Every year we took a group shot." I bend forward toward one. "Sixty-four," I point to the legend. "That's Paul in the middle next to Akiko."

"What are those, may I ask?" He points to a shelf full of video cassettes.

I smile. "I recorded all of Paul's big broadcasts. The John Paul II interviews, the Berlin Wall, Colin Powell after the Gulf War. They're all here."

"I know how I'll be spending my evenings." He runs his finger along the spines, neatly hand-lettered with topic and date. "Yeltsin, 10-16-92 – the Yeltsin debate?"

"It didn't start out that way but things got out of hand..."

"...and they end up shouting at each other."

"Then the apologies, the hugs, all on camera. Ever hear what happened after they left Yeltsin's office that night? Not many people know about that."

Jonathan shook his head.

"As Paul told it, it involved a considerable amount of vodka and the worst hangover he ever had. Remind me, I'll tell you later."

Jonathan puts the cassette back. "Paul Bernard was a hero to my generation of journalists. Some say he was a more effective Secretary of State than the real one."

"I don't know about that, but he told me he'd get calls from the White House asking him to carry a message. Or telling him to back off, depending. Everybody respected him, those who didn't hate his guts, that is. Then came the Iraq business – very ugly, that.

"My sense is the harder people beat on him the more he dug his heels in."

"You got that exactly right."

* * * * * * *

GUS, WHY IS IT SOME OF OUR EARLIEST RECOLLECTIONS are the most vivid? Because the child isn't yet burdened with the baggage of reason? Or is it the drama of seeing, hearing, touching for the first time? To this day a singular sound or scent or color can summon those first experiences to mind. Proust had his madeleines, I offer you my first-grade schoolroom.

Sunlight streaming through the patched brown shades, a long hooked pole for raising and lowering. Tree shadows stirring, a movie screen where nothing happens and everything happens. Above the blackboards, maps of the United States, the Holy Land, Ireland, Rome. Saints' pictures, Christ Child on a ledge, his plaster gown falling in folds from a raised arm, faint smile beneath the gold leaf crown. Our teacher's face, ruddy above the shapeless habit which provokes the curious or, some said, filthy minds of her charges. What *is* black and white and red all over? Most amazing, the triple chin forced by her high collar, and that starched white bib. Does she take it off to eat? Does she eat at all? None of us has ever seen this. If not, she wouldn't need to go to the bathroom. For all we know she doesn't!

The long day proceeded into afternoon and her robes were covered with chalk dust from filling the blackboard with incredibly precise handwriting, example to us all, every letter identically inclined, every loop the same, every line parallel. "Piece," "receive," "neighbor," "weigh." The sound of young minds being stretched. Ssstamargramary, for that was her name, peered over the small faces, some attentive, some not, continuous motion, sunflowers in a breeze. This afternoon her face had attained a new hue.

"The rule in this case, what is the rule!" Not a hand. "Someone must know!" She cracked her pointer against the blackboard. "Omer Arsenault!"

Omer and I sat side-by-side in the middle of the room. His face was a triangle, slanting down to a severely pointed chin. His ears were adult-size, cupped forward like handles, which is how some of the older kids treated them during recess. This feature accounted for his nickname, Dumbo, which was unfair, for Omer was plenty smart, though he did often panic. At this moment his face was frozen in the downward position, as if the surface of his desk was the most interesting thing he'd ever seen. The boy behind him whispered but too late. Omer looked up, shaking his head.

"I knew it yesterday, I really did, but I can't remember it."

I shrank in my seat until my eyes were at inkwell level. I wouldn't put my hand up against Omer, not for anything would I do that. I squeezed my eyes shut, but when I opened them Ssstamargramary had me in her sights. "Well, class, luckily there is one person we can always count on. Paul, give us the answer, please."

I stood, swallowing hard. "'I' before 'e'..." I began inaudibly, "except after 'c.'"

"Louder! Everyone wants to hear you!"

Sure they did. "'I' before 'e' except after 'c'," I mumbled and sat down quickly.

"And... and... on your feet again. The rest, please."

"Andinwordssoundedaylikeneighborandweigh." Score one for the class brain.

"Thank the Lord *somebody* in here pays attention!" Her mocking voice enveloped us. "Class, what would we ever do without Paul?"

I sat down, ears burning. After a minute I snuck a look at Omer. His chin was trembling and a thin, wet trail tracked down his cheek. In front of him, Tony Marino was applauding, a smug grin on his pudgy face. Next row, Tommy Clark was making four-eyes at me. Look who's talking, I thought loudly, don't need eyes to tell when you're around. Not for nothing did we call him Skunkweed.

I was the youngest kid in first grade and the only one with glasses, not counting two girls. The girls had their own separate classroom and teacher. Bad enough I was one of the shortest and, I say reluctantly, smartest boys, but those glasses were a killer. Pink horn-rims, the kind that turn amber after a few months. I was already on my second pair! This first classroom was the crucible for that insatiable desire to please adults which bedeviled my young life. I longed to be ordinary and fit in, but as I learned and absorbed I distanced myself from others, others whose offhand attitude I admired, carefree spirits who might have been my friends but were not.

I could read, and pretty hard stuff too, before I ever set foot in St. Teresa's. This alone was enough to make me a freak or, as Ssstamargramary put it, an "outstanding pupil." Same difference. I also shone in Deportment, was never kept after, never confined to that cool, dank cellar room with the cartons of milk and Coca-Cola stored for lunch. Sadistic grown-ups had conspired to set me apart, designing not a child but an adult in a child suit. It was like they needed a small, compliant version of themselves as pathetic reassurance of who knows what.

A lot of what we learned was interesting. I loved geography. Augusta, Maine on the Kennebec River. Hartford, Connecticut on the Connecticut River. The Grand Canyon. Teak floating down the Irrawaddy. Australia's peculiar animals. But nothing could top a book about the Panama Canal that a well-traveled friend had given my mother. There was one page, actually this one particular picture, where two dark-skinned women look straight at you and the only thing they have on is... grass skirts! This astonishing sight prompted me to approach my father.

"Who are these people? And what are those... things hanging off them?"

"Those are natives, *ti-Paul,*" he stammered. "That's how... how God makes natives." The truth came out later, but Panama fueled my curiosity about what might lie over the horizon. Or under, as the case may be.

Religion occupied much of our time. First time I peeked into the thick, soft-covered catechism book I thought, neat! A question-answer game, page after page. How wrong I was! Every night, twenty sets of questions to memorize. Spelling and arithmetic mattered, but in the most solemn tone Ssstamargramary said this little book was something far, far greater, our guidebook to eternal life. Even the music we studied, most of it, was for Church. Chant, with little square notes.

So all right, why was I put on this earth? Why did God make me? What kind of person does He want me to be? All of a sudden I had answers to questions I had never asked. My world, the only world I knew, to which I was attached with a mostly pleasant bond, was a stepping stone to something else, and a slippery step at that, a place of sorrow and danger for piling up credits for the next life. Disobey the commandments of God or His Church? Better you had never been born! Heaven! Hell! Eternity! More than forever, if you can imagine, which you can't, so don't even try.

I was astonished to learn the dismal legacy of our first parents which somehow led straight to me. It was unsettling to learn about my evil tendencies, worse yet, that they were about to erupt. I had shown some limited talent for getting into trouble, but never had I felt evil or ashamed. Yet there it was in writing and the person of Ssstamargramary. All God's children are connected to each other under Him, but what was supposed to be a beautiful and happy time had turned to ashes. Literally.

> O God I am not worthy, that Thou shouldst come to me.
> But speak the words of comfort, my spirit healed shall be!

Not worthy? That made no sense. Punished for things that happened long before I was born or my parents or my grandparents. But I was reminded of certain indisputable facts. I had the dark hair and eyes of my father, didn't I? A fact. Some unfortunates were deformed or sightless from birth, I was not. A fact, though I'd never met anybody like that. Some people were rich men's sons but I was not. A fact. The Divine Plan touches every one of us, and just because I had nothing to say about it doesn't make it unfair. God is the Creator, I am the creature. Big difference. If God had wanted my opinion, He would have asked. But to my vast relief, I discovered our weak human condition is not the end of the story, not by a long shot.

> I believe in God the Father almighty, Creator of heaven and earth, and in Jesus Christ His only Son, our Lord... crucified, died and was buried... rose from the dead... seated at the right hand of the Father... will come again to judge the living and the dead...

The God of Abraham and Isaac, of Moses and David, the one with long gray hair and flowing robes, He turns out to be the only true God. And astonishingly, He so loved the world He sent His only Son to heal our sin and help us to heaven. God acts, we conform. The try counts but results do too, and there'd better be plenty of those or He'll know you're faking. He knows everything. Even before it happens, He knows.

What a world! How wonderful to be part of it!

TRAINING INTENSIFIED as we prepared for our First Holy Communion. Sister Perpetua, our second grade teacher, looked on as the pastor questioned, prodded, explained. Father Donnelly was tall, with a shock of thick white hair. His voice was low and chalky but Sundays when he wound up you had no trouble hearing him, even in back. He wasn't gloomy like Father Maloney, but sometimes he exploded for no particular reason. My mother said he talked too much about money. Here also began my acquaintance with Latin, the mumbling from the altar I had only a foggy idea about. *Et unam, sanctam, catholicam et apostolicam Ecclesiam...in remissionem peccatorum.*

I finally figured out what it meant to believe. If people you know really well tell you something it must be true, especially if they're all saying the same thing. Your parents, the nuns, the priests, especially the priests. Things written in books can be believed, but you don't know the people who wrote them so better you listen to who you know. This belief thing is complicated, but fortunately there are people whose job it is to steer us straight.

Never was I asked whether I believed. It never entered my mind I might choose not to believe. The nuns and priests expected what they told us to stick, and with me it certainly did. Saints and angels, the Blessed Virgin, bells and candles, I believed in them the same way I believed in the air I breathed. Later, I was surprised to meet normal people who disagreed with what to me was so obvious. Back then I didn't know anybody like that, having heard only vaguely about such people. From my haven I felt sorry for them, whoever they were, missing out on the joy of my wonderful world. No wonder they were lost. I'd have been lost too, without the divine roadmap it was my privilege to inherit. I figured, if God wanted their opinion, He would have asked.

With the big day nearing, arithmetic, geography, all worldly concerns were set aside. How does the Sacrament of Penance remit sin and restore to the soul the friendship of God? What is the Holy Eucharist? Why did Christ institute it? And the question that bothered me most – how can the wafer look so different from what it has become? Father Donnelly had the answer to that one, too – it is a mystery. If we could see God, there'd be no need for faith, would there? If we knew everything God knows, we would ourselves be God, which deserves no comment. I closed my eyes. What is mystery? Does it have color? Is it like the sun that helps you see but if you stare at it you go blind? No, mystery can't be like that because light reveals things. Mystery must be dark. Black.

Once when I was small, I bought a vanilla cone from the truck that drove down our street ringing a bell. It was a hot day and my cone began to leak. I licked so hard the scoop fell off and onto the sidewalk. I put it back on the cone but now there was this little puddle on the sidewalk. Here's what I could never understand. To this very day, through rain, snow and countless feet, there exists a chalky white patch in that very spot on the sidewalk in front of Malloy's house. Was this a mystery? Or is mystery tied up only with religion? I thought of asking Father Donnelly but didn't have the nerve.

With so much at stake I couldn't fail, I wouldn't fail. How much time we spent in church I don't know, but we were there early and late, rising, sitting, kneeling in the cavernous space, dark except for a few lights and candles and the red lamp telling us Jesus was present in the tabernacle. The radiators clanged against the chill, and sweet incense hung in the air. Wooden pews that turn sticky in the heat of summer were cool and smooth, grooved from generations of fingernails, wads of gum under the benches.

The girls whispered and giggled and my friends fooled around, but that ended when our teacher came up the aisle with her weapon, two pieces of hard wood hinged with a rubber band she'd snap to warn of a rap on the ear or across the knuckles. Tall, sandy-haired Father McAdam was in charge. He was the only one of our priests you dared talk to. Younger than the others, he helped with the CYO. It was strange seeing a priest shooting baskets, though he always wore black pants in the gym, I guess that was a rule. When they weren't snapping those knuckle killers, the nuns fussed over Father McAdam, especially the girls' teacher, who was kind of pretty, which I also thought odd.

I was fifth in line as our class lined up in the center aisle. The girl beside me was quite a bit taller, which would have been embarrassing except my attention was on the back of Margaret Foley's head. I was taller than Margaret, which was fortunate, because I was in love with her. When she walked, her banana curls swayed side to side and even from behind I could picture the freckles on her face. I'd never really spoken to her because we didn't see the girls much and you wouldn't be caught dead at recess talking to one. My brother Jim was big enough to get away with talking to girls. My only chance would have been at dismissal when everyone filed out to the march music from the loudspeaker on the side of the school building.

Sometimes I could have walked near or even beside (but not with!) Margaret since she lived up my way. But I didn't. Most days Father Donnelly paced up and down Pope Street in his black windbreaker, hands behind his back, making sure our lines were straight and nobody got run over, but really looking for crimes to write in his notebook. Walking a girl home was serious because it set in motion a whole chain of events, none of them pleasant. No one knew of my crush on Margaret and I wasn't about to ruin my sweet, sad secret by doing anything dumb like talking to her. Anyway, what would I say? Girls were strange, unfathomable creatures (not my sister, that was different) and Margaret Foley the most mysterious of all.

Shuffling toward the altar I watched Margaret return, her eyes fixed prayerfully on the tips of her fingers pointed to heaven, palms together. So perfect, she was. I held my breath... our shoulders nearly touched. She smelled beautiful, like soap. Now it was my turn to kneel on the hard rubber pad. My chin barely reached the rail. For this final rehearsal, Father McAdam was giving out wafers, unconsecrated, of course. The hum grew louder. Omer, then Eugene Sullivan who always whined he was taller so should be behind me. Finished with Eugene, Father McAdam's server jammed the cold, hard, plate against my Adam's apple. *Corpus Domini nostri Jesu Christi...* he traced the sign of the cross with the small white host...*custodiat animam tuam in vitam aeternam.*

Amen, I replied. May the Body of our Lord Jesus Christ preserve your soul unto life everlasting. I opened wide and stuck out my tongue. What a letdown! It was a piece of... cardboard! Oh well, maybe tomorrow it will be different. This was only practice, after all.

At confession I went through my catalogue of sins, then it was five Our Fathers, five Hail Marys, say a good Act of Contrition. The Fourth Commandment came in for special attention, also the time I took Jim's baseball after mine went down the sewer and didn't give it back until he found it in my closet. For all the mean things he did to me, I wasn't sorry at all, which as you know creates a whole new problem on top of the first one.

At home, preparations were well along for the celebration. The kitchen was fragrant with apple and cinnamon. Aunt Moira was sitting at the table drinking coffee. My favorite aunt, always had a nice word and a smile, dark as my mother was fair, and taller. She lived up Chalkstone Avenue past the golf course. Her husband, Uncle Eddie the policeman, told great jokes but people said he drank too much and had an awful temper when he did. One time I rode my bike to their house to deliver something and through the window I saw Aunt Moira crying, sweeping up a mess of broken dishes. I left whatever it was on the step and took off. Uncle Eddie was a sergeant. He used to be a lieutenant but they said he got into some kind of trouble at work.

"How did it go," my mother asked, "your confession."

"I hope you had something interesting to tell," Aunt Moira laughed, tapping her cigarette against the ashtray.

I shrugged. "I don't feel any different."

Aunt Moira nodded, "I never do either."

"You're not supposed to feel different!" My mother wiped her hands on her apron. "What's different is how your soul looks to God."

I opened the fridge for a look but there was a gaping hole where the shelves usually were. Looking around I saw why, a giant ham, thick, round and tapered to a stub, sitting on top of the stove in one of those heavy blue speckled baking pans. The skin was x'd all over with little brown things sticking out of it. "As soon as the pies are done, in it goes." Baking into the evening, then a warm-up for tomorrow's feast. Low and slow where pork is concerned. If my mother said that once, she said it a thousand times.

Grandmother Kelley would be at the party but not Grandfather Kelley who died before I was born. Many cousins, all older, since my parents were last in their families to marry. My father's parents still lived in their little town in Canada but *Mémère* had been sick. They'd send a card, they always did holidays and special events, and there'd be other cards with bills. Ones and twos for sure, if I got lucky a few fives. It would go into my savings account at the Old Stone Bank in Olneyville but I'd keep a little out for essentials. I liked my bank a lot. It looked like a bank, old and stone.

The mail was late but not to worry. Most days, Francis O'Rourke, our mailman, stopped for a "quickie" at the Melody Lounge which was conveniently located in the late morning of his route. Sometimes I was home from school and still no Francis. When he showed, I could smell the quickie as he handed me our magazines and letters. Francis had been delivering mail so long nobody complained except to him. Francis was one of the many Men who plied their trades in our neighborhood. Henry The Milk Man. Pete The Egg Man who doubled as The Chicken Man and at Thanksgiving, The Turkey Man. Arthur The Garage Man. Mario The Garbage Man. The Rag Man clattered by every Tuesday in his horse-drawn wagon, wearing a top hat and a suit coat winter or summer. He was my favorite Man though I didn't know his name because for some reason we never asked him to stop.

After dinner, my father was relaxing in his red leather chair, smoking his pipe and reading the paper. Sprawled on the floor I sorted my picture cards. I had decided by team was better than by name. Williams and Pesky and Doerr would now be together as in real life, Sain and Spahn of the Braves and so on. Some of them had wonderful names, especially Spahn, Warrrren Spaahhhnn. Just like my bank, his name was exactly right. It sounded like he pitched, slow, graceful, with a leg kick that floated up and above his head. "Spahn and Sain and pray for rain," they said all last summer though Cleveland killed them in the Series.

We'd been to a couple of games, my father and I. The first time he picked me up at school and as I got in the waiting car I couldn't help smirking at the other kids slaving away. My mother fixed it with the nuns. They knew her because she did all kinds of work for the school since she didn't have a real job. She even knew Father Donnelly personally, though she didn't like him. Somewhere on Route 1 we pulled off the road and broke out the lunch she had packed. Ham on white bread, the good kind where you can see your fingerprints. For me a thermos of milk, coffee for my Dad.

My first game was against the Yankees. My mother won the tickets by calling a radio station and giving the name of some song, the kind with no words that didn't interest me until much later. Our seats were down the first base line and about the fifth inning the shade came across and it got cold. We were so close to the field you could even hear the game, that wonderful, milky sound when the bat's sweet spot meets the ball dead on, fast balls popping the catcher's mitt, the umpire's calls, the players yelling at him and everybody else.

The Yankees, the despised Yankees. Okay, I admit I had Yankee cards too – Raschi and Rizutto and Berra, staccato sounds, harsh to the ear. Our neighborhood used to be Irish but it was mostly Italian now and I had many friends and enemies with names like that. Wops, my father called them sometimes, not my friends but their parents, but only when they weren't around. I didn't know why wop was so bad but my friends went crazy if I called them that when we were having a fight, usually just names and shoving but sometimes punches. Wop. It got them going every time.

But it was the Irish my Dad really lit into. Drunks and bums, good for nothing but talking and drinking. I remember one time he told Uncle Eddie the Irish were the most arrogant people ever walked the face of the earth, staggered is what he actually said. "And your unions, damn bunch of socialists! The only part of you that works is your mouth!" Now his finger was in Uncle Eddie's face. "And your so-called failin' – what a load of crap! Rummies is all you are!" That's when Uncle Eddie asked him to step outside.

After that my mother didn't talk to my father for a long time. For her part, she scoffed at his plodding Canucks – nothing above the neck, no literature, no music, no theater. "If excess be the price of culture," she would say, "then I welcome excess!" How could such different people have ever got married?

Speaking of Uncle Eddie, when I mentioned cousins coming to my party, I forgot the twins, Martha and Mary. They didn't count, being girls. Of course my sister was thick with them.

Many kinds of people lived in our neighborhood. As I said, my parish, St. Teresa's, was mostly Irish and Italian with a few French families. You were in the parish your house was in, so we belonged to St. Teresa's, St. Teresa of Avila which is in Spain. There was the French Church, Our Lady of Lourdes, and the Polish Church whose name I was never clear about. The names up there had a lot of cz's and ski's. Holy Ghost was in Federal Hill, the really Italian section where we rarely ventured. One time thieves stole a gold crucifix from Holy Ghost. The parishioners wanted to call the police but the pastor said, no, I will make a phone call. Next day the crucifix was back, good as new. My mother had bad things to say about the mob but at the time it seemed a decent thing for them to do.

We were all Catholics, of course. Some Protestants lived in the area but I didn't know any. The children of Protestants went to public schools and we felt sorry for them because they were in error and didn't have the sacraments or God's grace. Jews I knew nothing at all about except they killed Christ and were still paying the price. Chinese and Japs? Cartoons in the back pages of the *Bulletin.* It never occurred to me they might have churches, too. For me the world was either Catholic or non-Catholic. I had the same pride being a Catholic as I did being American. It was something precious, something everyone would have wanted if they really understood things. America, America! God shed His grace on thee! Just as God was a Catholic, deep down I knew He was an American, too.

My mother never missed a chance to rail against politicians. She had gone to school with some of them and said their hat size was bigger than it had any right to be. My father liked to remind her that living on the same block as the ward chairman brought certain benefits – garbage collection, snow plowing – and anyway, when you're in business like he was you need to get along with people, not knock them all the time.

Most of their fights were over religion. My mother had nothing good to say about the big-shot bishop downtown and our parish priests except Father McAdam, yet she never missed Mass and we always had fish on Fridays, deep-fried hard and brown or finan haddie creamed and cratered in mounds of mashed potatoes. My father said bad things about her saying bad things, but he often slept late Sundays then ambled down to the shop to get caught up for the week. Some nights he disappeared there too, and my mother would read, enjoying some peace and quiet, she claimed, though I noticed she didn't turn the pages as fast as usual and sometimes seemed out of sorts.

IT WAS ABOUT EIGHT. My mother was in her room, recovering from her labors. The house was filled with the friendly aroma of ham. Suddenly I heard noises, a car outside. There were footsteps and voices. Before the doorbell rang I was at the door.

"Ti-Paul! Ti-Paul!"

I couldn't believe my eyes! Tante Jeanette! And Uncle Albert! *"Ça va, mon petit?"* he said, hoisting me in the air. "My, how big you got!" Uncle Albert was a giant, with a rough, leathery face that scratched mine as I flew up over his head. From my perch I looked over his shoulder... not one car but two!_And more people coming up the walk! Laughing, Uncle Albert put me down. "Ah, *ti-Paul,* you're so heavy you give me a rupture!" That pleased me. I was still trying to break fifty pounds but had been stuck a long time at forty-six. His laugh boomed up at you from way down near his shoes. I really liked Uncle Albert. My father was at the door, beaming, as everybody threw their arms around everybody else. Uncle Albert was my father's oldest brother and Tante Jeanette his sister. She was always smiling, I swear, even in pictures. She was also tall, though of course not as tall as Uncle Albert.

"Entrée! Entrée!" My father waved everybody in. Tante Geneviève, Uncle Albert's wife, as tiny as he was tall, squeezed my hand and kissed me silently on the cheek. She didn't talk much, I remembered that from the last visit. In all, nine people including cousins I'd never even heard of. Just then, my mother appeared, finger marking the place in her book. She had this funny look on her face.

"Albert! And Geneviève! My, this is a surprise!"

One by one she greeted our visitors so I got to hear the names again. Cousin François was a younger copy of Uncle Albert, and two men who didn't look much older than Buddy Malloy next door, plus their wives. As usual, no kids my age. The women all were wearing nice clothes, dresses and sweaters, and the men had on plaid work shirts and baggy pants. My mother was staring at the tracks on the carpet.

"We heard something about tomorrow being *ti-Paul's* big day," Tante Jeanette was saying, her face red and shiny as she tousled my hair, "so we come by to say hello. And Catherine! *Jolie! Si jolie!"* Catherine had slipped in behind my mother. She was always slipping in somewhere.

My father was counting heads. "How long on the road?" he asked. Not waiting for an answer, he yelled at me through the hubbub, *"Ti-Paul!"* He hardly ever called me that, "two chairs from the dining room."

Well, I had to move four chairs because he forgot my mother and Catherine. Jim was out, as usual. Conversations criss-crossed the room which suddenly seemed small and inadequate. By the time I dragged the last chair in my mother was in the kitchen, opening bottles of Narragansett – that's beer – and boiling water for coffee. I couldn't figure out why, but she kept shaking her head and looked like she was going to cry.

In the living room, my father was sitting with Uncle Albert. My father was the oldest of *les Bernards américains,* as they called themselves, so he was in charge of parceling out the visitors among the local clan. My uncle kept nodding and waving his hands and saying "way, way." Once in a while he'd throw in a "you bet!" and an "oh boy!" and nod even faster. His English sounded a lot like my father's French. My mother placed a bottle on the table beside him with a coaster. She was big on coasters.

The plan, they'd stay two nights, then hit the road Sunday, arriving back in Québec for work the next day. Farmers and mechanics they were, who my father said never took a day off in their lives, even weekends, so it was a big deal they came all this way just for me. I noticed my father heading for the phone with my mother on his heels. She was waving her hands like Uncle Albert then she disappeared into the kitchen.

"Ti-Paul!" Tante Jeanette was beckoning me over. She was holding a small package wrapped in white paper tied with a red ribbon. "Here! For you!"

I took the package and turned it over in my hand. *"Ouvrez! Vite! Vite!"*

I knew enough French to undo the ribbon and tear off the wrapping. Of course my nosy sister was there taking it all in. When the paper fell away I saw a small, thin box. I lifted the lid... it was a watch! A real watch! With a leather band! "We was afraid maybe you had one already," Uncle Albert was saying, but I shook my head. My heart was beating fast. "Waltham," the dial said in gold letters. It also said twelve-fifteen. For as long as I could remember I could tell time and it wasn't twelve-fifteen. I stuck my thumbnail under the stem and started to pull it out like I'd seen my father do. Tell the truth, I had tried that a couple of times with his watch when he left it out, though I never dared touch his pocket watch, the one he wore on a chain with his best suit and vest, the brown one. "Here." The watch disappeared in my uncle's palm. He fitted it to my wrist, inserting the little gold point in the band.

"Always put it on before you wind it," Tante Jeanette said, "over the bed is best."

I pulled out the stem, a real trick with one hand, and set the time by the mantle clock, seven fifty-two. "I've been wanting one a long time," I said.

Tante Jeanette beamed. "Don't wind too far. When it feels tight, stop."

As my mother replaced Uncle Albert's empty Narragansett she nodded at the watch. "I hope you've thanked them properly."

Tante Jeanette winked. She knew I was getting to that. "Fiona, something for the house." She handed over a larger package with the same wrapper as mine. My mother opened it – a tin of maple syrup with a picture of trees and a red maple leaf.

"How nice. We'll have it for breakfast tomorrow."

"Non! Non!" Tante Jeanette shook her head. "Save it! It is for you to enjoy!"

"We'll see," my mother replied, placing the container on the table next to Tante Jeannette, kind of like a trophy.

A few minutes later Catherine came parading in with a platter of sandwiches but they were gone before it got to me. Luckily she was right back with another plate. I grabbed one, the meat still warm from the oven, butter melting into the bread, that good kind with the fingerprints. I was feeling great when I realized – we're eating my ham! There won't be any left for tomorrow! After a couple more bites, though, I decided it was okay. My mother would take care of everything, she always did. Besides, fasting from midnight meant a long wait for my next meal. So I did what I had to do. I reached for another sandwich.

4. THE GOOD TIME THAT WAS HAD BY ALL

"THOSE COMMENTS ABOUT THE IRISH – I suppose they're nothing new to you, Gus."

"You got used to it. And don't you love that comeback? Nothing above the neck. I welcome excess! Quite a lady, and attractive too, though I met her only the once."

"Your interest in slavery – did being Irish have anything to do with that?"

"Let me say, the British were very much a topic of conversation around the dinner table. I didn't make the connection with how blacks are treated here, that came later."

"Speaking of underdogs, you count the Jews as an oppressed people, surely."

"Of course, though when they're on top they seem to forget what it's like with the boot on their neck."

"Paul came to a similar conclusion."

"And it made him unpopular in some quarters."

"We'll come back to that. I must say his Christ-killer remark is disturbing."

"That's a seven-year-old talking, Jonathan. Be patient, we'll get to that, too."

Over lunch I ask Jonathan a few questions. Turns out he hasn't been altogether straight with me. He's doing this piece for *The New Yorker,* all right, but he's a free-lancer, not on staff as he led me to believe. Not that there's anything wrong with free-lancers, but I am disappointed in him. "What else have you written?" I ask.

"Things for *Esquire* and *Harper's. Vanity Fair,* the *Times* Sunday Magazine. A few years ago I did a big piece for *Playboy* on NBA teams signing kids out of high school. That made some waves. You see it?"

"I haven't looked at *Playboy* in years," I laugh. "Never could get past the pictures and after my interest peaked, so to speak, there was nothing left to hold me."

"They've always had great articles and big-name fiction – Ian Fleming, Nabokov."

"Sure, sure. And I know a really good bridge for sale. Anything else for *The New Yorker?*"

He shakes his head. "They have a staff guy who covers the same territory so I don't hear from them that often. This article was my idea, I brought it to them."

So, I think to myself, this is a very big deal for you, Jonathan Bernstein, though I won't embarrass you by saying so. "How come you became a journalist?"

"It was my major at Columbia. I minored in History, you'll be happy to hear."

"You wouldn't have known Hofstadter, you're too young."

"Jacques Barzun, I took courses from him."

"Dick and I got together at conferences and the like. Well, I wish you well with the article. Whatever I can do," I say, raising my glass which, by the way, was Poland Spring.

"You've already been a big help."

That is true. He wouldn't stand a chance without Paul's letters and notebooks. With recent events, it has occurred to me other people might be wanting a look at them too, so I make a mental note to call Paul's assistant – Susan, I think her name is – and ask her about the stuff in his office. I'll need to go through that too.

"I went over my schedule last night," Jonathan says, his brow furrowed. "This is going slower than I expected. You have Jennings set to record – right?"

"I told you I did." I know Jonathan is under pressure but he is already starting to get on my nerves.

"By the way, do you still have the *Times* obit?"

"Of course. And a *Globe* and the Providence paper and our local rag though they didn't have much. Why do you ask?"

"I must have misplaced my copy."

This does not augur well, I am thinking, but I keep my mouth shut.

At six thirty we turn on the television. Near seven the tribute to Paul comes on. At the end the screen fills with Peter Jennings' lean, handsome visage. "In coming days there will be other tributes and retrospectives on the life of our colleague, Paul Bernard. Tonight ABC was privileged to present this brief look at a giant in the news business and a close personal friend. For everyone at ABC News, I'm Peter Jennings. Good night."

Jonathan looks puzzled. "Rewind to the ambush part," he says. It's essentially the same footage I taped that first night. I fast rewind then inch it ahead.

"I have ETVN's tape too, if you want to see it."

"I will, but there's something odd here. Okay, stop it – there!" Jonathan gets to his feet and goes up to the television. "That's the convoy," he says, tapping the screen with his finger. "Three Humvees, an SUV, and Paul's is the only one hit! Everything else is untouched! You can't tell me that's a coincidence!"

I spread my hands. I don't know. I don't disagree, but I don't know.

"Somebody knew Paul was in that Humvee!" Jonathan's eyes are bright.

"Maybe," I say, "maybe not. More likely it was just bad timing."

"That was no coincidence, Gus. Somebody targeted Paul. I'm going to find out who, and why."

Good luck, I think to myself. Jonathan says shut it down which I do gladly. I have seen more than enough.

"Jennings said there's nothing new on the attackers. I'd hate to be them if our guys ever catch up with them."

"A chance in a million. It's their turf. Turf beats technology every time."

****

I WAS FIRST UP AS USUAL, 6:15 by my new watch. Dead to the world, Jim was rolled up in a blanket on my floor. He'd come in late, banging and grumbling about them giving his bedroom away. Every square foot of the living room was covered with relatives, my father slumped in his chair, Uncle Albert on the couch snoring, his legs draped over the end, his feet on a table. As a precaution Grandmother Kelley's mother's china lamp had been put on the floor. I opened the fridge and there it was – my ham. A forlorn carcass with a few scraps of meat. I stared longingly at the orange juice pitcher, the milk, the eggs. My stomach was complaining when my mother appeared, yawning and fussing with her hair. "So, you're ready for your big day?"

"I'd rather have something to eat. Like Dad." My father didn't fast before he went to communion, something he called a working man's exemption.

She filled the kettle. "May that be the worst cross you ever have to bear."

"I suppose." Something else had been bothering me. The year Catherine was born, when my parents remodeled the attic into bedrooms they added a tiny bathroom but mornings when the five of us were trying to get out it was a real squeeze. "How'll we all get ready in time?" I asked.

She smiled, another one of her not-quite-a-smile smiles. "With your father's relatives, bathing is not a high priority. Here," she gestured toward the table, "sit a minute." By now the kettle was whistling. She filled the coffee pot and put the lid on, the rest went into her antique teapot, the one with the little shamrocks.

"You're such a good son..." she began, sitting down opposite me. The coffee was pinging into the metal pot. "...so good at school and never a bit of trouble." What she really meant was, not like Jim. She stared at me, her lips pursed. When she was serious like this, she looked exactly like those pictures from her plays. "Tell me, do you believe the things they're teaching you? I mean, do you really believe them?"

I was puzzled. What a strange question.

"If you had to walk to the end of the earth for your Faith, would you do it?" She paused, "well, would you?"

"I guess so," I replied. "Sure."

"Why?"

"Well... I suppose... it'd be the right thing to do?"

"Paul, listen to me." She placed her hand on mine, "within every person are two forces, fear and love. Fear loses its power when the person ceases to be afraid. The person who loves, that person stays the course, he accomplishes great things. The Father Donnellys of the world, they rule by fear," she said, shaking her head. "The world is cruel and men are weak, but never, never let those who carry Christ's message tarnish it for you. It's too pure, too fine to lose over the weakness of a few men." Her eyes were ablaze. "A black robe is proof of nothing. The best priest is the one who steps aside and gets out of God's way."

The dripping had stopped. The pungent smell of coffee filled the room. "Some day you'll understand. It's sad, but the severest tests of your Faith may come from the very people God chooses to entrust with it." She sat back and sighed. "But enough. You are young and this is your day. Just remember, your Faith can be a strength and joy, but the time may come when the price you pay for it is very dear."

THE DAY STARTED OKAY. Sunny and warm, scent of flowers, young voices in song, even the organ playing was okay. Shirts and ties and those short pants they made you wear, the girls' white dresses, Margaret, stomachs growling in the quiet moments. Only one thing went wrong but it was a beaut. I was returning to my bench after receiving communion and tried wetting the cardboard with spit so I could swallow it. Never, never chew! But now the warm soggy lump was glued to the roof of my mouth! I began twisting my jaw different ways, using my tongue to peel it off, but when I looked up there was Margaret Foley at the end of her row, laughing! Laughing at me! Seconds after qualifying for eternal life through Jesus Christ our Lord and Saviour, I wished I was dead. That was the only disaster I knew of. Nobody stood when he should have knelt or threw up or fainted, nothing like that. But then, what happened at home...

My mother started out planning a big affair with everyone we ever knew but, not so much for parties, my father put his foot down. For my part, the bigger the better – more cards, more money. In the end they invited a couple dozen, but the northerners threw everything off. The dining room was now too small for a proper sit-down dinner, even sticking us kids in the kitchen. Then there was the Great Ham War, though my mother recovered quickly, phoning her sisters who arrived after church with platters and dishes. In fact, she managed to transform our dining room table into a lavish buffet of roast beef, potato salad, cole slaw, hot rolls – you get the picture. And there, all by itself on a huge platter in the center of the table, the carcass, tied with a green ribbon and bow. Take that, Julien!

Tante Héloise was there, my father's sister who lived in a tenement with her friend Tante Marie who wasn't really my aunt. Tante Héloise was fat and jolly and never married. Though younger than my father, Tante Héloise had always looked old with her frizzy hair and shapeless dresses. She arrived with Uncle Antoine and Tante Roseanne. Aunt Moira and Uncle Eddie also, and of course my two dumb girl cousins, already holed up with Catherine. Grandmother Kelley came with my mother's sister Aunt Mary Elizabeth Finnegan and Uncle Paddy and their two boys, my mother called them, cousins Steve and Terry, who weren't boys at all but out of high school and out of work too, according to my father neither of them able to keep a job. They were tall and bulky, with red hair and freckles. Uncle Paddy used to work for the phone company but suffered an injury whose particulars nobody seemed to recall.

"Deadbeats, the whole bunch," my father said, shaking his head.

Grandmother Kelley was extremely old and walked with a cane. She lived with the Finnegans – actually they lived with her – in the tenement she owned in North Providence. They said Grandfather Kelley made a lot of money during Prohibition. He'd been in the Merchant Marine in World War One and owned a boat I'd seen pictures of. For a time when my mother was young they lived well, part of the city's burgeoning Irish elite, then came the Depression. One day they found Grandfather Kelley floating in the Providence River, his feet bound, one end of the rope frayed where the police said the weight broke away.

Having a taste for the good life, my mother had scratched and clawed to attain a position in local cultural circles, then everything changed when she met a handsome Canadian who with his brother owned a business which, by the day's standards, was prosperous. Julien Bernard saw her picture in the newspaper for *Hedda Gabler*. A bouquet of roses appeared backstage and they were on their way.

"First play I ever went to," I heard him brag more than once. "Last one, too."

I guess she figured over time she could smooth the rough edges, small price to pay for security and a home and a base for her artistic ambitions. But then came the little ones, one, two, three, and her discovery that Julien's unlettered coarseness was central to the man and beyond repair.

When we arrived home from church, my brother Jim volunteered to bartend. No surprise, there. More than once I'd caught him sneaking a beer to his room. Now he shuttled between house and the ice tub in the garage. My father had laid in a store of Hanley's Ale for the Irish guests who preferred it to 'Gansett. He loved to provoke my mother by singing the Hanley's jingle, same as "Rose of Tralee." It wasn't so much that he butchered it – everybody knew he couldn't carry a tune – it was his slurring the words and wobbling as he sang. At least he had sense enough to back off when my mother set John McCormack on the Victrola for Grandmother Kelley. Whatever her mood, the sound of his voice would cause the old lady's eyes to close and she would move her lips and hum, reliving happy times.

"Being this is a religious event we'll be havin' to shut your people off, Fiona. Three bottles and not a drop more," my father said the day before as he and Jim lugged in the Hanley's cartons, "three an hour, that is." She didn't appreciate that.

I hung around the front door greeting guests, accepting presents, mostly cards, which I didn't mind at all. After a decent time I darted upstairs and spread the haul on my bed. Twenty three dollars! And more to come in the mail! By now everybody had a glass or a bottle and my aunts were herding people toward the food. Leaping in, I secured a large portion of roast beef. After stuffing myself, I went out to the screened porch where we sometimes set up cots for hot summer nights. Outside, Uncle Albert and Uncle Antoine were talking with my father under the basketball hoop he had built for Jim and me. They were smoking and sipping 'Gansett and looking gloomy, all of them. Uncle Albert was leaning against the post under the basket.

"Too bad, Julien, too bad... " he was saying, shaking his head. I leaned forward to hear. "We was hoping you had some work for Pièrre. Hard as hell that boy works, honest and sober, he would do a good job for you, any job." He sighed, "things are not good at home, *mes frères*. The farm don't pay, there's no other work. You heard they're having a baby, him and Céline. I don't want them to leave but I don't blame them."

My father shook his head. "It's no picnic here, Albert. I laid off ten people last week. Machine tools went to hell after the war, no sign of them coming back. "By summer we'll be laying off another fifteen, twenty people," my father added, "skilled workers, them, machinists. That's less jobs for everybody else."

"What about the mills? You know the people run them."

"The mills!" Uncle Antoine spat on the ground. "You come through Allens Avenue? Or Olneyville? Shut down, all of them, the windows broke, boarded up."

Uncle Albert ground his cigarette in the dirt. "*Eh bien.* At least I tried."

"How's *Mémère* doing?" Uncle Antoine asked.

Mémère was sick with cancer. From the snapshots she was a small woman with white hair. She visited when I was born and had never returned. Uncle Albert shook another Chesterfield from his pack, tapping it against his lighter. "A matter of time. The pneumonia took it out of her last winter. We're just trying to keep her comfortable." Inhaling deeply he snapped the lighter shut. "One of these days you be getting a call."

All of a sudden there was this loud crash from inside the house.

My father looked up. "What the hell...!"

I rushed back in. There in the middle of the living room was my cousin Steve, sitting in the wreckage of Grandmother Kelley's mother's lamp. Glowering, Pièrre stood over Steve. My mother was at the door, her hand to her mouth. Steve was rubbing his nose. His face and shirt were spattered with blood. He got to his feet. "C'mon, frog!" he yelled, "what're you afraid of, frog?" The two of them began to circle. My father put his arm in front of my mother. "Let it run its course," he said calmly.

"Not here! Not in my house!" She was staring at the shattered lamp.

"Let them have it out, 'long as it's just the two of them." My father glared at Terry Finnegan who was jawing with Pièrre's brother Mathieu.

Suddenly Steve made a rush at Pièrre, butting him in the stomach with his head and driving him into the couch. Pièrre let out a loud "OOOF!" and they fell, rolling together on the floor. Now everyone was screaming. Steve was on top, pummeling Pièrre, but Pièrre rolled him over, driving his knee into Steve's chest. Now he had him in a headlock.

"*Salaud!* Take it back! Take it back!" Pièrre was smaller than Steve but he was wiry. Now he was grinding Steve's face into the carpet, smearing blood all over it. "Filthy *cochon!* Apologize, damn you!"

Despite his bulk Steve was quick and the better wrestler. Suddenly he exploded out of Pièrre's hold. "Not on your life!" he shouted. Now they rolled the other way across the floor, crashing into the fireplace screen which collapsed over them. Steve was on top with his hands around Pièrre's neck, banging his head against the flagstones. Pièrre's eyes bulged, his face was purple and he was making little gurgling sounds. Suddenly a figure darted forward. Céline! Holding a 'Gansett above her head, she danced around with little steps, looking for an opening, then CRASH! Down it came, right on Steve's skull! Moaning and holding his head Steve crumpled into the fireplace. The room fell silent.

Céline rushed to Pièrre, father of her unborn child, and bent over him, cradling his head in her lap. He was rubbing his throat, gasping for breath. Now everybody was milling around. Steve's eyes opened. Dazed, he shook his head and sat up, trying to figure out what had hit him. Why that bottle didn't break I'll never know. Through the other guests' legs the warriors spotted each other. By now my father was beside Steve, lecturing him. Steve tried to get up, but fell back. After a moment he rose to his knees and slowly crawled on all fours over to Pièrre. Pièrre opened his mouth. "Apologize!" he croaked.

Steve rubbed his head and inspected his hand for blood. "Yeah, well, that was the beer talking, I guess." He stuck out his hand. "For a frog you fight pretty good."

Pierre hesitated, then took Steve's hand. "You ain't half bad, yourself."

A great cheer went up.

In tears, my mother was on her hands and knees putting the remains of the heirloom in a paper bag. Grandmother Kelley clucked on. Each clan ministered to its hero, mopping his face with wet towels. Catherine was already scrubbing the carpet. Aunt Moira motioned Aunt Mary Elizabeth Finnegan into the kitchen. A mellow mood began to settle over the house.

The doorbell rang. "Hey, Julien!" somebody yelled. "C'mere!"

My father elbowed his way to the door. I followed, thinking it was more cards, but it was a policeman! In uniform! And at the curb right outside our house, his cruiser!

"Bernie!" my father exclaimed, "what brings you here?"

The policeman had his cap in his hand. "Sorry to disturb you, Julien, but we had a report of a large amount of noise in the vicinity. From your house, in fact."

"We're having a little party. It's my son's First Communion." He smiled down at me, "isn't that so, Paul?"

I nodded, looking up at the policeman's badge. He had a black leather holster on his hip. There was a gun inside – I saw the handle! What an amazing day!

"I got to ask you to tone it down, 'else I'll have to make a report."

"There'll be no more cause for complaint." My father reached into his pocket and extracted a bill, folding it into his palm. "By the way, I'm curious, who made the call?"

The policeman nodded at the house across the street.

"That figures."

Everybody called them Old Mr. Southworth and Old Mrs. Southworth but I knew them only as shadows moving behind screens and curtains. My mother brought supper for Old Mr. Southworth whenever Old Mrs. Southworth went into the hospital which seemed quite often. Nothing wrong with their hearing, though.

"Next time, invite the old folks," the policeman winked at me, "then make all the noise you want."

My father reached out and shook the policeman's hand. The bill disappeared. "Good advice, Bernie, we'll do that."

The policeman put his hat on and gave us a salute. "Just keep it down so everybody gets along."

As he went down the steps I caught a glimpse of Old Mr. Southworth ducking away from his window. The policeman opened the door to his cruiser and my father patted my head. "Let this be a lesson to you, *ti-Paul.* It is important to have friends in the right places. You never know when it'll come in handy."

STANDING ON THE STEPS, I heard something happening. We went back inside – on the arm of the couch was Uncle Albert, tuning his fiddle. My father broke into a big grin. The last time the Bernard clan visited I was dragged to a dance at the Mongenais Club next to the French Church and was bored out of my mind until Uncle Albert sat in with the band and started playing. It was really something, this bear of a man with the huge hands making magic from a little piece of wood, his heavy shoes thudding out the beat.

"Fiona! *Allons! Venons!"* Uncle Albert yelled across the room. "A duet! Just for you I learned some Irish tunes!"

My mother was moving around the room, picking up dishes. Her jaw set, she shook her head firmly.

"Aw, c'mon! Just a coupl'a songs!"

"You go ahead, Albert. I'm not in the mood."

His face fell. I was disappointed, too. It was fun hearing her play the piano with other people. Usually she played alone and sang, from old books with German and French words, sheet music with blue covers and men and women in canoes under the moon, or Molly Malone and Galway Bay her mother always asked for. But this time it was not to be.

Then Uncle Albert unwound and put the fiddle to his chin, and the room quieted. He began sawing away, first a slow number then a fast one that everybody clapped to. Next the Irish Washerwoman and Aunt Moira stepped forward, kicking up her feet. Nothing ever kept her from having a good time. She collapsed into a chair out of breath. The music went on. People sat on the floor, singing. I thought maybe I should take piano lessons like my mother wanted. Catherine had since she was five and I had to admit wasn't bad. I liked music but hated the idea of being inside on a nice day. Maybe later when I was older.

Around three, everybody began to stand and stretch. After much fussing with coats and hats, dishes people brought and so on, the house began emptying out. Outside under the hoop, Uncle Albert had his hand on my father's shoulder. My father was nodding. A few minutes later, I saw Tante Jeanette carrying her suitcase into the living room. What was happening? My father came back in, looking gloomy. Uncle Albert was shaking his head.

"No, no, better we get back tonight. Rest up tomorrow, be ready for the week."

Cousin Céline came up to me. "Thank you for letting us be part of your big day," she said, giving me a kiss on the cheek. Céline was small and pretty and smelled nice. Tante Geneviève put her arms around me. "Come see us, *ti-Paul,* we be disappointed if you don't." They filed out to their cars, luggage piled into the trunks, a lot of hugging and tears. I looked around. I knew Jim had taken off, but... "Where's mom?" I asked.

My father frowned and shook his head.

After the cars pulled away, I went looking for her. My search ended at the bedroom door. Catherine saw me standing there. "Ma was really mad about the lamp and the fighting and Dad didn't stop it and the police came. It was so *embarrassing!*" She tossed her head, "I bet you don't even know how it started!" She was right, I had no clue.

"Steve made a joke about Tante Geneviève's moustache, and Pierre..."

"Her what?"

"Her moustache, fool! You mean you never noticed it?"

Sure, there was a little dark fuzz there... actually if you thought about it, it did look odd, but it wasn't a moustache. Women didn't have moustaches. I didn't know what it was.

"Pièrre told Steve to take it back, but he wouldn't, that's what started it! See!"

Well, I didn't blame Pièrre. If somebody made fun of my mother, I'd fight him, too.

"And who ever heard of people coming to visit and not telling you ahead," Catherine was going on. "Of course Ma wouldn't play the piano! How could he even ask? Good thing they left, if you ask me! Good riddance!"

First up next morning, I did my usual house patrol. My parents' door was closed but this early that was normal. What wasn't, finding my father on the couch in a blanket, his legs over the arm like Uncle Albert's the night before, but this morning no lamp on the floor, no lamp at all. Chin in hand I sat on the stairs, pondering the remains of my perfect day

5. A NINE-YEAR-OLD SUMMER

JONATHAN LOOKS UP, PUZZLED. "I'm surprised how important religion was to Paul," he says. "I wouldn't have expected that."

"Those days, that was par for the course. The parishes, the parochial schools, they were immensely powerful. Totally different now, with Vatican II and the unraveling of the American Church. But I give old Pope John credit. He ran a risk, but sometimes overreaction is better than no reaction. The jury's still out – it will be for centuries."

"Politics was my family's religion. My mother was a red diaper baby. She and my father met at Columbia in the Sixties."

"Ah, Columbia – we watched you from afar. But as for religion, there's no guarantee that conformist pressure will work. The individual determines the outcome surely as a glass shapes the water it holds. And if it's all genes and wiring, what's the point, anyway? I will say this, though, dissent has its price. And when what's at stake is eternity, every inch you stray from the path magnifies the guilt and fear."

"Not exactly how I see it."

"Nor I, not since I figured out which end was up. Some people take it on themselves to redefine the game so nothing means the same. They call that growing in the Faith, but to me that's simply dishonest. You're in or you're out. I'm out, though hope springs eternal, and incidentally, it's a lot less demanding than the other two. All right," I say, sliding a pile of folders toward Jonathan. "Today we start with one of Paul's infrequent letters. After 9-11 we talked by phone but he had no time for correspondence."

Everyman TeleVision Network
419 West 13th Street
New York City, NY 10014

October 1, 2001

Gus,

I found a couple of spare hours so here's your next installment. You really need to get down here and go through the rest yourself.

Next week I'm in Paris. The French will be key to whatever Washington does about bin Laden, at least they should be. I need to know more about their thinking.

As I pulled this together it occurred to me, these reminiscences are similar to your young religious experiences, or as you called them, impositions. As for me, one thing is clear, everything was foreshadowed. The acorn does indeed possess the oak.

We need to talk about where this business of yours is going.

All the best,

Paul

****

ON COMPLETING FOURTH GRADE, a few weeks before my ninth birthday we acquired a dog. We always had cats – strays who saw a life commitment in a dish of milk, but dogs didn't fit my mother's concept of a home, particularly carpets and furniture. I grew up loathing carpets and furniture nearly as much as cats. My nose was always in a book and my father thought a rowdy animal might straighten me out. Girls read and had cats, boys were about roughhousing and dogs. True to form, though, after his announcement I headed for the library and checked out as many dog books as I could carry. Dogs, Breeds of. Dogs, Care and Feeding of. Dogs, Diseases. Dog, History of. That Sunday afternoon we headed for the country, the newspaper clipping in my pocket:

> BEAGLES for sale. Pups, six weeks, 3 males 2 females,
> variety colors, markings. Shots and wormed. AKC regis.
> Irresistible. $35. Lincolnwood Kennels. Lincoln 2828B.

Thirty-five dollars was a fortune, an indication of the peril my father thought I was in. I loved Lassie, but my mother wouldn't abide the hair. But a kid two streets over owned a beagle, a compact, friendly animal with acceptable hair. And so it came to be.

King was a wiggly black and brown fur ball who mostly slept and ate and messed. I fixed a box with a blanket and put it beside the kitchen stove so the pilot would warm him at night. The first night he whined so miserably my father put a hot water bottle and a clock in to settle him down.

A beagle named King? I settled on the name before my mother nixed the collie idea. Here was a creature with no name until I pronounced one over him. Now it was on his tag and he was beginning to answer to it. Disconcerting, such power over another creature. I knew how Adam felt setting up all those animals with names. One of the men in my father's shop built a doghouse I painted white with red trim and ninety-three, our house number, on the front. We set it under the spruce trees behind the basketball hoop. King was an outside dog, though I could have him in the house as long as I dealt with the inevitable.

Every summer we piled into the car and visited some relative's house. To qualify as a vacation it had to be a somewhat distant relative, about fifty miles at least. North was the preferred destination. As a driver, my father was *fou,* everybody said, never stopping except for gas. We always had to get there in one day, which meant an exhausting ordeal usually ending at Bic where he grew up. By the second time I went, *Mémère* had died. My father and mother went to the funeral but we didn't because of school.

This summer was extremely rainy and our lot a sea of muck, so Omer and I spent hours on his porch working jigsaw puzzles and playing picture cards. King mostly slept, though sometimes he'd yawn and pull a card in for a chew. One morning on my way to Omer's an airplane flew right down my street, so low I could read the number on the wing. Circling under the clouds, all of a sudden it dropped behind the trees. I held my breath, waiting... but it never came back up! I yelled at Omer to come on. It took him several blocks to catch us, King and I were running so fast. But nothing! No plane on the golf course, no plane up a tree. No police cars, no fire trucks, no sirens. How disappointing! Later I wondered if what I was really chasing was excitement, disaster. A sign of things to come? That night for the first time I had a dream which visits me to this day. In it I spread my arms and soar, swooping, turning, racing my shadow over the ground. Whenever that dream appears, the next morning I wake exhilarated, ready for anything.

RAINY DAYS MEANT BASEBALL ON THE RADIO. I was still a year away from getting on the school team but I hung around their practice and helped with the bats and equipment. I hoped to make it my first try. When it rained here it rained in Boston, so the Braves or Red Sox, whoever was home, were rained out and I'd listen to telegraphic recreations of games from other cities. For some reason it always seemed to be the Cubs and Cardinals. Or Cincinnati. Maybe it didn't rain as much in that part of the country. The telegraph clacked as Jim Britt described somebody thousands of miles away stealing second or dumping a Texas Leaguer into short right. I always wondered how much of it he made up.

I was the next-to-smallest player. Only Omer was shorter. Then there were the glasses which kept people from noticing how good I was, which was not all that great, if you really need to know. Most of my hits were chipped to the opposite field, and I did not have what they called sure hands, tending to close my eyes on hard grounders hit at me. But what I lacked in ability I made up in desire and, of course, there was nothing about the game I didn't know. I had my own Official Major League Baseball Rule Book and could tell you how many innings for an official game, the height of the mound, the score of a forfeit, and so on.

Our games started by catching the bat, then you and the other captain went hand over hand up the handle and around your head three times and you got first pick. We played ball all summer, all the time, mostly with a dirty, scuffed ball. The cover would fall off and you'd wind it with friction tape and douse it with baby powder which left a slippery, sweet-smelling ball for a few innings. Long fouls to right landed in the street bordering the lot, where every fifty feet or so there was a long, narrow opening in the curb perfectly located to swallow a well-hit ball. Once in a rare while somebody showed up with a new ball, birthday present or paper route money. A taped ball was no big deal but a new ball in the sewer called for retrieval measures involving a crowbar, rope, a flashlight, and one very unhappy player. Lot rules – that miserable job fell to the fielder if it was his error that let the ball get into the street. Next came the hitter, who complained don't blame me for a good hit. As a last resort and the usual result, the ball's owner. Not fair, but realistic.

One day we were short a player when Genie Sullivan didn't show. About the third inning this tubby kid, Murph, who thought he was hot stuff, shouted, "Benny!" I looked around and saw a slim boy with dark curly hair approaching. I'd had never seen him before. "You're on their side!" Murph yelled, pointing at me. The kids snickered as the new kid made his way to right field where the weakest fielder was put because fewest balls were hit that way. It turned out Benny was not very good, in fact he was awful. Balls hit right at him he missed. One fly went through his glove and got him in the face. He didn't know what to do with the bat either, holding his hands exactly wrong. Though I joined in ragging this newcomer I pitied him. Too close to home, much too close.

Benny lived the next street over from the lot. His last name was Kaplan, and his family just moved from New York. As the summer went on we became good friends. He never showed up at the lot again, and I learned his lack of ability was matched only by his lack of interest. When we played together there was rarely anybody else around, which made me wonder if he had many friends. I always went to his house, for some reason he seemed reluctant to come to mine though once in a while he did.

His father had a job downtown which he left for every day in a suit and tie. Mr. Kaplan spoke in an accent different from our Canadians but he also mixed in foreign words. Benny's house was bigger than ours with a giant oak in the back yard. One day his father built a platform, nailing planks together in the crook of the limbs then bracing it with two-by-fours. "Not too many nails," he warned, "we do not want to damage the tree." We spent a lot of time there playing ship or spy, games of imagination and high ground. One rainy day we dragged a tent up there but Benny's parents wouldn't let us stay overnight because he walked in his sleep.

Their house was dark, with old pictures and a strange object I'd never seen before, a silver candle holder with a bunch of branches, plus other things they used on Friday nights. Saturday mornings he went to religious school he called "schul." He was studying for his "Bar Mitzvah" which sounded a lot like Confirmation. He let me try on the beanie he wore to schul. During the week he went to Sennott Street School. Benny was my first public school friend. He was also the first Jew I had ever known.

We didn't talk about my Church or his either, which he called "Temple." Why not, I don't know, since I was proud of my religion. Though maybe that was it. My world was so comfortable I saw no need to explore outside it. When you live in a house whose rooms are perfect in every way, what is the use of windows? But actually, I was curious how these normal-looking people could believe in anything as odd as the Jewish religion, especially considering their ancestors killed Our Lord and Savior. How could they act so calm since without the sacraments they would never get to see God? Somehow, though, it didn't seem right to question Benny. He wouldn't have a good answer and I didn't want to embarrass my new friend.

Everyone in Benny's family read a lot, even his father. There were books all over the house, plus a newspaper with strange lettering he said was Yiddish. They had a lot of pictures in the living room and he said, yes these are my relatives but most of them are dead, killed by the Nazis. He told me many Nazis were Catholics, which made me angry. I knew Catholics wouldn't kill old people and children, but he said sure they did. My mother said it wasn't as simple as that, and when it came to cruelty the Nazis had nothing on the British.

One day I was having lunch at Benny's house. As his mother set my sandwich down she stared at me. "Paul, how do you come by those eyes?" she asked, "whose child are you?" What a peculiar thing to say. I started to explain about my family, but she smiled then said something even weirder. "Those dark eyes, Paul. You are one of us."

I'D BETTER SAY SOMETHING about my brother Jim. To start with, he got all the attention. My father made a big deal out of him getting his name in the paper after a game. My father had left sixth grade for the family farm, dispatched to the U.S. a year later to work in the mills and send money home. With no childhood of his own, he was making up for it with a double dose for number one son, crafting with favors and praise the boy he always wanted to be.

Jim lived without boundaries. He thought he could do anything, anytime, and with my father behind him, he was right. Girls called him at home. I know because I sometimes answered the phone. He'd flash a roll of bills at me, always a five on the outside, despite no after-school job and an allowance not nearly big enough for everything he bought. His closet was full of clothes and was always telling me, shape up, Paul, if you want to get anywhere you've got to look sharp. The kids he hung around with, a couple of them owned cars and they spent a lot of time cruising. He bragged, the day he got his license he'd have one too.

Jim owned the world, talking loud and getting into fights at school, which bothered my mother tremendously. She kept her distance, as if she feared Jim's wild energy. My parents had struck a deal. Jim was my father's domain, Catherine my mother's. So far from my father's idea of what a boy should be, I fell into my mother's sphere of influence, though in reality I was invisible, the family Switzerland. This had advantages, for bad as it made me feel, it gave me space to enjoy my solitary, orderly pastimes. I envied Jim's easy athleticism, his confidence and good looks, and though I would have liked his companionship, he had no time for me. Our paths diverged as we became more of what we were, ever more different.

One day in August my father called from work. He'd forgotten his lunch, would I bring it to him? He had something to show me too. I found the bag in the fridge and set out for his shop, wondering what was up. Passing my school I thought that in less than a month I'd be entering fifth grade. I didn't consider myself a big shot, though I stood first in my class and had a stellar reputation with the nuns that helped me not at all with my friends. What I excelled in, they cared nothing about. Grades didn't mean that much to me, either. They came so easily I didn't see the point, but I sensed if you're going to spend that much time on anything, you might as well do it right. This practical approach would carry me along until I figured out what I was doing, more or less.

I proceeded downhill along Manton Avenue past Clift's Variety, provisioner of picture card gum and comic books, past Virgilio's where I had my first slice of flat bread with tomato and melted cheese in a greasy wrapper that later became such a big deal, past the dry cleaners, past Francoeur's where I watched myself watching myself watching myself from a high leather chair, the spring shearing producing summer's crewcut, past the tap rooms, their sweet, dank odor spilling onto the sidewalk, open early every day though later on Sunday for sad-eyed men and women on stools hunched over their drinks. But not my father. Not even a quickie on the way home. He had class.

You approached the brick building that was my father's shop by a steep driveway angled between two mill buildings, one abandoned, the other with only a few cars outside. It always thrilled me to see the sign on the roof – Bernard Bros. Tool & Die. Somehow, his work belonged to me, and I to it. From the parking lot you could see across to Merino Park beyond the railroad tracks, beyond the willows and brush and the brackish, foul-smelling river. Merino, where winters we played hockey, terrorizing the girls, my sister and cousins, as they skated backward and did spins. We helped them spin, all right. Merino, home to St. Teresa's baseball. I was already obsessed with my tryout. On my knees each night, I pounded my glove and pleaded with God, aware I was testing His patience and power to the limit.

Walking into the reception area I waved at Miss Grenier, a stout older lady who'd been with the business since it started in the Thirties. A distant relative, she'd been in the States a long time. Her gloomy face and dour expression are permanently etched in my memory. She nodded as I opened the door to the corridor where my father and Uncle Antoine had side-by-side offices, black letters on frosted glass.

JULIEN BERNARD – PRESIDENT
ANTOINE BERNARD – VICE PRESIDENT

I peered into Uncle Antoine's office but he wasn't in. My father's door was ajar and I heard voices so I knocked. No answer, so I knocked harder. "Who's there?"

"It's me. I brought your lunch."

"Well, don't just stand there! Come in!"

My father was seated at his desk. Lorraine, his secretary, was standing by his chair, brushing the front of her dress, kind of pulling it down. Sweeping up some papers she floated past me with a big smile, which reminded me of something my mother said about perfume, that its presence should be felt but not smelled. That didn't make any sense to me. Isn't that what perfume's for, to be smelled? But I have to admit Lorraine's particular perfume was extremely powerful, in fact, the room reeked of it. If it had been my office I would've opened a window, that's for sure.

My father had two secretaries, Lorraine and Mrs. Lamontagne. Mrs. Lamontagne was another of those other people who'd worked for him forever. His bookkeeper, she knew everything about the business. As well as being my father's personal secretary, Lorraine helped out in front. The person in her job changed often, younger women who left to get married and have kids. This day I thought how pale Lorraine's hair was, white, really, which recalled another of my mother's comments, about women who bleach their hair. Everyone knows what kind of woman does that, she'd say, scowling at my father, and we know what they're after. Her hair would have made Lorraine look old except she was pretty and not at all fat which you could tell since her dress was very tight. I don't know, maybe it shrank.

"Ti-Paul!" My father waved me into the chair in front of his desk. As I said before, he rarely called me that, but the shop was one of those times. "I've got something to show you, something-you-will-not-believe!"

It had been a dull day, nobody around, and I ended up on my hands and knees clipping grass along the edge of the driveway, a dreary, pointless task. I placed the sack lunch beside my chair. My feet easily reached the floor – I was pushing five feet.

"There!" he said, inserting his gold pen in its holder and blotting a paper. "We'll give this to Mrs. Lamontagne then we're off!"

He dropped the bag into a desk drawer. "That can wait," he said, plucking his hat from the hat rack. I followed him down the corridor through the heavy metal door to the factory side of the shop. I always liked watching the machines, some going up and down, others side to side or in circles, punching holes, slicing, bending, filing. Most of them were quiet which these days wasn't unusual. We passed the timecard rack which could hold a couple hundred cards but these days had a lot of empty spaces. I often heard my father and mother talking about how bad business was. But today he was in a really good mood.

"Pretty soon, *ti-Paul*, pret-ty soon! Before long, this place'll be hopping, just like the old days!" He bent down and put his face close to mine. "I'll tell you something not even your mother knows. We just landed a contract from one of them big jewelry makers! A ve-ry big contract! First time we've ever been able to crack them." He nodded. "The other news you'll hear about soon enough."

"There's more?" I asked.

He paused. This time his face was serious. "It looks like we'll be having another war. Them Orientals are up to their old tricks – this time it's the Koreans. They better watch out or we'll kick their ass again!"

Wow! This was the first I'd heard about another war.

Our car was in the first parking space, in front of the PRESIDENT signpost, a black Plymouth we'd had a long time. If things pick up, I thought, maybe we'll get a new one! Soon we were driving through the Olneyville business district down the hill. We turned into a side street and pulled up in front of a store with the sign QUALITY RADIO SALES AND SERVICE – ALL WORK GUARANTEED. The front window was full of radios and victrolas and dead flies and bees on the sill with a lot of crumpled paper. As we opened the door a chime sounded and a man pushed his way through a curtain from the back room.

"*Ça va,* Julien!" It was my father's friend, Mr. Lemieux. He ran the Mongenais Club Christmas party every year.

"*Ça va,* Roland, damn good, in fact."

Mr. Lemieux was a short, balding man with a lean face and a heavy beard and something that shocked me every time I saw it, something that wasn't even there, his right arm. It had been shot off during the war, they said, in the Battle of the Bulge. He was another hero of the neighborhood, though seeing this incomplete person, in an odd way it made you feel worse than Cosmo or cousin Maurice who didn't come back at all. I once asked my father how Mr. Lemieux could repair radios and he said, lucky thing, he was left-handed to start with. When he was working Mr. Lemieux strapped on this fake arm with a metal hook. Unbelievable how he could move things around and pick them up with that hook. Today he didn't have the arm on and the sleeve of his short-sleeve shirt flapped as he moved. I always wanted to see what it looked like, some kind of stump, I figured, but I never dared ask.

"So, *ti-Paul,* you ready for the big show?" Mr. Lemieux asked.

No idea what he meant but I nodded anyway.

"*Allons-y!* Back this way. Just got it in this morning."

He led us through the curtain to this amazing indoor junkyard, thousands of radios and other stuff in every state of disrepair. Next to the workbench a calendar lady in a red swim suit gazed down on us from August. "Here it is!" he said proudly.

There it was all right, in front of Mr. Lemieux' workbench, a... I didn't know what it was. Some sort of cabinet like our living room radio except bigger and with a round window and a bunch of dials. I ran my fingers across the cool glass.

"First one in the city," Mr. Lemieux said, winking. "The Dumont man's a friend of mine. Here, let's start it up." He turned one knob and fiddled with another that had little numbers around the edge... circumference, that is. This knob clicked when he turned it.

"This is television, *ti-Paul!*" said my father, looking extremely pleased with himself.

Now the box was hissing and giving off a tone. The window grew lighter and a design appeared, several circles and a star with a black arm, a white arm and two shaded arms, and the words WJAR-TV - Providence - Channel 10. "That there's the test pattern, they's nothing on that station til later," Mr. Lemieux said, reaching for the numbered dial, "but look here!" He turned the dial through several clicks. The test pattern disappeared and what was this? The window was fuzzy but I saw a baseball field, with a pitcher at the top of the window! Near the bottom, a catcher and a batter! I leaned forward.

"It's Ted Williams!"

"You bet!" Mr. Lemieux said, fiddling with a V-shaped thing on top of the box. As he moved it around, the picture faded, then returned. "This here's the Boston station. Comes in okay with the rabbit ears. When I hook up the roof antenna we'll get rid of that snow."

Ted Williams, my idol, here in this... this box! "Two men out, last of the first, here's the three-one pitch." Williams swung and the ball disappeared through the upper right corner of the window. Suddenly the picture changed and you could see the second baseman flip it to first for the out. Again the picture changed and a Narragansett sign appeared. The announcer started talking about seedless hops and all, just like radio except you could actually see somebody pouring the beer. It rose in the glass and foamed over. I felt my father's arm on my shoulder. "Well, how do you like it?"

I was speechless. It was a miracle!

He glanced at his watch. "I gotta get back but maybe Roland will let you watch a couple innings."

I looked at Mr. Lemieux, "Can I?"

"Sure, you bet. You're the first one, my own kid hasn't even seen it." Mr. Lemieux dragged a stuffed chair over. I watched until the fourth when I had to go back up the hill for my own game. When I left it was Sox three, Tigers nothing, thanks to Ted's homer with two on his next time up. I don't remember anything about my own game.

The next week a red QUALITY RADIO SALES AND SERVICE – ALL WORK GUARANTEED truck appeared in front of our house and two men staggered up the steps with a huge carton. Of my friends I was the first to have a television. My father moved the furniture around so we could all watch it. We began having more company. Television changed our lives – only later did I come to realize how much.

ONE EVENING AFTER DINNER I wandered back to the lot. This older kid named Jerry Shields was sitting on the rock in back of home plate, smoking a cigarette. Jerry was on the basketball team and smart, an altar boy, even. My mother was friends with his mother. I took a seat next to him on the rock. "Want one?" he asked. He held up a pack of Luckies, big red circle with a black rim. I had never smoked before but I thought, why not? I'd seen lots of people smoke – my mother and father, Jim snuck them in the back yard all the time – so I knew how it was done.

He tapped the bottom of the pack. A new pack, they were in there tight. I pinched one out, which kind of messed up the tip. I put the other end in my mouth and Jerry handed over his matches. I tore one off and struck it, holding it against the tip, breathing deeply. Suddenly I coughed and the match went out. Jerry nodded. "Windy, ain't it?"

Another match. This time I kept my mouth closed and was able to get the thing going. I puffed a few times then took it out of my mouth. The paper stuck to my lips. "Great," I said, my mouth hot and dry, "really great. Thanks."

Jerry looked at me. "Not inhaling tonight?"

"I was getting to that."

I raised the cigarette to my mouth and sucked, letting the smoke collect in my mouth, then inhaled. Again I began to cough. The fit went on until my eyes were watering like crazy. So were Jerry's. He couldn't stop laughing. "It's a rotten habit, Paul." He ground his butt under his foot. "Take my advice, don't start." A few minutes later he lit up again, this time with special flair. I was in awe of Jerry. He knew how to do things – practical, manly things. Something had been on my mind for a while. "Jerry," I said, "mind if I ask you something?"

"Be my guest," he said.

I hesitated. Again I'd be showing my ignorance but this I needed to find out. "The word 'fuck.' I was wondering, any idea what it means?"

Jerry started to speak but held up. "I could tell you," he said, "but I won't."

"Why not?"

"It's a bad word. You don't say it around people, especially grownups."

"Come on. I won't let on you told me."

"No," he said, inhaling thoughtfully. "Besides, you'll find out soon enough."

He knew but wouldn't tell me? I'll find out? "At least tell me what it's about."

He blew a cloud my way. "Girls and babies. That's all I'll say."

Girls and babies. So that was it. But what did that mean?

Looking back, it was fitting. My first cigarette, same time as my first talk about sex, though I didn't know that's what it was. I had stumbled across an idea of great power that could have made me rich and famous. Too bad the advertising people beat me to it.

6. THROUGH A STAINED GLASS, DARKLY

I AM HEADING FOR THE DECK when the phone rings. "Professor Flynn?"

"Speaking."

"This is Susan Leone, Paul Bernard's assistant. Sorry to bother you but it's about Paul's papers. I had a call yesterday from a lawyer for Rudolph Latimer, you know, LTN. He said he was sending somebody to pick them up. Says they're Latimer's property and they want them back."

"That's ridiculous! How do they even know about them?"

"Beats me, but he said Paul worked on them when he was on Latimer's payroll so they belong to LTN."

"That's bullshit! ... Sorry."

"I'm familiar with the word. I told him to buzz off. He said ETVN would be hearing from him at a more appropriate level. The asshole! What a nerve!"

"We've never met, Susan, but I love you already."

"Paul always spoke well of you, too."

"We need to make sure those papers are safe. They're Paul's personal papers, they're nobody's business."

"And now they're yours. He dictated a document making you his literary executor."

"He never told me that."

"He never got around to signing it. I don't know if that matters, but I have the tape."

"How much stuff is there?"

There is a pause. "Sixteen boxes, would you believe."

"No wonder it was taking him so long. Where are they now?"

Another pause. "Professor Flynn, you owe me – you really owe me. My roommate and me, we moved them last night. They're in our spare room, in Cobble Hill, you know, in Brooklyn. All we have is a little car, one of those minis. Three trips, it took. I got to bed at two-thirty."

"Susan, you are something else."

"That call really shook me up. I didn't want Paul's stuff sitting here. No way Latimer or his asshole lawyer's going to get their hands on them, not if I have anything to say about it."

"You used to work for Latimer."

"Twenty-three years. I came over to ETVN with Paul. "

"What about ETVN? Will they claim them too?"

"They're cool. There's no love lost between them and Latimer, you can imagine."

"Well I owe you. What about dinner for you and your friend at a nice place, a very nice place?"

She laughs. "That'll do, for starters. No, seriously, I'm happy to do what I can for Paul's memory." She was quiet a moment. "I hear you're working with some writer. To me the important thing is give people a chance to know the real Paul. He was a peach."

"Whatever you do, hold onto those boxes. I'll talk to my lawyer. Larry Cahill, he's in Boston. He'll take care of everything."

"You want me to send them to you?"

"Hang onto them for now. I'll call you when I reach him."

"Okay. Nice to meet you finally, even if it's on the phone."

"Likewise, and count on that dinner. I can't believe you did all that."

"No problem. I work out at Golds, three, four times a week. I figure that was my weight training for the week."

"That lawyer better not mess with you."

"That's for damned sure."

I look at my watch. Cahill won't be in yet but Jonathan is waiting. I'll get him started, make the call mid-morning. We sit down over today's batch. Jonathan leads off. "There's that Christ-killer comment again. Gus, he's old enough to know better."

"He's just repeating what he's been told. That was the Church's position for centuries."

"I'm sorry but I have zero tolerance on this subject."

"I hear what you're saying, but a child is exposed to many things. You'll agree Paul was no anti-Semite, in fact for a long time he was a great friend of Israel."

"That's true. Well, at least he's made his first Jewish friend. I guess that's a start."

"You know, I identify with that Benny – he couldn't care less about sports. I felt the same at his age, though I always followed the Red Sox. But Paul's interest was personal, he wanted desperately to play the game."

"Doesn't sound like he was that good at it. His brother was the athlete. Siblings can be so different. My brother and I, you'd never know we were related."

"I had five, and four sisters. Remember Cabbage Patch Kids? No two alike."

* * * * * * *

IN FIFTH GRADE religious study remained the big deal, as we were preparing to become soldiers of Christ. I had decided to take Maurice as my confirmation name. But a second focus had emerged. This year's teacher, Sister Mary Francis, sensed that God wasn't the only one who'd hold us accountable for what we knew. Geography, my favorite, continued putting flesh on the dry bones of History (sorry, Gus – this was before I met you), every map, every new country a treasure. And what a relief to set the math tables aside and work on real-life problems. How

I would use any of this I had no clue, but it was dawning on me that learning for its own sake might be a good thing.

Well into April and sooty snow lingered in the corners of our schoolyard. One Monday morning we were summoned to the auditorium, the whole school. Assemblies were special occasions, for a movie when we'd sold enough raffle tickets for St. Teresa to meet its diocesan quota, for example. But this morning there was no screen, no projector. The principal, Sister Superior, Philomena of God, was on the stage along with Father Donnelly.

"Children, I have very sad news." She looked even grimmer than usual. "Your classmate Eugene Sullivan has died. He has drowned." A hush fell over the hall. Genie Sullivan! Impossible! "His body was found in the Woonosquatucket River this morning."

Genie was in my grade, one of my special friends. Just Saturday, a bunch of us went down to Merino to see if the field was getting dry enough for tryouts. Now I remembered... he was missing from class today, his name read off as absent.

Sister Philomena paused. "Father Donnelly will now lead us in the rosary, for the repose of Eugene's soul." Father Donnelly said you never know when your time is coming so be ready. I hoped Genie was ready, but who's to know? How can you be sure, yourself? We pulled out our rosaries... the five sorrowful mysteries, of course.

The funeral was Thursday. There was a closed coffin at the wake which, this being my first one, I learned was unusual. They said Genie's body was bloated from being in the river and smelled very bad. They put his picture on top of the casket in a gold frame. Next day, the church was packed. Many times I have heard the *Dies Irae* sung magnificently, but our young voices on that sad morning echo in my memory. Candles flickered, like Genie's life. The incense rose to greet his soul. It was hard to think we would never see our friend again, not until we met him in heaven. After Mass we went back to school. It was a long time before we laughed again.

These days much of the news was about Korea. At night we gathered around the television as John Cameron Swayze invited us to sit back, light up, join the Camel News Caravan and watch the war. I liked the attack planes best, Skyraiders, screaming over the tree-tops, dropping those tumbling canisters then you'd see this tremendous ball of flame and oily smoke on the ground. That was napalm, and it killed everything it touched. The color pictures in *Life* gave you an idea how hot it was. Once in a while you'd see a picture of some North Korean burned to a crisp. Good thing it wasn't anybody who mattered, Jim said, like an American. This bothered me, though I couldn't say exactly why.

I was older now and my scrapbook was a thing of the past. For my eleventh birthday I was given a camera, a Sears Tower Special I carried everywhere. Film was so expensive I mostly practiced, framing shots and capturing action, panning for cars to blur the background and give the impression of great speed. The pictures I did take, the best ones, I put in a photo album, sliding the corners into triangular pockets I glued to the coarse black paper. I'd write a caption, just like in the *Bulletin* but in white ink – what was happening, when it happened and so on. I had already staked out a windowless corner of our cellar for the darkroom my father promised to build me.

Television brought the war close. That remote part of the world was important, we were told, because there we were up against the evil of atheistic Communism. Russia had the A-bomb and we couldn't trust them not to use it. Then there were the Chinese hordes. To me all this was confusing and troubling. How could my country, my home, be attacked? How, if we were as powerful as everyone said and under God's special protection?

We practiced against the blinding flash that could come any moment. Without warning the school siren would sound, like a fire drill but an uninterrupted wail. We'd drop everything and dive under our desks, covering our heads with our hands. Not until the all-clear, a series of short blasts, would we crawl out again. Some kids thought it was a joke, a fun way to break up the day, but I knew better – I'd seen it on TV. If a little napalm did that to a person, what would an A-bomb do? Or an H-bomb if Russia ever got one of those! I showed my father ads for bomb shelters but he wasn't interested. That's what a basement's for, he said, and anyway, when your number's up, it's up.

Civil defense, spiritual defense. Extra prayers Pius XII himself wrote for the conversion of Russia. Strange as it seems, we came to love our enemy. The day our prayers were answered, Russia would be like us and nobody'd have to worry about being annihilated. A couple of nights a week our church had special Novenas to Our Lady of Fatima who possessed a special power for this perilous time. Let my father scoff, I knew my next breath could be my last.

Not everything was so serious, of course. During recess, roughhousing was the name of the game. Picture cards were big, too. From our knees we'd sail them up against the school wall, beat up cards only – you never saw one with crisp edges and corners, still smelling of pink gum. A few were off limits, Williams and DiMaggio and Musial. If only we'd known enough to keep them! Johnny Wyrostek, Eddie Waitkus, that kind of card you saw everywhere, also football cards which were inferior even when brand new.

We collected everything, traded everything. Superman and Batman were the most common comic books, The Heap the oddest. Pepsi caps with state outlines under the cork, Hoodsie lids with movie stars covered by peel-off wax paper (girls collected these) and foil from chewing gum you'd roll up, trying for the biggest ball. It was a sad day the grocery began selling aluminum wrap, debasing an important collecting art. Some improvement!

Horse chestnuts were the best. Dangled from a shoelace, five whacks for you, five for the opponent, then back and forth until one of them breaks. Legend has it, one time two nuts exploded at the same time but nobody I knew ever saw that happen. Squeeze the lemon, needless to say girls were excluded, and while there was no reason they couldn't compete in horse chestnuts or picture cards, they'd no sooner be seen doing that than a boy jump rope.

By this time a light fuzz had appeared on my upper lip and chin. I figured in a couple of years I'd be shaving. Jim started when he was twelve. I'd also developed little brown hairs on my chest like my father who had a lot of those and darker, also on his shoulders and back which he liked to show off when we went swimming at Scarborough or Olivo's near the my parents' friends' house in South County. One day I came home pretty scraped up, I don't recall why, and after taking a bath and drying off my mother put ointment on the bruises. I noticed her inspecting my chest, then she reached out and traced something with the back of her fingernails against my chest and stomach.

"Have you ever noticed those hairs of yours form a cross? It may be a sign," she said soberly. "I've heard for a boy this may be the sign of a vocation."

I grimaced. The nuns were always dropping hints and sometimes one of the priests would promote the idea, but however my life spun itself out, being a priest would be no part of it. I was surprised my mother even mentioned it, she had such a dim view of priests, most of them. Seeing my reaction, she smiled. "It would be below your potential, but there is the will of God to consider. There's always room for a good priest – if nothing else, you'd raise the average."

Jim was in his freshman year at La Salle and already a big shot. He started his first jayvee game at tackle and late in the game with the team way ahead the coach put him in at fullback to see what he could do. Needless to say, he scored, in fact he scored twice, one on a long run he said winded him so bad he barely made it to the end zone. Jim smoked a lot more than my parents knew, which I thought was dumb for an athlete. By mid-season they'd moved him up to the varsity and he even got his picture in the paper a couple of times. The Frosh Phenom, they were calling him, a shoo-in for All-State next year.

By now I had a better but still maddeningly approximate idea what "fuck" meant. You must realize, we had no opportunity to observe the female body and even pictures were hard to come by. One day I lined up with my nickel to inspect this picture book a couple of eighth graders were showing around, when Sister Philomena swooped in and confiscated the book and all the proceeds. Luckily she didn't notice who was in line exposing himself to the occasion of sin. Word was, there was a medical book in the downtown library I needed to take a look at. I'd already checked out our book about the natives I mentioned before, but those grass skirts covered what I was told were the most interesting parts.

My father was no help at all. He said I was still too young to understand. But my body was acting in ways I suspected had something to do with that mysterious activity called fuck. I told him about waking up with my thing hard which really worried me. I must have some disease nobody will talk about because it's so terrible. He said don't worry, all it means you need to take a leak. When I woke up in that condition I made a special point of visiting the bathroom but it didn't help. Finally somebody had pity on me and filled me in. Of all people, my brother.

"Why didn't you ask me before?" He sounded hurt. "I'd of told you."

Armed with this startling new information, I began looking at girls differently, especially Margaret. I started paying more attention to new features she was developing, though those baggy uniforms were no help. My sister was changing too, but no way I would think about her that way. Every month she and my mother disappeared in the bathroom, something about her not feeling well. Not long after, Jim showed me how to jerk off, and this exciting new activity opened expanses of pleasure and remorse. Now I understood what the priests were driving at when they said keep your hands out of your pockets. I never believed those stories about going blind, or acne which I had in spades anyway, but mortal sin and eternal damnation got your attention. If Lent lasted the whole year it still wouldn't be enough to atone for my decadence. I had this mental picture of the devil catching my guardian angel and throttling him.

Jim said I took everything too seriously. I didn't think so. The whole point of life is to make yourself a better person in the sight of God, which means doing what He commands and avoiding what he forbids, even when it seems impossible. Here, as with everything, I struggled while Jim just bopped along, going his own way.

OF COURSE I WAS AN ALTAR BOY. Maybe it was my looking like some kind of jayvee priest that pushed my mother over the edge with that vocation stuff. The job had a lot of variety. Low Mass, High Mass, Solemn High Mass, saints' days, feast days, different color altar cloths and vestments for weddings and funerals, Month's Mind, Novenas, Stations of the Cross. Weekday seven o'clock Mass was my favorite, compared to the Eight or on Sunday the Eleven. Getting out of bed in the dark was a struggle, then the twenty-minute walk to church, but I loved it. I usually arrived after old Mr. Drury who unlocked the doors and turned on the lights and heat. Mrs. Drury would be laying out the vestments in the sacristy, filling the cruets with water and wine and arranging flowers on the altar, picking out the wilted ones. The servers' changing room was used for storing equipment, heavy candleholders we dragged out for funerals and during Lent, the kneelers (*prie-Dieu* in the French Church) for weddings, extra racks of blue and red votive lights, plaster statue of St. Francis with the bird's head missing. I wondered how that happened, probably a plaster cat.

The Seven was quiet and peaceful. It attracted the faithful Irish and Italian ladies, bulky or frail in their black cloth coats, hats and tie-shoes, plus a handful of men going to work or getting home from the night shift, sometimes a policeman or fireman in uniform. That early in the day you felt especially close to God, because He knew what you went through to get there. When everything was ready, the priest and servers assembled at the sanctuary door then strode to the center of the altar. Briefly dropping to his right knee, the priest rose while we stayed on our knees for the prayers at the foot of the altar.

In Nomine Patris, et Filii, et Spiritus Sancti. Amen. That one you know.

Introibo ad altare Dei. I will go in to the altar of God.

Ad Deum Qui laetificat juventutem meam. To God, the joy of my youth.

I didn't understand much Latin until I studied it later, but comprehension wasn't the idea. What mattered was accurate, timely recitation. We were encouraged to use prayer cards, laminated five-by-sevens with prompts for the novice or the forgetful. Understood or not, the stately cadences resonating in the expanse of the church conjured up their own images, creating an overwhelming sense of piety and proportion.

The opening prayer didn't fit, for I was not having that joyful a time, in fact, my relationship with God was troubled. Later, as it became even more complex, those tender years looked good by comparison. In a world bent on its own destruction, the steadiness of the liturgy, the progression of the Church Year from birth through death to renewal, was a sanctuary of security and sanity. Sadly, even that would change.

Our movements were orchestrated, no room for mistake or invention. We practiced until we could do them in our sleep. Short of stumbling over the Latin, nothing infuriated Father Donnelly like being out of position or missing a step. As I said, Father Donnelly was a thunderstorm – one minute he'd explode, the next he was okay. With Father Maloney we were always on guard, he was so gloomy and hardly ever spoke to you. It got to the point you thought more about not messing up than what the Mass was supposed to be about. Sundays, after reading the gospel in Latin, the priest approached the pulpit for the sermon. If it was Father Donnelly, you could count on hearing about the new roof the church needed and how the price of heating oil is going up. Since those days I've encountered many ornate pulpits, even gold-plated constructions resembling space capsules in those early Japanese science fiction films, but St. Teresa's was simple, a plain wood lectern atop a short circular staircase.

Though my family were long-time parishioners our name didn't appear on the list sent around each year showing how much everybody gave. A few years earlier a box of envelopes arrived in the mail with our name on them for depositing in the Sunday collection. My mother sent the box back with a crisp letter. Of course my parents always put something in the basket, and I suppose they were generous enough, but to her it was nobody's business what we gave or anybody else either. That was between the person and God. It's a fine pastor, she maintained, who embarrasses the poor and encourages the rest to boast. If you want to report something for us, she said in her letter, just put down zero. Instead we were deleted.

The heart of Mass is the consecration. The priest washes his hands, says some more prayers, then the bells are rung. *Sanctus! Sanctus! Sanctus!* Now, the most solemn moment of all, changing bread and wine into the body and blood of Christ. Here I have to tell you about Father Maloney. He would roar through the Mass at breakneck speed, but when he reached this part he slowed to a crawl, almost a stop. His hands shook as he held the host. *Hic...est...enim ...Corpus ...meum.* For this is my Body.

I do not exaggerate when I say it took him at least a minute to get through those five words. Watching him start and stop, start and stop, I wondered if he was overcome by the importance of the moment. At last he would genuflect, straighten, and lift the host over his head. Then once again he hunched over, inclining the chalice toward his face and speaking into it. *Hic est enim Calix Sanguinis mei, novi et aeterni testamenti, mysterium fidei, qui pro vobis et pro multis effundetur in remissionem peccatorum.* For this is the Chalice of my Blood of the new and eternal covenant, the mystery of faith which shall be shed for you and for many unto the forgiveness of sins. Two full minutes. Father Maloney had been a chaplain in Europe and people said he got shell-shocked which I figured explained this strange and troubling behavior. When he got through this part he was fine and we raced ahead to the prayers for the dead and the living and what you were asking God for. Then it was the *Pater Noster,* the Our Father, and we were ready for communion. As you're walking beside the priest you have a chance to check out where your friends are sitting, who's lining up to receive, and so on.

This is as good a time as any to mention it. It's one thing to get a hard-on when you were serving, usually there's time for it to pass, but there were two deadly exceptions. When you were moving the Mass book from one side of the altar to the other – for at least fifteen seconds, I timed it once, you were out in the open with both hands holding the heavy book. Anybody with an eye in their head could see something was happening under your cassock that wasn't on the program.

Then while assisting with communion. Here, the groin area of all but the very shortest boys was several inches above the altar rail. Picture it. There you are, standing right in front of a person with this... thing practically in their face. For me, a glimpse of Margaret Foley was all it took, but most of the time it just happened. It had a mind of its own, I tell you. I had no idea what anybody else thought because speaking about such things was off-limits. But it was mortifying. You knew everybody was laughing at you or thinking you were a sex fiend. You can tell me the hole in your tooth feels bigger than it really is, but believe me, some things are plenty big enough for everybody to see.

For funerals the altar was draped in black and the priest wore black vestments. You used lots of incense, the server igniting the charcoal in the bottom of the censer then holding it open as the priest sprinkled what looked like birdseed on the glowing coals, from which would arise this beautiful, pungent smoke. The soul of the faithful departed flies up to heaven. Eugene.

One funeral I remember vividly was for a soldier killed just before Ike stopped the Korean War. After putting everything away, I changed out of my cassock and surplice then remembered I'd left something in the sacristy. I was surprised to see Father Maloney there – he was supposed to be on his way to the cemetery. He had strewn his vestments across a chair and was just sitting, staring straight ahead. He must have thought he was alone, for here was this tough, grizzled man, a retired Colonel, the priest who struck terror into the hearts of altar boys, the person you couldn't talk to without him biting your head off, and he was crying. Crying! His eyes were red and tears were streaming down his cheeks. He was smoking and his hand shook so badly he could hardly lift the cigarette to his mouth. When he noticed me, he looked surprised. Then his face softened. I had stumbled upon a part of him nobody knew. Instead of exploding he gave me this odd smile. and he sighed.

"War is a bad business, Paul," he said. "A foul, evil business."

I was shocked. He had been in the Army. How could he say that? He wet his lips and took a long drag on his cigarette, then he said something I will never forget.

"How sad God must be, watching His children kill each other."

7. LOVES LOST

CAHILL SAYS WE NEED TO GET HOLD of that paper Paul didn't sign and the dictation tape. He'll call a lawyer friend in New York. Two days later he phones me to say it's tucked away in their conference room – Carter, Delfino & Samuels LLP on Park Avenue South, a few blocks up from Madison Square Park. Steve Samuels is an expert in something I thought was a joke the first time I heard it, "intellectual property." Possession is nine-tenths of the law – I don't need pricy lawyers telling me that.

Every day after we wrap up, Jonathan heads for Bar Harbor to clear his head and pick up the *Times*. My three-day home delivery apparently isn't good enough. Tough. Today he throws the paper on my desk, open to the editorial page. "Look at this!"

PAUL BERNARD'S DEATH is the lead editorial. "The *Times* believes the Army must investigate promptly... open process... important questions needing answers." It goes on, "the congressional investigation called for yesterday by Senator Clinton and Representative Nadler is an appropriate way to put pressure on the Army for a prompt resolution." It ends by urging the media to hang together on this or they'll hang separately.

"How about that!" Jonathan said. "A little heat from Congress won't hurt."

"It'll go nowhere if the Republicans don't go along and they won't."

Nearly a week Jonathan has been here but I still don't know what his plan is for completing his work. I tell him about the sixteen cartons but not how they got to where they are. Or the Latimer flap. Time enough for that.

"I just got a message on my cell," he tells me. "My editor wants to see me Monday."

"How come?"

"I'm not sure. They said there's more interest in my article after what happened to Paul. I'll bet they're thinking of expanding it. I've got some ideas about bringing in the investigation. I fly out Sunday, be back late Monday."

* * * * * * *

PASSION AND COMMITMENT ISN'T ALWAYS ENOUGH. I was cut from the team. Only on my second try the following year did I earn the prized gray flannels with "St. Teresa" in green across the chest, number nine on my back.

Even in that collection of less than stellar athletes I did not excel. Oh, I started a lot of games, and at my best position too, second base, but puny hitting and an erratic glove did me in. My father called it quits after the season opener. I went oh-for-four and booted a grounder to let in the winning run. As I left the field in tears he put his arm around my shoulder. By nature, he said, some people (Jim) are better than others (me) at certain things (everything that matters). Said he'd see me at home, he had to get back to the shop. Right. The last thing I needed was advice on how to fail. Why couldn't he just say I needed more seasoning? Or wasn't that infield in lousy shape? The businessman through and through – clear-eyed, results-driven, no wishful thinking for him... or for me.

That summer I went to camp for the first time, CYO camp on a lake in the far west part of the state. The past few summers had been a nervous time, with people worried you could catch polio swimming or if you got chilled. One kid a year behind me nearly died of it and was in a wheelchair, they said for the rest of his life. But now they'd discovered the Salk vaccine. At first I objected. Why can't I hang around like I always do, work on my batting and fielding, read? But being benched the last two games – for a fifth-grader, if you can believe it – gave me perspective.

Never before had I really looked at the horizon, or appreciated that clouds did more than fill the gaps between buildings. Canoes and snakes and birds, lying on a float, all the food you could eat, campfires, stories and singing, kids from all over, and the first portable radio I'd ever seen. Sports, too, softball, three-on-three basketball, running and swimming races, ping-pong. Winning wasn't the point, which was a good thing when it came to swimming which I was not that good at. Everybody wore the same red and white camp T-shirt, no ribbons for coming in first, every day you changed sides. I even went on the optional all-day hike to a lake cars couldn't drive to, packing lunch and swim trunks in my knapsack. It was beginning to dawn on me, maybe I wasn't such a terrible athlete after all, that baseball had blinded me to simpler, more attainable pleasures.

I began that final year at St. Teresa's part King of the Hill, part Ivan the Terrible. I was bored out of my mind, too long in one place. From the first day I made a pain of myself, fooling around, making loud, often rude comments. My classmates were astonished. Though my work was exemplary, in Deportment I was a grave disappointment. Finally my parents, both of them, were summoned for a conference on the topic: "What Is Wrong With Paul?" After the meeting I noticed my father looking at me differently. Perhaps I wasn't the marshmallow he had taken me for. I thoroughly enjoyed his confusion.

Our eighth grade room had more desks than pupils and Sister Georgina positioned me in the last desk, two empty rows away from the others. The front desk belonged to Stevie Burns, the dumbest and meanest kid in the school. It was a peculiar tribute to be lumped with him, though I didn't like him or his friends and refused their overtures. Stevie was one of the few kids at St. Teresa's from the Project, a public housing sprawl off Manton Avenue which after its opening deteriorated into what my mother called the worst slum in the city. Buildings in disrepair, broken-down cars, littered sidewalks, poorly clad kids running wild, police there all the time, a blight on the neighborhood. She forbade us to have anything to do with the people who lived there. Our standing in the community required that we avoid bad families. Unemployment, welfare, delinquency, no man in the house or if a man, not the husband – those were the indicators of bad. A Project address was an automatic.

My advancing years brought on a family crisis. It was assumed that St. Teresa's boys would attend La Salle Academy, the French Christian Brothers School where Jim went, and the girls, St. Xavier's, where Catherine was in her first year. At this tender age we were hardly prepared for atheistic teachers, not to mention the perils of a co-ed institution. My friends and I weren't so much worried about the impact on our immortal souls as being known for attending Mt. Pleasant, the huge public school a half mile from our house. Only dolts, troublemakers or those too poor to afford La Salle attended Mt. Pleasant, is how we saw it. Project kids went there, the ones who went anywhere, that is.

The nuns pushed La Salle hard, particularly its science program. Everybody said our country needed engineers to stay strong and I thought that might be the thing for me, designing bridges, televisions, even planes. I demolished La Salle's entrance exam and a personal letter from the principal, Rev. Bro. S. Jerome, congratulated me on my admission. My mother begged to differ. To her, the Brothers offered an inferior education and until recently, I'd displayed no need for their vaunted disciplinary skills. She had a different plan.

My mother was a graduate of Classical High in downtown Providence which, despite being public, attracted especially capable students – many from well-off or accomplished families – skilled in music, drama, the arts. Their sports teams were terrible except for those where individual excellence counted, like tennis. Classical was on a par with Moses Brown, the private prep school on the East Side, and miles ahead of Mt. Pleasant, Central, Hope and the other public schools. It was co-ed, which offered the intriguing prospect of getting to know girls, perhaps well enough to ask them out, possibly even (a radical idea) as friends. My mother saw Classical as her last chance to mold me into an educated, cultured person.

Though my athletic career was kaput, I was reluctant to break entirely from that milieu. Plus, if I attended Classical I would need to make all new friends and take a bus to school. Benny was going to Classical, a plus, but not enough of one. In February, to my mother's everlasting disappointment, I mailed my acceptance to La Salle along with my father's check for $125, half the first year's tuition. By now I had settled down and was in an advanced math group working with concepts in Algebra and Geometry.

ONE APRIL AFTERNOON, trudging up my street I looked ahead... police cars! In front of our house! I started to run. As I neared I saw a policeman leading Jim down the steps, another one talking to my father. They were putting Jim in the police car! He flashed me a grin and winked, then the door shut and off he went. My father had already disappeared into the house. My mother met me at the door. Her eyes were red and watery. "It's Jim. He... he may be in trouble," she said in a trembly voice, "they're taking him in for questioning."

"But why? I asked, terrified, "what'd he do?"

My father appeared at the door. "Marty's on his way to the station."

"Who's Marty?" I asked.

"Our lawyer." I didn't even know we had a lawyer. My father looked down at me. "Paul, I'm going to tell you something you do not repeat. You understand me? Do not repeat what I tell you."

I nodded. He paused, searching for words. "Some girl is saying Jim... forced himself on her. Him and two boys. Says they had their way with her."

"Well, did they?" I asked, unthinkingly.

"Of course not!" His face got red. "It's a damned lie but the little tramp's parents went to the cops. I'm on my way downtown, make sure they don't do anything stupid." As he turned to leave he wagged his finger at me. "Not a word!"

My mother squeezed his hand and they walked together to the car. When she returned I couldn't contain myself. "This girl, who is she?" I followed her inside. She reached in a drawer for one of my father's Chesterfields. I hadn't seen her smoke for a while, she'd been trying to quit. "Someone from the Project." She snapped the match. "No one we would know."

"Who were the others?"

"Billy Moore, for one. No surprise there," she drew the smoke in hungrily, "and somebody named DiMaio. He supposedly goes to Mt. Pleasant." Billy Moore was on the football team with Jim. They were always driving around in Billy's red convertible. His father was a car dealer and had his picture in a big ad in the Sunday paper. She shook her head, "I have never trusted that Billy Moore, not from the day I laid eyes on him." Her eyes began filling with tears.

I was puzzled. "Why are you crying? Dad said there's nothing to worry about."

"I don't know, Paul... I just don't know. Even if it's not true, it's so shameful, police coming to our home, being treated like common criminals." She reached for her purse. "I need to go see my mother." She wiped her eyes and ground out the cigarette.

I threw my books on my bed then came back downstairs. The telephone cord led under my sister's door. I banged on it and pushed it open. Catherine was sitting on her bed, her legs folded underneath her. "You little turd!" she yelled at me, covering the mouthpiece. "Can't you see I'm on the phone!"

"Until I opened the door, I couldn't."

"Well, you can now! Get lost! And close the door!"

At sixes and sevens I roamed around the house, thought of starting my homework. While I was inspecting the fridge, Catherine appeared. "Sorry I yelled, but next time, knock."

"I did knock," I replied.

"You're supposed to wait."

She had me there. "What is going on?" I asked.

She flopped down at the kitchen table. "Her name is Gloria Russo. She's a sophomore at Mt. Pleasant. A friend of mine has a friend that knows her. She's from the Project."

"Dad said she's a tramp."

"Dad is so stupid! Jim this! Jim that!" She tossed her head angrily. "Well, this time big brother has really gone and done it!"

"Done what? What do you mean?"

"Come on, do I have to spell everything out for you?"

I flushed. "Jim, he'd never do anything like that. He wouldn't, would he?"

"He is a boy, isn't he?" She leaned forward on her elbows. "Look. Everybody knows about him and that Billy Moore, what they do. The wonder is somebody had the nerve to say something. Maybe because it was three of them, I don't know."

"Jeez."

"Supposedly they were out cruising and that creep DiMaio knows this girl so they pick her up and supposedly there's a lot of beer in the car and they go to Merino and park and, well, after a while they did it to her. All of them."

I was floored. This couldn't be true.

"I guess she was really messed up, her clothes were torn and everything and she smelled of beer so her mother said where have you been and she told her everything."

"Dad said not to say anything."

Catherine sneered. "There's not a person in the whole city doesn't know already." She shook her head morosely. "Makes you feel great, doesn't it?"

That hardly described it. What would become of Jim? Of our family?

It was late when my father returned with Jim in tow. I was upstairs when the car pulled in. I raced down, my mother and Catherine already in the kitchen. "Well, that's that!" my father announced. "There is no problem, absolutely nothing to worry about. The lying little slut!" Jim was standing there, absolutely still, white in the face, staring at his shoes. My father poured a drink from the whiskey bottle they kept in the dining room but rarely used. He took a big swallow, then another.

"She and that DiMaio! Ha! They know each other, you bet! They been going together! So the boys pick her up at her job and they drink a little beer and leave them off at the Project. Big deal!"

He looked sharply at Jim who still hadn't moved a muscle. "What happened between her and that DiMaio, that is no concern of ours!" He took another swallow. "Only thing, the police are taking it much too serious. It's a lie and they damn well know it!" I looked into my father's eyes. Between rounds – bloodied but defiant. Zale or Graziano or Sugar Ray from the TV fights. Quick on his feet and powerful, that was my dad.

My mother finally spoke up. "Well, what next?"

My father took a cigarette from his shirt pocket. She motioned at him and he shook another out of the pack. "They'll have to finish the investigation but Marty's on top of it."

"Our name won't be in the papers, will it?" she asked.

He shook his head. "They're all juveniles." My father glared at Jim then shook his head really hard, as if trying to clear it. "Aaggh! It's so ridiculous! That kind of girl is trouble, the way they dress, the big come-on, dragging good kids down to their level. A little Project tramp, that's all she is!" I glanced at Catherine who was staring at the floor, her mouth a thin hard line. Suddenly my father reached over and punched Jim on the shoulder. "Cheer up, Jimbo! It's not your fault! Everything'll turn out okay!"

That seemed to loosen Jim up. He looked pleadingly at my mother. "I didn't do it, ma. Honest, I didn't do nothin.'"

Never had I heard that tone of voice. It was obvious my father had talked to him in no uncertain terms before the ranks slammed shut. My mother stood up and gave Jim a kiss on his cheek. "You're a good boy, son. Your father's right, everything will be fine." She swept her hand around the kitchen. "Now, to bed! All of you! Tomorrow's another day."

During recess next day one of the Project kids, a seventh grader I barely knew, came up to me wearing this big grin. "What's this I hear, somebody's brother's in big trouble?"

"What're you talking about?" I replied warily.

"Don't shit me, Bernard – him and his friends knocked up that girl."

"You're lying! Jim didn't do anything like that!"

"Oh, no?" He looked at me belligerently. "You people, your big houses and fancy cars. Too good for the rest of us til we got something you want, like a little pussy!"

"Hey! Cut that out!" I stepped up next to him, shoving my face in his. We glared at each other, then he turned.

"Aw, why bother," he said over his shoulder as he walked away. "You're not worth the trouble. The cops'll take care of it."

During the day I noticed kids in little groups glancing at me. At my desk I thought of all those afternoons I'd spent at Merino, at practice, how at times my eyes would be drawn to the bushes behind first base and the trees behind the bushes, the deep, cool woods and the lane where kids and girls went and did things to each other, terrible things, wonderful things. Then I'd spit in the pocket of my glove and bang my fist. Hum boy hum boy hum it in no stick let 'im hit it no stick no problem. No problem, Jimbo. No problem at all.

That night we sat down to dinner, the five of us. It was eerie. Nobody mentioned what was on all our minds. After supper, I wandered into Catherine's room where she was lying on the floor doing homework and listening to the radio. *Secret Love.* Doris Day. I kind of shrugged and looked hapless, my way of asking what did she think about things.

"Some kids were talking about Jim today," she said. "I almost got into a fight. Can you believe it, me, a fight?"

"Me too," I replied. She turned the radio off and told me to shut the door.

"Jim's in more trouble than mom and dad are letting on." Her face became serious. "They took him out of school today. He was in a lineup..."

"At the police station? But nobody identified him, right?"

"...and two cops were here and went through his room. You know that red checked jacket of his, they took it with them. I'm worried, Paul. Dad was down there all day with the lawyer."

I hesitated. "They wouldn't... he won't have to go to jail, will he?" It hurt even to ask.

She took a deep breath. "My friend told me her family is really mad. They said somebody's going to pay for this."

The rest of that week was truly miserable. Each day more people were in the know. A couple of my friends tried to cheer me up, saying I must be a real stud too, how about showing them some tricks, that kind of thing, but that only made it worse. On Wednesday a three-line item appeared in the *Journal* – several boys questioned about a sexual assault on a fifteen-year old girl. No names, but there it was, in black and white.

A week went by. The next Friday night my father called us all together in the living room. Jim wasn't there, he hadn't been around much since this started. "I want you children to know what is going on." My father still had on his best suit which he wore every day to make a good impression at the police station. "Our lawyer met with the District Attorney. They were trying to make a case to charge Jim and the others with rape..." My sister gasped, "...but they didn't have any proof, besides, that kind of girl, anybody can have their way with her, they know that for a fact, so we made a deal, we would plead guilty to assault. They gave Jim a suspended sentence. The others, too."

"Suspended sentence?" Catherine asked. "What does that mean?"

"It means that's the end of it but he has to check in with a probation officer and he'd damn well better stay out of trouble."

"And thank God our name won't be in the papers!" my mother exclaimed. "Jim has been a foolish, foolish boy, but he needs our love and support," she looked at Catherine and me, "and I want you to give it to him. Generously. He is paying for his mistake."

"That's for sure," my father added, somberly.

"But he's not going to jail," I interjected.

My father shook his head. "It's La Salle. They're... they might expel him. Marty knows the principal but if that doesn't work," he spread his hands, "all that hard work, the chance to make a name for himself, gone. Down the drain." My father looked across the table. "Fiona, this would be an excellent time for some of those prayers you're so good at."

As it turned out, Jim wasn't expelled or suspended but what they did was devastating. They took away his extracurricular privileges. No football. No All-State. No college scholarship. Our lawyer went before the alumni association which gives the school a lot of money, Billy Moore's father weighed in too, but the decision stuck. According to the principal, the boys were fortunate. Their attitudes must be reformed, otherwise this sordid affair will have no value for anyone. Soon after, I heard my parents arguing, the worst fight I ever remember. Nothing was broken, it was the passion in their voices. "Over my dead body!" my mother screamed. "Rather you rip out my heart!" Dad wanted Jim to transfer to Mt. Pleasant for his last year so he could play football, something might come of it.

"This is the boy's life, Julien! Not some game! You drop him in that snake pit and mark my words, he'll not come out alive!"

"Three years of those damned Brothers. Did that keep him from doing what he did?"

"If it weren't for the Brothers where would he be now! No, Julien, I cannot,

I *will not* give my consent!"

So it was decided, Jim would finish La Salle. He was quiet around the house, no swaggering or cracking jokes, but beneath the sullen exterior he was really hurting. He'd lost what he loved best and had no way to get it back. Everybody knew what happened and the talk would start again when the varsity took the field in the fall minus their star fullback. Already resigned to living in Jim's shadow, now it wasn't his success I'd have to contend with, but his shame.

One night a few weeks later my father came home early, more depressed than usual. He could hardly speak. What's wrong, my mother kept asking. Finally he spat it out. "The jewelry account... half our business. They canceled it today."

"No! How could they!"

"Traficante... their President. I got a letter... said they couldn't honorably do business with us any more."

"Those hypocrites! It makes no sense."

My father sighed. "It makes perfect sense. Marty checked it out. That girl Jim was involved with. You have any idea who the mother is?"

My mother stared at him blankly.

"She's a Rosati. Big Anthony, from Federal Hill. She may be a black sheep but she's family." His eyes bored into hers. "They're paying us back."

ON A BRIGHT SUNNY JUNE DAY I graduated from St.Teresa's. I was called up in front of the packed church. Top student award, English prize, Math prize, it would have been embarrassing, but despite being an exceptional student, I had a lot of friends. Everybody knew my heart was in the right place. Many of my classmates, even a couple of the girls, even Margaret, signed my autograph book, adding funny drawings and sayings. We had a party at home, cake and ice cream, just the five of us, King had wandered off which he sometimes did. Catherine was being especially nice, she and Jim went in on a portable radio for me. Midway through the doorbell rang and I got up. Nobody there but there was a box on the step. Stuck under the green and orange ribbons, an envelope with my name. I picked the box up, it wasn't that heavy and shaking it, I went inside. Something bumped around inside.

"Another present!" my mother exclaimed. "Why didn't you ask them in?"

"Nobody was there."

"Well, don't keep us waiting, open it!" Catherine said. I ran my finger under the envelope flap. There was no card, just a folded-up piece of paper, ragged along one edge like it had been ripped from a notebook. Puzzled, I unfolded it and read.

On his graduation day, for Paul the brother of James the rapist.
Memento Mori.

James the rapist! My heart leapt into my throat. Everybody crowded around, staring at the paper. I looked at my parents. My mother's face had turned white. "Julien!" she said in this fierce voice I'd never heard before. "Take it outside!"

"But..."

"Take it outside! NOW!"

I followed my father through the door. He placed the box on the cement in front of our garage door and stripped away the paper. With his pocket knife he slit the wrapping tape. *"Sacre Bleu!"* he said softly.

I couldn't see. He was in the way. I peered around him... He tried to hold me back, then his arm relaxed. "Go ahead, Paul. Look, but make it quick."

Blood! There was blood everywhere! I moved closer...staring up at me was King's head! KING'S HEAD!!!

"OH, NO! NO! NO! NO!"

I slumped to the ground, sobbing uncontrollably. That's all I remember. When I came around, my mother was bending over me, tears streaming down her face, whispering, over and over, "Memento mori...memento mori. Remember, man, you too must die."

8. NEON INTERLUDE

JONATHAN LEAVES TOMORROW. He seems uptight but we plow ahead and manage to put in a good day. At one point he looks up from his reading, shaking his head. "Can you believe somebody doing that to a little kid?" he says.

"Paul took it very hard, one time he told me the story. At least he learned something from it though perhaps not enough. National purpose, historical necessity, the glory of God, whatever you call it, Jonathan, it is always a living, breathing person on the receiving end. There is no such thing as a crowd of victims, people die one by one. Just ask the families. The big shots of the world never learn."

"You were a military man, how can you talk that way?"

I smile. "That is precisely why I talk that way. Just like that priest, that chaplain. For me, war is the absolute last resort. Odd, isn't it, that's the old Catholic teaching. Did I mention, Akiko was Buddhist – she lived through the firebombing. Being on a lucky ship I was spared the misery she saw but it had its effect on me."

We put in a good day and morning, then he excused himself to get ready. I insisted on driving him so we piled into the Volvo and proceeded up the road toward Bar Harbor Airport which is actually in Trenton, nowhere near Bar Harbor. A half hour later I watch the little jet scream down the runway and lift off, heading for New York and the offices of *The New Yorker* Magazine.

* * * * * * *

FOR A LONG TIME I'D WAKEN with a start. Eventually the nightmares faded but to this day the shock has not, that someone would do that to a little animal. Evil. More real to me than Adam's sin ever was. My parents said they'd get me another dog but the memory of my friend demanded that I grieve. It troubled me too, that I blacked out. Only for a moment but it scared me to think there was a page in my life of which I knew nothing. I vowed never again to disappear to myself, and aside from one slip it didn't happen again until years later. Oddly, the bright spot that summer, Jim went out of his way to be considerate. Though I desperately wanted to, I couldn't bring myself to blame him. It was somebody else, one mean, twisted person. Would I have returned the favor in kind? Good question.

The police said they could do nothing and that's exactly what they did. Oh, they took the box away, and they returned it a few days later. The policeman who came to our door said it was the mob but the note was no help and nobody was talking.

Omerta. I buried King's head beside the doghouse, putting a wooden cross I painted white on his grave.

Again I went to CYO Camp, this time two full weeks. The country saved me, plus learning I would meet up with many camp friends at La Salle.

Things were bad at home. My father had to lay off more people, even Lorraine – no great loss there, my mother sniffed. Every day the tension between them asserted itself in new ways. Grownups were so unpredictable. Who would have thought my mother would be the one to rally round Jim? They grew closer as my father withdrew to spend all his time trying to find new business, he and Uncle Antoine even driving to Wilmington, Delaware, to follow up a lead. All I could figure, her first-born was a part of her spirited nature she couldn't deny. As it turned out what saved us was, of all things, the Russians.

I was now reading the newspaper front to back and had a good idea what was going on in the world. The Supreme Court had ordered Negroes admitted to regular schools and people expected trouble in the fall. I read about the McCarthy hearings. In our parish McCarthy was a saint and I had to admit he had a point when he said why should Americans join an organization that was out to destroy us? But what I saw on TV was a shock – the slippery look, the exaggerations. This raised an important question for me. If you find a person is lying about one thing, what else might he be lying about? How can you know he's telling the truth about anything? I still don't have a good answer for that.

Dad and Uncle Antoine had been getting up at dawn and driving to the General Electric plant north of Boston, returning late then turning right around next day to save money on a hotel. But after months of worry, a contract came through to sell G.E. tools and machinery for making jet engines. In August they began setting up equipment to produce the parts to make the engines to power the planes to protect our country. That summer we would have no vacation, rooted to the spot as my father tried to salvage his business, but one night soon after they got word of the contract, he burst into the house, grinning from ear to ear.

"Ti-Paul! Would you like to see New York?"

New York!

He flopped down on the sofa. It was great to see him happy again. "When this new work starts I won't have a minute," he stretched his legs and clasped his hands behind his head, "and we never celebrated your graduation right, did we?" My mother walked into the room, smiling. She knew. "Mrs. Lamontagne got the reservations today. Two rooms! One for us," he winked at my mother, "and one for you kids. A week from Wednesday we drive down then come back Sunday night."

The day before our trip, my father came home early. He had this sad look on his face. "What a shame, and just before our big trip," he said, shaking his head. "It's the car. No chance in hell it'll make it there and back."

My heart sank. Our trip was off. He sat down, elbows on the kitchen table, chin in his hands. There'd been talk about engine work, also the differential, whose function I grasped only vaguely, was said to be slipping. But this was no reason to call off our trip!

"The train! We can take the train!"

He shook his head, "Can't afford it, not if the car needs an overhaul."

As I sulked, King's face flashed in front of me. Tears weren't far away. My father pursed his lips. "But maybe there is a way," he said, standing. "Let's go outside, *ti-Paul,* maybe the fresh air will give us an idea." I followed him out and... what was this! In our driveway, a car! A bright red brand new car! As my father stood by, arms folded, beaming, I ran my hand over the fender. Never had I touched anything so smooth. "Not bad, eh?"

"Can I get in?"

"Sure! Why not? He opened the door and immediately I was engulfed in this wonderful aroma. I patted the seat cushion and slid behind the wheel. So many dials and knobs! I looked around. Lots more room in back, too. The interior was gray and red. We always had a black car, up til now. Red! This was unbelievable! "Move over, *ti-Paul,* let's go for a spin. We need to break it in, right?"

He backed down the driveway and we drove to the turnaround, circled, then paraded down the street. I'd never seen my father drive so slow. Neighbors waved and he leaned out the window and waved back. Suddenly I realized. He wasn't shifting! "It's an automatic!"

"Damn right! Nothing but the best for Julien Bernard and his family!"

He rolled up his window. "Close yours," he ordered. I looked at him, puzzled – it was a hot day. "Go ahead." As I cranked the handle he reached down and turned a knob. All of a sudden there was this WHOOSH! and a blast of hot air hit my face. "Give it a minute."

It started to feel cooler... I put my hand against the vent. It was freezing! He grinned.

A few minutes later we were turning onto Fruit Hill Avenue, crossing into North Providence, heading toward the real country. "Can I steer?" Sitting on his lap I had often steered on the two-lane roads when there wasn't much traffic.

"No way," he laughed, "not in this car. Not til you get your license."

"But if I can't use the car, how'll I get my license?" I was planning on my learner's permit the day I turned fifteen.

"We'll keep the Plymouth, that's how. Anyway a shift is better for learning. One of these days Catherine'll want to learn too, though girls aren't that interested in cars." He leaned back and stretched his arms, caressing the steering wheel. "The worm has turned, *ti-Paul.* Yes indeed, the worm has turned."

THE NEXT DAY WAS FULL OF EXCITEMENT. Crossing into New York, I soon caught my first glimpse of Manhattan, tall thin silhouettes stenciled in the haze and heat. Jim was full of his what's-the-big-deal routine. Mr. Expert had been here on a school trip. We paid a toll and were on what the signs called FDR Drive. I noticed this steam rising from building roofs. "Cooling towers," my father explained, "for air conditioning."

We drove along a narrow, shaded street, crossing broader streets and swiftly moving traffic. First Avenue, then Second, then Third... I got the picture. When we turned onto Fifth, I craned my neck and looked up. You couldn't see the tops of the buildings, you could barely see the sky between them. Stone and metal walls dwarfed *la famille Bernard's* tiny red raft as it plunged down the canyons. After more rights and lefts we pulled off the street and wheeled under this canopy with JEFFERSON HOTEL on it.

"Made it!" My father turned to us with a big grin.

A man in a red and gold uniform opened my father's door. "Welcome to the Jefferson," he said, tipping his hat, one of those tall shiny hats you see at fancy parties, pictures of them, that is. On this hot day he looked ridiculous but I figured somebody must be impressed. Another red and gold man helped my mother out. My father handed over the car keys and a dollar bill, motioning toward the trunk.

"Thank you, sir." The doorman's partner was placing our suitcases on a little two-sided wagon. We entered the gold and red lobby. The clerks behind the counter wore gold and red striped shirts and ties, even the women wore ties. "The Bernard party," my father announced in a loud voice, "we have a reservation."

One of the men began flipping through some cards, then he picked one out. "From Providence? Two rooms, four nights."

"That's right," my father nodded, "at your best commercial traveler rate."

The man looked down at Catherine and me, Jim was already cruising the lobby. He frowned. "Sir, I'm afraid that rate is available for one room only."

My father had his elbows on the counter, leaning toward the man. "We were promised that rate for both rooms."

"I'm sorry, sir, hotel policy is one room only at the special rate. There must have been some mistake."

"There is no mistake," my father interrupted. "I am President of a large company and you guaranteed my secretary that rate for both rooms!" The back of his neck was getting red. "If you will not honor your commitment we'll have to take our business somewhere else!"

Catherine and I looked at each other. Such a fine hotel, how could we find another as good? By now our luggage was right beside us in the little cart. It belonged here, we belonged here. My mother was tugging at his arm. He turned toward her. "Fiona," he said loudly, "if these people can't keep their word, it is not a place we want to stay."

The clerk was getting frazzled. "A moment, sir, I have to speak with the manager."

"You do that," my father said as the clerk disappeared through a door. He looked at us. "Don't worry, *mes petits choux!* If this doesn't work we'll stay somewhere else."

My mother was shaking her head. "Julien! You said everything's booked! You said we were lucky to get this reservation!"

"Relax, Fiona. You got to play the angles."

"Angles? You mean we really don't have that rate?"

"Shhh!" he put his finger to his lips. The other clerks were silently flipping through their papers and cards.

"Well, I never!" She stomped her foot and strode across the lobby, flopping down in a chair and crossing her legs.

My father winked. "Keep your eyes open, *mes petits,* you'll learn something."

A couple of minutes later the clerk returned. "This is extraordinary. We always note special rates on the guest card." He held up our card. "You see, it says one room only. But this one time we will make an exception, possibly whoever took the reservation made an error." The clerk slid a form in front of my father. "Two rooms, twenty-seven dollars per night for each," he added sourly, "instead of our standard rate of thirty-five."

My father smiled. "This is good. This is very good."

Catherine and I looked at each other with relief, though, I thought to myself, what I just saw looked an awful lot like cheating.

Our room had two beds and a cot (guess who got the cot). We had to promise Catherine not to look. Fluffy white towels, too, little bars of soap in gold and red paper, a shower separate from the tub and not just on a hose like at home. In the corner was a television and a phone. Our parents' room was next to ours with a door in between. While they unpacked, Catherine and I began calling in orders from the room service menu, holding down the button. My mother rushed in all upset, then she laughed. If you hadn't already figured it out, this was my first time in a hotel.

The plan was, everybody could pick something they especially wanted to do unless it was too expensive, and everybody else would go along with no complaining. No surprise, my mother chose a play, *Cat on a Hot Tin Roof,* which was interesting, especially all the yelling. Catherine went for the Rockettes at Radio City Music Hall. Jim picked Yankee Stadium, Yankees vs. White Sox. Mickey Mantle belted home runs his first two times up. My father said he'd enjoy everything since he was paying for it all.

I would have said the ball game myself, but for once I acted cagey and let Jim go first. Mine was the cheapest, all it cost was a couple of souvenirs. The United Nations might seem an odd choice, but I'd done a term paper on it and wanted to check it out. There wasn't much going on, the General Assembly wasn't in session and the Security Council had no great crisis going, but I was happy just walking around. We went on a guided tour and I saw where everything happened when it did happen. I came away with a wooden stand with flags of the countries. The African delegates were fascinating to see, some in colorful robes, some with faces so dark they had a bluish sheen. I heard native languages but also English with a British accent and a French one as well. These people seemed different from the Negroes I'd seen at home. None lived in my neighborhood, not counting the Project where there were a few, and none attended our church. I'd seen some downtown and on the bus though I'd never spoken to one personally. What I would say to a Negro? What he would say to me?

Our last night, my mother and father went to a double feature, leaving us on our honor and with permission to order dessert from room service, two dollars each, tops. About eight-thirty we were watching TV when Jim punched me on the shoulder, saying follow him to our parents' room. "Let's me and you go out," he whispered, "some things I want to show you."

Great idea! Our after-dinner family strolls had been fantastic, like being inside a light bulb. "But how can we? We're supposed to stay here."

Jim gave me his sideways look. "What they don't know won't hurt them. Anyway, we'll be back in plenty of time."

"What about Catherine? What about her?"

"Leave little sister to me." He led the way back to our room. Catherine looked up. She knew we were hatching something. "Me and Paul are going out," he announced blandly, "you know, get some air, that kind of thing."

"But the parents said stay here! If you go I'm coming!"

"Well, you can't! This is men's night out."

"Oh, yeah?" Her eyes narrowed. "I'll tell on you!"

Jim smiled. "Listen, Catherine," he said gently, "this means a lot to me and Paul. Be a good kid and shut up. I'll make it worth your while."

"How?"

He shot a glance at me. "You can have our desserts, both of them. So how about it?"

That stopped her but not for long. "I want money, too," she said, scowling.

Jim laughed. "Okay. A dollar."

"THREE dollars!"

"Two."

"Three! Or I tell!"

"Okay, okay," he grunted. "Three."

Five minutes later the revolving front door of the Jefferson Hotel spun us out onto the sidewalk. Jim lit a cigarette. "This place me and my friends found, you got to see it."

"What kind of place?"

"You'll see soon enough." Striding away he yelled back at me. "C'mon! Let's go!"

A couple of paces behind, I was one with the steamy night. Millions of people on the street, so alive, so different from home. Department stores, clothing stores, jewelry stores, books, toys, restaurants, delis with sandwiches and drinks, signs in Benny's Yiddish. Every few blocks we came upon a stand with fruit and vegetables stacked in wooden trays right out on the sidewalk. "Getting close," Jim announced after a lot more walking.

As we turned the next corner this odd feeling came over me that I'd been in this very place before. "Where are we?" I asked, puzzled.

"Times Square. There's the ball you see on TV."

Of course! It was daytime, the signs, light in motion, people everywhere. I was pleased to see Times Square, but sensed there was more to the plan. Jim had slowed down, looking for something. "It's around here, I'm sure," he said. We waited for a light to change then crossed, dodging a couple of cars that didn't even slow down. He turned to me. "Now, listen, leave everything to me. I'll do the talking, they ask you anything, tell them you're eighteen but you forgot your I.D. Got that? You forgot your I.D."

I nodded, not knowing what was going on. We approached a brightly lit theater building with a lot of light bulbs winking on and off. A man in a dark suit wearing a movie-type gangster hat was standing in front, then there was this sign –

☞ LIVE! ✰ NUDE DANCERS! ✰ LIVE! ☜

Hanging back, I noticed a large glass case on the wall beside the entrance with pictures of women without anything on. Jim went up to the man like he'd known him his whole life. The man made a gesture and Jim reached in his back pocket. The man squinted at his wallet, handed it back. Jim pointed at me and the man motioned me over. "Let's get a look at you, sonny, I need to see your I.D."

"I... I forgot it. I left it in the room."

He scowled. "You're not trying to pull a fast one, are you?"

I swallowed hard. "I'm eighteen," I croaked, "I'm small for my age."

The man shook his head. "No way, sonny. I let you in, I lose my job."

Jim jumped in. "Thing is, he smokes a lot. He used to be bigger than me! Two packs a day! Since he was eight!"

"That kid's eighteen," he rasped, "I'm the man in the moon!"

"But I tell you..."

"Beat it!" The man stuck out his thumb like an umpire. "This here's a high-class establishment. We don't want no trouble."

"But..."

"Scram!"

We skulked back to the street corner. "Damn!" Jim frowned and looked around. We were right in front of an all-night restaurant, a Needix. "Listen," he said, pressing a couple of bills into my hand, "wait in there, get an ice cream or a hamburger or something. I'll be back in half an hour, hour at the most. Okay?"

I nodded. What choice did I have?

"Sure you'll be all right?" he said, edging away.

"No problem." I felt disappointed. I went into the Needix and ordered two hot dogs and an orange drink. I spotted a newspaper which after a minute I grabbed and began reading. The *New York Post*. It was smaller than the *Journal* and the pages went up and down. I read the sports then started at the front and worked through the whole thing. Still hungry, I ordered a sundae to make up for the dessert he talked me out of, fudge sauce and nuts, whipped cream and a cherry. Another twenty minutes, still no Jim. I decided to leave. Walking slowly toward the theater I observed the man who had turned me away.

"Best show in town!" he was yelling, "No cover! No minimum!" Whatever that meant. But nobody was going in and not that many stopped, either. I took a deep breath and went up to him. "You again! You don' understand English or what? I tol' you to get lost!"

"I'm waiting for my brother," I replied.

"Your brother." The man's face softened. "Okay, wait, but don' give me no trouble."

I walked up to the pictures of the naked ladies which close up I saw weren't totally naked, there were these little stars on their chests and a piece of glittery cloth between their legs. Each of them had autographed her picture – Candy and Monique and Bambi and maybe eight others. The penmanship was excellent. I could hear music from inside.

The man lit a cigarette. He offered me one. "No thanks," I replied.

"I didn't think so." Lighting up, he nodded at the pictures. "So whaddya think? Pretty good, huh? Like what you see?"

"Oh, sure," I replied. I didn't want to hurt his feelings, but he was right, too.

"Here we are," he sighed, "me and you, you're the only person in this whole friggin town wants to see my show and I can't let you in. Ain't that rich!" A couple of minutes passed and so did a lot more people who didn't stop. The man looked at me and shook his head. "Bummer," he said, "I don' believe this shit." Suddenly he looked left and right, then put his hand on my shoulder. "Here. C'mre." He steered me toward the heavy dark curtain at the doorway. "Go on, take a look. But be quick." He pulled the curtain back.

The room was dark except for dim lights and a small stage. This woman was up there, and far as I could tell, she had nothing on except that little cloth and a belt with bills sticking out of it and high heel shoes. She was wrapping herself around this pole like you see in fire stations, moving in time with the music though I wouldn't call what she was doing dancing.

"That there's Cheri," the man whispered hoarsely, "she is really hot!"

How can she be hot, I wondered, with no clothes on to speak of. Now she was down on the floor, crawling toward the edge of the stage and heads that were looking up at her, then the music stopped and she stood and picked up this little pile of clothes and threw a shirt over her shoulders. People started to leave. Somebody was coming up the aisle, it looked a lot like Jim. It was Jim! I backed out and the curtain flopped shut.

Jim emerged, slitty-eyed in the glare. ""Say, Paul, whadd're you doing here?"

"I ran out of money."

"Too bad they wouldn't let you in," he said with a scowl.

I looked at the doorman. He winked.

"Great show," Jim said, walking away, "those babes are stacked but, boy, they rob you blind! Price of a couple of beers you could buy a whole case at home!" He pulled out a pack of cigarettes and fished around inside. "Damn! My last one." He balled the pack in his fist and heaved it into the street. "Y'know, Paul, something you just don't unnerstan,"" he said, lighting his smoke, "you just don't unnerstan' how easy you have it."

"Me easy! What are you talking about?"

"I mean compared to me."

I couldn't believe this! How many beers *did* he have!

"Having to live up to Dad. Push, push, push, all the time push, that is no picnic... I mean, it wasn't. I dunno what'll happen to me now." He sighed. "You, you just bop along, mindin' your own business. Lots of times I just wished I was you."

I stared straight ahead. I had no idea he felt that way. Jim's eyes were moist. "I been a shit to you sometimes. Sorry, Paul," he put his hand on my shoulder, "sorry." He crushed the cigarette under his heel. Fumbling around he pulled out a small crumpled wad. "Next time I'll fix you up with a real fake I.D like mine. I am beat," he hiccupped, "let's get a cab."

We were back with time to spare. Catherine was on the floor watching TV, her room service tray littered with dirty dishes. As soon as his head hit the pillow Jim was sawing wood. Catherine and I stayed up with an old movie but my parents came home and turned it off. Do I need to tell you, that night on the cot I had some very enjoyable dreams.

9. BRAVE NEW WORLD

WHEN I PICK JONATHAN UP AT THE AIRPORT the sun has just set. In the car he says barely a word. Now facing each other across our work table, his face is grim. "I don't believe those people. They want to take the project away from me."

"You can't be serious! Why would they do that?"

"They said Paul's death makes it such a big story they want somebody with more experience to handle it. You've heard of Seymour Hersh?"

"Of course." Pulitzer Prize winner, the man who broke My Lai.

"They want to give it to him, the whole thing. I'd write up my notes, cash their check and hand everything over to the big shot. Probably has a book contract already."

"And you've done all this work."

"Tell me about it."

"So how did you leave it?"

"For once I held my ground. It was my idea, after all, I brought it to them. Long story short, they're going to split it up. I keep the bio. Somebody else'll do the death, the investigation – Hersh, I suppose. We're still at three parts but I can live with that." He slumped in his chair. "It's been a day and a half. Got anything stronger than Chardonnay?"

"Jack Daniels Black?"

"Perfect."

I start to get up. "No, let me," he says.

"I'll have the usual."

After what seems like an hour he returns. "Sorry," he says, handing me my drink. "I'm quietly going crazy. You know I appreciate everything you're doing."

"Of course. Right now this is the most important thing in my life."

"That makes two of us." We touch glasses. He rolls his in his hands, rattling the cubes, then downs it in one gulp. "Not to be maudlin, but the last few years things haven't gone so well. This assignment is really important – it could get me going again."

"I had a suspicion," I say. I think of leaving it at that, but the hell with it, I think. "You're not as good a liar as you pretend to be, Jonathan."

He flushes. "What do you mean, liar?"

"For an old guy I'm pretty good on the Internet and I checked you out yesterday. Only thing came back the last five years was that *Playboy* article and a couple of things for *Ladies Home Journal*."

He lowered his eyes. "Did it say I got fired from the *New York Post*?"

"I didn't see that."

"Thank God for small favors. Yeah, I had a run-in with them. A story about corrupt judges. They said their attorneys wouldn't let them run it which I did not believe, not for a minute. I had them dead to rights and sources willing to go on the record." He is silent, still avoiding my eyes. Finally he looks at me. "If you want to call it quits I could understand. Sorry. I should've just kept my mouth shut."

"Jonathan," I put my hand on his, "I like your passion, but let's not have it get in the way. If this story is half as big as we think, your ambition will take care of itself."

"I appreciate that," he says, looking directly at me, "very much."

He goes inside and returns with a refill. We sit in silence. "By the way," I say, "I enjoyed your *Playboy* article. And I'm not much of a basketball fan."

He smiles, the first today. "That makes me feel better. You read it online?"

"While I was at it I looked through the rest of the magazine, too. I figured, why not? Got me to thinking, maybe I'm not as over the hill as I thought."

"Gus, you're younger than I am."

I laugh. "Now that makes *me* feel better!"

"Did you do any work today?"

"The New York trip, some other stuff. The father had good instincts. That trip was just the right thing."

"And our man is showing signs of life."

"Oh, Paul was no ice cube. Thing is, he learned early how to say no, even to himself. Very unusual for a young person, that amount of self-control. Even for a Catholic."

* * * * * * *

THE STRANGENESS WAS OVERWHELMING. If I belonged anywhere in the world, this, my first high school classroom, was not it. A kid sauntered in as if he'd been here his whole life. When another brushed past, I took a deep breath and stepped in. Taking a seat in the rear, I looked around. A few familiar faces from camp. Everybody looked confident and intelligent. At the front a Brother sat at his desk on a heavy wooden platform, towering above us, reading. Occasionally he looked up and stared out at us. I wondered how tall he was. When the clock hit eight-thirty, he stood. He wasn't that tall.

"Mister," he said, pointing to a kid near the door, "will you shut the door."

He had a long, bony face with furrows each side of his mouth and deeply recessed eyes. My impression was a hound dog needing a shave, a weary hound at that, which I thought odd, this being only the first day. He wore a priest's cassock, at the neck a starched white bib split in two. "I am Brother A. Robert," he began in a deep, husky voice, "and, gentlemen, as of today, you are La Salle boys. Three hundred forty-eight of you, the Class of 1959. God willing, that same number will be here four years from now." He put a hand to his chin, then asked nobody in particular, "What is a La Salle boy?"

No response. It didn't sound like a question, anyway.

A slight smile. "Come, gentlemen, that's an easy one, but all right, let's think about it. Consider our motto, that of the French Christian Brothers of Jean Baptiste de La Salle. *Religio, Mores, Cultura.* Religion, Morals, Culture. That's it, in a nutshell." He leaned forward. "We expect your time here will strengthen your love of Our Lord and Saviour, and mold you into educated young men, but let me warn you, we have very high standards..."

Suddenly the door opened. A tall boy with a shock of red hair above a pink face tiptoed toward an empty seat near me. Brother Robert called out, "What's the matter, mister? Lost? Or just late?" He nodded at the clock.

"Sorry," the boy mumbled.

"Perhaps you would favor us by introducing yourself." He looked down his nose at the miserable creature. "In other words, mister, what is your name?"

"Michael Grady." The boy was very thin.

"We'll let it go this time, Mr. Grady, but be aware, tardiness is noted on your record and reported to the Principal." Brother Robert peered down at us. "Mister Grady happens to be the first one to mess up, no doubt there'll be others. Take a seat, Mister Grady."

The boy sat down next to me and let out a long breath.

Brother Robert closed his eyes. "As I was saying, La Salle has the highest standards of any school in this city, and if that is not to your liking, I invite you to leave right now. Don't waste our time and your parents' money." He pointed at the door. "You think I'm joking? Go! Cross the street to Mt. Pleasant or Central, because, gentlemen," he banged his fist in his hand, "here we teach the qualities – that – make – you – *different!* That distinguish you from the boys in those schools. Oh, they'll gain skills, but those young men will miss the opportunity to deepen their faith, to form themselves into young Catholic gentlemen. So get it into your thick skulls, you are fortunate indeed to be here. We expect you to work hard and follow the rules, because if you don't," he smiled, "if you don't, we have ways of encouraging you."

Jim.

Now the Brother was standing. "I am your home room teacher and your teacher of English. Class begins promptly at eight-thirty," he said, glaring at Michael Grady and reaching for a thick, gray-covered book. "This is your textbook. Loring, *Survey of English Literature.* You may find a used copy in the bookstore, but they go fast. Cover your Loring because you will use it a great deal. By tomorrow I will expect you to have read these pages..." he walked to the blackboard and wrote, Loring, pgs 12 - 24. "Tonight's assignment is a commentary and several excerpts from *Beowulf.*" Brother Robert looked around the room. "How many of you have read *Beowulf?*"

No hands went up, certainly not mine. "How many of you have *heard* of *Beowulf?*"

One hand, tentatively, at the front of the room. "Yes!" Brother Robert motioned a pudgy, dark-haired boy to his feet. "We stand for recitations, mister."

"It's this story about a wolf," the boy said in a reedy voice, "at least I'm pretty sure..."

Brother Robert closed his eyes. "What an interesting answer! It certainly sounds like a story about a wolf." His voice was soothing, encouraging. "Now, mister, what is your name?"

"Andrew McCaffrey."

The boy stood basking in his success, unaware everyone was sizing him up, the first volunteer. Brother Robert ran his finger down a list of names. "McCaffrey... McCaffrey... Andrew... Ah, here you are! Well, Mr. McCaffrey, your answer is ingenious, though I must say it's not correct. In fact, you haven't the faintest idea what you're talking about!"

The boy's face darkened. He began to collapse into his seat.

"No, no, Mr. McCaffrey, stand until you are told to sit!" He leveled his chalk at the boy as he shrank before our eyes. "Mr. McCaffrey, I single you out only because you had the temerity to say what was no doubt running through many of your classmates' minds."

Brother Robert sniffed. "The fact is, I would be astonished if you or any of your classmates had even heard of *Beowulf*, let alone read it. Some schools don't get to it until junior year and many not at all. Let this be a lesson. Keep up with your assignments and you won't have to guess. And for goodness sake, if you don't know an answer, say so! If I'd called on you, Mr. McCaffrey, that would have been different, but why volunteer if you're just guessing? It's a waste of everybody's time.

"One more thing. I will assume that all of you can read and write. Your skills will improve, we will work on the essay, the short story and so on, but I assume you bring the basics to this class. You may be seated, Mr. McCaffrey."

Brother Robert opened the text. "Most of our readings you'll be seeing for the first time. Now then, by tomorrow you will understand that *Beowolf* is the only surviving Old English heroic epic, the greatest poetic achievement of Anglo-Saxon times. Curiously, the poem is set in Denmark and England is not mentioned at all. Who can tell us what other English masterpiece is set in Denmark?"

This time nobody ventured an answer.

The Brother smiled. "This year we will pay a visit to Hamlet, Prince of Denmark. Remember the name. Shakespeare, William Shakespeare." He wrote it on the board. "You'll be hearing a lot of him. Now, as to epic poetry – first, the definition."

Nearing nine-twenty, Brother Robert shut the text and came around his desk, leaning against it with his elbows. "As we finish today, gentlemen, a piece of friendly advice. La Salle is like nothing you've ever seen before. You are responsible for assignments, you may be tested without warning and I expect order and attention at all times. In return, I will treat you as the young Christian gentlemen you are supposed to be. Is that clear?"

We nodded.

"After a short break I will depart, and another teacher will take my place. At nine-thirty Brother Adalbert will begin your instruction in Christian Doctrine.

Now, I have for each of you a copy of your daily schedule." He picked up a stack of papers and fanned them out to be passed back. "Questions?"

A hand went up. "Brother Robert?"

"On your feet, Mister Cos-tan-ti-no." This boy had spoken earlier. I still hadn't opened my mouth.

"What's the deal with lunch?"

Brother Robert coughed. "A useful question, though rather inelegantly put. *Mens sana in corpore sano,* as it were. Now, lunch period..." he consulted the schedule, "...lunch is twelve-thirty to one-twenty in the cafeteria. Bring your own or buy one there. Don't believe everything you hear, the food is quite good. Now, if you will excuse me."

Brother Robert stepped down from his platform and circled the desk, opening a door beside the blackboard. He disappeared inside, closing the door behind him. I looked at Michael Grady. We shrugged. Suddenly the lid blew off, everyone talking, getting up and stretching. A couple of minutes later the door opened and Brother Robert emerged. The class settled momentarily as he gathered an armful of books and papers and rushed from the room, his cassock flapping behind.

The day passed quickly. Brother Francis, a wispy-haired youngish man with horn-rimmed glasses. At ten-thirty, Brother F. George for Latin. He was old and hunched over, which fit, Latin being a dead language. Next, a burly lay teacher, Mr. Mello, who coached hockey and owned that liquor store. Civics – American Government From Colonial Times. Algebra and Biology, also study period which this first day we used for buying books. P.E. twice a week. Never had I walked around with so much money, twenty dollars, but when the bookstore was finished with me there was hardly enough left for a coke.

Under our burden of books we struggled up the hill that seemed much steeper than a few hours before. It had been a pulverizing experience. Even I, the scholar, was pensive and gloomy. Worse comes to worst, I thought, I can always work in my father's shop.

"First day and I'm already flunking Algebra," Cosmo grumbled, "I didn't understand a thing." Cosmo was in the second Science class which was for kids who weren't that well-prepared or smart. Naturally I was in the first class, 1D. The ideas were familiar from eighth grade advanced math, though more complex. "You'll help me, Paul," Cosmo said, "right?"

"If I can."

"Come on, you know more than the teachers!"

"Commercial math's a pain," observed Omer, "and how do they expect us to learn all the parts of those plants? Anyway, who cares?" A large book slid out of his stack and landed in the street. "What'd I say?" He held up a brand new *Fundamentals of Biology,* a corner of its cover crushed. "I'm jinxed."

That night I searched for clues that my fear of failing might be misplaced. Algebra and Latin put me at ease somewhat, also Christian Doctrine and its question-answer format. Everybody said how tough La Salle would be... might they be wrong? I hadn't volunteered once nor was I called on. I was thinking maybe I can go the whole four years and not say a word.

After the worrisome start, things improved. My first quizzes were excellent and the white cardboards I scotch-taped stamens and pestles onto earned me A's. Grasshoppers, crayfish and, it was rumored, a cat, were on our victims list. The volume of work was huge and more complex than anything I'd ever seen but I made it through the first month. As I mentioned, La Salle was a huge sports school, their teams always written up in the paper, but I gave sports a pass. P.E. was the way to go.

"You can't study all the time," my mother remarked one night. "Do something with photography, you like cameras so much."

She was a mind reader. I had already scoped out the camera club, which had a darkroom and an enlarger, but film cost extra. My puny allowance wouldn't handle it. A camera with a fast shutter and a good lens, even a used one like the Leica I coveted at Ritz Camera downtown, was beyond reach. After a lot of thought I decided to apply for a job at our neighborhood grocery. DiLorenzo's Market hired kids for after school and Saturdays. Frank Pezzulo, a 1D classmate and nephew of the owners, worked there. My father was all for it, but my mother dissented.

"This year is for getting your feet on the ground and making a good start. A job can wait til summer."

"Then that's it for the camera club," I moped.

"Perhaps we can help," she said. "Possibly your allowance could be raised, if you helped more around here, that is." Great. More windows, more raking, who knows what else. But if that was the price, I would pay it and more. How much more I didn't let on.

And that is how I learned about f-stops, lighting, depth of field, developing, enlarging, cropping, dodging, printing and the rest. Our advisor was the Chemistry teacher, Brother C. George, a short, humorous man with permanently stained fingers. For me, the best part of the darkroom was being able to control the whole process, start to finish, camera to final print – adjusting, fixing mistakes, experimenting. Many club members were also on the school newspaper, the *Maroon and White,* which would get my film paid for. But I decided to wait until I was sure my good start wasn't a fluke.

Jim and I didn't cross paths much. In the corridors he was civil. At home he helped me some to learn the ropes, though not that much since he was on the business track and just squeaking by. He was talking about enrolling in a junior college with a football team – if he did well maybe have a chance for a scholarship to a regular college. Game days, he paced back and forth, smoking right in the house, his enormous energy denied the release the speed and violence of football had afforded. He and Billy Moore were barred from practices, too. After supper, out the door he'd bolt.

I forgot to mention, Jim was going steady. "A good girl and a proper family," was my mother's concession to the reality that Sheila Rourke was wearing her first-born's class ring on a chain around her neck. Sheila was a junior at St. X and a friend of Catherine's. Miss Cupid herself, she had introduced them. "Boy, do you owe me," Catherine often reminded Jim. "Be nice or I'll tell her what you're really like!" Jim was always at Sheila's house in Cranston, next town over. Too proud or lazy to take the bus, he talked my father into letting him borrow the Plymouth.

My first football came in early October. I don't remember the game but the event stands out clearly. The night before, a storm had ended a miserable stretch of heat and humidity that left me drenched on reaching school. On game night Omer and Angelo and I set out on our usual route but blessedly, no books. We left the crowd converging on the City Stadium half-shell, lit up for Mt. Pleasant's first home game, then down the hill to our game. Our game. Doesn't take long to become attached.

Under the floodlights Alumni Field's turf was a brilliant emerald, and beyond, a sliver of moon floated in the sky. I'd seen a few night games at Braves Field but this was much better. We sat in the rooting section, far from the action due to the track ringing the field in front of the grandstand. Our team was in home uniforms, white shirts with maroon numerals and matching pants. Players waiting to go in warmed up, stretching, throwing the ball around. The subs huddled on the bench in their hooded ponchos.

I can still see the ball lofted into the dark sky then falling back through the lights, though this could have been any number of games, I'm not sure. What I do remember is the girls parading back and forth in front of the grandstand, chatting, moving on, reappearing a few minutes later. These so-called fans showed no interest in the game. Why bother going, I would have said not long ago, but now I knew why they were there and from my safe distance I felt their presence keenly.

Near the end of the half, Angelo yelled he was hungry. He was always hungry. So we threaded our way down the steps to the refreshments beneath the stands. Needing to take a leak I told Omer to get me something to drink. Now, Omer's parents were as big on coffee as my mother was on tea. Without fail Mrs. Arsenault offered me a cup whenever I was at their house. I always refused, the bitter taste made me gag, so here is wise guy Omer pushing a coffee at me. He said that evened up what he owed me, but at a dime a cup it didn't even come close. "I didn't know how you wanted it, so I put milk and sugar in," he smirked.

I couldn't hold the cup, it was so hot, then I figured it out, easing up with one hand then the other, like throwing it back and forth, but carefully. The moment the warmth surged through me I became a lifelong coffee addict. At the beginning it was the milk and sugar that did it, though they went by the boards long ago. Angelo was stuffing his second of three hot dogs into his face.

"Eggplant casserole tonight," he said, surrounding a bite. Enough said.

The three of us began walking, more like swaggering back to our section. We fell in behind a bunch of girls who kept looking into the stands and giggling. I followed their eyes up to several boys on their feet, whistling, one of them shouting something I couldn't hear over the band that was assembling for the half-time show, fooling around. Coffee in hand, feeling rather sophisticated I started up the steps when... oh my God! Margaret Foley! She was with some tall kid and they were... they were holding hands! And the way she was hanging onto him, it wasn't just for balance. He had to be a senior, a junior at least. My heart sank.

Just the other day I had been thinking, I wonder how old Margaret's doing, haven't seen her since graduation, she's probably having a hard time of it, being new to St. X. Alas, here was my answer, a six-foot two, seventeen-year-old answer. The distance between us closed. "Hello, Paul," she said, smiling at me. Jeez, she was wearing lipstick! I mumbled something and kind of hunched my shoulders as we passed. And suddenly I realized, I was ashamed of my friends! Mustard-covered Angelo, triangular jughandled Omer. The second half I spent sneaking glances around but mercifully didn't spot her again.

As the fall deepened my confidence built. Surprisingly, with all the science, Civics emerged as my favorite subject. I enjoyed seeing how everything fit together, our country and its government, how fortunate Americans are with our boundless resources and God's special friendship. But with this bounty comes responsibility, I learned, to bring democracy to others, show them also how to become free and prosperous. Like my Catholic Faith, it cried out to be shared. I was humbled when I realized, with the enormous number of people in the world what were the odds of my being born a Catholic and an American, both? Clearly, Someone was looking out for me. Looking back, I see this as an early sign of the dilemma that would come to haunt me – patriotism versus religion. More on that later.

I had many new friends and reveled in the give and take, the competition, the humor. Omer and Angelo and I were still close, but from the camera club I was becoming friendly with Norm McDermott, two years ahead of me. He was also on the school paper and pressing me to join. Later, I told him, next year for sure. Another new friend was Terry Grimes, a Negro kid from East Providence. He had a tough bus ride and long hours, playing jayvee football and running indoor track. Terry was the first Negro I'd ever known. He was quiet, but had this sly sense of humor that takes a while to figure out then it hits you in the face, it's so hilarious.

Jerome Barnes lived near Terry and was in Omer's business class. Jerome had a sort of sour disposition and I heard him complain the only reason people were friends with Terry was because he was an athlete. He'd say things like why am I at La Salle, maybe next year I won't be back. Another Negro played varsity football but as far as I knew, they were the only three in the school. A number of other students were dark-skinned – Walt Gomes, for one, his parents were from the Cape Verde Islands. In fact, by the end of summer many Italian friends like Angelo were pretty dark, themselves.

At first I didn't understand why Jerome felt uneasy, but as the year went along I heard kids using the word nigger, kids I wouldn't have expected it of. Terry never spoke of this but he was writing a term paper on school integration in the south. His family was originally from Mississippi or if you want to be accurate about it, he chided me once, Africa.

Terry had a quick mind but with all his time at practice and on the bus, he was failing Algebra, so he asked me to help. It made me proud to see my friend on the field, a hint of what it would have been with Jim. Terry knew I was Jim Bernard's brother and the first time it came up, he went out of his way to say what a terrific athlete Jim was, too bad what the school did to him. Actually, everybody had only good things to say about Jim. The cloud I expected to follow me around was simply not there. I was free to make my own tracks. When second quarter results were posted in January, I was in the top three of the freshman class, along with a boy from Immaculate Conception and one from St. Pius, both in the classical class, 1A. We hadn't met though I knew them by sight.

Athletic pretension a thing of the past, I enjoyed P.E. basketball, and our hockey on the pond at Merino. A couple of times friends and I drove to a lake where you chased a puck forever across the ice, the cold snapping at your face. I wasn't a great skater, my ankles were weak – good thing I had that stick to lean on – but those were wonderful days. High school hockey was in Rhode Island Auditorium, a ramshackle building on North Main Street near the Anderson Little store where my father bought me my first suit that I outgrew before hardly wearing. I could go on about the swift, slashing play, my headlong insane Canadian ancestors, how fog blanketed the ice on warm spring evenings, the fact that later I would adopt the New York Rangers, my only treasonous act as a Boston sports fan – but that's not why I mention hockey here. As the season progressed we kept winning and there was talk of the New Englands which pitted the six state champions against each other. When we downed hated rival Burrillville in the state finals, tickets went on sale for the playoffs.

"We better get our tickets," Omer said, walking to school.

I looked away. "I'm not sure I'm going."

"Not going! How could you not go!"

"You go ahead. I'll get one later if I change my mind."

"If you say so," he replied, kicking a rock.

Here's why I wasn't sure. Margaret Foley was out of the picture but there was this other girl, Joan McGrath, also a St. X freshman. She'd been in my St. Teresa's class though I didn't spend much time on her, I'd been so obsessed with Margaret. I asked Catherine about Joan, actually several times. Finally she confronted me. "If you're so interested talk to her yourself!"

A few days later I again approached Catherine. "Let's say, a person wanted to take another person out. How would I... I mean, how would a person go about it?" Brilliant.

Catherine had been on a few dates, nobody that impressive but that was her problem. She'd been reading *Seventeen* since she was twelve. "It's not that hard, stupid!" she said, helpful as always. "Just call her up and ask her!"

"I'm terrible on the phone. And you're on it so much I never get a chance."

"Look. Talk to her after Mass. I think she goes to the Nine with her family. Just tell her you want to see her for a minute."

Well, I already knew she went to the Nine. That's why I had switched from the Seven except when I was serving, which I had pretty much retired from. I set my strategy. What I needed was a way to lure Joan away from her family and if the ploy happened to work, something to say. I had no idea if she was interested in hockey. If she wasn't, that'd be that. I mean, why would anybody go out with a person if it wasn't to something she wanted to do in the first place? Would a movie be better, I wondered, but I had no idea what kind of movies she liked. No, it had to be the game. The New Englands would be impressive and I could snow her with my vast knowledge of strategy, the players, and so on.

Sunday next, I took up a position behind a pillar midway up the right aisle, watching Joan and her family walk in the front door and seat themselves in the first row. The whole Mass I was totally distracted. During the recessional hymn, I elbowed my way through my row and to the rear of the church. Quickly down the steps, then a U-turn along the sidewalk and up to the front where the McGraths would exit. I positioned myself a few feet from the door. People were starting to file out. Finally, Mrs. McGrath, a stout woman in a bright blue topcoat emerged, followed by Joan's little sister and... there she was!

Joan was shorter than me and had brown hair, the kind that hangs straight down, this day under a yellow hat. It was nearly Easter. She had freckles around her nose though not as many as Margaret. I took a giant breath. "Joan." I cleared my throat and said it again, louder. "Joan!"

She turned around. "Why, Paul, hello." She was beside her father. "You know Paul Bernard, daddy?"

"Sure thing. You're at La Salle, aren't you? How're the Brothers treating you? I'm class of twenty-nine, myself." He was tall and heavy-set. I wondered how two large people like them could be the parents of a normal-sized person like Joan.

"Good, sir, very good." I stared at Joan. "I need to talk to you a minute," I said rapidly under my breath. Her family began to sidle away. I motioned her away from the crowd. "Joan," I began, "what I want to know... how would you like to go to a hockey game Friday? With me, that is?"

She smiled. "Sure! That'd be fun!"

She said YES! "I haven't got around to getting my license yet," I went on, cleverly avoiding the fact I wasn't old enough anyway, "so we'd have to take the bus... if you don't mind, that is."

"What time?"

Time? Time! I was so sure she'd turn me down, I never thought what time. Rapidly I calculated backward. Faceoff at seven-thirty, an hour for the bus... "How about six-thirty?"

"Okay. You know where I live?"

"Sure." Actually I didn't, not exactly, I'd look it up in the phone book. I kicked myself later – why'd I have to say that, look so eager.

"Well, 'bye, then" she said with a big smile, "see you Friday."

"Friday. Yes. Friday."

I retraced my steps, turned at the corner and crossed in front of the church, gazing up at the stained glass window above the entrance, at the turquoise tower with the gold cross. "Thank you, God," I said. "Thank you!"

Heading up Manton Avenue, step assured, bearing suave, I paused in front of Dunning's Drug Store, staring at my reflection when it dawned on me. Three hours with a girl, five, with the bus... the game would sort of take care of itself, but what about the ride there? And back? How do I fill up all that time? How do I say good-night? By the time I reached home I was a nervous wreck. What had I gotten myself into?

After a week of torment Friday night arrived, cool and rainy. I brushed my teeth and changed into my best shirt and sweater. My parents had been very good about it, Catherine too, considering. Only Jim gave me a hard time. "Don't do anything I wouldn't do," he said, whacking me on the back, "'course that doesn't rule out much, but seriously, if you need advice about anything let me know."

Yeah, sure. You'd be the last one I'd ask.

The McGraths lived on the bottom floor of a two-story tenement. As I said, it never bothered me that Omer or Angelo or my other friends lived in tenements, but standing there in my wet raincoat, I was disappointed someone as pretty as Joan lived in a place like this. I climbed the steps and rang the bell. She appeared at the door and seeing my umbrella, turned around and propped hers inside the door. "No need for two of these," she laughed.

As we walked to the bus stop, waiting for the bus, we talked about her school, my school, people we knew. She didn't know the first thing about hockey, which didn't surprise me, most girls don't, so I filled her in. What to look for, the rules and so on. The time flew. It wasn't that awkward at all. During the game I snuck glances across at her and it certainly looked like she was having a good time. We went for coffee and a doughnut and ran into a bunch of her classmates but she didn't seem at all embarrassed. The game was excellent. La Salle jumped out to a two-goal lead over the Connecticut champ, Hamden, but they roared back and it was tied four-four at the end of regulation. After a couple of narrow escapes, Tom Mainelli, our captain, broke in alone and lofted the puck over the Hamden goalie. The crowd went wild! Could I get away with a hug around the shoulder, I wondered, with everybody celebrating and all, but the moment passed before I could decide.

Getting off the bus at the foot of her street it was really pouring. I raised my umbrella and reached it across, over her head. She nestled close to me and took my arm which fairly drove me wild though I knew it was because she didn't want to get wet. How would I bring the evening to a close? Standing on her porch, I saw lights behind the curtains.

"Thanks a lot," she said, "I had a really nice time."

"Me too."

"I've never been to a hockey game before. It was really fun."

Then there was this long silence. "Well, thanks again," she said with a kind of funny smile, opening the door and disappearing inside.

Beneath the shelter of my umbrella, I turned toward home, filled with thoughts and emotions. In a way the evening was less than I had hoped, but exhaling deeply, I pronounced it a success. It could have been a lot worse.

We made it all the way to the finals before falling to St. Dominic's, the Maine champ. I went to the rest of the games with Omer. I thought of calling Joanie, but it bothered me that Omer had avoided me when we ran into each other in the boys' room the game I took her to. Maybe I'd ask her to a movie, anything but Westerns, she said, which would open up new possibilities like holding hands. But for now I decided to back off. No need to rush things.

FORGET FIRST APPEARANCES. 1D was not the sedate collection of scholars that so intimidated me that first day. And Brother Robert was not an ogre but a kind, gentle man with a severe case of nerves. In fact, why he missed the last two years, he needed time off – from students, that is. As the year deepened and our true colors appeared he became short-tempered but was never mean. Even from my seat halfway back in the room, I could see his hands tremble. He often clasped them together to disguise his shakes.

Teachers had a faculty lounge for smoking and there was a room in the basement for sophomores on up. I mention this because Brother Robert was the worst smoke fiend I had ever met. His breath about knocked you down, the fingers on his left hand – he was left-handed – were yellow-brown, and you could smell smoke on papers he handed back. As the year went on, his trips to the closet behind his desk became more frequent. One day after class a kid poked his head in there. He backed out, coughing violently, and everybody crowded forward for a look. There was this huge ashtray with a couple dozen butts and not even a chair, just a light bulb on a cord. It made me sad Brother Robert had to smoke standing up. From then I looked for the cloud of smoke as he opened his door and emerged, sedated and ready to take us on.

During this first year, I developed a very important skill, how important I didn't realize at the time. Eight to eight-thirty was quiet time for review, completing assignments. Though I was a good class citizen, I found it impossible to be silent. My work was always finished ahead so I'd get up and wander around, talk with my friends. First few times, no problem, then I got nailed.

"Mr. Bernard," Brother Robert said, calling me to his desk, "this has gone on long enough. Give me a hundred words on the Wife of Bath's Tale. You have fifteen minutes." We'd read Chaucer the previous week. At least he picked one of the best parts. I pulled out a pad and began scribbling furiously. As the buzzer sounded I rushed through my conclusion and handed it in. "Thank you very much, Mr. Bernard." Next day, same thing. "A hundred words on the Presidency under Eisenhower." Next day, "last night's basketball game, I assume you were there, a hundred-fifty words will do." Fifteen minutes later I filed my report on our rout of a good Hope High team.

If I was caught early I'd have to whip off two hundred, but late in the period a hundred would suffice. A couple of times he called for a poem. The day after we studied *haiku,* those seventeen syllables were the only assignment I couldn't finish. Sometimes my work came back with notes, but not always. He trusted me to do a workmanlike job. It became a game, one Brother Robert enjoyed, too. Though I didn't know it at the time, learning to meet these deadlines was the best thing that ever happened to me.

10. SATURDAY'S HERO

I HAD BZ ON WHILE I WAS SHAVING," I say. Jonathan and I are just settling into the study. Another rainy morning, too wet for the deck. "Some General's telling Congress to bug off, let the Army handle the investigation."

"No surprise there. Incidentally," he laughs, "I notice you've stopped complaining about seeing the *Times* on a daily basis."

That is true, I even suspended my subscription for the duration. "It fits the urgency you've introduced around here."

"My apologies for disturbing your routine."

"Don't worry about it. Speaking of urgency, how about Paul's deadline training?"

"Outstanding, and I say that from experience."

"I take it they extended yours. You and your editor are still on speaking terms?"

"Oh, sure. It's one particular prick tried to pull a fast one. My guy backed me up."

"Incidentally, how are you doing? I'm ready to read."

"Another week, I'll have something presentable."

I reach for the next stack of material. "A couple more high school sections coming up. I don't know about you but I like seeing the young man being tested, making his way."

"Testing," Jonathan grunts. "I'm well acquainted with that."

* * * * * * *

"EH, CUMPAR'!"

Sweat stinging my eyes, I wrestled a case of canned peaches onto the conveyor belt. "Move it!" the figure at the top of the stairs yelled, "I don' got all day!" I jabbed the button and the cartons began their ascent to the shopping level, to the fine ladies and gentlemen wheeling their carts in air-conditioned comfort, ignorant of the poor souls toiling in the heat and dust below. "On its way to you, Tone."

I wiped my eyes on my sleeve, muscling up the No. 6 Canned Peas, Heinz Ketchup, Mott's Applesauce, Cott ginger ale, pale dry and golden. I'd like to mix it all together, I muttered, slamming the last of my crazy stew onto the belt. Beefaroni.

Saturday afternoon was Pit time for DiLorenzo's junior workers. A hundred-twenty down there. Smart of them, no thermometer on the wall. I ought to bring my own. Only thing kept me going was the Leica, the thought of my finger on the focusing ring, my eye to the eyepiece, but until my deposit grew to seventy-five dollars, in the display case it stayed. At a buck-thirty an hour that meant a lot of Pit time. Years later the *Inferno's* sulfurous realms brought canned pears to mind, and Sisyphus' hill, it looked a lot like that conveyor belt.

My hours were Friday four to nine and all day Saturday, also Thursday nights. When some kid's family went on vacation I got extra time. The more the better. Sundays the market was closed, Friday nights were the most sociable. As a bagger I enjoyed seeing what people bought, how much they spent. I became an actor, a master of the significant pause. After putting the customer's bags in the trunk of her car (men never used baggers) I'd stand there and smile. Usually it was a dime, a quarter was exceptional. Younger women tended to be more generous. The old ones, crotchety and some of them so huge you wondered how they'd ever squeeze behind the wheel, they had this strange idea a thank-you was enough. Maybe in the old days, but this was 1956 and things were darned expensive.

One pretty, dark-haired woman with two little kids drove a red Fairlane convertible. She was always good for a quarter. Sliding behind the wheel her skirt would creep up her leg and when I shut the door and she'd give me this long stare, finally squeezing my hand and pressing a coin into it. I guess I was more muscular from all that lifting, but my underdeveloped imagination didn't put this particular two and two together, not at first. Also it threw me off, her being married and a mother at that.

My usual restocking partner was Frank Pezzulo. Tommy and Phil (Tomasso and Filippo) DiLorenzo owned the store their father Guiseppe started. Guiseppe was about a hundred and ten and still came around to complain that the boys were doing everything wrong. We griped about the rotten conditions, the pay, the torture chamber those slave drivers stuck us in. A store legend had a family of tarantulas nesting in the canned Sicilian tomato crates. Supposedly one time a crate was dropped and splintered, and a bunch of them scattered in all directions, but I never saw one and neither did anybody else I knew.

This particular Saturday Tony Andreozzi, Tone, grabbed me as I punched in. Frank had called in sick so he had to work The Pit with me unless they brought in someone else which they wouldn't, being so cheap. Tone had worked his way up at DiLorenzo's and he protested Pit duty, but today he found himself at the top of the stairs, barking at me through his cigarette. Fat chance he'd come down and give me a hand. In fact more than once he bawled me out, saying don't work so hard, you'll make everybody else look bad. The younger kids looked up to Tone. At nineteen he was a man with a life. Tall and swarthy, he often stood at the mirror next to the time clock, combing his pomaded hair and sharpening his D.A. He wore tight T-shirts that bulged at the left bicep where his Luckies were rolled up even if the shirt had a pocket. Suede shoes matching his pegged pants completed the look, rust or dark blue, unsuitable for heavy lifting, like their wearer.

Tone was Captain of the DILORENZO MARKET – FINE MEAT AND PRODUCE panel truck, green with gold block letters, both sides. He made deliveries for elderly shoppers and women like my convertible lady. Then there were the girls who hung around, never buying anything. You'd see one or another in the truck, perfecting her face in the rear view mirror as Tone finished loading. First time I rode with him on a delivery I noticed the pillow and blanket in back. With a job many would kill for plus tips and side benefits, Tone was proof even a Mt. Pleasant dropout could make it big.

The owners' youngest sister Maria was in charge of the registers. Maria was plump and cheerful, somewhere between thirty and forty, hard to tell. Her marital prospects were a topic of loud and frequent debate. "You see that guy checking you out?" This from Tone, the expert. Maria had just rung up a middle-aged couple who were wheeling their cart out the front door. "If I ever saw a guy with the hots for you that's him, take it from me." Maria turned crimson and started in on the next customer. She had a really sweet disposition. The only time you ever saw her sad or mad was when they picked on her like this.

This was my first summer lost to duty, but griping aside, it was not a burden. Some of my friends gave me a hard time, Angelo especially, who made a big deal of my being an honorary wop. I was the only person in the store whose name didn't end in a vowel. People were always singing and whistling Italian songs, *Bacia Me Bambino, Way Marie* and so on. DiLorenzo's was a hotbed of rabid Yankee fans, insufferable at all times but impossible in the fall when they won the World Series. Thank God, Don Larson who pitched the perfect game that year was a Swede or something like that.

That summer I saw a lot of Benny. First time he came to my house my mother made a point of quizzing him about Classical, his classes, how much homework, all the time glaring at me. She told one and all my betrayal had ruined not just my life but hers as well. Like me, Benny had done a year of Latin, but his class read the entire *Aeneid* while we plodded through excerpts from Cicero and vocabulary drills. Next year he would begin Greek, and when you add in Hebrew I wondered how he kept it all straight. Benny wanted to be a historian because of what Hitler did to his relatives, which if people didn't pay attention, he said, could happen again. While I, scripted by my elders, would save our country through science. Better things for better living through chemistry, or physics, or math, whatever. It remained to be seen where I would alight, into which jar the specimen labeled Paul Bernard would tumble before somebody screwed the lid on and that would be that.

Everybody said technology was how our country solved big problems like the war. It made me uneasy that Benny truly loved History, in fact he was passionate about it. What did I love? Sports, true, but that didn't count any more. Photography, but that was just a hobby and, as my father reminded me at every opportunity a damned expensive one at that. For my mother, taking pictures was neither an art nor a science, and it certainly wasn't a sufficient outlet for the ability God had given me, with a large assist from Fiona Kelley. But first and foremost, taking pictures was not A Profession. And so it was, I found myself with no clear object for my hopes and dreams.

IT WAS A DIFFERENT PAUL BERNARD who showed up that fall, twenty pounds heavier and five-eight, meaning that six feet, my goal, was in sight. I was shaving every day, though only my chin needed it and not that desperately. I pondered my appearance, I admit, but to deliberately create a look like Tone, to mess with your natural self seemed somehow affected and wrong. Whatever I was I would continue to be, without artifice. I had recently heard the expression – "you make your own face." Puzzling. For my round face, the large dark eyes, what might that mean? But the real difference was my attitude. I knew I could make my way at La Salle as well as anybody and better than most, and it didn't hurt I finally acquired my Leica and was able to put it to work. Thank you, Pit.

French was my most personal course, not that we spoke it much at home. My mother's French dated from high school, embellished by songs and plays. Naturally it was graceful and Parisian. *Joual,* the patois of my father's *québécois,* she dismissed as coarse, rude and unworthy of her home. Of course, my father rubbed it in whenever he could.

Most of my classmates were nervous when they had to display their knowledge. I knew these Irish and Italian kids could pronounce *nous avons* or *les animaux* because they did when I practiced them, which they often asked me to. They did fine until it counted, then they'd mess up, it looked like on purpose. Some of them were against learning, especially anything different, as if the process was somehow unmanly. I discovered which of my classmates weren't afraid to be known as "brains." The other camp knew, too. Lines were being drawn.

Until now I haven't said much about religion at La Salle. It was pervasive but in a quite different way. During my first year I had quit the altar boy corps, uncomfortable around the younger kids and tired of the priests treating me like I was ten years old. So I was no longer immersed in church life, though it goes without saying I still attended Mass Sundays. Religion at La Salle was more about accumulating knowledge and, it was hoped, understanding the various aspects of our Faith, plus of course, character formation.

We learned why the Church was "One, Holy, Catholic and Apostolic" and about the Pope's infallibility. I was impressed to learn what a hell-raiser young St. Augustine was, and about the "Dumb Ox" Aquinas who had a knack with tough problems such as does God exist and how could the world be created out of nothing. We studied our Faith's opponents – Atheists, Pantheists, Materialists and Rationalists, also the Jewish religion and Mohammedanism. We were trained in the unfortunately-named art of "Apologetics," arguments to use against those people if we ever got the chance. Amazing, how the commandments, the sacraments and liturgy all fit together. The Brothers took this perfect whole to a level that made your head spin, adding explanations far beyond our old, childish ideas. Everything explainable, everything explained. Our most dangerous enemy, of course, was Communism. We rejoiced as the Hungarians rose up against the tyrant, but our hopes were dashed as tanks rolled into Budapest. We had seen the face of evil and it was not pretty.

We dwelt on Christian morality, rules for living your life. For every situation there was an answer and a rule that applied, and thanks to the sacraments, help when you needed it. The trick was finding the rule that applied, then applying it, again and again. Thus morality becomes second nature, you were forming a "right conscience" and becoming a better person. One, two, three – A, B, C. Trouble is, it wasn't all that simple. Compared with faith and reason, morality was a whole different ballgame.

My reading tastes expanded greatly, thanks to Brother Robert whom I had really grown to like. He cared about books and appreciated the few of us who did, giving us an outside reading list after pledging us to secrecy. "Keep this to yourselves, gentlemen. I believe your immortal souls are up to the challenge but around here I am in the minority." Some were already part of our underground library – *Catcher in the Rye, Lord of the Flies* – Others were on the Index of Forbidden Books, by nobody you'd ever heard of. Brother Robert had guts. Not that Holden Caulfield was such a great person, but it was thrilling to see in black and white things I thought about a lot and my friends must have also.

Though pure at the core, certain tentative and furtive areas existed around the edges of the school. Big Sal's Academy Variety was a hole in the wall a few blocks from the school that sold candy, soda, cigarettes, newspapers, magazines, and not just any magazines but on the wall below sports and fishing, movie magazines. *Photoplay, Modern Screen* and so on. Ava Gardner and Janet Leigh in low-cut gowns or bathing suits, leaning forward and showing a lot of what I learned was called cleavage. The black and white pictures inside were always better than the covers. It bothered me that Big Sal put these magazines near the floor, making a film fan such as myself struggle just to flip through them. Though maybe he wanted to see who cared enough about such things to make himself look ridiculous. YOU READ IT YOU BUY IT, the sign said, but nobody paid any attention. There were also certain comics like *Wonder Woman,* featuring female heroes or women in distress and not much else. Big Sal's was an occasion of sin, and no less so if you told yourself you were going in for a Coke or a candy bar, because God knew why you went in and He knew why you stayed.

One stormy Sunday our pickup game fell apart, so Omer and I decided to hit a movie. I wanted to see, *Fire Down Below,* or more precisely Rita Hayworth in *Fire Down Below,* which I had researched at Big Sal's. I'd never gone as far as to see on the big screen what was so intriguing in small doses of black and white, but when I told Omer there was this great action picture at the Majestic, for want of a better idea, he agreed.

It was everything I'd hoped and more. From time to time I glanced at Omer who sat transfixed but with this frown on his face. As we walked to the bus, he was quiet. Finally he said, "I don't think we should have seen that." I knew what he meant because I had a hard-on the whole two hours. At confession the next Saturday, to my own sin I had to add one that made me feel guilty and ashamed. I had led a friend into an occasion of sin. For all I knew, I had set him on the slippery slope to damnation. This was the first time my weakness hurt someone else, and I felt as sorry as I had about anything, ever. I vowed never again to invite anybody else along on my cloudy and uncertain course.

MY JUNIOR YEAR BEGAN ROUTINELY ENOUGH, but a thousand miles away the Governor of Arkansas tried to block Negro students from Little Rock high school and it took President Eisenhower sending federal troops to get them in. The pictures in the *Journal* and on TV floored me. People full of hate, screaming at little kids, spitting on them, throwing rocks. Kids my age running a gauntlet up the steps and into the school. I went looking for Terry Grimes.

"This surprises you?" he said. "Just shows you don't know what's going on."

"I admit, I had to check where Arkansas is."

"No, no, I'm talking right here. Scratch the surface in Providence R - I and you get Arkansas. Maybe even worse, 'cause white people here hide it better. Keep you off balance, you never know where you stand."

"C'mon," I replied, "nothing like that would ever happen here."

"Like I told you, you don't have a clue," he said with a thin smile.

I didn't accept that, but it was on my mind when I sat down to write that fateful column. Midway through freshman year I had joined the *Maroon and White*, wrote a bunch of news stories and had some photos published. This year I asked Norm McDermott, now Editor-In-Chief, and got the go-ahead to write an occasional column. In this one I asked what would it be like if instead of being at La Salle, we were students at that Arkansas high school? How would we have acted? As Catholics, clearly we couldn't be in the racist camp, but what if we just stood around and did nothing? I wound it up this way (I've kept a copy all these years).

> If we had been there, how would we have acted? Hopefully as La Salle men we would have stood tall and supported these brave kids. But on our calm campus far from that troubled scene, do you or I really know what we would have done? Easy to say we'd do the right thing, but how can we be sure?
>
> Well in fact, there is a clue, a test we take right here every day. How do we treat those among us whose skin is a different color? Or our classmates who don't drive the finest car, or any car at all? Or who don't live in that great a neighborhood? Do we go out of our way to be friends with them? Or are we afraid of what "the others" might say? Do we go our own way, stick to our own crowd and say nothing? Give it some thought. I know I am.

Although students put the *Maroon and White* together, the Brothers had the final say on what went into it. A few days after Norm submitted my column to our faculty advisor, I got a note summoning me to a meeting in the Vice-Principal's office. I had a hunch why. Brother Adalbert was sitting behind his desk. Brother William, our advisor was there, and Norm. The office was imposing, dimly lit with blinds drawn against the bright afternoon sun. Brother Adelbert was tall and broad, built like a wrestler, completely bald, his eyebrows permanently knitted in a scowl. Not for nothing was he the Dean of Discipline. I'd never had any business with him, though from Jim's ordeal I knew his reputation. He told me to be seated, then handed me a piece of paper. Sure enough, it was my article, double-spaced, neatly typed with a couple of eraser smudges, just as I had handed it in.

"I'm told this is your work, Mr. Bernard."

"Yes, Brother, it is."

"You know we can't publish anything like this. Were you not told at orientation that news and opinion must pertain to matters pertaining to the La Salle community?"

I shook my head. "But this is about La Salle. It's about how we need to see what's happening and not ignore it."

"We have never printed anything like this and we're not about to start now." Brother Adalbert's face relaxed and he leaned forward. "Paul, personally I agree with what you say, I even admire you for putting it so well, but there's a time and place for everything and this is not it." He sat back and steepled his fingers. "We have to avoid causing unnecessary strain in our community. Everyone here gets along and it's my job to see that continues."

In the silence that followed, I replayed my conversation with Terry. I felt my neck getting warm. This was wrong, not letting people think for themselves on something this important. Suddenly I knew what I had to do. "So you're not going to let it run," I said, looking at Brother William.

"I'm sorry," Brother William said, holding out his hands, "but that's our decision." His face brightened, "but give me another column by Friday, we'll hold the presses for it."

I nodded slowly, looking for the right words and the courage to say them. "I'm sorry too. But if that's the way things are, I'll have to resign from the paper."

Brother William frowned. "What did you say?"

"I said, I resign from the paper. I'll clear out my desk this afternoon."

"Why would you do that?"

"You say the *Maroon and White's* a student newspaper, let it be a student newspaper." Now I was up to my neck in it. "If it's not a student newspaper, it's wrong to call it one."

Brother Adalbert exploded. "Watch your tongue, young man, or you'll find yourself on suspension."

Norm had been silent til now. He had encouraged me when I told him about the idea but his concern was how the students would take it. It never crossed our minds the Brothers might refuse to print it. Norm had a squeaky, high-pitched voice but a reputation for being fearless. He turned to Brother William. "You know we're going to have to redo our front page."

"What do you mean?"

"An Editor of the *Maroon and White* resigns over a censorship issue. That's a major news story, and no question it pertains to the La Salle community..."

"But you can't..."

"...and people will ask why, so we have to print the column as a news item."

Brother Adalbert pointed his finger at us. "Very clever! I'll bet you cooked this whole thing up, the two of you."

Norm shook his head. "Not at all. Farthest thing from our mind."

"Watch it, mister, or you'll have the shortest tenure of any editor in history!"

He laughed. "Sounds like another story in the making."

Brother Adalbert stood up, his face lighting up the room. "You two are dismissed. I mean, leave! We'll let you know about your discipline. Rest assured there will be some."

Norm and I walked out, not looking back. "Jeez," I said, "what'll we do now?"

"Hey, don't worry, they can't afford to let this get out." He laughed. "They're right, we couldn't have written a better script if we'd tried. Going down to the office?" he asked.

"Yeah," I replied. "I said I'd get my stuff – guess I'd better do it."

It wasn't like I could avoid telling my parents, bringing home a gym bag full of gear and dumping it on my bed. My mother was outraged. "You did absolutely the right thing, Paul. Never have I been prouder of you! They should send that idiot Adalbert back to the Middle Ages where he belongs!" It was all my father could do to keep her from driving to the school and beating on the Brothers' door, but true to form, he was practical.

"Things have a way of sorting themselves out," he said, pulling on his pipe, "but let's see if we can't help them a little." Beneath his composure, he was still nursing his wounds from the battle to save Jim. "Paul, get me the phone book."

He leafed through it then picked up the phone. "Dave LaPointe," he said firmly. "Hello, Dave! *Comment ça va,* you old bastard! *Bien, bien.* Well actually not so good. We got a situation at the high school, maybe you can give us a hand."

Dave LaPointe was the *Providence Journal's* ace photographer. He and my father went back a long way. Thanks to Dave I had visited the newsroom a few times, even went on assignment with him once. My father recounted what had happened, then fell silent a moment. "Yes, yes, that's the way to go. I'll owe you one if you can pull this off. Right... right. *Merçi bien. À bientôt, mon ami.*" He turned to us. "Here's what we're going to do. Dave knows your Brother William pretty well and he's got this idea..."

"What idea?"

"Hey," he said with a merry look I rarely saw, "let's let Dave handle it. His editor doesn't wear a black dress but he has to work around him sometimes, too."

Later that night the phone rang. It was for me. "Paul, Brother Robert here. I just heard about your little problem, news travels fast in our community. I'm not surprised what you wrote, I saw a lot of your writing when you were a freshman, you'll remember. Nor does our reaction surprise me." He coughed several times, then cleared his throat. "Sorry. What I'm saying, La Salle is a great place but once in a while it needs to be shaken by the scruff of the neck. I'll do what I can to see it comes out right. Don't worry, and whatever you do, stick by your guns. As we say in the trade, keep the faith."

What a great person, I thought, putting the phone down. All of a sudden, my knees weren't so wobbly.

A few days later Brother William collared me in the corridor and said they'd decided to run the column with a statement that it was a personal opinion and did not represent the views of the paper, La Salle, or the Brothers. He seemed a bit sheepish but didn't say any more so I figured, let well enough alone. When the paper came out, the "it didn't represent the views" part was missing. The column ran on the editorial page over my name with "A Personal Opinion" in bold. Otherwise there it was, word for word. I moved my equipment back to a big round of applause. Norm shook my hand and clapped me on the back. I told him I was grateful how he backed me up. He grinned. "I figured I'd be cleaning out my desk too, but we heard somebody put the pressure on. Know anything about that?"

I thought a moment then shook my head. "Not really... just glad to be back." I put the treasured Leica back in my desk and locked it. When I told my father, he nodded knowingly and shook my hand. That was all. Some people told me they'd read the column, a few thanked me, it made them think, some said it took guts to do it. Some sideways looks too, but Terry Grimes took me totally by surprise.

"I saw what you wrote." He glared at me. "Why'd you do it?"

"I wanted to get people thinking. Like what you said made me think."

"No way! That was between us two, but this? In the paper? Just 'cause you see something on TV that makes you an expert? This has been going on for-ever! Where you been, man? Rosa Parks, Martin Luther King, ever hear of them? And by the way, who appointed you to fight our battles? I sure didn't."

"I never said you did," I replied, my face reddening. "Anyway those are my words, not yours. It's my name on it."

"But that's *my life* you're messing with! And Jerome's! Plus the grand total of two other Negroes in this place. Did it ever occur to you, you could make things bad for us, doing something like this?"

"Bad?"

"Yes, damnit!" He shook his head. "Look, we get along okay, you and me, but what I'm saying, some kids have it in for us, they'd like nothing better than see us back in the jungle. That's what I'm trying to tell you. Given the chance, that type person is just as bad as those Arkansas honkies, and here you go stirring them up! We're on trial, we're out front here, acting twice as good as everybody just to keep it together. That is one heavy load, bro, one very heavy load." Terry's eyes glistened and he seemed on the verge of tears. "I don't want anything happening to me and my brothers. We're just trying to get by. Get along, get by, get out."

I was floored. I took a deep breath. "Terry, most of the people here are decent. If they think about these things they'll be on your side These are the people I wanted to reach. I'll take your word there are others, too..."

"Take my word? TAKE MY WORD! You ever been called nigger? You ever had fuck you black boy painted on your locker like Jerome? Next time stick to stuff you know. Don't go sticking your nose in other peoples' business!" He turned and strode away.

That night after dinner I confronted my mother, Catherine was there, too. I forgot to mention she had started at Brown and was living on campus, though she came around often.

"I thought I was doing the right thing," I began, "now I'm not so sure."

"True, as a family we don't really know any Negroes, not to socialize with, at least. I hope you and Catherine will do better along those lines than we've done..."

"My friend Genevieve, she says Brown is the friendliest place she's ever been."

"Good for her," I said, "what about the others, how do they feel?"

"I don't know the others well enough. Anyway, Mama, how can you say what Paul did is right or wrong? People look at the same thing differently. According to Hume..."

My mother shook her head. "You surprise me, Catherine. Have you forgotten morality isn't measured by results but principles? Clearly what applies here is love your neighbor as yourself for the sake of God."

I shook my head, "but if my neighbor's not interested...?"

"That doesn't alter the fact you need to try, you have to make people aware of evil and cruelty. In fact, with your position of influence, it would be wrong not to try."

"I don't know. I just don't know anymore."

"Well, I do. Thinking isn't enough, you have to act! Catherine, you have opportunities your father and I never had," she glowered at me, "as Paul will if he makes the right choice for *his* college. Make the most of them!"

11. FROM THE CHRYSALIS, IN A MANNER OF SPEAKING

"THAT BLACK KID SURE BROUGHT PAUL UP SHORT," I observe. "No good deed ever goes unpunished."

Jonathan nods. "When you wander into opinion, you're asking for trouble. That's happened to me when I was least expecting it. Here Paul knew he was getting personal, he just didn't expect that kind of reaction."

"It could have made him gunshy but I saw no sign of that later."

"He learned a lesson. Be fearless but not stupid, that's another way to say it."

Over dinner Jonathan is more pensive than usual. I ask what is wrong.

"I'm still pissed. I can't get over losing that part of the story."

"I hear you, but Paul's life is more interesting than his death could ever be."

Jonathan shakes his head. "If it bleeds, it leads. A celebrity? And intrigue? Together the two halves make a fantastic story. But you know, if they give it to Hersh I'm thinking he's not going to have an easy time of it. He burned a lot of bridges with My Lai, military sources, I mean."

"That was decades ago."

"People have long memories when you show them up."

"Ah, come on, an old pro like him's got an address book a foot thick. He'll always find somebody with a grudge that's willing to talk."

Jonathan has this funny look on his face. "Maybe it's not too late."

"What're you saying?"

"I could still do it on spec. As far as the magazine's concerned it's no skin off their nose, not if I give them what I'm under contract for."

I feel bad Jonathan won't be working on that part of it. I feel bad *I* won't be working on it. Much as I hate to admit, it would be sweet to help find the bastards responsible. Is there anything I can do, I wonder. I'd better look into that and damned quick, too.

****

AS MY SENIOR YEAR BEGAN, the battle over "Paul's future" was in full cry, but I had already made one big decision. Pour X into Y you get Z, design a bridge that'll stay up – someone else could worry about such things. I'd been caught up in the Sputnik lamentations but as events unfolded I was more interested in how we dealt with the Russians than how they got the thing up there. When I told Benny about my load of History and Government he laughed, telling me welcome to the club.

Jim was engaged, and my mother appreciated Sheila's healthy influence on son number one. He was growing up despite himself, apprenticing for a plumber and going to school nights for his license. Right after high school he joined the National Guard to stay out of the draft. He drilled weekly in the red brick armory on Cranston Street near Tante Héloise's house and went to camp in the summer. He still spent time with his buddies, but not as much. Football was in the past as, apparently, were thoughts of college. These days he swung from a shorter but sturdier chain.

It interested me that Catherine's non-Catholic environment wasn't the end of the world. She still went to Mass Sundays, at the Newman Center. We had interesting debates, thanks to a Philosophy course she was taking. Everybody had followed the accounts of Pius XII's death and the election of John XXIII. One Sunday night shortly after the new Pope's election we were having dinner at our house. Somebody asked me how the La Salle community was taking the change.

"One of the priests studied in Rome, he has great stories about what happens on the inside, the politics and all."

"No," my mother said, "the Holy Spirit playing politics?"

"Everything's political," my father said. "Anything can be bought will be bought." "I meant what I said as a joke, but I certainly wouldn't go that far!"

"You say God works through men, Fiona, that's how men are. No better, no worse, no exceptions."

"You don't mean money changes hands," Catherine ventured.

"No, but say you're a cardinal and you want so and so to win. If you want my vote I'll expect you to come across when there's something I need."

My mother shook her head. "How you men can steer an interesting discussion in the most boring direction. I want to know, what do they think of the new Pope? He certainly looks to be a man of the people."

"He's from a humble background," my father replied, "his family were farmers. Can't be all bad."

"A nice change from the so-called princes of the Church," my mother sniffed.

"He's almost eighty," I added. "Some people say he's an interim Pope, they couldn't agree on somebody who'd be there a long time."

"See, what'd I tell you," my father grinned. "Politics."

"People are saying he might surprise people," I went on. "He has a habit of doing the unexpected."

"Not to change the subject," my father pointed his finger at me, "you saw our troops just left Lebanon. Would you say we did the right thing going in there?"

"It's a friendly government and was in danger of falling, so I'd say, yes."

"You won't be writing any critical editorials, I take it." My comment calling Korea a tie still rankled him.

"This is different. We did the job and we got out. That's the way to do it."

"I don't see why we mess in other countries' affairs," Catherine added.

"It's nothing new," my mother said, "we've been doing it forever."

"Who runs a country matters," my father said. "We don't send troops for no reason but if a friend needs help and we have something at stake, that's different."

"It just doesn't seem right to get mixed up in somebody else's business."

My father frowned, "Sometimes their business is our business, too. That Nasser is a bad actor, cozying up to the Rooskies like that. If you ask me, they're behind all the uproar over there, no question about it."

At my mother's insistence I applied to Harvard and Brown, as well as Holy Cross in Worcester, forty miles west of Boston. Harvard was impressive – the tradition, the stately buildings, the famous graduates – but word came, no scholarship. My father said he'd swing it if I really wanted, but a few days later Holy Cross came through with tuition, room and board, though I'd have to work in the dining hall as part of the deal.

I have to admit, the prospect of leaving the Catholic cocoon was making me nervous. While most of the Brothers fed my fears, once again Brother Robert stood above the pack. Welcome the unknown, he said, that's where the most interesting things happen. What a great person, I thought, but I also thought, easier said than done.

My decision came down to this. In addition to gaining knowledge, I wanted the next four years to deepen my Catholic beliefs and tune them up for real life. And so it was I cast my lot with the Jesuits and Holy Cross.

Our family was doing all right except for one thing, but it was a big one. With success, my father had become more remote than ever, having less time for us. I sensed he felt we sapped his energy, interfering with more interesting and important things. Also, better able to read the signals, I knew there were other women. I recall the sadness in my mother's face when it grew late and he still hadn't come home. What went on between themselves they kept from us. I went along, minding my own business, feeling sorry for my mother, and for him, too.

But spurred on by Catherine, mother was stirring, working on persuading herself the time was right for a return to the stage. Thriving at Brown, Catherine had already been in several plays. I admired theater without appreciating it, considering entertainment thin gruel for people of serious mien. It took me much too long to realize that art is also a handmaiden of truth, that it may illuminate the human heart far better than endeavors that tackle it head-on. That aspect of Brother Robert's genius was still lost on me. I'd had glimpses, recently with *On the Road,* last year's clandestine choice, but like so many things file this one under "opportunity lost."

Military service was now on my mind as classmates talked about registering for the draft. Next year, when I turned eighteen, I'd have a Selective Service Card in my wallet too, and a student deferment. I put aside the ROTC materials that came in my acceptance packet. I'd gladly serve my country when and if, just not yet.

I'd never tested the Saturday night school dances but the prospect of my senior prom pushed me into it. I had taken Joan to a couple of movies but the last time it was really awkward. When I slid my hand across, hers just sat there. Jim clued me in on hand-holding, that it meant more than it seemed. If a girl really held your hand back, squeezing it or rubbing it, this was an invitation to take the next step, which was put your arm around her. If she leaned against you or put her head on your shoulder, well... But Joan's limp fish stopped me cold. I finally pulled my hand back and sat, distracted and miserable, through the film. *April Love,* ha! I called her once more and she said she was going steady. Actually made me feel better. I wished her luck.

So on a chilly early December evening, Omer and I set out. Omer had on his shiny rust-colored jacket but I didn't say anything. We were nervous enough already. I had to talk him into going but I figured the Brothers wouldn't run these things if they weren't okay. I had on a gray tweed sport coat, the kind with brown leather buttons you never button and new loafers that began killing me the first block. "This is such a waste of time," he said as we passed Mt. Pleasant. "I can't dance, what's the use?"

"Just do what everybody is doing."

Easy for me to say. I didn't know how either. One time my mother offered to show me how. She was a great dancer, I'd seen her at weddings and so on, but I said no thanks, that would be too weird, I thought, dancing with your mother. All I knew was what Catherine taught me the one time I let her try which was also the last time.

I told Omer, think of a square on the floor. Step ahead with your left foot, then move your right foot up to it and across, then back with the left – something like that. You do this over and over. The girl does it backwards.

"That is so dumb!" he shouted. I found it hard to disagree.

Fifty cents wasn't a fortune, but we stopped to think it over. Why pay anything for an awkward and painful couple of hours? Omer shook his head, "I can't do it." Then *Ain't That a Shame* began to filter through the half-open door... that did it for me. I pulled out a dollar and handed it to the kid I knew who was the guard. He gave me back two quarters and pressed an ink stamp onto my wrist. "Go to the bathroom, show this to get back in. Leave the building you don't get back in."

This seemed reasonable. If I left, I wouldn't want to get back in.

"C'mon, Omer," I said. "Look, if it's that bad, we'll leave."

He sighed, reaching for his money. "Okay, you win."

I'd never seen the auditorium so lit up. It made our assemblies look like midnight on a moonless night. We found ourselves in a crowd of boys beneath the overhanging balcony in the back of the room. The girls were from all over but the boys were from La Salle, all of them. The Brothers said they couldn't be responsible for outsiders, but it was really to improve the home team's chances. We spotted several clots of girls as we sauntered through the crowd, toward where the dancing was happening. The lines of girls stretched along each side of the room. I nudged Omer. "There they are." Suddenly I had this image of Buzz Sawyer pointing out a formation of Jap planes to Hotshot Charlie. Why? These girls weren't the enemy, were they? They were playing slow music that would fit my box step, so I set off toward one of the lines, Omer trailing behind.

Before I go on, let me explain something – what I was looking for. In a girl, that is. It didn't happened often, but what made me look a second time and a third, was a really pretty face. And nice hair, particularly if it was long. I didn't have much experience with girls' bodies because of those loose-fitting clothes I've mentioned – that's probably why their faces interested me so much. This may sound weird, but it was like shopping for shirts, which I was forced to do at the start of every school year. Walking down the rack, I'd look for a color I liked, such as white or blue, and a pattern, such as striped. What the material felt like didn't matter until I came to a shirt with the right color and pattern. Then I'd check out the material. Anyway, that's what I was looking for.

As I walked along I kept my eyes open for a pretty face, preferably a small and interesting one like Ann Blyth or Piper Laurie. Being behind the girls as I was, I couldn't see their faces too well so I had to break through the line then casually turn and look around. I worked my way nearly to the end when all of a sudden, there she was. A little shorter than me, long dark hair, a small nose and large eyes and, well, the most beautiful face I'd ever seen. She was talking to some other girl but mostly just staring out at the dancing. I edged closer. She had this kind of sad expression as if she wanted to dance and didn't know why she wasn't. I looked around to see who was waiting to pounce but nobody else was even sizing her up! I elbowed Omer. "What do you think?"

He moved out to get a look, then came back. "You better make your move fast. Boy, is she stacked!"

Stacked? Honest to God, I hadn't even noticed. She was wearing a sweater that wasn't all that tight but now that I looked he was right, but as I said before, for me the face was what mattered. And so there is no misunderstanding, let me say my standards were extremely high. At times I worried why some of my friends seemed so successful with girls but I rationalized that by thinking there were plenty of girls I could ask, but not many met my standards. It wasn't that I had to be in love with somebody to be interested in them – not exactly, but close. My glasses had a lot to do with this. They gave me this serious look, because glasses imply a person is studious, which in my case happened to be true, though not to the exclusion of normal interests like sports and so on. And a person who was serious about things, or at least looked serious, had to act serious, he couldn't fool around as much, if you know what I mean. So when that kind of person asks a girl out, it means something.

Shake, Rattle and Roll was on – too fast. I looked around. A couple other kids in the area now. Finally, the last few bars... please let the next one be slow. I took a deep breath and exhaled, when Mr. Tambourini the History teacher came over the microphone – he was acting as deejay. "We'll take a break now. Be back in ten minutes."

Ten minutes! No way I could just talk with her for ten minutes. At least when the music was on you didn't have to say that much. Omer was pulling at my sleeve. "Let's get a coke."

"Go ahead. I'm going to hang around." I wasn't about to let her out of my sight.

I was happy to be rid of Omer so I could concentrate. The crowd began to thin but now a couple of guys, seniors, were lurking, pointing at different girls and making obnoxious remarks. The object of my desire was still there with her friend. All of a sudden she turned and our eyes met. I looked away. When I looked back she was looking away but then she quickly looked back to see if I was looking back, which I was. I thought I saw her smile... she said something to the girl next to her and they giggled. Were they laughing at me? Now I was watching like a hawk... one more laugh and that was it, she'd never know what she missed. I must have been there a couple of minutes but they just went on talking so I figured it was something else.

Where was Mr. Tambourini? Where was Omer, though I didn't really care. Finally, the music started again. *The Great Pretender*. Perfect! I steadied myself and closed in, brushing back my hair and straightening my glasses with my finger. Some kids were already dancing. I noticed she was quiet again, just staring at the floor.

"Uh, excuse me." She looked at me... God, was she beautiful. "Would you like to dance?" I expected her to say no. I mean, I wouldn't have blamed her, but then...

"Sure."

She stepped onto the floor and turned to see if I was there. She had done this before. "My name's Sandra." My hand was around her waist. Her hand was on my shoulder. I fumbled to get hold of her other hand and started my box to the music.

Owowowowowoyesss! I'm the great preetennderrrr...

"I'm Paul Bernard. I'm a Senior here." I wished I were ten years older.

"I'm at Saint X, I'm a Junior." Turned out she even knew Catherine slightly. I asked her what courses she was taking and so on, and we danced on, my box acting well, she doing hers backwards. I began thinking maybe it was time to try my other step where you pivot and turn ninety degrees. The one-eighty I hadn't yet mastered.

"It's been warm, hasn't it," she said. "Do you think it'll ever snow?"

"Yeah, but I don't mind. I have a pretty long walk. It's better than freezing."

"I take the bus usually."

"Where do you live?"

"Warwick."

Warwick! The other side of the earth. "How'd you get here tonight?"

"My friend's boy friend has a car."

"You're here with some girls." Omer flashed through my mind, but I quickly decided let him take care of himself.

She was quiet for a moment. "We saw you looking at us."

"I... I was trying to figure out if you wanted to dance."

"That is why we came, you know," she smiled. It made her look even prettier, if that was possible.

"I meant with me..."

At this she laughed out loud, then recovered quickly, "I'm sorry, I wasn't laughing at you but you know, you're really funny."

Whatever I thought of myself, being funny wasn't part of it, funny in the sense of, well, fun. I hoped she didn't mean the other kind of funny. Suddenly she put her arm around my neck and came closer, now my glasses were brushing her hair and I couldn't even see her face, which was nearly resting on my shoulder. I could feel her... bosom, I guess you'd say. When you're with your friends or thinking about things there are words for it but when it's a girl right in front of you... Omer was right, she was big.

Then... damn! Here it comes again, a mind of its own. At least it wasn't an occasion of sin this time, I wasn't thinking about anything and we were hardly touching except where she couldn't help it but still I decided to back off. I didn't want her thinking she'd started something like I did between Omer and Rita Hayworth, but then again, this is what you hope happens, up to a certain point but not beyond if you follow me. I moved my feet back from hers a little. This helped but it was awkward. I wondered what we looked like. She was still holding me around the neck, tighter than ever. The image of an open ladder, side view, came to mind.

I'm wearing my heart like a crown...pretending that you're still around.

When the music stopped she let go but didn't leave. Like I said, it was very bright out there and Jim told me the Brothers sometimes actually separated kids. Leave room for the Holy Ghost, they'd say, stuff like that.

"Want to dance again?" She smiled and nodded.

I was looking around to see if somebody would try and ace me out and, strange thing, this guy standing next to us with his arm around a girl was staring at Sandra and the girl he was with had this really angry look on her face. I turned the other way and another guy, his girl was tugging at him. Sandra seemed flustered. She knew guys stared. Thankfully the music started and I resumed my box, less nervous now but troubled by what I'd just seen. "You come to these a lot?" I ventured.

"Not very often." She paused as if to say something. There was this sweet, sad expression on her face. "They, well, they're usually not much fun."

That was the last thing I expected her to say. Being so beautiful and all, she ought to be the most popular girl in the whole place, then again, when I first saw her she wasn't dancing. And what Omer said, the first words out of his mouth, and these guys staring at her... she was embarrassed because she looked so great! Maybe guys were so overcome by her looks they were afraid to ask her to dance, or for a date, the kind of guys a nice girl like her would want to know. Suddenly this wave of confidence came over me. If what Sandra wanted was an ordinary person who wouldn't try to do anything or at least not that much, somebody she could be with and not worry about things... I glowed inside. This was me to a T.

We were out there a long time, some fast dances too, talking about everything, even between the numbers. She liked baseball – unfortunately she was a Yankee fan though her being Italian I could accept that. Ianello was her name, she was the oldest of seven, all boys but her. At the break, she said she had to check in with her friends which I understood, she'd come with them, after all. Omer found me. He was looking pretty gloomy. "You were dancing a lot. With that same girl." He acted like I had stabbed him in the back.

"That is why we came, you know."

"I'm going to leave. Acne. I have no chance. It's too bright in here."

"Did you try?"

"I don't want to talk about it. I need to go to the bathroom."

I looked back at Sandra... she was talking with her friends. I wanted to keep her in sight so I could find her right away when the music started, but if she liked me, I figured, or at least didn't mind me that much, she'd be there when I returned. So Omer and I went and got a couple of cokes. "That girl... what's she like?"

"Oh, I don't know, she goes to Saint X. She's from Warwick."

"That's a long bus ride."

He read my mind. If things went well I would definitely ask her out. He had this sly expression on his face. "I never was that close to anybody that big," he said. It seemed Omer had developed this obsession after the Rita Hayworth incident though it wasn't all my fault, he'd probably been thinking about it already. "You were dancing close... did she rub them against you?"

I glowered at him. "You have a dirty little mind, don't you."

He laughed. "Don't we all? What are you, some kind of statue?"

A statue I was not. Suddenly the music was on again. I had to get back. "Come on, you'll do better this time," I said. Even if Omer was a sex fiend mentally, he was still my friend. I was relieved his hang-dog expression was back. We returned to the spot I'd left Sandra but... where was she? Her friends were gone too. I looked around frantically. Suddenly my heart sank. She was on the floor with Harry Croft, a loudmouth jock, a real jerk. He was wearing his letter sweater, naturally. They were dancing back and forth when suddenly he grabbed her around the waist with both hands and pulled her in really tight. I tensed. I felt like going out there and punching him though he was six-three also who was I to watch out for Sandra, I'd just met her and maybe I read her wrong. After a few seconds of groping, she shoved him away and stomped off the floor. She and her friends put their heads together then Sandra and this other girl started to leave. They passed close to me but Sandra had her head down.

Omer saw her, too. "Why didn't you stop her, lover-boy?"

"Omer, you really are a shit."

Well, that was it. Fed up with "La Salle boys," she had left. And the evening had started so brilliantly. I began shuffling toward the exit when I saw Sandra and her friend coming back. I stepped in front of her. "Sandra," I said. Her eyes were moist and red.

"Hi," she said, blinking and looking away.

They were playing a really fast song but throwing caution to the wind I gestured and she smiled and led me to the floor. I'm not very good at this, I said. She said don't worry, I'll show you how. It turned out to be a fast box with a lot of turning and when I let go of her she spun around before re-entering my happy, confused orbit. When the set was over I asked if she'd like a coke and she said yes. We were sipping in the lobby NO BEVERAGES FOOD SMOKING ON FLOOR and I told her about myself. She also liked to read and had a nice camera, not as good as the Leica but better than my old one. We went on, back and forth until finally she looked at me in this funny way. "You know," she said, "you're different from the others."

Normally this would have been discouraging, but I figured, that is I hoped she was talking about Harry Croft. "I don't mean that in a bad way. It's nice. You're nice."

Nice? Nice! The next set was all slow numbers, and she put her hand around my neck and held me close when we danced which drove me wild so I fell into the ladder again. During *Good Night Sweetheart,* I asked for her phone number. I committed it to memory which wasn't that big a deal except my mind was filled with thoughts and feelings so I repeated it a couple of times. "Shall I write it out for you?" she laughed, but I replied crisply, "West 5524R. Right?"

"Right!" The music stopped and she said she'd better get back to her ride. I said I'd call, she said she'd like that. She liked Westerns, too. Walking out, Omer made another crack but I let it go. The most beautiful girl in the world had just given me her phone number. Outside we ran into Terry and Jerome. Terry and I had long since mended fences but Jerome was his same morose self. "Why do I bother with these dances?" he said. "Damned waste of time. Last time you'll see me here."

"You were dancing a lot," Terry said to me. So people had noticed.

Jerome gestured toward the crowd, "What do you think'd happen if I asked one of those white chicks to dance? Not that any of them'd say yes."

Even Terry was glum. "Why don't they ever invite some colored girls?"

"That's the trouble," Jerome went on, "damn Brothers...all talk, no action."

Terry burst out laughing. "No action, that's for damn sure! No action at all!"

Well I got my license. My mother drove a hard bargain – you want the car, you take dancing lessons. So twice a week for six weeks I climbed the stairs to Arthur Murray's in a Westminster Street office building. I stared out the window over the shoulder of this woman old enough to be my mother as she initiated me in waltz, rumba, tango, swing and perfected my fox trot. All of a sudden my box had lots of company.

Several times Sandra and I got together, movies and, you guessed it, a hockey game. The most we had done was hold hands because we'd never really been alone and I didn't know how she'd react anyway. It made me nervous that these excuses were about to disappear. Prom night, my parents beamed as, resplendent in white jacket, plaid tie and cummerbund, I drove off in the old Plymouth, corsage on the seat beside me. I debated, wrist kind or the kind you pin on, and went with wrist as safer. Pink sweetheart roses. We looped back for Angelo who was taking a Mt. Pleasant girl. I don't remember much about the evening but what happened at the end I will never forget.

I'll be the first to admit we were late. We stopped at a diner then drove Angelo and his date home. I shut off the motor and turned off the lights and there we sat. Sandra slid over toward me and I put my arm around her shoulder. When I turned to face her she came closer... closer...and... we kissed. I put my other arm around her and we did it again, longer and harder. Times like this I wished I didn't wear glasses but I couldn't take them off because that would send the wrong signal to a girl like Sandra. She still thought I was different in a nice way, but that night I didn't feel at all different or nice. I was hoping, sort of, I'd have the grace to stay pure, with this wonderful girl who wasn't that kind of girl at all, but there we were in what can only be described as a clinch. Suddenly, there was this blinding light. We jumped apart.

"Oh my God," she said. "Oh my God!"

Next thing the door opened and this face looked in. Her father. It smelled like he'd been drinking. "Way past your curfew, young lady," he rasped, shining his flashlight at us. "Let's go. You've said enough goodnight already." Sandra looked at me, this wretched expression on her face, and without a word she slid across to the other side. He slammed the door, and I was left to watch my pink chiffon dream trudge up the walk and disappear into the house behind an old man and his bathrobe.

I really wanted to see Sandra again. I practiced disguising my voice in case somebody like her father answered. I thought of hanging around her school, too, but I did neither, I'm not sure why. A couple of years later, I heard she got married and moved. That night, that agonizing night, I was so unhappy. God help me, I said, lying awake, the first girl I ever liked who liked me back. You better help me, God, I sure can't help myself.

Next Sunday I was totally focused. Body of Christ, Blood of Christ. My mind began to wander... where in the Bible do we see the sixteen-year old Jesus? What did he feel like when he looked at girls? Did he wonder what they were like under all those clothes, or did he already know? Did he ever get a hard-on? Did he accept pleasure knowing it wasn't his fault (often it isn't)? If not, how can you say he was a real boy? And if he wasn't a real boy, how could he be a real man? There is no mention of these things that preoccupy boys, girls too, I supposed, though I knew nothing about what they dream of. Why couldn't Jesus show me the way, not leave it to a bunch of men in black?

I felt like I was shrinking into myself, becoming an observer. On the sidelines, peering through his lens, notebook in hand, Paul Bernard reporting on life, his life. It made no sense. Though if you thought about it, perhaps that was just as well.

PART TWO

KNOWLEDGE

12. LINDEN LANE

I DIDN'T SLEEP WELL, first cold of the season plus a sore throat for good measure. The headache that woke me at three is still there but I'm not going back to bed if that's what you're thinking. Tough it out. I slide a folder over. "In this next part keep a close eye on Paul's new mentors. The Jesuits come across as more intellectual but the biggest difference with the Brothers is their emphasis on rationality."

"Rationality? In the sense of common sense?"

That's a laugh, I think, reaching for the box of Kleenex. "No. Confidence in the intellect, confidence to penetrate the mysteries of this world and the next. Religious faith in philosophical clothing, Aquinas through the Jesuit lens." As I wipe my nose I'm thinking Jonathan is a neophyte in such things and a slow learner to boot, but I go on. "The Jesuits and the Brothers both admit limits to human reason. That's where the famous leap of faith comes in. Remember my mentioning that?"

He nods.

"The Brothers make the leap sooner and with less confidence. Theirs is a gloomy outlook, Jansenist – you might look that up – not so different from Calvin's predestination. Very much in line with the quietude of Paul's Canadian forebears and their immigrant sons."

Jonathan's eyes are beginning to glaze over. I think I will take a nap after all.

* * * * * * *

FROM THE FRONT STEPS of O'Kane Hall I watched our car disappear through the trees lining the entrance road. My mother's teary farewell was the genuine article. Even Catherine, who had come along, seemed pensive. I was disappointed my father begged off at the last minute. The first twenty he gave me I chalked up to good will, the two he shoved through the car window had guilt written all over them.

After an hour unpacking I took time to explore the view from my fourth floor window. Holy Cross is built on a sizable hill, Mt. St. James, with the football stadium at the bottom, dorms and classroom buildings on up the slope and topped by a parking lot and farm fields. Following an orientation we plunged into the bookwork. I was set with the standard array of courses, slotted into a "high achieving' group," which I'll get to later. A long, excellent day. I knew I was going to like this place. But first I want to share an experience that stands out after much else has faded.

It wasn't one of my finer moments, or anyone else's for that matter, maybe that's why I remember it so well. My new friends and I were packed into the upstairs room of Putnam and Thurston Restaurant, attending what was billed as a "smoker." There was plenty of that, all right, but that's not what the event was about. Three beers in an hour, a new record, had left me lightheaded. "Hey, beer is food! It's good for you!"

"Had enough," I mumbled. My eyes had taken leave of each other, wandering off in different directions.

Dennis Healy was a thin-faced Irish kid from Scarsdale who lived a few doors down from me. Eighteen was the "drinking age" in New York, so he had experience. Here, it didn't matter – I could have been prodigy of twelve and been served. "All right then, I'll stand you to a scotch." We pushed through the mass of bodies to where an older gentleman in a tuxedo, wilted shirt and clip-on black tie was standing. "What'll it be, gents?"

"Two scotches, one with soda, one with... Paul, whaddya want in yours?"

I'd never had a mixed drink. "How about... coke?"

"Scotch and coke!" Dennis stuck out his tongue. "Bleagh!"

I thought a moment. "It's called a Brown Russian." I'd heard of a Black Russian. This seemed a reasonable try.

"A what?" the bartender frowned, setting two glasses on the bar.

"Brown Russian. It's big in Providence. I'm from there."

The bartender grimaced. "That figures. Well, whatever works."

Dennis clinked his glass against mine. "Up yours."

"You too." One sip told me why nobody'd ever heard of a Brown Russian. As soon as we moved away I began looking for a place to dump it. "So whaddya think so far?" Dennis asked. We men of the "entering class" had been on campus a week.

"Great," I said.

"Me, I'm not so sure," Dennis replied as we attached ourselves to a group of corridor mates, other New Yorkers, a couple of Chicago kids and one from Medford, north of Boston. No sign of my roommate, Frank Cormier. Frank was undecided whether to come along. He was from St. Dominick's in Lewiston, one of La Salle's big hockey rivals. His real name Jean-François, so we had something important in common.

Back at the dorm I navigated the stairs unsteadily. It wasn't yet ten, lights-out having been extended this Friday night. Frank was already dead to the world. As soon as I flopped down, the room began to rotate. I congratulated myself on taking the first bus back, the only smart thing I'd done all night.

I awoke with a start, on top of the bed, still in my clothes, light on. My new clock said two-fifteen. My mouth was parched and I needed to take a leak in the worst way. The room had stopped spinning but now I had this splitting headache. So I hadn't just fallen asleep, I had passed out. I went to my dresser, found my toothbrush and a bottle of aspirin and stumbled toward the bathroom.

What hit me first was the overwhelming stench. Chunks of yellowish-brown barf dripped from the first sink onto the floor. I held my breath and moved down the row... the next two were also fouled. I set my toothbrush and paste on the last sink and plodded to the urinals, avoiding barfprints at the toilet stalls, then took what had to be the longest leak of my life. Back in my room I undressed, dropped my clothes on the floor and fell back into bed.

Next morning, I awoke surprisingly clear-headed. I was ashamed at losing control, passing out. I took a deep breath. Okay, I screwed up... go on from here. This will not happen again. What others did was up to them. Not that I was better than anybody else, but I had to be who I was, whatever that was.

I wondered what our corridor priest Father Raymond thought about it. He surely knew this stuff went on, and the people running the college. I watched the bulletin boards but there was no admonition, none at the corridor rosary, none at Mass. The attitude seemed to be "boys will be boys," as if this bizarre behavior was part of our preparation, as I would learn they were so fond of saying, to take our places as leaders of society.

ADJACENT TO "THE QUAD" was our community center, Kimball Hall. Residents took meals in the dining hall but day-hops didn't share this bonding experience. And bond we did, over basically decent food with the occasional varicose chicken leg with yellow sauce over rice. Some considered the food unfit for human consumption and ate out often, but I have mostly fond memories of the sights and smells and tastes. It helped that I waited tables. Waiters had first dibs on food before the steam table did its number, solidifying the spud, wilting the bean and congealing the "loaf." Only athletes ate better, exceptionally well on game days – steak and egg breakfasts. A lot of student body officers and top students were waiters, and during off-season a surprising number of athletes as well. Right away I got to know a lot of interesting people, and from all four classes, too. Ordinary work (I hesitate to call it humble) can be not only respectable but respected. I also learned, if you want something done right, ask a busy person to do it.

School spirit was legendary, and friendliness official policy. Everyone was expected to say hello or good morning, even if they didn't know the other person. There were no fraternities, social or residential. One legend has a priest walking along reading his breviary – prayerbook, that is – when, greeted by a new freshman, he replied, "Fuck you, sonny," then continued on. Turned out it was a senior who had gotten hold of a cassock and a collar.

Dress was conservative – suits, sport jackets charcoal gray or Harris Tweed, blue blazer and ties for class and official occasions, golf shirts and Bermudas for informality, chinos, oxford cloth shirts and crew neck sweaters, desert boots or dirty white bucks. There was considerable economic diversity – some from wealth, others relying on scholarships and loans, but like La Salle, almost everyone, student body and faculty alike, was Catholic. Everybody was male and nearly all of us were white. We were all products of a good to excellent high school or prep education.

What differences there were, however, mattered mightily. Irish or Italian, New York or Boston, aesthete or jock. Classicist, humanist, scientist or businessman. Dean's list or gentleman's C. Nothing, of course, compared with the diversities I discovered later, what some few of my fellows from the inner city knew even then.

Beyond a grassy expanse near the campus' eastern edge stands St. Joseph Memorial Chapel, not a chapel at all but a massive structure that put my parish church to shame. One of Holy Cross' hallmarks was the closeness of the faculty and students, reinforcing the link between academics and the spiritual life. We were led in the classroom by the same men who offered the holy sacrifice of the Mass, two sides of a single coin. Some were better teachers than others, but then, which of us was the student he might have been?

That first Sunday, Mass was celebrated by the college President, Rev. J. Walter McBride, S.J., an eloquent orator, best I'd ever heard. From the pulpit Father McBride greeted the Class of '63, warning that a great deal is expected of Holy Cross men but assuring us that the college community stands ready to help. He told us to look forward to the freshman retreat, a four-day affair in October he promised would "open our eyes like nothing we've ever seen," which, as it turned out, was a serious understatement.

13. SPIRITUAL EXERCISES

LATE AFTERNOON AND I AM FEELING BETTER. The cold tablets helped, plus a bit of down time. Around four Jonathan returns with today's *Times*. "Here we go," he says, "page 8. 'Yesterday General Philip Parsons, commander of U.S. forces in Baghdad, responded to calls for an investigation of the attack that killed journalist Paul Bernard. He said the Army has already initiated its inquiry and he is personally committed to getting to the bottom of the incident.'"

"That'll be the day," I say.

"Deplores the loss of life – I'm paraphrasing here –news organizations know the risks... no guarantees. Random, no reason to believe otherwise. Okay, here we go. 'General Parson admitted no one from the ambush party has been identified though the Army is following several leads and will keep the press informed.'"

"That's the best they can do." Jonathan slams the paper down. "Totally useless."

"The military isn't meant for detective work. Think surgery with boxing gloves."

* * * * * * *

ON A CHILL OCTOBER EVENING three hundred sixty young men filed past the massive wooden doors of the college chapel. Inside, candles flickered, the air heavy with spent incense. From the spacious interior came an overwhelming impression of stability, the arches and columns less about soaring praise than accountability, responsibility. Fittingly the church was named for that most solid of saints – St. Joseph, bedrock of the Holy Family.

At precisely seven-thirty, a short, moon-faced priest emerged from the side of the sanctuary, genuflected, and mounted the pulpit. "For those of you I haven't met," he began, "I am Father Barry, the college chaplain. I welcome you men of the Class of 1963 to Holy Cross, and extend best wishes that your four years will be holy and fruitful. Now then, to retreat means to withdraw, to regroup and emerge stronger. From this moment, for four full days, excepting only your prayerful responses here, you will observe silence, complete silence. You will speak with no one. All classes, labs and extra-curricular activities are cancelled."

We looked at each other. The oddity of this enterprise was sinking in. "A successful retreat is hard work, so if you find yourselves sailing through the week you're not getting it right. As a young man Ignatius of Loyola served the Crown of Spain as a military officer. As a man trains for a race or a battle, he authored his Spiritual Exercises for those wishing to strengthen themselves for the battle for their immortal souls. For make no mistake, gentlemen, you are in a battle for that most important prize of all, eternal happiness. To succeed you must train hard and go beyond your limits. As St. Ignatius was a soldier, so also you must be, in the service of Christ."

The priest pointed over our heads. "If some emergency compels you to break your silence, do so to one of the priests. Of course, you don't ignore an attack of appendicitis," a smile played about his lips, "but a word to the wise. From long experience my colleagues and I can distinguish a compelling reason from an excuse. Finally, a word about your retreat master. Father William Ronan has been at Holy Cross longer than any of you have been alive. He is one of our most respected and learned faculty members, but his real love is this freshman retreat he has conducted the past twenty-three years. I pray these few days will mark the time when, once and for all, you embrace sanctity as your way of life. Finally, let me wish you good luck and godspeed."

As Father Barry stepped down another priest appeared – tall and lean, a purple stole about his neck, shadows from the dim light marking his long face. I looked at my seatmate and we shook our heads. Never seen him before. He settled into the pulpit. "'I will go unto the altar of God,'" he began, "'to God, the joy of my youth.' Words from the Book of Psalms, Chapter 42, Verse 4. In the name of the Father, and of the Son, and of the Holy Ghost."

"Amen," we responded, making the sign of the cross.

Pulling on steel-rimmed glasses, he went on. "Our Lord said it best. 'What does it profit a man if he gain the whole world but suffer the loss of his immortal soul?' My dear young men, your most important task in life, the only job that really matters, is to prepare yourselves for eternity. Ecclesiasticus warns, 'Remember only thy last things and thou shalt not sin for ever.' So simple, so obvious. Sixty, seventy years versus eternity! As we are painfully aware, however, knowing and doing are not the same."

Deep and sonorous, the priest's voice reverberated through the half-empty church. He spoke deliberately, pausing often. "Each day you are surrounded by temptations designed to distract you from the task of saving your souls. Make no mistake – Satan is real, and he is a wily and formidable adversary. Do not underestimate his intelligence or his resolve. He presents the good things of God – food, drink, material goods, friendship, love – in a guise calculated to damage your immortal soul.

"These few days we will meditate on The Four Last Things – Death, Judgment, Hell and Heaven." The priest stared down at us, two bright discs obscuring his eyes. "At that all-important moment, when you are called on to account for your life, what will the condition of your soul be? First, however, close your eyes and imagine what it is like to die. You have been ill," he went on softly, "in and out of the hospital. Now exhausted, ready to let go, you lie at home. Your loved ones surround you. Medication has eased the pain. The parish priest has given you the last rites. Picture the scene, see yourself in it." The priest paused. "Then again, it may be quite different. Sprawled on a battlefield halfway across the world you cry out in agony, your body riddled with shards of metal. Feel the pain, hear the screams, smell the burning flesh... your flesh. Or..." he paused again, "there you are, driving home to your family, rich, successful, in your prime, when an oncoming car swerves and you know something very bad is about to happen. The point, as Our Lord warns, you will know neither the day nor the hour.

"Will you be calm and confident? Or furious at squandering your chance to serve the Lord? The agony! The shame! A wasted life passes before you and you tremble, for it will be thumbs down for all eternity," he chops the air with his hand, "and there is absolutely – nothing – you – can – do – about – it! Worst of all, it did not have to be this way. You gasp an act of contrition," the priest spreads his arms, "and who knows? The infinitely merciful God may take pity. But is that how you want it to end? A last-minute escape from a life of sin? Better to know that although your life wasn't perfect you did your best – when you turned away you came back to the path. As you stand alone before the all-knowing God, which will it be? 'Come, blessed of my Father, take possession of the kingdom prepared for you from the foundation of the world?' Oh happy soul, hearing those words! Or will it be, 'Depart from me accursed ones, into the everlasting fire prepared for the devil and his angels!'"

The priest pointed his glasses at us. "We resume tomorrow at nine. Spend this time in prayerful contemplation, clear your mind of the clutter. Now repeat after me the prayer of St. Ignatius that sets forth so clearly why we are here. "Soul of Christ, sanctify me," he began. Only a few spoke up, nobody wanting to be first. "Body of Christ, save me. Body of Christ, save me." More joined in now. "Blood of Christ, inebriate me." I glanced around... some smirks, but we were into it now. "Blood of Christ, inebriate me!" We went on, "...in the hour of death call me, and bid me come to Thee, that with Thy Saints I may praise Thee, forever and ever. Amen."

I stayed behind, asking God to help me make a good retreat. I prayed for my family, particularly Jim, asking for the strength to love him in spite of everything.

MORNING OF THE FIRST FULL DAY. After a cold rain the day dawned bright and sunny. The mood seemed lighter. "'In the beginning was the Word, and the Word was with God; and the Word was God. He was in the beginning with God. All things were made through Him, and without Him was made nothing that has been made.' Words from the Gospel according to Saint John, Chapter 1, Verses 1 through 3. In the name of the Father, and of the Son, and of the Holy Ghost."

"Amen."

Father Ronan shuffled some papers then looked up. "Our task this morning is to make a start on purging your souls of sin, but first we need to understand who you really are. 'I'm James. I'm Italian. I'm seventeen, from New York. I'm a math major at Holy Cross. I'm a Roman Catholic.' Good answers, but insufficient. In the sight of God, James, *who are you?* Our Faith gives us the answer. You are a creature of God, plain and simple. Without God's spontaneous, loving act of creation, you would be nothing. No wants, no needs, no rights, no duties. The fact is, you simply would not exist. Nor would you know anything is amiss, for there'd be no 'you' to be aware of anything! All right, what's the proper way to react to this truth? With humility, gentlemen. Humility to acknowledge your insignificance when it comes to what really matters. And the courage to accept who is in charge."

I tried to imagine what it would be like never to have been born. No sights, no sounds, no memories, no hopes, no plans. But how do you think of nothing? What does it look like? This... void, I shuddered, it's way beyond me.

The priest was going on. "From this truth another follows. Since you are the creature, you are not God, you cannot be God, you never will be God. You nod your heads. That's so obvious, why even mention it? Let me tell you why. Remember all those times you played God, pretended He wasn't there? Those times you set your course contrary to God's plan? Another name for this is pride, thinking you can go it alone. Now notice, gentlemen, we've just touched on the spiritual disorder known as sin. Ecclesiasticus tells us, 'Pride is the beginning of all sin, and it shall ruin him in the end.'"

The priest looked out over our heads. "As St. Paul so truly observed, 'I do not the good that I wish but the evil that I do not wish... I see another law in my members warring against the law of my mind and making me prisoner to the law of sin that is in my members.' Sound familiar? My dear young men, why this predicament? Wanting to love God but pulled powerfully by our lower instincts. Adam's and Eve's pride – there's that word again – their pride led them down that path. Oh, they so wanted to be like God! But they were driven from the Garden, consigned to toilsome labor and sorrow, to eat bread in the sweat of their brow until they return to the soil whence they came. And sadly for us, the sins of that father and mother were indeed visited upon their descendants, for each of us is dust and unto dust we shall return. Each of us is tempted, and in our weakness we fall.

"Long before the sin of our first parents, disorder and evil were in the world. Created in grace, the most privileged angel in heaven, Lucifer's pride led to his fall and instantly grace became malice. His formidable powers enable him to this day to do great harm to the sons of Adam. God wants men at His side for eternity, but the devil and his dark angels compete tirelessly for those same men. With these foes no holds are barred, they play for keeps."

The priest put his glasses down and fell silent for a moment. "When we think of Hell, what first comes to mind is fire. A burn is painful but time and care will cure it or *in extremis,* death ends our suffering. But what of the fire that never ends, the fire from which the damned know no escape, not the briefest cooling breeze? Your parched lungs gasp for breath, the torrid, sulfurous fumes fill your nose and mouth. Close your eyes and visualize this place of eternal misery, this place with no exit. Your body is wracked with pain, but the mental torment is far worse. Cries and wails fill this infernal region, the damned blaspheming against Christ and His saints. They know what brought them to this place – pleasure, greed, preferring earthly things to God's friendship." The priest leaned over the pulpit and shook his finger. "WRETCHED SOUL!" he thundered. "BITTER, MISERABLE SOUL!

Aware every instant of your eternal suffering, THIS DID NOT HAVE TO HAPPEN!"

His tone became more confidential. "From time to time, we lose something of value, a sum of money, a watch or the like. We feel stupid and inadequate, but," he shrugged, "we can replace such things. Even when a loved one dies hope consoles us, our hope of reuniting with that mother, that father, that friend in paradise. Imagine the pain of knowing that never again will you enjoy the company of that loved one, never again will you see your family and friends. Realizing that the vision of God, the presence of the loving Creator, is lost to you FOREVER! And through your own choice! 'Abandon all hope, ye who enter here.' I put it this way – you made a deal with the Devil and you lost. Did you ever lose!"

"Eternity." He paused and steepled his hands, leaning his chin on his fingertips. "Thought much about eternity lately? Remember your catechism? It was a start, but let's see if we can't do better. You're standing on a beach. Waves lap ashore, water spreads across the sand and seeps back. The sands seem endless. Ask yourselves, how many grains of sand does that shore hold? If you started today, how long would it take to count them all? A year? A hundred years? A thousand?" He smiled. "Then consider, this beach is but a small part of the shoreline. There's sand in Mexico and Central America. Our west coast has a lot of sand, not to mention other continents and islands, full of sand, all of them. How long would it take to count the grains? A million years? Say a billion, for argument's sake. So one day in a far millenium, or billenium, you finish. Time for a well-deserved rest! Well, I hate to tell you, but we just heard from the boss and he says you've got to start over again – from the beginning. And when you finish that second tally, do it over and over, again and again.

"Try this. Compared to eternity, the time this monumental task takes is as one single grain of sand compared to all those grains of sand on all the shores of our earth! So then, is this eternity? I think not. Not even a pale approximation.

"How many stars are there? On a clear winter night, on a mountaintop, you look up. Unbelievable! So dense, and ours is but one of countless galaxies reaching who knows how far into the deep recesses of space. Are there an infinite number of stars? Would it take an eternity to count them all? To travel to all of them? To repeat the journey, again and again? Each of us a speck in the universe, our bodies composed of the chemical compounds and electrical energy we see everywhere. We are part of the continuum of the material world, and it is thanks only to our intellectual and spiritual powers we have any chance to discern, however faintly, the meaning of eternity. The shackles of our flesh hold our intellects back, but you know, perhaps this is good enough. Shouldn't even an imperfect idea of eternity motivate us, no, *compel us* to avoid eternal suffering and deprivation?

"My dear young men, this is your time and place to be tested, you will have no other. Will you commit yourselves to getting it right? Commit yourselves now. TODAY!" He looked out over the lectern. "This afternoon read the Book of Genesis, Chapters One through Three. At the back of the chapel there are stacks of bibles. They are for you, to be your companion your four years here at Holy

Cross. Now join me in the prayer Our Lord taught us. Our Father, who art in heaven, hallowed be Thy name."

We joined in heartily. "Thy Kingdom come, Thy will be done, on earth as it is in heaven. Give us this day our daily bread, and forgive us our sins as we forgive those who trespass against us. And lead us not into temptation, but deliver us from evil. Amen."

Again I lingered. What if I could trace myself back, trace the earth, the universe? Everything came from something that was there before, it didn't come from nothing. There had to be a beginning. At that moment, a great comfort arose in me. This beginning wasn't some abstract idea or blob of matter, it was a Person, an all-powerful Person who cares for us, cares for me in the most intimate way. Amazing, totally amazing. Thank you, God.

EVENING OF THE FIRST FULL DAY. I was sitting in my bench, thinking how the loud and garrulous among us burden the rest. For me, this enforced quiet was a welcome break from the mindless banter. Sports, girls, drinking. Drinking, girls, sports. Again I was gravitating toward people who weren't afraid to show their interest in things of the mind. I looked up... Father Ronan again.

"'I know that my Redeemer liveth," he begins, "and in the last day I shall rise out of the earth.' Book of Job, Chapter 19, Verse 25. In the name of the Father, and of the Son, and of the Holy Ghost."

"Amen."

"Let us move to the Gospel's message of good news. One of the devil's best tricks is to portray evil as glamorous, appealing. He even fooled the immortal Dante who, for all his genius, couldn't make his *Paradiso* nearly as interesting as the *Inferno*. It's not news when the boy scout conveys the little old lady across the street. Murder and mayhem trump kindness every time. A current author puts it well: 'The snake had all the lines.' In fact, he still has a lot of them. If you accept the artist view, what's the big deal? Lounging on clouds – white sheets, cherubs, harps and so on. Doesn't sound all that great, does it? Could it be that our eternal reward is nothing but a negative, avoiding the torments of hell? That would be worth the effort, but happily our Faith tells us there are even better things in store for the just man. That most noble activity of the human soul, knowing and loving God, will be fulfilled in a way inconceivable on earth. The blessed will see God directly, clearly, distinctly, in the words of St. Paul 'face to face,' the creature and his Creator, bound through love and praise. We'd like to know more, but this Beatific Vision is a mystery and we simply have to await our experience of it. However, it is a revealed truth of our Faith and a great comfort to us."

Father Ronan paused. For the first time his face was animated, happy. "Aquinas teaches that perfect happiness is the true and supreme end of man. St. Augustine said, 'Thou hast made us for Thyself, O God, our heart is ill at ease til it find rest in Thee.' Even our most sublime human moments, relationships, events, are clouded by the certainty they will not last. The universal human experience of pain and loss make this plain. Sadness is ever the frame of our joy. But in heaven our happiness is everlasting, for God is eternal and our souls immortal. No more fear of loss, and that's not all – the blessed soul enjoys the company of Christ, the angels and the saints, as well as his dear ones. At the Last Judgment each soul will be reunited with its own glorified body, purified according to God's plan.

"Man's error brought sin into the world. Theologians say that is why a man was chosen to help undo the harm. But no mere human could accomplish this, so God sent His Son into the world to assume our human nature and expunge the stain of original sin. My dear young men, sin confuses us, offers us unworthy models of what to be and how to live. His Son shows us what a man can be, should be. The life of Jesus opens a window onto heaven, showing us not only how to get there but why it's so important to try. So let us together open that window. St. Ignatius called this part of the retreat the Illuminative Way, where our souls are enlightened and we are inspired to imitate Christ by making His virtues our own. Is Christ one of your heroes? If not, I would like to think after this week He will be.

"Picture Earth before the time of Christ. The nations varied in dress and bearing, some white, others black, brown, yellow. Some at peace, some at war. People weep, people laugh, some in good health, others sick, some being born, others dying, and not one person living or who ever lived, *not one single person* with a chance for heaven! All nations, all people in darkness, cut off from God. Then, Miracle of Miracles, His Son embarks on His mission of redemption.

"But why to Nazareth in Galilee? And of all people, why to Mary, daughter of Anna and Joachim? The prophets foretold some of this, but why did God put such ideas in their heads? We simply don't know. The fact is, God ordained that His Son would become man, a specific individual in a specific place, at a specific time. The miracle of Christ shows that God does not stand apart from human history, but is involved in the most intimate way, sustaining us as individuals, day in and day out. 'Not a sparrow falls to the ground without your Father's leave.' Matthew, Chapter 11, Verse 29.

"Next let us meditate on the Holy Family's flight into Egypt. Joseph the caregiver seeks to avoid Herod's wrath and protect his wife and the Child. An unexpected journey of about a week along the old caravan route between Palestine and Egypt, the newborn infant at Mary's breast, the little family nourishing itself with what food and water they can carry, unprepared, exhausted, sleeping on the ground. What courage and perseverance! Close your eyes and see the three travelers journey into exile in a foreign country.

"You young men will identify with this next story. Every year at Passover the Holy Family went to Jerusalem, but on the trip back when Jesus was twelve his parents lost him. They lost him! They thought he was in the caravan with relatives and friends but he wasn't. After three days combing Jerusalem, they found him in the temple, 'sitting in the midst of the teachers, listening and asking them questions. And all who were listening to him were amazed at his understanding and his answers.' Were his parents relieved? Absolutely. But Mary lets Jesus know in no uncertain terms the sorrow he has caused them. 'How is it that you sought me?' he replies, 'did you not know that I must be about my Father's business?'

Then the Gospel says he returned with them to Nazareth 'and was subject to them.'

"Honor thy father and thy mother," the priest went on. "Words to live by, even as you set out on your own adult lives. One final comment. That temple scene is our last look at Jesus until his thirtieth year. I wish we could have seen how Jesus dealt with the trials of young adulthood, the situation you're in, but that was not to be. However with Jesus' example, with the sacraments and the Church's teachings, you will make it through."

Yes, I thought, I would have appreciated something more.

"Tonight read in Thomas à Kempis' *The Imitation of Christ.* Pick up your copy in back of the church. This treasure of spiritual counsel is about achieving serenity and inner peace. Read Book One, 'Admonitions Useful for a Spiritual Life,' and now let us acknowledge Jesus' mother, our mother and our advocate. "Hail Mary, full of grace! The Lord is with thee. Blessed art thou amongst women, and blessed is the fruit of thy womb, Jesus. Holy Mary, Mother of God, pray for us sinners, now and at the hour of our death. Amen."

MORNING OF THE SECOND DAY. Wide awake, one of those times you know you'll never get back to sleep so why try. I dress and go out into the darkness. The tower clock says twenty past four. Lying low in the eastern sky is the grayish-pink band that will become the dawn. I'd been beset by dreams I don't remember. I pass Fenwick, kicking up damp leaves. The chapel door is locked so I climb the rise to the Jesuit cemetery which I haven't yet explored. Tablets row upon row, clean and tidy, impressive in a creepy sort of way. I sit on a stone bench and stare at the markers. My breath stands out before me. What will it be like to stop breathing? To be still forever like these men who just the other day ate, drank, laughed, cried? Ricardus J. Cleary S.J. *Natus* 24 Aug. 1888, *Obiit* 4 Mar. 1952. Petrus R. McElwain... Paulus F. X. Dunn.

I breathe in deeply... fifteen seconds... twenty... thirty... OOOF! Another of my life's billion breaths explodes into the chill air. What was it like for these men? What will it be like for me, laid out in a box when they shut the lid? In the dark I panic but can't scream because I'm dead nor can I dry my tears, for besides being dead my arms are pinned to my sides... never did like tight spaces claustrophobia I suppose then more bumping lifting tilting I hear an engine running more jostling and voices I fall falling then wait for the dirt I know is coming I was there for Eugene a clot thuds on the wood over my head two three four five six the sound is softer now dirt falling on dirt then everything is quiet. Quiet.

I shake my head... this retreat business is getting to me. Ridiculous, I think, why worry? There's a chance I won't feel anything at all. Father Ronan's non-being – can't rule that out altogether. Or maybe I've already met Jesus and he's invited me to live with Him forever which means I am peering down at that group of mourners, my sister and brother, father and mother if they're still around, wife and children, whoever they turn out to be. "Don't worry!" I shout, "everything's fine!

It's wonderful!" Or I am looking up from that other place and being trapped in a box is the least of my concerns.

Suddenly I have the feeling I'm not alone. I look up and in the half-light I see a figure moving toward me. For a moment I wonder if I'm dreaming but the hairs on my arms tell me I am not. My first instinct is to flee, I am an intruder, after all, then I think, what's *he* doing here? The tall figure draws closer... rooted to the bench I see... it's Father Ronan! He nods silently, passes, then stops and turns. "Would you like to serve my Mass?"

That's it, of course. It would be an honor, I think, but...

"Don't worry, the responses won't break your vow."

He knew! Well sure, two days straight I've been sitting twenty feet away from him. Or maybe I just look like a freshman. I nod.

"Well, let's get to it."

He leads the way out of the cemetery, I trail behind. At a side door to the church he takes out a key ring. I follow him down a set of stairs to a small altar in the far corner of basement room where he opens a cabinet and fishes around. "These'll fit," he says, tossing a cassock and surplice to me. After he finishes robing – the color of the day was green, I remember – we stand at the bottom of the single step before the altar. He bows. I kneel.

In Nomine Patris, et Filii, et Spiritus Sancti. Amen. Introibo ad altare Dei. Ad Deum Qui laetificat juventutem meam. The responses return... how long has it been? He moves at a respectful pace. I feel calm, serene. After the final prayers, he turns and makes the sign of the cross over me. In silence we disrobe. Nearby two other priests suit up. When everything is put away, Father Ronan stretches out his hand. "No need to say anything, Paul, but thank you. It's a treat to have a server."

Paul! I smile and shake his hand. A big hand, a firm handshake.

"I'll be here a bit longer but feel free to be about your day."

I slip on my jacket and leave. How did he know my name? So composed, he is here... where does he get that fire we see? I can tell he enjoys terrifying us. I can see him in the nether world with tour guides Virgil and Dante and I smile. The tower clock reads five-fifty.

A FEW HOURS LATER and we took our places again. Father Ronan appeared and mounted to the pulpit. Nine o'clock... I'd already been awake half the day. As always, he gazed into the cavernous church, left to right, front to back, but for a moment his eyes settled on me and he nodded, the hint of a smile on his face. "'Now when the centurion saw what had happened, he glorified God, saying, "Truly this was a just man."' Words taken from St. Luke's Gospel, Chapter 24, Verse 47. In the name of the Father, and of the Son, and of the Holy Ghost."

"Amen."

"The Spirit led Jesus into the desert. After fasting forty days and forty nights He was hungry and the devil came to Him and said, 'If thou art the Son of God, command that these stones become loaves of bread.' But Jesus answered, 'Not by bread alone does man live, but by every word that comes forth from the mouth of

God.' Bread, earthly goods are for man to use, to nourish and support him, not enslave him.

"The devil then took Jesus into Jerusalem and set him on the pinnacle of the temple. If you are the Son of God, throw yourself off the roof, for Scripture says God has given the angels care for His Son so no harm will come to Him. Jesus replies, 'It is written further, "Thou shalt not tempt the Lord thy God."' Jesus refuses to dignify the devil's arrogance.

"Finally, from a high mountain the devil showed Jesus the glory of the kingdoms of the world, all yours if you will bow down and worship me. But Jesus said, 'Begone, Satan! For it is written "The Lord thy God shalt thou worship and him only shall thou serve."' Jesus' mission is not about political power and glory, a message forgotten even by some Church leaders in times past." Father Ronan leaned over the pulpit. "Why do you suppose Jesus let Himself be challenged? I would say He did it for us, immersed as we are in temptation, so we might take solace from His struggle."

Images of the Holy Land came to me... Jerusalem, villages, the desert. Never been to that part of the world, I thought, never been anywhere. Our country has great deserts – Painted Desert, Mohave. There's something about the idea of a desert – barren, harsh, arid. Tough people. Survivors. Perfect place for a test of wills. Am I a survivor? How do you become a survivor, I wondered. Maybe these few days are a start.

"Returning to Galilee, Jesus began preaching and healing the sick. One day on a mountain near the Sea of Galilee, Jesus sat with his disciples and began to teach. "'Blessed are the poor in spirit for theirs is the kingdom of heaven. Blessed are the meek for they shall possess the earth. Blessed are they who mourn... they who hunger and thirst for justice... the merciful... the clean of heart... the peacemakers... they who suffer persecution for justice' sake.'"

Father Ronan looked up. "Jesus tells us, align yourselves with the less fortunate. Later he goes even further. I was hungry and you gave me to eat. I was thirsty and you gave me to drink. I was a stranger and you took me in, naked and you covered me, sick and you visited me. I was in prison and you came to me. Then the inevitable question, 'Lord, when did we ever see you in need?' and His astonishing answer, 'as long as you did it for one of these, the least of my brethren, you did it for me.' You did it for me! Clearly, your chances for heaven depend on what you do for those around us who suffer and are in need.

"Jesus says a rich man enters the kingdom of heaven only with difficulty. So what are we to do? 'Do not lay up for yourselves treasures on earth where rust and moth consume, and where thieves break in and steal. But lay up for yourselves treasures in heaven... for where thy treasure is, there also will thy heart be.' Did you hear that? *Where thy treasure is, there also will thy heart be!* Yes, the person who takes Jesus seriously has two strikes against him in this world. And yes, the race we run is unfair. Despite the beauty of the earth, despite the saintliness of many, this is a tough world, not a nice place. Fallout from original sin is everywhere. Mendacity, cheating and selfishness abound, the gap between the 'is' and the 'ought' dishearteningly wide. So do you play it smart, having one set of values for Sunday, another for the rest of the week?" Father Ronan shook his head. "No, you can't divide life like that. Keep the commandments, Jesus told the young man seeking the way to eternal life, but then the difficult part, 'if thou wilt be perfect, go, sell what thou hast, and give to the poor... and come, follow me.' He looked down at us. "You shake your heads. Impractical, you say. That's what the young man in the story thought too, and he went away sad. Father Ronan stared down... I felt he was looking directly at me. "Will you young men go away sad?"

His words troubled me. You need to live decently, take care of your family, but how, if you maintain your principles? How reconcile the "is" and the "ought" and not be destroyed by the effort? Here, at least, in this land of God's bounty, there must be a way.

The priest backed away from the railing. "Let us turn now to the Last Supper. Today I want to focus on the two disciples who clouded that evening." He steepled his hands and raised them to his face. "Since that time and forevermore, the name Judas signifies 'traitor.' At the start of the meal Jesus shocked his disciples. "One of you will betray me." The disciples crowded around. 'Is it I, Lord?' Who could possibly think of betraying the beloved master? 'Is it I?' When it was Judas' turn, Jesus replied simply, 'Thou hast said it.'

"Everyone knows the story. Judas did indeed hand Jesus over and Peter denied knowing Jesus, but notice what happened next. Peter wept bitterly but he came back strong. Not only did Jesus forgive Peter, but gave him a hugely important job. Judas? Realizing what he had done, Judas returned to the priests and elders and flung the blood money at them, but despair overcame him and he 'went away and hanged himself with a halter.' As far as we know, Judas didn't reconcile with Jesus, but who's to say? That is between him and the Lord. If asked, Jesus would have welcomed Judas back. No sinner is beyond the pale. Once again, Jesus' character and life are our guide. Forgive those who trespass against us, difficult though that may be.

"This afternoon, meditate on Matthew's Gospel. Now let us say together the wonderful prayer of St. Francis. "God grant me the serenity to accept the things I cannot change, the courage to change the things I can, and the wisdom to know the difference."

EVENING OF THE SECOND DAY. The air was fast escaping the balloon. Some of the guys were sneaking out for pizza and beer, the rule of silence was fading fast. That afternoon in my room, I finally had it with the noise. I went up to a group in the corridor and put my hands over my ears, shaking my head.

"Lighten up, Bernard! It's the middle of the afternoon, for Chrissakes." Fran McNulty, one of the offenders. "Too bad we're not all perfect like you."

"Thanks for the advice," I blurted out. Damn! My ears reddened at the slip.

I left to a chorus of laughs. Somebody else mumbled, "no, thank you, Saint Bernard." A third guy barked. I flipped them the bird. No more effective but quieter.

Father Ronan was on time, as always. A new cardinal virtue, I thought – punctuality. "'The Lord appeared to Abraham," he began, "and He said, 'I am God the Almighty. Walk in my presence and be perfect.'" Words taken from the Book of Genesis, Chapter 17, Verse 1. In the name of the Father, and of the Son, and of the Holy Ghost."

"Amen."

Be perfect. Right.

"As we near the mid-way point of our retreat, let me remind you why we spend so much time on Jesus' life. Simply put, to achieve your heavenly goal you must model your life on His. Tomorrow we will conclude our reflections on Jesus' life, but tonight, in preparation for your confession Thursday, we're going to make a trial run at examining your consciences. Your lives need fixing, so let us get about the task. Close your eyes, concentrate, and bring to mind your failings and sins."

I swallowed. This was always difficult. Father Ronan bowed his head. "We thank you, Lord, for bringing us here. We accept your invitation to improve our lives, and we are prepared to face our faults openly and honestly. We ask for the grace to confess our sins, we ask for true sorrow and repentance, we ask your help to remake our lives after yours.

"I am the Lord thy God," he went on, "thou shalt not have strange gods before me. Do I make time for God, acknowledge Him through frequent prayer?" A lengthy pause. "Second commandment, thou shalt not take the name of the Lord in vain. Have I used the name of God or Jesus in anger, lightly, carelessly? Ungrateful worm, how could I presume to dishonor His sacred name?" Another pause. "The third. Thou shalt keep holy the Sabbath Day. Through my fault have I missed Mass on Sundays or Holy Days of Obligation? Is Sunday a day for work or routine instead of the special day set aside to pay homage to Him?

"Do I honor my parents? Or do I treat them as beneath their sophisticated son and his friends? In family arguments do I act as peacemaker? Do I visit older relatives, assist them in their need?" This was a tough one. My father working so hard, my mother sacrificing her talent to the family's needs, sometimes I took them for granted. What about Catherine? Jim? Did I meet them halfway or wait for them to begin treating me right, which would be a long wait?

"Fifth commandment, thou shalt not kill. Have I fought with someone, caused physical harm without just cause? Have I harmed myself through alcohol or other excess? Have I wished another harm, been angry or resentful? Have I led another into temptation, endangering his immortal soul?" Omer. I'd confessed it right away, what else could I do? Wasn't the rest between Omer and God?

"Sixth. Thou shalt not commit adultery." I felt his eyes on my soul. "Have I engaged in impure acts, whether with a girl, a woman, with myself or, God forbid, with another boy or a man? Have I taken pleasure in impure thoughts, living the sin in my mind? These sins debase and enslave us and cause us to treat others as objects instead of persons deserving our respect and kindness. Even impure acts that we think of as private are not. They make establishing satisfying and healthy relationships more difficult. When you are married you must avoid the use of contraceptives. The act of procreation is central to God's design. Deliberately closing off the opportunity for new life is a serious sin." He looked up. "This commandment is important, but don't fixate on it to the exclusion of the rest.

"Thou shalt not steal. The ways of violating this Commandment are subtle and varied. Have you cheated others out of what is rightly theirs? Do you live up to your agreements? Are you establishing a habit of sharp dealing that can lead to serious dishonesty? If you become an employer, will you pay a living wage? Whether you are caught in dishonesty is not the point. The properly formed conscience catches itself. And as sin has its origin in pride, it also springs from an unhealthy attachment to the things of this world.

"The Eighth. Thou shalt not bear false witness against thy neighbor. Few of us see themselves as liars, but take a closer look. Have you injured someone's reputation? Do you shade the truth when it's to your advantage? Do you tell one person one thing, another something else? As with stealing, lying about small things begets dishonesty in larger ones. Jesus said that when Satan tells a lie 'he speaks from his very nature, for he is a liar and the Father of Lies.' Recall that Satan's lie to Eve led to her sin and our downfall. Lying and pride are closely connected. Pride is the engine and lying the fuel that makes it go. The prideful person can't abide being caught in an error, can't stand to have his so-called image tarnished. The morally weak person lies to avoid danger, as Peter did when he denied Jesus. In our competitive world, winning and acquisition are everything for the prideful man, the means don't matter. As Thomas à Kempis observed, 'How many perish daily in this world by vain cunning, that care little for a good life nor for the service of God.'

"Now let us turn briefly from falsity to its cognate virtue, truth." I sat up straight... pay attention! "Jesus is the light of the world. St. John's Gospel tells us that everyone who does evil hates the light, and does not come to the light, that his deeds may not be exposed. My dear young men, it is essential that you cultivate respect – no, not just respect, *a passion* for the truth!

"Moving along, thou shalt not covet thy neighbor's wife, nor his goods. Jealousy of another's position or good fortune can be a cancer on the soul, robbing you of your own proper measure of success – worse yet, it can lead to sinful retaliation. The most helpful virtue in this connection is trust, trust in God's care and His plan for you. Remember the lilies of the field. Jesus cautioned, 'do not be anxious, saying what shall we eat? or what shall we drink? or what are we to put on? But seek first the kingdom of God and His justice, and all these things shall be given you besides.'

"The Commandments of the Church. Have I attended Mass faithfully on Sundays and Holy Days of Obligation? Have I fasted and abstained on the days appointed? Have I confessed at least once a year? Have I made my Easter Duty, receiving the Blessed Sacrament at that time? Have I contributed to the support of the Church? And, for the future, do not marry within specified degrees of kindred or at forbidden times.

As Father Ronan stepped back from the railing we let out an audible sigh. After pausing a few moments for our banging and rattling, he went on. "I have a piece of advice for you. The single most effective way to steer clear of sin is to avoid the occasions of sin. You're intelligent, you know the places, the magazines, movies, the people even, that are a problem. Ask your confessor's advice in dealing with these all-too-appealing trouble spots. Prayer and regular use of the sacraments will toughen you for the next temptation. In the heat of battle, as you are being dragged down, ask God to come to your side."

"Your attentiveness has been exemplary," the priest nodded. "Continue examining your consciences and look forward to the most humble, most unconditional confession you've ever made. And now, make a good Act of Contrition." Together we said the familiar words. "Oh my God, I am heartily sorry for having offended Thee. I detest all my sins because I dread the loss of heaven and the pains of hell, but most of all because they offend Thee, my God, who art all-good and deserving of all my love. I firmly resolve with the help of Thy grace, to confess my sins, do penance, and amend my life. Amen."

"For this evening's spiritual reading, *The Imitation of Christ,* Book Two. Meditate prayerfully on the section, 'On the Gladness of a Clean Conscience.'"

I was enjoying my few minutes alone after these sessions... should make it a regular thing, drop in and visit with Jesus from time to time. No agenda, no ceremony, just time spent with a friend. Going back over what Father Ronan said, what I came up with – passion for the truth isn't just some lofty idea. I need to recognize the day-to-day places where it's needed.

THAT EVENING AFTER DINNER, Frank was at the library. Taking a break I was looking out the window when there was a knock on the door. Visiting had fallen off, at least for those of us still observing the silence. I was surprised to see Dennis Healy. As I greeted him with a wave, he handed me a piece of paper. I unfolded it.

'I need to talk to you. Important!' I raised my eyebrows. He took the paper back and pulled a pen from his shirt pocket. 'PLEASE!! I need to talk to you!' He was clearly in pain. I pulled Frank's chair over, then shut the door and drew mine up.

"So," I said, "what's going on?"

"Sorry to do this." He looked more gaunt than usual with bags under his eyes. His skin, sallow at best, seemed almost yellow. That first night at the smoker told me he might have a drinking problem. "You don't mind, I hope," he said, pulling out a pack of Marlboros and picking the ashtray off Frank's desk. "I haven't been keeping the silence," he gestured at his note, "but I figured you were. You're good at that type thing."

That wasn't a compliment. He was in the group I faced off with earlier in the day.

"Well, here's how it is," he said, leaning forward in the chair, his hands on his knees. "I got this girl pregnant. She wants to have the baby but she's afraid to."

"Ah," I said, startled. Why is he telling me this? How do I talk about it? "Sorry to hear that," I offered.

"Not half as much as I am."

"Do her parents know?".

He laughed wryly. "They're totally pissed. They want her to have an abortion. Big Catholics, big family, big house but it comes down to what'll the neighbors think. It's all set for next week." He lowered his head. "It isn't right, it just isn't right." Anguished, he looked at me, "I may be a shit but I'm not a murderer."

I stared back. "Why are you talking to me? We hardly know each other... and look at this afternoon."

He took a drag on the cigarette. "I can't talk to those guys, they don't know the time of day. Father Raymond? He'd get my ass kicked out of here. Confession? Six Our Fathers and six Hail Marys? Six million's more like it."

"Your parents?"

He stubbed out the cigarette. "They are nowhere when the chips are down. You know, it's not like I figured you have a lot of experience with this kind of thing..."

"You'd be surprised," I said.

"What?" he asked, raising his eyebrows.

"Never mind. Another time."

He lit another cigarette. "Look. You probably know what people say about you, the people I run with anyway – they think anybody that's such a straight arrow can't be for real. They're very good at bad-mouthing people behind their back."

This was no surprise but still it made me feel bad. Consider the source, I thought, but something he said... "You said '*they* think.' Are you trying to tell me something?"

"There's more to me than I let on," he replied with a thin smile. "You might say I'm an acquired taste. I'm sorry about this afternoon, McNulty and all."

"I didn't see you objecting."

"See, that's partly why I'm here. I... I like how you stand up for what you think. I'm not the only one, either."

I sat back. "I didn't think anybody noticed."

"You'd be surprised. You've probably figured out I'm into the herd mentality thing but I thought, if you talk this through with me, it might help."

"Give me a minute." It just dawned on me, I never found out what happened to that girl Jim and his friends got in trouble over. At the time we were so fixated on saving him.

"The girl," I ventured, "you're willing to marry her?"

"Yeah. Even before this happened we were talking about that."

"Ask her again. Maybe she will."

"My father'd kill me. He has plans for his eldest son. God does he have plans."

"Eldest son," I said beneath my breath. I stopped to think, trying to figure out what to say next. "Okay," I finally said, "how about this. Tell her you'll marry her if she has the baby. Since you love each other, maybe that wouldn't be so bad."

"That would royally screw up my career."

"But doing the right thing has a certain ring to it, *n'est-ce pas?*"

"What?"

"Old Indian expression. White man get squaw in trouble, white man get her out." For the first time he smiled. I thought of Jim and Sheila, how my parents liked her. "My guess is the parents would come around. There's money to get started?"

"Oh, yes, money is not the problem." Dennis looked dubious, gloomy.

I thought I'd try to lighten things up a little. "Well, there you go. Advice to the lovelorn. I'll have to work up a column for the *Crusader* along those lines."

"I doubt they'd publish it."

I laughed. "Don't bet on it. I have experience in that area, too."

He stood. "I still don't know what to do, but thanks. This helps a lot."

As he started to leave, I thought of something. "You know, it wouldn't hurt to see one of the other priests. Father Ronan, maybe?"

He held out his hand. "Maybe. Thanks, Paul. This is between us, right?"

"Of course."

I sat on the edge of my bed a long time. Who was I to give advice? The only thing I felt comfortable about was telling him to talk to somebody with experience. But it felt good. Apparently some people thought well of me, though they couldn't bring themselves to say so. I had a hard time getting to sleep, lots of things running through my mind.

MORNING OF THE THIRD DAY. Father Ronan put his watch on the lectern "Jesus answered Simon Peter, 'Where I am going thou canst not follow me now, but thou shalt follow later.' Words taken from the Gospel of St. John, Chapter 13, Verse 36. In the Name of the Father, and of the Son, and of the Holy Ghost."

"Amen."

"The examination of conscience is often followed by discouragement. You may think reforming your life is just too difficult. If you find yourself at this low point, it means you are taking your retreat seriously. The grace of God is with you, and your spiritual mentors are too, every step of the way. As we resume our meditation on Christ's passion and death keep this in mind. Jesus suffered and died for *you.* Not for some vague concept of humanity but for the person who looks back in your mirror every morning, that person who fails often but is sorry and makes amends. Because of your sins Our Lord went to his Passion and death. You are the reason Jesus hung from that cross."

Father Ronan closed his eyes. "Picture Jesus at Gethsemane. A 'country place,' the Gospel writers say, by tradition an olive grove, a short walk from the site of the Last Supper. Awaiting His trial, Jesus' humanity is on plain display. He takes Peter and James and John with Him for support. Such a typical human reaction, to be with friends in times of difficulty. Then Jesus begins to be troubled, 'My soul is sad,' he tells them, 'even unto death.' 'Wait here and watch with me,' he says, and removing Himself a short distance falls on the ground, exhausted, and begins to pray, 'Father, if it is possible, let this cup pass away from me.' As the hour approaches, what does Jesus do? He begs to be spared! How human is that! But He resigns Himself to His Father's will. 'Yet not as I will, but as thou willest.'

"In a while He returns, and what of the trusty sentries? Asleep. No stranger to disappointment, Jesus asks, 'could you not, then, watch one hour with me?' In the cool night he feels very much alone, but even so, aware of our frail humanity, he offers a kind comment. 'The spirit indeed is willing," he says, "but the flesh is weak.'

Soon a crowd with swords and clubs appears, sent by the chief priests and elders. According to plan, Judas comes up to Jesus and greets Him. Jesus is seized and taken away, but not before He restores the ear of the high priest's servant that Peter had rashly cut off. 'Put back thy sword into its place,' Jesus tells Peter, 'for all those who take the sword will perish by the sword.'

"Jesus is brought before the high priest. 'Tell us whether thou are the Christ, the Son of God,' Caiphas demands. 'Thou hast said it,' Jesus replies, 'nevertheless, I say to you, hereafter you shall see the Son of man sitting at the right hand of God and coming upon the clouds of heaven.' 'He has blasphemed,' Caiphas crows, 'what further need have we of witnesses?' Guilty as charged, sentenced to death! The Roman procurator, Pilate, ignores his conscience. The consummate politician, he takes the easy way out, putting Jesus' fate in the hands of the crowd. They roar their verdict: 'Let him be crucified!'

"Pilate has Jesus stripped of his clothing. He is made to bend over, his wrists bound to a post. Pilate's soldiers flog him with a leather whip... the sharp metal turns his neck and back into a mass of bloody welts and gashes. When they finish, the soldiers drape him in a scarlet cloak, give him a crown of thorns and a reed for a scepter. 'Hail, King of the Jews!' they cry, spitting on him. With the reed they drive the thorns deep into his skull.

"Jesus takes up the cross, two heavy wooden beams lashed together, the Roman way of executing slaves and brigands. Jesus falls. He meets His Blessed Mother. Imagine her feelings on seeing her child, for He was in every sense her child, suffering so cruelly. A man, Simon, is forced to shoulder some of the weight and helps Jesus complete the cruel walk up to Golgotha, the Place of the Skull. Jesus falls again. He falls a third time.

"Finally, Jesus is nailed hand and foot to the cross, it is raised and secured in the ground. On his left one man hangs, another on his right, robbers condemned to die. 'And from the sixth hour there was darkness over the whole land until the ninth hour. But about the ninth hour Jesus cried out with a loud voice, saying, *"Eli, Eli, lema sabacthani?"* My God, my God, why hast thou forsaken me? Then Jesus again cried out with a loud voice, and gave up his spirit.'"

Father Ronan stepped back from the railing and lowered his head. There was not a sound. I closed my eyes and saw Jesus' suffering, his death. I opened them, looking around at the stations of the cross, those I could see.

A few minutes went by. "My dear young men," Father Ronan began again, "Jesus has given us the supreme example of love. Not selfish love but love in action, love fulfilled. 'This is my commandment, that you love one another as I have loved you. Greater love than this no one has, that one lay down his life for his friends.' Take Jesus' example to heart, and whatever the world says or does won't drag you down. You will live forever with this friend who loves you so much he gave his life for you. That is what heaven is all about.

"Heaven." Father Ronan smiled. "If Jesus hadn't risen from the dead, the critics would be right – our expectations would be wishful thinking, nothing more. As St. Paul put it, 'If Christ has not risen, vain then is our preaching, vain too is your faith... for you are still in your sins. Hence they also who have fallen asleep in Christ, have perished.' *But it did happen!* What a stupendous event! 'The angel said to the women, "Do not be afraid; for I know that you seek Jesus, who was crucified. He is not here, for he has risen even as he said... Go quickly, tell his disciples that he has risen."' Jesus appeared to them, 'and they came up and embraced his feet and worshipped him.'

"After visiting with His disciples, preaching and giving His final instructions, Jesus was taken up into heaven and sits at the right hand of God. He will come again in glory and the tribes of the earth 'will see the Son of Man coming upon the clouds of heaven with great power and majesty.' And he will set the sheep on his right hand but the goats on his left, then his Father will hurl the damned into everlasting punishment but welcome the just to everlasting life." Father Ronan took off his glasses and put them on the pulpit.

"Today, please look through the *Lives of the Saints*. Joseph, Thomas Aquinas, Ignatius, Francis of Assisi, as many others as you can."

EVENING OF THE THIRD DAY. Those saints couldn't have been more different, some others I took a look at too. Disappointingly little is known about Joseph. The young Ignatius, like Augustine before him and Francis, for that matter, a wild man early. Aquinas, the towering genius. Francis and the simple, gentle things of God's creation. Amazing, all finding their niche and thriving under the same roof, catholic with a small 'c.'

Father Ronan was already in the pulpit, I didn't see him come in. "'I am the way, the truth and the life, no one comes to the Father but through me.' Words of Our Lord, my dear young men, from the Gospel of St. John, Chapter 14, verse 6. In the Name of the Father, and of the Son, and of the Holy Ghost."

"Amen."

"All of us have close friends. One of the best things about Holy Cross is the lifelong friendships you make here. At some point most of you will meet a special young woman who will become your wife and best friend. Now let me ask – who among you would deliberately reject such wonderful friendships? Stop washing, stop brushing your teeth, go around in dirty, foul-smelling clothes? Would you train your tongue to be unkind, caustic, vicious?" The priest smiled. "Of course not. That makes no sense.

"We've looked at Jesus' character through his life, words and acts. Now we understand better what kind of person he is, why he is worth having as a friend.

And so I ask you direct, why would you do anything that risks losing Jesus' friendship in heaven? You shake your heads, but consider this. With a single mortal sin you can lose Jesus' company for all eternity. All eternity! A single venial sin can deny it to you for eons as you suffer in purgatory to overcome its effects.

"There's a very practical lesson here. If you really, truly want to be with God and his Son, you must hate sin with all your heart, all your mind, all your will. Not sin in general, but *your* sins, and not only hate but fear them, as well as the occasions of those sins.

"Now, one of Ignatius' goals in designing this retreat was to help you discover that root failing from which all your others flow and how to deal with it, also that special virtue which can best help you conform your life to God's will. Is there one key weakness that makes you an easy target for Satan? A key vice from which all your other faults spring? If so, what is it? Is it drink? You're not so young or sheltered, you may already have trouble with alcohol. Does the mindlessness that accompanies excessive drinking loosen your inhibitions and make you easy prey for sin? Have you driven drunk, putting yourself and others in harm's way? Have you fought and brawled? What about unchaste actions? Ask yourself, is alcohol the root cause of my difficulties?" I thought of Uncle Eddie, the friendliest, funniest person you ever met, but a terror after he'd been drinking. And that smoker...

"Perhaps you're not tempted by alcohol," he was going on, "though be vigilant, for it can come on as you grow older. Could your key vice be an unhealthy attachment to the things of this world? Those of you from so-called privileged backgrounds know what the striving for wealth and possessions can do to people. Others of you, your failing so far may be desire or envy. I single out this vice because a tendency toward acquisitiveness may develop into the full-blown disease once you get a taste of the world's material rewards. Acquisitiveness is tied to the seventh and eighth commandments, for often it leads to cheating others out of what is rightfully theirs and lying to make things 'come out right' – that is, the way you or your boss wants them to.

"Let us next mediate on which virtue you have greatest need of, so you can nurture it in your souls. This may be the virtue opposite to your key vice or failing. For example if obsession with unchaste thoughts or acts is dragging you down, concentrate on purity. Or it may be a virtue you already have in good measure that you can make an even more meaningful part of your lives. Speak about this tomorrow with your confessor."

Father Ronan paused, inviting us to relax a bit. There was a lot of noise as we shifted in our seats... heavy stuff, close to home. "This morning we spoke of discouragement. Well aware of our frailty, Jesus does not expect us to go it alone. He left us the help we need, His Church, the Holy Sacrifice of the Mass, the Eucharist and the other sacraments. The price of admission is a humble and sincere commitment to follow His will for you. Talk with Jesus as you would a friend, which is another way of saying – pray. Pray as the Psalmist prayed, 'O Lord, teach me to do Thy will.' What a joy to know you have everything you need for a holy life. You have only to ask.

"Tonight turn again to *The Imitation of Christ,* Book Four. Meditate on approaching Christ in the Blessed Sacrament in a worthy and reverent manner."

Sitting in the bench I thought everything over. What particular weakness sets me up to sin? Not drinking. Impurity? Sometimes at night thoughts come to me and I would get to feeling lonely and the pressure was so much I sinned with myself. I usually fight it off but when it happens I feel bad. Is that my root failing? Possibly, though it doesn't occupy me that much. What else? I went carefully through the commandments but couldn't think of another sin I fell into that often or seriously. On the virtue side I had no doubt. Honesty is number one. Honesty, passion for the truth, this will be the soil from which everything grows that I want to be and become.

MORNING OF THE FOURTH AND FINAL DAY. "'O Lord, rebuke me not in thy anger, nor upbraid me in thy wrath. Have mercy on me, O Lord, for I am weak. Heal me, O Lord, for my bones are troubled and my soul is troubled exceedingly.' The Book of Psalms, Chapter Six, Verses Two through Four. In the Name of the Father, and of the Son, and of the Holy Ghost."

"Amen."

Father Ronan put his hands on the railing. "The end is in sight. Those of you who have applied yourselves these past few days, I congratulate. But unfortunately, in the quiet of your souls, some of you know you haven't made a good retreat. This morning you can make up lost ground. Perhaps some worry has distracted you, if so this is an opportunity for insight. What is it about that worry that you couldn't put it down for even a few days? Talk with your confessor about it, man to man. God wants you back as a friend. No one is so evil or so deluded that he cannot reform and repent, but you have to want to do it.

"Now please kneel." The banging sounded through the building as we lowered the kneelers. Almost over. "In your own words, in the silence of your hearts, ask God for the grace to examine your consciences sincerely, for the wisdom to know your evil tendencies, to know where you have sinned."

Father Ronan paused. "Now pray for the grace of a good confession, asking God for the courage to admit what you have done and how serious it is. Do not rationalize, do not make excuses. Be open and honest. Ask for sincere sorrow that you have offended Him and the Son who gave His life for you. Mean it when you promise to change and to live a life worthy of His friendship.

"A word about repentance. Today you will make a good confession. You will leave here on top of the world, in the state of grace, friends with Jesus again. Yes, it's a wonderful feeling, but don't get cocky. Together you and Jesus landed a good blow on the Devil but the fight isn't over. Satan isn't through with you. There's a lifetime remaining – your lifetime.

"Now, I want to say what a privilege it has been working with you these last few days. I pray I have had a part in bringing you closer to Jesus and His Father, and that I will get to know many of you in the coming months and years. Now, if you will stand and move to the confessionals."

Built into the side walls were a dozen dark wood enclosures. Picture three phone booths joined together, a cut-out in the center door covered by a thin curtain. When lit, the priest is in. The compartments are covered by heavy drapes you draw aside entering and leaving. We stood and stretched and milled around a few minutes. Several priests appeared to move things along. I walked to the back of the church and over to the side right aisle, pausing randomly at the last confessional. 'Rev. William Ronan, S.J.' the plaque said.

I frowned. He'd recognize my voice, for sure. When it comes to such personal things, anonymous suits me fine. I was about to move on when it struck me – it's more than a coincidence, the cemetery, now this. I took a seat in the pew and awaited my turn. All of a sudden this huge wave of discomfort swept over me. I thought I had everything under control but now this... apprehension that I'd missed something important. I went through the commandments again, couldn't find anything. My anxiety increased. Now I was third... the line was moving fast. Sweating profusely I raced through everything again. The last person rose and went in. Low voices, the drone of absolution, then the drape parted and in I went. On my knees I waited for the other side to finish then the little door slid open and there he was, in silhouette. I hesitated, trying to collect myself. Finally he asked softly, "Is anyone there?"

"I think so," I blurted.

"Well, then, shall we get to it?" he said.

My face flushed. For the next couple of minutes I ran through my list. Nothing exceptional. I'd never been one for discussing complications in the confessional, but as I finished it occurred to me maybe this was different. "Father, what I told you is all I have to tell," I ventured, "but outside, just now, I had this feeling something was missing and it really bothered me."

"You have nothing more to confess, but you've missed something?"

"That doesn't make any sense but yes."

Father Ronan was quiet a moment. "Should we speak about your great failing and virtue? Perhaps that would help us get at it."

"The virtue part I'm pretty sure about," I went on. "Honest and direct, that's how I want to see myself. I figure that's my most important virtue."

"That's fine, but realize it gets harder as you go along. What about your worst failing?"

I paused. "I really don't know what to say. I get tempted by impure thoughts but I don't think about them all the time, it doesn't drag me down like you said. The fact is, nothing really stands out."

"So on the one hand you value honesty above all other virtues, but on the other hand you don't have any important failings, just a lot of little stuff. Is that it? Is it possible I'm talking with a saint?"

I choked. "Not hardly."

"Almost sounds like it, though I wouldn't know, I've never met one." Father Ronan chuckled. "Now, listen. I'm not trying to be hard on you, but I think you just gave us a clue. I'm going to say the prime candidate for your greatest failing is complacency, spiritual complacency. With a dash of tepidity sprinkled in."

"I don't understand..."

"What I'm hearing, you think your spiritual life is in pretty good shape. Sure, take comfort that you're not sinning left, right and sideways, but where's the passion that you might not be doing the best you can?"

I nodded... never thought of it that way.

"The trouble with complacency, it keeps you from growing spiritually, from reaching the next level of God's friendship, then the level after that, and on up the ladder. And speaking of honesty, since you brought it up, if you're not facing up to the fact that you could do better, are you really being honest with yourself?"

"I guess not," I replied.

"If you don't *try* to do better, you won't *do* better. Don't settle for average, for 'good enough.' If there's as much in you as you seem to think, your goal should be nothing less than spiritual perfection and a life of works to match it. Not that you'll ever get there but the effort is crucial, in fact that's a big part of the reward. For your penance say the Sorrowful Mysteries. If you ever want to talk things over, I hear confessions Thursday evenings or come by Beaven III, you know where it is. Now make a good Act of Contrition."

Into the brilliant mid-day sun. After kneeling so long I was stiff. Usually after confession I feel light, on top of the world, but not today. After an agonizingly slow start my life has gained a measure of self-confidence. I can't afford to lose that, but if I have so far to go and such a difficult path ahead... this will take time to sort out. Spur of the moment the best I could come up with was – if Jesus is such a friend, he'll be there for me. Then again, I thought, that should be plenty good enough.

14. FAMILY CIRCLE

"THAT RETREAT BUSINESS, GUS, I don't know what to make of it."

"How much of it did you follow?"

Jonathan pauses. "Not enough. I'm trying to relate it to Judaism. Some similarities – I mean they're both about your relationship to God, but the details couldn't be more different. It's too complex – they're both too complex. I hate to use the word gullible, but that's what comes to mind when I see Paul tracking the party line like that."

"Impressionable I'll buy, not gullible. And for your information, a lot of people who still call themselves Catholics consider that hellfire and damnation stuff outmoded. All to the good, as far as that's concerned, though there is a loss of seriousness I find troubling. Whatever religion is supposed to be, folksy and friendly ain't it. And very significant, Paul's comments about truth and honesty, they'll bear close watching as we go along."

"But how can he maintain a 'passion for the truth' yet hold such doctrinaire beliefs? The priest picked up on that – didn't he say Paul wasn't being honest with himself?"

"That wasn't his point, but if you're asking can truth and faith be made consistent, the answer is maybe yes, maybe no. Incidentally, don't get the idea you have to solve these conundrums. What you need to understand is how *Paul* dealt with them. You saw how he was conditioned to give his superiors the benefit of the doubt, but that changed, and a good thing too. Some people are born skeptical, he wasn't. It took him a long time to get there.

"But back to religion. When it comes to an all-seeing, all-powerful Being, sure, who wouldn't like to think when you shuffle off this coil there'll be somebody welcoming you into a better life? My goodness, nothing would compare with seeing my dear Akiko, even my parents, though they were often a trial. Thing is, Jonathan – if there is a heaven, I'm not sure how welcome I'd be, anyway. I haven't exactly followed the party line, as you call it. For instance, I've often said a God that permits the atrocities we see every day, men against each other, nation against nation, earthquakes, floods and all – if He can't prevent these, well, he's not so almighty, is He? If He can but won't, He's a monster. You can't have it both ways. Half a God is no God at all."

Time to put it down for a while, take a break. I'm thinking, we've been at it almost four weeks and I still have no idea where Jonathan is, his organizing, his writing. Again I invite him to share a draft with me.

He shakes his head. "That's not how I work. I'm one of those people who needs to know the end of the story before I can settle the rest down."

"I didn't understand that. That puts a big burden on you, not writing as you go along."

"Oh, I'm writing, all right. It's just not in shape."

"What's happening with the investigation part of the story?"

"It's Hersh, all right. Word is he'll be in Iraq next week." Jonathan shakes his head, "it's discouraging," he says with a far-off look in his eyes. "No contacts, and even if I did, where would I find time to work on it?"

I don't know the answer but it reminds me I need to make a call. I look at my watch. Tomorrow, for sure.

****

MY PARENTS PAID A VISIT in mid-October. Parents Weekend. Penn State game, dinner at a "fine restaurant" my father researched, which turned out to be Putnam & Thurston's. I had vowed never to set foot in that place again but here I was, chauffeured in the family Cadillac like I was any kid from Scarsdale or Lake Forest.

Jim and Sheila were now engaged, with a June date. My mother fretted that they were too young, but there was no denying Sheila had straightened Jim out. He now had his apprentice plumber's license and they were apartment hunting. Sheila was in nursing school, working nights at the hospital. Dark-haired and pretty, she had a fearless sense of humor and was one of the few people who could cut Jim down to size and get away with it. Over dinner, I learned Catherine had opted to major in English Lit and was thinking of high school teaching. They told me Benny was at Columbia. His parents had moved back to New York. "As for me," my mother said, "we're in final rehearsals – a week from tonight we open." My father looked at the ceiling and rolled his eyes. "The *Bulletin* promised us a nice spread, pictures, too. I'll send you the clipping," she said, smiling. "A long time between engagements, as they say."

"Nervous?" I asked.

"Not really."

After coffee my father lit a cigar. My mother grimaced as he leaned back and puffed away. "That's so disgusting," she said, "how can you stand it?" He winked at me as if I were in on the secret. I wasn't. I thought they smelled terrible, too.

At the Communion Breakfast after Mass next day, Father McBride spoke of his pleasure welcoming the fathers and mothers, and how he knew Holy Cross students are such fine men. "In our philosophy program we put great emphasis on the principle of causality, and each year we see it validated when we meet you parents."

"What a wonderful speaker your Father McBride is," my mother gushed afterward, "so erudite, and all those classical allusions!"

"I didn't follow half of what he said," my father grumbled. "A tenth at best."

My mother glared at him. "Well, I for one am pleased Paul is able to rub elbows with men like that. I may even change my opinion about his choice of college, if that is typical."

The day ended with a "social" in the Field House at the top of the hill featuring the college dance band. We sat with Frank's family and I got to practice my steps with his sister without having to impress anybody. She was nice, but that was all. I had to dance with my mother, of course, who remarked on how I had improved. Within the privacy of the dance floor she confided in me. "Do you understand how you can still love someone yet not even like him any more?"

"I don't know, that seems kind of tricky."

"It is. You'll have to live a lot longer to understand it."

"I noticed Dad doesn't seem too interested in your play."

"Interested!" she snorted. "I'll be getting a lot of attention and he has a problem with that. Between us, it's spelled j-e-a-l-o-u-s."

"Will he go see it?"

"At this point I couldn't care less. I hope you come down, though. It would be nice if you knew something about this side of me which, I assure you, is only going to get bigger. You know, Paul," she went on, "when you're my age and you have a glimpse of the other side of the hill the view is scary. This little hobby of mine, it's a way of staying on top a bit longer. You asked if I'm nervous." She smiled, "I lied. Of course I'm nervous. I wonder if I still have it in me. But the director is kind, he's brought me along slowly. I did some Shakespeare way back when, but these will all be university people. Mess up and they'll catch you on it, no question. It's a stretch after all this time but I've got it down. I'll be fine."

"Which play is it, again?"

"The Comedy of Errors."

"You'll do well," I said, "I'm sure of it."

I wanted to hear more about how things were with my father but I didn't ask. The two of them danced some that evening and they looked fine together, in fact aside from a few pointed comments, the weekend seemed amicable, but who knew where they were headed? As he loaded their suitcases in the car my father asked, whether I'd given any thought to the summer. I replied I hadn't.

"I'd like you to work for me, get to know the business. I'll pay you real money."

This was a real surprise. I had hung around his "shop" plenty when I was younger but had never thought of working there. "That's good of you to offer," I replied.

"I'm not doing you any favors," he said. "You can help me a lot. Besides, I'm not going to be around forever – maybe you'd like to give it a look."

I had no interest in a business career, especially my father's business, but I guessed I could stand it for a summer. It couldn't be any worse than DiLorenzo's which I wasn't going back to on a bet. And I certainly could use the money. "What would you want me to do?"

"Let's talk about it at Thanksgiving. If you don't want to I'll find someone else."

I WAS IMMERSED IN THE CAMPUS SCENE, enjoying my courses and making friends. I scored well on the first set of exams and spoke in class discussions. People began turning to me for help with assignments. Sports and spirit were a big deal, but the crowd I ran with had other interests. Collegians preferring *Don Giovanni* over Saturday football? Hard to believe, but there it was. With a foot in both camps, I was on our corridor intramural team and looking forward to basketball in the winter.

By eight o'clock our corridor was a very active place – you could tell even through the closed doors. Student reps roamed the dorms selling all kinds of stuff – cigarettes (Marlboros, mainly), neckties, grinders (same as subs). But every day odors would waft up through the leaky old building from the basement Chem labs and hang around. Rotten eggs was sulfur dioxide, vinegar acetic acid, and banana, my favorite, meant somebody was working with butyric acid. Memories of high school, and a reminder that Chemistry and I never mixed that well.

Weak speaking skills confined me to Intermediate French, though with language lab six hours a week they were improving fast. Our enthusiastic young teacher, Father Bourassa, suggested Frank and I speak nothing but French one evening a week, so even Philosophy and Religion got the treatment *français*. We were well into the *grand livre* of the semester, Camus' *La Peste,* and anticipating the summer's extra-credit *très grand livre,* rumored to be *Nôtre Dame de Paris*. My first venture into Political Science was a survey course examining different types of governments. We contrasted the results of 1776 with the very different French experience, and compared our republic against the Romans, a sobering exercise. We studied ancient Egypt's theocracy, the Greek city-states, monarchies, and hybrids like England's. Then there was a European History survey course. History is crucial, I had come to discover – the indispensable raw material for the other social sciences which would be thin gruel indeed without context. Benny introduced me to this insight though it took someone else to make it come alive. More on him later. I also had an Introductory Econ course, macro the first semester, micro the second. English was "Prose & Poetry," from old friend Beowulf to *Portrait of the Artist,* Wilfred Owens, Yeats, then back across the Atlantic second semester with Longfellow, Cooper, Poe, Whitman, Twain, Wolfe, Fitzgerald, Faulkner, Steinbeck, Hemingway. Brother Robert would have been proud. But why no Salinger?

Philosophy offered Logic the first semester, then Epistemology. I had been eagerly anticipating these, but as the year went long, I knew something was missing. Logic did help us reason clearly and spot fallacies in arguments. While the course text was clear (as well it should have been!) with plenty of examples, disappointingly, there was no mention of the big names – Plato, Aristotle, Descartes, Kant, Nietzsche. Instead of letting us learn from the greats, our text doled out hyper-critical snippets about "isms" – Subjectivism, Materialism, et cetera, so contrived it was laughable.

Let me say, though, the substance of what we learned was convincing to me then and still is. A world of material objects exists and they are the starting point of our knowledge. The mind tries to understand what exists from the outside-in, not the other way around. Whether that's the best or only way to explain it is a whole other question. We finally did get around to folks outside our circle, usually not sympathetically. And credit where it's due, I managed to acquire some tools for separating fact from fiction that have stood me in good stead. How to distinguish truth from falsity? How is knowledge conveyed from one person to another? Authority versus reason. A start, but a good start.

One afternoon my neighbor and chem major J.J. Malot pushed my door open. With him was a slim young Asian man about five-four, from his garb a priest, the smallest, youngest priest I'd ever seen. "Father Trần," he said, "this is Paul Bernard I told you about." Then turning to me, "Father Trần's from Vietnam, he's getting his Masters' in Chemistry. He'll be here a couple of years." Chemistry was one of the few Departments to offer an advanced degree.

"Good to meet you," I said, moving a chair toward him. "You are a Jesuit?"

"No, I am no intellectual," he replied, in excellent, slightly accented English.

"I told Father Trần you're a former scientist turned bureaucrat. Father Trần speaks French, of course." From Woonsocket, J.J. spoke flawless French.

"I thought I should like to meet an expert in the science of government."

"I'm hardly that," I said. "Just a beginner."

"I am myself recently ordained but I have opinions, as I'm sure you do."

"Oh, opinions I have many," I laughed.

"You may know something of my country," the priest said, "the French leaving several years ago and the troubles that persist."

"Not that much. I would like to know more."

J.J. looked at his watch. "We'd better get going."

"A pleasure meeting you," the priest said, getting up from the chair. "Let us plan another conversation in the near future. *A bientôt.*"

"Absolutely. *Bien sûr,*" I added with a smile.

So young, that priest! But why Chemistry, and why so far from home? His part of the world I knew almost nothing about. Teak forests, rice paddies, exotic images from my earliest school years. I recalled an ignominious French defeat a few years ago and withdrawal from the region they had governed many years. I had some homework to do.

I RAN INTO DENNIS HEALY OFTEN, but since that night he unburdened himself he hadn't said a word about his situation. But one evening in the dining hall he signaled me from a couple of tables over. "You in tonight?" he asked.

"I expect so," I replied, balancing my tray.

"I'll stop by, if that's okay."

I tried to read his expression but no clue. At eight he showed up at my door. "Thank you for helping me," he said, sitting down. "Somebody else will be thanking you too."

"What do you mean," I said, puzzled.

"There'll be a baby after all." He swallowed hard. "After we talked I told Susan we could get married if that's what she wanted, but we decided the timing was wrong. A couple weeks later she called me, there's a nun close to her family, long story short she'll have the baby and put it up for adoption. A Catholic Charities outfit – hush-hush, very respectable, nobody the wiser."

"Her parents?"

"Not happy but not insane like they were. I'm on their permanent shit list but what else is new?" He looked hard at me. "Things turned out better than I expected." He sat back in the chair and let out a long sigh. "Susan, how she handled the situation, I got to know her a lot better." He stared at me for a minute. "I really do love her, a lot more than I thought, even."

"You can't marry her and keep the baby?"

He shook his head. "I'll have to be satisfied we didn't do something really terrible. He smiled wanly. "I learned a lot about myself, too, not all of it good."

I nodded. "But not all bad either."

He stood up and put his arm on my shoulder. "Listen, I mean it – talking with you made a big difference." He turned and left the room, closing the door quietly behind him.

I stared out the window a long time, couldn't concentrate. Finally set the clock for 4:45, pick it up then. I hoped Frank wouldn't make too much noise coming in.

I'D FINALLY HIT THE SIX FOOT MARK and was tipping the scales about one-seventy. Not bad for the runt of the litter. Our first intramural game, I caught a couple of balls so I got to play more. O'Kane IV was outstanding all year and just before Thanksgiving we found ourselves in the championship game against the Juniors from Bevan II.

Three solid days of rain and the field was a quagmire. I couldn't feel my fingers for the cold. Down by three points, fifteen seconds left, my next-door neighbor and second team Connecticut All-Stater Dick Murray called my play in the huddle. I would streak downfield, fake toward the sideline then cut back, hopefully arriving at the goal line same time as the ball. We lined up in the mud, forty yards from the touchdown that would give us the championship, a glorious first for a freshman team. Hut one - Hut two - HIKE!

Off I went through the muck. At the twenty I feinted right then cut left. I left the defender behind but when I drove my foot into the mud I lost my sneaker! Gimping along, at the five I looked back but no ball. Upfield I saw why – a pile of bodies. My heart dropped, they had Dick trapped. There goes the season. Suddenly somebody squirted out of the pack – it was Dick! He faked one tackler, then another, then he was in the clear!

Trouble... the guy who'd been covering me had a bead on him. I picked a line that would bring me between the two of them, Dick down the middle, the defender angling in. As I slogged closer I shouted, "Left foot! Left foot!" To have any chance, I had to push off my left foot, the one with a shoe. As the gap closed I lowered my body and threw myself at my opponent. I went down, he flew over my head. As I raised myself I saw Dick cross the goal line. Then I heard a roar! Cheering! My teammates, the crowd on the sideline, everybody was running. They had Dick on their shoulders then a couple of guys grabbed me and lifted me too. They were carrying me off the field! Dick and I threw our arms around each other. "What a block!" he shouted, "that was one great football play!"

"Aw, shucks," I said, grinning broadly. I'd never been happier in my life.

"But what were you yelling at me? I couldn't hear you."

"Yelling?" What was he talking about? Then I remembered. The sneaker. "Oh, nothing, just trying to psych myself up."

I never did find that sneaker, but its mate has a place of honor all these years. A 10D, still caked with mud from an afternoon long ago. I'm looking at it now, Gus, as I write these lines.

MY ROOM, MY REFUGE. Red Sox pennants, baseball shirt, summer camp photos, picture of my King. Hardy Boys, Tom Swift, *Gulliver's Travels*, untouched for years, athletic gear, clothes closet needing a serious pruning. Every time I came back, the room, the house felt smaller. As I lay in bed Christmas morning, my feet over the end of the bed, it occurred to me if I stayed away maybe this shrinking would stop, I could still time's wheel. My Mom, my Dad, we'd all stay just as we are. But then, I thought, why would I want that? It's not like things are that perfect and anyway, I want to see everything, do everything, and for that I have to get older. And if I get older, everybody else does too. So much for that idea.

I hadn't been in the house five minutes and my mother had her clippings spread out on the kitchen table. "Great fun," the *Journal* called it. "Fine Shakespeare. A tour de force!" "Fiona Kelley Bernard, too long absent from the local stage, made her triumphant re-entry in the complex role of the Abbess Amelia, wife to Aegeon, the merchant of Syracuse."

I bent down and scrutinized the picture. "I'd know that beautiful lady anywhere, even in that funny nun's outfit."

"My friends said to watch out, the stage can be habit-forming."

I smiled. "Bad...very bad."

"Actually, it is, habit-forming, that is." Her radiant face said it all. "It was wonderful, I'm sorry you missed it. We're doing *Cat* in the spring. That'll be fun."

"Just like our New York trip," I said.

She smiled. "That seems so long ago."

I hesitated... but we were alone here, so why not? "How did Dad deal with the play?"

"I was surprised," she replied, "he even came to a performance, the last one but at least he showed up." She shook her head. "I admit it took a lot of time – the rehearsals, getting my lines down and all."

"Don't apologize. This is something you love, he ought to be cheering you on."

"That's nice of you to say." She fell silent a moment. "Your father, he has so much baggage it's hard to have a conversation. I don't know how much longer I can take him... ignoring me. It's rude and disrespectful, after I basically gave my life to him and you children." Her eyes filled with tears.

Embarrassed, I put my arm around her. "Don't worry, you'll be fine."

She wiped her eyes. "See, there you go, my steady hand. She kissed me on the cheek. "I'd better wash my face," she said, "everybody will be here soon."

The Christmas table was old times. Roast beef and Yorkshire pudding, ham with raisin sauce, candied yams, endless vegetables, and pies! French apple, mince, pumpkin. Cider, beer, wine. My mother put to shame the quite good try the dining hall made the night before the break. Tantes Héloise and Marie were there, Aunt Moira also, cousins Martha and Mary, still friendly with Catherine though they had gone a different direction, holding down secretarial jobs. Uncle Eddie had been living apart and was not well, his liver, they said.

The night before we exchanged presents in front of the tree before heading out for midnight Mass. Sheila was the new face at the table, with her gift of lighting any room she entered. The engaged couple had spent Christmas Eve at her family's. When they announced the wedding was set for June 6, my remark about D-Day was not appreciated.

"Chip off the old block," my father said, toasting the newly licensed plumber. "I cut and bend metal, Jim makes sure it keeps us dry." A few minutes later he raised his glass again. "And I want all of you to know Paul will be working in the shop this summer. Who knows, maybe we'll make a metalworker of him yet." It was true, I had agreed to cast my lot with Bernard Bros. Tool & Die. Nothing better out there and I stood to make a bundle, $1,200, plus a bonus if I did well. Silently answering his toast, I had absolutely no desire to follow in his footsteps. Next summer, I vowed, I'll find something better.

"How did your exams go?" Catherine asked.

"Hoping for the best. We hear in January, right after we get back."

"Me too. I'm not the scholar you are, though. I've settled into a "Ladies' B."

"That like my Gentlemen's C?" Jim asked with a crooked smile.

"A smidge better."

"I don't want to hear that, Catherine," my mother said. "A little more application and you'd have straight As. You certainly have the mental ability."

"The genes, that's what you're saying."

"Now, that's uncalled for."

"You don't understand what it would take to go from Bs to As. No more theater, no more Irish dancing. You of all people should sympathize with that!"

"There's enough time to do it all, just do it a little better."

It was a relief to be back at college, exhilarating in fact. The house, the family were getting on my nerves, which made me worry how would I get through the summer. Late one day I heard grades were in. In my mailbox I found an official letter, also something from the Dean. My hands shook as I ripped open the envelope, then it occurred to me, why does this matter so much? What if I fall short? But there it was, the "Scholarship Report" for Bernard, Paul, term ending January 6, 1960. All As! Every one of them! Economics an A (okay, an A-) English an A, French an A, History, Philosophy and Political Science, I couldn't get over it. In my excitement I forgot the Dean's envelope. It was a personal letter, informing me I had attained the Dean's List and that my 94.37% grade average ranked me second in the Freshman Class! Second! Unbelievable! It turned out a classmate named Tom Devaney, a Classics major from Cincinnati, was first with 95.09% and got his picture on the front page of the *Crusader* along with "top students" from the other three classes.

My fear of failing assuaged, it was time to go down to the student newspaper, the *Crusader,* and offer my services. Charlie Carroll, the News Editor, looked over my *Maroon & White* portfolio. "Not bad," he said, "but why do you want to do photography and writing both? How'll you fit us in? We publish every Thursday, rain, snow, gloom of night, you know the drill."

The Managing Editor, Rudy Fossett, wandered by. "Your interest honors us," he said bowing deeply. "Our humble publication has never had a 'top student' on staff. We're not sure how to handle it, actually." I was taken aback by this welcome until they looked at each other and laughed. "Hey," Rudy said, shaking my hand, "welcome aboard the slave ship. Can you start today?"

"Sure, why not?"

"All right! I have a couple of photo shoots for you. As for the writing, we start rookies slow and edit them heavily. Let me say the best style manual is just spend time with our back issues. Come on, let me introduce you to the others. You've seen the darkroom, over behind the chapel?"

"I already checked it out."

"We'll get you a key, you'll be needing it."

I inherited the extracurricular activities beat which, along with sports, took up most of the space allotted photos. The guy who had it quit the week before. My old Leica was holding up fine and I had the use of a couple of telephoto lenses courtesy of the camera club. And by sheer coincidence, Father Ronan was faculty advisor. It turned out he had worked a couple of years for the *Boston Globe* before going into the priesthood. He remembered our meeting that chilly October morning, and we were on our way to becoming friends.

As for girls, I took the coward's way out, plunging into my studies and activities, avoiding the time and trouble of the chase. Except for the occasional bout of introspection, I really didn't miss it. I diverted myself with Kimball's free films, some good ones, too – *Lawrence of Arabia, Bridge on the River Quai, Damn Yankees.* My classmates' success with girls never ceased to astonish. Every weekend a bunch of them hopped in their cars and headed for Marymount or Manhattanville or Newton to see their steadies or try their luck at mixers that showcased the new talent. For me that scene was overwhelming, especially since the male freshman of the species wasn't in much demand. And I certainly wasn't about to backslide into the high school talent pool.

The highlight of my so-called social life came from an unexpected quarter. Campus groups hosted functions and needed people to wait on table and clean up. I worked several of these. The Military Ball was a colorful though bizarre experience, seeing my peers in formal military dress. But what took the prize was the Senior Ball. I had two tables they put together – a big group from New York which took its fun seriously. The outcome of four long years was no longer in doubt and graduation only days away. Letting-hair-down time.

Every table had several bottles – champagne, wine, scotch. A very good band, Les Elgart. As the evening wore on, the waiters mostly just hung around, not much going on. On toward midnight, this one guy was slouched half-out of his chair, half-asleep, too. His date, a pretty Manhattanville junior named Elaine, I learned that early, seemed bored out of her mind, her back to him, talking across the table to the others. Suddenly he sat up, put his hand over his mouth and bolted for the exit. Elaine didn't seem that surprised. Maybe she was used to it. She waved me over. "Paul, be a dear and get me some ice water."

I brought a fresh pitcher and poured her one. She smiled and motioned at the chair vacated by her errant knight. "Take a break. You've been on your feet all night." I sat.

"So, are you having a good time?" she asked.

I shrugged. "How about you?"

"Whaddyou think," she replied. She'd had a few, herself.

I had noticed she was wearing a diamond. "You're engaged."

She spread her fingers and looked at the ring. "Indeed, that does appear to be the case." She took a sip of the ice water then looked at her hand again. "Yes, I am engaged."

"If you don't mind my saying, you don't seem that excited."

She looked at me blankly. "Ted and I have known each other since we were three. Ted and I have gone steady since high school. Ted's parents and mine belong to the same country club. Our fathers golf every Sunday. Our mothers are in a bridge group. What can I say? It's fate. Or a fucking lack of imagination." She was quiet for a moment. "Look," she finally said, "he's a good guy, he just can't hold his liquor. It's something we need to work on. He'll be at NYU Law so we'll see each other more often."

"When's the wedding?"

"June. Next year."

"Ah," I said. "My brother's getting married this month."

"And where will that happen?"

"Providence. That's where I'm from."

"Providence. Been there on the train many times but I never got off."

"Nobody does. It's a good place to be from. Everybody leaves who can."

"And never goes back," she said solemnly.

"And never goes back," I replied solemnly. Did I really mean that, I wondered?

"And when will you be leaving?"

I laughed. "When I finish here. If things break right."

"That's a few years off."

"Yes."

She smiled. "You have beautiful eyes. Wanna dance?"

Fraternization with guests was not encouraged but there was no rule against it, exactly. Then there was the boyfriend who'd be back any minute, but why not? As we stepped onto the floor, my thoughts returned to that Military Ball. Tonight it's my turn, I in my crisp, high-collared white jacket. It was a slow set and we didn't so much dance as sway. She put her arms around my neck and pressed her body against mine. Booze and boredom, nothing personal, but it felt nice anyway. We didn't speak, what was there to say? Present tense, no past, no future. The band had just begun *Moon River/Theme from Picnic* when I felt a tap on my shoulder. It was Ted. Ted the lawyer.

Elaine and I separated and she rippled her fingers in a wave. My fellow waiter Alex Murtaugh collared me. "Didn't know you were such a ladies' man."

"You learn something every day."

"They're from Larchmont, next town over from me. His family's filthy rich, hers even more. Father's a big Wall Street lawyer. You know the Cravath firm?"

"Never heard of it."

"They're getting married next year. Remind me, I'll send you the clipping."

"Don't bother," I said, peering out at the dance floor.

At the evening's end, my guests came across with tips, expected but appreciated. Ted the lawyer came up to me. "You know, when I saw you two I was really pissed, then I thought, what the hell, I asked for it." He had this crooked grin on his face. "I wouldn't have blamed her if she left without me. Anyway, it was kind of a wake-up call. Thanks."

"It's not like there was anything to it."

"No matter," he said, "I have a tendency to think the worst of people. They say that makes for a good lawyer. Here," he held out his hand and pressed a bill into mine. "Spend it on anything but booze."

"Thanks," I said. "Good luck with law school."

He grimaced as he headed back to the table. I snuck a look at the bill. A hundred! Amazing! Maybe life in the present tense isn't so bad after all.

15. LEAD US, LEAD US NOT

"JONATHAN! THAT'S ME HE'S TALKING ABOUT! The indispensable raw material of the social sciences. Though it's a whole lot more, too, of course. Good lad!"

"Congratulations."

"Thank you. And is that flower pot real or in my head? I can play that game but I refuse to waste time on crap like that. You've heard of Dr. Johnson?"

"Of course."

"Dr. Johnson was right to kick that rock. There's your answer – the rock kicks back!"

The phone rings.

"Gus! How the hell are you!" I hold it at arm's length, it's so loud.

"I had quite a time tracking you down, General Riggs. You're a hard man to find."

"That's the way I like it. How are you, Gus? Where are you? How long has it been?"

"Taking your questions in order, Dennis, I am well. I am in Maine. And the last time I saw you was in my office. You were a Captain, if memory serves, twenty, twenty-five years ago. You've certainly climbed the ladder."

"A rare case of talent rewarded. Maine," he says. "We used to refuel in Maine."

"That is now Bangor International Airport and less than an hour from my house."

"I'd stop by except we have no need to refuel there any more."

"When did you graduate, remind me."

"'Seventy-two then straight into the Army. I was in ROTC, you'll remember."

"You missed Vietnam."

"I had orders but it was over before I got there. I was sorry to hear about Akiko."

"Thanks. Yeah, that was hard."

"But you're doing okay. Why'd you move?"

"I couldn't stand it any more. I took retirement the next year and came back here. The property here was in the family, nobody was using it so I took it off their hands."

"Listen, I've got a meeting in five minutes, why don't I call you back."

"I'll talk fast. You weren't in the house when Paul Bernard was, were you?"

"We missed each other. That was a shocker, what happened. I disagreed with a lot of what he said but give the guy credit, it took balls to put himself on the line like that."

"I'm working with a writer on an article about Paul. I know it's out of channels but can you get him a contact? The events, the investigation, he needs to learn more about that."

"There's a procedure for credentialing. Let him use it."

"It's complicated. He's doing a story for *The New Yorker* about Paul's life but not his death, if you follow me. Another guy's doing that. He's a free-lancer, he has no affiliation. It's unusual but you know the ropes, I'm sure."

"Do I ever. I've been up to my eyeballs in Operation Iraqi Freedom since the first shot. I coordinate between Pentagon and field, among other things."

"I didn't realize you were so involved. You can probably guess my position on the war but I hope that won't color your answer."

"I expect you still have the same old liberal hang-ups."

"If nothing else I am consistent."

"Consistently wrong," he laughed. "I used to think I could bring you around but I gave it up as a lost cause."

"Good decision. So what do you say to my proposition?"

"My first reaction is it's a non-starter but let me check around."

"I'd appreciate it. I know this is irregular."

"Incidentally, who do they have on the other part of the story?"

"Seymour Hersh."

The phone fell silent for a moment. "You know, maybe we could use another point of view. Give me your number. I'll get back to you."

* * * * * * *

I HARDLY RECOGNIZED MY FATHER'S SHOP. With a state grant they'd taken over the building next door, gutted and renovated it, combined the two and installed modern equipment. He waved his hand around the metalworking shop. "We were hanging by a thread," he said, "now we've got the most modern shop anywhere! We employ two hundred, pay well, health insurance, a retirement plan, need to stay a step ahead of the union. Every time we start doing okay they make a push to get in."

"I always wondered why Tool & Die on the sign but you call it a machine shop?"

"Tool & Die sounds more scientific, and don't think that didn't help when we were after the state money. But you're right, basically we're a specialized machine shop. You know, I used to hope Jim might come in with me but that's not going to happen."

"I'll give you what you need this summer."

He put a hand on my shoulder. "That means a lot. Since Antoine retired I've had to carry it all. Look, you have your life and I know this isn't it. Just give me a couple good months." His eyes were moist, unusual for him. "Come on, let's keep moving."

He led me into a room of drafting tables lit by crooked-neck lamps, people bending over blueprints and drawings. "We put the customer's specs into drawings, accuracy to the thousandths of an inch. We'd go down the tubes if the people in this room didn't do the job, so we hire good people and supervise them very close."

A couple of draftsmen waved at my father. "How goes it, Mario? *Come sta?"* he said. A short, balding man took off his glasses and looked up. "My son Paul. He's helping out this summer."

"Nice to meet you," the man said, shaking my hand. "Holy Cross, right? I have a nephew wants to go there, maybe he could talk to you sometime."

"Sure, any time," I replied.

"Who's that for?" my father asked, glancing at the drawing. "Coro?"

"That line of bracelets they're coming out with for the fall." An array of drawings and photographs were mounted on a corkboard wall above his desk and a model of the bracelet sat on his bench surrounded by measuring tools. My father stood back. "All this equipment but it's guys like Mario that make it happen. We have a lot of artists in here." He laughed, "this is a working museum, not like that stuff your mother goes for."

We passed through a heavy steel door to a narrow corridor, then through a second door into a large room where the noise hit me full force. Men in safety hoods bending over metal lathes, sparks flying. A man focused the arc of his welding torch on pieces of metal in a jig, joining them into one. The hammering and cutting was incessant. Everyone but us was wearing large aviator-style earphones. "We'll spend more time in here," he shouted, "but you get the idea." As we turned to leave my father pointed to a big sign on the wall.

382 DAYS WITHOUT AN ACCIDENT
SAFETY IS NO ACCIDENT

Ears ringing, I backed out of the room.

"Never had a fatality, knock on wood. One time a guy got careless and lost a finger. This would be a dangerous place if we didn't stay on top of things."

We were approaching the familiar office area. A stout, white-haired woman sat at a desk pecking away at a typewriter. "Morning, Mr. Bernard," she said, barely looking up.

"Morning, Miss Grenier," he replied, thumbing the mail, "you remember Paul."

A big smile came to her face. "Of course, how are you? You surely have changed. You'll be spending some time with us, I hear."

"I'll be doing more than that, I hope," I said with a laugh.

"Come on back," my father said. "You can use Antoine's office for now." He unlocked the door and pushed it open. There was a musty feel to the room. "Use the desk, the phone. Anything you need, let Miss Grenier know. I need to get caught up then I'll be back to get you started."

I slid the wheeled chair back and sat down behind the desk. He stood at the doorway a moment, nodding. "You look good there. Two months now Antoine's been gone."

"What's he doing with himself?"

"After the last heart attack the doctor said take it easy. A little fishing, the garden, you know. I think he made a mistake quitting, you got to keep busy or you go nuts. I have a feeling he'll be back. That's my excuse for not replacing him, not that I ever could."

"Where's Mrs. Lamontagne?"

"In Canada visiting family."

"There was a younger woman, a receptionist, what was her name..."

"There's a lot of turnover in that job. What did she look like?"

"She had this really blond hair, almost white."

"Lorraine! She hasn't been here for years! She's got a couple kids, lives in Fall River. Actually, the last girl left a few weeks ago so we're looking to fill that position. Maybe you can help with the interviews," he said, winking.

After he left I inspected the office, looking at the pictures and plaques, the souvenirs, the picture of Maurice and his P-38. I raised the blind and opened the window, looking at the back parking lot. A small green car was circling, searching for a space, a good sign. An old gent in a blue uniform was walking around, keeping an eye on things.

My father came back with a stack of files and set them on the desk. "Get familiar with these. The red folder's a lawsuit. We fired this guy, caught him taking drawings home and copying them. Selling them! Somebody tipped us off or it could have been a disaster. We turn him in, then the crook sues us! Idiot! We made what they call a counterclaim, get our costs covered at least, if we're lucky."

"A couple of my friends are thinking about law school."

"You could do worse," my father replied, "lawyers make good money but there's a lot of sleazebags too." He lifted a thick folder out. "The union file. We expect they'll try for an election this summer and you'll be part of our team to beat them off. Who knows, maybe this'll be the start of your legal career!"

"Sounds like I have my work cut out for me."

He beamed. "This is just the beginning, *ti-Paul.* Like I said, I don't pay good money for nothing, not even to you."

"Mr. Bernard." At the door was a young man in his early twenties. About my height, short dark hair, wire-rimmed glasses, he had a manila envelope in his hand.

"Simon!" my father replied, "Come in. I told you about Paul, he's working with us this summer. Paul, meet Simon Benoit."

A firm handshake. I instantly liked him. "Simon's automating the shop for us. He's Pete's son, you know, my friend that wired our house."

Simon opened the envelope. "We just got the punch cards back." He took out a stack of cardboard cards, removed the elastic band and spread them on the desk. There were holes in them, all over. "This computer system will make the machines more productive. They'll work to spec each time, faster and more accurate than the human hand and eye." I picked up one of the cards and ran my fingers over the holes. "My job – I'm the tech rep assigned to develop the program."

"We interviewed a couple different outfits," my father said. "It's a total coincidence he's Pete's son. They're designing the system soup to nuts – 'turn key,' they call it. If everything goes well, we're looking at phase two for more shop operations, our office systems too – payroll, parts inventory, all that."

I looked at Simon intently. "How did you get into computers?" I asked.

"I studied it in high school then got hired and went into their training program."

My father nodded. "I used to think I knew about machinery but this stuff's way beyond me. That's why we're paying you such a bundle of money, right?"

"I won't comment on that," Simon laughed, "I just do what the client wants. The cards came out great, Mr. Bernard, just what we asked for."

"How about a presentation to our team today, say at eleven. Paul, you attend too."

Simon gathered up the cards. "See you at eleven."

As the summer went on I became immersed in the work. I helped on the legal issues but was mainly involved with the computers, part of the team bringing the new system "on line." In a few weeks they had a test running on a metal-cutting machine in a small back room with sealed windows and a powerful air conditioner. They were aiming to complete this first phase by the end of the year.

THE WEDDING WAS THE BIG SOCIAL EVENT of the summer. Eddie Phelan, one of Jim's high school cronies, was best man. I was an usher. Billy Moore attended but Sheila put her foot down and excluded him from the wedding party. She got wind of the bachelor party Eddie was planning and Jim wisely sent regrets. During the ceremony a hung-over Eddie had trouble finding the ring, the priest and everybody standing around as he rooted through his pockets. Catherine looked better than I'd ever seen her in her peach-colored bridesmaid dress. Sheila's older sister Moira was maid of honor, swollen with her first child.

Sheila's father was a Cranston police sergeant. Don't call me a police officer, he said, I'm a cop and proud of it. At the reception he told a couple of Little Sheila stories I bet she wished he'd forgotten. The K of C Hall was packed, a hard-working three-piece group making the music. My mother was on the floor nonstop, even my father ventured out for a couple of sets. My mother pointedly observed there were attractive young ladies present and I danced a lot with one – a cousin of Sheila's, from New York, out of range.

By seven the festivities had wound down. The suitcases were lifted into the Cadillac, though I'm sure my father was having second thoughts as he saw the string of cans tied to the rear bumper. The newlyweds made their adieus, then clattered off for their week at Niagara Falls. Later I was on the back porch at home staring at nothing in particular when my father came out and sat down. "So how's it going? Looks like the work agrees with you."

"That computer stuff is interesting. Simon really knows his stuff."

"You mean not everybody has to be a college man to be smart?"

I laughed. "Of course not! Look at you!"

"Yes, look at me," he said, pointing to his rumpled tux shirt, half unbuttoned. "What's that they say? A self-made man but a product of poor workmanship."

"Come on, you don't mean that."

"You're right, I don't, not for a minute." He looked out over the yard, "but today makes me feel old. I never thought I'd see Jim settled down. God only knows where he'd be if it wasn't for Sheila."

As we fell quiet the crickets began their song. "You know," he went on, "it's time to go north. Been a couple of years for me and *Pépère* isn't getting any younger. I thought maybe the end of August." He leaned forward in his chair, "I was wondering if you'd like to come along, just the two of us."

"Me? What about the job?"

"I'll get the boss to approve it." He put his hand on mine. "Look, we need to do more things together. You're my only son, now. Jim belongs to Sheila." He shrugged. That's the way it is. We'll hit Québec City, Montreal too. Montreal is a very special city."

"Sounds like fun," I said.

He looked at me out of the corner of his eye. "And you don't know the half of it."

16. O CANADA!

WOULDN'T YOU KNOW, today I get a letter from Paul's former wife. What are you up to, Gus, whatever it is I want in. Not one of my favorite people. I love his kids, it was good to see them at the funeral, but how that woman produced such fine children is beyond me. Shows how much Paul brought to the table, or bed, as the case may be. I bet she and Latimer got along just fine. Concerned about her reputation, she is (I'm quoting), what might be said about her. Well she ought to be, and of course if there's money floating around she'll have her hand out for it.

Her letter made some reference to the divorce settlement. I sent the thing to Cahill. I have no time for her bullshit. I better ask Cahill about that literary executor business, too. If there's to be a fight I want it on my terms. I'm also thinking I should push the issue with Dennis. Jonathan is climbing the walls.

* * * * * * *

OUR PLAN, HEAD NORTH along the migration route of *les Bernards québécois.* "I invited your mother, you know," my father said as I watched her disappear in the rear window, "she said no." She knew his heart was set on this unprecedented one-on-one and for her it was no contest – a week of relatives, his relatives, versus time to herself. I drove the first leg, now Dad was at the wheel slicing through the fields and pine forests of Maine. I asked if he was up for a French session, feeling nervous about my upcoming competition with the fast-speakers.

"Ouais, ouais!" he replied, *"J'ai besoin de la pratique, moé-même."*

His off-center French fascinated me. Father Bourassa told us the powers-that-be had tried for years to eradicate *Joual,* in their view a national embarrassment. *Joual* was at the intersection of politics with economics, he remarked, here an issue of haves versus have-nots. He implicated history as well, identifying spelling and forms of speech traceable to dialects outside Paris. Many settlers emigrated from those areas, notably Normandy and Brittany. I made a note to ask Father Trần how this played out on the other side of the globe.

The northern third of Maine sped by. At the little town of Knowles Corner we turned onto SR 11, a two-lane road leading straight to the border at the St. John River. Traversing New Brunswick, an hour into Québec, we came upon the town with the crazy name – Saint-Louis-du-Ha! Ha! When we stopped for coffee the counterman said there are lots of theories but nobody knows for sure why the name. I was the only one who seemed to care. After eleven hours on the road we checked into a hotel overlooking the marina in the busy industrial town of Rivière-du-Loup. We stopped here, an hour short of our destination because our hosts were early-to-bed types. This night, so was I – out before my head hit the pillow.

I was awakened by my father on the phone to his brother in Bic. All was in readiness for our visit. Another way of saying it, we would slide right into their normal workday. The sun was full in our faces as we drove east along the St. Lawrence, and as we neared his boyhood home my father became really excited. Wheeling into the driveway he leaned on the horn, bringing Uncle Albert and Tante Geneviève to the porch. It always made me smile to see her Mutt and his Jeff, so jolly, full of life. *"Bonjour! Bienvenue!"* she said, throwing her arms around me. "You get bigger every time we see you!"

"Bonjour," I replied, kissing her on the cheek.

Albert threw his arms around my father, then stepped back and began pumping my hand. *"Ti-Paul, si bon de te voir!"*

"Merci, c'est bien d'être ici," I ventured. I was determined to keep it up.

"How long since we seen you, two-three years?" she said.

"More like five," my father said.

"Well, come in! *Faites comme chez vous!"*

"We added on since you were here," Tante Geneviève said as we unloaded the car. "You'll be in the new part, but only two days you're staying? You can't stay longer?"

"I need to show Paul Québec City and Montreal too," my father replied, "and Friday I got to be back. You know he's working for me this summer?"

"Poor kid," Albert said, punching my shoulder. "How's the slave driver treating you?"

"Bien, bien," I said. "He's easy, I have no complaints."

"And college, what are you studying?" Tante Geneviève asked.

"A little of everything. They're big on Philosophy and Religion."

"Ah," she nodded her head, "very important, especially the Religion."

"I'm majoring in Political Science. You know, Government."

"Pièrre works for the government, you two will have lots to talk about. A few years ago he moved the family to Rimouski and took a job there."

"Last time I saw Céline she was going to have a baby."

"Par ici" She led me to the living room. "Here," she said, picking up a picture, "little André's First Communion." A boy in short white pants and shirt, the trademark family eyes peered from the frame. Céline had put on weight. "Anne is the oldest, eleven," Tante Geneviève said, pointing to a dark-haired girl almost as tall as her mother. "She was that baby." I sneaked a look at Tante Geneviève's upper lip. No hair. The problem had solved itself... or been solved.

"We'll cook outside if it don't rain."

"Where's *Pépère?"* my father asked.

"In town for supplies," Albert said, "he'll be back anytime."

"Still driving, is he?"

Tante Geneviève nodded. "That'll be the day he stops driving,"

Albert lit a cigarette. "Seventy-eight last week and not sick a day in his life."

"Knock wood," my father said. "Good for him."

I changed into my old clothes – they had a full day planned for us. Behind the house lay the land that had supported three generations of Bernards. Potatoes, corn, beans were the mainstays, a small herd of cows whose milk they sold through a co-op, brown-egg chickens. Break-even was an excellent year. Albert's youngest son Philippe took courses at Agricultural Extension in Rimouski, and under the watchful eyes of the old-timers was experimenting with new irrigation techniques, new crops. Last year he successfully introduced soybeans, they said, this year, sorghum wheat.

A half hour later, relaxing in the front room with a lemonade, through the screen door I saw *Pépère* wiping his shoes on the doormat. The door screeched and banged shut. Tante Geneviève rolled her eyes. The bane of women everywhere, but her smile told me she knew I was in the other camp, the slammers. *Pépère* was a tall, rangy man with a lined face and a full head of white hair. He wore scuffed work boots and a white T-shirt under denim bib overalls. When he and his first-born, Albert, stood side by side, except for time's asterisk they were twins – the original and a copy minted some twenty years later.

"Qu'est-ce qui se passe?" he said, stepping into the room. "Ah, this must be the new hand!" he said, coming up to me. *"Ti-Paul!"* He grasped my hand firmly. *"Bienvenue!"* My father gave him a big hug. "*Bonjour, papa,* it's been a long time."

"Ouais," the old man replied, "much too long."

After the greetings *Pépère* directed all able-bodied men to report outside immediately. Sitting in the driveway, an ancient pickup truck, its fenders crinkled, the back window cracked. Piled high in the truck bed, visible over the side slats were bags – there must have been fifty of them – demanding to be unloaded. "We'll drive to the barn," *Pépère* said, "you men meet us there. Get in, *ti-Paul.*" I started for the passenger side. "No, the other side."

"You want me to drive it?"

"What the hell you think I mean?" he said with a scowl.

"I never drove a truck before."

"First time for everything. You drive a stick?"

"Sure."

I slid behind the wheel and got acquainted with the controls, then looked out. Uh-oh. There it was, right in front of us – the Cadillac. No way I could back out, either. I made very certain the gearshift was in neutral, then turned the key. The engine rumbled to life then settled to a noisy thrum. Standing next to his pride and joy, looking ready to throw himself in front of it, was my father. I didn't have the heart to meet his eyes. I rode the clutch into reverse and pressed the accelerator, inching us backward and turning the wheel away from the Cadillac.

Pépère nodded. "First gear, upper left."

An 'H,' same as our Plymouth. A couple of leaps and we were off, clearing the Caddy with room to spare. We circled the house. The barn was a distance away, a large red building with a pitched roof. As we neared, *Pépère* pointed to the open door. "Take 'er in."

Blinded from the glare, I eased into the dark barn.

"Turn here," he said, pointing to a clear area. I brought the truck to a stop.

"Formidable!" Pépère said with a big grin, slapping me on the knee.

I set the handbrake and jumped down. My father and Uncle Albert were coming in the door. Uncle Albert punched me on the shoulder. "Good job!"

My father was shaking his head, he had this funny grin on his face. He and Albert clambered into the truck bed and began tossing sacks overboard. I was indeed the designated hauler. *Pépère* pointed to the far wall, about twenty paces away. "The feed goes there and the fertilizer along the wall." By the label, thirty-five pounds for the feed sacks, sixty for the fertilizer. Lift... steady... walk... drop. Lift... steady... walk... drop. The piles grew. Lift... steady... walk... lift... drop. Lift... stagger... walk... stop. Mesmerized, I was no longer in cool, sunny Gaspé. This was the Pit, this was ketchup and canned pears and tarantulas. A nonstop hour and I was finished. Literally.

"See why we're all in such good shape." Albert wiped his face with a bandanna, "not even counting the plowing and harvesting."

I grimaced, trying to catch my breath. This summer had been the least physical stretch of my life.

We broke for lunch. Thick slabs of homemade bread, ham and chunks of cheese, lemonade, a chocolate cake. For good measure, a bowl of apples, more cheese.

While we were working, Tante Jeanette had slipped in. She lived alone about a mile away. For years Geneviève and Albert had tried to persuade her to move in with them but she valued her privacy. After the inevitable hug, she stood back and looked at my naked wrist. *"Ti-Paul,* you still have that watch from your First Communion?"

I rarely wore a watch in the summer. "Sure do, in my drawer at home," I replied. It had been there a long time, supplanted by a better Bulova, but I wasn't about to tell her that.

Midway through the afternoon cousin François arrived with his wife Margot and their two little kids. They had driven up from Trois Pistoles, a half-hour back toward Rivière du Loup, where he owned a service station and car repair. The house was starting to fill up. I was thinking I should take a shower but my father said this summer water was tight so just wash, and anyway, who cares? By five a couple dozen people were milling about the back yard. The rain was holding off so it would be a cookout.

That iced Molsen my father handed me really hit the spot. Beer is for good company, I thought to myself, not a competitive sport. About six, Pièrre and Céline showed up. As we visited, he told me about his studies toward an Economics degree from the University of Québec – night courses, correspondence courses. I wondered how he handled that kind of load and a family, both. I asked if what he was studying was any help in his government job. He ran a unit that processed applications for assistance from *les chômeurs,* people out of work. He began to explain when François wandered by.

"Paul! What're you up to? Long time no see."

"That's for sure. Great part of the world you have here."

"'Long as you don't have to make a living. Of course, if you can't make a living, my brother here'll put you on the dole."

Pièrre flushed. "François figures if somebody loses his job that's tough. That's what families are for, to pick people up."

"Couldn't have said it better, myself," François replied. "Me, I work seven days a week, ten-twelve hours a day. You call pulling a car out of a ditch in a blizzard fun? And that's my savings in there. Why should I support some bum who don't even try?"

Pièrre looked at me, shaking his head. "The people I see, months they've been looking, some of them years. The wife and kids, they're supposed to starve so Mr. Hard-Ass here can pay less tax? He even objects to the health benefit, if you can believe it."

"That's enough," François said, "we don't want Paul to get the wrong idea."

"Or the right idea," Pièrre retorted, his mouth in a line.

After dinner, Uncle Albert tuned his fiddle to Philippe's guitar and the singing and dancing began. It turned out, *Pépère,* the sly old dog, had a girlfriend. Widow Frechette was a family friend who lost her husband about the time *Mémère* died. They visited back and forth often, talking, playing cards, they even went to the movies in his pickup. It was something to see, these old folks having such a good time.

The next day we piled into cars and went to Ste Anne de Beaupré for Mass. Twentieth Sunday after Easter, the priest meditated on Christ's sacrifice and the Eucharist He left for our strength and consolation – *le pain du ciel, la coupe du salut.* The sermon lasted all of three minutes. Simple, direct, to the point. Like his congregation. Like *les Bernards canadiens.*

The quiet Sunday afternoon was a nice break. During the party Uncle Albert had asked if I'd like to work on the farm next summer. I said maybe I would, wondering why we hadn't thought of that while I was in high school. Later I noticed *Pépère* rocking on the front porch and sat down beside him. "It is good to see you, *ti-Paul.* Come more often, next summer, *bien sûr.*"

"I would like to, it's very peaceful up here."

"Peaceful!" *Pépère* spat on the floor. "An outsider's word! You don't hear peaceful in the winter around here. This is a hard place, *ti-Paul,* it wears a man down. If he ain't hard he doesn't survive. Your father is a hard man. He has what it takes." He added, nodding, "you got half as much, you be lucky."

As I was getting ready for bed, I caught my father writing a check. "I help out a little," he said sheepishly. "Many years I felt bad not being able to do anything."

We left about eight the next morning. Albert and Philippe came in from the fields to say goodbye. It was a cloudy day, with a chance of rain, according to the radio. My father was driving... he had this grin on his face. "Let me ask," he began, "what were you thinking when you drove the truck with the Cadillac right there? You looked terrified."

"That makes two of us. I saw you, too."

"I was proud of you – you did it." His eyes took on a faraway look. "You know, up here you learn a lot, stuff you don't get in books. It's a simple place but demanding."

"You have to be hard to survive, you mean?"

"That's about right."

Flipping around the dial, Radio Canada had an update on the U.S. election. The Republican, Nixon, had injured his leg and might have to undergo surgery. He still led Kennedy in the polls, but his absence from the campaign could boost the young Bostonian. "What do you think of Kennedy?" I asked.

"Young, inexperienced, but I think he can learn. Anyway, I never liked Nixon, just don't trust the man."

"Do you think a Catholic can win?"

"Rhode Island for sure, the rest of the country? Beats me."

EARLY AFTERNOON WE ROLLED INTO QUÉBEC CITY. As we neared, we saw our destination, the Chateau Frontenac, towering from a bluff over the river. It put that New York hotel to shame. A beautiful big room, we had, and what a view! Beyond the city walls we saw the Plains of Abraham where the British won the battle for French Canada. Success came dear, however, for soon the centuries-old power struggle erupted again and led France to side with the American colonists.

Under our umbrellas we strolled the cobblestone streets of Old Québec from the *Haute-Ville* to the *Basse-Ville* and slipped into l'Église Nôtre-Dame-des-Victoires to see the famous stained glass. Some years later when I came across Willa Cather's *Shadows on the Rock,* it brought me back to the sights and sounds of Québec City. Later still, living in Paris, I remembered this happy time. And I most certainly remembered Montreal.

After checking into our hotel in Montreal we went for a long walk, then had an early dinner. I was settled in my bed with *Nôtre Dame de Paris.* It was a real treat to enjoy the great author in his own language and in a similar milieu. I was so engrossed I hadn't noticed my father on the phone. "She'll be back when?" I heard him say. "Okay, I'll call then. *Au revoir.*"

"What was that?" I asked.

"Nothing," he replied. "Checking on a friend."

The next day, our last day, we signed up for a tour of the city which lasted until late afternoon. Back in our room after dinner I figured we were in for the night, but about nine my father told me to get myself together, we were going out again. "So late?" I asked.

"You're not a night person, I take it."

"I don't know what I am." I peered over my book at him.

He looked me up and down. "How about changing into your good pants and a proper shirt, and while you're at it brush your teeth. When was your last shower?"

"This morning. Why? Where are we going?"

"You'll see."

On the balmy evening the sidewalks were crowded with people out strolling. Actually, I was glad to be outside again – Hugo could wait. My father was a couple of paces ahead so I kept walking into his cigarette smoke. He looked back at me several times. "You doing okay?" A moment later, "Everything all right?"

"Why do you keep asking?"

He looked ahead again. "No particular reason."

Puzzled, I continued on. We turned onto a tree-lined side street of stately townhomes, each joined to the next. Halfway down the block he stopped and looked up. We were in front of a four-story brownstone, number 96. "Ah, this is it," he said, flicking his cigarette into the street. He climbed the steps and rang the bell. As we stood on the landing he shifted his weight from one foot to the other. A moment later a young woman opened the door. She was, without question, the most beautiful girl I had ever seen. Long dark hair, full red lips, she was wearing a low-cut blue dress.

"Julien Bernard," he said. "I'm here to see Hélène."

"*Bienvenue.* Come in, she's expecting you. I'm Madeleine," she said, looking at me and smiling. We were ushered into a high-ceilinged room with red wallpaper that looked like velvet with a raised pattern, plush chairs and a sofa, paintings and photographs on the walls, soft music playing on a phonograph. "Make yourselves comfortable," she said, "I'll get Hélène."

"What is this place?" I whispered. "Why are we here?"

My father put his hand on my arm. "Look. I know I haven't been the world's best father, I haven't, you know, talked to you about things like I should have." He sighed. "I have no idea where you are with women but just in case I want to get you started right."

I couldn't believe what I was hearing.

"Just be yourself. Do what comes naturally. These are good people, you have nothing to worry about."

"Damn you, Julien Bernard!" A tall, heavily made-up woman strode into the room. She wore a dark blue shift that flowed over her ample figure. Fifty? Sixty? Lovely, in a faded sort of way. She must have been something once. "You're a naughty boy, neglecting us," she said, throwing her arms around him then pushing him back for a better look. "How many years this time?"

"No excuses," he smiled, "guilty on all counts."

"And this must be Paul," she said extending her hand, a ring on every finger, bracelets up her wrist, "I'm Hélène."

"Pleased to meet you," I choked.

"If you hadn't guessed, I'm the Mother Superior."

I laughed nervously. She put her arm on my shoulder and kneaded it with a firm hand, her bracelets jangling. "Relax! You're among friends. Would you like a drink?"

"Two glasses of red wine would go well," my father said, nodding at me. We each took a chair as she went to the corner of the room and opened a cabinet filled with whiskies, wine, liqueurs. She took down three goblets, uncorked a bottle and poured a generous portion for my father and me, half an inch for herself.

"1952 Chateau St. Emilion. Only the best for my old friend and his son. *Salut,*" she said, touching her glass to my father's, then to mine.

"Salut." He reached toward mine, adding, *"et toi, aussi."*

As we sat, other women, girls, passed by the doorway. Every so often the doorbell rang and a man was ushered in. In my high excitement I was in no position to take part in a conversation but I gathered my father and Hélène had grown up neighbors in the Gaspé. Later he would tell me her acting career in the big city didn't pan out. Landing on her feet, so to speak, she married an elderly admirer, and on his demise came into a sum she used to stake herself to this... business. My father was telling her about our visit to the old homestead, Jim getting married, Catherine, me, everything but my mother. Keep on talking, I thought, keep on talking. But finally...

Hélène turned to me. "Paul, you met Madeleine earlier."

"Yes," I said. The drowning man going under.

"She would like you to call on her," she said, "top of the stairs, first right."

I knew it. My father raised his glass. I stood and tamely made my way from the room, furious. What was the man thinking? This isn't some family outing. I looked up... and I saw Father Ronan on the top step. Flames rose about me, sulfur burned my lungs. The screams of the damned rang in my ears. With a shudder, my body climbed the stairs, catching a glimpse of my immortal soul going the other way.

First room on the right. The door was ajar. Sighing deeply I rapped and pushed the door open. The room was dimly lit. Madeleine was reclining on a four-poster bed, a mound of pillows behind her. She had shed her gown and was wearing only her... underwear. *What in the world am I doing here? This isn't what I want. This isn't how I want it to happen.*

"You could close the door," she said, sitting up. Of course. Close. The door. She smoothed the bed with her hand. "Come. Sit." I sat. "Paul," she said, *"c'est un si beau nom, intelligent, fort."*

"Merci. Madeleine is very beautiful too... the name, I mean." I reddened. How dumb... did I really say that? She smiled, a very nice smile. I was doing my best not to stare at her but I couldn't help sneaking looks. It didn't help that the two of us were reflected in a big mirror across from the bed. It was like being in a movie, one the movie magazines wouldn't touch. I tried to avoid the mirror but couldn't. My lower regions were coming alive.

She put her hand on mine and smiled. "Your first time, I can tell..."

I nodded. She smelled of perfume, some kind of flower.

"...there is no hurry," she was going on. "Hélène told me to be especially nice to you, but that will not be a problem, I didn't expect you'd be so tall and handsome."

It almost sounded like she meant it. "Would it be okay if we just talk a while," I said, "you know, get to know each other?" It took all my strength not to say, "first." I was glad I had only one sip of that wine.

"Whatever makes you comfortable." She reached to the night table, lit a cigarette, took a long drag then held it out to me. I noticed her lipstick on the tip.

I shook my head. "I... I gave them up."

"Smart as well as good-looking," she nodded.

"I try to stay in shape. Smoking really cuts into your wind."

"Oh, you are an athlete? What is your sport? Around here hockey is the big thing. Are you *un hockeyeur?*"

I thought a moment. "I play a little football."

She nodded. "A dangerous sport, like hockey."

"That's why it's important to stay in top physical condition," I lied.

She smoked silently a while, then ground out the cigarette, then reaching over, she lifted my glasses off. "What are you doing?"

"I want to see what you look like without those glasses."

"I'm pretty nearsighted."

She held the glasses up to her face. *"Mon Dieu!* They give me *le mal de tête!"* She put them on the table beside the bed and turned, leaning toward me. *"Tiens.* Now let's see about those eyes. *Ah, bon! Fantastique!* So large and dark. I've never seen such large, dark eyes. They're so, *comment dit-on,* so intense."

"It runs in the family. I have it more than the others."

"I wouldn't want you angry at me."

"Not a chance." I was relaxing a little. Without my glasses I couldn't see the mirror, though out of focus the highlights in her hair, her smooth skin, her neck and breasts were even more beautiful. My hard-on kept reminding me it was waiting. For some reason I wasn't embarrassed, but I had to keep the conversation going. "Do you mind if I ask, how long have you been, you know..."

"Doing this for a living? That is what you mean?"

"Actually, yes."

"Not so long, a couple of years."

"How did you get into it?"

"It has to do with money, or rather not enough money. Does that answer you?"

"I wouldn't expect you do it just because..."

"...because I like it? No, I'm not *une nymphomane,* if that's what you mean, though it can be enjoyable when you're with a nice person, like yourself." She looked down at my crotch. "And it appears you like me, too," she said reaching over and rubbing me lightly. I put my hand on hers. That was the first time I had touched her.

"Sorry... I'm not quite ready," I heard myself saying.

She pursed her lips. "Maybe I was wrong. Maybe you don't like me after all."

"No, that's not it." I took a deep breath. "You see, I was... I'm kind of saving myself for the right girl."

"Ah, the right girl." She was silent for a moment. "Someone from a good family. Someone who has been saving herself for you. Someone you can see as the mother of your children, that is what you mean?"

"I guess," I replied, "though when you say it that way it sounds kind of dumb."

"God protect us from his saints," she said under her breath.

"What's that?"

"Never mind." She lit another cigarette. "So you are thinking, what is a nice girl like me doing in a place like this? Or perhaps you're thinking I'm not a nice girl at all."

"Couldn't you find another way to make money?" I said intently. "Maybe I could help you figure out something else to do..."

"I do have a life, you know," she said sharply. "I finished *l'école secondaire,* I take courses to get that job you so much want me to have. Hélène is my good friend and there is no other way I can make enough. Department store, office work, waitress, I've done it all. You see, I don't have a daddy to fall back on."

I flushed. She looked at me severely. "What I do have is a little girl to take care of. I have my looks and my body and I'm not ashamed to use it. I do what I have to."

"I'm sorry, I didn't mean to make you feel bad."

She snorted. "Make *me* feel bad? Come on! Hélène runs a high class place – lawyers, professors, judges come here. I even had a mayor once, for God's sake, from somewhere in Manitoba. Then there's the normal guys who save up for one fun night a year, them I like much better. One time this priest comes in, without his collar, of course, how was I to know? He didn't treat me to his sermon until he was finished with me."

"Sounds hypocritical."

She stubbed out her cigarette. "So you're not going to play the hypocrite tonight."

"What do you mean?"

"I should get dressed." She stood and picked up a light robe, slipping it over her shoulders. She came back to the bed, stood in front of me and put her arms around my neck. "You're going to let me off easy," she said, stroking the back of my neck, "but you're not leaving without something to remember me by."

She pressed her lips onto mine, then played her tongue across them. My lips parted and she put her the tip of her tongue in my mouth. I had my arms around her and, unbidden, my hands drifted along her brassiere toward her breasts, when suddenly she pulled away.

"Okay, Paul," she said with this funny look. "You want to save me from a life of sin? Well, don't bother. I'll do it for you. Never fear, your morals are intact." Her face softened, "But we proved one thing, didn't we? You are made of flesh and blood – that's a start, at least." She opened a drawer and scribbled on a pad of paper. "If you're ever up this way give me a call," she said, tearing off a sheet. "We'll go out for a milkshake or something. If I'm not here Hélène will know how to reach me."

She stuffed it into my pants pocket, stopping to feel around in there a few seconds.

"That makes me feel better," she said with a dazzling smile. "See, you do like me, after all!"

Returning to the hotel my father hung back, waiting for me to say something. Finally, he couldn't contain himself any longer. "Well, how did it go?"

I wasn't about to give him any satisfaction. "Perfect," I said enthusiastically, staring ahead, *"Merci mille fois."*

"Pas de quoi. She is one lovely young woman, that Madeleine."

"How about you?" I asked, looking sideways at him.

"Ah. Hélène is an old friend. We talked. Friendship is a wonderful thing."

"You seem to know everybody."

He smiled, "Only people that matter."

On the drive back we were both spent. I wasn't angry any longer, in fact I was calm. So like my father, this was – size up the situation then barge ahead. His remark about friendship made me think of my mother. Duty, pain, sickness, children, these come with the territory, but that kind of sharing isn't enough. Friendship – was that their missing ingredient? As for Madeleine, I had to admit, in an odd way I admired her. Fortunately it wasn't my place to judge her, though I'd done my best to muddle the issue. Something important was dawning on me. Plug real people into those moral equations, right and wrong get a lot more complicated. Not like the textbooks, not at all.

I couldn't blame my father, either. Once I figured out what he was up to I could have left. I said the right things, did the right things but, face it, I enjoyed this... occasion of sin. No other way to describe it. Drawn by the beauty of the flame, its warmth held me. Deep down, escape was the last thing I wanted. Even my relief at having survived was colored by a measure of disappointment. The paper with Madeleine's number? I kept it in my wallet. Sometimes when I felt bad I'd take it out and look at it. Just knowing it was there gave me a warm glow. I wonder what ever happened to it... and to her.

17. DIGGING IN

"I NEVER HEARD THAT STORY. Paul didn't share that sort of thing with me."

"I'm sorry, but I still don't see how a person gets himself so wrapped up in denial."

"Well, keep at it. You shake your head. All right, given the chance he had..."

"I think you know my answer."

"Well, everybody's different. I have to say that father's instincts were good – a clean, safe, classy situation. By the way the *Globe* says they've appointed somebody to run the investigation." I hand Jonathan the paper open to the page.

"Captain Robert Martinez. And it'll be at Fort McNair. That's near D.C. isn't it?"

"Right. They're playing it close to the vest. I better call Dennis today."

* * * * * * *

THE JUDGE DISMISSED THE CROOK'S LAWSUIT, and every few weeks Simon would extend his magic to another part of the shop. But the union secured enough signatures for an election – that one really worried my father. I asked him to keep me posted. "You helped a lot, I hope you learned a few things too," he said with a wink on my way out the door.

Spending so much time with him, I learned a big part of my father's insensitivity was from moving so fast and focusing so hard, mostly for the family's benefit. Luckily, my mother had *Cat* opening in October, voice lessons and a piano refresher as well, and was looking forward, in a way, to becoming a grandmother in April. She had this image of herself as forever thirty... well, maybe thirty-five. "I'll love having a little person around," she said, "but being a grandmother is not my persona. If it were, how could I play Maggie?"

I plunged into a heavy second-year schedule. Frank and I opted to room together again and found ourselves at the end of a Carlin III corridor next to a six-person suite. The day I moved in, I heard banging and poked in to see what was happening. A tall, dark-haired kid I knew only by sight was moving a large picture around, trying to hook it on a nail. "Damn!" he said, setting it back on the floor. "Wire's too tight. Hold it for me, will you?"

I placed the picture against the wall as he fumbled around. "Got it!" We stepped back and admired our effort. "Fabulous, isn't it?"

What I saw, a group of naked, angular... women, I guessed they were. "What is it?"

"You don't know? Surely you recognize the style."

"Sorry," I said.

He shook his head, "Picasso, *Les Demoiselles d'Avignon. 1907.* A seminal work in the development of modern art."

"Why didn't he finish it?" I asked, digging him back.

My neighbor looked at me as if I were from another planet, then burst out laughing. "Pat Harrington," he said, extending his hand, "actually Paidraic, but nobody uses that."

"Paul Bernard. You know a lot about art."

"A fair amount. I'm in Classics."

"Political Science here. What's that one?" I pointed to another print standing against a wall, a muddy pink and gray scene with boats and a sunrise, or sunset, couldn't tell which.

Pat rolled his eyes. "You're serious, aren't you? *Impression: Sunrise.* Claude Monet, 1873. One of the world's most famous paintings."

"I was afraid you'd say that."

He shook his head. "I recommend Father Rooney's art appreciation course."

"That is an area I am entirely ignorant of."

"How about music?" Classical music was coming from a radio on his unmade bed.

"Somewhat better," I said, thinking I probably had a few music genes from my mother, though they'd been recessive so far.

"Where'd you go to high school?" he asked.

"La Salle, in Providence. You?"

"B.C. High."

"That's Jesuit. That must have given you a good start for this place."

"Not really. In fact papa's parting words yesterday were shape up or ship out."

I hoped he wouldn't ask how I did. "I'd better unpack," I said. "I live next door."

A few words about what I had coming up. Introduction to Political Thought. Plato and Aristotle, Augustine, Aquinas, Hobbes, Locke, Rousseau, the *Federalist Papers,* de Tocqueville, Marx and Engels. We'd end in the twentieth century – *Mein Kampf,* Koestler, Lippmann. American Government would put our system under the microscope, and Sociology complete the social science menu. English, Rhetoric & Shakespeare – writing and argument, the Bard, and history's great speeches, prompting my mother to say it's about time. We'd read a dozen plays, sonnets too. French was vocabulary-building and high-speed comprehension, with a generous slice of big names, Montaigne, Pascal, Zola, de Maupassant, more Hugo. Second semester, the moderns – Camus, Sartre, Gide. My *voyage à Québec* had bumped my conversation to the next level.

Philosophy was Metaphysics, the "philosophical study of the real." We would finally meet the great minds we had bypassed freshman year. Following Aristotle and Aquinas, though at some distance, the modern Scholastic position was "moderate realism," a middle-of-the-road approach, which credits the mind while acknowledging its limitations. We would audaciously set about proving God's existence and something about His nature.

In our first session, Father Downey called on Chris Sheehy, my next-door neighbor from San Francisco. "The Principle of Sufficient Reason is central to this exercise. Would you remind us what that Principle is?" We had discussed it the day before.

Chris had a wild mop of curly hair and a problem with pressure. "Everything has its suf-suf-sufficient reason. That is, whatever it n-n-needs for being what it is, it has." By now everyone was used to him.

"Isn't that just stating the obvious?"

"I was won-wondering that m-m-myself." This brought a laugh. "I mean, wh-why do we have to invent something called a 'principle?' If something's, say, a hor-hor-horse, of course it has whatever it takes to be a horse."

"Anybody want to venture an answer?" Seeing no hands, Father Downey went on. "Yes, the world got along fine without Principles before the Greeks invented them. They are a convenience, to help us organize our understanding of the world." The priest put down his book. "The notion of the contingent being. Who will begin the discussion? Mr. Bernard?"

I'd been over this last night. "Whatever comes to be is contingent," I began. "And since at one time it didn't exist, existence is not one of its necessary features."

"Examples."

"This room, everybody in it. Once none of this existed and neither did its component parts. We're all contingent."

"It follows, does it not, we depend on other beings for our existence? Could all these other beings be contingent, Mr. Bernard? You owe your existence to your father and mother, your ancestors. The wood in your desk came from a tree, which came from a seed, which came from another tree, and so on. Is that a satisfactory explanation?"

"They're all contingent themselves, none of them necessarily exists."

"Can't you go back indefinitely? Infinitely?"

"You'd still be talking contingent beings. Multiplying the size of the series doesn't change the fact they all depend on something else."

"And what might that something else be?"

"It would have to be non-contingent, incapable of not existing."

"In other words, a necessary being. What else?"

"It wouldn't depend on any other being. It would be independent of everything else."

"And as the last being in the chain of causality, or strictly speaking the first, it would be the cause of everything else, independent in its causal activity, a Primary Cause. And unlimited, because if limited, it would be just another contingent being. So, an Infinite Being. Summing up, to account for the world and everything in it, we need a primary cause, one that is necessary and infinite in Being. In other words..."

"God," I interjected.

He nodded. "Gentlemen, we've just seen St. Thomas' second proof of the existence of God, the argument from efficient causality. Remember it – you'll be seeing it again."

OFFICIALLY IT WAS 338 CARLIN but to everyone it was "the Sixpack," and in two weeks it had been transformed into something remarkable. The walls were covered with Pat's Monet and Picasso, original oils by another resident, Bill Rossi, in the far corner a tall wooden fish, now a lamp, found in a Greenwich Village junk shop. To the pallid hue of the walls was added an undulating tricolor stripe that encircled the room – green-white-red over Rossi's bed, green-white-orange for the Irish guys, broken by Freddy Aust's black-red-gold, the *bleu-blanc-rouge* over Pat, in honor, I learned, of his French-born grandmother. The final touch, a chandelier, in place of the standard-issue globe, a genuine fake Tiffany according to Ed Dolan and heavy enough to avoid sitting under. These guys were artists, not engineers. Dolan, a pre-med, might have known what he was doing, but nobody wanted to take the chance.

Why Sixpack? You're right, it didn't fit. My neighbors' "Christian Brothers Winecellar" was a cavity under a floorboard, crammed with wines and whiskies for special occasions which at times, but rarely, included the opposite sex. Female visitors were *verboten.* So "fornicatorium," one of the suite's other names, was a stretch, though I suppose on occasion "vomitorium" fit. I often stopped by for sociability and conversation. The day we started on proofs for the existence of God I happened in. Pat was holding forth.

"Kant says you can't prove the existence of something from your idea of it. If all you experience are contingent, limited things, you can't reason to an all-powerful being, infinite, necessary and so on. Too big a stretch."

"Not so," I countered, "the second proof says there has to be an adequate explanation for all those contingent, limited beings. You can't go back ad infinitum. And what can that be except the being that was there first, that caused them in the first place? In other words, the First Cause, the Primary Cause."

"But what about the attributes of your Primary Cause?"

"Well sure, they're expressed in negative terms –that's the best we can do. Infinite equals 'not finite.' Necessary means 'cannot not exist.' To that extent Kant has point, we are bound by our limitations."

"And Revelation's there to fill in the blanks," Ed added.

Pat scowled. "Very convenient, *mein herr.*"

Bill Rossi broke in. "What about Pascal's Wager?" We had just covered this in class. "Gentlemen, place your bets!"

"I go with Pascal," Ed Dolan said. "If you're wrong and there is no God, no big deal. If you're right, infinite happiness. That's an easy one."

"As usual, you miss the point," Pat replied. "To quote my friend Paul, one morning you wake up and decide God exists because it's to your advantage? Faith doesn't work that way, it comes from inside, from the heart."

"Luther says it comes from outside, if at all. The free gift of God. Some get it, some don't. Tough guy. Calvin, too."

Pat shook his head. "Say there is a God and he's watching your tricky little game – he'd be totally pissed! Man, you just bought yourself a one-way ticket to hell."

"Of course there has to be follow-through!" Ed retorted. "Once you place your bet, then you live the life God wants you to live. Moral, just, kind. Otherwise, yeah, you're a hypocrite and you deserve what you get."

"What you give up isn't trivial, either," Bill Rossi said. "Pleasure isn't all that bad..."

"Damn right!"

"...and if you bet wrong, you miss your only chance to have a good time, here or hereafter."

"Bummer."

"I'll drink to that."

Pat was quiet for a moment. "When you think about it, why does a person need God to do the right thing? If there is such a thing as natural law, which I understand they'll prove in a couple of weeks, then moral action stands on its own. I shouldn't need an eternal reward not to kill my sister or to help somebody who needs it."

"It makes for a better society."

"It keeps you out of jail."

"In fact," Pat went on, "religion, our own included, has promoted some of man's worst atrocities. Maybe we'd be better off without God, just go with the natural order."

"We don't exactly have a choice. If the Man's there, he's there."

"You have to admit the threat of hell packs a pretty good punch."

"Not good enough, if you know your history."

"What it comes down to," Pat said, "brother Pascal is peddling heaven insurance." He held up a copy of the *Pensées* with the cover a drawing of a man with long curly hair and a beak of a nose. "I ask you, would you buy a bridge from this man?"

MY WORK ON *THE CRUSADER* went well, articles and photography both. Halloween night I got a call from our Editor-In-Chief, Ray Perkins. "What are you doing tomorrow afternoon?"

"I'll be at the Kennedy speech." Cross & Scroll, the student impresarios, had landed candidate John F. Kennedy thanks to an alum who was a big Kennedy backer. A hectic day for the candidate – a $5,000-a-plate luncheon in Boston and a Hartford rally with a stop at Mt. St. James in between, including an interview for *The Crusader*.

"I want you to help me with my interview. Al just came down with appendicitis, he is under the knife as we speak." A senior reporter, Al Jarvis owned the juicy news stories. "Meet me at the office in half an hour."

Twist my arm!

Kennedy was everything I expected. Slim and tanned, he wore a classic dark gray pinstriped suit. Charm, energy, confidence, masculinity – he had it all, along with a firm handshake. We sat at a small conference table, the others standing. One of the candidate's handlers began by saying they'd have to cut the interview short, they were running late.

Unfazed, Ray began. "Senator Kennedy, you and the Vice President have been going back and forth in the polls. What do you expect your margin of victory will be?"

That broke up the room. Kennedy leaned back and smiled his enormous smile. "You never want to peak too early, and I'm pleased to report we've managed to avoid that." More laughter. "But seriously, we see this as a very tight election. We're counting on the northeast of course. Nixon will be strong in the West and Midwest and away from the big cities where we have the advantage."

I was scribbling fast. Ray looked up from his notes. We had gone over his questions last night and if Kennedy expected softballs he was in for a surprise.

"According to news reports you were applauded in Houston by that ministers' association when you said you'd resign the Presidency if you had a conflict between your religion and the office. My question, wouldn't that be unfair to the voters who elected you? The American public will be counting on you despite any claims from your religion."

"Fair question." Kennedy paused. "My belief is it would never come to that, but if it did I'd have to make a choice. One option would be to step down, but that assumes a most extreme situation. In fact, I can't conceive of circumstances where it could happen."

After a few more questions one of Kennedy's crew pointed at his watch but Ray wasn't looking. "From your voting record you're a civil rights moderate – evolution over revolution, if I can put it that way. How does that square with your brother bailing Martin Luther King out of jail after the lunch counter incident in Atlanta? Doesn't that align you with the these activists' hardball tactics? Or was his call really about the black vote?"

I looked around. Our public affairs officer was cringing.

"Where'd this guy come from?" Kennedy said, grinning. "Ray, I think the *Post* has a job for you – except forget that, you'd be too rough in my press conferences. But seriously, Reverend King is one of our country's finest men, one of the great leaders of our time. He speaks for a large constituency unfairly denied their rights and economic opportunity. I don't condone everything he says or does but I fully support him getting his message across. It's no secret we are actively seeking the support of the black electorate across the country, and yes, we hope they will rally strongly behind us."

This time Kennedy looked at his watch. "Okay, one more. Give me your best shot."

Ray paused. "The vice presidency is hardly the 'bully pulpit' the Majority Leader is used to. Can you two really work together for a common agenda?"

"Lyndon has a great track record. He will be a major force in getting our legislative program passed. Together I think we'll serve the American public well if given the chance."

"And that chance is enhanced by his following in the south and southwest?"

"No question about it. Good policy says put your best team on the field, but good politics says it has to be electable. I think our ticket is that. We'll see in about a week. Thank you." Kennedy was standing. A fast round of handshaking and he rushed out the door to the auditorium. Ray and I beat it over to our reserved front row seats. As we left the interview room Ray stopped to light a cigarette. He took a couple of deep drags then put it out. "Well, what do you think?" he asked me.

"Is there a Pulitzer for college reporting?"

"Let's write the story first."

And so we did, front page of the *Crusader,* with a joint byline, very decent of Ray.

That encounter started me thinking about a Washington summer job, and as the new administration rolled out one exciting program after another, led by the Peace Corps, it appeared other young people were thinking the same thing.

For a paper in American Government I analyzed FDR's First Hundred Days against the gloom and misery that swept him into office. Banks failing, people starving, jumping out of windows. I had no idea how bad things had been. If God had shed his grace on America, in a fit of insanity somehow we had thrown it back at Him. "The only thing we have to fear is fear itself..." What FDR said next is less familiar but no less important. He warned about "nameless, unreasoning, unjustified terror which paralyzes needed efforts to convert retreat into advance." I couldn't believe how people dug their heels in when the old order was so clearly inadequate. And what a strain on our democracy, Roosevelt assuming powers never imagined, let alone authorized. Some said the cure was worse than the disease.

Two other big questions I could only touch on. What conditions justify the President to alter constitutional processes and restrict protected rights? The other, even with the recovery it took another war to restore the nation to health – do we need wars to thrive? To survive? I had a feeling I would face these issues again. I was reluctantly coming to the conclusion that our country wasn't as perfect as I had been led to believe. We're a work in progress, I wrote. Let's hope we progress in the right direction.

As I was writing this paper our French class was finishing *La Peste.* What a contrast! The will of Americans roused, versus this allegory of French collaboration, ordinary men and women struggling against their so-called leaders, inertia, ignorance and cowardice. I was beginning to see that literature, great literature, might actually have something to say.

PAT AND I HAD BECOME FRIENDS and we'd decided to room together junior year. Washington's Birthday weekend he invited me to visit his family in Boston. The Harringtons lived below Charles Street in a town home overlooking the river. Pat told me his father was continually badgering him about going into the law and disparaging his interest in art. Mr. Harrington was a partner in an old-line Boston law firm before jumping to First Massachusetts Bank as their top lawyer, a few years later becoming President. I told Pat his father seemed kind of aloof but he said not to take it personally. "He's like that with everybody."

Unfortunately Pat's *grand-maman* was away, I was looking forward to meeting her. Pat told me that as an eighteen-year old she had married a cavalry officer headed for the front, and made a widow by the Battle of the Somme. After the Armistice she fell for a wealthy Chicagoan on the Grand Tour and they were wed in Paris. The groom's family offered him a choice: return to the family business or be disinherited. So the newlyweds settled on a large estate in Lake Forest on Chicago's gold coast. Eleanor, Pat's mother, was their only child. Widowed again some years ago, Madame Baldwin, Élodie, had recently moved to Boston and occupied the suite of honor in the household. This weekend *grand-maman* was in Chicago meeting with her attorneys over sale of the Lake Forest estate.

Pat mentioned his twin, Meg – Meghan – but he made her sound like Catherine so I didn't pay any attention. It turned out she and Pat were very different. His personality was sharp as his pointed nose and jutting chin. Meg was willowy, with light brown hair, soft features and a wonderful smile. Saturday morning the three of us were sitting on the patio after breakfast, sun slanting through the limbs of an oak in the neighbors' yard, enjoying the first warm spell since November. It had snowed the previous week, same storm that paralyzed Worcester with twenty-two inches, and traces remained in the shady corners of the yard. Mrs. Harris, live-in helper and companion to Élodie, put the last of the dishes on her tray. "How you people can sit out here is beyond me," she clucked, "I'm shutting the door behind me, if you please."

"No problem," Pat said, adding as she disappeared into the house. "I love her dearly but she is not one of my favorite people. Is that possible?"

Meg smiled. "No, but you're by nature impossible so it's all right."

"Ouch," he said, snapping his head back, "that smarts." He turned to me. "Do you and your sister act this way?"

I set my coffee down. "All the time. This is very familiar."

"You have the brother gene, too," Meg said.

"Only thing that keeps us sane around the female of the species," I said. "We're actually very chivalrous. I am anyway."

"That's even worse," she said. "A woman shouldn't have to rely on a man in any circumstance. That's what *grand-maman* says."

"*Grand-maman.* We called ours *Mémère,*" I observed.

"Called?" Meg asked.

"She died some years ago."

"I'm sorry," Meg said. "Where did she live?"

"In Canada, in the Gaspé."

"That's supposed to be very beautiful."

"I was there this summer. It is quite a place."

"They say Mt. Tremblant is the best. Do you ski?"

"Never have."

She looked at Pat. "Maybe we could invite Paul to North Conway."

"You better have a sense of humor," I said, "I've never tried it."

"How do you spend your summers?" Meg asked me.

A funny question, I thought, then I remembered the Harringtons had a house on the Vineyard they used as a base for their summer travels. A bit different from DiLorenzo's or Bernard Bros. Tool & Die. "Mostly I've been putting money aside, though this summer I was thinking about a job in Washington..."

"JFK personally offered Paul a high-level position," Pat said.

"Dream on," I replied, making a face.

"Daddy's family and the Kennedys lived in the same parish way back when," Meg said, tossing her head. "So have you found anything in Washington?"

I shook my head. "I'm giving it a pass. Probably next year."

This is why. I'd heard about students making four, five thousand dollars in a summer selling encyclopaedias. I'd never pictured myself as a salesman but the prospect of so much money was tantalizing. Though I decided to keep it to myself for the time being.

Pat stood up. "I'm headed to the MFA – Museum of Fine Arts to you," he said, nodding at me. "Interested? It's the last week for the Van Gogh."

"Think I'll take a rain check."

"Paul's come a long way in terms of art appreciation," Pat said to Meg. "Of course, considering where he started that isn't saying a whole lot."

"You mean considering where you are. That's hardly a fair comparison."

"You're right. Sorry, Paul, bad joke."

Half an hour later Meg and I were walking along the Charles, crossing over Storrow Drive on the footbridge near their house. There was ice on the river, thin sheets with dark patches extending out a distance. "How do you like Radcliffe?" I asked.

"It's okay. I had my heart set on Barnard but I didn't get in. Being so close to home's a pain."

"What are you interested in?"

"Maybe literature. My problem is I like everything but nothing well enough."

"My sister's doing English Lit at Brown, she's a junior. She's thinking of teaching, probably high school."

"She must be a saint." Meg looked at me sideways, "speaking of which, are you sure about rooming with that brother of mine? He can be awfully hard to get along with."

"Don't worry, I can hold my own."

"You'd better. What's ahead for you after college?"

"Probably an advanced degree. I'm leaning toward Political Science."

"Do you get to Boston much?"

"I'm planning to be here more. The MFA, you know," I laughed. "Not to mention I'd like to see you again."

She thrust her hands into her pockets. "Most of Pat's friends aren't my type but you might be the exception that proves the rule."

THE RITUAL PACKING OF THE BELONGINGS was well along. Almost everyone was gone but I stayed an extra day to clean up some things at the *Crusader.* Suddenly I noticed Father Trần in the doorway. "I came to say good-bye," he said. "I've finished my studies and tomorrow I leave for home."

Over the two years we'd had some frank talks about what was happening in Vietnam.

"Here, please sit down," I said, pulling over Frank's former chair.

"I didn't want to leave without a word with you. When you become a person of influence, a senior official in the American government, let us say, I want you to remember what I tell you today." He seemed tired, dark circles under his eyes. "I am worried about my country. The Army again tried to overthrow our President Diem, and the North Vietnamese, their so-called National Liberation Front is more aggressive all the time. I fear them, but what I need to say, I fear your government even more."

"Why do you say that?" I was puzzled.

"I worry that you will abandon my people to the Communists. In the south we Catholics are such small numbers, that will wipe us out. Those people will stop at nothing, spare no one." I had learned he was the scion of a prominent family allied for generations with the French and the Diem dynasty.

"Why do you think that?" I asked. "We're promising additional aid to your country. Our Vice President just got back from a visit."

"That is well and good, but I worry that your government will not follow through. When I saw the uproar over the Bay of Pigs, it caused me to think deeply, and I concluded that whatever promises your government makes, one cannot be sure the American people will stand behind them when difficulties come."

I pictured those Cuban exiles on the beach, abandoned to Castro's wrath. "Not one of our finest hours," I said, shaking my head. "Growing pains for Kennedy, let us hope. Don't judge us from that one mistake. Our country is better than that."

"I hope so. Well, I see that you're busy..."

"No, not at all..."

"Here, I want you to have this." He reached into his shirt pocket and pulled out a card with his name and phone numbers on one side in English, the other in Vietnamese. "These are Saigon numbers. This," he said, pointing to a number written in ink, "this is the organization that sponsored me here. If all else fails they may be able to find me."

I looked at him quizzically. "If all else fails...?"

He smiled and nodded. "If all else fails."

Standing, he put his hand on my shoulder. "My beautiful, wounded country needs me, so I go to it. I hope we see each other again, my friend. May God be with you."

18. KNOW THYSELF...

"WHICH WAY DO YOU BET, GUS?"

"Bet? Oh, you mean Pascal. I'm a yes, definitely a yes."

"But as one of those people said you need to follow through – that's where I'd have trouble. That Kennedy business was interesting," Jonathan went on, "especially in light of his conversation with the Vietnamese priest. And it's about time he met somebody he's interested in."

"By the way, I called Paul's assistant, told her we'll be down to look at those papers soon." I still haven't let Jonathan know about Latimer or Paul's wife. Maybe the problem will go away, but I'm not counting on it. "And she gave me a piece of good news. ETVN may have an inside source for the Army investigation."

"Did she say what kind of source?"

"No, but their interest in this goes far beyond the news value."

"That makes three of us. Did you talk to Dennis today?"

"I left a message."

* * * * * * *

WE PULLED OFF THE ROAD after the New London bridge and were sitting, idling, as our driver scanned his map. "Gotta go back. We missed the turn."

"Aw, shit."

"Where'd you get your license? You sure you got a license?"

"Hey, the guy sells books, for chrissakes, don't mean he can read a map!"

"Knock it off or get your own ass back to Providence!" This from the driver.

Twenty minutes later I was standing on a street corner in Groton, Connecticut, the submarine base town. Ranch houses, new lawns, scraggly trees, freshly asphalted streets, gleaming crosswalks. I put my briefcase down and mopped my face with a handkerchief. Third week on the job. Here's why I was here.

COLLEGE STUDENTS! EARN BIG $$$$$
Encyclopaedia sales R.I. and S.E. Mass
Car provided. Guaranteed top earning
Flexible hours – time for sailing and golf
Information call ELmhurst 1-7652

When I reported to their downtown walkup office, I discovered the facts. Car provided? A team leader piled us proto-Lomans into a station wagon, drove an hour and scattered us around a "high prospect" neighborhood. Earnings guaranteed, as long as you sold a ton of books – all on commission. Flexible hours, sailing and golf? Nine to one-thirty we worked the phones for appointments then at three off we went. A round of golf in an hour? I didn't even play golf. A sail if you lived on the water, but then you wouldn't need the job in the first place.

Still, I signed up. I could earn more money with the Hamilton-Frey Encyclopedia Company Inc. than anywhere else, potentially. My first morning calling I secured three appointments out of sixty calls, not a good ratio – in a minute I'll tell you why. The first three days they put us through a training program that was actually quite good. We got familiar with the product, twenty large maroon leatherette volumes plus an annual "yearbook" update and a research service, great for school reports. We role-played, watched films of great salesmen in action. We practiced the "close." Never ask, "want to buy an encyclopaedia?" No. It's "mahogany or walnut for the bookcase?" But first you have to get in the house. Nobody would ever admit wanting to buy an encyclopaedia, so we stressed the educational survey we were embarked on. On our return we duly filed our survey forms in the office. I think I know where they ended up.

Inside, you jotted answers on a clipboard – number and ages of children, school performance, then the fateful question: "If I could show you how to improve your children's grades, you'd be interested, wouldn't you?" Invariably the answer was yes, and you were off and running. Though first you had to retrieve your briefcase from the bushes near the front door where you'd left it as a precaution.

You're wondering what happened to my vaunted commitment to truth and honesty. Good question. To stay close, I had to make a few changes to H-F's sales approach, changes I didn't mention to our Sales Manager, Mr. Spaulding. Obviously I couldn't deny I was selling something. If they asked me straight out I'd say yes, and I'd tell them what it was, too. This got a lot of phones hung up but those who didn't were better prospects, what Mr. Spaulding called "pre-qualified," though he would have had a fit if he knew what I was doing. I also refused to say tonight is your absolute last chance for this special offer. Come on! If a person called back and said they wanted a set of books, there'd be somebody on their doorstep before they hung up the phone.

The H-F sales force was four guys who did this for a living, plus three college students still hanging in, all the others having quit. One of them felt so bad about this one family's raggedy kids he gave away his Preview Volume and Sample Volume Five (F - G). After firing the guy Mr. Spaulding had to drive to New Bedford to retrieve them. My favorites were the old timers. Joe Wilson, fox face with a thin moustache, a chain-smoker. Aluminum siding, roofing, storm windows, pots and pans, Florida real estate, cemetery plots, if it could be sold he had sold it. My first day I went with him to observe. Oh, was he smooth – no way I could touch him, but I had my own style. Sincerity, youth, my glasses even. People trusted me. Plus I spoke credibly about college, which was impressive to working people wanting something better for their kids. With Joe, it was check to see you still had your wallet when he left.

Then there was the guy we called "The Sheik." Ed Khouri was of Lebanese descent, dark-skinned, heavy-set with a bushy moustache and a wardrobe of shiny suits that must have been tremendously hot. "It's a lot hotter where I'm going," he'd say. Ed had two obsessions – women and food, and a million stories about each. I accompanied him one day and watched his eyes light up when we came upon this great looking woman alone in her house. He liked working Quonset Point with its Navy wives pining away for their husbands at sea. How he had any energy left for selling books you had to wonder, though from the reports on the bulletin board he was H-F's best producer.

The Sheik delighted in showing us how to tell if a woman wanted it, versus one it was a waste of time to try. How they dressed, coming on to you with low-cut blouses, tight skirts, heavy makeup, using your first name right away or calling you honey. Sitting close on the couch when you broke out your Preview Volume. His astute point – don't sell the homely ones short. They're often more appreciative than the others.

This steamy afternoon, after recovering from the ride I began knocking on doors, "cold calling." My first appointment wasn't until six, ninety minutes away.

"Good afternoon, is your mother at home?"

A boy of about five answered the door. "Whaddya want?" I could see his sister lurking inside the doorway.

"I'm taking a survey." I showed him my clipboard.

He slammed the door. A moment later a lumpy young woman in a dirty apron opened the door. "Whatever it is we don't want any," she said, brushing back a tangle of hair. The little girl was hanging off her, pulling at her.

"We're doing an educational survey today, speaking with your friends and neighbors. If I could have five minutes of your time."

"Can't you see I'm busy?"

"You certainly do look busy," I said affably. "I'll just stop by after dinner."

"Don't bother," she said, slamming the door. I guess it ran in the family.

I retrieved my briefcase from the bushes and headed for the next house. The garage door was open and a man's legs were sticking out from under an old Chevy, a '46. "Hello," I said. No response. "Hello," I said, louder.

The man slid out from under the car on a wheeled dolly. He looked up and squinted. "Who the hell are you?" he asked.

"I'm Paul Bernard. We're doing an educational survey today, speaking with your friends and neighbors. About five minutes would do it."

"Goddamned fucking salesman," he muttered, disappearing back under the car.

I turned and trudged down the driveway. Times like this made you feel like hunkering down over a coffee and a book until it was time to go home, but luckily there were no places like that in these high prospect neighborhoods. To my astonishment, the second week on the job I sold three sets of books. At a commission of thirty-five percent, I calculated my earnings as $312.90! Less tax withheld, of course.

Veteran salesmen got the best leads, coupons sent in from newspapers and magazines. As a reward for my good work I was given one of these, but somebody had scrawled across it, "Booklet Only! No Salesmen!!"

I looked at Mr. Spaulding. "What am I supposed to do with this?"

"You're thinking I gave you a piece of shit, right?"

"Actually, yes."

"This is a very good lead. It shows these people care."

"But not to see me, apparently."

He coughed. "Sometimes one of our guys pisses off a prospect. Go out to this house, ask for Mr..." he took the coupon back, "Mr. Carvalho. Tell him you're from H-F's Complaint Department. Here's what you say. Our company takes its reputation seriously. Somebody on our staff must have offended you. Tell us what happened so we can make amends." He spread his hands. "Works like magic. You can't miss."

"But I'm not from the Complaint Department."

"You are now." He gave me back the coupon. "Find out what went wrong, take notes then go into your pitch. Give me a report along with the contract you'll bring back. Believe me, Paul, this lead is worth its weight in gold."

I knocked on Mr. Carvalho's door. This was in Fairhaven, near New Bedford. An unshaven man with glasses on top of his head answered the door. "Mr. Carvalho?"

"Yes."

"My name is Paul Bernard, I'm with Hamilton-Frey, their Complaint Department." I pulled the coupon off my clipboard and handed it over. "We just received this."

"That's me all right," he said, frowning. "You look like an intelligent kid, how is it you don't read?"

Unfazed, I went on. "Apparently somebody did something to offend you, we want to find out what happened and correct the situation."

Suddenly he broke out laughing. "Nobody offended me. I teach fifth grade, nothing can offend me. Come on in, bring your briefcase, too," he said, pointing to my case in full view beside the barren steps. His wife asked if I wanted a drink. "A coke would be great, if you have it."

They sat on the couch, me in a chair in front of them. Thanks to our training I could now read upside down. I noticed he had a set of H-F in a bookcase along with a lot of other books. He saw me looking at them. "Fifteen years old. The yearbooks are useless. I just wanted to see what the new edition looks like." He paused. "Let me tell you something. When I was in college I sold H-F myself. I can still give the pitch by heart, so I thought, why waste everybody's time, though I figured somebody would show up." He held the coupon up. "Worth its weight in gold, isn't it?"

We laughed, our complicity sealed.

"Since you're here, go through the spiel. I'm curious what they have you kids saying these days."

I went through my pitch, showing him my Preview Volume, my sample Volume Five (F - G), the colorful oilcloth sheet with the life-size picture of twenty books in a walnut bookcase, some sample research reports.

"So what're the damages these days?"

I hesitated a moment. Highly unorthodox, but I had a hunch. "Two ninety-eight," I said, "fifty dollars down, an invoice for the balance comes with the books."

"How long for delivery?"

"Two weeks but for an additional charge we can get it to you in five days."

"Two weeks would be fine. Whaddya think, Norma?"

My heart leapt. Number four!

She nodded. "Okay," he said. "If my good wife will get the checkbook we'll do some business with this gentleman." A few minutes later and another coke I was congratulating them on their decision, accepting his check and giving him a copy of the signed contract. "Nice job," he said. "I enjoyed your presentation. Brought back memories, some of them good."

"Thank you, I appreciate that and your order."

As I turned to go down the steps he stopped me. "By the way, tell your Complaint Department I said hello," he winked, "if you can find them, that is."

Midway through the summer a carton arrived at our house. When I opened it, I found a complete set of H-F, my name in small gold letters on each cover, and a letter from the President of H-F. Pretty neat, I thought, but Joe Wilson took me aside. "You know why they put your name on them? You probably think it's some kind of honor."

"That's what it looks like."

"What it is, it makes it harder for you to sell them."

Oh. Oh well, they'll come in handy anyway.

My parents were impressed, my father saying door-to-door sales is one of the toughest jobs there is, good training. Out early, back late, six days a week.

IN THE SPRING my mother developed severe stomach cramps, which led to tests and an operation. Thankfully the cyst they removed was benign. The near-miss threw a scare into my father, who'd been a model of patience and dedication since. Maureen appeared in mid-April, a tiny Sheila, heaven-sent for my mother who was feeling fragile and mortal. Her Maggie had been a triumph, more great reviews, but she'd miss the spring production. As for Jim, it was something to see this bear of a man, which is what he had become, with his little daughter. Catherine graduated from Brown with honors and would be off to Columbia for a masters in teaching, having practice taught in Providence schools her senior year.

Before I started with H-F, I had taken a few days in Boston to see Pat and Meg – well, really Meg. The family was preparing to open the Martha's Vineyard cottage, as they called their sprawling twelve-room house on the ocean at Oak Bluffs. I had a standing invitation which I hoped to take them up on later in the summer. Pat was puzzled when I mentioned my upcoming sales career. "It seems a waste to work at something just for money, no intellectual stimulation at all."

"It's not my first choice," I admitted.

I'd been more interested in Meg's reaction. She'd held several jobs, volunteering at Mass General, fund raising for charities, others. "Just because I don't have to work doesn't mean I don't want to work," she said, "but it's nice to be able to pick and choose." She smiled at me. "Be careful not to make too much. You know what they say, every great fortune begins with a crime."

Harringtons included, I wondered, but didn't ask.

Summer's end didn't find me at the Vineyard, but I did get to meet *grand-maman.* On a drizzly day late in August, she held court for Meg and me in the parlor. Madame Baldwin was a small woman with snow-white hair, once auburn I was told, bundled in a complex twist. Her face framed lively eyes, a bony nose and lips permanently pursed in a position of superiority. She started right in on my Canadian roots.

"'*Les provinciaux,'* we used to call you, that is when we called you anything at all." Her English was heavily accented, even after years in the U.S. "At least your French is passable," she commented, "not that barbaric patois that offends the ear."

I hoped she was joking but didn't think she was. *"Je vous remerçie.* My French professor has his doctorate from the Sorbonne. He also is of Canadian ancestry," I added defiantly.

"You cannot do better than *la Sorbonne.* How well do you know Paris?"

"Not at all, though it's on my list."

She frowned. "Paris on a list! *Impossible!* Paris *eez* zee list!" Madame was quiet a while, looking at me, then Meg, then back again. "You two are very attractive, *très gentils."* I noticed Meg stifling a laugh.

"I take that as a compliment."

She shook her head. "You must learn *les Françaises* do not give compliments, we speak the truth. If it is pleasant, *c'est bon.* If not, so be it."

Mr. Harris, the other half of the husband-wife team that cared for the family, appeared at the doorway. "It's two o'clock, *madame.* We should be going."

Madame looked at me. "So nice to meet you... Paul, it is, *n'est-ce pas?* I hope we see you here often." Meg offered to help her up but she waved her away. *"Au revoir,"* she said, extending her hand to me. I pressed it lightly between mine.

"À bientôt," I replied.

"Ah, oui! À bientôt! That is much better."

After she left Meg broke out laughing. I asked her what was so funny. *"Grand-maman* has said that to every boy I've ever brought home. For her, marriage is a woman's only proper state."

"You mean it isn't?"

She wrinkled her nose. "Oh I do like a sense of humor. By the way, I'll bet you can't guess where Mr. Harris is taking *grand-maman."*

"No, where?"

"To Filene's Basement. Every Thursday. You should see the bargains she brings back. You'll have to give me your sizes so she can put you on her list."

"What list? I AM *zee leest!*"

Near the end of the summer I tallied my earnings – thirty-two hundred dollars. Not bad, though I didn't have the heart to calculate the hourly rate. The time/money equation had visited itself with a vengance. Little personal life, no reading to speak of, no music (I was finally getting interested, even thinking of auditing a music appreciation course), and I got Pat's point – life without intellectual stimulation is indeed barren.

ANOTHER YEAR. The routine was now familiar, though Pat said he really needed to crack the books. I told him I'll believe that when I see it. An occasional visitor was Father Gene Boyle, a young philosophy professor and a friend of Pat's. He used to drop into the Sixpack and join the spirited debates. By reputation he was a tough grader, borderline unfair, though in person he seemed okay. Other than Fathers Trần and Ronan, he was the first priest I had come to know informally. I finally got to the point of calling him Father Gene, though I couldn't bring myself to call him Gene, as Pat did. I never could call Father Ronan Father Bill.

My course load was so heavy I hardly noticed when Roger Maris broke the Babe's record the last day of the season, against the Red Sox, of course. One of my best courses was Psychology. No lab work, not a single observation or experiment, nor did it follow Freud, Jung or any of the moderns – this was Scholastic Philosophy through and through, building on Aristotle, with improvements by – who else? – old friend Thomas Aquinas. Taking off from the spiritual nature of the intellect's activities – universal ideas, judgments and reasonings, ideas of self, time, space, causality – we infer that the principle from which they proceed, mind or soul, must be spiritual, independent even of the body it animates. Thus, the argument goes, the individual soul survives the body's death and dissolution. Moreover, its personal identity remains intact and is connected by conscious memory with its past life.

Heady stuff. To me, it explained things better than the alternatives, though I still worried about wishful thinking. And religious pre-conditioning. But everything considered, I figured a say, eighty percent chance was good enough.

I continued on the *Crusader,* though I could see journalism wasn't in the cards for me. It was gratifying to see my work in print, but I wanted to accomplish something with my own life, not just report on other people's. Beginning of the second semester, I said I needed to reduce my time commitment. Terrible timing – that was the day they threw a surprise party to honor my cracking the top spot, first in my class, and the traditional photo on O'Kane steps with other three top finishers. It turned out well, though, for they created a new position, roving columnist. I would propose topics and take assignments as able. A departure and one I appreciated greatly.

"WHAT A SIGHT!"

A crystal clear day, bright sun, not a breeze. I gazed across the valley at the peak of Mt. Washington and the giant bowls below. "Glacial cirques," Pat observed, "Tuckerman Ravine and Huntington Ravine, the Great Gulf Wilderness on the right. Here's a tip. Whenever you don't understand something about the mountains, say 'the glacier did it.' Though in this case it really did."

Meg, Pat and I were at the top of Wildcat Mountain, having just ridden the chairlift up from the base. "Enjoy the day while you can," Meg said. The forecast was for a rapid buildup of clouds and snow by mid-afternoon.

My first time on skis. When we arrived, Pat and Meg had a run while I rented equipment. Shuffling along at the bottom of the beginner hill resplendent in my new outfit – white turtleneck, red sweater and parka with white arm band – I saw them coming at high speed. Just before the collision they stopped, spraying me with snow.

"Ready?" Meg asked.

"So it seems." When they invited me for the long weekend I accepted eagerly, but as I eyed the mountain towering above us a wave of second thoughts set in.

"Don't worry," Meg said. "You're reasonably well coordinated."

Pat jabbed at the ground with his pole. "First thing, you learn how to fall down."

"Not a problem. Next lesson."

"No! How to fall and not break your leg. You see, if you're afraid of falling you'll be afraid of speed. And if you're afraid of speed you'll never be a good skier."

After a half hour demonstration, falling and getting up, snowplow sliding, turning and stopping, Pat said it was time for the beginner hill. We went up and down a few times and I was feeling good when Pat announced, "He's ready for the top. Let's do it."

"You've got to be joking." She had this horrified look on her face.

All my fears were back. "What is this 'top' stuff?"

He turned his tanned face toward the mountain. I couldn't even see the top. "That top," he said quietly, pointing his pole almost vertically.

Meg shook her head. "This is crazy."

"Thanks for the vote of confidence. I agree with you."

"Look," Pat said, "there's an easy trail all the way down. It's no harder than the bunny hill, just longer. You're skiing under control, that's what counts."

A struggle was going on inside me, male ego versus self-preservation instinct, humiliation factor included. Meg shrugged. "Okay," I said, "let's give it a go." They showed me how to get on and off the chairlift, a trick the ski magazines don't warn you about, and we rode to the top, my panic rising with every vertical foot.

"Just remember your snowplow turn," Pat said as we stood on the summit. "See you at the bottom!"

"That's not fair," Meg said, "we'll ski down together."

"Just kidding," Pat said quickly. "Would an instructor abandon his pupil?"

"Depends on the instructor."

As the Polecat trail unrolled I was able to get a nice rhythm going. I fell a few times but no big deal. Meg and Pat let me go first then bombed past in great swooping turns and stop below. About halfway down Pat reached in his backpack for a bota bag, demonstrating his long-arm technique, then I gave it a go. At the bottom about ten-thirty, soreness was already setting in. Pat was anxious to go up again. "You two go ahead," I said. "I'll mess around on the beginner slope."

"You're sure?" Meg said.

"Absolutely. I'll perfect my technique."

At lunch I signed up for a group lesson from a real instructor. Mid-afternoon I met up with Meg and showed off my new stem turns. We hit one of the intermediate trails and I navigated well enough, which I would not have thought possible a few hours before. As dusk fell we were walking through the parking lot in a light snowfall. What a great day! Thank you H-F, for making this possible. I was sore all over, a happy sore.

"By the way," Pat said, "if I were you I'd get rid of that parka."

"Why should I? It's a perfectly fine parka." Even with the wine stains.

"You notice what color the instructors wear?"

"Sure, I was just staring at one for an hour."

"Identical to yours. Very common color for instructors."

"You mean..."

"Right. You don't want to give the profession a bad name."

Meg was cooking dinner at their North Conway house, another "cottage," though only eight rooms. Pat burst into the kitchen to say John Glenn was in orbit, circling the earth. He broke out a bottle of champagne and we stepped onto the deck, looking up at the stars and lifting our glasses to the long-awaited exploit. I was growing very fond of Meg, the first girl I had kissed whom I could also see as a friend. Things were moving nicely but don't put her on the spot, I thought to myself. Slow and steady wins the prize.

A FASCINATING COURSE that spring was Natural Law – Man and the State. Under the tutelage of Professor Plunkett, recently arrived from Georgetown, we put Natural Law, another scholastic mainstay, under the microscope. "You first find the concept of an unwritten, unchangeable law in the Greek poets," Pat commented one evening. "'The unchangeable unwritten code of Heaven, that is not of today and yesterday but lives forever.' You can thank my classical education for that."

We learned that the religious aspect harks back to the Church Fathers, Augustine, even St. Paul. Aristotle adds the idea that reason is the master of man's existence and actions, his intelligence capable of discovering moral principles that dictate how he should act. Here we bump up against the idea of free will. Aquinas later formulated the supreme and universal principle this way – "Do good and avoid evil." Not "live comfortably," not "make a lot of money," simply do good and avoid evil.

"That's bullshit," Pat observed. "It's meaningless or so obvious it adds nothing."

The course then explored how natural law affects men's attempts to govern themselves. Our main text was by Jacques Maritain, one of Scholastic Philosophy's leading lights. We also read Augustine, Aquinas, Hobbes, Locke, Rousseau and other big names. According to Maritain, the State tends to grow its power beyond proper limits and make self-perpetuation an end in itself. The State often sees the individual as existing for the State, which is exactly backwards. Maritain had kind words for democracy, calling it the highest, most moral political form yet devised, and was a fan of the U.S. Constitution. The State must facilitate work and property, political rights, civil virtues and the life of the mind. The goal is decidedly not to ensure the material convenience of scattered individuals, each absorbed in his own well-being and enriching himself. Politics is essentially about civilizing and culture.

Writing post-war with Communism ascendant and the wounds from Hitler and Fascism still fresh, Maritain condemned the totalitarian state. It suppresses the people's means of supervising and controlling the State's actions. In its paternalistic view, the people are infants and don't know what's good for them, though of course the leaders do. Now, after real-life Communist aggression and atrocities, Maritain's analysis put a footing under what I had always been told, that free nations have constantly to be on guard against Communism. Give an inch, it'll take a mile, the yardstick too, if you let it. In contrast, the first axiom of democracy is to trust and respect the people.

I concluded that Maritain's approach was sound, and began to formulate a hypothesis. The time to see what a government is really made of is when it's under duress. I tried the idea out on Pat. "Makes sense to me, tell me more."

"In a crisis what becomes of the big things government is supposed to take care of? Security, civil rights, people's ability to know what's going on? I'm thinking about a scientific study comparing how governments act in normal times against how they act in crisis. Put some 'science' back into Political Science."

"When will you find time to do all this?"

I laughed. "Good question. Maybe it'll end up being my doctoral dissertation."

The course emboldened me to treat a controversial situation in one of my first Crusader columns – Israel's trial of Adolph Eichmann. After discussing his abduction and whether he could get a fair trial in Israel, I focused on the defense that he was just a bureaucrat following orders, that is, following the law. I didn't have too much trouble dismissing this claim. Neither did the Israeli court.

BY EASTER I WAS PUSHING HARD for that Washington job. Dr. Plunkett put me in touch with a State Department official, Peter Moretti, a former student of his at Georgetown. Moretti sent me a ticket, which brought me one April morning to Providence's Hillsgrove Airport. Boarding the plane I had mixed feelings. Here I was, almost my last year of college and this was my first time on a plane! Some of my classmates lived on airplanes. This summer Pat would be back in Paris then on to southern France and Italy, Spain and Portugal too. Oh, well, I sighed, my turn will come. As we lifted off, I watched the houses and cars grow smaller, then we turned and set course for Washington. After a ham and cheese omelet with a muffin and fruit, I relaxed over my cup of coffee. This is the life.

On landing I took a taxi and less than four hours from home I was meeting with Mr. Moretti. He was stocky and dark-haired, a graduate of George Washington University Law School, according to a plaque on the wall. As we talked he flipped through my application. Why Government? Why State? I explained my interest in international relations, another great course I took. Europe? French roots, Irish heritage.

"Fluency in French is a big plus. Can you carry on a normal conversation?"

"Yes," I answered, knowing there was still room for improvement.

"Consider getting another language too, especially if this turns out to be more than just a summer job."

More than a summer job? I liked the sound of that. But there was more. "If we offer you the position you'll be working directly with me. We keep long hours but nobody complains about being bored, and we have a bunch of really hot issues going..."

There was a knock on the door and in walked a tall, gray-haired man in a white shirt, sleeves rolled up, tie loosened. "Sorry to butt in," he said, nodding at me, "but do you have that Algeria correspondence file, Peter? I can't seem to find it."

"It's right here," Moretti said, reaching for a folder on his desk.

"I'll take it back, if you don't mind."

My paper for the International Relations course last fall was on Algeria. Under tremendous pressure, de Gaulle had agreed to a ceasefire in the eight-year-old war that had nearly blown his government apart. Moretti gestured toward me. "Bill, meet Paul Bernard. We're talking about the intern position. Paul, this is Undersecretary Dempsey."

I stood and the man reached over and shook my hand. "We're preparing for a meeting on the Hill," he said. "The senators want assurance that we're encouraging our NATO ally to extricate itself from that godawful mess they're in."

Moretti pointed at the file Dempsey was holding. "Paul's an expert on France and Algeria, Bill."

"Excellent! Just what we need. Good meeting you, hope to see you around."

After he left, Moretti said that takes care of the courtesy call. "Bill and RFK are personal friends, which gives us great access." He leaned forward, "let's cut to the chase. We've decided to offer you the position. It's a GS-12 paying $9,200 a year. The dates would be 20 June through 20 August."

I did a quick calculation. Ninety-two hundred divided by twelve, times two – far less than last summer, not even counting living expenses, but this summer is about a lot more than money.

"Let me know by Friday. If you don't want it we have someone else in mind."

I smiled. "I've thought about this already. I'll take it."

"I like a man who can make a decision," Moretti said, standing up and shaking my hand. "Let me walk you over to Personnel, they'll take you through the paperwork. Don't be discouraged, you'll learn that Washington runs on paper."

On the flight back I looked over the list of projects I'd be working on, plus a reading list. Terrific stuff. Outside the American Airlines terminal, as I descended the plane's stairs, I saw Catherine waving at me. She'd taken time from her Easter break to pick me up. "Congratulations!" she said. I had called home to give my mother the good news. By now everybody knew. I was a family celebrity, it seemed.

"Let me try something out on you," I said to her. "I'm thinking I might want to get a car. It'd save me money and be more convenient than the train or bus."

"Didn't you like your flight?"

"Flying's expensive. I saw what the ticket cost."

"When I got mine Dad helped with the down payment. I bet he'd do that for you – all the money he'll save on food he'll come out way ahead."

19. ...NOTHING IN EXCESS

ABOUT MID-MORNING DENNIS CALLS BACK. I can barely hear him over what sounds like traffic noise. "Before I give you this," I think he is saying, "you need to swear you never heard it from me."

"For me swearing comes easy. Talk louder."

"I'll hang up and get to a better place." A moment later he calls back. "Better?"

"Some."

"It'll have to do. Your writer friend, what's his name? Can he be trusted?"

"Jonathan Bernstein. You don't have to worry about him."

"I'll need to see what he writes before he sends it in. You both okay with that?"

"Yes." I figure that won't be a problem with Jonathan. What's his alternative?

"Okay. Bernard Syzmanski, that's S-Y-Z-M-A-N-S-K-I. Colonel Syzmanski, he works for me. Have Bernstein call him tonight, eight sharp. Here's the number." I fumble for a piece of paper. "It's a cell phone, the disposable kind."

"This is all very hush-hush. I'm impressed."

"I'm on one of those too. Into the dumpster after we hang up."

"What's Syzmanski's involvement?"

"That I can't tell you. Why I didn't call you sooner, he's in Iraq every other day. He lives at thirty-seven thousand feet."

Something doesn't add up. "I take it he's not part of the official investigation."

He chuckles. "Still the old fox, aren't you."

"How are you and Sy Hersh getting along?"

"Don't try my patience, Gus."

Something else I need to ask him. "I appreciate your doing this, Dennis, but you're not doing it just for me and it's not about Hersh, either. What happened? Wasn't your Captain Martinez up to the job?"

"Roberto is an excellent officer, one of my best." There was a pause on the line. "Between us, the problem was he's too good."

"If you don't mind my saying, I'm beginning to smell a rat. What do you think? Do you buy the official line?"

Dennis laughs. "C'mon Gus. Have your guy call Bernie tonight."

* * * * * * *

THE GLOVER PARK SECTION of the District borders Georgetown and, not to mince words, it's cheaper. I stopped in front of a two-story row house with a big front porch on 39th St. NW, set back and up a rise, my home the next two months.

"Hey, Paul! You made it!" It was Matt Wallace, my classmate who had also landed a job at State. Two rooms and use of kitchen, living room, yard. "Welcome to our humble abode," he said, lumbering down the front steps. A good guy, with his small head and thick torso, your basic eggplant shape. "Want a hand?"

"Sure. Is Mrs. Ravenal around?"

"Charlotte?" He rolled his eyes, "wait til you meet her. Charlotte is one piece of work."

"What do you mean?"

"You'll see. I don't want to spoil it for you."

My old Plymouth sat at the curb, recovering from a long day on US 95. I say "my" because my father flat-out gave it to me! With you kids out of the house we don't need it, he said. I had my eye on a newer, sportier number but was happy to save the money and have the company of the old family friend. Aquinas got it wrong – this car has a soul, and as my father said, keep it long enough, it'll be an antique. Looking at Matt's bright red Impala I thought that day has already come.

After we carted my possessions to the second floor, Matt went on a store run. I was sitting on the porch steps taking a break, when this tall, elegant white-haired lady came up the walk. "You must be Paul," she said in a heavy accent. "I'm Charlotte Ravenal." She shook my hand with a firm grip, then sat down next to me. "Tell me all about yourself," she said, removing her white gloves and reaching in her purse for a cigarette. Exchanging histories I discovered she was from New Orleans, her family emigrating from England in the 1760s to South Carolina, relocating a century later as the Civil War came on. She'd been in Washington since college, rising from clerk to a policy position at State, retiring years ago. She even had a hand in planning for the League of Nations, I was impressed to learn.

After a while she excused herself, then Matt re-appeared with several bags of groceries. I lowered my voice, "Charlotte's okay. What're you talking about?"

"The accent, for one thing."

"It's different but so what?"

"Not different, bloody strange. I can hardly understand her."

"Since when is Brooklyn the King's English?" Matt was from Flatbush.

"Awright, but wait, it gets better," he glanced at his watch, "it starts about now. I lost track how many Bourbons she had last night. She's world class."

"You kept up, I trust."

"To a point. I go upstairs to read, coupl'a hours later I come down, she's still at it, sitting by her stereo. Beethoven."

I would discover the composers changed but bourbon and branch water was a constant. Only the first day, but I already liked old Charlotte, looping about the house, humming Mozart, mellowing by the hour.

I WAS SPENDING A LOT OF TIME ONE-ON-ONE with Bill Dempsey. My burgeoning expertise on France/Algeria was useful to them. Factional fighting continued in the newly independent country, and despite a cease-fire the FLN was still terrorizing colonialists who were fleeing the country in droves. What should

U.S. policy be on recognition? What were our national interests? In addition to Algeria, I had several other interesting files including rebuilding bridges to our NATO allies after the Bay of Pigs fiasco.

Each day Matt and I drove to a dusty lot near G.W. University and walked to work, skirting the site where in a few years the Watergate complex would rise. At the flag-draped lobby I headed one way, he the other. Matt was in the Far East Bureau of the Agency for International Development. Vietnam, Thailand, Cambodia, Laos. This will be fascinating, he told me, I can't miss, but he soon learned otherwise. Buried in minutiae, he was assigned to track aid expenditures against dollars authorized. Also help revamp the agency's filing system. Bor-ing. When I asked what was going on in his countries he shrugged. "Read the papers, that's what I do." He had no exposure to the issues and neither, it seemed, did the people he worked for. "Strictly administrative shit. You hope the higher-ups know what they're doing, but I have my doubts. Ever read *The Ugly American?*"

"No." I knew it was written by a Political Science professor, of all people.

"*The Quiet American?*"

"It's on my list, too."

"Move them to the top. It's important stuff."

I was luckier, dealing with people and policies that mattered. Thrilled to be even a junior member of Kennedy's team, I embraced his youthful, vigorous vision of our country's future. I got to know a couple of people on Senator Pastore's staff, as Bill regularly brought me along on his trips to the Hill. When I shook the Senator's hand at a reception, he asked about my father and said how pleased he'd been to recommend me. Unfortunately, Matt told me, his application had gone in the door with no push, nobody important to speak for him.

The summer was great. Tons of people my age, plenty of parties. Movies too – *The Manchurian Candidate, Lawrence of Arabia* – and at evenings at home with Charlotte and her "Bourbon Classics." I heard a lot of music. She loved jazz too, had a stack of old 78s – Django Reinhardt, Stephane Grapelli, Bix Beiderbecke, Sidney Bechet. Sometimes I awoke at night and she was still downstairs, listening to the FM jazz station. One night she invited us to accompany her to Charlie Byrd's Showboat Lounge on 13th Street, a marginal neighborhood but that didn't faze her. I was totally absorbed watching the musicians play off one another and the audience in the intimate, low-ceilinged space. She introduced us to Byrd and I began listening for him on that late-night program.

Near the end of our summer a friend of Matt's invited us to a bash in the Dumbarton neighborhood of Georgetown. A hot, muggy night, as most of them were, we could hear music blaring as we trolled for a parking space. There must have been two hundred people in the house and the patio. A bunch of Aussies lived here, grad students, embassy staff, some with normal jobs. At the door somebody shoved a can of Foster's at me and I established my sipping pace. One of the hosts, Peter Adamson, was interested to hear I was at State. "I'm a press officer with the Embassy," he said in a drawl, half-Cockney, half-cowboy. "You got anything to do with us folks down under?"

"No," I replied, "Europe's my beat."

"Ah, the Old World," he laughed. "Some of us got out by choice, others they gave a shove. There's beef on the barbie," he said, pointing through an open door to the patio where I could see island torches flaming. "Help yourself, be at home!"

Straightaway my jacket and tie came off. Matt had already glommed onto a girl so I went upstairs to check out the deck, cooler and less crowded, and the neighboring backyards. I sidled up to a loud knot of people. "Eisenhower a Communist? That is moronic!" This from a preppy guy about my age, longish blond hair, tortoise shell glasses, prominent chin. His antagonist, in blazer and bow tie, was shouting back.

"Your Ike was a dedicated, conscious agent of the Communist conspiracy! Why didn't we take Berlin? He let the Red Army get there first, that's why! At Columbia he fell all over himself pandering to Communists. Dulles' containment policy? Pusillanimous, that's the only word for it. We should have pulverized the Soviets when we had the chance."

"Are you finished?"

"I am not! That so-called Farewell Address, no real patriot would slander our armed forces like that. Military-Industrial Complex! At least his agenda's out in the open now."

The waspy-looking guy shook his finger. "You conveniently forget he said *we need* the armed forces and the defense companies. His argument was against the rise of misplaced power. Get that? The disastrous rise of misplaced power. What good's security if it destroys the liberty it's supposed to secure? I was there, I heard him."

"Bully for you," the other said, downing the last of his drink. "I've had enough of this. Young Americans for Freedom, you call yourselves, more like Young Americans for Surrender." He was still muttering as he brushed by.

The WASP looked at me with a big grin. "Those guys are so predictable."

"Which guys?"

"The Birchers, of course. Alex Gardner," he said, extending his hand.

"Paul Bernard."

"Are you in college? Grad school?"

"A senior at Holy Cross. How about you?"

"Harvard, also a senior, I'm a national officer of YAF. Hey, we started a chapter at Holy Cross last year. Kevin McManus – you know him? He's the President."

"Sure, very well." Kevin was a History major from Connecticut. I did a *Crusader* article on his YAF activity.

"We have high hopes for the Catholic colleges. There's a natural affinity between Catholicism and us as far as personal freedom and big government are concerned. Where do you stand on these issues?"

"We have to oppose Communism – that's a given. As for big government, some jobs only the federal government can do – national defense, of course, and somebody's got to look out for the people at the bottom. But even good governments get arrogant, start thinking it's more about them than the people. I agree with you there, you have to watch that."

"Who did you support in the last election?"

"Kennedy. I would have voted for Kennedy."

He frowned. "Hmmm... maybe I had you pegged wrong. You realize Kennedy can screw things up with the best of them, he's shown that."

"But he's done a lot of things right too, the Peace Corps, for one. And I felt very uneasy about Nixon. He's not a person I would like to see as President."

"I agree with you but sometimes it's a lesser of two evils sort of thing. We're already pointing to sixty-four. Keep an eye on Goldwater from Arizona. *Conscience of a Conservative,* it's worth a look. Well, take it easy, good to meet you," he said over his shoulder, "must get back to my crowd."

I was going to ask if he knew Meg but he was gone.

It was a productive evening. Two phone numbers I wished I had earlier in the summer. "I got three," Matt said.

Charlotte was still up, of course. I looked at the record jacket on top of the stereo. Brahms Variations. Brahms Saturday evening. "This one is a theme by Haydn," she said. "So elegant, one of my special favorites." She held her glass out. "You wouldn't mind getting an old lady a smidge more branch water?"

"Old lady? None of those around for miles."

"My, you boys are chivalrous tonight," she said with a coquettish smile. I went over to the cabinet where she kept her supply. "Since you mention it, another touch of Old Grand-Dad would go well too. Whiskey's like men. Find a good one, stick with it."

I fetched the bottle and poured it slowly. "Say when."

"That word is not in my vocabulary. How did your evening go?"

"Very well," Matt said, "a houseful of Aussies and their friends."

"Ah, those boys certainly know how to enjoy themselves. A bit crude but you can't beat the spirit."

Brahms' Variations had run their course. I thought I'd play a little joke on her. "Got any Beach Boys?"

She looked at me blankly. "Beach boys? Those kids that sell umbrellas and chairs?"

"The California sound. It's like rock and roll."

"Cabinet, lower right."

I slid the stereo door open... unbelievable! Chubby Checker, Fats Domino, Chuck Berry. On top, the Beach Boys' new single! And who knows how many more 45s and 33s and old 78s in the stack! She was laughing. "Don't just stand there, put something on."

I removed Brahms and inserted Beach Boys. What a woman. I think nothing she does can surprise me, then she comes up with something like this. Surfin' Safari, flip side 409. Now she was out of her chair, moving with the music. Darned good, too. Charlie got up and we made a threesome, dancing until the record was finished.

"Put on Chubby Checker."

She showed us her twist, kind of half-speed but all the right moves. "You know his name isn't Chubby Checker? Ernest Evans. Chubby was a takeoff on Fats Domino."

"Is there anything about music you don't know?"

"Of course. One never stops learning."

"More?" I asked as the record came to an end.

She eased back into her chair, out of breath. "Enough. I don't want to make my friend Brahms jealous." As I looked for the next Brahms in her pile she became quiet. "I'll be sorry to see you boys leave," she said, a sad look on her face, "as I said, find something good, you stick with it."

The week before I had received a letter from Meg. After six weeks at Mass General she and Pat were making their way across southern France, destination Rome. I'll have to get up to Boston before the end of the summer, I thought. Want her to see the old Plymouth – that'll test our relationship. Big decisions coming up for me. Peace Corps? Maybe an African country where my French would give me a leg up. Don't know, though, I thought nervously, grad school might be the best way to go.

THE RECEPTION HALL WAS CROWDED, late afternoon sun slanting through the tall windows, silhouetting the flags of the nations. Glass in hand, I was standing next to Pete Moretti, at this thank-you event for the summer interns. "We've enjoyed having you this summer," he was saying. "There'll be a place here for you when you graduate." We'd already had this conversation and I told him and Bill I probably would pass for now. A few years down the road, it could be very interesting. About a half-hour in, a Deputy Assistant Secretary whose name I didn't catch was at a podium set up in front of the flags.

"It's been two months since we welcomed you, a very fast two months. We appreciate your good work and we wish you well in your studies and hope to see many of you again. Now I'd like to introduce the architect of our nation's foreign policy, our leader at the Department and I'm proud to say, my good friend, Secretary of State Dean Rusk."

The applause was long and loud. A tall, balding, moon-faced Georgian, Rusk had an academic bearing, had once been a professor. A strong believer in military action to counter Communism, a "hawk." Kind of an odd emphasis for our statesman-in-chief, I thought.

"Let me add my thanks and good wishes to those of Assistant Secretary Murdoch. You've been here at an important time in our nation's history. This summer, diplomacy played a key role in helping our NATO ally, France, resolve her crisis in Algeria. We are working with the U.N. toward a speedy resolution in the Congo. On many fronts the forces of liberty are being tested by the Communist enemy, Vietnam, for one. Despite reports to the contrary, our efforts to help the South maintain its independence are succeeding. We are lucky to have Ambassador Nolting and General Harkins..."

I felt a hand on my shoulder. It was Matt. He shook Pete Moretti's hand, I had introduced them earlier, and motioned me to follow him. We walked to the back of the room. "You wanna hear something rich," he said, slurring his words, "the straight skinny?"

"You've had a few."

"Had a little lunch, my fellow file clerks and me. Actually not that little."

He was talking loud. "Hadn't you better keep it down?" I said.

"What've I got to lose? My future isn't in this fucking place, not how they screwed me over."

"You don't want to get a bad reputation."

"Better than none at all, but anyway, I got to drive, that'll be my excuse." He poured his drink into a plant. "What Rusk's saying is horseshit. Absolute horseshit!"

"Tone it down." A couple of people were looking our way.

"By accident I got a look at this top-secret memo. I tell you, we are up to our ass in alligators. If the war's going so damn well, why do they keep sitting on people who say it isn't? Officers. Reporters. Don't make waves, that's the name of the game."

"I wouldn't be so sure about that..."

"Trust me. I saw it in black and white. Tell you what, I'll make you a bet. Hundred bucks. January one, check with me. And bring money. I know what I'm talking about."

By the first of October I had settled on grad school, Political Science. Harvard headed the list, top-notch faculty, law school, Littauer for public administration. It would also atone with my mother for past sins. During the summer I visited Georgetown, and on a more affordable scale, UMass Amherst. One day I was talking with Father Ronan. He suggested something completely off the wall. "I have an old friend on the faculty at Berkeley, let me put you in touch with him. You never know what might develop."

"I wasn't thinking that far away."

"It's one of the best universities in the world. I suspect they're tops in the social sciences but Gus can fill you in. He and I were classmates at B.C."

And thus I made the acquaintance of Professor Doctor Augustus F.X. Flynn. Although in the History Department, he knew Cal's Political Science faculty well, he said in the first of several letters back and forth, he'd recommend it to anyone. And based on what his friend Bill Ronan said, he would recommend me to them as well.

As I put my applications together it became clear, even with financial aid I'd be in debt the rest of my life or longer. My father said he'd back me and even my mother agreed this career direction suited me, or should I say, her concept of me. An interesting wrinkle, Professor Flynn and his wife rented rooms to students, so that could take care of housing if I choose Cal. I mailed my applications and sat back. In March I'd hear who wanted me, and how much. So it would be more school... a lot more. What would emerge after this extended incubation, I wondered. After its extended life in the academic cocoon, what would the butterfly look like?

20. *AVE ATQUE VALE*

WHEN I CONFRONT JONATHAN he pleads freedom of the press, prior restraint and everything else. In the end he relents. He has no choice. At precisely eight we make the call. I'm on our office phone, Jonathan, the portable.

"Yes," a voice replies.

"This is Gus Flynn and Jonathan Bernstein," I say. "Colonel Syzmanski, I take it?"

"Hang up. I'll call you back." There is a click on the line.

"Careful, aren't they?" Jonathan says.

A moment later my phone rings. "Gus Flynn," I answer.

"I hear good things about you."

"You come well recommended, yourself," I say. "Jonathan Bernstein is also on the line. He's the one doing the article."

Jonathan breaks in. "A pleasure, Colonel."

"Forget the title," comes the crisp reply. "Make it Bernie."

"Okay, Bernie," Jonathan says. "Where do we begin?"

"We begin by meeting and it's got to be next Tuesday. No offense, Professor, just the two of us. You know the Marriott in Crystal City?"

"I've been there," Jonathan replies.

"Outside the front entrance, twelve-thirty sharp. I know what you look like."

"Okay," Jonathan replies, surprise in his voice. "How do I reach you?"

"You don't. If you don't hear from me by Monday night, we're on."

"Let me give you my cell number."

"I have it. See you then." Click. The conversation is over.

A few seconds later Jonathan shows up in my office. "How does he know what I look like? How'd he get my cell number?"

I chuckle and shake my head. "I'd be worried if he didn't."

"Why are these people helping us, Gus? What's in it for them?"

"All I can say, I've known my contact for years and trust him implicitly." As for Jonathan's question, I don't know the answer, but I have a pretty good hunch.

* * * * * * *

"I NEVER THOUGHT I'D STOOP SO LOW." Pat was heading out the door with three large envelopes under his arm, his law school applications. When he first told me it came as a surprise but his explanation didn't. "Papa say no law school, no money."

"What are your chances of getting in?"

"All too good, I fear. Can you believe me last year, on the Dean's List? It's all your fault, those good habits of yours. Then the matter of influence, which is to say, Papa."

In October the world came as close to nuclear war as it ever had, the superpowers facing off over Cuba. JFK announced a naval blockade, then it was thrown to the Security Council before being resolved. After the fact we learned there had indeed been nuclear warheads in the country – tactical, for use against an invading force. Kennedy was also tested at home, sending troops to the University of Mississippi to quell riots over James Meredith's enrollment. Four years after Little Rock, not much seemed to have changed.

During the missile crisis, I was proud of Pope John for speaking out. He had just convened the Second Vatican Council, the first such gathering in a century. A simple, unaffected pastor, not a theologian or disciplinarian, John was refreshingly unimpressed by papal trappings. Asked why a Council, his answer was to throw open a window. *Aggiornamento!* The Church's leaders need to see out, the people need to see in. From now on, mercy is the watchword. Forecasts of doom are to be rejected. Good for him, I thought, but frankly, I didn't see the need for updating. If anything seemed out of place I figured it was because I hadn't understood it well enough. And some said open windows are risky – something bad might blow in, you might fall out. I was curious to see how would go.

A couple of courses bear mentioning. Communism – Theory and Practice examined this phenomenon that had bedeviled my young life. We circled back to Plato, the early Christians, More and American utopianism, looked at the kibbutz experience. I learned it was Marx and Engels who initiated the aggressive, godless strain that would end in violent revolution and triumph of the industrial proletariat, which crystallized in agrarian Russia, of all places, under Lenin and the Bolsheviks. Stalin and the wartime alliances followed, then Mao, Eastern Europe, and the Cold War including our irksome Caribbean neighbor. We studied critiques. Orwell and Huxley, Koestler, Hayek, von Mises, Ayn Rand. Set against Russian totalitarianism, the western democratic systems, dignity of the individual, the right to practice religion, own property, meaningful elections. I was particularly offended how Marxists twisted the idea of truth. Whatever advances the program, whatever greases the historical wheel, that is true and acceptable. The useful slander, the necessary lie – not far from the useful liquidation. But the infallible leader needs the tools, must have the tools.

The big Philosophy course was Ethics, with Father Tully. We debated the Principle of Double Effect, a source of guidance where an act has both good and bad results. Four conditions. First, the act has to be morally good, at least not inherently wrong. "Mr. Harrington, give me an example of the first condition."

Pat took his pen out of his mouth. "Removal of a cancerous uterus from a pregnant woman." The night before while reading I gave thanks my mother had come through her ordeal. Pat was going on. "The operation is a good act. It gives the woman a chance to live, though it causes the death of the fetus. The assumption is the fetus wasn't developed enough to live on its own."

"A hysterectomy, yes. What about the second condition?"

"The person must intend the good effect, not the bad one. Here, the death of the fetus is an unwanted but unavoidable effect of the operation." Pat put his pen down. "You know, Father, I have a problem with that."

"And what might your problem be?"

"To me it's splitting hairs to say I intend this effect but I don't intend that one, when you know both are going to happen."

Father Tully raised his eyebrows. "You deny the distinction between a consequence you will and one you merely foresee?"

"I don't see the difference. If you foresee a consequence, you will it."

"Aquinas is clear that there is a real difference between the two."

"But we can't use the argument from authority. We're supposed to figure it out ourselves." Father Tully reddened. Pat had a way with the inconvenient remark.

"That is so," the priest said patiently, opening a book to a marked page. "So let's take a look at Aquinas' reasoning. 'Nothing hinders one act from having two effects, only one of which is intended, while the other is beside the intention,' that is to say accidental. He goes on, 'moral acts take their species according to what is intended,' that is, not what is accidental. Do you see now, wanting something to happen, desiring its advantage, is very different from accepting it while wishing you could avoid it?"

"No." Pat paused. "I guess I just don't operate."

"Then both the woman and the fetus die, Doctor Harrington. A bad result all around."

"I guess so, but I'm still not convinced."

On this one I was with Aquinas. To me the distinction seemed real enough. What troubled me was the potential for abuse, for rationalizing something you've already decided to do regardless. I recalled Pascal criticizing the Jesuits for pandering to the whims of the powerful and wondered if Double Effect was part of the problem.

"Mr. Sheehy. The third condition. Use Mr. Harrington's example."

"The good effect must be p-produced directly by the action. In other words it can't be p-p-produced by the bad effect." Despite his problem Chris knew what he was talking about.

"Explain that in terms of causality."

"Well, if X causes Y, then Y causes Z, th-th-this is wrong." There was a ripple of laughter. Well, he usually knew.

"You mind rephrasing that?"

Chris was silent for a moment. "If you kill the fetus by s-s-say c-crushing its skull to make it easier to take out the uterus, th-th-that is wrong."

"Yes. Because you intend to kill directly, and you do kill directly, as a means to take out the uterus."

"And the end doesn't j-j-justify the means."

"Correct. How about the last condition?"

"The benefit of the g-g-good effect must outweigh the h-h-harm of the bad one. Saving the m-mother is more of a good than the fetus d-d-dying is bad."

"How do you determine this?"

"I'm not sure. The m-m-mother has other responsibilities, people are c-counting on her, the fetus, w-w-well..."

"You balance benefits against harms. In the end the good has to outweigh the harm."

"That's not s-s-so easy to do."

Father Tully smiled. "The beginning of wisdom. Rules are one thing, applying them quite another. Mr. Bernard." I sat up straight. "The bombing of Hiroshima and Nagasaki. What were the two main effects?"

Uh-oh, I thought, this wasn't in the text. I started slowly. "First, the deaths of all those people. The other... to weaken the will of the Japanese so they'd surrender. Shorten the war and save the lives of our troops."

"All right. Let's look at the conditions. Was dropping the bombs a morally good act? Or at least morally indifferent?"

I paused. "I'd say indifferent, or possibly good. Either way it meets condition one."

"Is that so? Can dropping bombs ever be a bad act?

I'd never thought about this before. "I suppose it could."

"Incidentally, why is dropping a bomb any different from firing a gun at someone? The fact you can't see your victim doesn't make a difference, does it?"

"I wouldn't think so."

"What about the second condition?"

"The good effect was intended, to shorten the war."

"Did the good effect follow directly from the bombing?"

I paused again. "The effect on their government took longer to work its way out but I'd say it was direct enough to count."

Father Tully frowned. "Look at the sequence of events. A. Bombing. B. Civilian deaths. C. Surrender. Is it possible *that* could have been the sequence of causality?"

"You mean, did the deaths produce the change of heart and the surrender?"

"Precisely. What if we meant to kill those people as a demonstration?"

"That'd be using a morally bad means to get the good result."

"Incidentally, what's the point of the fourth condition?"

"Proportionality," I said. "The good has to outweigh the evil." I paused again, uncomfortable. This thinking on your feet was tough. "The number of dead was high but many would have been killed in an invasion, too."

"Were you aware Truman waited all of *three days* before dropping the second bomb? Was that long enough to see whether the first one would have done the trick? Did we have any indication the Japanese might be preparing to surrender after the first bomb?"

"I don't know the history but three days does seem kind of quick."

"What if we could have avoided dropping any bombs and still got the surrender?"

"Then that's what we should have done."

Father Tully put his hand to his chin. "Did you know there was a debate at the highest levels, whether to drop the bomb offshore as a demonstration?"

"In terms of Double Effect, that would go back to minimizing the harm, avoiding it altogether if you can."

"That seems intuitively correct. Which condition does that play into?"

My concern about rationalization was rearing its head. "If you could have avoided the evil effect but didn't, that's pretty close to intending the evil effect."

"Are you still so sure the second condition was met?"

"I guess not."

"Incidentally, does it matter that almost all the victims were civilians?"

"That might influence whether the first condition was met or not."

Father Tully nodded. "It might even determine whether the bombing was a bad act in itself. How much of the context you import into the definition of the act is important. Define the act narrowly you get one result. Define it broadly, you can get quite another. Have you considered our firebombing of Tokyo? Or Dresden? Bomber Harris, ever hear of him?"

I shook my head.

"He worked for Churchill, look him up."

Father Tully came around his desk and settled back against it, folding his arms. "Mr. Bernard, I put you on the spot, but I want everybody to squirm. Clearly, gentlemen, we condemn the Japanese and Herr Hitler for Manchuria, for Guernica, for the indiscriminate bombing of Rotterdam and London, and of course they started the whole mess in the first place. But here's my point. If something is morally wrong when our *enemies* do it, what makes it right when *we* do it? Does the United States of America have some sort of privileged moral status? Is whatever we do justified? If that is what you think, what possible basis do you have for that position?"

He lowered his head a moment, then looked up. "Gentlemen, I've been asking all the questions, so it's only fair I tell you what I think. I'm convinced that dropping those two bombs was morally wrong. Our government failed the tests for correct moral action and deserved to be condemned." And with that he dismissed us.

I was shaken. As a child how proud I'd been of my country, of our new weapon that ended the war with a stroke. Later, realizing its monstrous power, I began to be uneasy, but never did I doubt we held the moral high ground. Now, I guessed I'd better find out why Truman did what he did and not something less.

As I walked back to the dorm I thought, if these acts are wrong, where do we as citizens come in? We have a say in our government that people in totalitarian countries don't. Our officials represent us – in a real sense, they *are* us! Besides celebrating the end of the war, how did Americans act? Did we demand answers? Were the questions even asked?

When leaders keep secrets, what can citizens do? What if they flat-out lie to us? How much can government say without tipping off the enemy? On the other hand, I knew of no exemption for governments from telling the truth. They are no more than individuals acting together, and no better. Was Double Effect in play here? This whole thing was confusing, disturbing.

OVER THANKSGIVING I VISITED THE HARRINGTONS. The nights had turned cold but we were enjoying a stretch of glorious warm days. Meg and I were relaxing on the patio, watching the last of the leaves spiral to the ground. "I've finally made a decision," she said, looking very pleased with herself. "I'm going to be a doctor!"

"A doctor! I had no idea. Your volunteering, I thought it was just..."

"Just a rich girl's hobby?"

"That's not what I meant..."

"That's okay, but no, I've made up my mind and this is what I want."

"What about med school, about getting in? You've taken hardly any science – you'll be up against people who've been preparing for this all their lives."

"The Dean and I worked it out, next semester I start piling on the science. But you're right, I need time to pull it together. Do you want to know what my specialty's going to be?"

"You figured that out too?"

"Infant pediatrics. One doctor particularly, how she cared for them was inspiring."

I gave her a kiss on the forehead. She put her head on my shoulder, then backed off, her eyes moist. "I'm hoping you'll be here to cheer me on but I hear rumors."

"I need to escape the Catholic orbit."

"You can do that here."

I nodded.

"So here I'll be, sniffling and shoveling and you'll be basking in the sun, surrounded by all those cute girls." She was quiet a moment. "It's your first choice? California, I mean."

"Possibly. Everything being equal," I squeezed her hand, "which it never is."

I didn't see much of Pat that weekend, but had an interesting visit with *grand-maman.* Saturday afternoon I ran into her in the kitchen, an unaccustomed sight. There was a brick of cheese and slices of baguette on the breadboard. "What are you making?" I asked.

"*Croque monsieur...* a tomato and cheese sandwich, normally *grillé.* What sets French cooking apart are the ingredients – only the finest, freshest ingredients, and believe it or not, the simplicity. May I make one for you?"

"*Bien sûr,* that would be great."

"By the way, I've been meaning to ask how you and Meg are getting along."

I never knew what to say when she started down that path. "We continue to be good friends, perhaps a *soupçon* more."

"If I may be so bold, I've had my eye on you for her. You look very good together. Perhaps you should consider, *comment dit-on,* a closer relationship."

"All in good time," I replied with a smile.

"Meg is a very attractive young lady, a fact not lost on her other suitors. She tells me you are interested in government."

"I'm starting a doctoral program in the fall."

"I have had the best of both worlds, living in this country but with the good fortune to return often to France. Let me ask you something I have never understood. Why do most Americans have so little interest in the things that matter so much to *les Françaises?* For you making money is everything. You strive so hard but to what end? Simply to strive more. Or drive a bigger car. Or live in a bigger house. Culture, the arts, the intellect, enjoying the good things of life, these are a distant second. Why is that?"

"You're not the first French person to think Americans fall short. De Tocqueville noticed it many years ago."

"Of course. But I am asking what you think."

"We rush around more a lot but don't forget this is a nation of immigrants. People with little or nothing come here for opportunity, for the dream of progress, or the illusion, depending on how things turn out."

"But opportunity brings anxiety."

"True. When given the chance to move up people think they'd better go for it or someone will grab it first. And like it or not, money is the ticket of admission."

"Too often that upward movement turns out to be sideways, or downward, and your famous competition! Pah! You crow about it as if it were a good thing in itself. Sports prepare the young person to compete in life and so forth and so on, but after all what is the point? Isn't cooperation better, people helping one another?"

"The theory is, competition produces better products at lower cost so more people can benefit. But you're right, the system is cruel to those who fail."

"Often the old ways are perfectly fine, in fact better than the new ways. Your attitude is, if there's no pot of money at the end, why start down the path?" She put her glass down. "I am very discouraged the way this country is going."

"I wouldn't be so quick to condemn it," I replied, a little piqued.

"Quick!" she snorted. "I have studied this country for forty years!"

Meg appeared at the door. "Sounds like a lively exchange!"

I nodded. *"Grand-maman's* critique of American society."

"At times I oversimplify things," she observed. "Just let me enjoy a proper meal and my glass of wine, I'll be all right."

"Merçi pour le croque monsieur," I said, winking at her.

Meg nodded. "The way to a man's heart..."

"That depends on the meal," *grand-maman* said unsmilingly, "and the man."

Over Christmas, I narrowed it down to Harvard and Cal. My mother, fully recovered, was apprehensive. "I love Catherine and Jim," she said over coffee one morning, "but you're my special one, you always have been."

Catherine was in her first year teaching at Classical High, my mother's alma mater. Jim and Sheila had two babies, a third on the way. He was in line to earn his plumber's license, and whenever his short-lived athletic career was mentioned, people remembered him for the right things. My mother poured another cup for me. "Who knows, perhaps you'll be a great statesman," my mother observed, "a Senator, even."

"I'm not cut out for politics. Too much compromise. I saw that this summer."

"That's true of everything," she replied. "But I am pleased you didn't choose business. That would have been beneath you."

"Dad's done damn well by us." I didn't disagree with her but I wasn't buying even a backhanded slap.

"True," she went on blithely, "but that's in his blood. You're different. You have a finer nature and the chance to do great things. That doesn't come along often. It would be a shame to waste it." She took another sip. "So, when do we get to meet your Meg?"

"She's not my Meg. For now she's a good friend and that's all."

"You've been to her house many times. It's only fair you invite her down here. You're not ashamed of our little place, are you?"

I flushed. "Of course not. But when you introduce a girl to your family, that sends a message I'm not ready to send."

"I see it rather as a test. The kind of girl a young man spends time with says a lot about him. That information about you I don't yet have."

"I'm sure I'd pass your test," I laughed.

Back after Christmas, I had just thrown my suitcase on my bed when there was a knock on the door. It was Matt Wallace. "Ready to talk?" he asked.

I shook my head, puzzled. "Dean Rusk. Remember?"

"Oh, yeah, now that you mention it."

"Today's *Times*... seen it yet?"

"No."

"Well, take a look. There was a battle outside Saigon, town name of Ap Bac. We lost a bunch of choppers, got our asses kicked, in fact."

"What kind of talk is that?" I said, irritated. "Sounds like you want us to lose."

"It's honest talk." He fell silent. "Of course I want us to win, whatever that means. What I'm saying, the people in Washington are feeding us a line. See what the military comes out with the next few days, not to mention our favorite department of government. You'll think we scored a smashing victory instead of, well... I won't say it again. The bullshit level remains high and it's climbing all the time."

Matt was right. The American commander in the Pacific called An Bac a triumph, claiming the South Vietnamese Army had forced the Vietcong to abandon their positions. But according to the news reports, it was the enemy inflicting heavy losses on our much larger force, then disappearing into the swamps to fight another day. Very confusing. Matt's words as he left my room stayed with me. "Paul, this bothers me a lot. What's happening over there is exactly what happened to the French, and you know how that ended."

LATE MARCH I LEARNED I'd gone four for four with my applications. Harvard came through with a good package but California and a change of scenery was very appealing, plus a fellowship and loan meant I could cover all my expenses.

After I made my decision I was feeling nostalgic. The prospect of overturning everything weighed heavily. Sometimes just thinking about it, my stomach tightened up. The winter had been bone-chilling and the first warm Saturday Pat put a bottle of wine in a paper bag with bread and cheese and we walked out along the ridge behind the dorm and spread a blanket in the cold, hard grass. He tuned his radio to WCRB, the Boston classical station. Live from the Met – Manon Lescaut, Renata Tabaldi. At our feet lay the campus and beyond, the city of Worcester, dingy, boring Worcester, which few of us loved but most, including me, had accommodated. The aunt who against all odds grows on you, the one you fall in like with.

Pat pulled out the corkscrew. "I'll be glad to get out of here. Oh well, at least the next three years I'll have Boston." As expected, the news from Harvard Law had been positive. He poured the wine, glass goblets of course, no paper cups for Pat. *"Salut!"* we touched glasses, "nothing like a good Bordeaux." He took a sip. "All good things come to an end. So it's the left coast for you. Meg will be disappointed."

"I called her when I decided. She took it in stride."

"She's going to have her hands full. She wouldn't be fit to live with."

I laughed. "That's not an option we were considering."

I placed my glass on a flat spot on the ground and lay back. Eyes closed, Puccini wafted around me. I opened them... puffy clouds racing across the deep blue sky. Take your time, I told myself, look around, enjoy everything, every single thing about this place, this moment. A light breeze caressed my face. I glanced over at Pat. He was absorbed in thought. "What will become of us?" he said, "so many plans... how will it all turn out? Where will we be in twenty years? Thirty?"

"I'll tell you something if you promise not to laugh."

"I never laugh."

"I have this feeling... what I end up doing will make a difference. Somehow the world is going to be a better place for my being in it."

Suddenly Pat jumped to his feet, breaking into a cracked falsetto. "Vee vill chenge the vorld! Vether it vants it or not!" He cupped his hands to his mouth. "EEEOOWWW!!! EEEEOOOWWWW!!!" He looked down at me. "See! I made a difference! Because of what I did nothing will never be the same. If I'd sneezed, I would have changed the world too."

"That's not what I'm talking about, nut case."

"So what *are* you talking about?"

"Well, that's the problem, I don't know. But someday people are going to look back and say, you know, he did really good."

"The world's so fucked-up, more power to you. All I know is I'm going off in the wrong direction and for all the wrong reasons. Tell you what... " he downed the last of his wine, "...twenty years from now, let's meet back here." He patted the ground. "This very spot. Nineteen and Eighty-Three. You'll leave your wife and two-and-a-half kids in New York..."

"And you'll leave yours in Paris."

"I'll drink to Paris, but family? I'm not cut out for family." He lifted the bottle from its grassy saucer and poured the last of the wine. "But this humble scholar is grateful for your kind words. Perhaps there is life after law school."

We touched glasses again. "A deal. Nineteen Eighty-Three."

"April one, Nineteen Eighty-Three." He took a swallow, then suddenly burst out laughing, spewing wine over himself. "I'll be here, will you?"

"Of course. You can count on me." I held up my right hand with two fingers crossed.

Worcester spring was upon us, drizzly days with Mt. St. James often in the clouds.

I was in line to graduate second in the class, which meant I wouldn't be valedictorian but no big deal. I was pleased, so was everybody who had pinned their hopes on me, not to mention their money.

I realize I haven't said much about the spirit and color of the Cross, the sports. These were a big part of the experience, for some the most important part. I enjoyed this aspect, Gus, but as I stitch this together for you, what meant most was the intellectual life, the great courses, the spirituality, and of course, those I shared these with. My critics had a valid point – I was, still am, of too serious a mien. At times lighthearted, but that has never been my strong suit.

A word about WCHC. The Station Director, my friend Ed Murray, asked me to do occasional commentaries and interviews and I did a dozen or so during the year. I interviewed Father Tully about the first-ever nuclear test ban treaty. It turned out he was quite an expert, and as he pointed out, this was only a step, since the treaty wasn't signed by France or, more worrisome, China, and it didn't extend to surface testing. I interviewed Father McBride on the death of Pope John XXIII, and drew him out on Paul VI's elevation and what it meant for Vatican II. Sadly, he said, John was given too little time to shepherd his grand enterprise, and his successor didn't seem to share his enthusiasm. I thought of asking Matt in for a session on Vietnam but decided not to risk it. And thus my journalistic and broadcasting career drew to a close. They belonged to my youth, and I was ready for other things.

I duly graduated, throwing my mortarboard tassel to the "completed" side. The prom committee broke the bank for Lester Lanin. Pat and I doubled with Meg and Pat's friend Amanda Cabot... yes, those Cabots. A Mt. Holyoke junior with blonde hair down to her waist. They said girls ironed it with wax paper to get it so straight and shiny. I wanted to ask her but I didn't. We put them up at the Bancroft and it occurred to me, this would be a great time to make a move on Meg. We dabbled but didn't do anything we'd be sorry for in the long run or ecstatic in the short. After two drinks, without a word we both switched to soda water.

For pocket change I filled in at my father's shop here and there, but I was focused most on my great adventure. Pat promised to return from Scandinavia to accompany me across the country. Meg's days were packed with make-up courses but we managed a few visits. She steered me to a double feature at the Brattle, *All Quiet on the Western Front* and *Paths of Glory,* bookends from the war to end all wars. The suffering they portrayed was disconcerting. Less sanguine, I was – my faith no longer blind faith. I knew more about our mistakes, though I still believed our good intentions and our know-how were a positive force.

The reading list from Cal's Political Science Department dominated my summer. Much if it was new to me. One book, Michael Harrington's *The Other America,* jumped off the page and I picked it up. I found he was a Holy Cross alum who had worked with Dorothy Day. I hadn't realized such poverty and suffering existed in my own country. The aged, minorities, agricultural workers and what he called "industrial rejects." With Negro grievances, a lot of wrongs needed to be righted here at home. Some disputed his statistics but he maintained, properly, I thought, that no one will be hurt if we see the problem in its most pessimistic light. Optimism, though, could lead to complacency and inaction.

Mr. Harrington reacted predictably. "If people don't like this country, let them leave." He bragged he hadn't read the book nor would he, excusing me on grounds of professional duty. "I won't make time for such idiocy... he's a disgrace to the family name."

In July I received a letter from Professor Flynn congratulating me on my admission to Cal and formally inviting me to lodge at his house where "the cooking is second only to the conversation." His wife, Akiko, joined in wishing me well, he said, and they would be pleased to host me in the upcoming academic year. Their students stayed on several years, so it was fortunate they had an opening. I wrote back, accepting his offer. The price was right, and it seemed an interesting place to live.

In August another letter arrived, from Benny Kaplan whom I hadn't seen since he moved back to New York. He was about to embark on a doctoral program, and where else but Berkeley! He'd heard through the grapevine I'd be there and was looking forward to catching up. I called him in New York and after trading messages we connected. He said he had visited the campus and it was spectacular, so was the History Department, and yes, he knew of Professor Augustus Flynn. We made plans to meet.

And so, with these civilized exchanges I turned the page, not knowing what lay ahead.

21. YOUNG MAN GONE WEST

IT'S THE SATURDAY BEFORE JONATHAN'S WASHINGTON TRIP and we have decided to spend the weekend reading. We need to speed things up. I have to say, I approach this Berkeley material with mixed emotions. Revisiting that time is not going to be easy.

* * * * * * *

FROM ALL ANGLES the physical beauty of San Francisco overwhelms, Toledo without El Greco's macabre touch. When I arrived in sixty-three, the glass and steel shafts of today were but a mote in some architect's eye. "The City" still boasted the most Mediterranean of American skylines – sunwashed pinks and blues and yellows, modestly scaled buildings rising and falling with the remarkable hills. On East Bay afternoons, San Francisco is silhouetted against the sun as it starts its tumble through the Golden Gate.

Ten days on the road, Pat and I, every day, every minute, a new experience. Faithful Plymouth jammed to the roof, suitcases and boxes in the rear view mirror. Our first leg bisected Vermont, then we circled Montreal (Montreal!), crossed southern Ontario and dove back into the U.S. at upper Michigan. A day off in Glacier Park gave us a hike to a stream where I froze my face in water seconds from the snow. At a bonfire I heard real folk music – Appalachian songs, English and Scottish melodies. A guitarist from Minnesota told me to keep an eye on a friend, he was going to be really something. His name, Bob Zimmerman. We shot south through Idaho, bleak Nevada and on into the Bay Area. The first few days in San Francisco would be at Pat's Uncle Al and Aunt Betty's on Russian Hill, at the foot of a street he told me I would not believe. Then on to Berkeley for me, back to Cambridge for Pat. Not once the whole time did he mention law school.

The night we arrived, I opened my window in the old Victorian and peered out at the Golden Gate and the headlands. Ten o'clock, and the fog had driven the temperature down to fifty. Al said the Bay Area's natural air conditioning system kicked in, something about low pressure inland and a cold current offshore. I flopped on the bed and opened my ragged copy of *On the Road*. My highs and lows weren't quite Kerouac's speed, but it felt good having this *copain* along. Fog horns sounding, I unfolded the letter I was using as my bookmark.

My Dear Paul,

We're so pleased you'll be staying with us. Your check arrived yesterday. I'm enclosing a map to our place which is not easy to find. Like the University, somewhat disorienting at first, but there are ways. Akiko joins me in wishing you safe voyage. We look forward to welcoming you soon.

All the best,

(signed) Gus

Professor Augustus F.X. Flynn

I had time to think on the long trip. Lots of questions. What was so bad about where I was, what I had been? As we neared the west coast it dawned on me, my first twenty-one years had already become my "former life!" A sturdy lifeline to my youth was recovering in Al and Betty's garage, but I must say that venerable machine was a willing accomplice to my apostasy. Sorry, Parmenides, Heraclitus wins this one hands down.

Why this place? Well, the University, for one. For another – the climate, not too hot, not too cold. San Francisco's eccentricity, its Mark Twain and Emperor Norton, the confluence of east and west. Zen, Gertrude Stein, who Pat said spent part of her youth in Oakland, and of course the Beats. All this held a strong appeal. I lowered the window against the chill, but it was the excitement that made me shiver. Falling asleep, it occurred to me – for someone on a short leash his whole life to break out with a bang wasn't all that weird.

Pat's relatives treated us like kings. First, a wine country trip north to Napa. I'm glad Mr. Harrington wasn't stopped on the way back. Next day Pat and I toured Chinatown where I had my first encounter with dim sum, then to the City Lights where Pat said the Beat saints occasionally hung out. No Kerouac today, but I bought a copy of *Dharma Bums,* and from the proprietor, Lawrence Ferlinghetti, his *Coney Island of the Mind.* Walking back, Pat steered us to the top of that street above his uncle's house – "the crookedest street in the world." Lined with flowers and trees, Lombard Street counts seven switchbacks in its short plunge. Two days of San Francisco's hills and my lungs and legs were seared big time.

After showering I wandered into the Harrington's third-floor solarium. A pair of stiff scotch and waters in our hosts' hands was the sign that the sun was indeed over the yardarm. Or under, whatever. Al had been a Marine in the Pacific War, a Brigadier General. I took a glass of Napa Chablis as Betty (Cal '31) steered me to a telescope trained on her alma mater, challenging me to find its most famous landmark. I groaned when she confirmed those were indeed hills surrounding the Campanile.

Al had other words for the school, said the place was crawling with Commie pinkos and going to hell in a handbasket if people didn't wise up. She just shook her head and smiled. I dismissed Al's comments as a west coast version of his brother's blather. In a while the four of us strolled out to dinner, then hopped a cable car to the waterfront and the Buena Vista Café for an Irish coffee, which that establishment claims to have invented. My first look at San Francisco convinced me the place ran on alcohol.

That night I slept fitfully, at one point slipping on my bathrobe and returning to the solarium. I admired the lights of the East Bay, my home for the next X years. Leafing through a large illustrated book I read that "Cal" was the University's flagship campus, nearly a century old. Over the years seven others were added, and more were on the drawing board. Berkeley is named for the Anglo-Irish philosopher who viewed the westward march of civilization with great hope. After perhaps an hour, getting sleepy, I closed the book, gazing again at the shaft of light across the Bay, beckoning to me.

AUGUSTUS F.X. FLYNN LOOKED EXACTLY AS I HAD PICTURED HIM, a florid face topped by a white mane, bushy eyebrows, short of stature with an angled gait as if leaning into the wind. To this portrait, I now could add a gruff exterior and the Irish gift of gab. In a closet somewhere, I thought, there's got to be a green suit and a clay pipe. I had him pegged about fifty but he looked and acted older.

Professor Flynn, "Gus, to you," ushered us into a high-ceilinged room with wood beams and an immense flagstone fireplace in the corner. Full-length glass doors opened onto a magnificent view of the City and the Golden Gate. "It's good to meet you, and your friend. Harrington, you say. Any chance you'd be from Southie?"

"My father was, though he managed to escape. I grew up on Beacon Hill."

I noticed Gus' eyes narrow. So, apparently, did Pat, who quickly added, "I have plenty of aunts and uncles still in Southie."

"Well, isn't that a comfort," Gus replied evenly.

Looking out, I spied a tall peak north of the bridge. "What's that mountain?" I asked.

"Come on," Gus said, "let's take a look." He slid a door open and we stepped outside onto the planked deck. I was about to comment on the view when a large Irish Setter came out of nowhere, put its paws on my shoulders and started licking my face.

"Monty! Down! Bad dog! Bad dog! Down!"

I pressed my knee firmly into his stomach. The dog backed off, made a complete circle then plopped on the deck with an abject expression. I bent down and stroked his long auburn ears, chucking him under the chin. "Don't feel bad, boy, you just surprised me."

Gus was grinning. "This is Monterey Jack, Monty as you have gathered."

"What a great-looking animal," I said. The dog was up again, sniffing at my legs.

"His mother's inside somewhere. She's Alice. That's short for Alice. Fourteen, give or take, this guy's six."

Recovered, I asked again about the mountain.

"Mt. Tamalpais, in Marin County. Twenty-five hundred seventy one feet. From the top you can see everything in the Bay Area that's worth seeing, on a clear day even the Sierras."

Down in the yard I inspected the shrubs, flowers and trees, including several towering eucalyptus that gave off a pungent aroma. A hedge ran the width of the property with a metal fence behind. Marking the corner, a stand of redwoods, and beneath them a doghouse – an A-frame. Looking back, I took in the house, a sprawling two-story redwood and glass structure that was bigger than it first appeared. "It's a Maybeck," Gus said expansively, "he was on the faculty here. Dates from the Thirties."

I heard steps on the flagstones... a petite woman was coming up to us. "Ah," Gus said, smiling and inclining his head, "this, gentlemen, is Akiko. Left to right, my dear, Mr. Bernard, Mr. Harrington."

She had jet black hair pulled back into a bun, a black turtleneck and slacks, an enameled pendant with a Japanese character hung from her neck. Her tawny skin was perfect, not a wrinkle or blemish. The color of her lips matched the pendant, her nails also. The dog went over and calmly lay down beside her.

"I am so pleased to meet you," she said, extending her hand to me, then Pat. As she nodded, her gold and red earrings sparkled in the light and her bracelets made a light jingling sound. "Paul, I know, but your name is?" she asked, turning to Pat.

"Pat. Padraic, actually," he added, glancing at Gus.

"You found us easily, I trust."

I laughed. "We'd still be driving if it weren't for your map." Coming up University Avenue, the patchy mid-morning fog burning off had given me my first glimpse of the campus before our climb through the terraced streets to Tamalpais Avenue. "What does the pendant signify?" I asked, looking at the character.

She held it up. "It's the word 'tomo.' Japanese for 'friend.'"

They met in Tokyo during the occupation, I learned. He was a naval officer attached to the American Embassy, she an interpreter. With a degree from the University of Washington, she had returned to Japan as war broke out in Europe, teaching in a Maryknoll school in her native Kyoto before moving to the big city just before Pearl Harbor.

We climbed back to the deck where Akiko had set out a pitcher of iced tea. Her effortless, graceful movements had a calming effect. Gus was telling me about my new roommates. "Four this year, a full house, though some years we have only three. We had a young married couple once but that didn't work out."

Akiko nodded. "There was no privacy. The poor things, they were practically newlyweds." Her English was perfect, her voice bell-like.

Gus nodded. "Now as to this year," he took a sip from a tall glass and raised it to me, "we have you, of course..."

I raised my glass in reply.

"Hamid al-Rashid, he's Iranian, an undergraduate which is unusual for us. What year is he in, Akiko?"

"Sophomore," she replied. "Hamid is from a very old family, he says if you go back far enough there is royalty."

"He's declared a major in World Literature," Gus was going on. "Bill Porter is in his second and as he often says, thankfully final year of getting an MBA. He went to Long Beach State. Bill's a bit older, twenty-five, I believe..."

"Twenty-six," Akiko corrected.

"After college he did a stretch in the Army. Bill is, how shall I say, Bill is not the most diligent student. Last but not least there is Hiroshi Suzuki, we call him Hank..."

"Hank is always practicing his English. I never get to speak Japanese."

"He's finishing his dissertation in Nuclear Physics, don't ask me what, I don't understand that stuff and it's probably classified anyway. We don't see much of him here. He has a sleeping bag at Livermore, puts a lot of miles on that car of his."

"Most honorable Toyota," Akiko said with a laugh. "This year everyone has a car. What do you drive, Paul?"

"An old Plymouth. I bet it has more miles than Hank's."

Gus spread his hands. "That's the crew, though nobody's here now. As I mentioned, you're lucky we had an opening. By the way, when you see Bill Ronan, give him my best."

Later in the day I moved my belongings into my tiny room. The built-in shelves wouldn't hold all my books so the rest would remain in cartons in the cellar. Pat sniffed around the house. That's really why he came along, to get a feeling for my new life. I offered him a ride back but he called a cab. Next morning he'd be bound for the airport.

"Best of luck the next three years," I said as he opened the cab door and tossed his backpack inside. "I'll see you at Christmas, anyway."

He put on his first-year law student face. "I am not looking forward to this."

Back in my room I tested the bed which was on the small side but hard, the way I like it. Down the hall, a bathroom Hamid and I would share, and in the kitchen two refrigerators, one for the Flynns, one for the rest of us. My room had a window looking onto the tree-lined street. Even in full sun it would be dark, but I wouldn't be here that much in daytime. All in all I was pleased. The excitement mounted.

GUS OFFERED TO ACCOMPANY ME to the campus. I had met only Bill Porter. Hamid came in late and was still asleep. Hank never showed at all. At eight-fifteen we set out. The streets and sidewalks were damp from the fog. As we walked along I noticed it was downhill the whole way. The end-of-day return trip would be a workout. Through gaps in the trees I could see sun on the flats below. "North Side, there's not much action," Gus said. "Rarely do you see a table."

"A table?"

Gus stopped. "You don't know about the tables?" I shook my head. "My, you are an innocent," he said, resuming his walk. "Well, let me offer you Political Activity 101. The Bay Area has always been big on political theater. It was once a wide-open port – unions, longshoremen and so on. You've heard of Harry

Bridges, of course. The city of Berkeley has a long history with radicalism, even the International Communist movement, though at core it is conservative, with a strong liberal element."

Communism. With all the attention I'd given Communists I'd never met one.

"So it figures the University would attract people with an affinity for causes. Away from the Bay Area, the state is right-wing. Sometimes things happen here that drive the powers-that-be wild, including the Regents who run the place. You have to register, right?" He looked at his watch. "I'll walk you to Sproul."

I nodded. "Go on."

"I go off on a tangent once in a while. Like I said, never a dull moment around here. What were we talking about?"

"You were telling me about tables."

"Ah, yes. The Regents have a rule against student political activity on the campus, any political activity, for that matter. You can't raise money here, you can't hand out literature, if you're a candidate for office you can't campaign here. In fifty-six Adlai wasn't even permitted to speak."

"That makes no sense."

"What else is new? Back in the Thirties the Communists were involved with some student organization and the University President didn't like it. How students get around it, there's a strip at Bancroft and Telegraph that belongs to the city, so they apply for permits to do those things out there. Card tables with literature, everything from Young Republicans to Maoists. You can't walk through there without somebody pushing paper at you."

"Is there much of a Communist presence these days?"

"The Party backs some of the far left student groups but it's harmless." Gus looked at me quizzically. "Why, does that bother you?"

"Communists are trouble. I'm surprised you take them so lightly."

"They've never been a problem in this country, though not for lack of trying. The only thing they've succeeded at is stealing some secrets, but then we're not exactly squeaky clean there, ourselves. Look, in spite of what you hear, Berkeley is not Moscow or Havana. You see kids, even professors, talking up Castro and Mao. Little Chés. It's like a letter sweater – it sets you apart, which to some people is important. I've known real Communists, in the unions, other places, tough guys, some of them, but they can be handled."

"The other end of the spectrum, the Birchers, what about them?"

"They're here too. But don't get the idea it's all politics. The Poetry Society and the Flying Club are big, in fact anybody with anything to sell is out there, though the political types get all the attention. A few years ago some kids got themselves washed down City Hall steps in San Francisco – at the HUAC hearings. Surely you've heard of HUAC."

"Even I have heard of HUAC."

"The politicians were fit to be tied. Got to put a lid on the University, they said. A whipping boy, we are sometimes. What those people fail to understand, demonstrations are to activists as football is to universities."

"Come again?"

"Demonstrations means crowds, crowds mean funds and publicity, and not least of all, they provide sociability. These groups give students a social life. In spite of the Neanderthals, demonstrations are here to stay."

We were walking through a broad plaza with trees in cement planter boxes, people sitting on benches, standing around, walking in all directions. The sky had turned a hazy blue, still nippy, but the morning fog was nearly gone. "Up the hill's the Campanile." Now I could see it was actually a grayish stone. "And that's Dwinelle," Gus said, pointing right. "Classrooms, offices. Mine's in there. Beyond it, California Hall and the Chancellor. In theory he runs the place which would be tough under any circumstances, but when your boss is right next door forget it. Clark Kerr's the President, his office is just off-campus.

He just published a book about something he calls the multiversity. Kerr is not universally admired. A lot of people think he's pushing bigness and depersonalization, departing from our teaching mission."

"This is discouraging to hear my first day here."

"Sorry but facts are facts. One complaint you hear a lot, the University is so intent on making its students useful economic units it's more an arm of government than the grove of *academe* some wish it were. Well, the University *is* an arm of government! We're not some serene collection of scholars, we are an agency of the State of California no less than the Department of Motor Vehicles. It happens our job is to train young people and do "useful" research on agriculture and forest management and so on. Incidentally, that includes weapons research."

"There's something to be said for giving graduates the skills to get jobs."

"That is true, but often the price is failure to educate the whole man, or woman. Then again, if the country were run by philosophers, nothing would ever get done. You've opted for Political Science but my advice is take as much History as you can. Otherwise your science, political or otherwise, is pseudo – no facts, no context, no foundation. But don't get me wrong, despite its faults this is a great University, one of the very best. The people who love it work hard to keep the philistines at bay."

We were passing under a heavy metal arch. "Ahead is Sproul Hall, named for that President I mentioned." My destination was another imposing edifice topped by orange tile, fronted by four heavy columns. Across, more buildings and a long seating area. "The Terrace. People hang out there. A lot of coffee is consumed, politics, poetry, you name it. Come on, I'll show you the tables."

We came to a fountain, people sitting around its cement rim. "Ludwig's Fountain, this is called." A boxy, four-story building stood beyond. "That's the Student Union."

"Who's Ludwig? Another President?"

Gus chuckled. "Don't I wish. No, Ludwig's a real mutt, a German Short-Hair. I don't see him now but he'll be here. Thinks he owns the place, for all I know he does." We were approaching a busy intersection with pedestrians dodging cars and busses. A kiosk was placarded with notices of concerts and speeches, apartments for rent. Only a couple of tables in sight. "Not much going on now, but come back at noon." He squinted into the sun that was beginning to warm my back. "Okay, time for me to split."

"I'd better get in there before the lines get too bad." I had noticed a steady stream of students going into Sproul Hall as we passed and none coming out.

"Lines. That's the multiversity for you. It's forgotten how to do the simple things. Well, good luck. See you tonight."

After two hours waiting and filling out forms, I was officially matriculated at the University of California, Berkeley, for its Ph.D. in Political Science. With a little time to kill I wandered into Sproul Plaza, as it was known, soaking up the sights and sounds. I'd been worried my so-called wardrobe would look out of place, but my new chinos, button-down shirt and loafers fit right in. A little before noon I headed across to Wheeler Hall, climbed the stairs and went in, looking for room 202. Beside the door was a small sign, "Assoc. Prof. Don Morrison." The door was ajar. I knocked and looked in.

"Come on in!"

A sandy-haired youngish man in an open-necked shirt and chinos, got to his feet and reached over the desk. "Don Morrison," he said, gripping my hand, "and you are..."

"Paul Bernard."

"Nice to meet you. Welcome to Cal. Have a seat."

He shuffled through some files then selected one. "Let's see, 3.95 gpa, excellent. Holy Cross, that's Boston? Never been there, should do that sometime."

"Worcester, but you can skip that. Boston's great but nothing like Berkeley."

"Everybody's first impression of Berkeley is correct." He looked up from my file. "You know the Ph.D. takes four to six years, now let's see... what interests you in terms of fields?" He read for a moment. "You've singled out Political Philosophy and International Relations. The two fit nicely." He turned a page. "High-achieving in French... we encourage everybody to pick up a second language."

We pored over the catalogue and laid out a program of courses and seminars not just for my first year, but the second and third as well. He insisted I take what was called the "Integrated Course In the Social Sciences" but defer it until my second year. "The Political Science part is taught by Eugene Burdick, you've heard of him."

"*The Ugly American* and *Fail-Safe.*" By now I had taken Matt's advice and read them.

"I disagree with everything he says but the man is a brilliant teacher, someone you should get to know."

Don identified some gaps in my resumé, notably Statistics, though I didn't see that as a problem. He said a course in International Econ was a must. For a second language I chose German, figuring I'd try to acquire some facility in Russian as well. "Oh," I said, thinking of Gus, "I'd like to fit in a couple of History courses, audit them at least."

"Don't know where you'll find the time but give it a try."

We covered housing, my financial situation, my deferment, getting a card and study carrel at Doe Library next door. Finally he asked, "have we forgotten anything?"

I shook my head. "Seems like we've covered it all."

He stood and shook my hand. "Then I'll see you in my seminar." He reached behind his desk. "Here's the reading list. This'll get you off to a good start."

"Political Theory from Aquinas to Mao," at the top of the thick sheaf of paper. "Looks great," I said.

Back in Sproul Plaza, a world of new sensations – crackling clean air, fragrant, bright colors. I sensed a buzz of energy and purposefulness but my overall impression was calmness, which surprised me. Many of the girls, women, were attired in skirts and penny loafers, though more wore jeans with shirts, sweaters and sneakers. That there were females at all was a shock. Some of the most conservative-looking students were from the fraternities and sororities, bastions of outdated attitudes, Gus called them. The first few days my head was on a swivel, so many pretty girls. I figured I'd meet some soon.

As they said, Berkeley offered something for everyone. The Rathskeller in Larry Blake's was a "Greek" hangout with excellent burgers, its on-campus counterpart, the Bear's Lair, in the Student Union Building. On the Terrace lots of ordinary-looking people were eating lunch, reading, mixing easily with the beards and sandals. Telegraph Ave offered an incredible array of bookstores and cafés for the intellectual and arty. I dropped into Caffé Mediterranean but left after downing my espresso. It wasn't my kind of place, but I could see Pat holding court, debating *Howl* or Genet or *The Bicycle Thief*. As for me, I had to fight the temptation to binge on used books and paperbacks for my growing library.

Thanks to Cal's financial package, I could afford my own phone, and the first time it rang it was Benny, whom I'd left a message for at Hillel House. We had agreed to meet at Ludwig's Fountain. I wondered if we'd recognize each other, it'd been so long. I was checking my watch when I heard a familiar voice. "Paul!"

"Benny!" We threw our arms around each other then stood back and laughed.

"You haven't changed at all!" he said. "You're not a skinny little kid any more, you're a skinny big kid." He smiled. "Only joking."

"You don't look so terrible, yourself." Benny was taller now, about my height. He wore his dark hair long, down to the collar. Most astonishing, though, was the moustache and goatee, neatly trimmed in the style of V.I. Lenin.

"We do our best. Let's get something to eat. How about the Terrace?"

"I left my sandals at home."

"They'll take your money anyway."

We seated ourselves at a table along the wall overlooking the steps to the Lower Plaza. "So," I said, "what have you been up to?"

"All kinds of things. We moved. I spent four years at Columbia."

"That's a lot of living in a few words."

"And now you're doing Political Science! Will wonders never cease!"

"I've got a terrific program. What's yours look like?"

"European, twentieth century, the Jewish experience. Nothing new there."

"That was always number one with you."

"There is no number two. How about yourself?"

"I'm leaning toward international with a minor in theory. I had a job in the State Department a couple of summers ago. It was a real eye-opener."

"Don't tell me you want to change the world."

"As soon as I figure out how. And what to put in its place."

"I don't deny my ambitions. I spent time on a kibbutz. I want to help that fragile country survive – no small order, given the hate that surrounds it. Even here there's so much anti-Semitism, we have to be constantly on guard."

His words brought me back to the many hours I spent in his home, up the street from mine. His ebullient father, his mother who loved me like a second son. "Your mother and father, how are they?"

He looked away. "My mother died last year."

My heart sank. I could see her now, the large dark eyes she thought mine so resembled. "I'm sorry. I didn't know."

"We didn't make a thing of it." His eyes were damp. "She was sick a long time."

I put my hand on his. "You have my sympathy. I wish you had called me."

"I should have, she would have liked to see you." He brightened. "And your family?"

"Talk about not connecting. Catherine was at Columbia same time as you. She got her Master's in Teaching. She's back in Providence teaching at Classical."

"Of all things. My old school."

I filled him in on Jim, life after La Salle, his family, my mother and her performing career, my father's success. I even confided something about their difficulties which I had never told anyone. It made me feel good to share that, especially since they seemed to have patched things up some. I asked if he was still going to temple and he said yes, though not as often as he should.

"Your note said you're living at Gus Flynn's place."

"Yes. It's a good situation. He's quite a character."

"You don't know the half of it."

"What do you mean?"

"He's one of the most outspoken faculty, plus he advises some of the radical groups which makes him a pariah or a hero, depending. Everybody says he is a great teacher. I'll let you know – I have a seminar with him this semester. Were you at the Washington march?"

"No," I replied. I didn't mention that marches weren't my style.

"I've never seen so many people in one place. King's speech was fantastic."

"I saw it on television." I remember watching the event and feeling guilty I hadn't followed up my early columns with anything of consequence.

"Hey! Look who's here!"

A tall girl with a mop of red hair was standing beside Benny. He pulled her face down and kissed her, then steered her into the chair between us. She had large brown eyes and freckles, a slight frown on her face at repose. "Hello," she said, "I'm Leah Jacoby."

"Paul Bernard," I said.

Her handshake was firm, borderline masculine. "Benny's mentioned you." She turned to him. "You are such a gentleman, Benny, thanks for introducing us."

"Leah is my good friend, my very, very, *very* good friend." I noticed her powder blue Columbia sweatshirt. "She followed me out here."

"Bullshit! You followed me!"

"But I applied first."

"We got here at the same time." She looked at me, "actually we drove across the country. Despite that we're still speaking to each other, if you can believe it."

"Are you a historian, too?"

"Hardly," she answered, "Sociology. Somewhat less rigorous."

"We're kindred spirits, then – I'm in Political Science."

"She's a musician, too," Benny said, "a brilliant cellist."

"I hope you have a big car."

She wrinkled her nose. "A Beetle."

"I know the feeling. I couldn't see out my back window."

"You have a back window? His doesn't."

Benny nodded. "That cost extra."

As we talked I learned that Leah had a brother, Gideon, also at Berkeley, a grad student. They all lived in the Co-op – Cooperative Housing – on the north side of campus. After a while Benny looked at his watch. "We'd better make tracks," he said to me, "but let's get together soon. Come to Hillel, we'll show you around." He looked at Leah. "Paul's an honorary Jew. My mother did everything but have him circumcized."

I reddened. Leave that one alone.

THAT EVENING AKIKO PUT TOGETHER a welcome dinner. "A rare event today," Gus was saying as we seated ourselves around the table. "We had a Hank sighting. Some big experiment he has going – he says things'll settle down soon but that's what he always says." I declined a glass of wine for the green tea Akiko said was so good for you.

"You start classes today, Hamid?" Bill Porter asked.

"No, Thursday."

Bill seemed a solid citizen, though from his conversation, as Gus intimated, not that intellectual. Hamid was different. Bookish, medium height with brown skin and dark eyes, a wispy moustache seeking a foothold on his upper lip. His black hair was combed straight back above a fine-featured face with regular, almost girlish features. His bearing seemed tentative, which I credited to my presence. The evening I arrived, I had knocked on his door and introduced myself. I couldn't help noticing his closet, absolutely chock full of suits, though his daily attire was typical undergraduate. Before Berkeley he had been at Eton, one of England's elite schools. At his parents' request, Akiko had taken him under her wing.

His father was an oil executive and his mother at home with eight children, of whom Hamid was the second-oldest. His British-inflected English was excellent, slightly clipped. Without explanation I would have taken him to be Indian. I conjured up scenes of bedouins, Lawrence of Arabia, the desert I had never seen. Wrong. He was a city boy, from Tehran. I confessed how little I knew about his country. "I studied Persia in biblical times but if you could catch me up on the last two thousand years."

Hamid smiled. "Everyone knows our ancient history and everyone knows Mossadegh and the Shah, but nothing in between."

"I understand your father's a petroleum engineer," I said.

"He was with Anglo-Iranian back when it was Anglo-Persian, now is Deputy Oil Minister. He hoped I would follow him but I have no interest in engineering and less in oil."

"You're studying literature. Why Berkeley?"

"I liked their interdisciplinary approach. I could have taken my degree at Cambridge or Oxford but California intrigued me and it has not disappointed..."

Gus interrupted. "Paul, you're aware Hamid's country was the scene of one of the more deplorable chapters in American foreign policy."

"I know something of it. Tell me more."

He put his cup down. "The West has meddled in the Middle East for decades – it's all about the oil, of course. In fifty-one the prime minister was assassinated and Parliament elected Mohammad Mossadegh, free and fair. Mossadegh had been pushing nationalization and even the Shah also wanted better control and compensation so he went along with it. Of course this drove the Brits up the wall..."

"Income, prestige..."

"Exactly. Mossadegh was a canny guy. With the help of the local pro-Soviet party he managed to marginalize the Shah. Of course the Soviets had been nosing around Iran forever – oil, naturally, and their age-old dream of warm water access. A dirty word, nationalization, and when you combine it with a Soviet presence, it was a setup for Dulles and the hardliners. In fifty-three the CIA and the Brits orchestrate a coup against Mossadegh, but it fails. The Shah decides this is an excellent time to tour Italy. A few months later we try again and this time it works. In two days, who's back but the Shah. He claps Mossadegh in prison and replaces him with a friendly general." Gus took a deep breath. "So much for our commitment to elections. We're all for them except when we lose. Hamid's father and I had a good tangle over that one, I'll tell you."

"My father is a man of principle but also practical."

Gus shook his head. "Your father worked for the Brits, then Mossadegh, now the Shah. He is, how do I put this charitably, a survivor."

"Survival, I think, is a very practical principle."

"I'll display my ignorance again," I said, "but what is Iran's language?"

Hamid smiled. "Simple question, difficult answer. Iran has many, composed as it is of ethnic groups reflecting our border regions. Kurds, Turks, Armenians among others, and of course the Arabs historically overrunning the country from time to time. Are you aware Iran has a sizable Jewish population? For the most part in the large cities, notably Tehran. Native Persians, so to say, are of Aryan ancestry, in fact that's the origin of the name Iran. People make the mistake of thinking Arab and Persian are the same. They are not. I am Arab."

"And your language...?"

"Arabic, although Iran's principal tongue is Persian, also called Farsi. Everyone learns Arabic as the universal tongue of the Near East, or as westerners call it, the Middle East. I speak English, obviously, Farsi, French and Spanish fluently, to a lesser extent German and Italian."

"What about religion?"

"I am Muslim, of the Shi'a branch, which is the official state religion." Hamid laughed. "And now you know everything about me and Iran there is to know."

"Hardly. I look forward to learning more."

"It will be my pleasure. We Iranians are very proud of our country."

22. GETTING TO KNOW YOU

"A LEPRECHAUN! HE CALLED ME A LEPRECHAUN!"

"Gus, I don't know what you looked like then but if you permit me to extrapolate..."

"You too, Jonathan? You too?"

"C'mon, you have to admit..."

"I admit to nothing."

Now we're both laughing. "Can we go on?" Jonathan says. "Our hero has reached Berkeley, you'll admit that, at least. He called the campus calm. That surprises me."

"Most of the time it was, but there always was an undercurrent of ferment."

"Which student organizations did you advise?"

"The History Graduate Association, of course. SDS too, very interesting bunch. Born in Michigan but our kids put the Berkeley stamp on it."

"What about the violent offshoots? The Weathermen?"

"That crap is wrong and dumb and I told them so. Oh, I worked with Snick too, Student Non-Violent Coordinating Committee. I had a friend at Ole Miss I put our kids in touch with for sixty-four, but that's getting ahead of the story."

"What did you think of Pat, Paul's friend?"

"My kind of kid. He spoke his mind, went overboard sometimes but better that than the opposite."

"And your first impressions of Paul?"

"Truthfully, I had reservations, he was so quiet. He grew on me, needless to say. Had a tremendous inner strength though it took time to see it. A matter of confidence, I think."

"By the way is that guy *the* Hamid Rashid?"

"The very same."

"That's impressive. Did they keep in touch?"

"They did. I saw him occasionally as well."

"Was this Paul's first encounter with the Middle East?"

"I believe that's right, except for his Jewish friends, of course. As you know, he became something of an expert. It started right there in my house, for which I take full credit."

Jonathan leans back in his chair. "After my meeting with Bernie we really need to get down to New York. I'm worried, after Berkeley the material is sketchy, we need more. And things are going to get crazy, all the interviews I have to do. Something this complex can fly out of control."

"We'll hold it together."

"You know, I'm nervous not knowing who your contact is. These people are going out on a limb for us. Why are they doing that?"

"My guess is their guy is coming up with something the brass can't stomach."

"Which they don't want to get out. A bombshell, in other words."

"So to speak, Jonathan, so to speak."

* * * * * * *

IT WAS GOOD TO BE BACK in the academic mix. Hamid volunteered to help me with German. He was an amazing linguist. I was hoping my brain was elastic enough that these hard-edged new sounds wouldn't crowd out my hard-earned French. International Econ wasn't offered until spring so I signed up to audit a Philosophy course for fun. Father Tully said Berkeley was known for its analytic approach and a Theory of Knowledge course might be interesting. The professor was a tiny British woman, Professor Markham.

I was soon on a first-name basis with a number of students. Art Tedeschi, Don's teaching assistant, was affable and approachable. A bespectacled Chicagoan from Loyola, he and I had the Jesuits in common. Art's dissertation was well along, an exploration of Locke's influence on the founding fathers. In Philosophy class I struck up an acquaintance with a tall, frizzy-haired New Yorker, a transfer from Manhattan College named Mario Savio who was amassing credits to qualify for a doctoral program in Philosophy.

I noticed a cute blonde, Stephanie Rogers, in German the first day and made a point of sitting beside her. A senior from Redwood City, she was majoring in Botany, working weekends in her family's nursery business. A definite possibility. Phil Ryder, from Don's seminar, was a recent Political Science graduate from Woodland, north of Sacramento, and my best source for campus lore. Phil was shocked to learn I hadn't yet been to a Cal game and said he'd remedy that before long.

The next Saturday night, after a winding drive through the hills above Berkeley, I spotted a mailbox marked 160-162 Panoramic Way and pulled off the road onto a dirt ledge. All along the narrow street cars were parked at crazy angles. How could a fire truck make it through, I wondered, noticing the sign, EXTREME FIRE DANGER. Brush fires were common in the late summer and fall before the rains. Eucalyptus again, a dirty tree strewing bark and seed pods everywhere. Faithful Plymouth was still chugging along but I had put off servicing, concerned they'd find something I couldn't afford. Soon after the grueling trip a banging developed under the hood that was especially bad on the steep hills. I even treated it to some high-test but it didn't help.

I walked down a driveway crammed with cars and along a stone pathway. Laughter and music were coming through an open window on the top floor. Walking into a small kitchen, I saw a bunch of people standing around. A girl with Orphan Annie hair was removing a tray of hors d'oeuvres from the oven. Bags of chips, loaves of bread and bricks of cheese littered the countertop, jugs of wine, soda bottles. The room was hot, though the doors and windows were wide open. "Welcome!" A young man with a dark crew cut slid off a stool and stuck out his hand. "Ari Gordon. I live here, and you are..."

"Paul Bernard, a friend of Benny Kaplan."

"Then doubly welcome! Help yourself to wine, there's beer in the fridge, soft drinks if you prefer. Ice's in that bowl over there."

"How about a glass of wine?"

He pointed to a stack of plastic glasses. "Heaven helps those who help themselves. Benny's upstairs, worker bees only down here, right, Rita?"

"Right," said Orphan Annie, wiping her forehead with the back of her hand. "As you see, the kitchen attracts the best people so you're welcome to stay."

"That sounds good. Let me say hello to Benny first."

Leaving the kitchen I ascended a circular staircase to a crowded room with exposed beams angled under a pitched ceiling. A balustrade ran the length of the room with a dropoff to the first floor. The west wall was floor-to-ceiling windows, two stories high. Beyond a stand of trees I could see the lights of the flatlands and a dark expanse beyond, the Bay, and a necklace of lights I figured was the Oakland Bay Bridge. In the distance, San Francisco showing off. Huge speakers boomed out Peter, Paul and Mary. Horizontal beams crossed the room under the rafters with a swing hanging from one of them. An indoor swing! And on the swing who but Leah! I went up to her and said hello. Legs dangling, she was sipping what looked like orange soda.

"Benny's outside." She gestured with her cup toward the back of the room.

After chit-chatting and pushing her a while I eased through the crowd, into a yard framed by hedges, a strong scent of magnolia in the air. Several groups of people were standing around, talking. Spotlights hung off the walls and looking up, one caught me square in the eyes. Blinded, I stepped into the shadows a moment and had a sip of the sweet wine. I sidled up to one of the groups and still couldn't see much but in the next group I thought I heard Benny, near a tall, broad-shouldered shape and a girl with long hair.

"'Say, Benny," I ventured.

"Paul! Long time no see. Here, meet Gideon and Rachel. This is Paul Bernard, my oldest friend here tonight."

The tall shape extended his hand. He turned out to be a redhead with a beard. "Gideon Jacoby. You don't look that old."

"I'm Rachel Levy," the girl said. Vision returning, I saw a pretty girl with a pert nose, dark eyes, a large, generous mouth. She was wearing a long skirt and a peasant top. I took her hand. "Pleased to meet you," I said.

"Same here," she said looking up at me. "So how do you and Benny know each other?" she said, still holding my hand.

"If you can believe it, we lived on the same street when we were kids."

"Back East, that would have been. Leah and I were friends at Columbia and we all transferred out here. So here we are."

"Where the action is," Gideon said.

Benny grinned. "Gideon's also a grad student in History. We met on a kibbutz, summer before last. He's an Israeli..."

"At heart. I'm really from Jersey City."

"...and Leah's brother. Now you know everything."

"It seems very incestuous."

Benny shook his head. "Confusing, yes, incestuous, no."

By now Leah had joined us – a remarkable resemblance. "Let's sit over there," Gideon said, pointing to a bench beside a pool with lily pads and leaves.

"Quite a place, this is," I said.

"It's a whole compound. There's another house down by the driveway and a little cottage in back. Probably two dozen people live here."

"Who owns it?" I asked.

"You met Ari?" Gideon asked. "His father's a real estate developer, bought this place so Ari'd have a cheap place to live. And as an investment, of course."

"Cheap!" Leah exclaimed, rolling her eyes. "It's a fucking palace."

"What I mean, dear sister, he doesn't pay anything."

Benny jumped in. "He earns his keep, managing the place. And it's great for a party, a lot better than Hillel."

I looked hard at Gideon. First impression he seemed direct, no nonsense, a person I could get to like. Benny's comment prompted me to ask when he had lived on the kibbutz. "Summer before last, just a month but the best experience of my life. Leah steered me to it because Gideon was there."

"I've been spending time in Israel off and on since I was a kid," Gideon said.

"What was it like? The kibbutz I mean."

"It was one of the first kibbutzim," Benny answered. "Degania, at the southern tip of Yom Kinneret – Sea of Galilee to you. I did farm work, worked the fields, planted, harvested, tended the cattle and the chickens. If there was a job, I did it."

"I've done some research on collectivist movements," I said. "I'm curious how that part of it worked, you know, property in common, common meals."

"Great in theory," Gideon replied, "but it doesn't always work out. We were out to create a new type society, everyone equal, nobody taking advantage of anybody. At this kibbutz children were raised apart from their parents with special nurses and teachers."

"Did that work?"

"Not altogether. In a fundamental way that sort of thing goes against nature."

"Interesting," I said. "I'd like to talk with you more about it. Oh, there's one other thing, if you don't mind a serious question."

Rachel stood. "I need another drink, I'm not into serious tonight. Coming, Leah?"

"No, I want to hear this."

"I'll be back," she looked at me, "maybe."

I was sorry I drove her off but I went on. "Were you in Israel during the Eichmann trial, Gideon?"

"Yes. Why do you ask?"

"I followed it, did a paper on it. I focused on his defense that he just followed orders, did his soldier's duty, whether that should have been enough to get him off."

"And how did you come out on that question, may I ask?"

"It had to fail, of course. You're responsible for your own acts. If you're given an order to do something morally wrong, you have to disobey it."

"If you're in the Army, you realize that's an excellent way to get shot."

"Never been in that position but I hope I'd have the guts to do the right thing."

"Nor have I," Gideon said. "I trust Israel to have more moral fiber than that..."

"Don't count on it," Benny jumped in. "A small country surrounded by mortal enemies, it very well may have to test the limits. Look at the U.S. Our history's full of atrocities in the name of security and order. The Japanese internment – we panicked, we overreacted. The slave trade. Democracy is no guarantee a government will behave right."

"I disapproved of Eichmann's kidnapping," I went on. "It showed a troublesome disregard for international law. Would you have taken part in that kidnapping, Gideon?"

His eyes narrowed. "Without the slightest hesitation. Nobody was about to hand that monster over, least of all Argentina. Why do you think he was hiding there in the first place?"

"You see," Benny said. "A case of necessity trumping morality."

"Not trumping," Gideon replied, shaking his head, "redefining."

I glanced in the direction Rachel had disappeared. "I didn't mean to put a damper on the evening."

"Don't worry about it," Gideon said. "I am never immune from a serious discussion except when I'm asleep, and even then, oy, do I have dreams."

Benny broke in. "Before you arrived we were talking about the picket next week. We're starting to put the screws to local businesses to hire more Negroes and pay them fair. Job discrimination's the hot issue this fall. A San Francisco Mel's is the first target."

"Mel's Drive In?" I asked, surprised. I'd been to the one in Berkeley, a hamburger joint modeled on carhop eateries but without the roller skates.

Benny nodded. "We'll hit the Berkeley Mel's next, after that the car dealerships and we're working on a plan for supermarkets and hotels. All these places, their hiring and pay practices are abysmal. And discriminatory."

"Why Mel's? That seems like small fish to fry."

"Everybody knows Mel's so it'll be news, plus one of the owners is running for mayor of San Francisco. If we worry him enough he might make concessions that'd start the ball rolling. Interested?"

I thought for a moment. New here, trying to get off to a good start, I couldn't afford a time-consuming commitment, besides, I'd never done anything like this before. "I don't think so," I said. "I've got too much on my plate now, but I wish you well." I looked at my empty glass. "Think I'll get a refill."

I caught up with Rachel. She was watching two girls sitting on the swing, pumping their feet out over the railing. "Let's hope that rope holds," I said coming up next to her.

She looked at me quizzically. "You're too serious. Anyone ever told you that?"

"Actually, I have heard that."

"It doesn't bother you?"

"Not really. Why? Does it bother you?"

She laughed. "I wouldn't tell you if it did. How about relaxing, letting go?"

"For me that would be a new experience."

"I might be persuaded to help," she said, raising her drink to her lips.

"Sounds like a good plan."

"Plan?" She shook her head again. "See, you're too cerebral."

"Sorry. I guess that's the way I'm built."

"You're a perfect fit for that crowd," she said, nodding toward the door.

"Meaning?"

"Meaning they're too serious – Gideon, Benny. Leah the passionate radical, she's the worst. I know she lost family in the Holocaust but there comes a point when you put it down and get on with your life."

"I haven't heard her talk about that."

"You will. Behind every bush there is danger. Same with her politics, everything has cosmic implications." She made a fright face. "Help! The forces of evil are out to get me!"

I looked around. People were dancing. The Beach Boys, my comfort zone. I nodded toward the dancing. "How about it?"

She smiled. "Why not?"

"You getting used to California?" I asked as we began moving to the music.

"Not really. I've lived here most of my life." It turned out her family was old California – Swiss-French. Lévy, though the European moorings were long gone.

"How do you like Cal compared with Columbia?"

"It's okay but I'm thinking of dropping out. Been here all of two months and I'm ready to leave. Can you believe it?"

"Why would you do a thing like that?" I asked.

"The classroom suffocates me, it always has. I'll bet you love it."

"I'd better. I'm on track to be a professor."

"I couldn't stand that."

"If you leave school where will you go? What would you do?"

"Oh, I'll stay here," she said. "I'm in the Mime Troup, I've been with them since high school except my time in New York." I'd seen a flyer with the name. "We give shows in the parks. It's not silent mime, more classical theater – farce, topical, political. Everything's original, more or less. See, I'm not immune to politics, I come at it my own way."

"I'd like to see one of your shows sometime."

"We're in Golden Gate Park Sundays. Other places, too."

"Are you in the Co-op?"

"No, I share an apartment with some people. South of campus, Derby Street. The low-rent district, no-rent if you're lucky. Most hill people avoid it."

As we danced I was finding this free spirit was everything I was not. If I were definition and clarity, she was ambiguity, masks, make-believe. By the end of the evening we had reached a truce. I would stay serious because I couldn't help it, but not too serious. And Rachel would be herself. "Nothing I can do about that, either," I said.

She laughed. By the end of the evening we had made a date to see the new Fellini film, *8 1/2*. I said I'd catch her act in Golden Gate Park. Maybe, I thought with some excitement, maybe opposites do attract.

I HAD BEEN GOING TO MASS at the Newman Center, a rambling wooden building on Dwight Way, south of campus. The first Sunday I was bowled over by the diversity – Chinese and Japanese, Negroes, Africans, Indians, Latin Americans, others I couldn't place. My mother's varicolored dream, though I didn't yet know any of these people, or, for that matter, that many others. After Mass, as people gathered for coffee and doughnuts, I stopped at the bulletin board. A welcome dance for new students – that might be fun. Weekend retreats, flag for the future. A call for Mass servers – I don't think so, then a series of evening discussions caught my eye. Vatican II Update. That, I would be interested in. During the summer I had pretty well lost track of church news. As John XXIII had thrown open some windows, so had I, coming to Berkeley. Choosing a room with a window is to be open to what exists outside, but I knew I'd need luck and God's help in this place.

BENNY, GIDEON AND I MADE OUR WAY around the police barricades. We were on our way to see Madame Nhu, the last stop on her tour to rally support for the beleaguered Saigon government. In my orderly, contained life I'd never seen such aggressive protesting and shouting or police in such numbers. War opponents had failed in their attempt to prevent her appearance, in fact classes were cancelled to accommodate it. But now they were urging people to disrupt the speech. Her husband the President's brother and a key advisor, the "Dragon Lady" was acknowledged as the power behind Saigon's throne. She'd been the public face of the spring crackdown against Buddhists flying their flag on Buddha's birthday, this on the heels of a similar Catholic celebration the government actually endorsed. More protests followed, with round two marked by that astonishing photograph of an elderly monk immolating himself in a busy Saigon intersection. This was followed by more "Buddhist Barbecues," Madame Nhu's felicitous term, the protests spread and the lady continued railing against the demonstrators, calling the monks Communists and Communist dupes. "Hooligans in robes. Let them burn and we shall clap our hands."

We showed up early at Harmon Gym, a good thing, for a lot of people had to stand outside and listen on loudspeakers. The speech was an anticlimax, though it was impressive seeing a world figure up close. She drew polite applause and a lot of hissing and booing but to the campus administration's relief, no eggs like at Harvard and Columbia – or worse. As we walked back across the campus, I said I didn't hear anything new. For a long time she's been saying the Communists are behind those monks.

"Well, aren't they?" Benny asked.

"Sure they are. That's what they do. Destabilize, then move in for the kill."

"She said we're abandoning them, that American liberals are worse than Vietnamese Communists."

"You don't expect a reply to that, do you?" I laughed, but I remembered Father Trần's comment – identical. I wondered how he was faring. I should write to him.

In August, old warhorse Henry Cabot Lodge had been sent to Saigon to replace Ambassador Nolting, and highly placed U.S. officials were now complaining about the Diems' ineffectiveness and corruption. Signals were being sent.

"She's made the war a big issue on the campuses," Gideon said, "though not what she intended."

Three days later a group of dissident Army officers led a successful coup. Diem and his brother were assassinated in the back of a truck carrying them to promised safe passage out of the country. Madame Nhu escaped their fate because she was still in the U.S. Although her trip wasn't convincing American audiences, it did save her skin. Matt's warnings also came back to me. I had no doubt that our goal was honorable, but it was looking like a far harder challenge than we had bargained for. Was Matt right? Could we end up like the French?

Philosophy class. Mario and I exchanged greetings as I fished in my backpack for the course text and my notes. I glanced at the old-fashioned clock above the blackboard, five to eleven, then spotted Professor Markham. She was standing quietly in the doorway, then she stepped in, but she didn't close the door as she always did. She walked slowly to the desk and put down her briefcase. Her face was ashen. "I have terrible news." Her voice quavered... it was even smaller than usual. "Your President has just been shot."

What did she say?

Everyone stared... *I didn't hear her right...* tell me I didn't hear her right. "Your President has been shot. It just happened. It's on the television. He's been rushed to the hospital, they say it is very serious."

We looked at one another – bewildered, stunned, helpless.

"It... it would be inappropriate to go on. We shall resume Tuesday next." With that she picked up her briefcase, turned and left. I looked at Mario, he looked back at me. "This is beyond belief," I said.

He nodded. "Let's see what we can find out."

We walked out onto Dwinelle Plaza. People were coming and going, apparently word hadn't gotten around though I noticed some people in small clusters talking. We started for the Student Union, it had a television that was always on. As we mounted the steps people were coming down, some with vacant expressions, some with tears streaming down their cheeks. Inside we joined the crowd. Peering through layers of people I saw the somber visage of a newsman and leaned forward to hear.

> "...injured by one or more gunshots to the head, apparently fired from some distance. Preliminary reports from Parkland Hospital where the President was rushed indicate his condition is very grave. It would be a miracle if he survived according to one doctor we spoke with, who saw him being carried into the emergency room."

Mario and I looked at each other and shook our heads. I felt tears welling up in my eyes.

> "Texas Governor John Connolly, riding in the front seat of the limousine, was also hit, though his wounds don't appear to be as serious as the President's. Mrs. Kennedy was apparently unharmed, in fact she climbed up on top of the seat beside her husband and used her jacket to try and stem the flow of blood."

Somebody switched the channel. Walter Cronkite was on the screen, just lifting a pair of heavy horn-rimmed glasses to his face. He looked down and began to read.

> "From Dallas, Texas, the flash, apparently official, President Kennedy died at one p.m. Central Standard Time." He took the glasses off and looked up and across the room. "Two o'clock Eastern Standard Time, some thirty-eight minutes ago."

"I'm getting out of here," I said.

"Let's go to the Terrace, get a coffee, be around people."

We sat in the bright sunshine. Neither of us felt like talking. "What can you say?" Mario had a chalky voice and a pronounced stutter that intruded into normal conversation but vanished when he was excited, as he was now. As we both were.

I looked off into the distance. "The winds blow fiercest about the loftiest peaks."

"That's good. That's very good. Who said it?"

"I don't know. Shakespeare? For all I know I made it up."

"Death is a fact of political life." Mario steepled his fingers in front of his face.

I took a sip of my coffee, then put the cup down. "I met Kennedy once, interviewed him for our college paper. Just before the election."

"What did you think?"

"Smooth, articulate, energetic. A visionary, but I wondered if that was style over substance. He had some great ideas but he wasn't that different from what went before. The passion – how much of it was really him, how much for effect?"

"Being a politician you can bet most of it was for effect."

We were quiet for a while. "In a way this is payback," I said. "Three weeks ago the Diems, now this."

"The Diems I didn't lose any sleep over. Medgar Evers, that's different. Losing a good man like him, that was a tragedy. And the four little girls in that church. Horrible."

I nodded.

"Political killings are old hat. The hypocrisy of our system makes all this very predictable. However many followers a man has, it takes only one enemy. Evil in the world is a fact, right here in the U.S. You're Catholic, you know about sin. Your good liberal tends to forget that. The fact is, our system is rotten to the core."

"I don't buy that," I said, shaking my head. "We've accomplished tremendous things, giving people from everywhere the opportunity for a good life. Nothing like the United States has ever been tried before. A work in progress but it's still a great country. Trouble is, from time to time the experiment blows up in our face."

"Good life, you say," Mario said with a hard, bitter laugh. "A lot of people aren't invited to that party. Look what's happening in the South, what has always happened in the South." He squinted into the sun. "You know, today is too much of a coincidence to be just a coincidence. Where do they murder him but in Texas? And who is there to take his place but the biggest, baddest Texan of all."

"Whatever LBJ thought of Kennedy he'd never be involved in anything like this."

"Well, then, who? The Russians? The Cubans? The Mafia?"

"Cubans and Russians I can see, but the Mafia?"

"Why not? Stranger things have happened. He was a womanizer, too. Maybe that's part of it." A couple of his friends came over and sat down. He introduced me but after a while I decided I'd rather be back at the house with people I knew.

Walking across the campus was eerie, looking into grim, sad faces. Arriving back, I peeked into the living room. The television was on, Gus and a couple of the others watching. I backed out, wanted to collect myself first. On the way to my room I noticed a message with my name pinned to the cork board in the hall. My mother. I called her back and she was all weepy, how terrible, she said, what will happen to us? What will this cowboy Johnson do? I was happy to hear her voice but didn't really want to talk about it. I had no answers. "You sound good," she said finally. "And you're all right, you're really doing all right? Could you use a little more money?"

"No." I laughed for the first time all day. "I better go. Tell everybody hello for me."

Gus looked up and nodded as I appeared in the living room. I sat down in the chair next to his. "I just came from the campus. Complete shock."

Hank the absentee was sitting on the couch. Gus was slouching in his favorite soft chair. Bill Porter was in the corner of the room, reading a magazine. They held hands up in greeting.

Gus was expounding. "The fourth of our Presidents to be assassinated, first in half a century. Even in such a violent society you get complacent, you almost believe we've turned the corner, but we never will. I met JFK last year when he spoke at Charter Day, so Paul, you're not the only one to meet him."

"What did he say?"

"Oh, we talked a bit about Boston, Southie, but there wasn't time..."

"I mean his speech."

"I have a copy somewhere but as I recall he enumerated the Cal graduates working for him – Rusk, McNamara, Glenn Seaborg who's a personal friend of mine, McCone. He said he was upset when he realized his New Frontier owed as much to Berkeley as Harvard."

"You called us a violent society. Second time I've heard that today."

"It's a fact. Violence at our birth – don't forget we are the product of a revolution. We endured a civil war, one of the bloodiest in history, draft riots, a thousand killed or hurt in New York alone. Our expansion west? Violence against native people in the name of manifest destiny, violence to promote the railroad land grabs. Violence against Mexican and Chinese Californians run off their land by greed in the pursuit of gold." Gus was getting red in the face. "Vigilantism... sounds very American, doesn't it? Violence against newcomers, Jews, Catholics, the Irish. Violence against Negroes in the South, not to mention the shameful acts that brought them here in the first place. Violence against unions and unionizing, plus, it must be admitted, violence by those promoting unions as well, and I haven't even touched on plain old criminal violence."

Bill Porter turned around. "Do you condemn our country?" he shouted. "Are we so rotten we should scrap it and start over? That's what people around this place want! That's their goddamned agenda – is it yours?"

"Of course not," Gus replied evenly. "But we are not the great country we claim to be, and we never will be if we don't clean up our act. Our ideals are the light of the world, but how we practice them is a disgrace." He shrugged. "Other countries see the hypocrisy, don't kid yourself they don't. What about our tradition of militarism, our martial character? It's like we need a bloodletting every few years, a foreign escapade when one of our corporations gets its tit in a wringer somewhere."

I'd never heard such a perspective and it didn't go down well. "So Bill's right. You think we are beyond saving."

"No. But it will take years, decades of strong, intelligent, consistent leadership. Something this country has been lacking in a long time."

"What about JFK?"

He shook his head. "Beneath the smile, the charisma, he is – was – a mainstream politician, perfectly willing to use force and lie about it. Look at the Bay of Pigs. Look at the late, unlamented Diems. Look at our current war, though they're afraid to call it a war. No, JFK was no statesman. He was an opportunist and not all that competent either. Domestically he had better instincts, a vision even, I'll give him that."

"If you think our society is violent," I asked, "what about the French Revolution? That was neighbor against neighbor. What about Lenin? The Bolsheviks?"

"I'm not comparing us against others, I'm comparing us against ourselves, and I say violence is American as apple pie, so don't be surprised when you get a slice of it from time to time." He nodded at the television. "Or society is complex, a settler of new lands, an open door for newcomers. They butt heads with the entrenched – is it any surprise sparks fly? All this makes the task of civilizing, of governing very difficult. I doubt we'll ever grow up."

Gus was quiet a moment. "Let me give you a peculiarly American example. Our romance with the outlaw. Despite the myth that we're a peaceable people, we admire violence and that steps everything up a notch. What is the Second Amendment but a hedge against state monopoly of violence? A vestige of the founders' distrust of a strong central government, an idea that survives to this day, though that battle's long since been lost." Gus turned to our Japanese roommate who had been listening intently. "So, Hank, tell us what you think."

Hank shifted in his chair. He talked science readily but otherwise was rather reticent. "I am not in a position to comment," he began. "I do not know your history well, also, as a guest of your country I am thankful for the opportunity to do my research and it would be discourteous to criticize. The Japanese people, I will say we are quite different from what you describe. We do not so readily exhibit our feelings as Americans, our violent tendencies for the most part we keep to ourselves."

He looked away a moment. "The militarism in this century that led to such suffering, that was highly exceptional for modern times and we hope will never be repeated. But your talk of union riots and draft riots, of citizen against citizen – this is very foreign to me. I do not understand it at all."

The next day, Saturday, our debate raged well into the evening as we kept one eye on the television. Lyndon Baines Johnson had been sworn in aboard Air Force One before takeoff for Washington just hours after the fateful event. A photo that would become world-famous showed a stunned Jackie, still wearing the suit her dying husband had bloodied, standing at LBJ's side as he raised his hand.

The authorities had arrested a twenty-four year old drifter, a high-school dropout named Lee Harvey Oswald and were preparing to charge him with the murder. He'd been caught in a theater after fleeing the sixth-floor window where they said he did his deed. A high-powered rifle was found in the room. More about Oswald was coming to light. A self-proclaimed Marxist, he had spent time in Russia, was married to a Russian woman and, very puzzling, had been a U.S. Marine. As the day wore on, the news having spent itself, it dissolved into comment and interpretation.

I woke about nine, planning to go to the Newman Center. In bathrobe and slippers, coffee cup in hand, I wandered into the living room. Gus was already there. "Take a look, they're moving Oswald to maximum security. Why the hell'd they wait this long?"

I stood next to his chair. The Sunday *Chronicle* littered the floor. A recent addition to the household, the large color TV was tuned to a black and white broadcast. A number of burly men in light Stetson hats were hustling a short man through what the announcer said was the basement of the police station. Outside, an armored car waited. "Oswald?" I asked.

Gus nodded.

The prisoner had on a dark V-neck sweater and a white shirt, collar out. Looking closer I recognized him from yesterday's pictures, a small-featured face that somehow seemed cruel and mean, though my observations were colored by the heinous act of which he was accused. As the grotesque parade shuffled forward suddenly a figure darted in from the right. There was a loud bang. Oswald's face, now in plain view, twisted in surprise and pain, his mouth agape as he bent forward.

"He's been shot!" the announcer cried. "He's been shot! Lee Oswald has been shot!" Pandemonium broke out. Oswald and the assailant were surrounded by police, officials wrestled the shooter to the ground. The announcer was going on. We watched the chaos a while longer. Doubtful Oswald would survive, they began to say, serious wounds to the stomach. Then the TV cut away to preparations for JFK's funeral in Washington. The networks would replay that Oswald-Ruby videotape many times that day. They were already calling it the first-ever live killing on television. Gus shook his head. "Congratulations are in order. Another milestone reached. Guns, guns, guns – it's all about guns."

Church! I almost forgot. Better get moving. I can still make it, maybe. JFK can use my prayers and now, apparently, so can the man they say killed him. First Joe Jr., now another cross on the family's Calvary, beside them the thief who stole JFK's life. No one will ever forget where he was the day John F. Kennedy was shot. "How about coming along?" I asked Gus. I knew the answer but with the events of the last few days, why not?

He shook his head. "Haven't been in years."

"It's time then," I said. "Don't you miss it at all?"

"No, but you represent me. If there's any good to be got out of it, you'll get it."

Later that afternoon I ran into Bill Porter in the living room. For once, finally, the television was off. Bill was relaxing with the *Chronicle's* Sporting Green section. He was an interesting guy, I was finding, more mature than most students, perhaps because of his military experience. "Nothing but bad news this weekend," he said, pointing to the headline: BIG GAME – STANFORD 30 - CAL 13. "That's three in a row." "Did you go?"

"Doesn't appeal to me much, especially when it's not your own school. Oswald died."

"So I heard. Gus was really getting under your skin the other day."

"Mine and everybody else's. I'm surprised somebody hasn't punched that guy out a long time ago. He loves to set people off."

"It's not just that, he's so critical of our country. Sure, I don't know history like him but I have to believe he's being selective. Whatever our shortcomings, this is still the best place on earth to live. If not why would do people still come here?"

Bill nodded. "Amen to that. My mother's family moved here from Mexico. They worked the fields, kids included, I'm not ashamed to say, moved north with the seasons. A hard life but a paradise compared to what they left – that's what they say and I believe them. Finally got enough together to buy a little place. They put every single kid through high school. My mom ended up with a job at Douglas Aircraft, that's where she met my father."

His story answered a question I had about his looks, the dark hair and dark eyes, swarthy skin. Bill went on, "I only had two years active duty but I came out of it with more respect for this country than I went in. I was happy to serve, give something back."

"Were you in Vietnam?"

"That didn't heat up until I was out, though knock wood, the way things're going it may get me yet. It's getting dicey for my Reserve unit."

Something had been on my mind. "One thing about Gus I haven't figured out, he was a naval officer but he is so dead set against the war..."

"He's not anti-military if that's what you mean. His quarrel is with Washington. I happen to disagree with him on that too, but no, he is definitely not anti-military."

"I got a first-hand look at Washington a couple of summers ago. There's truth to that saying about watching sausage being made."

"I hear you, but if you like sausage you've got to accept how it's made."

"Come to think of it, I do like sausage. Maybe I'd better find a different example."

23. FREEDOM YEAR

"DO YOU THINK THERE WAS A CONSPIRACY?"

"I never thought Oswald was just a kook acting alone, but the conspiracy evidence wasn't persuasive either. Seeing what's happened to the Kennedys since, you have to wonder if there wasn't some dark cloud following them around. Sins of the father sort of thing, though that would be inconsistent with Occam's Razor."

"Occam's what?"

"William of Occam. Fourteenth century Franciscan. Got it now?" Jonathan looks more confused than before. "Try this. Don't make the explanation more complicated than what you're explaining. K-I-S-S. Keep it Simple, Stupid."

"I see."

"I'm not so sure." I stand and stretch. "So tomorrow's your big day."

"Bright and early. In fact I'd better call it quits and get ready."

Next morning Jonathan is up and out before I even start my coffee. I must be growing used to him, for today I am at loose ends. For a change of pace I decide to take the morning to get caught up on Iraq so I go online and start surfing. I'm getting better at this.

It is early October in the Year of Our Lord 2003. Cool as it is here, the Middle East is torrid and not just the weather. Sure, we knocked over that statue, but Saddam's still on the loose. They'll probably find him sitting on a pile of WMDs, which to nobody's surprise are also missing. Difference is, we know there really was a person called Saddam Hussein, or still is. On the plus side, two of his sons are dead and they've captured cousin "Chemical Ali," engineer of the attack on the Kurds in ninety-one. Nice to see the family business doing so well. And the Governing Council we appointed has been sworn in. As to that, we shall see.

The lawlessness in the streets, and our military standing by! The violence is becoming endemic, yet the geniuses in Washington maintain this isn't a real insurgency. They're so big on word games. What did they expect, throwing a hundred thousand armed men out of work? Humiliated, desperate for money, food, some semblance of a life.

A couple of weeks ago the head of the U.N. Mission was murdered. A truck bomb. From all accounts Vieira de Mello was an up-front guy, stark contrast to our "liberators" hiding in their bunkers. The suicide bombings continue. Iraqis perish, those patriotic or foolish enough to work with us. Our so-called leadership didn't believe in working the grass roots, trying to understand the Iraqis. Well, they're paying the price now. Our plan? No plan. That was beneath them too. Arrogant, self-righteous – it's Vietnam all over again, even worse because we had that monstrous example to learn from. No wonder Dennis is climbing the walls.

* * * * * * *

A FEW TIMES I HAD VENTURED into the city, but this year's Christmas shopping would be done at the campus store. My parents bought me a plane ticket so I didn't have to choose between penury and staying put for the holidays. Christmas week was a blur, landing in a snowstorm after a connection in Chicago. My return was on a nonstop from Boston, which set up a visit with the Harringtons my last night.

One week in Providence was more than enough. I brought drafts of my papers due soon after I got back, but there was always an excuse. The highlight of my visit was Jim's little family. The baby, Mikey, six weeks old with a shock of black hair and a powerful set of lungs, Mark, nearly two, crawling faster than most people run. Maureen was already in pre-school as Sheila tried to piece her professional life back together. I told them being an uncle was so much fun I was hoping they'd go for four soon. Sheila's dirty look said it all. Worried about Vietnam, Jim was trying to get out of the Guard and my father was pulling strings. Family hardship sort of thing.

Catherine had a new boy friend, Tom, a biology teacher at Classical, a guy in his thirties who was working on a Masters at URI. Entomology. He seemed okay, but I thought, in a protective kind of way that surprised me – he's not up to her standards. He was actually kind of boring. Bugs and boring – maybe the two go together.

Boring, my mother never had been, she wouldn't know how. La belle Fiona was in not one, but two plays. *The Threepenny Opera* at a community theater near Brown would bring back her singing. She was also rehearsing Behan's *The Hostage* for a new repertory company to be housed in Trinity United Methodist Church. In that one she would play Meg (there's a coincidence!), proprietress of a Dublin rooming house which doubles as a brothel. I had a good laugh, wondering what my father would think of that. Speaking of my father, I detected a unsettling weariness in him that was new.

"I'm thinking of selling the business," he explained one night as we sat in the living room. "If you're around this summer I'd like you to help sort it out."

Pat was his usual self, grousing about law school. "Civil Procedure's the absolute worst. What a waste of time, trying to figure out how to get somewhere I don't want to be in the first place."

"Where's that?"

"Court."

The only relief, he said, some assigned cases were truly bizarre. Lady dies after finding a mouse in her Coke bottle, that sort of thing. Against Pat's dark maunderings, Meg was happily juggling a full load of Biology and Chemistry plus med school applications. I caught her up on my doings out on what her father called the "left coast."

"At least you're still the same person," she said.

We talked about the assassination, I told her about my roommates and the Jewish crowd I'd been initiated into. Pat had told me on the Q.T. there was another guy in the picture, a second-year law student, and if I wanted to make a move I'd better go for it. I felt bad but was in no position to get serious. That evening we three took in *La Strada* at the Brattle. Anthony Quinn as Zampano, the carnival strong man. Gelsomina. The Fool. One of the all-time great films, then dinner at the Wursthaus. Heavy film, heavy dinner.

FOR MY INTERNATIONAL RELATIONS PAPER I chose the division of Berlin, Ike's restraint that led the Birchers to paint him as a Communist. Finished that, I turned to Don's seminar, building on my work on Communist movements and adding insights from the kibbutzim. Between everything else, I crammed for the German final. One afternoon I hooked up with Benny and Gideon on the Terrace.

"Snick wants students to go to Mississippi this summer to register Negro voters," Gideon said. "Rigged literacy requirements, phony I.Q. tests, poll taxes, intimidation – we need to give those people back their confidence. We'll flood the sovereign state of Mississippi with thousands of students from all over the country." He nodded at me. "Everything we do will be strictly legal but things could get ugly. There were threats against the Freedom Ballot work last year and that was just a trial run."

"People set in their ways..."

"It's more than that. This is going to blow the lid off the white supremacist way of life, and the better we do it the harder they'll come down. Think Freedom Riders times ten... times a hundred."

Benny nodded. "We're talking people denied their humanity, the fundamental rights you need to live and function. So, Paul, can we sign you up? You missed the fun at Mel's and the Sheraton Palace. Time to get involved."

Some of those protests had turned into sit-ins with students arrested, dragged out of buildings. Gains were made but I felt I made the right decision to stay out of it. Breaking the law was not the way to go, not my way. My first reaction to Gideon's offer was discomfort. Never had I done anything remotely like this. Still, I thought, I claim to be sympathetic... is that just lip service? The thought made me uncomfortable. "Let me follow it a while, see how it develops."

"Follow it!" Gideon shouted, "we want leaders, not followers! Your landlord knows all about this, ask him!" We talked a while longer, I stuck to my guns, such as they were, then as we were leaving Gideon asked, "By the way how is it, living with the eminent Professor?"

"I'm still trying to figure out what makes him tick."

Gideon nodded. "I just stumbled across something interesting. You've heard about the loyalty oath situation?"

"Some."

"In the Forties the Regents went nuts – McCarthy kind of nuts. They made University employees sign an oath denying they belonged to the Communist Party et cetera et cetera. A lot of people signed but some refused on principle, others never had anything to do with the C.P. It got a bunch of them fired, including some very distinguished scholars."

"What does that have to do with Gus?"

Gideon smiled. "He signed the oath."

"You're kidding!"

Gideon shook his head. "I suspect he's been trying to live it down ever since."

Amazing, I thought, I need to find out more. But it didn't seem right to bring it up in his home so I just let it hang. The following week when he invited me to lunch at the Faculty Club, though, I decided to raise it if the situation seemed right. "Since you're going to be a professor," Gus said, "you should get a feel for the perks. Meet me in my office, we'll walk up together."

I arrived at his office early. Dwinelle second floor, the first time I'd been there. The door was ajar so I knocked and stuck my head in. "Paul! Be right with you." In a few minutes the door opened and his visitor left, looked like another grad student. "Working on my latest tome," Gus said, shaking his head. "It's not easy to find the time, there's so much going on. Thank God for Research Assistants."

The room was tiny. Every wall was lined with books, papers and folders covered every surface. He swiveled around in a handsome leather chair that seemed too large for the space and told me to have a seat. "Let's give the crowd time to thin out. Nothing worse than a lunch line of hungry academics. So, how are you getting along? How's the program going?"

"Fine, I think. I handed in my last seminar paper yesterday. The one on Communist movements, for Don Morrison."

"Oh, yes, Don, good man. Were you pleased how it came out?"

"By chance I came across something really good. I've gotten to know a fellow who spent a couple of years in a kibbutz. He gave me some insights into the tension between community ideals and the practicalities. You may know him, Gideon Jacoby – he's in Snick."

"Big red-headed kid with a beard. He is very good. He turns out a lot of those position statements you see on leaflets – the theoretician, if you will."

"He's in this group of Jewish kids I've gotten to know thanks to my former neighbor Benny Kaplan. Benny's in your Slavery seminar."

"Oh, sure, another very bright youngster. How were you neighbors?"

"If you can believe it, we lived on the same street, then his family moved back to New York and we lost track of each other until we reconnected here."

"Gideon must have told you about Freedom Summer."

"He's trying to enlist me. I support what they're after but I'm just not sure."

"Give it some thought. They're committed to nonviolence, though the people down there certainly aren't. The way I see it, if you believe strongly it's important to take a stand, as much for your own self respect as the cause, sometimes. But I sense you have a good heart..." I noticed him looking intently at me, suddenly he laughed, this sharp, unfunny laugh. "Listen to me pontificating." He was quiet for a moment. "You know, I feel like I should come clean with you. It might even do you good to hear what I have to say."

My heart leapt into my throat.

"Years ago, the late Forties it was, this campus tore itself apart. No, let me say it straight, a bunch of ultra-conservative politicians out for a fight maneuvered us into a position where we tore ourselves apart. You've heard of the loyalty oath business."

I nodded.

"I'll spare you the gory details but long story short, I ended up signing the goddamned thing." He averted his eyes. "Went against everything I believed in, everything I stood for. Worst thing I ever did in my life." He fell silent, deep in thought, in recollection.

I finally got up the nerve to ask. "Why'd you do it?"

"I was up for tenure." He shrugged. "It wasn't the money, we could have managed." He fell silent again. "I lost dear friends," he said. "Some of them were fired and moved away, others I've had to face all these years. Everybody knew I had betrayed something very dear." His eyes became moist. "Not a day goes by I don't kick myself. Worst thing, it wasn't necessary, not necessary at all."

"What do you mean?" I asked, puzzled.

"Akiko was new here, we had just embarked on our wonderful adventure, I didn't want to hurt her, risk uprooting her, but what I did was even more devastating."

"I don't understand."

"I lied to her, Paul! I lied! I said, oh, it doesn't matter, it's no big deal, I'll just go ahead and sign. And she believed me. Later she found out signing that piece of paper tore me up so bad it practically killed me." He shook his head ruefully. "Was she ever angry! Never cross a Japanese woman – they're worse than the Irish, if that is possible. Worst argument we ever had. I didn't trust her, didn't respect her, didn't think she had a mind of her own, didn't give her credit for loving me. First and only time in our married life we went to bed without patching things up. Very bad. When you get married you'll understand what I mean. She said if I'd confided in her, she would have stood by me. 'Whatever happens we will be fine as long as we have each other,' she said. Her exact words."

Eyes still glistening he flipped through some folders on his desk. "I hope I didn't embarrass you and please, don't let on I told you."

"Of course not."

"How do I conclude this sermonette?" His face became severe in a way I had never seen. "Be faithful to what you believe in. And when you're in love, give the person you love a chance. Do not underestimate her. If you're with her, really be with her."

"I appreciate your telling me this," I said. "I can see it wasn't easy."

"Some people wonder why I spend time with the Gideons of the world, young people on fire for a saner, juster existence. Why do I help them through the bullshit university politics? Why do I help them raise money?" He nodded. "Maybe now you'll understand."

"You've been living down a mistake."

He shook his head. "I think of it more as living up to something. Better late than never." He reached for his jacket. "Give Mississippi some thought. If you're not ready, so be it, but don't underestimate yourself." He came around the desk. "There is one more thing."

Good God, I thought, what more can there be?

He put his hand on my shoulder. "I'm starved. Let's go eat."

We headed up the hill to the club. Gideon was right, but I sensed there was more.

As the spring wore on Gideon stepped up the pressure. Over a thousand young people would be joining with Negro youth from the South. Living in Negro homes, becoming part of their communities. Going door to door, engaging local people many of whom would be distrustful and afraid.

"Door to door, that much I am familiar with."

"We have to be prepared for anything," Gideon said, "though if they force me I'll take a couple of those rednecks with me. In my non-violent way, of course."

One day I ran into Mario and he let me have it. "You call yourself a Catholic? It's time you start proving it! Words without actions are as sounding brass and tinkling cymbals. Saint Paul, First Corinthians. Check it out."

I felt guilty but I needed a focused summer to get on top of my work. By March, I had scored an undemanding summer job in Brown's library that would give me time to lay out my doctoral thesis. The passage to Berkeley was upheaval enough for one year. After much thought and prayer, I told Gideon no. My friends would go to Mississippi and I would return home, inching toward my own contribution, whatever it might turn out to be. I gave Benny my Rhode Island address and phone number again. He said he'd write.

MY SECOND BERKELEY SEMESTER was a repeat of the first, with more confidence. I progressed in *die deutsche sprache* and added International Econ. I had to cut Professor Markham loose, but I would never forget the look on her face that awful day. Rachel was no longer at the University, though she did finish the semester. She was splitting time with the Mime Troup and a couple of jobs that paid the bills. Her family was really upset at her dropping out – they were barely on speaking terms. I'd been down Telegraph Ave many times but one evening Rachel offered to give me her private tour. After the third shop with incense so thick you could cut it, I asked what was up. "It's for atmosphere," she said – this in a shop of South Asian wares, Nehru jackets, batik scarves, bead curtain separating a mysterious back room, probably a supply room – "or to cover the pot."

We had dinner in an Indian restaurant, on cushions, from a low table, and afterward strolled, stopping for a girl on a dulcimer and a skinny guy plucking a banjo. I had come to like Appalachian music – fourths and fifths, minors and majors, young love, unrequited love, early death often by drowning – and tossed a quarter into his case. A lot of people greeted Rachel by name. "I used to work in Cody's," she said. "One summer I practically lived on the Ave, I spent so much time here."

The cafes were crowded, beards in earnest conversation. From the signs, lots of homeless and hungry, one guy with a tiny girl in a tattered dress, she couldn't have been more than three, "a family down on our luck." Emaciated souls with sunken eyes rose up, then drifted on, glassy-eyed youths with their all earthly possessions in a backpack. Though tranquil, there was an edge of desolation and despair that made me think, for some of these people, panic or worse is not far off.

About nine we descended a set of stone steps into a low-ceilinged bar. First thing I noticed, they were playing very good jazz, Coltrane, Miles Davis. The room was bathed in blue light, the walls and furniture glowed blue, the upside-down glasses in racks above the bar shone blue. A number of young people, also blue, some in a state of serious undress, sprawled across sofas and soft chairs, the scent of incense overpowering everything. Rachel winked. "Atmosphere. It's still early," she said, looking around. "Things don't get started here til ten-thirty, eleven." She spotted a long, low sofa with a couple entwined on its corduroy cushions, a pretty Negro girl and a bluish-white guy with a thin face and long, scraggly hair. Rachel went up to them. "Hi Randy hi Tonya."

"Rachel," the guy said, looking up, "c'mon in, the water's fine."

"This is Paul," she replied as they disengaged and moved over.

As I sank into the overstuffed cushions I could tell my knees were in for more abuse. A young woman in a very short, tight skirt came over. She bent down in front of me and set a couple of paper napkins on the table. I couldn't help notice her bare breasts, didn't even try, as her loose, low-cut t-shirt fell away. "Hi Rachel," the girl said.

"Hi Linda. This is Paul."

"Hi. What'll it be," she said with a smile.

"The usual," Rachel replied.

"Make that two," I said, watching her walk away. "You have nice friends."

She pulled across an ashtray full of butts. "Linda's our token intellectual. She's getting her master's in Art History – Medieval Church Art."

"Will wonders never cease."

"Don't judge a book by its cover."

"Or lack thereof."

"I saw you looking at her, or should I say leering."

"Looking, yes, leering, no. Well, looking intently, I'll accept that." I sat back, wondering what I had ordered. The music put me in mind of good old Charlotte. Rachel reached into her purse, a knit bag with a drawstring, and pulled out a little pouch. She unfolded it, several skinny cigarettes in a heap of brown shavings, raising her eyebrows. I shook my head. "To each his own poison."

She twisted the ends of a joint. As I fished around for a match, stringy-haired Randy reached into his jeans and brought out a lighter. Rachel got it going then took a deep drag, holding the smoke a long time. Our neighbors also lit up. "Have a drag," Rachel said.

"No need," I said as the smoke drifted across. I'd seen her do pot before though never with the Jewish crowd. In Berkeley there was little chance of getting caught as long as you didn't embarrass the police into doing something. To me, drugs were a curiosity, a dusty window into the world of Kerouac and the Beats which I found attractive, in an oblique sort of way.

We sat around, talking, listening to the music. Randy was an anthropologist, a grad student, Tonya another would-be actress – films she said, some modeling. Her hair was so short you could plainly see the shape of her head, which was a very nice head indeed. This style from certain parts of Africa was beginning to catch on. Disconcerting at first, it had a way of growing on you. The room was filling up. Now they had a new Dylan album on. I had trouble with some of his songs. *Masters of War,* for one, and *With God On Our Side.* They went too far, but politics aside, his music was compelling, if you could stand the raspy, irritating voice. He was saying something important, even though you disagreed with it.

After a while I began getting sleepy. Rachel was on, I don't know, her third joint, and I was thinking tomorrow's a big day, I have to lead the discussion in Don's seminar, it would be a good idea to look over my notes tonight. "You want to stay?" I asked Rachel.

Her eyes were kind of vacant. "'Course," she said. She waved her hand around the room. "Don' worry, I'll get a ride, these people are my frens."

I made my adieus and left. The smoke had made me woozy and in the car I felt a sore throat coming on. When I got back to the house, I took a long look at my room. Bed, desk, chair, books. Lamp, clock, radio, phonograph. Family pictures, crucifix propped up on the desk. Simple, spare, just how I liked it. Lying on the bed staring at the ceiling I felt guilty not getting on my seminar notes but I had some things to sort out. Rachel went out with a lot of guys and was no innocent when it came to sex. I replayed the night a few months ago when she invited me in after a movie and there we were on her couch kissing and the front of her shirt was open and she was leaning all over me but when her hand reached my thigh I grabbed hold of it. This wasn't the time, nor the place nor, I had come to realize, was she the girl. I thought about Montreal. Madeline had reasons. Rachel was all about Rachel, and that bothered me. Father Ronan came to mind. What would he say about Mississippi? I could call him but I thought, no, this one's mine to do.

WE LANDED IN PROVIDENCE ON SCHEDULE, seven-ten local time. During the flight I plotted my strategy. I would hold my ground, carve out plenty of time for my work. Not cave to family pressures. As I entered the terminal I heard myself being paged. An agent handed me a slip of paper. "Meet us at Miriam Hospital right away. Mother."

The cab screeched to a stop in front of the hospital. At the reception desk I learned my father had suffered a stroke. He'd been operated on mid-afternoon and hadn't yet regained consciousness. I raced to Intensive Care on the fourth floor where my mother and Catherine were sitting in an alcove. "I'm so glad you're here," my mother said, throwing her arms around me, her voice husky.

"What happened? Is he going to make it?"

"He passed out at the office. Thank God for Miss Grenier, she had him here in twenty minutes."

"They said downstairs it was a stroke."

She nodded. "They operated but he's still in the coma." Her eyes filled with tears. "I don't know what we'll do..."

Catherine put her hand on her shoulder. "Mom, we have to stay positive."

"You're right," she said, wiping her eyes, "pray and be positive."

Ten o'clock, no developments. I said I'd stay so my mother could get some sleep. Catherine would go with her. I tried to get some shut-eye in a hard plastic chair. No luck. Long ago I'd tossed the cup of sludge from the corridor vending machine. I'd eaten almost nothing all day and by the time I realized that, the cafeteria was closed. I'd be on their doorstep at six. Jim would bring my mother back later.

I must have slept some because when I heard the nurse's voice I didn't know where I was. "Mr. Bernard," she was shaking me gently, "Mr. Bernard." I looked up.

"You'll be happy to know your father is awake."

"Awake," I said. Things were coming into focus. "That's good news."

"It's very good. He's reasonably alert, considering." I nodded and rubbed my eyes. She sat down next to me. "He's suffered some damage, there is considerable weakness on one side. The next few days we'll run tests to determine how extensive and what to do about it. But for now the doctor says he's out of the woods."

"How long will he have to be here?"

"Typically two weeks, possibly more. The tests will tell."

"And then..."

"Then there'll be a period of rehab which will be rather intense."

"That he can do at home?"

"You're way ahead of yourself. Be thankful he's alive and out of the coma."

"Can I see him?"

She shook her head. "We want him to get some sleep, healthy, natural sleep. No excitement. Later today."

I looked at my watch. Four-fifteen. I'd promised to call mother if anything happened but I decided to wait until morning. Last thing we need is two sick parents.

They kept him in for three weeks. There was significant paralysis on the right side and he was able to speak only with difficulty. His mind was as keen as ever and his memory unimpaired, but it was painful seeing him so limited. After stablilizing his medication the process of therapy would begin, and it would occupy him a long time to come. He would be in a wheelchair for months, perhaps years, perhaps forever.

It was devastating. Our tough, energetic dad, never sick a day in his life, now this. We rallied round, letting him know even half a father like him was twice as good as anybody else. Fortunately the business was pretty well able to run itself. He vowed he'd be back in a week, but of course that didn't happen. The real effect was to accelerate his plan to sell and get out. It also meant my role would be more central than I had thought, and much more time-consuming.

The next Monday I started my library job, on my lunch hour shooting over to the hospital to begin sorting through the myriad of details. Through slurred conversations, gestures and handwritten notes, we plowed ahead. The doctors objected, but he insisted on conferring with his advisors, his lawyer Marty, the V.P. from Industrial National Bank who handled the company's account, his CPA. After he was discharged I changed my work hours to finish at two-thirty. When I realized my summer was now odd man out I was furious, but before long I came to my senses. At least I'd kept my rotten reaction to myself.

Francis O'Rourke had lost a few steps himself, but he was still doing the job. When I happened to be home I looked on as he sorted the mail, hoping for a letter from Benny or Gideon, smoke swirling about my head from Francis' cigarette, dangling from his mouth on all but the rainiest days. As he handed me our packet and removed the butt, a trace of paper stuck to his lower lip. I could smell the quickie was still part of his routine. Blessed are those who honor the old ways, for theirs is the kingdom of memory.

One week went by, two weeks. Every morning I looked in the paper for something about Freedom Summer, every evening on the news. In late June, a full ten days after its postmark, a letter from Benny arrived. Their Ohio training was finished and they'd soon set out for the Deep South.

> I'd be lying if I said I wasn't afraid. We expect one hell of a reaction, White Citizens Councils, the Klan. I feel part Negro after our three weeks. As much as possible we're trying to see the world through their eyes. The locals will hate us, and realistically, even the people we're trying to help will think we're from a different planet.
>
> Have we had workshops! How to handle insults. What to do if a mob starts yelling and screaming. Non-violence is number one, be polite, don't mouth off. No surprise, Gideon had trouble with that one. What if the cops whack you around. They're making us bring bail money if you can believe it.
>
> There's a camp meeting every night, we go over the program then sing. It's good there is this lighter side, it's so intense. Have you ever really listened to Blowin' in the Wind? It's our anthem, that plus We Shall Overcome. There are so many Jewish kids it looks like Panoramic Way. The hora, Hava Negila, etc.

etc. By the way, Gideon is very proud of Cal. We have more volunteers than any other university, just like the Peace Corps. Mario says hello.

Well that's all for now. I need to write my father. He is an insane worrier. He was against my going but he and my mother taught me too well. Leah sends her love, Gideon sends his best. Need to be clear who is sending what.

Your friend, Benny

P.S. My address is RFD 3, Meridian, Miss. They say this is one of the easier towns.

The library was so relaxed I had time to study after all. My thesis ideas were sketchy but I was developing those old concepts about governments under stress. Benny's letter made me feel bad, but I didn't see myself as Hamlet any more. You can't do everything, and what I was doing was worthwhile, if not spectacular. The evening I received Benny's letter I glanced at the TV as Walter Cronkite broke into a program to announce that three civil rights workers had disappeared – in Meridian, Mississippi! The three had set out to visit a church the Klan had torched as payback for hosting a Freedom School. The local sheriff was saying they'd stopped the three for a traffic violation, brought them to the county jail then released them. No word from them since. It wasn't my friends. Some locals claimed the disappearance was a plot to discredit the white community, that the three were sitting in Chicago or Cuba or wherever Commies hide out, drinking wine, smoking pot and laughing their heads off. SNCC said the Klan was trying to terrorize the program. Within days their burned out car was found – then, no word at all.

In another brief note Benny said SNCC had been besieged by demands that sons and daughters be returned, though few had left. Under pressure from some influential parents, LBJ pushed a reluctant J. Edgar Hoover to send federal agents to Mississippi. Some Negro commentators said this move, welcome though it was, showed who had the clout. When young Negro men disappear do the *Times* or *Gazette* take notice? Or CBS? Hardly. "My father panicked," Benny wrote, "but I was not about to let those kids down. Your prayers, goyish though they are, will be appreciated."

In a return letter I told of my father's illness, progress on my research. Benny's reply brought me to tears.

A month has given me perspective. Good as our training was, it never could have conveyed the extremes of good and evil. The families are welcoming but some of these people have never really spoken to a white person in their lives, let alone get to know one. Sleeping in their houses, sharing meals, being interested in them as persons, this has been the icebreaker.

It's disconcerting to hear people three times my age call me sir, but this is ingrained in the older folks. Many of them want to register and have their say but they're afraid. The white employers aren't subtle, threatening their jobs or worse. When I think of the danger I remind myself that I will return to my comfortable life but these people will still be here. They'll have to deal with what we've started.

The little kids are altogether different. After they get over their shyness they're like kids everywhere. The sky's the limit once they have the tools.

I've been called nigger lover and white nigger, but the one I like best is "Jew boy." I guess that fits but my Irish and Italian friends hear that too. I've been threatened but nothing serious. After a lot of collect calls I finally settled my father down. Of course I was less than candid, that would only have made things worse.

It is different here, no question. Somewhere between the nice things we take for granted and what I see here must lie a happy medium. How can our system be so smart about producing stuff and so dumb about distributing it? Answer me that, mister political science man.

Andrew and James and Michael are always in our thoughts. For what it's worth, the FBI is finally on the case. Nobody's talking but there are a lot of rumors, none of them good.

Gideon and Leah say hello. Leah is thriving, she is a natural teacher. You should see her with the little kids. You're missing a lot though at least you're there to help your father which is important. Give him my best.

Benny

In addition to Mississippi, an off-duty policeman fatally shot a fifteen-year-old Negro boy in a melee on Manhattan's Upper East Side and street battles erupted in Harlem, spreading to Bedford-Stuyvestant. Outbreaks followed in Rochester, Jersey City, Chicago, Philadelphia. Embroiled in a contentious campaign against the ultra-conservative Barry Goldwater, LBJ ordered an investigation of the riots. For the first time in our history of interracial conflict it was being said that Negroes, not whites, were the aggressors. It was disturbing, fascinating television, watching cities burn, storefronts smashed and looted. Shoved under the rug as a southern issue, "the racial problem" was now exposed for what it was. Martin Luther King pleaded for non-violence, but "Burn, Baby, Burn!" grabbed the headlines. Some said the Civil Rights Act LBJ forced through Congress was much too little, much too late. Others, that never would have been too soon.

The news from Vietnam was no better. Another coup ousted the junta that had overthrown the Diems. Then, at the end of July, one of our destroyers, the *USS Maddox,* patrolling international waters off Vietnam, was attacked by North Vietnamese gunboats and returned fire, sinking one of them. Several days later we learned the *Maddox* and a second ship, the *C. Turner Joy,* had been subjected to another unprovoked attack in the Gulf of Tonkin sixty-five miles off the North Vietnam coast. The next day carrier-based warplanes bombed torpedo boat bases and an oil depot. President Johnson went to Congress for the authority to intervene. We will seek no wider war, he said. We have no intention of getting tied down in a land war in Asia. His request was overwhelmingly approved.

On a quick visit to Boston, Pat warned me not to trust LBJ, there was more to this than met the eye. I begged to differ. "You've got to give him the benefit of the doubt. He knows what's going on and we don't." A Harris poll had found seventy-two percent backed Johnson. "That cowboy's got to prove he's as tough as Goldwater," Pat went on, "that's what's going on. I'm sorry, the timing is much too convenient."

Only later did I learn Pat was right and I'd been wrong, as to their sorrow so had many good men in Congress who essentially gave LBJ the blank check he wanted. Only two Senators had taken a stand, Morse of Oregon and Gruening of Alaska.

"What's your draft status these days?" I asked Pat. "My deferment's solid as long as I'm in the program."

"Mine's only three years so I'm fair game when I get my law degree. Listen to me," he said, a hang-dog expression on his face, "my law degree." He offered me a cigarette but I shook him off. "Still haven't taken up the habit, I see." He lit one and sat back. "I've been giving serious thought to packing it in and taking off for Paris, but I've grown accustomed to the finer things, like eating. Wouldn't my draft board love to hear I had the guts to stand up to the old man! 'Welcome, sucker,' or is it 'Greetings.' Do they still say Greetings?'"

My weekend with the Harringtons also featured Meg's review of my father's condition. Her prognosis was optimistic but she said he'll have to dedicate himself to getting better. "I'm no Christian Scientist but it's well documented that a patient's attitude has a lot to do with his recovery." Meg's big news, she was headed to Yale Medical in the fall. She was accepted at Harvard too, but said she needed a change of scene in the worst way. Her new steady, Clyde (can you believe that? Clyde!) was going into his third year at Harvard Law but the New England Thruway presents no barrier to lovers, if that's what they were. I sulked. As usual, nobody but myself to blame.

First week of August, the bodies of the missing men were discovered, in an earthen dam on a farm outside Meridian. Schwerner and Goodman had been shot in the head and Chaney savagely beaten. There were reports of panic among the volunteers. Mid-August I received another letter from Benny.

> Losing our friends was devastating. That and the harassment, the shootings, the bombings, the kidnappings, it has cast a pall over our mission. But now I understand that fear and resolve can abide together. And the acts of cowards in time bring them down. Something has changed and the Sheriff Raineys of the world know it. From now on, they'll be the ones looking over their shoulders.
>
> I don't know what the statistics will say but what we're accomplishing is beyond numbers. Negroes are not going to take it any more. And they know some white

people care about them enough to put our necks on the line. Paul, you missed the opportunity of a lifetime, wonderful and terrible both.

This will be my last letter, we're shutting it down soon. God be with these good people after we're gone. See you in the fall. As always,

Benny

IN JULY GOLDWATER RODE the right-wing bandwagon to the Republican nomination. Next month it was LBJ's turn, Atlantic City. The Democrats featured a fight by the "Democratic Freedom Party" to be seated as Mississippi's official state delegation. Amid hard feelings a compromise seated two members as delegates-at-large while leaving the white-only "regular" delegation as the official representatives.

My father was recovering well. He needed help to get out of bed and dressed, and weakness on his right side confined him to the wheelchair. His speech was still slurred and the right side of his face sagged, but if he continued to improve they said he might graduate to a walker by the fall. A sign he wanted to get better, he quit smoking cold turkey. The doctors didn't give him a choice, telling him two packs a day had a lot to do with his stroke. The physical therapist was introducing exercise into his rehab. He was learning to write left- handed while doing exercises for his right hand.

He'd been into the office only a few times, since getting him in and out of the car was such an ordeal. My mother set up an office in Jim's old bedroom. She had a phone installed, a new portable kind he could carry around, and a high desk his wheelchair rolled under. Miss Grenier worked next door in Catherine's old bedroom with a new desk, chair and typewriter, filing cabinet, and another phone.

The banker and accountant were running the numbers on the company's value. They hired an expert on selling businesses and by August a package was ready. Word was getting around that Bernard Bros. Tool & Die was on the block, and even before the official announcement an offer came in from a big Indiana tool works wanting to extend its reach.

These emotional months saw my father grow closer to me and I to him. He was progressing so well there was no need to postpone my return to Berkeley. And the more I worked on my thesis topic the more excited I became. I sure wouldn't be lacking for material. We don't always do the right thing or the smart thing, I thought, sitting in the plane waiting to take off. Often we make our problems worse. There's serious dysfunction in a system that permits, even encourages what we're seeing in the South. I had to credit Gus's point about American romance with violence, but rotten-to-the-core evil? That's going too far. I think it was Churchill who said democracy is the worst form of government except all the others that have been tried.

When they closed the plane door I gave a huge sigh of relief.

24. FAULT LINES

JONATHAN'S PLANE IS LATE. He doesn't get to the house until nine-thirty. I have Joseph keep his dinner warm, figuring he he'll want something. At the kitchen table he fills me in. Except for being out of uniform, he says Syzmanski is the professional soldier par excellence. West Point, twenty-plus years, gray crew-cut, decorated veteran of the Gulf War, military intelligence since then. "But the real news, are you ready for this, they shut Martinez down! They called off the investigation! Happened last Friday."

"Called it off! Why the hell'd they do that?"

"Like you said, Bernie thinks Martinez was taking it somewhere the higher-ups didn't want to go. But here's the real kicker, now they're starting *another* investigation! With some two-star in charge! Bernie says the guy's a real brick."

"What was Martinez coming up with? Did Bernie say anything about that?"

"No, but I got the sense it's what we're thinking. Paul was targeted."

"You mean they knew he was in that convoy, that vehicle."

"An Iraqi on our payroll knows the setup and makes a call – it had to be something like that."

I shake my head. "Hell, the place's is crawling with people like that, playing both ends against the middle. That'd be embarrassing, but it's no reason to mess with the investigation. It makes no sense."

Suddenly Jonathan pounds the table. "Gus! We've been missing something!"

"So? We miss a lot of things."

"No, this is important! Why would the insurgents target Paul? Why would they give a rat's ass about an American newsman and this one in particular? Take him hostage, I can see, but kill him?"

"I've been wondering that, too."

Jonathan shakes his head. "We've got to reach Martinez. I asked Bernie but he wouldn't touch it. Maybe your source can open it up for us."

"I'll give it a try."

Later in the day I call Dennis and leave a message. Inside ten minutes he calls me back. "You heard about the investigation."

"Jonathan just told me. What the hell is going on?"

"Disappointing, but not a surprise."

I get right to the point. "You need to put us in touch with Captain Martinez."

There is a pause on the line. "We go back a long way, Gus, but I can go only so far. I think we better talk soon, face-to-face. You need to know where I'm coming from."

We work through lunch then knock off for the day. A hard day, but by now Jonathan has come down to earth and our session is productive. "Mississippi," he's saying, "you encouraged your students to put themselves in harm's way. Didn't that bother you?"

"I worried about it, sure. But if a person believes in something and never goes for it, what good is it? Those kids were as prepared as it is possible to be."

"What about Paul? Would you say he wimped out?"

"I've thought about that a lot. You can only take on so many challenges and he was already in a sink or swim situation at Berkeley. I give him credit for that."

"What about his commitment to civil rights?"

"You have a point. Obviously he wasn't committed like Gideon or Benny. And he still felt like he had to control everything. You saw it when his father fell ill. His first reaction – something screwed up my plans. But he's learning to let go. Coming out to Cal was a start, the first time he took one of those famous leaps of faith."

"How about the next time?"

"That'd be getting ahead of the story."

Jonathan scowls. "I wish you wouldn't do that."

* * * * * * *

I'D BEEN BACK A WEEK, settling into the routine. Bill Porter had returned to Southern California and his place taken by Mark Hightower, another MBA candidate and Army Reservist. Mark was from Auburn in the Sierra foothills and had served in Vietnam. I asked Gus why he felt the need of military protection. He just laughed. I inherited Bill's second-floor room with a view of the Bay that made all the difference. I wondered how Mark would adapt to my tiny, landlocked room, but he said he could live with anything as long as it was dry and he wasn't getting shot at. He wouldn't be spending much time in the room anyway, he added, with drill one night a week and a girl in the City.

One night I told Gus my Freedom Summer friends were coming over and he invited himself. Akiko offered dinner but I opted for pizza and Chianti. At five-thirty the doorbell rang. "You're back!" I shouted as we clapped each other on the back. "You made it!"

"Our scars are not the physical sort," Benny said with a wry grin.

"I want to know everything," I said, ushering them into the living room. "By the way, Gus asked to join us. I told him yes, of course."

Gideon seemed agitated. "Good. I have something he needs to see."

When we were assembled Gideon pulled a piece of paper from his briefcase and handed it to Gus. "We just got this declaration of war."

"I heard something was in the works." Gus scanned the letter. "From: Dean of Students Katherine Towle," he read, "To: President, Campus Friends of SNCC."

"Everybody got one," Gideon said, starting to pace. "They can't do this to us, Gus. How can they expect to get away with this? We need our tables there."

Benny shook his head. "Suddenly the administration discovers the strip of sidewalk isn't city property, the University owns it! University rules apply. No more card tables. No political activity. Once again, law in the service of repression."

"We need those tables," Gideon said. "Without them we're dead."

Gus sat back in his chair. "I have good news and bad news. The bad news is you're dead. The good news, so is everybody else, from the Maoists to the Goldwaterites. The key thing, the administration needs to look like they're fair and impartial. Ban one table, they've got to ban them all. That gives you tremendous leverage if you use it right."

"We've been thinking along those lines," Bennie said, "a broad-based coalition."

Gus nodded. "Exactly. Be sure to involve the conservative groups, they have access to people the Regents listen to who wouldn't give you the time of day. Those politicians behind the Young Republicans want to get their message out as much as you do. It's an election year, that's in your favor."

The doorbell rang. Pizza delivery. We took a break to load our plates and refill our glasses. As the talk ranged back and forth, Gideon stressed that people who had spent the summer in Mississippi getting shot at are not about to let mousefart university rules get in their way. "They can't throw anything at us we haven't seen a thousand times worse."

That kind of talk made me uncomfortable. "If the University owns the property," I broke in, "it has the right to say how it's used. If the legal issue is just a ruse, that's different, but you don't know that."

Gideon shook his head. "Of course it's a ruse. What else could it be?"

"You're making a big assumption."

He reddened. "If you wait til you know everything with certainty, they win, you lose. The moment is past, your momentum is gone."

I shook my head. "You're telling me organizing is so important it trumps everything including the great majority of students who are here to get an education. I don't buy that. Besides this University is freer than any place I've ever seen."

"That says more about you than the University," Gideon countered.

"Okay, okay," Gus interjected. "Paul, you give the administration too much credit. The Regents encourage weapons research, the established order. That undercuts them when they say students shouldn't use campus facilities to promote social change. It's okay for the Regents but not when students do it? That's the level the debate should be conducted on. Only the most cloistered of my colleagues would deny there are legitimate uses of the University beyond classroom and laboratory. It needs to be kept in balance."

"I have no problem with that," I said, "but things are going to get sorely out of balance if one faction overrides procedures and good order."

"There's some truth to that," Gus said. "Anarchy is not pretty."

"It takes radical action to get the well-meaning liberal off his ass," Gideon shouted.

Leah's turn. "Obedience, civility, if they're casualties of the struggle so be it."

"Okay, enough." Gus turned to Gideon. "I'm meeting with a faculty group to see if we can't work something out. As far as the strip's concerned, you'll follow through for Snick and coordinate with the others. Let's talk, tomorrow night at the latest." He took a sip of wine and put his glass down. "Now tell me about your summer."

"What I Did On My Summer Vacation," Benny said, "A Third-Grade Report." Nobody laughed. "But seriously, it is absolutely amazing the progress those people made in a couple of months. They're off to a great start but it's going to take a lot more money and bodies. We can't let the administration shut us down."

Gus nodded. "Isn't what you did just a drop in the bucket? This struggle has been going on hundreds of years."

Benny was silent for a moment. "I would say the southern Negro has the best chance since the gains of the Reconstruction were lost. There's a real momentum. Lunch-counter sit-ins, the Freedom Riders, Selma, and what we did with the voter registration, what Leah did with those students."

Gus nodded. "The key is getting people organized so they can act effectively when you're not there. To me that's the difference you may make, and I stress the word may."

"The federal government will be crucial," I ventured, "intervention, pressure. Otherwise it's the lowest common denominator – states rights justify denial of rights."

"Well said," Gus added. "You sure you weren't in my seminar?"

WHEN I EXPLAINED MY THESIS IDEA TO DON he said the concept was good, but I needed to bear down on the comprehensives and start thinking about the oral. First things first. I had picked Public Law and Jurisprudence for my third area and it needed a lot of work. He suggested a program of directed reading in American History, and Gus said he'd be happy to supervise. It was also time for the integrated course in social sciences with Eugene Burdick, and once again Don mentioned statistics, so I reluctantly signed up for that, too. One more semester would do it for German, *jawohl!* Working with Don one-on-one, I'd sharpen Political Philosophy and we would schedule the exam for the coming spring, then the other two. Next summer I'd stay in Berkeley and grind, then the oral, and the dissertation path would be clear. Whew!

For fun, I signed up to audit a survey course in Asian Literature and Culture. Akiko was excited to hear this and I discovered she was not Christian, but Buddhist. "Though it's not very obvious, I'm afraid. I see how you might have missed this about me." I did know she was widely read in the literature of Japan and China.

Speaking of religion, first Sunday back I checked into the Newman Center. At a meeting later in the week I picked up news about Vatican II whose Third General Session was in progress. Progress? Heated battles raged internally over ecumenism and relations with Eastern Rite Churches, among other things. A proposal to alter the Church's historic position on the Jews' guilt for Christ's death seemed in danger of being scrapped, which would frustrate John XXIII's plea for healing. And in a controversial move, Pope Paul took birth control off the table until an expert commission he appointed reported back.

A FEW DAYS LATER I WAS CROSSING THE CAMPUS. As I neared Sather Gate I noticed tables – CORE, SNCC. Odd, I thought, they're not supposed to be here. A large crowd was milling about. Someone told me the administration had given out citations for manning tables against the rules. "But why so many people?" I asked a student.

"A lot of us signed statements we should be cited too."

"You're with one of the student organizations?"

He showed me his ALL THE WAY WITH LBJ button. "Young Democrats."

"What's been the impact on your organization?"

"We're hurting big time. Fund raising's way off. And it's a lot harder signing people up to get out the vote in November."

I nodded toward Sather Gate. "Even so, you've kept your table down, you're complying with the rules."

"If we show bad faith, it'll ruin our moral position," he shook his head, "like the administration. This has got to be solved politically. We're telling our members to get hold of their State Assemblyman and get this thing fixed."

I spotted Benny in the crowd and yelled to him. He motioned for me to hold on and a minute later he came over. "Paul, what're you doing here?"

"Why wouldn't I be here? I'm on my way to class."

"Oh, I thought maybe you had signed a statement." I looked at him sideways. "Just kidding. Not after how you were talking the other day."

"So what's the latest?"

"The deans are supposed to meet with the cited students today. We're demanding they meet with all of us, at last count that's over four hundred. We've all manned tables one time or another so if they discipline one of us, they've got to discipline everybody."

"You were hoping they'd change their position."

"They gave in on the tables but they're saying no organizing or fund raising. We can give out information, but that's not good enough. Typical liberal compromise."

"Keeping things together has its advantages," I said. "Anyway, it looks like your strategy's working. I just talked to a Young Democrat who's as pissed off as you are."

"I doubt that, but yeah, so far we're hanging together. Even the conservatives are with us – though in principle only, I hasten to add. They're 'opposed to trespassing and lawlessness as a means of protest,' if I remember the pat little formula."

"Sounds like my kind of people," I laughed. "Like I said, you have plenty of right to express yourself on the campus already."

"It's not Mississippi, but we have ways of making people show their true colors."

"Well, good luck, I guess," I said. "Stay out of trouble."

Benny shook his head. "Sometimes trouble's the only thing between you and where you need to go."

After German class, I wandered back to the Plaza. The crowd had grown. The mood seemed festive but snatches of conversation told me all was not well. "...deans were wrong to cancel the meeting..." So that's what happened. "...stay all night if we have to..."

After a while I'd had enough and went back to the library. About seven I packed up and returned to the house. I hadn't seen Gus for several days. Akiko said he'd been in meetings nonstop, seeking a way to permit political activity while giving the President and Chancellor a chance to save face. Preparing to walk to campus the next morning I ran into him downing a coffee on the fly. "Hold on a minute, I'll walk with you," he said. As we set out, Gus yawned. "Long week. The administration has moved but not far enough, and oh yes, in his infinite wisdom the Chancellor has now suspended the students."

"All four hundred of them?"

"No, just the leaders. Did you hear, a crowd spent the night in Sproul."

"You're kidding!"

He smiled. "Unless I miss my bet, what happens today will make yesterday look tame. By the way, I want to say you defended your position well the other day, in the face of stiff opposition, I might add. But speaking philosophically, which you are too accustomed to doing, I must caution you not to confuse the is with the ought."

"What do you mean?"

"Don't assume Kerr and Strong are some wise, impartial guardians of University values just because they ought to be. They work for the Regents who are political people, and they swim in the political sea. Sure, when nothing's upsetting the bosses, issues can be tackled more or less on the merits, but that's not now."

"Where do you stand in all this, you and the faculty?"

"The faculty's all over the lot. Some think we're out to destroy the University, but in my view those other interests the University serves are worth fighting for. Unfettered inquiry. Free expression. Appropriate on-campus support for important causes."

"But that's the issue! What is appropriate support? My point was, it's the administration's job to draw the lines. After all, they run the place!"

"There you go again!" Gus was shaking his head. "How can you say they're running the place when they take a different position every day. You can be sure they are bending to pressure. Sure, that disarms the critics but it provides very short term relief. A less savory name is blackmail, and blackmail is habit-forming. I've been around this place a long time, I know the signs."

"But you don't just flout the rules!"

"That's right. Civil disobedience is a decision to be made on a case-by-case basis. You can't make an omelet without breaking eggs."

"Tell me, Gus, where is it written you're entitled to an omelet whenever and wherever you want one?

We were still arguing when we reached Sather Gate and the stack of *Daily Cals*. The headline for the day: 700 SLEEP IN SPROUL HALL. "Probably a padded number," Gus said, "but this is an historic event, the first recorded 'sleep-in' ever. A new world record."

I saw my friend Mario was one of the eight suspended. "You know Mario, Gus?"

He nodded. "From Snick. He is a real firecracker."

The *Daily Cal* quoted Mario as saying the administration was "a bunch of bastards." I smiled... sounded like him.

I settled down for the day but got antsy around eleven and went back to see what was happening. Another big crowd, but now something was really out of place, a couple of tables right below the Sproul Hall steps – CORE and SNCC again. A leaflet called for a rally at noon. Just before noon a flurry of activity erupted around the CORE table, police and deans arguing with students. Standing on the back rim of the fountain I could sense the crowd growing restive, then I saw the police drag somebody toward a patrol car that had pulled onto the Plaza. The crowd surged forward but now he was in the car. "Sit down!" somebody yelled and everybody sat down where they were, instantly immobilizing the police car. When the crowd saw what they'd done, the mood lightened, people started leaning on the car, sitting on its hood, laughing and joking. Campus officials stood by, not knowing what to do.

As the afternoon wore on, one demonstrator after another clambered up to the car's roof, carefully removing their shoes, but so many of them the roof began to sag. They took turns with a mike the police provided to calm the situation. Mario had become the spokesman. His oratory was forceful and colorful and the crowd interrupted with applause, laughing at his jokes. He went on about the deplorable state of Kerr's knowledge industry. Others quoted Aristotle and drew lessons from the French Revolution. Periodically, hecklers who looked like fraternity men hurled insults and challenges from the fringe.

Hungry, I bought a sandwich and a brownie, then it was back to the library. This protest stuff was taking too much time and I wasn't even a protestor! Walking home about nine I fell in with some students who said a deal had been reached and everybody left peacefully, freeing the police car. When I got home Gus was slumped in his chair with a stiff drink. "This, I am pleased to say, is my second in less than an hour."

Akiko looked on, beaming. "Gus was right in the middle of everything, he led the faculty team that solved the problem."

"Don't exaggerate, Akiko. Participated yes, led no. Bought time yes. Solved no."

"The suspended kids'll go before a faculty committee. You see, Kerr needed to tell his bosses he didn't give in. They had three hundred police standing by, Berkeley cops, Oakland cops, Alameda Sheriffs, Highway Patrol, every law enforcement agency in the area. To Kerr's credit, he managed to hold off the assault until he made a deal."

"Hold it off? You mean he didn't send for them? Who did?"

"The details remain unclear, but come on, Sacramento's calling the shots. Yes sir, we really put ourselves on the map with this one."

"If Kerr saved face, what about the demonstrators? What'd they get out of it?"

"Respect, ill-will, everything in between. Waking up people who've never had a political thought in their lives. Time to work out a solution and a process for doing it – maybe." He poured himself another drink. "*Número tres,*" he said, raising his glass.

Next day I learned that like many of the protesters, the guy in the police car, one Jack Weinberg, wasn't a Cal student at all, though he had once been one. He was released and the University agreed not to press charges. By the end of his ordeal Mr. Weinberg had spent thirty-two hours in that police cruiser, no doubt another world record.

25. FREE SPEECH, OR SO THEY SAID

ANOTHER LETTER I DON'T NEED, this one from a lawyer says he represents Paul's ex. Burn before reading, I am thinking. This guy, Roger A. Goodhue, Esq., says his client is entitled to Paul's papers. I say welcome to the club. He cites language in the divorce settlement that gives her "ownership and control of all documents, papers, and memorabilia concerning events occurring during the period of the marriage." This sounds like a stretch but as I read on I come to the real point, "my client's entitlement to all income and profits from the use, sale or other disposition of any and all such property including literary or other media employment thereof." Already I dislike Attorney Goodhue as much as his client.

This means a trip to the market 1.5 miles up the road were I will fax the letter to Cahill, price of the call plus ten cents a page. It isn't the cost – I hate these machines. You'll never see one in my house. Invasion of privacy masquerading as progress, like that irritating little gadget of Jonathan's. I discourage faxing. There is little in life the good old U.S. Mail can't get there in plenty of time.

* * * * * * *

NEARLY LOST IN ABSORBING and self-absorbed Berkeley, the country managed to hold a presidential election. LBJ trounced his Arizona neighbor who won the Deep South and less than ten percent of the electoral vote. Democrats swept Congress as well. People wanted to see what LBJ could accomplish as President in his own right. He still denied any intent to widen the war. As to his predecessor, in September the Warren Commission issued its massive report, finding that Oswald acted alone, which would evoke criticism for years.

On the world scene, Khrushchev was toppled, replaced by Brezhnev. And, more fuel to the fire, China announced it had exploded an atomic bomb. In a dramatic development, unwelcome in many quarters, Martin Luther King was awarded the Nobel Peace Prize.

The protestors had given themselves a name, Free Speech Movement. Clark Kerr's name for its leaders was Reds, and though I supposed most weren't, his remark invited influential right-wingers to weigh in, among them Max Rafferty, the vitriolic Superintendent of Public Instruction and a U.C. Regent, and William Knowland, publisher of the *Oakland Tribune*. Daily rallies, often featuring Joan Baez. Pause for the music, stay for the politics. Sometimes in the thousands, the crowds buoyed the protesters and galled the administration, which let the rallies proceed to keep the peace.

In mid-November the Regents accepted a faculty recommendation to liberalize the rules and drop or reduce charges against the suspended students. Seen as a major victory for the FSM, people began staying away from the rallies, but the Regents had carved out an exception prohibiting "illegal advocacy." This move could split the protestors' ranks since only the civil rights groups employed civil disobedience.

Gus was around the house more, which I took as a good sign. One warm Saturday morning we were outside, he correcting blue books, I reading Wednesday's *Times* and doing my best to ignore the Statistics text on the deck beside me. After a while I noticed he had put down his work and was staring out toward the Bay. This was the quietest I'd ever seen him.

"Something's on your mind," I said.

He sighed. "Trying to figure out the next step. The irony is, if it were up to Kerr we'd already have an agreement, but he's just the meat in the sandwich. I'm afraid our poor liberal stands no chance against extremists of right and left who are out to knock heads, make a mess of everything."

"Figuring they'll be the ones standing at the end," I said. "I'm sounding like a broken record, but let me put in another plug for order. Without it, no teaching, no learning, no Faculty Club, no Big Game, no concerts..."

"But the other values, Paul! The other values! A citizen's right to change the system means nothing if he's denied the tools to do it!"

"The vote isn't enough? Then what was Freedom Summer all about?"

"No, in some situations it's not enough. Too slow, too uncertain. Sometimes you just have to find the beast's most vulnerable spot and attack."

"I take it there are still a lot of omelets to be made."

"You're catching on."

Emboldened, I decided to strike. "Tell me, Gus," I said, "why do these issues matter to you so much? Where does that fire come from?"

A stern look crossed his face then passed. "You know, these days I've been thinking about that a lot. As you said, I helped put some of our students in harm's way last summer and now it's happening again, right here on campus. Not as extreme, of course, but still serious. I feel terrible, the damage it'll do to the University, the disruption, loss of support in Sacramento, but this situation is not amenable to good will, not the way things are going. What's at stake is so important we have to bring it to a head."

"But why is it so important to you, personally?"

"You're a persistent bugger, aren't you?"

I nodded, pleased at a high mark from a tough grader.

"I'll tell you something not many people know. The fire, as you put it, my blessing and my curse, it all has to do with being Irish."

"Irish? How so?"

He was silent a moment. "We were a first generation family, I've told you that, many of the clan still in Ireland, and we stay close. Our neighborhood paper was pro-Republican, anti-British to the core. Parnell, Michael Collins, de Valera – they were my heroes, not ballplayers or movie stars. The pubs were full of talk, angry talk, fueled of course by the occasional pint, and people sent a lot of money back from their meager wages. Businesses, too, the clergy, prominent people. You see, hating the oppressor was our heritage, we drank it in with our mother's milk.

"What does this have to do with American civil rights? To be honest, I was no great friend to the Negro then, nor were the Boston Irish as a whole – in fact we didn't get along all that well. But I finally figured it out. The grandparents and great-grandparents of those Negro kids I saw on my way to school and never said hello to, what those people went through was every bit as bad as what the British did to the Irish. My ancestors were tortured, killed, starved out of their own country. Theirs were kidnapped, families destroyed, exported to a place which despite the humanity of some, was hostile and often deadly. 'As long as any man remains in chains I cannot be free.' I came to believe that. I still do."

"I see," I said.

"No you don't, not until you live through it. Look all you want but you won't see."

Day after Thanksgiving I ran into Mario. I hadn't seen him since he'd become a celebrity. "You're famous, Mario. I'd ask for your autograph but that would be tacky."

"I wouldn't give it to you anyway," he said wearily, "too many in circulation depresses the value. On that, at least, Adam Smith was correct." He swept his hand around the Plaza. "You know, I didn't ask for any of this. My problem is, I like Cal too much. I want it to be better, live up to its ideals."

"As long as you can organize and raise funds."

"Of course. That is non-negotiable."

"Where do you think this is headed?"

"If the administration would keep their word we could settle this in a minute but Kerr keeps changing direction. He is not an honorable man."

A couple of days later we learned that four leaders including Mario had received letters with new disciplinary charges from the police car incident. That afternoon I ran into Gideon going into the library. "Didn't think you had time to study," I said.

"I'm returning overdue books. Tough to do from jail."

"I hear there's a sit-in in the works." The campus was abuzz with rumors that the FSM leadership, of which Gideon was part, was planning a massive occupation of Sproul Hall. I'd also heard Kerr would have no choice but to use force, passing on the heat from the Regents and the Governor.

Gideon nodded. "You hear correctly. How petty these people are, how incredibly dumb. The naughty children must be taught a lesson. Well, this particular lesson is going to cost them dearly."

"Why not just keep negotiating? If you make a deal, amnesty'll be part of it."

He shook his head. "They don't want a deal, they want to show who's boss, but you see, that plays right into our hands. They are so out of touch, they don't realize the power of a sit-in. Let them bring in the cops. If heads get cracked so much the better. Every broken skull is ten converts. Maybe a hundred."

"That is one sick attitude, Gideon."

"Is it? From the sidelines how would you know?"

"An observer has the advantage of seeing both sides, all sides."

"Damnit, Paul! For once take a stand! This isn't some lab experiment, it's war! There are times you have to put down your pretense."

I felt myself getting hot. "It's no pretense, Gideon. When the time is right, for the right reason, I am perfectly capable of committing myself." He had hit a nerve but I wasn't about to back down. "Whatever your grievances are, Cal is not Mississippi." In an odd way it thrilled me that my friend had such fortitude, wrongheaded though he was. "This time I can't wish you luck, but I hope you get out of it in one piece."

"That is no longer a concern," he said, turning and walking away.

Wednesday, December 2, cool and with a bright noonday sun, after others had their say, Mario began to speak. Standing on the Student Union steps I couldn't make out every word but from published accounts, this is what my eloquent, intemperate friend said.

> "I ask you to consider: if this is a firm, and if the board of regents are the board of directors, and if President Kerr in fact is the manager, then I tell you something – the faculty are a bunch of employees! And we're the raw material! But we're a bunch of raw materials that don't mean to have any process upon us, don't mean to be made into any product, don't mean to end up being bought by some clients of the university, be they the government, be they industry, be they organized labor, be they anyone! We're human beings!"

To wild cheers, he went on.

> "There's a time when the operation of the machine becomes so odious, makes you so sick at heart, that you can't take part, you can't even passively take part, and you've got to put your bodies upon the gears and upon the wheels, upon the levers, upon all the apparatus, and you've got to make it stop! And you've got to indicate to the people who run it, to the people who own it, that unless you're free, the machine will be prevented from working at all!"

Joan Baez then stepped to the microphone, and more than a thousand students and supporters trooped resolutely into Sproul Hall behind an American flag, singing. We Shall Overcome. Singers and songs... Socrates had it right.

As I watched from across the way, it angered me, these people setting their own interests above those of us who are here for an education. Civil rights, yes, but there has to be a better way. So what if the large lecture classes aren't quite up to par? If the red tape and lines are maddening? Where is it written that everything has to be perfect? Fracturing the University won't set things right. It was discouraging, watching discourse and civility abandoned. Orderly they might be now, but a crowd is but a short step from a mob and no better than the beast, in Gus' terms, that provokes them.

The FSM held the cards but the administration didn't seem to notice. Now there'll be a whole new set of issues and a new dynamic. That is the way of the radical, I was learning. Create an intolerable situation, provoke a violent reaction, suck in the uncommitted. My guess, most of those filing into Sproul wanted most to show they could risk something of value for a cause. I trespass, therefore I am.

As I watched, a Maritain phrase came to mind. "Prophetic shock-minorities." The inspired few who show the masses a better way to right intolerable wrongs. Gideon and Mario, the FSM leadership – do they pass Maritain's test? No, I thought, their problems don't justify lawbreaking and violence. What of Reverend King and the civil rights leaders? Freedom Summer? There, I'd say yes. Their goals are supremely important, their adversaries the real offenders. Again I realized, when events swirl about you, it's not easy telling a true prophet from a false one.

In class the next day I learned that around three in the morning Chancellor Strong warned the occupying students to leave or they would be arrested. When he said "the purpose and work of the University have been materially impaired," a huge cheer went up. An Assistant D.A. advised Governor Brown to make arrests, based on a report of students trashing former President Sproul's office. The report was later shown to be false, but the hard line sent Edwin Meese III on his way. He would rise to Assistant to the next Governor of California, then U.S. Attorney General when that Governor, Ronald Reagan, became President.

The arrests took over twelve hours, those choosing to go limp being unceremoniously dragged down the stone steps, more like bounced, from what I saw on TV. Seven hundred seventy-three arrests, another new State record. Instead of waiting for the inevitable call I called home to let them know I was okay. "I'm sure you weren't in that crowd," were my mother's first words. "You can have principles without breaking the law."

"I've always thought so." I closed my eyes. "You trained me well."

"What is wrong with those people? I'd be surprised if you knew any of them."

I laughed out loud. "*You* know one of them and very well, too. The name Benny Kaplan ring a bell?"

There was a pause on the line. "That's right, Benny is out there... you mean he's involved in that awful stuff?"

"Up to his eyeballs." One of my Hillel friends told me Benny and Leah gone into the building. I'd have been surprised if they hadn't. "And they have a point, though I totally disagree how they're going about it."

"Well, I should hope you do."

"How's Dad?"

"He's amazing, every day he gets stronger. He's out at a meeting, if you can believe it. They're getting closer on the sale."

"Tell him I said hello."

Now Gus really did disappear. He went to Santa Rita prison to supervise. He conferred with faculty sympathetic to the students' cause. A newly established Graduate Coordinating Council had set up picket lines and called a general strike. Appalled at police violation of the academic sanctuary, many professors and TAs cancelled classes. My Statistics class was cancelled (no great loss, there) and I arrived at International Econ to find a note from the TA taped to the door. Many believed the administration's ineptitude and mean-spiritedness had lost it respect. People were looking to the faculty to fill the "vacuum of moral authority." Akiko told me Gus cancelled all his classes to work on a proposal.

Five days later I witnessed an amazing performance. The Greek Theater was packed for an "extraordinary convocation" called by President Kerr to try and regain the initiative. Gus was on stage in the second row. Down front in the audience were Mario and a number of FSM leaders. True to form, Kerr was even-tempered, but his comments came across as sarcastic and demeaning. Professor Scalapino, my Department Chairman, then outlined a proposal different from the one Gus and his group had put together. As he was concluding, I noticed Mario on his feet, edging toward the stage. As soon as the meeting was declared adjourned, he made a beeline for the mike. A cry spread through the audience. "We Want Mario! We Want Mario!" Suddenly two campus policemen tackled Mario and started to drag him away, pulling his jacket up around his ears. After frantic consultations he was released and led back to the podium, where he announced, simply, that the FSM was holding a rally that noon in the Plaza. Then he left. Smart guy, knowing when to stop.

The next month was stressful. Ignored by Kerr, Gus' group decided to circulate their proposal directly to the faculty. Within hours the whole campus knew about it and it took hold. In a dramatic evening meeting, the proposal was overwhelmingly endorsed by the Academic Senate and, after wavering, accepted by Kerr. The Regents named well-liked Martin Meyerson, Dean of the College of Environmental Design, to replace Chancellor Strong, who was bitter at what he saw as callous treatment by Clark Kerr. Acting Chancellor Meyerson adopted provisional rules that essentially embodied the FSM's agenda, and later in the year the Regents made them permanent. As for advocacy, the new rules provided there would be no regulation of the content of speech, only its "time, place and manner." And, amazingly, tables would be permitted not just at the famous strip of land, which was still on-campus or off-campus depending on who you talked to, but right there on the Plaza itself!

I'd been wondering whether Benny knew about my run-in with Gideon, so I called him and we agreed to meet. Leah was with him. "I can only stay a minute," she said, "but I want to see how you were doing. Rachel says hello, she hasn't heard from you."

"Yeah, well, that's how it goes," I said. "I've been pretty busy." I made a mental note to think about calling Rachel. "You must feel good how things went," I told Benny. This was my way of showing support as a friend but as far as I would go.

"It was a good win," Benny replied. "You cannot believe the sense of community we had in that building – it was like Mississippi all over again. We still have to go through the legal bullshit but our attorney says it'll be a slap on the wrist at the most."

Leah nodded. "I was worried we'd be suspended like for a semester."

"Gideon's okay?" I asked.

"Yeah. Excellent." Benny gave no hint he knew about Gideon and me.

Leah stood and gathered her books. "Got to go. Bye, you people." As she took her leave Benny and I went in to buy coffees to fend off the late afternoon chill.

"Were your parents worried you'd been arrested?" Benny asked.

"Not really, but I called them just in case."

Bennie sighed. "Well, old friend, maybe one day you'll see things our way. As a part-time liberal I'm trying to respect your view."

"How about your father?"

"My phone bill's going to be huge."

We sat for a while, gazing out over the calm scene. A few tables in their new locations, fewer than when I had walked through a half-hour earlier. The raw afternoon was draining political enthusiasm. "So what follows your glorious victory?"

"You can't guess?"

"If I could I wouldn't have asked."

"We have a war to stop, of course."

"To *stop?* We have a war to *win!* What kind of American are you, anyway?"

"A patriotic one, I trust." Benny shook his head wearily. "Here we go again."

CHRISTMAS NINETEEN SIXTY-FOUR. For the first time I would spend the holidays apart from my family, same for next summer. I was looking forward to an undisturbed time to work when I received the call. My mother would be out for a visit, and not just her, but Catherine and her boyfriend, and oh, if I know a nice hotel would I make reservations for them?

That explains how I came to be pulling into the parking lot at San Francisco International Airport and heading for the TWA terminal. I gave my mother a big hug, then one for Catherine and a hello for Tom whom I had met only briefly. He was tall and skinny, with a wispy moustache and a flaccid handshake. Hard to understand, but I figured he must have something going, for there on Catherine's ring finger was the big diamond. Entomology studies must pay better than Political Science, I grumbled to myself. We piled into the Plymouth, suitcases in the back seat squeezing the happy couple together.

"Just like old times," my mother said as we drove along. "What a wonderful car this was."

"Still is," I replied.

"What's that banging?" Catherine asked.

Leave it to her to notice. "It's going in for service soon," I exaggerated.

"I hope so," my mother said. "It'd be a shame for it to leave the family."

Crossing the Bay we shot up Ashby Avenue then turned left. "What in the world?" Catherine remarked. "Tennis in December?"

Stopped for a light next to the Berkeley Tennis Club we saw people hitting the ball, others watching from a small grandstand. I had taken Stephanie Rogers to a match there, Rosewall versus Laver, finals of a big tournament, very exciting.

"They do things all year round out here," I replied. It was a beautiful Berkeley winter day, sunny, in the low sixties.

We drove up a sloping road to the Claremont Hotel. "My, this is grand," my mother said, admiring the sprawling building with its majestic turrets and porches. "It reminds me of the Mount Washington. Did you know your father and I spent our honeymoon there?"

"This is a real resort, they have a pool, a spa, the whole works."

"Dare I ask how much it costs?"

"It's under the figure you gave me."

"How is that possible?"

"Well, it's kind of run down... but a real bargain if you don't look too close."

"You mean it's dirty?" Catherine asked.

"More like old and tired."

"Like me," Mother said.

"Never! You'll always be thirty." She wrinkled her nose. "Well, maybe thirty-five," I corrected myself.

Tom and I hauled the suitcases from the car. Seeing him toss them around I decided he wasn't weak, more like wiry. "It was either this or the Durant," I told my mother, "but that's really stuffy. Here you can walk around, see flowers, that sort of thing."

After dinner at Spengers in lower Berkeley, best seafood around, my mother and I were sitting in the hotel cocktail lounge, another one of those grand views. Catherine and Tom had borrowed the Plymouth to check out the City. Mother looked tired from the long trip. "They'll be out late," I said. "Won't Catherine wake you up when she comes in?"

She smiled at me. "And I thought you were the liberated one."

"What do you mean?"

"I have my room. Catherine and Tom have the other one."

I reddened. "I didn't mean to sound like a prude – I just didn't know. And that's all right with you?"

"Well they're engaged," she looked out the window a long moment. "It's not like I can do much about it. She's an adult, after all."

"Do you like Tom?"

She paused for a moment. "He grows on you. He's actually very sweet."

"What about Dad?"

"Nobody is good enough for his little girl."

"Have they set a date?"

"Probably late next year. He wants to finish his studies first. He's interviewing for jobs now, something in research."

We ordered a second drink, kahlua and vodka on ice that my mother really liked. She had already told me my father had graduated to a cane and had almost full use of his arm and hand, though he'd be working with a speech therapist for some time. "So how's the sale going?" I asked.

"Everything takes longer than you'd like but your father is optimistic. With this war business, companies like his are valuable again. He thinks it'll bring a lot of money."

"How much?" I asked. "A million?"

She smiled and shook her head.

"Five?"

"They say between five and ten."

I sat back in my chair. "That's amazing. That'll set you and Dad for life."

"It'll be yours after we're gone."

"Don't talk that way."

She took a big sip. "If you hadn't noticed, nobody lives forever."

"But you're healthy and he's doing better. We want long life for you."

"We're thinking if things go well, we could make a gift to the three of you sooner than later, help you get started in good style."

I had to admit it had crossed my mind, though this was way bigger than I had suspected. "That'd be nice, but I'm getting along fine."

"For a rainy day, if nothing else." She reached into her purse, "here," she said, shoving a bill into my hand. "This is for the use of your car. Take a cab back to your place. I'm going to bed before I fall asleep in front of you."

"If you insist."

"I'm looking forward to seeing your place tomorrow."

"I'll be sure my room is picked up."

"And the bed made?"

"Of course."

"You're such a good son," she said, stepping into the elevator.

The next three days I played tour guide. It poured the day I had the wineries scheduled so we got tickets to a Nutcracker matinee at the Civic Auditorium. At first I was irritated at my lost study time but decided to relax and ended up enjoying the break. My room, "small but neat," passed inspection.

Mother and Gus got along famously, swapping stories about the auld sod, the transplanted Irish. I was surprised to see Catherine, engagement ring and all, playing up to Lieutenant Mark. He was an strapping, outdoors kind of guy, a varsity athlete at "Sac State," in short, everything Tom the bug man was not. I liked Mark, not least because he shared my disdain for the FSM. "Spoiled brats, never wanted for anything in their lives. Don't know how good they've got it."

It was a teary farewell at the airport. "Look at me," my mother said, "I'm acting the fool." My eyes were moist too, in fact the only dry eyes were Tom's.

"I'll be back for a visit this summer."

"I'll hold you to that," she said as she turned to board the plane. "I'm happy to see you doing so well, among such good people."

"Say hi to Dad," I said. She nodded and waved.

AFTER MY TIME OFF I was a real whirlwind. My last semester of German – by now I could read research materials, though carrying on a conversation was a stretch. Statistics and I plodded along. It was every bit as bad as I'd expected and my attitude didn't help. I'd be lucky to pull a B, though I was getting a feel for the concepts. I figured if I ever needed statistical work I'd hire somebody.

The real fun came in Integrated Social Science. Burdick was a larger-than-life, Hemingway-esque presence. In bull sessions at the Bear's Lair, it was fun hearing about Hollywood and his celebrity friends. His heroes were rough and independent, "ugly" characters who outwitted bureaucrats and politicians then got swamped by the backlash of petty revenge. These conversations gave me a lifelong distrust for people who reject common-sense solutions out of hand. What is the hidden agenda, I learned to ask – who stands to gain? A useful framework for approaching the world, as it turned out.

Meantime I continued preparing for my first comprehensive exam, set for April. A weekly session with Don, reading and more reading, so much reading I was beginning to think I'd better have my eyes checked.

I fell so far behind in the Asian Lit course I quit trying to keep up, but by my bed I kept my well-worn haiku anthology and a book on Zen koans, dipping into them when I needed a break from serious activities. Not that the sound of one hand clapping isn't serious, perhaps I should say, my more purposeful activities. I vowed that someday I would return to my notes and reading list. From time to time Akiko and I talked about Zen and once I dared toss her a koan of my own construction.

"A student once asked his master, how do I attain enlightenment?'

She was quiet a moment, then stepped to the stove and picked up a pan of water that had just begun to boil, went to the sink and poured it all out. I stood there waiting for her answer, finally realizing she'd just given it. Nothing at all like my prepared reply. She laughed. "It pleases me you are interested in these things, but you are too logical, too cerebral."

"Don't you realize how much Catholic education I've had, Jesuits included?"

She shook her head. "The koan is a useful antidote to such rigid training. It is not rational, neither is it irrational. Vivid, concrete insights, they shock the mind into awareness more than a thousand explanations can."

I brought up the Beats, Kerouac, Snyder, Ginsberg. Were their koans and haiku a good thing or a bad thing? I knew her answer. Once I showed her my *Dharma Bums* and she left the room, returning with her own copy. "Whatever exposes Zen I favor, even in the hands of those who are not masters. Buddhism is, above all, approachable. Compared with the Catholic religion it is natural, there are no miracles, no secret rites. Each haiku, each koan must stand on its own. To generalize is not possible."

IN MARCH MY FATHER CALLED to tell me the business had been sold. Nu-Gem, a large Providence jewelry maker, was the buyer, one of his best customers. They wanted to make their own tools and dies in-house while expanding into a profitable second business line. "Guess how much we got for it," he said, slurring his words but not as bad.

"Just tell me."

"Three point five million!"

"That's great." But I thought, that's less than they were expecting. "We were hoping for more," he added, "but they wouldn't assume our loans so that had to come out of the proceeds."

"It's a great result. Now take some time off, go on a nice cruise or something."

"Your mother's always wanted to see Hawaii, maybe we'll do that when we wrap everything up."

"You can stop here and see Berkeley."

"That would be part of it. Absolutely."

He'd be staying on as a consultant to the new owners and was pleased he was able to extract a promise to keep the workforce together. "Some of these people, they spent their whole lives at Bernard Bros. Tool & Die. We had a higher offer from that Indiana outfit but I want to keep it local. I owed it to the community, how they stuck with us in the hard times."

"I'm proud of you, but I hope you're not pushing too hard."

"Never felt better in my life. I'm still not talking so good but they say that's a matter of time. Now let me tell you what this means for you." He paused. "Not much at first, I'm afraid. There's some cash coming our way but mostly we get Nu-Gem stock. It's better for taxes and if they continue to do well, it'll turn out great. We're working on a plan to spread some of it around to you kids."

I laughed. "I'm going to own a jewelry company, you're telling me?"

"You and a lot of others. Eventually you'll be able to sell the stock and make something on it."

"So my vow of poverty is out the window."

"You'll have to find some other way to make your point."

I remember the date of that conversation because that was the day the storm broke over the second FSM – the "Filthy Speech Movement," if you can believe it. Some idiot freshman parked himself on Sproul steps with a sign saying FUCK in big letters. He was arrested and charged with public obscenity. Some of the protest crowd tried to make it into a free speech issue and maybe it was, but to me it looked like a mindless effort to keep the pot boiling. Some Regents took notice, further embarrassing the Kerr administration.

BENNY'S WAR PROTEST became a fact, and Gus was in the thick of it. The August before, he was one of group of faculty signing a protest against the Gulf of Tonkin Resolution. In February, LBJ ordered bombing raids on the North as reprisals for a Vietcong attack on a military barracks at Pleiku. One night we were talking about the bombing.

"Theatrics," Gus said. "Bombing looks powerful as hell and it's seductive. People think it's a painless way to conduct foreign policy, a panacea. Just ask the Air Force, they'll be more than happy to tell you. Trouble with that line of argument, so-called strategic bombing doesn't solve a damn thing, in fact it's far overrated – history shows that. Look at Britain. Germany's war production actually increased after months of us blasting them. What you need to do is put bodies on the ground, a lot of bodies, and that is politically unpopular."

"Has Johnson trapped himself?" I asked. "After all, he got elected on a pledge of no Americans in Asia."

"Trapped? Only if you think he's a man of his word which he is not. If he sees his way clear politically, I don't put it past him to do just that." Sure enough, a month later three thousand Marines were landed in Danang to protect our airbase there. "I better start a tally sheet – the number's only going higher."

"Do you have a better answer?"

"I don't need a better answer. We shouldn't be there at all."

"You'd wait to draw the line until they're right on us? That's no good."

Gus waved me off. "That damn domino argument is no better now than when Foster Dulles first trotted it out. Come on, Paul, this is a war for national independence. These people destroyed the French, now it's going to be us in the barrel."

"But Communist China is backing the North."

"The enemy of my enemy is my friend? Sorry, but slogans just don't cut it. Those two countries have been at each other's throats for centuries. Just because the North has a Communist-type government doesn't mean China's about to invade Long Beach anytime soon. Supplies, assistance, sure, but helping a neighbor is one thing, taking on a great power quite another."

In March, the University of Michigan sponsored a "teach-in," a one-day event supposedly for students to study the war and the issues, and several other universities followed suit quickly. In April, SDS held a demonstration in Washington that drew a surprising 20,000. The next month a national teach-in on Vietnam was convened by phone from Washington and beamed to over a hundred campuses.

A week later "Vietnam Day" dawned in Berkeley, billed as thirty-six hours of speeches, songs and theater, an academic/political event. I dropped by Harmon Gym, thinking I might learn something. Outside, the Mime Troup performed. I spotted Rachel but didn't approach her. I missed Gus' speech, but somebody told me he drew a parallel between the civil rights movement and war opposition. I didn't see the connection. When people are denied their rights, sure, you object. But when the security of our country is at stake you support our leaders and trust them to do the right thing. I didn't buy Gus' low opinion of Johnson. Let him work through it, don't make his job harder than it already is.

The anti-American rhetoric flying around galled me – calls for revolutionary change, for rejecting our history, our way of life. Some of the speakers were against America more than the war. One I took particular exception to, someone named Paul Potter, from SDS.

> "What kind of a system is it that justifies the U.S. in seizing the destinies of other people and using them callously for our own ends? We must name that system and we must change it and control it, else it will destroy us."

My patience was wearing thin. Who is behind this one-sided farce? Who stands to gain? What exactly is that name Paul Potter is so careful not to pronounce? Democracy? Capitalism? Why so coy, Paul Potter, show us what if anything is in your head.

In a few short months, the Berkeley dissidents have left free speech, education and civil rights behind. The people pulling the strings have decreed Vietnam is the issue *du jour*. Benny was prescient, all right, either that or his crowd was controlling it from the start.

The more I listened, the madder I got. This "teach-in" wasn't about insights, it was for ridiculing our government. "Amerika" my ass! They're trying to undermine a nation that's so tolerant it guarantees even its enemies their say. This isn't about redressing mistakes, it's about some fundamental evil so terrible it can't even be named. It surely isn't about giving credit to the men who have died, who are still dying, to preserve the rights these people abuse. What I saw on the late news really sickened me, a march to the Berkeley draft board where they hung Lyndon Johnson in effigy and burned their draft cards. And who was out front? Young Socialist Alliance, a Trotskyite organization, no friend of our country's. Unbelievable. We're in Vietnam to prevent the spread of Communism and here it is in action, right before our eyes.

Two days later I sat for my Comprehensive Exam in Political Philosophy. I felt confident working through the three hours and was sure I had done well. A couple of weeks later, Don called to congratulate me. I had passed with high honors, Departmental letter to follow. One down, two to go. Despite the gathering chaos, for me the '64 - '65 school year had been most productive.

The previous year, I missed Gus and Akiko's traditional year-end party but this year I made sure I was around. It was the first time I'd have a chance to talk at length with Gideon since the sit-in and its aftermath.

"You disappointed me," he said over a glass of wine, "a no-show again."

"Sorry about that," I replied. "But I have to hand it to you, you showed up the administration. Your tactics really worked."

"One dumb mistake after another – they made it easy for us."

"They deserved what they got, so did you," I said putting my hand on his arm, a peace offering to my friend. But something else was on my mind. "Remember that rally after the Academic Senate vote, when it was clear you had won? Mario said something along the lines that now students have the right of free speech, they have to use it responsibly."

Gideon nodded.

"And he said he believed they would. Answer me this, how does that square with what I heard at Vietnam Day? That was the most one-sided bullshit I've ever heard."

"Aside from the fact nobody showed up to defend the government?"

"The deck was totally stacked. No way there could have been a fair debate."

"In a contest of ideas you've got to be willing to compete."

I shook my head. "That was not a good start for responsible free speech."

Benny and I visited, talking mostly about old times. He was interested to hear about the business and that I'd be coming into some money. "I always suspected you of latent capitalist tendencies," he said.

"You know what they say, rich or poor, it's good to have money."

"That has a nice ring to it. Groucho?"

"I have no idea."

During the party Mark came up to me with an intriguing proposition. He was putting together a hike in the High Sierra – how would I like to participate? Hamid had already signed on. On the trail a week, pack everything in, cook our own food, sleeping bags, the works. Thinking of *Dharma Bums* and good times in the mountains, I jumped at the chance. I didn't know how it would impact my summer research but frankly, I didn't care. After the year I'd had, I needed a break.

26. AN UNNATURAL HISTORY OF THE HIGH SIERRA

"HAVE YOU NOTICED THE CHANGE IN PAUL?"

Jonathan nods. "He seems to be moving to the right."

"I thought you'd say that, but it's not that simple. What I'd say, events brought out a conservatism that was always there. He couldn't abide the activist tactics and as you saw, we disagreed about Vietnam."

"Sounds like you nearly came to blows. Over the protests, the war."

"Oh, no, we always respected each other. Remember, Berkeley was a wake-up call for my young friend."

"But that talk about omelets?"

"Friendly sparring, nothing more."

"I suppose. Anyway, he was able to worm something out of you I wanted to know – where that passion for causes came from."

"Paul was persistent, even in those days. His mother, too – she had a lot of spirit. You can see where he got his feistiness."

"And here you are, a military man against the war. How do you explain that?"

"Well, there are military men and there are military men, just like there are wars and wars. First of all, I am not a pacifist, never was. Don't have the patience or I guess the courage of a Doctor King. If somebody's beating on my friend or my country I'm going to be there – hell, I *was* there! I wasn't drafted, I enlisted. You can argue FDR pushed Japan into the Second War but they were well on their way already. Vietnam, now that was totally different."

"You don't see a parallel between the two?"

"Only that both times too many people died. Otherwise, no, none at all. FDR was no paragon of candor but LBJ took the art of deception to new heights. The only way to straighten him out was in the streets. A healthy democracy emboldens people to be critical and gives them the tools to do it – to that extent Maritain had a point. The leaders hate it, of course, but there's always the chance they'll learn something. When you see a government claiming to be a democracy squelch dissent in the name of security or anything else, that is a nation that on the wrong side of the hill. The test is, does it bounce back and correct course. I like to think we will, though it's disconcerting how we keep losing our grip. It's a very good question why George Bush gets away with so much."

"What's your answer?"

"We're not the same country we used to be. We've changed, and not for the better. We'll get into that later."

"I was wondering, did coming into that money change Paul?"

"I don't think so. At the time I didn't even know it happened."

Just then the phone rings. It is Susan from New York. The other shoe has dropped. They received another letter from Latimer, high-level this time. "My boss, he kind of hit the roof when I told him what I did with the papers. What's your fax number?"

"I don't have one," I sigh. "There's a place up the road you could send it to."

"Is it secure?"

It's a mom and pop market, more soap than security. "I'll let them know it's coming." I give her the number. "Write confidential on top. Might help, might not."

"I shouldn't be doing this," she says, "but you need to know what's going on. I'm in so much trouble a little more won't matter."

The letter is on Latimer letterhead, from Senior Vice President and General Counsel Joel I. Shapiro, Esq. Joel I. Shapiro, Esq. says blah-blah-blah the papers are LTN's property and blah-blah-blah they will take legal action unless they're delivered to his office forthwith, meaning 5 p.m. next Friday. He ends the letter "Sincerely." I'm impressed. I figure it's time to clue Jonathan in so I show it to him and explain what has transpired. I tell him about Paul's wife, too. You should have told me before, he yells. You've got enough on your mind, I yell back. Why bring you in until I know it's a problem? Now it's a problem.

"Damnit, Gus! We've got to get down there right away."

"Calm down, Jonathan, our lawyers say Latimer doesn't have a leg to stand on."

"But I've got to see this material! We can't let them get it!"

"They won't," I sigh. Though I agree, it's time to get serious about New York.

* * * * * * *

FRIDAY MORNING, MARK AND I MADE OUR WAY to the Army-Navy store on San Pablo Avenue. When I asked what was on his list he smiled. "I am fully outfitted, courtesy of Uncle Sam. Didn't cost me a dime."

Ninety minutes later we piled my three bags into his Pontiac wagon. I'd been careful, but dropped forty bucks for leather boots with serious soles. Footwear is number one, Mark said – skimp there, you'll ruin the trip for yourself and everybody else. Paying for my purchases was only the start. How would I fit it in my pack? How would I carry it all? Mark shrugged. "If you want to see a real pack, join the Army."

Back up University Ave we met Hamid at the North Face. With Alpine summers and school trips to the Scottish Highlands, he was almost set. I knew North Face was top of the line, but forty-five dollars for a windshirt? Fifty for sunglasses? Watching Hamid plunk down a crisp hundred, Mark rolled his eyes. "The boy is in a different world." Hamid had told me Iran has very tall mountains, up to nearly six thousand meters (eighteen thousand feet) and he'd climbed most of them. We handled our food needs at the Coop Market. Near Yosemite we'd pick up fresh stuff for the first couple of days, the rest of the week we'd live off the dried. As we lugged our supplies into the house, I noticed Gus hanging around, watching. "What would you think about taking Monty along? He'd have a great time."

Mark shook his head. "He wouldn't. The rocks would do a number on his paws."

As the novice I'd have my hands full without looking after a high-strung animal. Seeing his disappointment I said, "How about if we walk him more when we get back?"

Next morning we were threading our way south on I-580, then the sweep east through the farms and suburbs of the San Joaquin Valley. This side of Manteca we picked up SR120 and three hours later rolled into Oakdale, the last sizable town before Yosemite. Hamid and I paid for the fillup and we shopped for steaks and sandwiches, packing them with ice into insulated bags. The first night we'd spend in a motel and be on the trail early. Mark and I agreed to share a room to keep the cost down. Hamid opted for a single.

An expert map reader, Mark had us each carry a map and trail guide. We leaned over the table as he tapped the map at a little patch of blue. "Vogelsang Peak tomorrow, then we return to Bernice Lake," his finger moved to a smaller blue spot. "We'll make base camp there."

"*Vogelsang* is birdsong," I offered. Two years of German, I finally had something to show for it.

Next morning we found ourselves on an easy trail beside a tributary of the Tuolumne River. Tracking Rafferty Creek we encountered cobblestones, then granite steps so tall I had to hoist myself up and swing my legs over. After fifteen minutes I was sweating profusely and my heart pounded. Another fifteen, a severe aching in my lungs set in and I fought for breath in the thinning air. Mark, in the lead, looked back. "You doing all right?"

"Great," I said between gasps.

"Relax, you're not having a heart attack. That tightness in your chest, it's perfectly normal first hour of the first day. Second and third days, too. Best thing is just keep going, though we can slow the pace if you want."

"I'm fine," I huffed. "Your interest in my welfare is appreciated."

I looked behind at Hamid, motoring steadily uphill, no strain, no pain... the kid's a machine. Mark had stopped and put his pack down, was pulling his sweater off over his head. "Have a good slug of water while you're at it. Don't wait til you're thirsty, you never can get enough water. How's your pack? Shoes?"

"Everything's good," I said, downing a long drink of water from my new canteen. Hamid leaned on his pack against a tree. Mark looked at his watch, one of those thick deals with sixteen buttons and dials. "The worst is behind us," he said, unfolding his map. "See these contour lines?" He pointed to a set of light brown concentric circles. "Close together means a big change of elevation. We just did this steep part here," he said, tapping a stretch that looked solid brown to me.

As we gained altitude the aspens gave way to conifers. Patches of snow became larger and more frequent, gleaming through the trees and brush beside the trail. I saw an occasional blasted trunk, though no areas of burnt trees yet. Fires from lightning were an issue here. In the distance a line of snow-capped peaks marched along – the Cathedral Range, eastern boundary of the Sierra with a steep drop-off to the arid country beyond. With my map, I ticked off Parsons Peak, Simmons Peak, Mt. Florence, and far in the distance the tallest of all, Mt. Lyell.

"Most of those are only a day hike away," Mark commented, "ten, twelve thousand footers. If they don't look that impressive it's because we're at ten thousand feet ourselves."

I shook my head. "They look plenty impressive."

In half an hour we came to Toulumne Pass and stopped again. A few minutes later the Vogelsang High Sierra Camp came into sight, a solid, comfortable shelter, the hulk of Fletcher Peak looming behind it. I remembered Pat saying the Appalachian Mountain Club ran camps like this in the White Mountains, "huts" they're called there. We cut down a path to Vogelsang Lake, deep blue backdropped by a steep, bare hillside. My legs were tired and I was relieved to see the shore where we'd stay the night.

After we finished setting up camp, Mark brought out a small metal rack, setting each corner on a rock, then squirted white gas on the sticks and branches underneath and carefully threw a match in. Adding larger branches, we placed foil-wrapped potatoes and corn in the blaze, broke out the ribeyes, dusted them with salt and pepper and placed them on the metal rack. Five on a side and they were done. A glass of wine would have gone well, but nobody wanted to pack the weight so we made do with water, and after dinner, boiled coffee strained through cheesecloth. A Coop brownie completed the feast. We could see fires from nearby campsites but were too tired for sociability, at least I was. Mark broke out his half-pint of Jim Beam and offered it to me but I declined. Hamid pulled out a thin sliver flask I had noticed before, unscrewed the top, offered it around and took a long swig. "Cognac," he said, "Rémy Martin."

"Nothing but the best," Mark observed, glancing at me.

I took a last sip of coffee and tossed the dregs on the ground. Time to turn in.

Next thing I knew I was listening in on an animated bird conversation. Lifting my head from my sweater-pillow I saw I was alone in the tent. I fished around for my watch... six thirty-five. Easing out of the bag, I pulled on my jeans and pulled the flap back. The area was suffused with a subtle glow. I smelled pine needles... and coffee! Mark was standing over the gas stove. At the edge of the clearing, Hamid was brushing his teeth. The air was crisp and cool. In the east, pale blue with streaks of orange rested on the hill above our camp. I stretched my arms as far as I could, leaning back to glimpse the fog in the treetops. How lucky to be alive and in this place! I smelled bacon frying and saw Mark opening the egg carton we had secured carefully to his pack frame. Soon there was a friendly spattering in the pan and chunks of bread were toasting over the fire.

An hour later our bags were rolled, the tent down and folded. We laid out our lightweight nylon packs and filled them with the day's essentials – hat, sweater, windshirt, and a coil of heavy gold rope Mark tied to his pack "just in case." We hung our big packs from the limb of a tree at the lake's edge to discourage bears and other critters. Mark began to walk away from the camp, looking around. "Over here!" he shouted, "this'll take us where we want to go," he said, pointing to a trail marker. VOGELSANG PEAK - SUMMIT 2.4 MILES. He looked at his watch. "Eight thirty, a good start. This climb isn't difficult but you want to allow enough time. It's a matter of respecting the mountain, which is another way of saying use your head."

We entered a meadow dazzling with wildflowers. With our light packs we were flying. Butterflies flopped lazily across the trail, yellow ones, pale green, white. I resolved to learn more about wildflowers and butterflies when I got back, though I knew I probably wouldn't. We wound through a stand of pines, and as we emerged the trail began to rise noticeably. I looked up at the towering mountain, a giant mound of granite with two peaks, rounded one to the right and a knife-edge ridge over to the pointed summit we'd seen from a distance. Never before had I climbed a mountain, and faced with the majesty of Vogelsang I wondered if this was the one to start with. "You sure we can make it across there?" I asked, pointing to the ridge.

Mark nodded. "We won't do anything too stupid."

We had reached a rock shelf – whitish-gray rocks, ledges and boulders either side, granite with dark-seamed volcanic deposits. Looking ahead, some of the rocks glistened in the sun, wet from the melting snow, rivulets ran everywhere and the footing was tricky. Larger patches of white appeared and a couple of times we traversed snow-filled gullies. I was thankful for my new boots, though they were a bit stiff. We were following a well-tended path with rock cairns and an occasional signpost. The late morning sun beat on my shoulders and my wide-brimmed Aussie hat. The trail steepened, and ahead, between us and the rounded summit I spied a wall of columns twenty or so feet tall, separated by vertical crevasses. "We'll go around that – right?" I shouted to Mark.

He stopped. "'Fraid not. Better brush off your tree climbing skills."

What tree-climbing skills, I thought, wincing.

"No sweat," Mark said. "You've done this thing before, Hamid?"

"Many times," he said, "the Alps are full of pitches like this."

Mark grabbed the top of a tall rock then put his boot into a waist-high niche and pulled himself up. Thrice more he did this, then he was standing on the rock shelf about ten feet up. He made his way over to a crevasse maybe three feet wide, kind of like a chimney, and shinnied up it, his feet and arms pressed tight to the sides, easing his way, extending his hands and grabbing with his fingers. In a few minutes he was on top of the outcropping. "The trail continues here," he grinned, looking down at us. "Just a matter of getting to it."

My turn. I hauled myself up the tall rocks with no trouble but in the chimney my feet kept slipping. I was just getting the hang of it, bracing myself in a solid position between the vertical sides when my head popped into the open and I hoisted myself over the lip and clambered to my feet. "Good job," Mark said.

Almost instantly Hamid was beside us. "The guy's a mountain goat," Mark said.

Hamid smiled. "Some fathers make their sons play soccer. We climbed."

About an hour more we attained the first peak which I would have thought a false summit but for seeing the contour from below. In our descent from the peak the path leveled off, the mountain falling away steeply on both sides. Close up, that intimidating knife-edge ridge turned out to be a path half a dozen feet wide though narrower in spots. On the ridge we encountered a stiff wind which made short work of the sweat I earned in the climb. Forty-five minutes later we closed in on the summit, scrambling over loose rock – "scree" – and winding through a field of small boulders. VOGELSANG PEAK - YOSEMITE NATIONAL PARK - 11,516 FEET.

After banging our canteens together, Mark pulled out a little camera and I set to work with my Leica. One of the shots is a great treasure of mine, the three of us next to the summit marker. In fact I'm looking at it on my desk right now. I say the three of us because another group of climbers showed up and everybody took pictures of everybody else. Then we descended out of the wind which was really blowing by now and broke open the last of our sandwiches. I noticed Mark scanning the sky. "See that," he said, pointing toward some wispy clouds high in the west. "Mares' tails, they're called. Rain by tomorrow."

Several times in our descent I threw caution aside and began hopping from rock to rock, trusting to gravity and my new boots. A definite Zen moment.

Under two hours and we were back at the camp, versus three and a half on the ascent. I was ready to take it easy and stay another night but no, we re-sorted our gear, slipped on the big packs and hit the trail for Bernice Lake. As I picked carefully down the rocky trail, my knees and legs began complaining for the first time. Forty-five tough minutes later we leveled off and at a signpost headed down the spur for Bernice Lake.

After setting up camp it was time for a swim but Hamid and I didn't last long in the freezing water. I inflated my air mattress and set it on a level spot by the shore and rested my pack against a tree, pulling out John Muir's *My First Summer in the Sierra.* An hour later I awoke with my finger in the place where Muir climbs a tree in a blizzard. Mark was still swimming back and forth. He told me he'd been in a special Army group, black ops, whatever that meant, which called for strong swimming skills. Mark was an onion. When you thought you knew him here came another layer, then another. He was one of the most competent people I'd ever met. He did everything and did it well.

Though Muir's book lay in my lap I started thinking about *Dharma Bums.* On my first reading, I was impressed by Kerouac's descriptions of trees and flowers and sky, his talk of enlightenment and quietness. Zen was new to me then. Second time through, an altogether different book – he and his friends racing around the mountains, madcap boozing and drugs, near-disasters. Compared to his manic crew our trio hardly made a dent in the wilderness.

The sun was sinking toward the rim of the mountains as we set about our meal. After his swim Mark caught two brown trout for dinner, to which we added freeze-dried potatoes au gratin and peas. As we lit the fire I saw people milling around a couple other tent sites, and before long a hippie guy and girl came by to borrow some matches. A young dog, a German Shepherd mix, was with them. I'd seen him splashing in the lake, retrieving a stick the guy kept throwing in. "How're his feet doing?" I asked.

"They're kind of sore," the girl said, "we're taking it slow." I noticed a bandage on one of his paws and thought, good decision on our part.

Mine was the last light off. As I put my head down I though how quiet it was, the trees rustling in the breeze, Mark breathing heavily, when all of a sudden this barking erupted. The shepherd. I'd like a dog again sometime, I thought, maybe one like that. The barking stopped and I was dozing off when it started up again, this time really loud and fierce for several minutes. Suddenly there was this CRACK! A few seconds later, CRACK!

I sat up in my bag, wide awake. "Whassat," Hamid muttered.

"Down! Get down!" Mark pushed me down onto the tent floor. I could hear him fumbling with his pack. "Stay flat!" he whispered. He wriggled out of his sleeping bag and crawled toward the front of the tent and untied the flap. A couple more feet and his head was sticking out. I lifted my head and saw something in Mark's hand glinting in the moonlight. The dog wasn't barking any more. It was perfectly quiet save for the wind in the trees. Mark crawled ahead some more. Now he was outside the tent... I saw him pad away in a crouch.

"What's going on?" Hamid said.

"I don't know. Sounded like a gun."

We stayed like this for ten, fifteen minutes. Finally Mark eased his way back into the tent and pulled the flap over. "Should I light the lamp?" Hamid asked.

"What, are you nuts?" Mark snapped.

"What did you see out there?" I asked.

"Not a hell of a lot. My bet is the dog smelled a bear, can't blame him for making a racket, that's his job, but..."

"Those were shots, weren't they?" I said.

"Yeah, that idiot hippie must have been trying to scare it off. Sounded like a thirty-ought-six. That'd make a nice hole in you."

"Jesus," I said. "What should we do about it?"

"Right now nothing, who knows if he's high or what. Stay low and go back to sleep."

"What if I have to pee?" Hamid said.

"Goddammit! Pee in your pants! I'll talk to him tomorrow. Now is not the time."

It took a long time to get back to sleep. When I awoke rain was beating on the tent. First up for a change, I pulled the tent flap aside and a got a faceful of rain for my trouble. I slipped on my pants and sweatshirt and felt around for my poncho. Socks, boots, everything where it ought to be. Simpler when you wear the same things every day. As I crawled out of the tent the wind was really whipping. No way we can hike in this. At the edge of the woods, I took a long, refreshing leak.

We ate cold cereal in the tent, taking a short cut of powdered milk on corn flakes then adding water which, let me say, I don't recommend. Coffee would await improved weather. We decided if the rain let up we'd head for the closest good climb, Mt. Florence – two of us, that is, for Hamid was complaining of a sore foot. There was some swelling but no apparent cause. We filled a plastic bag with cold lake water and told him to keep the foot elevated. He said he'd be happy to catch up on his reading. By ten the rain had stopped and we saw patches of blue so Mark and I set out. The walk in along the creek was easy and after we gained the high ground we sighted the summit of Florence and Simmons Peak to the north which we'd targeted for another day. The guidebook said three more hours to the top. Even in good conditions this would be pushing our luck, but the storm had deposited a sizable amount of new snow in the chutes and crevasses of our planned route. Mark and I looked at each other. "I don't think so," I said.

He nodded. "This isn't a contest. We've got a couple more days."

By the time we retraced our steps to Florence Creek, the day had warmed up nicely. We set our packs on a flat rock and broke out the last of the black bread and cheese.

I HAD TRIED TO RAISE THE SUBJECT OF VIETNAM a few times with Mark but he was reluctant to talk about it. He spent two years there, that's all I knew, except when we were planning our trip he'd mentioned being in the mountains, which made no sense based on what little I knew. But I thought I'd try again. "How come you were in the mountains in Vietnam? I thought our advisors were in the South, working with the South Vietnamese."

He smiled. "I could tell you there are mountains in the South too, which is true. What I will say, we have a variety of operations over there. Some of them, people know nothing about nor are they supposed to."

"Aha." I am thinking government secrecy. "Well, I won't push you on it."

"Wouldn't do you any good." He was chewing a piece of bread. "You know," he said between bites, "you know what really pisses me off about Berkeley? Those way those creeps hammer on the U.S. That free speech shit is bad enough, but giving aid and comfort to the enemy is totally unacceptable."

"It's getting to me too."

"Thing is, show the enemy you're weak, if he is at all intelligent you are in trouble, and believe me, those Vietnamese are plenty intelligent. Do not underestimate their smarts or their resolve, though let me be clear, I'm talking about the Northerners. The South, they're something else again. I'd call them a Chinese fire drill but why insult the Chinese? The North reads our papers, they see our TV, hell they've got people right here in Berkeley working for them. If they see us divided on the war, we might as well pack it in."

"It's no accident Vietnam is the issue of the day. People are orchestrating these protests – it's very deliberate."

"And why not? It's cheaper to win politically than on the battlefield. Sun Tzu says political change is less expensive and more lasting than military change and he's right. It's the way to go unless you're prepared to hold every position by force, which is impossible. And the North is patient, which is a pain in the butt to us, we're so tied to quick results."

"True, but impatience is the flip side of being a peace-loving country, at least at the average citizen level. 'I'll follow you, but only so far and only for so long.' Do you buy the domino theory?" I asked. "Ever talk with Gus about that?"

"Man, if I heard him on that I heard him a hundred times. Hell, yes, I buy it. The Communist is by nature aggressive and ruthless, but it's good strategy anyway. I don't buy Hawaii tomorrow, Long Beach the day after. That's ridiculous, what you philosophers call *reductio* something."

"*Reductio ad absurdum.*"

"There you go. But now, if you remember your World War Two, the Japanese took one country after another, worked their way down through Indochina. For that matter, once we got going ourselves we did the same thing. Assault the position, take the position, secure the position, move on. Encourage your friends, sabotage everything else."

"How'd you get into the military? Why didn't you make it a career?"

He laughed, "It's not like I'm a West Point wannabee. I needed cash and ROTC had some. I did my time and got out – well, these days the reserves aren't exactly out, not the way things are going over there. How about you? What's your situation?"

"On my current course I'll be twenty-six, twenty-seven when I get my Ph.D., so I'm safe unless they change the rules."

Mark shook his head. "Correction. You're safe because our kids are over there humping, doing a job you could help them do."

I reddened. "Poor choice of words. I'm taking things one step at a time. I'll do my share. Don't ask me how, not yet."

He nodded. "I didn't mean to put you down. These creeps and their high-sounding words, they're just protecting their own skin. I don't get the impression you're one of them."

"I appreciate that. I'm not."

"You're lucky if you can do it your way, though I'll say for me the Army was great."

"And you lived to tell about it."

"That is a big part of the program, I mean to tell you." He fell silent. "It never goes away," he said a moment later. "You're on automatic, it's always with you. Like last night in the tent – you saw it." He got to his feet. "Let's head out. Ever want to talk Army, let me know."

The hike back was familiar and pleasant. As we neared Bernice Lake, I asked Mark whether he had talked with our hippy friend. "This morning. He was trying to scare away a bear or what he thought was a bear."

"Did they actually see one?"

"No. They heard a lot of crashing in the bushes and Siddhartha was convinced."

"Siddhartha?"

"The Shepherd."

"Siddhartha," I said, shaking my head. "And you gave the guy some advice about firearms, no doubt."

"I reamed him out. You don't go around shooting up a public place. He said he fired it into the ground, I'll give him that much."

"Speaking of guns, I notice you have one."

"Don't leave home without it," he patted his pack. "Downtown Oakland or High Sierra, my little pal and I go everywhere together. Here, let me show you."

"No need," I said, shaking my head. I wasn't totally comfortable around guns. "Only gun I ever had was a Daisy at home. I guess that doesn't count."

"It's a start."

Back in camp we found Hamid in a lot of pain. His foot was red and swollen.

"You might have a bite," Mark thought out loud, examining the bottom of the foot with his flashlight, "there's a break in the skin I didn't notice before. He reached for his first aid kit. "That hurt?" Mark wore a grin as he poked around with a Q-tip.

Hamid nodded stoically, his teeth clenched.

Mark ran his finger over the wound. "I could use my knife but I don't want to screw with it. Let's put some disinfectant on." He opened a bottle of iodine tincture. "You're going to feel this," he said, rubbing some into the spot. Hamid winced but he didn't cry out.

"Ah, you probably stepped on something, that's the easiest explanation. You haven't been walking around barefoot, have you?"

"Not really," Hamid replied.

He put the back of his hand to Hamid's forehead. "Feverish?"

"I feel a little warm."

"I think we should get this looked at," Mark said. "Maybe I'm being an old woman but whatever it is we don't want the infection to get worse. You okay with that, Paul?"

"No! Don't cut the trip short!" Hamid shouted.

"Mark's right," I said, "you don't play games with something like this."

"Can you put weight on it?" Mark asked. Hamid stood up, balancing on his good foot, then he tried to stand on the other. Gritting his teeth, he moved around gingerly, walking lightly on his heel. "Can you make it out to the road?" Mark asked.

"I am from a line of Bedouins."

"There's no way you'll get that boot on," Mark mumbled, "we could wrap it, but..."

"I brought a pair of sneakers," I said. Mark touched his finger to his head.

An hour later we were on the trail, a loosely-tied sneaker on Hamid's foot. I sawed a tree limb and lopped off the branches, fashioning a walking stick for our patient. Mark and I moved weight out of his pack into ours. "At least we bagged one good peak," I said.

"And left plenty for next time," Mark added.

It was a slow go, stopping often to rest Hamid's foot. Not until three-thirty did I hear the first highway noise. After settling Hamid in back with his foot on the seat, Mark fired up the car. "Always hold my breath when it's sat a few days." The nearest emergency room was in the Valley.

The answer was a sliver of green glass lodged in his foot. It had gone straight in and it came back out only after half an hour's work, dicey because the doctor needed to be sure it didn't break and leave a fragment behind. Hamid was stoic, heroic even – he didn't cry out once, a lot better than I would have done. The nurse stuck him with penicillin and over his protest, a tetanus shot too. She was astonished he'd made it down the mountain on his own steam.

"I'm from a long line of Bedouins," he assured her. "Giving up is not in our nature."

"Bedouins. I remember them."

"Probably your second grade geography."

"Whatever." She ushered us out the door. "Good luck, stay well."

Before leaving the Valley, Mark relented and drove us around the valley, in time to see the sun disappear behind El Capitan and get a view of Half Dome bathed in golden light. Next trip back east I'd look for Yosemite from the air. "So, thank you very much," I said to Hamid.

"What for?" he replied, confused.

"If you hadn't messed up your foot we wouldn't have seen this."

We stopped for dinner at a café – we'd be getting back so late another hour didn't matter. When the bill arrived I pulled my wallet out. "Put that back," Hamid said.

"What do you mean, put it back?"

"I wish to pay," he said, "to make amends for spoiling our trip."

"We can't let you do that," Mark said, fingering a twenty dollar bill.

"Yes, I insist."

"Well okay, if you say so."

At the car Mark stopped and glared at Hamid. "You know, Hamid, you really piss me off."

Hamid's face dropped. "What do you mean? How can you say such a thing?"

Mark let Hamid squirm. "You should have said you were buying dinner."

"But, Mark, I *did* tell you!"

"Yeah, after we finished. If I knew ahead I would've ordered steak, not the damn meatloaf."

Hamid broke into a smile. "Ah, so we are still friends."

"Still friends. But next time don't go running around camp barefoot."

27. A TURN FOR THE WORSE

"WERE YOU SURPRISED, Paul taking to such strenuous activity?"

"No, not at all. He became a decent athlete after that less-than-impressive start. And did you notice how he took to Mark? Mark was an exceptional young man."

"They saw eye to eye on the war."

"True, and there I parted company with them. Domino theory – what a crock!"

"Hamid's an intriguing guy, a combination of stamina and – what would you say? Sensitivity?"

"Hamid was very perceptive. He certainly proved that later."

Speaking of people, I am thinking I need to call Dennis, set up a time to get together.

* * * * * * *

I PUT AWAY MY BOOTS and burrowed in, but soon I was having doubts. Halfway through the program and my resolve turns rubbery... not good. The long days and nights – sometimes it seemed a colossal waste of time. Did I really want to spend my life this way? But what's the alternative? Washington? The Government could use my help, I thought, anybody's help, the way things were going. If not the classroom, some sort of research job? I just didn't know. My hope of making a difference was looking pretty remote about then. What would Father Ronan say? Maybe Gus would have some advice.

Berkeley's style was also taking its toll. It was disconcerting, the vehemence of the dissent. As for Jesus and His example, that seemed irrelevant to these people. At times I wondered whether my first twenty-one years was all a dream. I missed the security of friends who shared the basics with me. Diversity was grueling, but more embarrassing, it had surprised me. I found it difficult to concentrate. Often I'd get up from my carrel and toss off a couple dozen push-ups. Deep breathing, a lot of coffee.

At least the material was interesting. I re-read the classics, also Communist, Nazi and Fascist texts. Churchill, Harold Nicolson, Aron, Morgenthau, Niebuhr. League and U.N. monographs. Kissinger and Kahn on nuclear strategy. Acheson, Berle, Laski, Kennan, Lippmann. Grotius, Suarez, Kelsen, Wheaton. Commentaries on war and Nuremberg. These kept me going, but were they anything more than wallpaper for my mental playroom?

Mid-July I made a fast trip east. My father had suffered another stroke, minor this time. Back in the wheelchair, he'd lost more weight and it showed in his face. The old feistiness was really gone now. He had the bat on his shoulder and he was waiting for strike three. Mother played her grim role, but emotionally spent, she seemed to have given up, too. My first night back we were having a late dinner, Dad had already gone to bed, and it occurred to me I hadn't heard anything about a wedding. "Set a date yet?" I asked.

Catherine frowned. "It's off," she finally said. "We called it off."

I was startled. "I'm sorry to hear that."

"Don't be," she replied quietly. "There are plenty of fish in the sea."

I glanced at her hand. No ring. Dumb not to notice that, really dumb. "Well, you made the right decision," I went on lamely. "You can do a lot better."

Suddenly Catherine put her napkin to her mouth. Bursting into tears she rushed from the room. "You didn't have to say that!" my mother whispered loudly.

I shrugged. "But it's true. He has no spirit. He's a limp fish, the way he shakes hands..."

"Paul!"

"What'd I do?" I asked, looking around.

She leaned over toward me. "Tom was the one called it off. *He* called it off! Last weekend, no warning at all. Just like that."

"Oh." I sat back. I felt terrible. "How can I make it up to her? What can I do?"

"Leave her alone. Disappear."

Good idea. But I had pretty well lost track of my friends. Omer, I heard he was in the Army. Angelo, no idea where he was. I ended up at a movie alone and in a rotten mood.

Next day I took my father out. Folding the wheelchair in the trunk, I headed the Caddie north on Fruit Hill Avenue onto the country roads we used to cruise in the Plymouth Sundays after church. Lots of development now, houses, apartment buildings, stores. We returned via Smith Street and La Salle. Dad said he was having such a good time, he didn't want to go back, so we climbed College Hill and ended up at Brown. "How about we park and get some air?" he said.

I found a space on the street and hauled the chair out. He tugged at the bill of the Red Sox cap I had given him many Christmases ago and we began wheeling along. "You know," he said, his voice growing stronger as the day went on, "I had doubts about Brown but it worked out for the best. You would have done well here."

"I'm happy where I am." I wasn't about to confide my troubles to him, he had enough of his own.

"Too bad you're so far away, it'd be nice to see you more often."

"Give me a couple more years," I said.

"Will you stay in California?" he asked.

"I doubt it, it's not my kind of place." New subject. "How's Nu-Gem these days?"

"They don't need me much, good thing, too. We should be able to free up something for you kids pretty soon."

"All contributions are gratefully accepted." Financially I was holding my own but there was little room for error. Passing under an arch I wheeled him toward an athletic field I noticed from the street. "I don't know my way around here. Catherine'd be a better guide."

He was silent for a moment. "She's going through a rough stretch." He nodded, "you know, it's strange, you and me, today."

"What do you mean?"

"I was always the one drove the bus. Now it's you. And Jim, of course."

"You helped me, I help you. You'll be back on your feet before long."

He shook his head. "I see through those doctors. Every time they say I'm doing great I subtract a couple more days."

"Come on, that's no way to talk."

"I'm going to church again, and your mother didn't even have to lecture me."

"I still go and I've got plenty of years left, knock on wood. Same with you."

He shook his head. "One more knockout, it'll be over. A TKO might do it."

"Let's head back," I said. The gloom was getting thick. "How about an ice cream? We passed a Baskin Robbins a few blocks back."

"I'm supposed to watch that kind of thing."

"If your days are so numbered, you might as well enjoy them."

He paused. "You know, you're right," he said brightly. "I feel better already!"

I sat on a bench, he in his chair, working on our cones. "Did I tell you Antoine is doing well?" he said. "He'd love to see you if you could make time."

"See, there you go. He did it, you can too."

He was quiet a moment. "What do you think about this Vietnam business?" he asked. Driving up Manton Avenue, as we passed Maurice's square he'd remarked how different things were these days, young people didn't have the patriotism they used to.

"I think we're doing the right thing. Sad but true."

"What's sad is our kids getting killed. From the TV I see a lot of people are against the war. That doesn't help."

"That's big out my way, but a lot of those people are out to cause trouble."

"The older I get the more skeptical I am about the government. I don't trust them any more. How long do you stay with a losing hand?"

"You think we're losing?"

He nodded. "Finish the damned thing and get the hell out."

A few days later I headed up to Boston. Pat was in France for the summer but I hadn't seen Meg for a while. Between first and second years of med school, she was her usual overloaded self, again at Mass General for the summer. I noticed she also was sporting a diamond. No date yet, they were waiting until she finished at Yale. When I told her about Catherine she made sympathetic sounds, then asked how I was doing.

"Three more years, give or take."

We were in a coffee house on Charles Street, she was going on about Pat, his dislike of the law in general and Harvard in particular. "I won't be surprised if he stays in Paris."

"That'll please his draft board no end."

"He says there's a way if the school approves a leave of absence."

"Keep me posted. I never hear from him."

Meg had to head for the hospital but that gave me a chance for some one-on-one with *grand-maman.* She never pulled her punches. The vinegar in her veins must keep her young, I thought. "I am so angry with your Johnson! Are he and his advisors stupid? We at least had colonies and interests, and of course *la mission civilisatrise,* but these people, what are they trying to accomplish?"

I took a deep breath. "Remember what the Communists did to your interests. Look at China's so-called wars of national liberation. A Vietnam under Communist rule and Peking behind it would be a disaster for the region."

"But I ask again, what is your interest there?"

"A great power has responsibilities but we can't do it alone. We need the support of friendly regimes that aspire to democracy. That's why we're trying to shore up the South."

"That is a very theoretical explanation to ask young men to die for."

"Perhaps, but the implications are very practical, very serious."

She was distressed to hear about my father, wanted to know about my mother's acting. As she saw me to the door she put her hand on my shoulder. "What troubles me, *mon jeune ami,* you deny me the satisfaction that our sacrifice might serve as a lesson for you. Your Johnson makes our suffering doubly painful. It was no use to France, it seems of no use to France's friends."

A week or so after my return, I received a letter from my mother.

> I'm relieved to tell you Catherine is recovering. She has an audition with Brown's drama department for a part in the fall. I'll get back to my own acting but I'm not quite ready. As they say, you only go around once. The cynics among us would add, if that, but I don't believe that for a minute. By the way, and strictly between us, Tom wasn't the right fellow. Obviously I couldn't say that when you were here. Take care, much love. Write soon and often.
>
> Mother
>
> P.S. I'm sending a little something. Have some fun with it.

A FEW DAYS AFTER RETURNING I did just that, lunch on the Terrace. Afterward I was walking around the Student Union when I noticed a crowd gathered about the television. Lyndon Johnson was just signing off, an unusual mid-day appearance. Something was up. A commentator appeared and said Johnson had just announced a 50,000 increase in troop level and was doubling draft calls to 35,000 a month. "'We did not choose to be the guardians at the gate,' the President said, 'but there is no one else.'"

That night, Gus brought out his scorecard. "Fifty-thousand today, plus the forty in April, that's a hundred-fifteen thousand and counting." He shook his head, "what'd I tell you? Bombing doesn't do it. It takes men on the ground, a lot of them."

Mark nodded. "Couple of years we'll be at half a million and it still won't be enough."

"Goddamn LBJ," Gus went on, "he wouldn't know the truth if it hit him in the face. But events are taking over. that'll strip away the pretense."

Mark said, "we differ on the strategy..."

"We differ on everything, Mark," Gus interrupted, "like whether we should be there at all."

"Okay, but from a tactical point of view, we're agreed you can't do it on the cheap. The worst of both worlds – you bog down, you lose men and the mission fails."

"What does this do to your reserve unit?" I asked Mark. He'd said rumors were flying about being activated, but LBJ had said no reserve call-up.

"Just delays the inevitable. How long, who knows?"

Word was going around that something calling itself the Vietnam Day Committee was planning a major demonstration. I reached Benny – he was in on it. Later in the month the *Daily Cal* printed an open letter from a group of faculty, arguing that civil disobedience would weaken the growing opposition to the war. I asked Gus why he didn't sign the letter.

"I won't associate myself with such a tepid response. Voters in the streets, millions of them, that's what our misguided leader needs."

"All this divisiveness, it's bad for the country."

"I have greater faith in the American people than you do. And by the way, don't forget we're at risk right now – at risk of becoming an outlaw nation, not to say spilling our blood and treasure for nothing."

I just shook my head. Futile to repeat my arguments. They cut no ice.

The next day I saw Benny. I repeated an argument some were making, that the anti-war protests could be hurting the civil rights effort. "Those hard-earned gains could be lost."

Benny stared at me. "Sure there's a risk, but the war is the real threat. With the bombing, the buildup, we're at the turning point. The American people didn't ask for this war, Paul – LBJ sweet-talked them out of voting for the warmonger." He paused. "You voted for Johnson, I take it."

"Yes. Why do you ask?"

"I voted for Goldwater."

"Goldwater! Were you out of your mind?"

"Not at all. I despise everything the man stands for, his militarism, his extremism, but I figured a Democratic Congress would keep him from doing anything too stupid."

"That makes no sense! How could you not support LBJ? He's been the Negro's best friend. He's done a lot more than Kennedy ever did."

He smiled. "I gave you only part of my reason. I don't trust Johnson. He tells you what you want to hear then does whatever the hell he can get away with. Goldwater, sure he's off base but he is an honest man, in fact candor was his undoing. Every time I pick up the paper LBJ proves me right. Don't you see, if we don't stand up now, we're giving approval for the war he didn't have the guts to ask for."

"But how can you risk all that progress? Desegregation? The Voting Rights Act?"

"The civil rights effort will have to maintain itself for a while. This crime in Vietnam needs to be stopped now."

"Crime!" I shouted. "The Congress of the United States authorized Johnson to do exactly what he's doing."

"The Tonkin Resolution? Come on, Paul, duplicity with a capital D."

I was really getting irritated. "Here's our President, playing a very tough hand, trying to do his job, and Benny Kaplan and company want to pull the rug out from under him. All that'll do is to drag the war out and get more Americans killed."

"Your good old endless war theory. Don't blame me – that's Johnson's policy, not mine. He doesn't have the balls to go for it, he doesn't have the smarts to call it quits." Benny shrugged, "but then I'm not about to change your mind, nor you mine."

I got up to go. "When's your show?"

"Thursday and Friday. Look for me on the news."

The Army had plans to charter trains to carry recruits to the Oakland Army Base, a key Vietnam embarkation point. With this ready-made opportunity, the local anti-war crowd set out to block a train, or garner publicity by attempting to block one. The first day Mark said he was going to check it out. I said I'd go along, I could use a break, maybe even catch Benny in action. We parked on San Pablo Avenue and fell in with a bunch of people carrying picket signs. Drawing closer I saw the protesters had strung up a banner across the track: STOP THE WAR MACHINE. When the TV arrived the protesters began chanting slogans and waving signs. GET OUT OF VIETNAM. YOU HAVEN'T KILLED YET, DON'T START NOW. UNCLE SAM WILL BURY YOU.

We were taking up a position alongside the track, down from the main knot of protesters, when I heard this call, "Mark! Mark!" A couple of young men, struggling under armfuls of signs. "YAFers," Mark said, "they're in one of my classes. Morning, Bruce, Alan."

"It's only right our side should be represented," the taller of the two said, out of breath. "How about a sign?"

Mark nodded, "Sure, why not?"

"There's a good selection today," he said, setting them down. "We're running a special on this one." OUR COUNTRY - LOVE IT OR LEAVE IT. He pulled the next sign off the stack. "This one's a collectors' item." EXTREMISM IN THE DEFENSE OF LIBERTY IS NO VICE.

Mark picked a KILL A COMMIE FOR CHRIST out of the pile. "I'll go with this."

"What about you?" they asked me. "Don't be the last on your block."

I hesitated, reaching for SUPPORT OUR TROOPS. "This says it well."

And that is how I got my picture on the front page of the *Oakland Tribune* and Mark, yours truly beside him, interviewed on the eleven o'clock news, KRON-TV, Channel Four. I actually used my sign as the train smashed through the banner, waving it at kids even younger than me peering out the windows, laughing, flashing Vs and thumbs-up. I didn't see Benny but a few days later I ran into him in the Plaza.

"So here's the publicity hound! Our P.R. director quit. You interested?"

"Sorry, wrong religion." I was relieved that despite the tensions our friendship still limped along. Mark and I also responded to Gus' mock eviction notices. Freedom of speech goes both ways, we reminded him.

Second day, an even bigger turnout, though I wasn't there. The police were becoming more aggressive, chasing demonstrators off the tracks, arresting some who boarded the train, and in a close call that gave me the willies reading about it, snatching a young woman from an onrushing train, a teacher who had camped on the track in her lotus position. I sent my picture home and got a letter from my father by return mail. Unheard of! He never wrote, but there it was, his handwriting, shaky and all. He said he was proud of me and to keep up the good work. Proud? Good work? Oh, well, if something I did made him feel good, so be it. Truth be known, it felt good to me, too, even if it was a fluke.

Speaking of letters, I located Father Trần's address and wrote to him before our hiking trip. Near the end of August this arrived.

Dear Paul,

Your letter gave me great pleasure. I have wondered what became of you. Please accept my mea culpa for not writing. I am pleased you continue your studies but surprised you abandoned the Jesuits. Berkeley is known here for leftist politics. I hope you remain safe, and secure in your faith.

No day here passes without a new atrocity, bombings, attacks on innocents. The whole world now knows what we have known, the Communists will stop at nothing. Nothing is sacred, nothing is safe. Our parting words I recall well, my fear your country would fail us, as in the end the French did. Your Generals Taylor and Westmoreland, I give them credit for trying. It is our own people who worry me now, their bickering and posturing. I have lost count of the number of coups and of course, the Buddhists scheme for their own ends.

I have been appointed assistant pastor of the principal church of Cholon, a much troubled suburb of Saigon. From your letter, before long you will become a professor. I have taught in our local university and hope you will also soon experience the joy of working with young people. I smile recalling our discussions, how theoretical they seem now. It would be good to see you again. I wish you well and wish you success. Prayerfully, in Christ and his Blessed Mother, your friend,

Rev. Trần Văn Minh

I read his letter several times. I wondered how he looked after the intervening years. I would reply but needed to compose my thoughts. "A professor," he called me. I felt uneasy reading that. I still hadn't told my family about the wavering.

THE SUMMER WAS MARKED BY MORE INNER-CITY TURBULENCE. L.A.'s poor, crowded Watts district was first, the forceful arrest of a Negro youth escalating into six days and nights of gang attacks, looting and destruction. As an *L.A. Times* reporter put it, the rioters are burning their own city now, "as the insane sometimes mutilate themselves." In the end, thirty-four killed, nearly nine hundred injured, four thousand arrests and forty-five million dollars damage. Chicago's West Side soon followed suit.

Cal was bracing itself for the new year and another round of protests, which now seemed endemic. Though in a heartening development, leaflets and rallies were starting to appear supporting our efforts in Vietnam. Without any classes, for me the start of the school year was a non-event. I simply kept on doing what I'd been doing, though more of it. I was now meeting twice a week with Don. I wanted to get through the International exam before raising my problem with Gus, but one day I ran into him outside Dwinelle, he invited me to lunch and one thing led to another. "I'm not surprised. Second thoughts are common."

"You're happy being a professor. It can be done, right?"

"It has served me well. And you know, there is variety in a professor's life, even a Political Scientist. Consulting gives you a break, and don't knock the additional income. I happen to love teaching and of course there's my research and writing – speaking of which, I have a book party coming up you'll be invited to."

"I'll be there. So, what do you think is going on with me?"

Gus was quiet for a moment. "How old are you?"

"Twenty-four."

"At your age I was second in command on a destroyer, then I ended up on MacArthur's staff. Amazing experience. You grow up fast under the gun, but why I mention it, everybody has a need for adventure, thrills, danger. I got it out of my system early so I was ready to settle down."

"You're saying..."

"No offense, I'm saying you haven't had much of a life."

I reddened. "Wait a minute!"

"I mean not yet. Look, if I said you've been on a short leash would that be unfair?"

I shook my head. "The most exciting thing I've ever done is come out here. Maybe the only exciting thing."

"It's obvious you need more of that. See the world, have some adventure."

I thought of Pat's sophisticated family, his European travels, but I didn't want to start feeling sorry for myself. "What do you suggest?" I asked.

"I'm not suggesting anything. Find a way out of your rut. Suck it up and finish your degree or take a break and do something different. Go somewhere you can use those languages of yours. Talk to the people in our counseling center, they're very good. Maybe they'll have some ideas."

In my carrel that afternoon I pondered my friend's words. Far from sating my appetite for adventure the west coast had done the opposite. In some ways Berkeley was too much, the contentiousness, the vile attacks on my country, in other ways it wasn't enough. Maybe he was right, I needed a break. But when? And of course, what?

A CONTEMPORARY REDWOOD AND GLASS JEWEL set alongside Strawberry Creek, Alumni House was a refreshing change from the campus' theme of stolid granite and orange. Of all times, Don chose today to tie up every conceivable loose end for my exam, now only a few days off. I was irritated at being late. Approaching the entrance I came upon an easel with a piece of foam board lettered in blue and gold:

U.C. PRESS PROUDLY PRESENTS
POLITICS AND CONSTITUTIONAL CHANGE:
THE RECONSTRUCTION AMENDMENTS
PROF. AUGUSTUS F.X. FLYNN

A second easel featured a blowup of the cover and a flattering old black and white photo of Gus. A modest crowd milled about, white-jacketed students circulating with drinks and *hors d'oeuvres.* Memories of Kimball. Scooping a pig-in-a-blanket and a square of spanikopita, it occurred to me, if I worked at it this could serve as dinner. I spotted Gus at a table signing books and talking, altogether in his element. I ran into Professor Shapiro from my International Economics seminar, the first Nobel Prize winner I'd ever met. Somehow we got onto politics and he commented that a national economy can afford only so much, even a wealthy one like ours. When war and social programs collide, he went on, invariably war prevails. If government tries to sustain both, runaway inflation takes over and everybody loses.

Armed with this insight I looked around for Benny but didn't see him. He was probably busy readying his next round of demonstrations, set for the same day as my exam. I visited with a number of people and finally was able to corner Gus. "What a great feeling to be finished! Exhausted but exhilarated!" He took a deep breath. "You doing okay?"

"Exam number two next week. I also hope to be exhilarated and exhausted."

"Good luck. But I'll see you before then."

I glanced at the stack of books, smaller than when I came in. "I haven't picked up a copy yet but I will."

"Don't bother, there's one with your name on it at home."

I came out of the exam with a splitting headache. It was very fact-oriented so my theorizing skills weren't that helpful. Tell the truth, I really sweated. I joined a couple of fellow-sufferers heading for the Bear's Lair. I'd been so focused I completely forgot about Benny's event. From what I saw on TV, today's teach-in was even more one-sided than the last one. As we left the Lair I saw the crowd in the streets, forming up for the parade to the Oakland Army Base but *sans* permit, I heard. Oakland officials feared Watts-type trouble since the route of the mostly white protesters would be through mostly Negro West Oakland. NO MORE WAR. STOP THE BOMBING. OUT OF VIETNAM. Nothing new.

Back at the house I learned that on encountering police barricades at the Oakland line, the leaders wisely turned the group toward downtown Berkeley where the event petered out. Next day they amassed larger numbers and again were turned away, but this time some Hell's Angels charged the parade, ripping banners and starting fights. The Berkeley police banged heads and after a while order was restored. I asked Mark if he'd been there, he said he was neither that interested nor that crazy.

I resented the in-your-face anti-Americanism but unfortunately it seemed to be working. The papers carried big spreads about nationwide protests, speculating that if this continued, the time-honored tradition of consensus behind a wartime President could be threatened. The *Times* reported a David J. Miller had burned his draft card outside the Army Induction Center in lower Manhattan, identifying Miller as a member of the Catholic Worker organization, Dorothy Day's group. I disagreed with Miller, of course, but he looked like a person who might actually be for something, not just knee-jerk against everything, plus he obviously had guts. Draft card burning had just been made a crime. He could, and did, end up in jail. There had even been immolations, one on the Pentagon steps, one in front of the U.N. Saigon West, I thought with a shudder. Complacency is no longer an option, if it had ever been.

A few weeks later I learned I passed, so it was now on to number three. Since my thesis would be an experiment of sorts, I needed data, so I started cataloging cases where our government had curtailed normal citizen rights. The Japanese internment was a natural. German citizens in World War Two, World War One as well, for that matter. McCarthy and the blacklists, for sure, and since Gus had been so open, maybe he'd help on the U.C. Loyalty Oath as a state government example. I decided to look at Vietnam too. Here we have censorship and news management – what about straight-out lying? LBJ was accused of lying when he denied receiving a North Vietnamese overture to negotiate, proving, his critics claimed, that he preferred military force over negotiation. That sounded far-fetched but I needed to explore credibility, secrecy, and the critical issue of how much can be said without tipping off the enemy. A new formula was starting to appear in the press, "plausible deniability." Lots of trouble behind that glib expression. My experiment also called for baseline cases, how freedom and government coexist in less stressful times. Or, if I could find any, wartime examples where the government didn't clamp down on civil liberties.

The war was getting grimmer. In November, hopes for a decisive conclusion were dashed when U.S. and North Vietnamese troops fought a prolonged and bloody battle in the Ia Drang Valley near the Cambodian border. Though the enemy lost nearly two thousand, U.S. fatalities reached a new high, over 250 that week alone. Of course the protesters feasted on the news, playing it for all it was worth. Some commentators suggested that before long, rising U.S. losses would prove more compelling to the American people than body counts and kill ratios. Pessimists worried that democratic liberalism was being undermined by the incompetence of its current practitioners. Faced with such failures, they asked, can it survive? More troubling yet, what would take its place?

The Sunday after the Oakland demonstration, the sermon at Mass dealt with – in the priest's felicitous phrase – "moral intersections," this one where individual conscience meets government policy, which he said these days is filled with fast and dangerous traffic. The Newman priests weren't afraid to stick their necks out. Father Fisher, the pastor, had been on top of the famous police car, urging a peaceful resolution. They preached on the war. This day the young priest, Father Garvey, commended David J. Miller for putting himself in that moral intersection, saying we all need time there, certainly the people running our government do. Lofty titles aside, he said, in the sight of God they are only people. The Millers of the world are vital – much as we may disagree with them, they force us to think. I learned that Roger LaPorte, the young man who set himself afire at the U.N., was also in the Catholic Worker organization. Father Garvey asked us to pray for his soul which I did unhesitatingly, and I was gratified he remembered the young Americans risking their lives in the cause LaPorte opposed with such finality.

Early December I returned for a Vatican II update, the Council having just concluded its work. The Bishops affirmed that Jews are no more responsible for Christ's death than Christians are. It's one thing to say so, I thought, what about the centuries of misery caused by the old attitudes? They laid a basis for reconciliation with other Christian Churches, Protestant and Orthodox. They affirmed that non-Christians can be saved – if they seek God and follow their consciences, they can't be blamed for ignorance of Christ and his Church. There would be new emphasis on an old truth, that God's people are an integral part of the Church. The laity will be a lot more involved... I couldn't wait to hear my mother's reaction to that one. Another change I had mixed feelings about and still do, expanded use of the vernacular in the liturgy. I know why they did it, but the Latin Mass was my bedrock, and though I had travelled little, I liked knowing I could be comfortable in any Catholic church anywhere. An important sign of the Church's universality, I was sorry to see it watered down.

DECEMBER 11TH, A FRIDAY. I just picked up my ticket for the trip home. My father celebrated Thanksgiving by trading his wheelchair for a cane, which, my mother's letter said, lifted his spirits tremendously. She and Catherine were taking the train to New York to see some plays, visit the tree, and stay at the Algonquin Hotel to rub elbows with literary history. The two of them had become very thick since the fiancée had bugged out (sorry, couldn't help that). I was in the throes of organizing my attack on Public Law, my last exam, set for April. With a tremendous amount of work ahead I was all too successful at finding excuses. I had just walked in the door when Akiko rushed up to me. "Your brother just called, call him right away." With a worried look she handed me a piece of paper with the number, our home number. Jim? I thought to myself. He never called me in his life.

I went to my room and picked up the phone. After half a dozen rings I was about to give up when Jim answered. "Paulie." My heart leapt into my mouth. He never called me Paulie. "I don't know how to tell you this. Mom got hit by a car. She's dead."

"Oh my God." I sat down heavily on the bed. "Oh my God."

"I'm sorry to be the one to tell you. Sorry."

"What happened?"

"Catherine called, she's all broke up. They were crossing the street, the car missed her but it got Mom."

"Jesus." My eyes were filled with tears. "Did Mom... did she suffer?"

"It threw her into a parked car. The cops said she was gone when they got to her. I don't believe it. She was just over the house Sunday for dinner."

"I looked at the picture of her and dad on my desk. "How's Dad taking it?"

"As good as you can expect. He's a pretty tough guy."

There was a long silence. "I'll get a flight tomorrow. It's too late tonight."

"Winfield's, I just called them, they're taking care of the arrangements. Catherine's still down there, she had to give the police a statement."

"Poor kid. It must be really hard on her." I paused. "Can I talk with Dad?"

"He just took a couple of pills, he's pretty groggy."

"Tell him I'll be there tomorrow."

"Right. Take care of yourself, Paulie."

"You too."

Akiko hugged me and said she how sorry she was. Gus put his arm around my shoulder, told me when he was away in the Pacific his mother died and he couldn't get back.

"She was a good woman," Akiko said. "She brought joy to everyone, from our brief acquaintance I saw this. Her spirit is safe but you need to take care of yourself."

The flight back was a hundred hours long. This can't be happening, I kept telling myself. We'd been resigned to losing Dad, but Mother! Cruelest of cruelties she goes first, and in such a stupid way. I prayed for her soul, asked this to be a wakeup to be kinder to each other, but the effort left me with a dry, ashen taste. I was angry with God for taking her, the light of our lives, for breaking the circle of our family.

Somewhere over the Great Plains, they said fasten seatbelts and for an hour we flew through the worst turbulence I have ever experienced before or since. Normally I would have had the seat arm in a death grip, but there I sat, utterly calm, staring out the window. In fact, from time to time I broke out laughing. Bring it on, God, I said, take your best shot. What more can you do to me? I tried to picture the funeral... the last one I'd been to was Eugene's, so many years ago. Finally the bumps eased. Now my small craft and I were in heavy swells. Closing my eyes, I spiraled down into a dark hole. I took a cab from Hillsgrove straight to the house. Everybody was there, crowded into our living room. I put down my bags as Dad hobbled up to me. He dropped his cane and took me by the shoulders. "I don't know what to say, son." He shook me gently. "I'm glad you're here."

"I'm so sorry. This is unbelievable."

"You know someday it will happen but..." Tears welled up in his rheumy eyes. "She was so full of life," he wiped his eyes with a sleeve, "so beautiful. It should have been me," he said. "Why didn't they take the cripple?"

I had no answer for that. "Where's Catherine?" I asked.

"Back at her place getting some sleep, poor thing," Aunt Moira said.

The wake was set for Wednesday night at Winfield's, the funeral for St. Teresa's the following day. The altar was adorned in black. Simple, beautiful, final. Incense filled the church, bearing my mother, my best friend, to heaven. Now pastor of a neighboring parish, Father McAdam, the young priest she so admired, returned to officiate. Burial on the cold, windy day at St. Ann's in Cranston in the Kelley family plot.

After the cemetery Aunt Moira did her best to thaw out the mourners with coffee and tea, sandwiches, coffee, drinks. A subdued gathering, almost gloomy, everyone still in shock. I caught up with aunts, uncles, cousins, all looking older but then, I supposed, so was I. Uncle Antoine and I got that chance to visit. Uncle Albert and Cousin Pièrre made the long drive, bringing condolences from the clan and a special greeting for me from *Pépère*.

I was glad Meg showed up, though I could have done without Clyde. He was now an associate in Mr. Harrington's old firm. Nice to see merit recognized, I thought. I meant to ask Clyde about his draft situation but didn't get around to it. Meg said she'd called Pat with the news and I'd be hearing from him. Sure, I thought, don't hold my breath. By the way, a letter did arrive and it was from Paris. I forgot to mention, his leave of absence came through and he was having the time of his life at the Sorbonne, hanging out in the Louvre.

The last night of my stay, Catherine and I met at an Italian restaurant in Federal Hill. She knew her way around the city well and said the area was more welcoming than it used to be, though I would always associate it with King. I was anxious to know exactly what happened, but reluctant to bring it up and ruin the evening. I needn't have worried because halfway through our first glasses of Chianti she started right in. "You're okay talking about this?" I interrupted.

She nodded. "Everybody's been trying to be nice, but I need to talk about it, get it out of my system." She took a deep breath. "We spent the day at MOMA, they had this wonderful Picasso exhibition, and we were trying to get a cab. We were out there in the rain, waving our arms, your typical sleety, unfriendly Manhattan rush hour, so I said we can get one at the Hilton. As we stepped off the curb the Wait signal was on, I'm holding Mom's arm, but nobody was coming so we went. Then it turns to Walk, that's what the police made such a big deal about, it definitely said Walk. I should know, I lived there two years."

She motioned me to refill her glass. "All of a sudden I see these headlights, two cars are racing to beat the light. I stopped in the middle of the intersection, I know not to trust New York drivers but Mom keeps going like it's her God-given right to cross the street on Walk. I yell, 'Stop, Mom! Stop!' but she keeps going..." She sniffed and wiped her nose with a handkerchief. "One guy stops but the other one comes barreling through, never even slowed down, the bastard." She lowered her eyes and fell silent. I thought her resolve had run out but she collected herself and went on. "She almost made it but it hit her and threw her up in the air. There was this awful sound, this crunch..."

"Jeez..."

"I went up to her..." Catherine's voice faltered. "I put my hand on her face... it was all bloody, her hair too. Her eyes were open but she was just staring. I bent down and took her head in my arms, I didn't know what to do, Paul, I didn't know what to do. A doorman from the hotel pulled me away, I heard them shouting call an ambulance. That's all I remember."

"You fainted."

"When I came to, all these lights were flashing, I remember thinking how pretty they were in the puddles, red and blue and white, then I started to cry. The police asked were we together, I said that's my mother and the cop said he was really sorry, there was nothing they could do. I guess I went crazy. They gave me a shot to calm me down."

"Did they take you to the hospital?"

"I wouldn't let them. The ambulance crew checked me over then a cop said he'd give me a ride. I called my friend Emily, we were getting together the next day. She wanted me to come up to her place, she was my roommate at Columbia, I don't think you ever met her, but I needed to be back at the hotel. She's such a good friend, she stayed the night..." Catherine looked at the bottle. "Pour me another?"

I tipped the bottle over but only a dribble came out. I looked at her, she nodded, and I signaled the waiter for another. "I never do this, I want you to know," she said.

"Me neither," already feeling tomorrow's headache. "The police are investigating..."

"A black BMW with a damaged left front. I called them yesterday, they're still looking for the bastard. I want him to hang by his balls."

"There's a surgical option I'd prefer, myself."

We went on another hour. I told her how sorry I was for my stupid remark. She said forget it, maybe she'd never get married, just cut her hair short and date girls, you can't trust men, if you have a few hours sometime I'll give you all the reasons. I laughed and shook my head. Finally I pushed my glass away. "Don't need any more, don't want any more."

"Let's settle up. Dutch?"

I had meant to pay but it occurred to me she might see that as a put-down. "Dutch it is." As we stood by her car I asked what she thought would happen next.

"I won't be surprised if Dad sells the house and moves to a place with care. He doesn't want to live with Jim, or me, for God's sake. As long as he can come and go he'll be fine. If something happens he's where he needs to be. We'll find something that works. Those places are expensive but he can afford it."

I had never felt closer to my sister, or Jim. The last few days he'd been great. We had finally grown up. My mother would have liked that, I thought. After a moment I broke out laughing. If I believe what I profess, I'd better say she *is* liking it.

28. THE GATHERING STORM

THIS AFTERNOON WHILE JONATHAN IS IN TOWN getting his *Times* the phone rings. It's Susan Leone again. "The fax come through okay?" she asks.

"Fine."

"I wanted you to know my boss told Latimer to pound sand."

"Couldn't happen to a nicer guy."

"I gave our attorneys Steve Samuel's name. They know each other so they were okay with him hanging on to the papers for now."

"Forget 'for now.' I am the literary executor, at least that's what you tell me."

"If push comes to shove that could be what gets ETVN off the hook with Latimer."

"But if ETVN's off the hook, who's on it? Me, that's who."

"There's some truth to that."

"Do the Latimer people know I'm involved?"

"I don't think so but it's only a matter of time."

I must have been muttering to myself because she asked me what I was saying. "You know what annoys me most about this business?" I tell her.

"No, what?" she says.

"If this keeps up I'll have to get a fax machine."

"Poor baby."

"Speaking of Samuels, we're getting ready to come down and look through the papers. Some time in the next couple of weeks, are you available to get us started?"

"I'll be here, just let me know."

An hour or so later Jonathan returns. We've fallen behind and have decided to work into the evening. Jonathan has settled down after his blow-up, and he's relieved to hear plans for New York are moving ahead. Finishing the Fiona file he puts the papers down and shakes his head. "That had to be tough on Paul, first his father, now this."

"They were very close. A fine lady, she was, spirited and grounded."

"What did you think about the father's comment about the war?"

"My gut tells me he was sincere. War made him a lot of money – you might think I'd fault him for that but I don't, I congratulate him for being an honest supplier. I despise the ones who cut corners, put our men at risk. There's another factor too, as they grow older most people mellow."

"Though not all, you for example."

"I'm not old enough, Jonathan."

"What about the mellow part?"

"Don't worry, when I go it won't be gentle into that good night."

"Looks like you weren't surprised, Paul and his second thoughts."

"Happens to a lot of kids. The dissident scene did get to him. In a more tranquil time my feeling is he would have stuck with the program, though at some point all young men need to spread their wings. Paul didn't want to hear that but it was true."

"That old lady in Boston, the grandmother, she's impressive."

"Absolutely! That *mission civilisatrice* she spoke of, it had flair but it was all about exploitation, no different from the others. Incidentally exploitation wasn't always a dirty word. Often both sides benefitted, though certainly not equally."

"Not to mention the chance for eternal life."

"See, you are catching on!"

"Thank you. What about thc anti-American issue? Your differences with Paul on that one seemed more a matter of degree."

"How do you mean?"

"You said you had confidence our system can take a beating and bounce back. But you both rejected the protesters supporting the enemy."

"That is true. Incidentally, I have never understood what 'Americanism' means, let alone its opposite. Such pieties always struck me as politically motivated and lacking content, but I also want to make a point about Johnson. Despite what I said, for such a smart guy, he did let himself get trapped. If he'd only played it straight he could have been a towering historical figure, one of the best, but it'll never happen."

"Father Trần seems like an interesting character. And by the way, don't forget your Reconstruction book, I want to see it."

"Thanks for the reminder. I'll bring it out tomorrow."

* * * * * * *

IN THE FALL OF SIXTY-FIVE Berkeley acquired a new Chancellor. Tough but fair, they said, Roger Heyns was a top administrator at Michigan, a Social Psychologist by trade. Good luck, Dr. Heyns, I said to myself, you'll need all the acumen you have to stay afloat here, surrounded by people for whom compromise is a dirty word.

The third exam was taking all my time. I got off to a decent start, but now my attention span was short and brittle. I found myself logging a lot of window time. At least the news from home was better. My father was finally taking his rehab seriously, walking an hour every day, and though his speech would never be normal, he was slurring his words a lot less. I told Catherine Mom's death seemed to kick him into action. She countered, saying it wasn't fair to think mother had been holding him back. That's not what I meant, I said, but if he's going to lick this thing he's got to do it on his own. Maybe he senses time's running out.

Catherine's hunch about the house was right. Dad hired a real estate agent, one of the clan, *bien sûr*, targeting early summer for a sale. Another old crony, a jack-of-all-trades, was remedying years of maintenance neglect. Soon I would have to face the unthinkable and clear out my room, say goodbye to my home. First, though, I had to get through the exam in May.

On Charter Day I trekked to the Greek Theater for U.N. Ambassador Goldberg's speech, wading into a sea of anti-war signs. The administration had let one of the protest groups distribute them, bowing to their threat to block the entrances. Looking at the sorry display I wished I had taken a sign and written my own message on the back. When the ambassador was introduced a lot of the crowd stood and walked out. Shameful treatment for an honored guest, but he showed his class by staying after the ceremony to debate the war, vigorously defending our policy. That evening also saw the famous Vietnam Day Committee dance Ronald Reagan would make so much of in his campaign, gleefully holding up a police report of three rock bands playing simultaneously (God forbid, three!), the light show, the marijuana, the dancers "twisting and gyrating in provocative fashion," in other words – his words – the orgy.

Reagan was so far off base. I had dropped into a dance concert at the Student Union the month before, and a couple of times crossed the Bay with friends to visit the Fillmore. Grateful Dead, Quicksilver Messenger Service, Jefferson Airplane. If some people wanted to fry their brains on pot and LSD, the new fad, let them. But the light shows, the ear-splitting music, the fantastic outfits more or less worn by the girls, it was all great theater and great fun. I even had one of those psychedelic posters, Grace Slick and the Airplane. Reagan was nothing more than an opportunist in an Uncle Sam suit – on this point the leftists were certainly correct – a glib front man for the state's wealthy elite.

Speaking of music, the local folk scene was moribund, crushed by the rock steamroller. Sergeant Pepper versus Peter, Paul and Mary? No contest. To his fans' dismay even Dylan went electric and we had "folk rock" hybrids like Creedence and The Byrds. Country Joe and the Fish, a Berkeley fixture, was *sui generis.* Earnest and melodic was out, ecstasy and altered consciousness in. A couple of radio stations played this music and from time to time I dialed in to hear the latest.

During the spring, anti-war opposition bubbled along with the occasional eruption. Over coffee one day Benny complained that the "mess at Berkeley" played right into Reagan's hands. "If he gets in, God help the University," he said.

"Isn't that what you want, make things so bad you can walk in and take over?"

"What I really want is to finish my degree before things come unglued."

Have your cake and eat it too, I thought, but in the spirit of amity I held my tongue. Shortly after the new year I had called Benny and told him about my mother. We declared a truce and resolved to focus on what we had in common which was, in fact, a lot. He also was through two exams and well along on his thesis plan. "Where do you get the time to study?" I asked.

"I need less sleep than most."

The hippies owned Telegraph Avenue. Once an eccentric fringe, they now were everywhere. I talked with enough of them to know they weren't interested in subverting society or even changing it. Their universe had little to do with the "normal" world. The pill offered risk-free sex, though oddly, there were children everywhere, particularly in the rural communes, a small-c communist movement. Mellow out, live in the moment. "If it feels good, do it," or in Timothy Leary's famous formulation, "tune in, turn on, drop out." The *Berkeley Barb* had the largest circulation of any local paper and I read it regularly. Though its politics were a turn-off it was a good source of information and the opinion pieces (they were all opinion pieces) well-argued. From its protest origins it had transitioned to hip, and had a keen interest in sex. Its classifieds left little to the imagination.

As flower power sprouted, again I found myself the observer – interested, bemused, occasionally fascinated. One time at the Fillmore, I spotted Rachel and went over to say hello. She was glassy-eye stoned out of her mind. She left the guy she was with, threw her arms around my neck and gave me a kiss that in other circumstances could only be described as passionate. Finished, she backed off and smiled. "I know you from somewhere, don' I? Wanna ball?"

The week before Memorial Day I sat for the exam, a three-and-a-half-hour ordeal. To relax, next day I pushed old Plymouth up the mountain to the Sierra Club lodge at Donner Summit, this side of Tahoe. Day hikes, family-style meals, a clean bunk, tame compared with last year's outing. I invited Mark and Hamid but they were busy. Hamid was headed for Columbia and a Ph.D. in Comparative Literature. I said I'd stop by and see him when I was back there. Mark had a job lined up in L.A. with RAND Corporation, some military project he couldn't tell me anything about. I learned later he was interviewing North Vietnamese POWs and defectors, trying to decipher the mood of the enemy. And I was headed home. The house had been sold.

AT THE AIRPORT Catherine filled me in. In a couple of weeks my father would move to an assisted living facility, everything provided, out beyond Greenville. She pressed for something closer-in but he said he always wanted to live in the country and if he was ever going to do it, he'd better do it now. He had the Cadillac fitted with hand controls, so he'd be mobile. I counted it a good sign that he was not about to give in to his limitations. Catherine said a young couple with three kids had bought the house. "It's weird to think it won't be in the family any more."

As we drove up my father was sitting in a chair outside the front door. He got to his feet, steadying himself with his cane. My arms encircled him easily. Catherine offered to cook dinner but he wanted to go out, so we compromised on Chinese take-out – our loss, she said. After dinner she washed, for old times' sake I dried. My eyes filled with tears and I had to look away, feeling my mother's absence keenly.

"Two weeks and I'll be out of here," my father was saying as he sipped a cup of tea at the kitchen table. "Believe me, I am ready." He offered to tour me around his new digs. "I'll even drive," he said, "if you're man enough to ride with me, that is."

"I think I can handle it."

Jim would tackle the huge job of dealing with my parents' possessions. Sheila lay claim to most of the furniture, she and Jim having just bought a house. Anticipating his portion of Nu-Gem stock, Jim was also talking about buying into the plumbing company as a partner. And now it was time for me to focus on the residue from my twenty-four years on the planet. I had outgrown my bed long ago, the desk would go, a couple of lamps I tagged for shipping. My Hardy Boys and Tom Swifts would pass to Mark and Mikey, also my Lionel trains, bike and assorted toys. My bat and glove, St. Teresa's uniform, important personal stuff, I would keep – the Little Prince and *le Petit Prince,* my dusty old Tower Special. Outgrown clothes were headed to St. Vincent de Paul, in fact there was so much stuff from the house they were sending a truck.

I sat on the floor, sorting. Late afternoon sun poured through my tree, shadows dancing on the curtains. The robins' nest was already full of baby birds. Pictures, albums, letters, souvenirs from trips to Canada, Maine vacations, clippings, reminders of long-forgotten events. Most of it hit the wastebasket, some I set aside. I had this idea that reminding myself where I had been might give me a clue where to go next. Last box... that big manila envelope. I slid the picture out, my namesake in his Army Air Force uniform. The browned, cracked obituary was in there, too, November 2, 1942. All Souls' Day. Years ago my father told me when it happened he called Dave LaPointe and a few days later the photo arrived in the mail. As I held the envelope something spiraled to the floor, the drawing from John Fawcett's "Rhode Island Heroes" series, modeled on the Spitfire photo in our living room. A hero, they called him. This stopped me cold. Here am I, same age as Maurice and what have I done? How will my nephews remember me, I wondered, my children if I have any. I shuddered... Vietnam makes heroes every day. I sped through the rest of the box.

That evening I told my father I had a favor to ask. I had Maurice's North Africa picture, the P-38, in my hand. "I'd like to have this," I said. "You'll still have the other one," I added, pointing to its twin, the Spitfire.

He gave me this funny look. "Sure, but why do you want it? You haven't looked at it since you were a kid."

I didn't know how to answer. After a moment I replied, "it's part of our heritage, something to remember us by."

"That's all?"

"That's all."

He nodded, his lips pursed. "If you say so."

That last night I tossed and turned, finally getting up at 4:30 and going to the living room to read. For some time I hadn't been sleeping well. Doubts about my studies, worry over my country's predicament, my anger at the protesters, but most of all I was upset at myself. My family had contributed. Maurice. My father and uncle, seeing the company through tough times. Here I am, the brain, more education than all of them put together and I'm not worth a fraction of what they were. That day I left my home for the last time.

The first night back I dreamt. Whenever I dream, no matter what it is or where, if there's a house in it, it's always that first home. My back porch, my yard, my living room, my room, my window, my tree. Make of it what you will, in the deep recesses of our being, mine anyway, childhood long outlives the child.

Catherine called the following week to give me Dad's new phone number. He seemed at loose ends, she said. The house sale went smoothly and I should expect a letter any day about the financial stuff. She had just gotten hers and I better be sitting when I opened it.

A few days later two pieces of mail arrived. The first one I had to sign for, a big envelope from Dad's lawyer. I skimmed the letter, saw that he was pleased to forward five hundred shares of Nu-Gem stock which I was free to keep or sell all or any portion of. He went on to say "for my planning purposes," my father's intention was to make a similar gift each year for an indefinite period. I had no idea how much the stock was worth, I'd have to look it up, but the other letter, from the Department of Political Science, was screaming to be opened. Eagerly I slid my finger under the gummed seal and ripped the envelope open.

I had failed the exam! I had FAILED! A blur of words... sorry to advise... very close... fullest consideration given. Contact your advisor.

IMPOSSIBLE! Paul Bernard doesn't fail! I sat down heavily, staring at the paper. How can this be? I worked hard, sure there were distractions but I dealt with them. Jesus! I better call Don, I thought, reaching for the phone but... what is his number? I know it like the back of my hand. I put the phone down. Take it easy, deep breath, go for a walk. Go out, get some air. I didn't even look at Gus on my way out. My face burning, I walked all the way to Grizzly Peak Boulevard then back down toward the Rose Garden. Sitting on a bench next to the tennis courts, I watched a couple of women hit the ball. Back and forth, back and forth – older ladies, pretty good. Suddenly a wave of indecision washed over me. Is this a message the game's not worth playing? I shook my head, hard. If I leave I'll go out on top. Next day I got hold of Don. He said I screwed up one part so badly the committee didn't feel they could pass me. Nor, for that matter, would it be fair to me. "Such consideration I can do without," I grumbled.

It turned out I had fallen short in not one, but two areas. One was comparing crimes with civil wrongs or torts, how each is remedied, prosecutions versus civil suits. Okay, I can accept that, I remember feeling uncomfortable with my answer, but the other was a total surprise – right in my wheelhouse, separation of powers, FDR's court-packing scheme. Don took me through their reasoning but my answer still looked plenty good enough.

Gus told me not to be discouraged. Don set the retake for the first week of October. Couldn't I take just the parts I had failed, I asked, but he said Departmental policy required the whole thing be done over. So again I plunged into the tepid waters of Public Law, driven by the need to redeem myself.

In my condition it wasn't until days later I got around to the other envelope. I looked up the stock price of Nu-Gem (NUG on the NYSE) and found it was a little under twenty dollars a share, which meant I had just come into ten thousand dollars! I never expected that much. I called my father that night to thank him.

"I hope it doesn't cool off your ambition, it's meant to help, not hurt."

"I think I can handle it," I replied.

He didn't ask about the exam and I didn't tell him. They knew I wasn't perfect, why remind them? Get through it, then tell him. I told Benny, though. He didn't lord it over me that he'd passed and already had a date for his oral. Somehow he managed to fit everything in while he changed the world. "Failing one isn't unusual," he said, "the social sciences are so subjective, grading's sometimes a crapshoot."

"I appreciate the vote of confidence," I replied, really meaning it. "So what's ahead for the fall of sixty-six, on the protest scene, that is?"

"The war continues, so we continue. Then there's the election. Can you believe, Ronald Fucking Reagan has an excellent chance of becoming Governor?"

"No small thanks to what you guys have done here. I can't wait to see what's up your sleeve this time."

NOW I REALLY DUG IN. Long days, long nights, no window gazing as I put my doubts aside and plowed ahead. By the end of summer I was ready, even eager. One day crossing Sproul Plaza I ran into a crowd of leather-jacketed, black-bereted young black people – don't call us Negroes any more – carrying signs for something called the Black Panther Party. They talked about the white establishment, how they would face down the pigs – the police – how Black Power would retake the streets of Oakland and every other city. Angry rhetoric, threats, violent images. I looked at the signs, names I'd never heard of – Bobby Seale and Huey Newton, though Stokely Carmichael was familiar from SNCC. Why were these people abandoning Dr. King? No good will come of this, I thought as I walked away, ears smarting. A new day was dawning, with a black and red sky. Anti-war chaos, now racial belligerence, the piece that will send Reagan to Sacramento and bring the right wing down on us. Poor Dr. Heyns, poor Cal. As I mounted the library steps Yeats came to mind. After the radicals have their way there'll be no center at all to hold.

I won't keep you dangling. I passed, and Gus and Akiko threw a party to celebrate. Benny and Leah were there, Gideon whom I hadn't seen in a while, Mark, visiting from RAND. Hank, insisting "two more years and I'm finished," though nobody believed him. Two new roommates, Sam Watson, a junior college transfer from Chico State, and Erika Schumann. Yes, Erika. Gus had finally relented and the house welcomed its first female boarder, not counting half of the short-lived married couple. After some redesign Erika ended up with a nice corner room to herself. She was from Austria, a grad student in Archaeology. When we were introduced I asked about her hometown, Linz. There was something about Linz...

"Hitler went to school there, his parents are buried near there."

"I see."

"People no longer hold him in esteem these days, if that's what you are thinking, though some remember the good things he did and discount the evil. Fortunately Linz can claim others of greater repute – Kepler, Anton Bruckner, Wittgenstein, for a few." I put Hitler on hold and turned the conversation in another direction. Skiing. That was more like it. Naturally she was an accomplished skier.

It was good to see Mark, though he was worried his reserve unit was about to be called up. "Question of when, not if. Sure you won't join us? We can use you."

Like Socrates, Gideon could drink everybody under the table, debating late into the night, but as this evening wore on the grape began making its presence felt. Gus had just made a nice speech and Benny was going on about Providence, how it was obvious early neither of us was much of an athlete. "The only difference, and this is important, Paul was devastated, but I never cared. I guess I knew myself better than he did back then..."

"He still doesn't have a clue," Gideon broke in. Everybody's heads turned. "I mean, how can a person who claims to be for the oppressed be such a tool of the establishment? Freedom Summer, he was among the missing. Sproul Hall? Same thing. The only sign he ever carried was on the wrong side of the tracks, managed to get himself on TV, though..."

"Hey, come on, Gideon," Benny said, "you know what happened there."

"No, that's okay." I went up to Gideon and put my arm on his shoulder. "Let him talk. He's entitled to his opinion," I said, "just like I am."

He yanked my arm away. "You? An opinion? How can you be for this war? How dare you support Johnson and his thugs?"

I took a deep breath. This wasn't the place for a fight but he was making it one.

"I happen to believe we have a duty to defend our country." I stood tall to Gideon, who was a big guy. "As for that bunch of thugs, you forget we elected them. If you don't like it, there's another election coming up. That's how to send your message. Don't pull the rug from under our men who're risking their lives for you."

"From this point on we take things into our own hands," Gideon said angrily.

"A government of men not laws," I shouted back, "and of course, you'll be one of those men. Chaos in the streets, threats, intimidation... that's not how we do things here!"

"Bull-*shit!* When the deck's stacked against you, that is *exactly* what you do here! That's how this system operates!"

I smiled. "That's part of the game, even I know that, but it sure as hell isn't the main part. Those boring little procedures for changing things – that's all that stands between us and chaos. Your way, it'll be rocks and bricks, then fists, then neighbors'll be gunning each other down. It took a long time to get where we are, Gideon. Trample on that system and you are starting down a long, dark path!"

Benny moved in and cut Gideon out of the group. I could see him lecturing him in a corner. Out on the deck I was shaking, I was so upset. Erika asked if I wanted a beer. On her way in she passed Benny coming out. "I apologize," Benny said, "that was highly inappropriate. I don't agree with you either but this isn't the time or place."

I slumped in a chair, totally fatigued. "I didn't need this tonight."

Erika appeared again and Benny left to go back inside. "Soon I must show you what good Austrian beer is like."

"You're on." I raised my glass, happy for a friendly smile.

She was quiet a moment. "What you said, I was thinking the world would have been spared much misery if ordinary Germans had stood up for their heritage, their institutions. My career will have me uncovering the bones of ancient civilizations." She shook her head. "What ruins will future archaeologists find in Europe? What will they find in America?"

One day in late October the phone rang. "Paul! This is Pat!"

"How the hell are you? Where are you?"

"Boston," he said. "You doing all right? Sorry to hear about your mother."

"Thanks," I said, "and thanks for the card. I'm working on my thesis. You remember my experiment, governments under stress?"

"Your what?"

"Governments under stress. We talked about it at the Cross."

"You still farting around with that thing? Send me a copy. I need to see what you do with all those good ideas I give you."

"How're you doing anyway? Are you back?"

"My draft board would like to think so but I've finally licked it. Just got some very good news. You remember that time I hurt my knee?"

"Can't say I do."

"Sophomore year. Ice in front of Carlin, bottom of the stairs? At the time it wasn't that big a deal but thank God I messed it up enough, it actually hurts like a sonofabitch sometime. I can even tell when it's going to rain."

"Your knee should be on the ten o'clock news."

"No kidding. Those little pieces of cartilage are all that stands between me and an all-expenses paid trip to a very bad place, but here's why I called. I just got a letter from this world-famous orthopedist and I quote. 'The patient's left knee is unreliable under stress.' Stress like carrying a pack and a rifle, if you get my drift. He says get it fixed surgically but even then the prognosis is not all that certain."

"Sounds like you could have written it yourself."

"Yeah, well my father had something to do with it."

"You and he are getting along? You going back to law school?"

"Hell, no. If this works I'm back to Paris next week. I've been working on a degree in Art History, I'll have you know, not just screwing around..."

"You've been doing some of that, I trust."

"*Mais oui!* No, to his credit papa has decided he doesn't want his only son coming home in a box, a thought I heartily second. He's even okay my not finishing law school. He doesn't like what I'm doing but he even admitted it might lead to a real job. Must be getting soft in his old age."

"I hear what you're saying about law. I had a snootful recently, no fun at all."

"Well, I gotta go. Keep in touch."

"You keep in touch! Still at the same address?"

"I'm in Montmartre now. I'll send it to you."

"That'll be the day. Say hello to everybody and congratulations, I think."

Shaking my head I hung up. Some things those black power people were saying came to mind, Vietnam being a poor people's war, a poor black people's war. Good work, Pat. Fall down and live happily ever after. Then I thought, it's not funny. I can face Gideon down, Benny, even Gus, I can criticize Pat, but talk is cheap. What am I doing about anything?

For the first time I ventured into the business end of the classroom. Don invited me to T.A. in Aquinas to Mao... had it really been three years? Being in charge was exhilarating and I found the students a challenge. The big surprise was the prep time, grading too, being fair but not a patsy. Art Tedeschi was pushing me to join the union. I declined, a good decision it turned out, for in December the radicals attempted another strike and had I been a member I would have had to cancel my classes. Striking was not my cup of tea, nor unions. Apparently enough others felt the same and the strike failed.

AT CHRISTMAS I MADE A QUICK TRIP to see my father. His strength and vigor were pouring back. He was doing light work around the complex – painting, carpentry. The Caddie was getting a workout as he often visited Antoine and Héloise and the grandchildren. I checked on his place, seeing his new life, how he spent his time. Even by my standards the food was mediocre. When I asked him if that's why he did so much visiting, he winked.

Driving by the old place it looked the same except for a hoop on the garage and a new name on the mailbox. I was tempted to ring the bell and announce this is not your home and it never will be, but I didn't. I called Boston, expecting to hear Pat and his golden knee were on holiday in the Alps. His mother surprised me – he was in Florence helping to clean up art damaged in the flood. What do you know, I thought, credit where it's due.

On New Year's Eve, Gus, Akiko and I raised our glasses to the falling ball. Akiko said 1967 is the Year of the Goat, a gentle, artistic sign portending harmony, tranquility and understanding. Since adopting the Gregorian calendar in the nineteenth century Japan celebrates the New Year on January first, she said, though the Chinese lunar calendar puts theirs in early February, same for the Vietnamese who have a lovely name for the first day of their year, *Tết Nguyên Đán,* "Feast of the First Morning," or simply, *"Tết."*

The election gave the political landscape a new look. Republicans gained fifty seats in the U.S. Congress, including one that made me proud of my semi-adopted state, Edward Brooke, the first black man ever elected to the U.S. Senate. Despite strenuous opposition from the radicals, also thanks to them, Ronald Reagan swept to the Governorship of California. Three weeks in office, Reagan showed harmony and tranquility weren't high on his agenda as he and hard-line Regents gave Clark

Kerr the boot. Kerr was quoted as saying he came into the President's job "fired with enthusiasm" and left the same way.

"Good for Clark," Gus observed. "He could have put his tail between his legs and gone quietly but he forced them to act." The Regents named an insider, Harry Wellman, a VP and Professor of Agricultural Economics, as Acting President. "Harry's basically been running the University for years," Gus said, "but don't count on him making waves – though these days maybe that's not so bad."

First week of February the faculty committee approved my thesis plan. The plan was the easy part, now I had to research and write the damned thing. If you'll bear with me, here's the start of a visual aid I was developing. We didn't give it to the thesis committee, though. Don thought they'd fixate on it and pick it apart before we were ready.

	GOV'T PROCESSES	SECURITY/ SAFETY	CIVIL RIGHTS	PRESS FREEDOM
U.S. EXAMPLES				
WW1&2 Internments/Curbs				
-- German/Italian-Americans				
-- Japanese-Americans				
McCarthyism: Blacklists				
U.C. Loyalty Oaths (state)				
Hiroshima and Nagasaki				
Negro/Black Voting Rights				
-- Southern States				
-- Northern States				
-- Federal Gov't vs States				
Urban Riots (local/state)				
-- 1964 Harlem/Brooklyn				
-- 1965 Watts				

VIETNAM - SPECIAL TOPIC? OR WORK INTO GRID?
-- Initiation - Tonkin Resolution and pre-
-- Anti-War Protests
-- Other
OTHER COUNTRIES???
France - Vichy/Deportation of Jews
England - Area Bombing of Germany. Dresden.
Russia - Gulags
France - African Colonies and Indochina
Belgium - African Colonies

I was afraid not enough reliable material was available on Vietnam. The "other countries" list was there to test my hypothesis that democracies do a better job living up to their ideals than other forms of government. Gus and I had some heated discussions on that one, and it was such a huge topic in itself I'd probably have to axe it.

Early in the new year the "counterculture" made a big splash. January 14, a bright, breezy Saturday, saw twenty thousand youths assembled in Golden Gate Park. Billed as a "Gathering of the Tribes" and a "Human Be-In," it was political rally, demonstration and drug festival all in one. Those who weren't stoned on arrival caught up fast. The police stood by, sensibly, hands in their pockets. Radicals wanted a political rally but were swamped by high times. When they finally gained the stage the crowd's attention was gone and soon so was the crowd. Long hair, beards, sandals, freedom, love, music – some ascribed the birth of the hippie counterculture to this event. An overstatement, but it gave young people as far away as Alabama and Maine ideas about an excitingly different way to live. In a few months many of them, "some flowers in their hair," would converge on the Haight Ashbury for San Francisco's Summer of Love. The older generation was freaking out as their imminent irrelevance came into focus.

On the other side of the globe, Vietnam was as intractable as ever. Our victories proved short-lived. Search-and-destroy missions knocked out Communist positions, devastated regions and killed many Vietcong, those who weren't forewarned to flee. Problem was, as our troops moved on, the guerillas seeped back, reclaiming their territory. The biggest broom is useless against the tide.

Gus showed me a letter he received from Mark. When Johnson decided to bite the bullet and call up the reserves, his unit would be the first to go. People were told to set their lives in order – jobs, families, mortgages.

A "Spring Mobilization" broke in San Francisco and a mammoth New York event with the old standbys – King, Spock, Carmichael. Dr. King had recently admitted the Great Society had perished in Vietnam, as Professor Shapiro had predicted, but in New York he went overboard, calling the United States "the greatest purveyor of violence in the world."

"An unbelievable day," Benny told me on one of our periodic get-togethers, "I even got my father to join me. We're talking middle America now... LBJ is in deep trouble."

"What were you people thinking! NLF flags! Collecting blood for the Viet Cong! Which side are you on? Glorifying those bandits makes a mockery of the non-violence you're supposedly for. And King's comment, that's just going too far."

"Yeah, well, consider he's in touch with a higher authority."

"A private line, no doubt."

Those who'd had it with the administration included not only newly-minted peaceniks Robert Kennedy and Eugene McCarthy, but others with a solid track record, like Senator Fulbright. I disagreed with Fulbright too, but he backed up his position with reasons, not just rhetoric. No way could you accuse him of opportunism.

During the spring Cal and other campuses encountered disruption against job recruiters for the CIA and Dow Chemical Company, the maker of napalm. To me, if somebody wants to interview for a job with the CIA or anywhere else he should be able to do it, and not just with recruiters "The Movement" happens to approve of.

I kept plugging away, finding lots of material on the Japanese-Americans, less on German- and Italian-American harassment, but enough for starters. What jumped off the pages was how so often worries about security and defense have fed a blanket paranoia. Obviously, in a nation of immigrants, some parents, grandparents were born in countries we are no longer friendly with. To me the key was how we individually identified dangerous people. Were our procedures workable? If not, what then? What was the impact of political pressure? And how did the courts handle what seemed a clear abuse of authority?

As I grappled with these questions, I tried to measure the political climate of the time against the real-life civics lesson unfolding in front of me. The dissent and lawlessness fomented by the Vietnam protestors didn't exist in a vacuum. The mood of the nation was being poisoned by people who had a very specific purpose. Standards of propriety were being obliterated, tolerance and respect overwhelmed.

As summer came on, a toxic cloud settled on the inner cities, then Negro unrest and resentment ignited the incendiary mix. In April Nashville exploded, May and June saw violence in Cleveland, Washington, New York, Minneapolis, Cincinnati, even San Francisco. The first weekend in July brought it home in a big way as, horrified, Gus and I watched gangs of Negroes roaming Boston's Roxbury section, looting, smashing windows, torching buildings, beating whites. By Sunday evening the police had put down the insurrection but seventy people were hurt and fifteen blocks of Blue Hill Avenue lay in ruins.

"This is hard to take," Gus said, shaking his head. I'd never seen him so angry. "Goddamn war! Goddamn stupid Johnson! He had it all right here!" he banged his fist in the palm of his hand. "Employment! Retraining! Education! Medicare! Then he bends over for the military and – surprise! What the hell did he expect? Damned chickenhearts, afraid of their own shadow!" He snapped off the TV. "Paul, look. If we do the right thing by our people, we have nothing to fear from the Russians, the Chinese, certainly not the Vietnamese. Of course that's the rub, often our government does not do the right thing. What pisses me off, Johnson was moving the country in a good direction, now he's blown it. If he survives he'll be so weak the selfish and greedy will have a field day and believe me, they know how to take advantage."

"You sound like FDR about fear."

"Old FDR knew what he was talking about." Gus put his finger to his temple. "It's all up here. Psychology. Confidence." He was quiet for a moment, then shifted in his chair and leaned forward. "But there's another explanation, Paul. Cynical, darker."

"Which is?"

"We need an enemy. We always need an enemy. If it's a religious enemy, and certainly Communism is that, so much the better. Why do you think that Cardinal from New York sponsored Diem? Why does he show up in Vietnam, parading around in those army fatigues? You think he's promoting our country's interests? Hell, no! It's the Roman Catholic Church plus, of course, his position in that august institution. He's using us, Paul, he's using us to beat back the godless forces of evil. *That's* his mission."

"But what's your point?" I knew Cardinal Spellman was a vocal supporter of the war, a man of influence, but so what?

"Let me lay it out for you. Point one. Communism is the mortal enemy. That's been drummed into us since we split with Uncle Joe. We're offered this choice: be a slave of Communism or be a cowed little child. Point two, the Catholic vote gets a hell of a lot of people elected, mostly Democrats. That translates into tremendous political muscle for the Church, so guess what's number one on their agenda. Anti-Communism! "Can't lose one square foot to Communism," they say, to which I answer, *bullshit!*

"Ever wonder why we didn't give a rat's ass about Hitler until it was too late? Why we were so quick to buddy up to Werner von this and Werner von that after the war? Why didn't the Church speak out against the monstrosity of Nazism? Because when it looked in the mirror what it saw was *its own face,* that's why! And now here we are stuck with timid institutions and eunuchs running them! Sickening, it is, absolutely sickening."

The next week Newark erupted, then Detroit. Eventually the pot boiled over and put out the fire. For now. LBJ appointed a study commission. Gus shook his head sadly. "Hearings, commissions, we do everything but deal with the problem. What a mess we are!"

In June we were treated to the "Six-Day War," Israel's decisive victory over Arab states and Egypt's Nasser. Israel gained control of the Gaza Strip, the Sinai Peninsula, the West Bank and the Golan Heights, moves that reverberate to this day. Through its proxy states, the United States and Russia had again faced off, though the quick end to the fighting limited the risk of a direct confrontation. I called Benny. He said he'd never been prouder. We agreed to meet on the Terrace, though our schedules prevented getting together until the six days had run its course. "Amazing display," he said. "That has to be one of the top performances of all time." Then a frown came to his face, "but not without its down side, I'm afraid. Those territories will be more trouble than they're worth, all but the Golan."

I was surprised at his frankness. "How does Gideon feel?" I asked.

"Keep it all, it's ours anyway. Flood it with settlers so we can never give it back."

"What about the refugees? They say huge numbers of Palestinians are being uprooted from the West Bank."

"We'll be living with that festering sore for years. Oh, by the way, Gideon is still pissed at you."

"*He's* pissed! He started it, right in front of my friends! Did he think I'd take that crap from him?"

"You caught him off guard. I wasn't surprised, still waters run deep. I wonder how deep yours are."

"I wonder too."

"How's your thesis coming?" he asked.

"Mired in research. You?"

"I hate to tell you but I passed my orals. And my first draft's about finished."

"You love what you're doing. With me, every day's a battle."

He looked at his watch. "Got to run," he said. "Don't worry, you'll do fine."

Don's advice was looking better all the time: keep it simple, don't attempt too much. I abandoned my plan to test democracies against other forms of government. Vietnam also missed the cut. Too bad the war and the protests couldn't be dispatched as easily in real life. Unable to fudge the numbers any longer, LBJ finally proposed an income tax surcharge. But Congress dragged its heels, and by the time it was enacted the budget deficit had tripled and the inflation spiral was accelerating.

The mood of the country was grim. Where would the whirlwind alight next?

29. YOUNG MEN, OLD MEN – VISIONS, DREAMS

"WAS REAGAN AS BAD as people make him out to be?"

"Every bit and more. Our esteemed acting governor tried to dismantle the world's finest system of higher education and damn near succeeded. I have no respect for that man. What he supposedly accomplished later, that's for another day."

Jonathan laughed. "Sorry I asked. Okay, back to Paul. Failing that exam – big problem? Little problem?"

"He was crushed, but he got over it. In fact, the work he did served him well later."

"Then there was that function at your house."

"Ah, Gideon'd had too much to drink. Gideon was something of a hothead, Paul had strong beliefs and that day they collided, though, as I say, the grape had something to do with it. Gideon wanted Paul with him but couldn't bring him around. That frustrated him."

"I was interested in your comments about fearmongers."

"It saddens me to see charlatans leading people by the nose. First they terrify – end of the world, nuclear disaster, economic collapse, you name it – then surprise! We have the solution – our party, our church, whatever. Mystery and secrecy are big, smoke and mirrors. Thing is, you never know if the clever charlatan delivers or not, because he's already on to the next round of scare and save. A neat scam – it's been going on ever since men first sat around a fire and looked at a chief, a king, a priest."

"Quite the cynic, aren't you?"

"Not at all. That is how power works, how it has always worked. Who sits at the finest tables, eats the choicest food, wears the best clothes? Who wears the funny hats?"

"Funny hats?"

"I kid you not, Jonathan, follow the funny hats. They lead unerringly to a society's power elite. A terrific phrase, by the way – my friend Mills beat me to it. And no coincidence, it's the scammers who profit the most."

Earlier in the day we worked it out that Jonathan and I will visit the New York offices of Carter, Delfino & Samuels LLP where Paul's papers reside. This will be an extended stay – at least a couple of weeks – I better make hotel arrangements. Jonathan offered me the use of his pad but I declined. A futon on somebody's floor doesn't do it for me.

ETVN's attorney has said if Latimer files suit they'll have to bring me into it. As literary executor I am what they call the "real party in interest." Steve suggested we could return the papers to ETVN, but I tell him no and hell no. Besides, if our case is as good as you say it is, you'll stick Latimer with fees, costs, the whole nine yards. He says he'll do what he can. I need to talk with Dennis, too – he owes me a call. Maybe I can get him to meet me in New York.

* * * * * * *

AT THE END OF SIXTY-SIX the troop level was at 375,000. By spring it approached 500,000, with casualties and deaths mounting. Prompted by the Joint Chiefs, the Senate Armed Services Committee convened hearings to pressure LBJ. The military was urging the amateurs to step aside and let them do the job. Johnson was chagrined at this unaccustomed sandbagging yet escalated his bombing of the North.

In the fall of sixty-seven, protesters filled the streets. A San Francisco-based group calling itself The Resistance advanced a simple proposition. Since the war is immoral, you are a murderer if you don't resist. Demonstrating is no longer enough, but the militants will make chaos in the streets the price of waging the war. Young people were increasingly receptive. Draft calls had increased tenfold, to 50,000 a month. Draft card turn-ins multiplied. The Bay Area contributed Stop the Draft Week, centered on the Oakland Induction Center, with a day set aside for open warfare in downtown Oakland. But it was left to Washington to host the main event, a march on the Pentagon which reflected the usual duality, peaceful protests and arrests, militant cadres bent on violence.

In November Robert McNamara resigned, likely under pressure, disillusioned, and reportedly close to a nervous breakdown. Also exiting was LBJ's friend and press secretary, Bill Moyers, unhappy with a boss whose credibility was in doubt. Mike Mansfield led a month-long visit to Vietnam, on his return warning that we were becoming trapped in an open-ended conflict. Others on the Hill stepped up the criticism, though Congress continued its funding of the war. In a startling development, Nick Katzenbach, Justice's Mississippi point man, now Attorney General, claimed it was outmoded for Congress to declare war – that the Tonkin Resolution is more than enough for the President to take such military action as he saw fit, period. I didn't like hearing this from the respected Katzenbach.

It was distressing, my country faring so poorly. Why were we no long able to shape events, solve problems? Why couldn't Johnson level with us? Even a national hero, Cassius Clay, now Muhammad Ali, came out against the war. He was stripped of his title and given five years for draft evasion. I agreed with Gus that Washington was doing a lousy job fighting the war and an even worse job explaining it. Then there were the faltering social programs once touted as the best chance for our problem-ridden cities.

Marches, speeches, TV, TV, speeches, marches... on and on and on. I read the papers and watched the news, but was drained to the point of not caring any more. No, I take that back, I cared too much. I just didn't know what to do about it. I wasn't at Cal to escape the war, but as my interest in the studies waned, how could

I justify staying out of it? I couldn't bear the idea of another Christmas in the library. Maybe some time at home would kick me into gear. First thing I did when I arrived was take my father to lunch. He'd been fighting a cold and was acting snappish. Back in the rental car I asked if he wanted to drive by his shop.

"It is not my shop!" he shouted. "Don't ever call it that! They don't need me! Nobody needs me!" Up to here with his gloom, I cut the afternoon short. Christmas would be at Jim and Sheila's, a big deal with lots of relatives. Maybe by then he'd lighten up.

Next day I pointed my rental car toward Worcester and Father Ronan, whom I had called from Berkeley. Walking toward Bevan, I felt my stomach jumping around. Shake it off, I told myself, this isn't confession, just two friends talking things over. I stood a while at his door... my knock echoed up and down the deserted corridor.

"Hello, Paul!" He took my hand, pumping it enthusiastically. More wrinkles about the eyes and mouth but still fit, still sporting the same steel-rimmed glasses.

"It's good to see you, Father." I still couldn't bring myself to call him Father Bill.

"Come in. May I offer you coffee? It's instant, of course." He filled the kettle at the sink and set it on his hot plate. "How's the west coast treating you? How many years is it now?"

"Four. Two more to go."

"And your thesis topic?"

"I'm looking at what happens to citizen rights in crisis situations. Japanese internments, the McCarthy blacklists, that sort of thing."

"I'm sure Gus is a help. I think of you two when I read about the troubles out there."

"He came out with a new book last year, he's involved with the radicals and trying to keep the peace too – a real juggling act. Akiko and he are salt of the earth, good people."

"I've never met her but give them my best. Your thesis sounds fascinating, I hope you'll let me read it."

I asked what was happening at the college.

"You see the alumni bulletin so I won't bore you with the headlines, so to speak, but let's see, Father Tully died. He'd been sick a while."

I frowned, remembering our struggles in Ethics. "He was a good person."

"Yes, God rest his soul. And Father Gene, he was a friend of yours..."

"More my roommate's, Pat Harrington."

"Ah, yes, the famous Padraic, how is he?"

I laughed. "He does two years at Harvard Law then throws it all over. Managed to get a 4-F for his knee. Long story short, he's in Paris studying Art History."

"Not everyone is cut out for the law, sometimes I wonder if anyone is. Father Gene, he left the order. Last we heard he was in New York, Greenwich Village."

"That's a surprise."

"Not if you knew him. Behind the cheery facade was a tormented soul."

The kettle whistled and he filled two purple and white mugs. "Milk? Sugar?"

"Black's fine."

He set the mugs on the table between us. "I appreciate your stopping by, it's a quiet time of year. Do I sense this is more than just a social call?"

"Actually, I could use some advice. You have a few minutes?"

"Anyone who travels three thousand miles has my full attention."

"Well, my problem – I'm having trouble staying motivated. No offense, I just can't visualize myself as a teacher – but nothing else really appeals to me either."

"I see," he said, steepling his fingers in front of his mouth. How often had I seen him do that. "You've spoken with your advisors?"

"At length. Gus, too."

"What did he say?"

I laughed. "Basically he told me to get a life." Father Ronan raised his eyebrows. "What he meant, get out of the rat race for a while, travel, see some new things."

"Everything being equal that sounds reasonable. Can you put your program on hold?"

"They'd approve a leave, but there is the little matter of the draft."

"Ah, yes. You didn't do ROTC?" I shook my head. "And how old are you?"

"I'll be twenty-six in June."

"Stick it out a little longer and you'll be past the draft age."

"I'm not going to use that as an excuse."

"What about enlisting? Some people find the service a broadening experience."

Enlisting. The last few months this idea had crept into my mind but for some reason I kept blocking it out. "I had family in World War Two and Korea," I said, "the First War too."

Father Ronan's eyes narrowed. "What is your opinion of this one?"

Just like him, I thought, right to the point. "The threat to our country is real. The fact things aren't going well doesn't alter that, though a lot of people out our way disagree, our mutual friend included."

"I didn't know moral philosophy was one of his strong suits."

"He is persuasive on any number of topics."

Father Ronan smiled. "Boston's a hotbed of opposition. Our community itself is split. Polls aside, I agree what we're doing is basically justified, though one aspect is particularly troubling."

"Which is?"

"What they call the body count. When we first got in we expected a short campaign, though if we'd paid attention to the French debacle, we would have known better. At any rate, we're three years in and have no plan for winning the war or forcing a negotiated peace."

"I hope you're wrong. But how does the body count enter into this?"

He smiled. "Let's go back to the basics – thou shalt not kill. In such a disorderly world it's comforting to know our principles don't change, but neither are they any easier to apply. Then as now, you must have a very, very compelling reason to kill another human being."

"Of course."

"And here, for some reason – lack of imagination, bad strategy, I don't know what – we've become entangled in a war of attrition. We define success by the number of enemy we kill or, according to the miserable math they use, the ratio of their dead to ours. Kill enough of them, eventually they get discouraged. That's seems to be our strategy."

"You have to kill the enemy or he'll kill you. That's elementary."

"My point is, has attaining our goal become so unlikely that by default, killing itself is now the goal? If so, we could no longer count this as a just war."

"I hadn't thought of it that way."

"I hadn't either but recently a quote from some general hit me between the eyes. 'Cold, calculated pursuit and destruction of people on the other side.' He said that's our plan. And there are always the casualties from high altitude bombing."

"But how is this different from other wars we've fought?"

"Perhaps it isn't. Perhaps we were mistaken there, as well." The priest looked at me hard. "Keep a close eye on this, Paul. When you're dealing with an act that's defensible only in extremely limited circumstances, a small change in the facts may force you to a different answer."

We talked more about the war, then Father Ronan said, "I'm sorry, I believe we've strayed from your reason for coming." He took a sip of coffee and leaned forward, balancing the mug in his palms. "Let's talk about what you want to accomplish with your life, then work backwards from there."

"The spiritual side is okay, it's those short-term lifetime goals."

"If it's any consolation I've heard that from thousands of young men." He sat back. "Let's sketch some possibilities. I remember you once were very good at journalism. And of course there's government work. Or some sort of research and writing."

As we went back and forth I grew more pensive. Finally I noticed we'd been at it over an hour. He saw me checking his clock and nodded. "Want to stop here? You know you can call anytime, and though it's becoming a lost art, you could write a letter, for goodness sake."

I thanked him for his time and took my leave. The conversation didn't clarify anything, in fact it re-opened something I thought was settled, the moral issue. I didn't agree with him, but when a thoughtful and holy man speaks, you listen. In a way I was relieved he brought the enlistment option into the open. One thing I knew, whatever direction I go, I'll be the one making the decision. No way would I ever let myself be drafted.

Christmas at Jim and Sheila's. The shock of last year's loss had worn off, and there were the children, energetically tearing into their presents. Dad was more like his old self, too. "Sorry I get cranky, and your coming all this way..."

"Don't worry about it. It's good we can be honest with each other," I said, but the words caught in my throat. The most important issue in my life I hadn't even mentioned. I wondered whether he sensed something. Before we parted he invited me to lunch. "We don't spend enough time together, we need to use these opportunities." At the Biltmore the maître-d' greeted him by name and ushered us to a corner table.

"You've come up in the world," I said.

"Marty and I, we came here a lot when we were selling the company. I said what're we doing here, Marty, it's too fancy, but he made a good point. When you're working on a million dollar deal, you got to act like a million dollars. Act small, you end up small. Besides the prime rib is very good."

I put my menu down, "Say no more. See, I do listen... sometimes."

"You always had a mind of your own. You're your mother's son, God rest."

During the meal I wondered how to tell him but worried what will he think, another change of direction. We went on, talking about everything else. Finally I had an idea. "You're healthy again," I said, "come on out to California. I'll show you around, you can meet Gus and Akiko. I've seen your place, only fair you see mine. I'll even make the bed."

He burst out laughing. "To hell with the bed. What do I care about the bed?"

I was still looking for a way in. "It's a pretty small room," I said, "there's a desk and chair where I work, a bookcase on one wall, a soft chair on the other side."

"Sounds okay to me."

"I've got pictures on top of the bookcase, one of you and Mom, Jim and Sheila and the kids, Catherine's graduation from Brown... and that picture of Maurice."

He looked at me hard. "You have something to tell me."

My heart skipped a beat. "I'm... I'm having a hard time concentrating. It's been going on a while."

"It's difficult, what you're trying to do, even for a studious person like you. How many years you been at it now?"

"Four-plus. At least two more."

He let out a deep breath. "I don't know how you do it."

"I might need to take time off, step back and look at everything."

"You can do that?"

"Oh, sure, they'll go along with it."

"What about the draft?"

"That's an issue."

"You're not the type to run off to Canada. I believe that leaves only one option."

"I've been thinking about that."

"Maurice?"

I nodded. "Maurice."

He motioned the waiter for more coffee. "The way things are going you'd find yourself in Vietnam pretty quick."

"I've been thinking maybe it's time to give something back."

"Our people have always served honorably. I was too old for the Second War or I'd have been there. You heard they let Jim out of the Guard?" I shook my head... I'd forgotten to ask. "Damned decent, him with a wife and three kids." He smiled. "Wouldn't that be a strange turn of events? *En fait, bizarre!*"

"Why strange?"

"If you went into the service."

"I guess it's hard to imagine me in a uniform."

"Not that. What I mean, your brother'd be at home with his family. Don't get me wrong, with all his responsibilities he did the right thing, but who would end up carrying the family flag but *ti-Paul?* Who'd have thought it? Who would've *ever* thought it?"

"You wouldn't think less of me?"

"Less!" he bellowed. "It would be great for you, for the country. I'd worry about you. In the end luck calls the shot. You're so big for control," he smiled. "When you raise your right hand you give all that up."

At his building I got out of the car and opened the door for him. "So, tomorrow you're on your way," he said.

"Yeah, I've got a lot of thinking to do. I might just stay put, you know, tough it out."

"I used to think life was pick one thing and stick to it, but when you get to my age things aren't as cut and dry. What matters, be sure what you go for is worth it. Well, whatever you decide I'm with you. I'd invite you in," he winked, "but my bed's not made."

We embraced. "Take care of yourself," I said, my eyes moist.

"You too, *ti-Paul,*" he said, shaking his head and smiling. "You'll do just fine, I know it. Who would have thought it?" He turned and walked up the path, leaning on his cane, still shaking his head as he opened the door and disappeared inside.

WHEN I GOT BACK I CALLED DON but he was away, wouldn't be back for a week. In our annual ritual, Akiko, Gus and I toasted the Times Square ball. Akiko said we were entering the Year of the Monkey, a most inauspicious sign. I didn't like the sound of that. A few days later I cornered Gus. He took a long time to respond. "You know," he began, "I suggested break out of your rut, see the world, have some adventure." He shook his head, "little did I know you'd take me so literally."

"I haven't made up my mind yet. Anyway, don't worry, it'll be my decision."

He sat back in his chair. "Let's think this through. If you enlist, chances are you'll be in Vietnam inside a year. Which service are you thinking about?"

"The Army. Keep it simple."

"Can't talk you into the Navy?"

"That's a longer commitment. If I do this I want to get in and get out, fast as I can."

He got to his feet and started pacing. "First and most obvious, it's a high-risk venture, no question." He stopped and looked at me. "It could turn out, your future is you have no future. You realize that, of course."

"Of course."

He resumed his pacing. "But if you happen to survive, and most do, it could be a very good move. You won't burn any bridges at Cal, they'll certainly welcome you back. And the service would open up other opportunities. You'd get a commission, of course."

I had been thinking about this. "That involves more time."

"Talk with Mark, or Bill Porter. You know how to reach them?" I nodded.

A few days later I caught up with Mark. "Nobody enlists these days," he said, surprised, "but I give you all kind of credit for considering it. Are we talking Army?"

"Yes. What about a commission?"

A commission would take longer, he confirmed, OCS, a reserve commitment on the back end. "No offense," he went on, "but you always struck me as an elitist. No, that's not right, what's the opposite of mediocre? That's what I mean."

"Why do you say that?"

"You have high standards, you're a quality person. You don't spend your whole life getting drunk and figuring out how to get laid."

"I won't argue with you there, but so what?"

"The relevance, sir, as an officer you'd be able to hang onto some of that refinement, some small amount, at least." I could hear him grinning through the phone. "Hey, look, as an enlisted man you'll meet a lot of fine people, but will they share your interests? From the neck up it's apt to get lonely, if you know what I mean."

"But this isn't a lifetime commitment. That's the point."

"That's true, but don't say I didn't warn you. Another thing, you have no clue what it's like taking orders from assholes and idiots. There's a lot of jerks in the officer ranks too, but as an officer there's fewer people above you, so simple math says you're better off. I can't wait to hear what you decide."

"Me neither." The opposite of mediocre, I mused. *Sounds* like a compliment.

Don wasn't surprised, he'd sensed I was cooling on the program. His advice, if you're going to change direction do it now rather than later. "A teaching load plus publish or perish plus a family, that's a recipe for disaster." He'd support the leave of absence, it'd be no problem.

One night I was settled in watching my little black and white TV, a recent purchase. I happened upon the Smothers Brothers, special guest Pete Seeger. His protest songs were even more biting than Dylan's, his Communist connections cause for concern. I was almost asleep when something made me sit up, something about a big fool. I listened closer. Trainees fording a river, they made it but the captain got stuck in quicksand and that was the end of him. Big fool. BIG FOOL! He was singing about LBJ! Fully awake, I snapped off the TV and sat there. A great sadness came over me. I felt terrible... my country, my President, sneered at, spat on. And why? For trying to do their best for us.

Next night, Gus and I were watching the evening news. Walter Cronkite's lead story was the seizure by the North Koreans of the *USS Pueblo*. "First time since 1807," Gus said. "Plenty of ships sunk but never one captured." Some senators came on, saying we should seize all ships flying the North Korean flag, wherever and whenever. Storm Wonson harbor and take back the *Pueblo*.

"What do you think we should do?" I asked.

"The naval officer in me hates to say this, but you do nothing unless the crew's in danger. Wouldn't you say we have our hands full already?"

Cronkite also reported on large-scale North Vietnamese attacks against our big Marine base at Khe Sanh near the Laos border. General Westmoreland said he was expecting this, it was good to engage the enemy in a stand-up battle, our kind of fight. Reinforcements were being rushed to the scene.

What happened next nobody expected. Most Vietnamese were celebrating the start of Tet. Shortly after midnight NVA regulars and Viet Cong elite units unleashed a massive, coordinated attack against Saigon and scores of other Southern cities. So much for holiday truces. We learned later that the Viet Cong had infiltrated the capitol, stashing arms and explosives around the city. Across the South they captured power stations and radio stations, assaulted embassies including ours, and gained control of large areas of the countryside. Khe Sanh didn't fall, but we fell for Khe Sanh. Did we ever.

Immediately, Westmoreland proclaimed a great victory. Actually, it did look like we'd beaten back the enemy, decimating the Viet Cong and recapturing most of the urban areas. Nor did the southerners rise up as the invaders hoped. But considering what we saw in graphic detail, words were no match for images of Americans in pitched battles, vehicles exploding, buildings afire, bodies in pools of blood, soldiers scavenging Viet Cong corpses.

During their occupation of the ancient capitol, Hué, the Viet Cong slaughtered many innocent people, civil servants, ordinary citizens, then in the battle to retake the city, the city was devastated. One Marine put it this way. "We had to destroy the town in order to save it." A couple of weeks later the *Times* ran another famous image, the pistol shot to the head of a prisoner, summarily executed by the chief of the South's National Police.

How can this be happening, people asked, you say we're winning the war. Vermont's Senator Aiken observed dryly, "If this is failure, I hope the Viet Cong never have a major success." Confidence in our military and our Vietnamese ally was at an all-time low. The military chiefs railed at the reporting, especially the TV. You're forcing us to fight with one arm tied behind our backs, and when we do something good nobody believes us.

But the fact is, we had been completely fooled, and as Father Ronan asked, what is our plan for winning the war?

I was so sick of our local radicals. After an impromptu rally at Bancroft and Telegraph that would have been sophomoric if it hadn't been so vile, several of them set an American flag afire. "Ho! Ho! Ho Chi Minh! The NLF is gonna win!"

That did it. I ran at them and yanked the flag away, stomping out the flames. I must have surprised them for I got it away easily, my prize and I leaving to a chorus of curses and boos. Free speech my ass. For an instant I thought of grabbing their North Vietnamese flag too, but thought better of it. Akiko put ointment on my hand and wrapped it in gauze. Gus examined the Stars and Stripes, charred and torn. In a few days the bandage came off, though the scar is still there. I still have the flag, too, singed in its lower right quadrant. Some years later I had it framed. Souvenirs of the Battle For Berkeley.

I got hold of Pete Moretti. State wasn't hiring but send us an application, you never know, something might open. I thought of having my father call Senator Pastore but kept putting it off and never did get around to asking. D.C. was looking like a dead end.

As the war situation worsened and protests grew, I saw Father Garvey becoming more rigid and self-righteous. One Sunday he launched into a tirade, telling the congregation no right-minded Catholic could support the rogue regime in Washington or be in danger of serious sin, his exact words. I kicked over the kneeler with a bang, stood up and walked out, muttering. Father Ronan's reasoned cautions were one thing, but I was not about to accept anything *ex cathedra,* certainly not from this guy. If I'd had a cigarette I would have smoked it right there on the church steps. Calming down, I meditated on Christ's choice, His unfathomable choice to entrust his Church to men like this one. I slipped back in for Communion, taking a direct route to Father Garvey who handed me the host without comment. After Mass I went into the common room where I noticed a couple of people staring at me. When I presented myself to the priest he greeted me by name.

"You have a problem with what I said?" he asked earnestly.

"You have some nerve calling patriotic Americans sinners!" I said loudly. "Where do you get your special insights these days? SDS? Progressive Labor Party?"

He flushed. "I can't believe I'm hearing this from you, Paul."

"I can't believe what I just heard from you. From now on kindly warn us when you're about to offer a political opinion. That collar gives you no corner on judgment or anything else."

"Perhaps you'd like to visit me in the confessional..."

"I don't think so," I replied. "We're doing the right thing in Vietnam. People who cut and run turn my stomach. And you have the gall to cloak it in morality!"

I turned and left the building. There were other churches in Berkeley, Newman's not the only game in town. My eyes stinging, I walked fast. Never had I spoken to a priest like that, not in all my appropriate, circumspect years. I was totally spent. No books, today, no focus, no patience. After wandering the campus I climbed the switchbacks to Grizzly Peak and my special flat rock. Having eaten little, as I neared the top I became lightheaded, but it passed and a sense of calm overtook me. It was a cool afternoon, the sun filtered by layered clouds. Staring at the Bay I thought of Jesus in the desert. What would He do? What would He have *me* do? Jesus backed his talk with action, but was Vietnam the moneychangers, or was it the woman taken in adultery? Justice or mercy? Which will it be?

As darkness fell I descended from the hill, my pace quickening as I neared the house. My hand shook as I dialed my father's number. After several rings I was about to hang up when he answered. "Dad, this is Paul."

"Paul! You doing all right, everything okay?"

"I'm going to enlist, Dad. You're the first person I've told."

There was a pause on the line. "I had a feeling..."

I waited for him to say something else but he didn't. "Well, what do you think? Am I doing the right thing?"

"Only time will tell," he replied thickly. It sounded like I had woken him up. "Come back safe, that's my only concern..."

"I know what I'm getting into. I'm not twelve years old anymore. All this academic stuff, it's pretty selfish when you think about it..."

"Teaching is an honorable profession, your mother was big on teaching. I miss her a lot," he said, "I'm sorry I wasn't a better friend to her."

"You did plenty well, Dad."

"Losing her so sudden I never told her how I felt. I never got around to telling her." After a long pause he asked, "What will you do now?"

"Damned if I know," I said, laughing. "Guess I better figure that out."

I REMEMBERED A T-SHIRT I once saw with the drawing of a little kid carrying a sack of books. Now the kid was putting the sack down. It occurred to me, never before had I made a complete break with anything. I also remembered after a class on Kierkegaard, I checked out *Purity of Heart is to Will One Thing.* What I recall, and I don't know whether it was in the book or if I made it up, the action a person takes to align himself with God's will is cheapened if he has a second motive. Personal advantage, money, friendship, even salvation. Single-minded is the only way. My effort here will change nothing in the big picture, but my country is in trouble and I have to do the right thing by it. No calculating the consequences. My life has been good because others did the right thing, now it's my turn. Pat's face came to my mind. I banished it, fast.

Next day I told Gus. He wasn't surprised. Akiko fell to fussing and worrying, then gave me some advice. If I got to the Far East which she hoped I would, and Vietnam in particular which she hoped I would not, I should learn more about Buddhism. Visit holy sites, talk with people. She said she respected my decision but it flew in the face of good sense, citing a proverb of the Ashanti People of Ghana – No one tests the depth of a river with both feet.

I put my arm around her. "I'm already in over my head."

"So it seems," she replied, hugging me back.

Whatever they could do, Gus told me, just ask. They would store my stuff. And don't worry about the rent, we'll find somebody else to take my place, he said, "your room, I mean. Nobody can take your place."

Monday I visited the Army recruiting office in Berkeley. Active duty a minimum three years, three more in the reserves... a very long time. Enlist longer, you can pick a specialty and avoid front-line duty, otherwise no guarantees. My inclination was, if I'm going to be in the Army, I want to be in the real Army, which means infantry. In any case you're going to spend a year in Vietnam, unless of course, you re-up. I said I'd go for the one-year tour and told them I wanted to be sworn in back home. They'd initiate the paperwork and transfer it to Providence but advised that I take the pre-induction physical here. The physical! I'd completely forgotten about that!

Resignedly, Don put the paperwork together, saying he'd hold it until I passed the physical. On the phone Mark asked if I had really thought it through. "Forget half of what the recruiters say, then disbelieve the rest, you'll have it about right. You realize infantry is the most difficult, the most exposed of all the services. You really up for that?"

"I think so."

"These days you're not so bad off going in at the bottom – a lot of lieutenants and sergeants are getting killed, not just grunts." I didn't need to hear that. He wished me well, send him a picture of myself in uniform. "You'll do fine, just don't think so much. The smart ones go crazy. Do yourself a favor, pretend you never finished eighth grade."

On the Terrace I started out telling Gideon it was too bad our differences had come between us so much. "Partly my fault," he said. "I expected too much of you."

I described how I had cooled on my studies, then sprang my bombshell. His eyes widened. "That must have been one tough decision."

"You got that right," I said.

"At times force has a lot going for it. The Six-Day War, the underdog fighting for its existence? No comparison with the obscenity we've forced on a small country."

"A small country that uses violence and terror, with powerful friends that do the same, two of them in the Nuclear Club. We're not talking David and Goliath here, Gideon."

"Yeah, well if you say so." He was unusually mellow. "I wouldn't have thought you had it in you," he said, shaking his head. "You're not the Canada or Sweden type, but to enlist? That is truly remarkable."

"In the end I couldn't not do it."

"That is how commitment happens." He raised his cup and we toasted life, *l'Chaim,* continued good health, luck, a big part of it, we agreed, peace and justice.

Two days later Benny and I were at the same table. "Gideon told me your news. Did you see this?" He lay today's *Times* on the table. MOST DEFERMENTS TO END FOR GRADUATE STUDENTS, read the lead headline. "It says you're okay through the fifth year then all bets are off."

"Fifth year from when?"

"From when you start. So this is our last year, my last year, I should say. You didn't know about this ahead?" he asked with a half-smile.

I pointed to the paper. "News to me."

"At least now you'll serve with a better educated group. Me, I better be sure my passport is up to date."

"Come on, you wouldn't do that," I laughed, "but you could go the C.O. route. Break out the tefillin! Quick!"

He shook his head and laughed. "Maybe M*A*S*H? Maybe I'll get to twenty-six first. Okay, enough about me... why *are* you doing this?"

I was getting tired of answering the question, but since I was the one who called the meeting... "Short answer, it's time to pay my country back. A matter of obligation..."

He rolled his eyes. "Spare me, please. You'll do your country a bigger favor if you stick around and fix what's wrong here. You'd end up killing fewer people, too. Doesn't that appeal to your Catholic morality?"

"We're in trouble here, we're in trouble there. I picked this one."

"Flipped a coin."

I laughed. "I have to say your anti-war movement had a lot to do with it."

"What do you mean? Don't try to pin this on me."

"The anti-American part, I cannot abide it."

Benny was silent a moment. "I'm not against America, I'm for a better America. You might like to know our organization has had some knock-down drag-outs on that one."

"Too bad you didn't win more of them."

"You have no idea how chaotic we are. It dignifies us to call us an organization. So when does this all happen?"

"I take my physical next week. If I pass I'll get sworn in in Providence."

Benny sat back. "Providence." He smiled, "Such a simple time, so long ago." He slouched in his chair. "I'll miss you, my favorite enemy... no, not enemy, debating partner. I'll have to make an exception for you next time I condemn the imperialist warmongers."

"I'd appreciate that." So my old friend and I parted, agreeing, as usual, to disagree.

At the physical, my myopia nearly did me in. I figured with the Army's manpower needs, anything short of a white cane would qualify, but no. Otherwise I was in good shape, five or so pounds over but the doctor said they'd burn that off me the first day. On the psychological test I went for the obvious answer like Mark said. Next day I told Don and a week later a letter arrived from the Department approving the leave of absence.

LATE FEBRUARY AND I WAS PACKING. I took a break and wandered into the living room, joining Gus to watch a somber Walter Cronkite review his recent fact-finding trip to Vietnam. "Pay attention," Gus said, "I have a hunch..."

> "To say that we are closer to victory today is to believe, in the face of evidence, the optimists who have been wrong in the past. To suggest we are on the edge of defeat is to yield to unreasonable pessimism. To say we are mired in stalemate seems the only realistic, though unsatisfactory, conclusion."

"What'd I tell you..."

"...it is increasingly clear to this reporter that the only rational way out then will be to negotiate, not as victors but as an honorable people who lived up to their pledge to defend democracy and did the best they could. This is Walter Cronkite. Good night."

Gus clapped his hands together and let out a whoop. "Goddamm LBJ just lost the country!" He raised his eyebrows. "Sure you won't reconsider?"

I stood up. "Doesn't change a thing, Gus. Anybody can win the easy ones."

It was too much to ask Gus to store the Plymouth, so with great sadness I put an ad in the paper and sold my old friend to a grad student from Wisconsin. Considering its condition I felt I should be paying him, but instead pocketed $175 in the deal.

Gus and Akiko drove me to the airport. We said a teary farewell when my flight was called. "Be safe," Akiko said, "come back soon."

"Absolutely," I said, putting my arms around her, "no problem."

Royal treatment at the other end, too – Jim picked me up and took me to his new house. "Can't wait for you to see it," he said as we drove away from the airport. "It's great! All that room and a fenced-in yard." I'd stay with them the six weeks before my reporting date. My father said how proud he was, even Jim had nice things to say about his brother, no longer the runt of the litter. He didn't say that but I knew he was thinking it.

First thing Monday I reported to the Army Recruiting Office. I was impressed they had the paperwork in order or, as I would soon learn to say, squared away. And so it was, along with eleven other young men of assorted shapes and sizes, all younger, I raised my right hand and my life changed forever. That night I called Gus to report in and get his views on the most recent shocker, LBJ's announcement that he was stepping aside. "You were right," I said, "about Johnson, that is."

"Yes, I suppose I was," Gus replied.

"I thought you'd be sky high. You sound kind of down."

"Exhausted is more like it," he said. "It's been a tough few years and there's more to come." He sighed, "I envy you, getting out and making a fresh start. Take care of yourself, and remember you always have a place here."

A week later we found more reason to grieve and the campuses and cities had another excuse to erupt, with the murder of Dr. King. Another good man gunned down – not a perfect man, but there's been only one of those. Leadership in this fractious time is perilous. Lift your head above the crowd and somebody's waiting to lop it off. I wouldn't miss the Berkeley scene, relieved to be entering a world where there was basic agreement on what had to be done, at least there had better be.

I practiced writing letters. I told Father Ronan I was up to the moral challenge and ventured an idea, that perhaps my decision might help expiate the country's guilt, make up for the bad things it does from time to time. Pat got a letter – I wish I could have seen his face. One for Meg, too. I thought about how we had cared for each other. If we had committed to each other, might I have been content with university life, not felt the need to put myself in this situation so foreign to me?

A phone call told me Father Trần was still in Cholon, last they'd heard. Trying to keep it light, my letter said I'd found a convenient way to visit Vietnam and would see him soon. Anticipating a little, I signed it Paul Bernard, U.S. Army.

Some time back I had bought a copy of *The Brothers Karamazov* but I'd never picked it up. Along with the Bible and *The Divine Comedy* I set it aside to bring. Whatever the Army would do to my mind I wanted to keep it in shape. Midway through my stay with Jim and Sheila, I cracked *Brothers* open and spent time with it each day. My last evening, after the house had settled from the farewell party they threw for me, I came to the Grand Inquisitor. Jesus a danger to his people? The Church allied with the powers of darkness? The Inquisitor's charges set my teeth on edge.

Next morning I packed my things. I unfolded the charred flag on the bed, looking at it a long time. Jim said he'd hold it. The reality was setting in. I would finally get my hands around the real world. In a U.S. Army uniform, yes, but steeling myself to be a soldier of Christ too, hoping against hope I was doing the right thing.

* * * * * * *

WE HAVE SPENT OUR LAST DAY on the deck, a gorgeous day in the north country. Jonathan seems a bit subdued. For the next few weeks we'll be in New York going over that material. For some reason, what we have here doesn't include anything about Paul's military service, a critical gap. I'm hoping we'll find it there. We'd better find it there. Jonathan also says he needs to interview something like a hundred people, then there's his so-called investigation which I doubt will amount to anything. At some point he simply has to put that aside and finish the article. He sets a glass of tonic water on the table.

"I'll really miss this place. I appreciate your putting up with me."

"After a bumpy start we did good work. Let's finish Berkeley, I need to pack."

"Same here." He ponders his notebook for a minute. "Paul says the anti-American protests put him over the top. What do you make of that?"

"I accept that it motivated him, though probably more on an emotional level."

"He prided himself on being so rational."

"A classic case of being driven by your assumptions – beliefs if you will. In his case, God and country."

"But it doesn't fit his persona."

"You're making it too complicated. As he said, don't overthink it."

Jonathan nodded. "Things were so chaotic. Maybe he just got swept up in it all."

"There's probably something to that."

"Revolution in the air. My parents used to tell me about it."

"Some of our radicals believed their time had come. Well, it hadn't, of course, anybody with half a brain knew that."

So it's on to New York. Jonathan leaves tonight, tomorrow I drive the Volvo to Portland and park it in a long-term lot. I will treat myself to a ride on the Amtrak. No need for a car down there. The second evening Dennis will join me for dinner. I'm going to insist on speaking to Captain Martinez. Why was he called off? What did he learn that was too hot to handle? Speaking of hot, Dennis told me on the phone another Iraq story is about to break, a big one. Didn't say what.

Next morning here I am, seat back, coffee in hand. I look down at the book in my lap, *John Adams*. Terrific writer, McCullough. I wasn't bad, but this guy puts me to shame. I eschew the Acela – too much money just to see New York forty-five minutes sooner. Ridiculous. Same Rhode Island shore out the window. Or maybe it's Connecticut by now. These days, far as I'm concerned, slow is better. None of us is getting any younger. I need time to think, arrange the pieces of this puzzle. I owe it to myself. I owe it to Paul.

PART THREE

BLOOD AND STEEL

30. BACK TO BASICS

WE ARE IN THE OAK ROOM, one of my all-time favorite watering holes. Vaulted ceiling, rich paneling, leather chairs, hansom cabs out the windows. Jonathan is pleased to join me for an early dinner, especially since I offered to pay. After arriving, I treat myself to a nap then a terrific room-service Manhattan, first one in years, then leaf through some odds and ends. Tomorrow early we meet in the lawyer's office for a first look. I have to believe Paul's Vietnam notebooks are there. I know he kept a journal.

Next morning I am shaking the rain off my umbrella in the lobby when I spot Jonathan waiting at the security desk. I stick my name tag on and we ride to floor twenty-seven. I've never met Susan Leone but I know her as soon as I see her in the waiting area. Fortyish, short and stocky, pleasant face, orange-dyed hair, also short. She breaks into a big smile.

"You must be Gus!" she said, reaching for my hand. "You look just like I imagined!"

"And what might that be," I say, preparing to feel maligned.

"You know, Irish."

"Well then, that's all right. Facts is facts."

"And this is?"

"Jonathan Bernstein," he says, extending his hand.

"Of course, pleased to meetcha." She turned to the receptionist. "Would you tell Mr. Samuels we're here."

After a minute, a tall man with a Van Dyke beard appears. He and Susan greet each other familiarly and he introduces himself to us. I would guess Steve Samuels is in his early fifties. "Follow me," he says. "This way to the famous cartons."

As we walk down the bright corridor I ask Steve if he has heard from Cahill. "We spoke yesterday. I don't know if you're aware but Susan gave me the executor document and the dictation tape for safekeeping. The ETVN lawyer's okay with that – we know each other well. Susan, I guess you were able to calm your boss down."

She grimaces and nods.

"The Latimer people are known for their bluster," he says, opening the door to a smallish conference room and flipping on the light, "just like their programming. After the initial shock, ETVN's not too concerned nor am I. Well, here they are."

He is pointing at an array of storage cartons, "banker boxes," on a conference table protected by a cloth. The boxes are marked in grease pencil – Basic Training, Vietnam, Homecoming, Newspaper Job, and so on. I count sixteen in all.

"You didn't tell me you were so well organized," I say to Susan.

"I can't vouch for what's inside – Paul kept that pretty well to himself. Originally there were a couple dozen but he already sent you a lot of it. He was starting on these guys when everything hit the fan – 9-11, that is. I have no idea how far he got."

"I'm three doors down," Samuels says, looking anxious to escape, "need anything, my secretary's Lisa. Coffee down the corridor, you passed the restrooms on your way in. Gus, let's talk before the day's out. I need an estimate how long you'll be here, plus we should talk strategy. Well, happy hunting."

I am going through the first Vietnam carton. At the bottom, under some manila folders are several spiral-bound notebooks. I open one – it is in Paul's handwriting. So's the next. Journals if I ever saw them. "We're in good shape," I tell Jonathan. "Here, take a look."

* * * * * * *

ABSORBED IN THE WINDOW VIEW, a few miles outside Westerly I bade my native state farewell. My book still lay untouched in my lap as we pulled into Mystic, the first Connecticut stop. Unheard of for me, I had overslept, and it took some virtuoso driving by Jim to get me here. Sprinting with suitcase and backpack across Union Station's marble floor I slid up to Track Three just as they were calling the six forty-five to Washington.

As we sped along, I wondered who else might be headed to Dix. On my way to the club car I spotted a few likelies. Back at my seat, the coffee made me drowsy and I nodded off. It had taken me hours to fall asleep last night. Five hours later, after a layover in Penn Station, we headed south. An elderly lady at the information desk in Trenton pointed out a green school bus with FORT DIX on a placard in the windshield. The driver, a stout black man in civilian garb, asked for my papers and I showed him my license and my orders with today's date, 20 May 1968.

The bus was stifling. I took a seat near the rear, lifting my suitcase into the rack and setting my backpack on the seat beside me. More guys filed in, including a couple I noticed on the train. Everybody younger than me. I thought back to that Oakland troop train, the fresh-faced recruits staring out the window – how ironic. I looked up. Beside me was a young man with a ponytail and earring, a thick gold chain outside his T-shirt. "That seat taken?" he asked.

I moved my backpack to the floor. "All yours."

The driver settled in, the door closed and the engine started. I reached up and pushed the window open the rest of the way. As we pulled away I looked at my neighbor. "Going the same place, it seems."

He nodded. "They nailed you, too."

"No, I enlisted."

He raised his eyebrows.

In a few minutes I saw LEAVING TRENTON and soon we were flying past set-back homes and small stores, barns, horses, cows, freshly planted fields. As the bus rolled along we bounced on the hard leather seats, cracked and shiny from decades of use.

"Shitful ride," he observed.

"It's firm, all right."

"Jake," he said, extending his hand.

I grasped his. "I'm Paul. Where're you from?"

"Normansville. Near Albany. You?"

"Providence."

"Never been there."

"I never been to Normansville."

"Nobody has."

"What'd you do there?" I asked.

"Pumped gas. S'all I could find after high school." He waved his hand at the interior of the bus. "But I'm finally outta there. How about you?"

"I was in school, getting a degree."

"And you enlisted. That doesn't make a lot of sense."

"I've heard that from people."

Jake stared past me out the window and we fell silent. I was on edge. After all the briefings and informational packets I still wasn't sure what to expect or how to handle it. I dozed fitfully, jostled awake by the driver's heavy foot. After a while we slowed and I looked out to see a military policeman waving us on... I felt myself tense. A moment later we stopped. We stepped out of the bus and milled about in the bright afternoon. We were in front of a brick building – FORT DIX RECEPTION CENTER. A uniformed soldier, a sergeant, appeared and gave us the once-over. "All right, men!" he yelled. "Fall in!"

We arranged ourselves more or less in a line and stood there, suitcases in hand, feeling out of place, me at least. The soldier nodded. "My name is Sergeant Oliver," he said crisply. "Put your belongings down and give me your attention."

Still wearing my backpack I looked around at the motley collection of young American manhood. Long hair, short hair, crewcut, Afro, greaser, tall, stubby, skinny, chubby, black, white, brown, pimples, glasses. "You will proceed into the Reception Station for your paperwork. Then you will be briefed on what to expect and how to conduct yourself at Ft. Dix. Let's get a move on. Fall out!"

We picked up our stuff and shuffled along. Inside I joined the tail end of a line, one of several. In a few minutes I was standing in front of a Corporal Hewitt, from his name badge, who issued me an Army ID number and ID card. I looked at my dogtag – Private Paul M. Bernard, 036165009, my social security number. For next of kin, after hesitating a moment I gave Jim. I found myself assigned to the 3rd Basic Training Company, Bravo Company. For nine weeks Barracks Foxtrot would be my home. "Report next door. Next."

I took a seat in a crowded lecture room. A beefy, crewcut officer at the podium introduced himself as Captain Pulsifer. Capt. Pulsifer punched his words rapid-fire – apparently there was no time to lose. "On behalf of the Commanding General of Fort Dix, Major General Rainey, and Lt. Colonel Charles Banfield, Commander,

3rd Advanced Infantry Brigade, it is my pleasure to welcome you to the United States Army."

There. I had done it.

"The next couple of hours I will brief you on the basics of Fort Dix and you will watch an orientation film. Then you will get haircuts, be issued your shorts and sweats, you will get set up in your assigned barracks. Chow is at 1830 hours then it's back to barracks for lights out which tonight is at 2100. Any questions?" He looked around the room. "Okay. Let's get started."

After the film we proceeded to a long, low room where recruits were separated from their hair. Mine wouldn't add much to the piles on the floor, heaps that an elderly black gentleman pushed around with a large broom. A short, dark man with gray-tinted sunglasses, Felipe Sanchez by his badge, originally from Manila and twenty-seven years cutting hair for the Army, he told me, threw a cloth over me. "We're gonna buzz it all," he said, and so he did. Then up and out and on to the next victim.

Barracks Foxtrot was about ten minutes from the Reception Center. Rolling my gear under one arm – bed linens, towels, new olive drab sweatshirt, shorts, T-shirts, socks, all army green, black sneakers looped over my wrist, still toting my suitcase and backpack, I fell in with the crowd.

"How'ya doing," one guy said, "it's Paul, right?"

I looked closer. It was my pony-tailed bus mate. "Jake! I don't recognize you."

"That makes two of us. I hope it grows back."

"Give it a few years." I noticed his earring had disappeared, too.

Barracks Foxtrot was in a cluster of two-story World War II wooden structures. I heard the base had modern barracks too, but hadn't seen any of those. As I walked in, the newly shorn were standing around, talking, goofing off, some lying on the bunks, two-story affairs of green steel tubing with thin mattresses and sagging springs. Every bunk had its precisely-folded green wool blanket. Foot lockers lined the center aisle. Metal folding chairs and multi-door metal wardrobes every few bunks. The floors were concrete.

"You just pick a bunk?" I asked a tall, skinny kid with a big case of acne.

"You kidding?" He pointed at a bulletin board next to the door I must have missed.

New to bunk beds, I didn't know which one to wish for but it pleased me to see my name penned in for a lower. My bunk was toward the middle of the long, low room and under a window which was good because it was stifling hot in here. On the bunk above, a pudgy, ruddy-faced kid dangled his feet over the side. The stubble on his head told me he used to be a redhead. I dumped my stuff on the lower bunk. "You here?" he asked.

"So they say."

He slid down to the floor. "Brendan Murphy," he said, extending his hand. "Everybody calls me Murph. I'm from the Bronx."

"Paul Bernard." I shook my head. "Only two people I've met, they're both from New York. I'm from Red Sox country, Providence."

"Jeez, we have a problem. I even worked at the Stadium."

"What else did you do?"

"Served time at Fordham."

I nodded. "Holy Cross here," I said.

"You finish?"

"Yeah."

"I flunked out." He waved his hand around the room, "which brings me here."

At orientation they said phone calls were a special privilege – you don't just make one when you feel like it. But this being the first night, after chow they let us line up for the three phones outside the mess hall. There was mail call too, but it wasn't clear how often, or when it would start. In the phone line guys shouted insults, mostly get the hell off and give somebody else a chance. I reached my father on the first try.

"You settling in?"

"Yeah. We got our haircuts. You wouldn't recognize me."

"I'll bet. What about the food?"

"It's all right."

"Made any new friends?"

"A couple. I'm working on it."

I wasn't trying to be curt but what was there to say? After a minute I told him I had to go, people were waiting. "Keep in touch. Don't worry, Paul, you'll do fine."

"For sure. Say hello to everybody."

BACK IN THE BARRACKS, about eight-o'clock – 2000 hours, that is – a burly black soldier appeared in the doorway, a staff sergeant if I read his stripes right. He glared at us, this collection of boys and semi-men in shorts, t-shirts, bare feet, then walked stiffly to the center of the room. Some of us stood, others just looked up.

"At-ten-HUT!" he roared.

I'd never heard anything so loud. We jumped to our feet.

"Good evening, gentlemen!" he roared, a piercing, high-pitched roar.

"Good evening, sir... good evening... " we fumbled.

His face reddened. "The correct greeting is Good Evening, Drill Sergeant!"

"Good Evening, Drill Sergeant," we intoned.

"What a bunch of pussies! I can't HEAR you!"

"Good Evening Drill Sergeant!"

"I STILL CAN'T HEAR YOU!"

"GOOD EVENING DRILL SERGEANT!"

He started walking between the rows of bunks, a stony-faced white sergeant with fewer stripes trailing behind. "Your accommodations are satisfactory, I trust."

"Yes Drill Sergeant!"

He stopped in front of a solidly-built black kid. "Isn't this a fine hotel, soldier?"

"Yes, Sir! Yes, Drill Sergeant!"

The Sergeant shook his head. "JAY-SUS! What kind of dumb-ass answer is that! What's your name, soldier?"

"Wayne Styles, Drill Sergeant!"

"That's Private Styles, Drill Sergeant!"

"Private Styles, Drill Sergeant!"

"Where you from, Styles?"

"Chicago. Drill Sergeant!"

"They have hotels in Chicago, don't they Styles?"

"Yes, Drill Sergeant!"

"You ever stay in one?"

"No, Drill Sergeant!"

"But you know what they look like."

"Yes, Drill Sergeant!"

"Ever seen a hotel like this place, Styles?"

"No, Drill Sergeant!"

"Not even close?"

"No, Drill Sergeant!"

"THEN WHY THE FUCK YOU CALL IT A HOTEL?"

"I d-d-don't know, Sir, I mean Drill Sergeant! I wasn't thinking, Drill Sergeant!"

"You sure as shit weren't! Get this through your thick skull, Private. You are in the United States Army! And this is a barracks! A BARRACKS! Not a hotel!"

"Yes, Drill Sergeant!"

He resumed his stroll, looking each of us up and down in turn. "I am Drill Sergeant Baldwin," he said, turning the volume down a notch, "and that is Assistant Drill Sergeant Rice," nodding at the younger man. "In a very short time we shall get to know each other very well, and two things I can assure you. Number One! Before you leave here, every one of you will hate my guts. By the way the name is B-A-L-D-W-I-N, in case any of you pussies care to make a complaint."

His high voice wasn't a tenor, exactly, more like his collar was too tight. Above the collar his neck was a hard roll of flesh. He thrust his chin forward. "NUMBER TWO! By week nine each one of you sad sacks will be something the Army can be proud of or you'll be on a bus back to whatever piss-poor place you came from."

He stopped at the bunk two down from mine. "What is your name, soldier?"

The tall, skinny kid with acne. Nathan, from Brooklyn.

"Private Berg, Drill Sergeant!"

The sergeant cupped his hand to his ear. "CAN'T HEAR YOU, Berg!"

"Private Berg, DRILL SERGEANT!" he shouted in a reedy voice.

"What happened to your face, Berg?"

"Nothing, Drill Sergeant. What does the Drill Sergeant mean?"

"He means it looks like a truck ran over it. Your face get run over by a truck, Berg?"

"No, Drill Sergeant!"

"Happened a few days ago, did it?"

"No, Drill Sergeant!"

"Then there's only one explanation. You jerk off a lot, don't you, Berg?"

The kid went completely red. "No Sir! I mean, not that much, Drill Sergeant!"

"Five, six times a day? That why you spend so much time in the crapper?"

"No Drill Sergeant!"

"Are you a kike, Berg?"

"No, Drill Sergeant! I'm Jewish, Drill Sergeant!"

"What's the difference, Berg?"

"Sir! Kike is a term of disrespect, Drill Sergeant!"

Sgt. Baldwin nodded. "Thank you for enlightening me, Berg, I didn't know that. Berg, I bet you like candy. Eat a lot of candy, Berg?"

"Yes, Drill Sergeant. I like candy."

"I bet you do. I bet you like O Henrys. You like O Henrys, don't you Berg?"

"Yes, Drill Sergeant! I like O Henrys!"

"How do you eat an O Henry, Berg?"

Berg paused. I wondered what Sgt. Baldwin was getting at. "You just put it in your mouth and... bite a piece off. Drill Sergeant!"

"You're lying, Berg! That is not how YOU do it! YOU put it in your mouth and suck on it, don't you, Berg? You suck on your O Henry like you suck a dick. You're a faggot, Berg, ISN'T THAT SO!"

"No Drill Sergeant! I am not a faggot!"

"Berg, you really piss me off! HIT THE FLOOR! Give me ten pushups!" The kid stared straight ahead, frozen. "GODDAMMIT, BERG! The only thing I hate worse than a lying faggot kike is a DEAF lying faggot kike! Hit the floor, Berg! GIVE ME TWENTY!"

The kid hit the floor. Twenty, no trouble. I was impressed.

"Twenty more!"

Berg looked up, then ripped off another twenty.

"On your feet, Berg." He got to his feet. "You trying to show me up, Berg? Think you're some kind of fuckin' ATH-A-LETE?"

"I played basketball in high school, Drill Sergeant!"

"I played basketball in high school," he mocked. "And were you any good, Berg?"

"Pretty good, Drill Sergeant!"

"Pretty good, you say. Well, Berg, seeing's you're such a big shot, whenever I tell the company give me ten, you will give me TWENTY. If I say twenty, you will give me FORTY. DO YOU UNDERSTAND ME, BERG!"

"Yes, Drill Sergeant!"

"And from now on the name isn't Berg, it's O HENRY! Got that?"

"Yes Drill Sergeant!"

"Let me hear it!"

"SIR! My name is O HENRY, DRILL SERGEANT!"

Sergeant Baldwin moved down the line. He stopped at Murph, next to me.

"What is your name, soldier?"

"Private Murphy, Drill Sergeant!"

"That figures. Ever told you've got a face like Paddy's pig?"

"No, Drill Sergeant!"

"Well, you do. Wipe that smile off your ugly puss."

He stopped in front of me. "What's your name, soldier?"

I stiffened. "Private Bernard, Drill Sergeant."

He narrowed his eyes. "You can do better than that, Bernard."

"Private Bernard, DRILL SERGEANT!" I shouted.

He looked me up and down. "You look uncomfortable, Private. Are you uncomfortable? Would you rather be someplace else?"

"No, Drill Sergeant!"

Now his face was in mine. "Why are you here, Bernard?"

"I want to serve my country, Drill Sergeant!"

"You have no idea what it takes to be a soldier, do you Bernard?" he shouted.

"No, Drill Sergeant! But I will learn, Drill Sergeant!"

"We'll see about that," he replied, moving on. I relaxed, a little. Every few bunks he let loose a torrent of abuse. I'd never seen people beat up like this. After half an hour he ended up back in the center of the room.

"LISTEN UP, YOU PUSSIES!" he shouted. "Reveille tomorrow at 0630. From then on it is at 0500. You will assemble in front of this barracks at 0700 in your P.T. gear and YOU WILL BE ON TIME! You dickheads do not want to get on my bad side, not the first day, not any day! In this Army there is an easy way – do what I tell you when I tell you! UNDERSTAND?"

"Yes Drill Sergeant!"

"There is also a hard way. Do not make me choose the hard way. After roll call we will proceed double-time to the parade ground for some good old-fashioned exercise." He looked at his watch. "Twenty minutes to lights out and when I say lights out I mean LIGHTS OUT! No flashlights, matches, candles, no means of illumination WHAT-SO-EVER! I will be back to check on you. I live right next door. Good night, ladies."

"Good night, Drill Sergeant."

Sgt. Baldwin came to attention, turned on his heel and strode from the room. Sgt. Rice lurked behind. We went about our business until lights out, then Rice left also.

As taps sounded I dropped onto my bed, exhausted from the long, difficult, exciting day.

Utter silence... for a while One guy started whispering, then a second, and soon everybody was in the act.

"Jesus! We gotta put up with that for two months?"

"S'matter, you a pussy like he said?"

"The man freaks me out..."

"Asshole, that's what he is!"

"Quiet! Don' let him hear that!"

"You know what they call him? Badass Baldwin. That's B-A-D-A-S-S."

"What about that other guy. Rice?"

"Looks like a real dickhead."

Murph leaned his head over the edge of his bunk. "I don't look like Paddy's pig... do I?"

"I didn't want to be the one to tell you... "

He laughed. "My father used to say that. Takes one to know one I told him."

Next door, Nathan was still fuming. "What that man said, it's just not right. I have a mind to report him."

"Forget it," I said. "It's nothing personal – he was showing off."

"Jerk off all you want, Henry, somebody else said. "We won't report you."

IT WAS BRUTAL. Pushups, pullups, situps, jumping jacks. Full-extension drops into more pushups and back up. Repeat... repeat... repeat... Drill Sgt. B-A-L-D-W-I-N birching and roaring the whole time. See Paul run. See Paul run in place. Run the parade grounds. Run until his lungs ache, run until he can't take another step. See Paul run some more. For the last half-hour the thought of food was all that got me through. I could see it, smell it, taste it. Finally he turned us toward the mess hall, running of course. Sweating profusely I held out my tray. Oatmeal in this compartment, watery scrambled eggs in that, cold burnt toast on top. Coffee, orange juice, apple. Poor fare by any standard, but I'd never had better.

Our 0900 entrance exam, a hundred guys, naked except for green boxer shorts, shuffling from station to station, prodded, poked, vital signs checked, every orifice despoiled, chair time with the dentist. Glasses off, I was no match for the eye chart. Glasses on, no problem. They handed me two new pairs with oversized lenses and green frames. Then the inoculation station. Nearing the front of the line I watched a rubber-gloved nurse deal with the guys in front of me. Left shoulder was the target *du jour.* The information packet listed diseases I'd never heard of. I forgot to mention, in one of the sessions they made it clear the next stop after Basic and Advanced was Vietnam, no ifs, ands or buts. No surprise either, though to hear it put so matter-of-factly gave me a chill. Smiling, the nurse beckoned to me. "This is gonna hurt me more than you," she said.

"That I doubt."

"Not afraid of needles, are you?"

I clenched my teeth. "There's always that first time."

Still smiling, Nurse Aguilar swabbed my shoulder with alcohol. "Feel faint or lightheaded, that's what those cots are for." She gestured toward an area cordoned off by a white curtain. "If you have to throw up go for it. Some people have that reaction." I tensed up as the needle found its mark. She made a bunch of checks on a large piece of cardboard.

"What's that?" I asked.

"Your shot card. Keep it on you."

The mental exams. I was warned not to overthink the questions so I didn't. As for the aptitude tests, unless they were playing some sort of game, I could have pointed my Army career any direction – clerk to cook. The language specialty continued to tempt me but I told the Sergeant who debriefed me, since I'm in the Army I want to be in the real Army. Infantry. Scanning my records he shook his head. "Keep an open mind and anyway you don't have to decide until later." When he mentioned if I extended I'd get more from the G.I. Bill, I had to stifle a laugh.

After lunch, more gear. Fatigues, shirts, pants, short-bill baseball cap, shiny black dress shoes, calf-high laced boots, a poncho, large rucksack and a duffel bag, compass, canteen, knife and sheath, entrenching tool. It reminded me of shopping for the Sierras except for one thing. For the first time in my life I owned a rifle – I guessed I owned it, an M-1 we'd use to drill. Later we'd be issued a state-of-the-art M-16 for marksmanship training. No ammunition yet, but I was all right with that. The way some of the others talked, they'd been shooting and hunting their whole lives. I stowed the stuff in my foot locker. By the end of the day those sawhorse racks standing in the middle of the room I'd wondered about were filled with rifles. The rifle that would become my best friend, I was told, my ticket back to the States – if I could get over being intimidated, that is.

Mornings left no time to shower, so we handled hygiene on the fly when and if. Communal showers left nothing to the imagination, though with glasses off I was spared most of the detail. Grabass, towel-snapping, high school P.T. all over again. In the barracks this guy I hadn't met yet pushed his way forward. A little shorter than me, blond buzz cut, big teeth filling a slit of a mouth. "'Ah wanna serve mah country,'" he said in a sing-song voice, "what kahnd of bullshit talk is thet?"

"The kind a bullshit question deserves." I shot back, feeling my ears redden. I turned toward my bunk, annoyed and disconcerted but not wanting a fight.

"We'll jes' see about thet," he said, sidling away.

I heard snickering behind me. "What's up with that guy?" I asked the guy across from me, a dark-skinned kid named Manny Fernandez, from Newark.

"He some kind of crazy, man – got a hair up his ass."

I learned Bobby Jenks was from Mississippi. Meridian, Mississippi. Wait til he finds out about Berkeley, I thought maliciously.

Mid-morning the next day we assembled on the parade ground. The physical fitness test called for ten pushups, ten pullups, fifteen situps and an eight-and-a-half minute mile. Surprisingly, I beat the target time by over a minute. We jeered our fellow trainees on. Several didn't make it. Names were taken, warnings given.

After lunch it was back to the parade ground, this time in fatigues, caps and boots. Names and assignments were read off and just like that, Private Bernard belonged to the 3rd Basic Training Brigade, 1st Training Regiment, Bravo Company – the Black Knights, "best damn Company in the whole United States Army." Sgt. Baldwin arranged us by height and I found myself in the last row beside Nathan, I mean O Henry. According to yesterday's physical I had hit six-one. Gratifying, indeed. Ten rows deep, four columns across, we stood at what passed for attention on the baking concrete of a May afternoon at Fort Dix.

"Bravo Company... A-ten HUT!"

Arms by your side. Head up, chin out, chest out. Heels together, toes at your forty-five degree angle. RIGHT FACE! LEFT FACE! ABOUT FACE! Right toe behind left heel, pivot smartly. PARADE REST! Saluting was explained in detail – when to, how to, who to. Sgt. Baldwin moved among us, shouting his peculiar brand of encouragement.

"Worst bunch of sad sacks I ever seen! O Henry, you sorry piece of shit! Shoulders back! That pitiful excuse for a chest, Bernard, stick it out! Goddammit, Clayton! No way I ever get near you with a rifle! Oh, man, what'd I do to deserve this bunch of pussies! Bravo Company, my ass – BULLSHIT Company's more like it!"

Standing to the side of our formation. "For-ward HARCH!" and we were off. "Lef-rye-lef... Lef-rye-lef. Moving up and down the line. "Lef-rye-lef...Yo lef-rye-lef. Close it up! Straighten them ranks. GODDAMMIT! Straighten them ranks! Steady cadence!" He beat his fist in his palm. "Together! Keep them columns straight! TOGETHER!" He strode to the front and started walking backwards. ""Call them columns? Straighten 'em out! Eyes on the head in front of you! Jesus H. Christ, what a sorry excuse for soldiers!"

Reverse direction. Left flank turn, right flank. "Wan-tup-threep-fo. Three-fo, yer lef. Three-fo, yer lef." I noticed we were nearing the end of the drill field.

"To the rear - HAR!" We made an about-face. Now my row led the pack. "To the rye flank - HAR!" Now I was on the outside. "To the lef flank - HAR!" Back in front. "Eyes lef! Eyes front!"

"I gotta girl lives on the hill!" Sgt. Baldwin broke into song. Damn good too.

"I gotta girl lives on the hill!"

"She won' do it but her sister will!"

"She won' do it but her sister will!"

"Sound off!"

"Sound off!"

"Sound off!"

"Sound off!"

"Sound off, one-two-three-four, sound off..."

"SOUND OFF!"

Up and down we went. "Right column - HARCH!" Tricky. Oblique turns. More column turns. Double-time. Sweating like a pig, my feet on fire. Boots, feet – a ball of pain. But in a weird way I had to admit – it was the most fun than I'd had in a long time.

"I don' know but I been tol.'

"I don' know but I been tol.'

"Eskimo pussy's mighty cold!"

"Eskimo pussy's mighty cold!"

"SOUND OFF..."

It's a game, I told myself, an intricate, costumed, game. After nearly two hours Sgt. Baldwin brought us to a halt at the far end of the field, the sun at his back and full face in our eyes. "Bravo Company...AT EASE!" He began pacing. "Some of you think drilling is fun and games. Or it's a bunch of bullshit. But get it through your thick skulls, DRILL IS DISCIPLINE! DRILL IS EXECUTING ORDERS!

INSTANTLY! AS A UNIT! No questions, no complaints! You got to trust your officers. We count on you doin' the right thing at the right time. The men in your unit count on you. Pick and choose what orders to obey, you fuck things up for the unit and be in a heap of trouble."

Feet apart, hands clasped behind our backs, we squinted into the bright afternoon sun.

"All right, men. Pick it up here tomorrow. Bravo Company! A-ten-HUT! To the barracks! Double-time... HARCH!"

That evening I popped blisters and covered them with a foul-smelling liquid to harden them. Next morning we awoke to a driving rain. Sure enough, at 0530 Sgts. Baldwin and Rice, ponchos and wide-brim hats with plastic covers, we in T-shirts, shorts and sneakers. Pushups, sit-ups then double-time. I figured maybe Sgt. Baldwin'd had enough rain, himself. Under an hour, we had toweled off and put on dry fatigues. My feet were much improved.

Luckily this morning we were scheduled inside. First briefing was the seven Army Core Values. Battalion Commander, Lt. Col. Mitchell led off. L-D-R-S-H-I-P. Leadership. Duty. Respect. Selfless service. Honor. Integrity. Personal courage. "Don't memorize it, live it! They're not the most important thing, they're the only thing!"

We watched a State Department film explaining why we were in Vietnam. It traced the French defeat and our involvement. Eisenhower, JFK, LBJ, Democracy. Our side came off a lot better than Mao and Ho, Hitler lookalikes. B52s and F-4 Phantoms. M-16s and the M-60 machine gun. Helicopters of various shapes and sizes. Army, Green Berets, Marines. The simplistic explanations hit all the high points. I wished I could have heard Gus review the film. Which reminded me I needed to get started on some letters.

We knew nothing about Sgt. Baldwin except he wore a 101st Airborne patch on his shoulder and was a "lifer" from Georgia. Late thirties, probably, close to twenty in, Wife? Kids? No idea. Apparently that's how he wanted to keep it.

Each day I got to know more people. The press made a lot of discontent and dissent in the Army, but so far all I saw was normal griping. About a third of the company were black, mostly from big cities. Wayne Styles I mentioned before, he'd played high school football and aspired to college but grades did him in. His Chicago neighbor, Fred McDaniel, was set on learning electronics. As I got to know these guys I came to appreciate that Cabrini-Green of the tough reputation had a human face too. Bobby Jenks and I kept our distance. Turned out he had a knack of rubbing everybody the wrong way, not just me.

BY NOW MURPH AND I WERE FAST FRIENDS and Nathan made it three. Murph's two Jesuit years had inspired an ardent skepticism. Pat Harrington without the erudite veneer. Nathan had been at Queens College, pushed into Physics by his family, but dropped out after a year.

"Why didn't you just change your major," I asked him.

"Needed to get away," he shrugged. "Change of scenery."

The three of us shared a passionate interest in baseball, and Nathan the Mets' fan made Murph odd man out. It was no surprise, the two guys I gravitated to had a brush with college. Mark Hightower had been right – many were rough-edged with limited interests, from small towns, many from the South or the inner city. But I caught flashes of real intelligence and saw a lot of mechanical know-how, cars and such, which gave them a head start, Basic Training being essentially trade school. Of course, some were simply your classic meatball, a type I was all too familiar with.

I took pains not to lord my learning over anybody – that would have been the kiss of death. For once I wanted to fit in, be accepted. One thing in my favor, my encyclopedic knowledge of baseball. What kid from Joplin, Missouri, like Eddie Clayton, could fail to be impressed that I knew Vern Stephens, later of the Red Sox, played short for the 1943 St. Louis Browns and hit third, behind second baseman Roy Gutteridge? We had no shortage of experts. Some knew the inner workings of a '49 Merc or the '57 T-bird like the back of their hand. The gun nuts couldn't wait to get hold of an M-16. Wayne knew everything there was to know about pro football. As a little kid he'd been a Bears' waterboy with an uncle on the team. I'd never heard of the uncle but didn't let on.

Not all our time at Ft. Dix was serious, only ninety-nine percent. Take hand-to-hand combat. The Training Pit was a clearing on the edge of the pine woods filled with coarse sand, heavy and wet from a drenching rain the day before we hit it. Our instructors gave us the picture.

"There will be times when you can not or do not wish to fire your weapon," Sgt. Baldwin led off, "because of noise or if you're at close quarters or out of ammo. But if you are skilled at hand-to-hand unarmed combat, you will be able to deal with the enemy. This is what we will work on this morning." We began practicing elementary wrestling moves on the ground with whoever happened to be nearest. "The object," Sgt. Baldwin said, "is to dominate your enemy and take him out, fast!"

After an hour of this we moved to another part of the clearing where a dozen large punching dummies, padded and weighted at the bottom, confronted us. One by one we were shown the proper way to make a fist, to punch. Athletic stance, knees bent, one foot slightly ahead, swing from the hips and shoulders, your legs power your fist forward. "The other hand protects your face, your abdomen."

The instructor steadied the punching dummy, shouting instruction and advice. I had to laugh – tall skinny Nathan reaching down to the dummy. Bobby Jenks attacked his with serious, rapid-fire punches. It looked like he knew what he was doing, unfortunately. Since that first night I figured he and I would tangle sooner or later. "Now pair up and form a circle in the pit." The plan was to square off and wrestle, open hands, no fists.

Murph and I had agreed to partner. I was looking around for him when I heard, "How's about it, asshole? You an' me." It was Jenks, jaw set, eyes shining. Okay, I told myself, it's sooner. "You're on."

We stood next to each other as the first pair took to the pit. "What is your problem, Jenks?" I said.

"Ah jest don' lahk yoah face," he said out of the corner of his mouth.

"Who said you had to?"

"Ah hear youah a college pussy,"

"College is correct. Negative on the pussy."

"Ah know yoah tahp. Youah all pussies."

We stood by as the first pair clawed and rolled around, an instructor hovering over them. At least, I thought, I've got four inches and a good twenty pounds on him. When the whistle blew the next pair went at it, then it was time for Mississippi Bobby Jenks and Rhode Island's finest to get it on.

On our knees, we faced each other in the sand. Jenks' expression told me this really mattered to him. The whistle blew and he began raining punches, real punches I had to fend off. A blow to the shoulder threw me off balance and I fought to stay upright. Digging a leg in, I went for his shoulder when suddenly he lowered his head and butted me in the chest, toppling me backward. Instantly he was on top of me, pressing my shoulders into the sand. Somebody yelled, "Come on, Paul! Get 'im!"

I exploded out of Jenks's grasp and rolled back onto my knees. Another fusillade made me cover up, then I saw an opening. I grabbed his wrist with both hands and jerked him toward me, hard. His momentum carried him forward and he fell. I twisted his arm and pinned it in back of him, turning him over and grinding his face into the sand with my knee. Now on top I easily pinned him. The whistle blew. Cheers broke out. Breathing hard, I stood and extended my hand. Other combatants clapped each other on the back but not this guy. He got up and shot me a look of pure malice. "Next tahm, asshole. Be ready." I walked away, brushing off the dirt.

As our first week drew to a close my doubts filtered to the surface. This was so foreign to me. Did I have the goods to make it through? Every day I hurt physically, some days it was mental. I toyed with failing some element of the program, making an end of it, but dismissed the idea. However badly I might do, wimping out was not my way.

Every night I slept like a rock, though no sooner had taps sounded than we were up again, groaning about another day. The close quarters would have made sleeping impossible except Sgt. Baldwin wore me out so much, even the constant twisting, turning, mosquito-slapping, cursing, muttering, snoring, farting and masturbating couldn't keep me awake.

Thanks to my mother I always knew how to make a good bed. Army way was the same as Fiona's way except for the level of perfection. Crisp hospital corners, sheets and blanket so tight a half-dollar dropped from three feet bounced back two. Brush your teeth by the numbers, up and down a full minute. Boots a high sheen, dress blacks spit-shined to a mirror finish. Everything in its prescribed place in its footlocker. The barracks? Spotless. Floor, walls and windows? Spotless. Beams and columns, wood scent long gone, reeked of the ubiquitous pine disinfectant. Grass cut, shrubs trimmed, walks debris-free. Cigarette butts field-stripped, gum a capital offense. As a basically orderly person, I identified with this mania, knowing it really wasn't about order, it was about control. Obedience and control in the service of discipline. One hot afternoon, Murph and I were in our shorts and flip-flops swabbing the latrine when the subject of chickenshit punishment came up. "This is all very familiar," I observed. "Did you have nuns in grammar school?"

"Eight years."

"Which ones?"

"Notre Dame."

"You too?" I laughed as a couple of the penguins flashed to mind. "These guys think Baldwin's tough. He could have taken lessons from them."

"Maybe he did."

"Nah, I bet he's a Baptist."

"Yeah, probably. And the priests, don't forget the priests."

The pressure to conform was relentless. It was remarkable, how focused they were on humiliating us into submission, and how obvious. Sgt. Baldwin was the hammer, we were the nails. Every day he'd give us a couple more whacks and deeper into the plank we went. The day would come, inevitably, when we would be nothing but shiny metal discs on a board, all the same. So long individuality, mannerisms, funny habits. Not for nothing was what we wore called a uniform.

I mentioned the latrines. Located in back of the shower building, a couple hundred healthy digestive systems put them under serious strain. Suffice it to say, thanks to our work details they were clean enough to eat off, a figure of speech. No partitions. Some long-forgotten military genius had deemed communal shitting good for bonding, in fact the whole food chain starting with common meals. No more private and personal. Everything was shared. As for quiet time, a moment to collect your self – not only no, but hell no! And they were working on that self part, too. I saw the psychology. Each day another piece of the personality falls away. Chip... Chip... Chip. Trim... Trim... Trim. Polish... Polish... Polish. All time and space was occupied. We ran everywhere, and when we didn't run we marched double-time, shouting and singing. If there is no time or place for thinking where can thought reside? Hint: Nowhere.

"If I die in a combat zone..."

"If I die in a combat zone..."

"Box me up and ship me home."

"Box me up and ship me home."

"Sound off!"

"Sound off!"

"Sound off, one-two-three-four, sound off..."

"SOUND OFF!"

TIGHT AT FIRST, MY NEW-ISSUE CLOTHES SOON FIT PERFECTLY. For a long time I had wanted to get in shape... what a way to do it! Midway through the second week we completed a five-mile run in combat boots, rifles and full packs, up and down the hills, through the woods bordering the camp, fragrant damp pine needles carpeting the earth, the closest to a nature experience Fort Dix offered. And experience it we did, several times a week.

By now we were drilling with the venerable M-1 which I was astonished to learn had been in service over fifty years. Manual of Arms from a stationary position: Order Arms, rifle vertical, barrel tip in your right hand, butt on the ground. Parade Rest, same but feet apart, barrel forward, the back of the left hand at the small of your back. Port Arms. Present Arms. Right Shoulder Arms. Left Shoulder Arms. Fifteen counts in all. The trick was transitioning smartly between positions which was difficult with the weight, then integrating the whole thing into our marching. Every slap, crack, step and thud in unison, Sgt. Baldwin by our side, haranguing, driving us on.

The Army makes boys of men, so goes the old adage, but I'd soon have to deal with something not so funny – firing range. There were other glimpses of reality, too. Fixing bayonets. Setting and disarming a Claymore mine. Hand Grenade 101 – proper grip of the grenade, "your own personal artillery support," how to arm and throw it. No live ammo so far, but what we were here for was coming into focus.

Written tests were big. Military history and heritage. Military justice. Pounding the Core Values. Communications. First Aid. Field exercises. Night maneuvers. Aerial photographs, map reading, navigation, compass. If you don't know where you are and how to get where you're going, you're a disaster waiting to happen. Luck has its place but only a fool relies on it. No less important is health and hygiene. In Vietnam the soldier's only reliable water is what he packs in, and figure that's going to run out. Canals used for toilets, laundry – you gonna drink that? Paddies fertilized with shit, even human shit. Anti-malarial pills, these little orange doohickies, once a week without fail.

"Your Vietnam climate ranges from extreme heat to extreme cold. It is a wet, miserable place. The monsoon lasts months. Constipation or diarrhea, take your pick. You are only as good as your feet and your feet are going to take a beating, count on it. Keep'em dry and have your mother send socks. Dysentery, leeches, malaria, jungle-rot – it's got all that, and we haven't even begun to talk about the enemy and his plans for you. Then there are the inevitable fuck-ups you'll bring upon yourselves."

I paid attention.

"You men love Army food, correct?" This from Sgt. DiNardo, a tall, dark-haired instructor with a Quartermaster Corps patch on his sleeve. Far as I was concerned the chow wasn't so bad, though what they said was true, the aroma of the mess hall gave no clue to what you were in for. Scrambled eggs, Salisbury Steak, shit on a shingle a.k.a. creamed chipped beef on toast – it all smelled the same. "A word to the wise, gentlemen. Compared to what you'll get in the field this is five-star. Enjoy it while you can."

Sergeant DiNardo took us through the provisions we'd pack in, how to get at them, how to heat them when and if. "Your basic C-Rat day begins with powdered eggs, you work up to beans and rice, hot dogs, mac and cheese, pork slices, tuna. No fresh fruit or vegetables to speak of, sorry 'bout that. To get at these delicacies, you will carry what is called a P-38 or 'John Wayne' on your dogtag chain." He held up a small can-opener with a short metal blade and a fold-out tooth. "Next to your rifle, your P-38 is your best friend. Base Camp mess in 'Nam, two-and-a-half stars."

The camp had an elaborate chapel several years old, used by all faiths. Two Masses on Sundays. After P.T., if I skipped breakfast I could just squeeze in the Seven. That first Sunday Nathan brought me a carton of milk and a piece of cold raisin toast, the price for refurbishing my immortal soul. As we got deeper into Basic the demands would grow and church a hit-or-miss affair. They said get used to it, the war comes first, God a distant second, if that. At least I maintained that little bulge in my left pants pocket. After college I'd gotten away from the rosary but as I packed for Basic it occurred to me this might be an excellent time to get reacquainted. I used it too, every few nights. I'd seen the Catholic Chaplain, Captain Tom O'Neill in his Army uniform, but hadn't met him yet. Made me think of old Father Maloney. If he could see me now! The Evangelicals were active, with flyers and posters for prayer services, Bible readings, brown bag lunches.

As we rolled into third week personalities took on definition. Crazy Horse, a guy from Idaho everyone had slated for a Section Eight, he talked in his sleep about chopping people up and cooking them. One night somebody put a tape-recorder under his bunk and brought it to Sgt. Baldwin. Crazy disappeared, we never saw him again. Another guy, Big Dick, had worked as a private detective. Francis Lavery from San Francisco, everybody called him Frannie, he had some non-standard underwear in his locker, claimed his girlfriend gave it to him but nobody believed that. Pete Borchart of Manchester N.H., was Booshit. Red Arsenault from Baton Rouge was Asso, no relation to Omer, I found out. As word of my academic career spread, a few people started calling me Doc. Others called me Bernie, but neither stuck. What's wrong with me, I thought. Never had a nickname in my life, can't earn one even in this place. Sgt. Baldwin picked a guy named Gene Wilson as temporary squad leader. Until he wrapped the band with fake Sergeant stripes around his arm Wilson seemed okay, then he started throwing his weight around – a frog full of fart, somebody called him. Overnight he was a pariah.

The Base PX offered everyday items at amazing prices. I bought a watch with multiple buttons and dials, an Omega that put a big hole in my wallet but I couldn't pass it up. The rec hall had ping pong tables, pool, board games, cards, magazines, a piano, a TV. Twice a week films were shown in the rec hall with a raucous macho commentary that was usually better than the film. We hadn't yet seen a weekend pass but I heard the area near the base wasn't much, bars and pickup joints, though some of the guys couldn't wait. Basketball was very big – we had an asphalted area next to the rec hall with half a dozen hoops and played a lot of three-on-three. Nathan wasn't kidding, he had a terrific shot and kept a ball in his locker that was in constant use during free time. Wayne was an excellent athlete, too. Though out of my league, I was part of the core group and played most days.

Since our match, Bobby Jenks had made himself scarce. Given his bluster and bravado, we were astonished what a disaster he was on the drill field. One time early on he turned left as the Company flanked right and ran his rifle head-on into the guy next to him. Six stitches. Next day he did the same thing, without injury except to his standing with Sgt. Baldwin, which was already rock bottom. Jenks' take on the Fifteen-Count Manual of Arms was an adventure, more like Eleven or Thirteen. One memorable day belonged to him. I saw it all, his row being right in front of mine. There he was, standing at attention... with no cap.

"Jenks, you idiot!" Sgt Baldwin bellowed. "You are out of uniform!"

"Ah know that, Sir. Ah couldn't find mah cap."

"You address me as Drill Sergeant! Have you forgotten that too?"

Jenks stiffened. "No, Drill Sergeant! Yes, Drill Sergeant!"

"Well, godammit! Which is it!"

"Yes Drill Sergeant, ah forgot to address you proper. No, Drill Sergeant, ah din't forgot mah cap, ah lost it."

"Get up here, Jenks!" Sgt. Baldwin screamed. "On the double!"

Jenks put his rifle on his shoulder, took a pace forward, turned and marched the length of his row, made another corner and came to the front. Sgt. Baldwin leaned in on him until they were eyeball to eyeball. "You playing with me, boy? Nobody in this Company loses their cap!"

Jenks's neck was a bright red. "It warn't easy, Drill Sergeant."

"You fuckin' dufus! Lose your cap now you JOKE about it!"

"Yes Drill Sergeant. Sorry Drill Sergeant."

"Jenks, you have no idea what sorry is! Twenty pushups! NOW! Then ten laps around the field! Double-time!"

In confusion, Jenks bent over and started to lay his rifle down.

"Jenks! You miserable bag of shit! You'd put your best friend in the dirt? Is your head up yo ass! SLING ARMS!" he screamed.

Back to attention, Jenks threw the rifle's sling over his right shoulder. "Goddammit, boy! You keep that rifle ON! You HEAR me? Do you com-pre-HEND what I am saying? The SHADOW of that rifle as much as touch the ground it's FIFTY MORE!"

I'll give Jenks this much, he was game. At parade rest, I watched out of the corner of my eye. He ripped off a dozen, fast, then at twelve he began to slow. At seventeen he stopped in mid-air, his arms locked, rifle on his back. One more quick one and again he froze in place. I was expecting him to collapse on his face but after a long pause, he strained through the last two. He got to his feet and stood at attention.

"Jenks," Sgt. Baldwin shouted, "you will now circle the parade ground double-time! You and yo little pink asshole keep runnin' as long as you see Bravo Company out here. NOW GET THE FUCK OUT OF MY SIGHT!"

While we marched, we watched Jenks circle the field. I thought of taking up a collection for a new cap but I said the hell with it, let him twist in the wind.

For most guys, comic books were the reading matter of choice. *Playboy, Hustler, Penthouse,* these served their purposes. The books I'd brought – Dante, *Brothers* – nobody gave them a second look. Not that I had time to read, some furtive tries under the covers but dead batteries killed that. Keeping up with the outside world was next to impossible. The rec room TV was never on the news, and all they had for magazines were old copies of *Time* and *Newsweek*. I wrote letters, to my father, Meg, Gus. We finally got our first mail and I had a few letters, but only Gus made any effort to update me, with a pile of Cal clippings. From time to time a whiff of pot outside or in the latrine brought me back to Berkeley. Word was some people were into the hard stuff but I'd seen no sign of that yet.

By my old standards I had regressed, but I had asked for it, after all. Nobody forced the Army on me. Though apprehensive, so far I was reasonably content. It was different, being around people pulling in the same direction, even if in a less exalted enterprise than I was used to. And don't think what we were doing was simple. Weapons, tactics, learning how to outsmart somebody who's out to kill you – that is plenty demanding. By the end of my third week I had barely scratched the surface.

As Sgt. Baldwin often observed, Basic is about the "how" of things. There is no room for the "why." Peel away the familiar, smash old instincts, grow new attachments, to your buddies, your unit, your Army. Slip into the mold, be a cog for the machine – tough, enduring, welcoming uncertainty and violence. How all-consuming this business of becoming a soldier is, I thought with some annoyance. It leaves no time or energy for anything else. I'll be hard pressed to keep up with the journal I started on the train.

Formerly a teacher in training, Pvt. Bernard admires this clever educational system, but while others cave to it, he will not. Drill, solidarity, the value of Selfless Service – these are supposed to bring it all together. But it happens Pvt. Bernard is not of a compliant disposition. Whenever he hears "Army Values," he remembers what he brought to this place – openness, understanding, empathy, love of God. None of them on the Army's list, he notes, but they're still on his, and there they shall remain.

Pvt. Bernard is uneasy when he considers the oath he has sworn, to accept whatever comes down the chain of command. If LBJ or his successor says jump, he has sworn to jump. If they say kill, as they most assuredly will, he must kill. An awesome leap of faith, squaring this with his Catholic, Christian values. One of those perilous moral intersections.

But Pvt. Bernard takes comfort in this thought. If I don't play your game, you can't control me. And if you think I'm playing it, I control you.

31. OF ARMS AND THE MAN

ONE MORE DAY FOR THE BASIC TRAINING MATERIAL. The crystal-clear early evening finds Jonathan and me on the sidewalk outside the lawyer's building. Cold and fatigued, I fish out my scarf and wind it around my neck. The day has been a strain – unfamiliar surroundings, the intensity of Paul's ordeal, which brings back old memories to me. It is especially hard to read, knowing where it leads. And the day isn't over – Dennis Riggs still awaits.

Jonathan prattles on. He's sometimes too distant, too clinical. "An amazing change of direction," he says, "academia one day, trade school the next." This is true, but so what?

A fast cab ride uptown and I greet Dennis in a little Italian eatery named Mimi's on Second Avenue around Fiftieth Street. I am not yet ready to tackle the subways. Dennis has put on weight in the face and through the middle, though he looks heavyset more than flabby. He's wearing a blue blazer and gray flannels, button-down shirt without tie. He still has his full head of hair, now the salt and pepper variety. "You look good, Dennis," I tell him, "excellent, in fact."

"And you, Gus, what can I say? What do you want me to say?"

"Tell me thirty years hasn't changed me at all. How's that for starters?"

"I won't lie, but you are holding up well. Clean air and pine trees must suit you."

"That they do, though the winters take it out of an old guy." I look around the place. "I thought you might've wanted to do room service, for security, that is."

"This works," he says.

A smile, and the hostess, an attractive woman with gray-blond hair and a German accent seats us at a table back near the kitchen. We won't be overheard, not with the crashing pans and music from the other end of the bar where a rotund gentleman with shaved head, earrings, bracelets and chains, in what we used to call a muu-muu (mumu? mu-mu?) was blasting away at a piano. Old favorites and patter in a southern drawl.

Dennis shakes his head. "I don't like hotel food. Been coming here for years. I recommend the chicken parm."

The Chianti in a basket is excellent, the parmigiana too. Dennis has a steak. Chit-chatting back and forth I wonder has he forgotten why we are here, but over coffee and a brandy he finally comes to the point. "Gus, let me say up front, I'm going to help you but you need to know my limits. I can't open the door to Captain Martinez. I'm already on a very long limb putting your guy together with Bernie. Just being here with you is a capital offense. From now on, look to Bernie. When this blows over we'll see about putting our friendship back in gear."

"I hear you," I say. "Go on."

"First off, Martinez. He's smart and persistent, fearless. I can't give you chapter and verse but he was on to something the powers-that-be couldn't handle."

"What about the new guy on the investigation?"

Dennis grimaced. "Ridiculous. But that's what they want."

"Why are you out on that limb at all? Why are you helping us?"

He takes a sip of the brandy. "You remember that trouble at Cal? That exam they said I cheated on?"

"Of course. And you were cleared. The Department issued a formal apology."

"Yeah, but it was humiliating. They said I was lying, until we brought that goddamn T.A. around. You made it happen, I'll never forget that."

"Come on, this isn't payback for something that long ago."

He nodded. "Not altogether. Ever since then I want to puke when I see somebody lying to save their own skin, or the organization's. You were in the military, you know what I mean. Close ranks, keep it quiet and protect the brass – at all costs protect the brass."

"That what's happening here?"

"Gus, this thing has cover-up written all over it. It's the same lying bullshit that got us into this war in the first place." Dennis reaches into his inside jacket pocket and holds up a thin envelope. "Swear to me by all that's good and holy you never saw this. What use you make of it, that is up to you. Bernie will do what he can but don't expect miracles."

"I won't let you down."

"We go back a long way and that's worth a lot." He hands the envelope over. "Read this, show it to your guy then get rid of it." He touches his forehead, "keep it here. And another thing, you'll need a secure phone. I'm going to send you a scrambler unit – it's state of the art but it won't work everywhere. Let Bernie know if there's a problem."

"Well what do you know, our very own Enigma."

Dennis laughs. "Enigma Junior's more like it."

"Enigma Junior. You're on."

He stands, lays a bill on the table and gets his topcoat from a rack next to the bar. "Don't get up," he says, shaking my hand. "Take it easy, old timer. Some day we'll come back here and laugh about this. I hope."

My friend threads his way through the tables, stops for a word with the hostess, drops a bill in the tip jar and is gone.

* * * * * * *

I HAD SEEN ALPHA COMPANY'S SGT. JOHANSSON mostly at a distance, but this week he'll be running our company's show as well. Tall, broad-shouldered, pock-marked, a red-blond crew cut and amber aviator sunglasses he wears even indoors. The one time I saw him up close I was struck by the tiny yellow-gray irises, beads really, the eyes of a predator. In repose his face was coarse and hard, the mouth set in a sneer, perfect for his sandpaper voice which left your ear raw and ringing. From Minnesota's Iron Range, the man was a Viking, his mission in life to create replicas of himself. Make your own face, indeed – Sgt. Johansson had taken over that job. In any other circumstance I would have gone out of my way to avoid a person like this.

Behind their backs people called Sgts. Baldwin and Johansson the evil twins, but we had by far the better of the deal. True, both of them ruled by wrath and terror, and true, we went to extremes not to cross either, not to screw up or be found wanting, but with Sgt. Baldwin you sensed somewhere inside there was a real person. His sarcasm and pettiness seemed more tactic than character, and occasionally you even glimpsed a touch of humor.

The pugil is a hard plastic rod, a weapon three-and-a-half feet long with heavy foam pads on each end and along the center. The combatant grasps his rod with both hands and advances, thrusting at the opponent's head and shoulders while kneeing, kicking, doing everything to bring him down. The pugil is meant to arouse the trainee's aggressive, martial instincts and raise them to a lethal level. The Lesson: when somebody is trying to kill you, you move first, fast, and with deadly force. Football helmets, hockey gloves, chest and groin protectors are worn. Serious injury is rare but concussion not unknown.

The day before, in front of a bunch of people, Bobby Jenks had challenged me to a rematch, with pugils. Long story short, he kicked my butt. Right off the bat he scored heavily against the side of my helmet, knocking me to the ground. The whistle blew. As I sat there shaking my head, trying to clear the cobwebs, Sgt. Johansson looked down at me. "Are you a coward, mister! Get up and fight!"

I slowly got to my feet and faced Jenks. A couple of feints and we went at it again. This time our sticks locked and he spun me around with a whack across the back of my neck, kneeing me in the groin as I went down. Whistle. More kind words from Sgt. Johansson.

By now I was getting hot, thinking this little asshole's not going to push me around. We circled each other again. I jabbed a couple of times, drawing him in, then sidestepped his rush, sticking out my foot and tripping him, giving him a belt to the head as he fell. Whistle. Point Bernard. Jenks got to his feet and gave me a long, searching look.

Next round was a struggle with much bashing and grunting, to the cheers of the onlookers. Finally Jenks slipped his stick through and landed a solid blow across my faceguard, snapping my head back. I didn't go down but the whistle blew anyway and Sgt. Johansson tapped Jenks on the helmet. "Winner!" he shouted, giving me a withering look.

We took off our helmets. Jenks's eyes glistened with satisfaction. A thin smile came to his face, a first. "Now weah even, college boy."

I patted him on the back with my pugil. At least he didn't skunk me.

Next day was bayonets. Same intensity, but here you have a real killing weapon, an eight-inch long Bowie-type knife called an M-7 attached to your rifle barrel. Of course, the opponent is just a dummy, for now.

"Listen up!" We sat on low benches in a clearing near yesterday's sand pit. Sgt. Johansson strode back and forth, camouflage shirt and pants, campaign hat, amber shades. He stopped in front of a metal stand that held two tires bolted together, the hub plugged, a pole sticking out hip-high, on top an object the size of a human head. A couple dozen of these devices were set up in the clearing. Sgt. Johansson pointed his bayonet at the pole. "This here simulates the enemy's weapon. You parry his bayonet with your rifle and move in for the kill." He stepped back, readied himself, then "HEEAAAAHHHHHH!" he exploded forward, sweeping the pole aside then one, two, three lightning thrusts, a head whack and a final slash to the groin. He stepped back, a crooked grin on his face. "No little gooks from this guy!" He almost looked sheepish, he was having such a good time.

"In combat," he went on, "if you are fighting with your bayonet you are already in a bad way, you're out of ammo or the enemy has overran your position. This is no time to be timid! LET IT GO! The objective is to terminate the enemy WITH EXTREME PREJUDICE! Do I make myself perfectly clear?"

A roar went up. "Yes, Drill Sergeant!"

Terminate? Extreme prejudice? Come on, I thought – say it like it is.

We affixed our bayonets, then one-by-one had a go. My first thrust, the bayonet stuck in the tire and I took forever to pull it out. "Too slow, soldier!" Sgt. Johansson yelled, "TOO SLOW! You are dead meat! Stick the fucker in! Stick it in, twist it out." He shoved his bayonet in then with a half-turn forcefully yanked it back. "Do it again! DO IT RIGHT!

My next attack was better. After the head butt I stood back to admire my work. A half dozen tries and he waved me aside. When we'd all had a turn we lined up for the course in the woods. Suddenly I heard a rapid series of gunshots. Sgt. Johansson was firing his pistol into the ground. "GO! GO! GO! GO! GO!"

We ran through the woods, screaming. I ran at the first dummy. "AAAGHHHH!" I screamed, surprising myself. I finished off the dummy, then it was over a four-foot hurdle and drop down into a half-buried pipe. I was having trouble getting through. "ON YOUR BACK! ON YOUR BACK! Lay the rifle down on your stomach LIKE WE TOLD YOU!"

I rolled over onto my back with the rifle on top of my flak jacket and shinnied through the pipe headfirst and out the other end. "There you go! There you go!" I picked myself up, dispatched the next dummy and continued on through the narrow barbed wire chute. There was gunfire now, automatic weapons! They didn't tell us about that! More dummies, obstacles, continuous firing. Ten minutes, I was back at the start, short of breath and drenched in sweat, throbbing.

Fred McDaniel finished right behind me. "Man, that does get the tension out!"

Wayne ran up, out of breath. "This is good!" he said, taking off his helmet and rubbing his scalp. "I'll have to remember this for the street!"

That night as I lay in my bunk I thought to myself, why didn't he just say 'kill?' That's what we're talking about here, pure and simple. I closed my eyes. Those long classroom arguments, my last talk with Father Ronan... so theoretical, so distant. Soon it'll be the real deal. Gary Cooper in the killing street, and no one but myself to blame.

WE HUDDLED IN THE BLEACHERS overlooking the parade ground, soaked from the steady drizzle. In less than a month these seats would be filled with people for our graduation, those of us who made it through. Sgt. Baldwin was taking us through the basics of the M-16A1 rifle we had just been issued. Care, use, safe operation. By the time we left this place they said, we would know intimately every part of the M-16, disassemble and reassemble it blindfolded in under three minutes. But right now it was the most foreign, most disconcerting thing I'd ever had in my hands. Beautiful in its own way, an *objet d'art,* but it was a gun and I didn't do guns. Up til now, that is.

"This week's Value is Respect," Sgt. Baldwin was saying, "respect for your weapon, respect for the enemy. Your rifle is your best friend, treat it that way! The enemy, know what he is capable of. On his own turf, he has a huge advantage. You underestimate him at your peril! Respect may keep you alive, gentlemen. Without it you haven't got a prayer!"

The rain had let up by the time we got to the firing range. We lined up and were issued two empty M-16 magazines and shown how to load them with live cartridges, 5.56 mm. My hands trembled as I lifted the slender, sharp-tipped objects from their boxes, fumbling the first couple as I slipped them into the magazine. I took a deep breath, then another. Slow down... get used to it.

As luck would have it, I was in the first group. Peering through the mist at the targets along a low grassy ridge two football fields away, not a chance, I thought, way too far. A set of six to the left, a twenty-yard gap, more to the right. On the side of the hill a wind directional flag hung limp, and next to the firing line orange smoke poured from a canister on a pole. Bravo Company's pennant, red with gold lettering, had been raised. Sgt. Baldwin briefed us about the target, a complex cardboard square with a grid, and a small human form with a four-inch circle on the chest centered at heart level, all mounted on a dark foam rubber pad, also human-shaped. Brand new, I thought, as we stepped forward.

Taking my position in firing lane number four I turned my cap backward and knelt in the wet sand, careful to keep my rifle off the ground. Behind us Sgt. Baldwin paced up and down. The Range Safety Officer was on the P.A. giving final instructions. "Firers!" he shouted. "Assume the prone position!"

First task, zero our weapons at the target. Three rounds to adjust front and rear sights. Then I focused in on the target, looking through the rear sight. Off one square to the left. A click clockwise on the windage knob centered it. Vertical was okay. "Lock and load!"

I rocked onto my side and shoved the magazine into the rifle, securing it with a firm slap then moved the selector lever into the semi position. Settling back into the prone position I steadied my left forearm on a cushion on the ground and curled my left hand around the thick knurled barrel. My instructor, Sgt. Hastings – everybody had one this first go – he adjusted my position, straightened my right arm to be parallel to the ground. Last three fingers around the pistol grip, forefinger lightly on the trigger... relax... relax... relax.

"Ready on the left!" Pause. "Ready on the right!" Pause. "Ready on the firing line! COMMENCE FIRING!"

I pressed my eyeglass lens against the rear sight, aligned front and rear sights with the center of the target... steady... breathe out... hold it... squeeze... CRACK!

The rifle went off before I was ready, giving my shoulder a sharp kick. The spent cartridge pinged out and flew past my head. They told us how stiff and sensitive the M-16 trigger was but it still surprised me. No slack at all, slight pressure's more than enough. Left and right was okay, but I was a little high. Adjust the front sight down, Sgt. Hastings said. I reached forward and turned the front windage knob down a click then settled back in firing position. This time just the slightest pull. Breathe out... hold it... squeeze... CRACK!

"Looking good," Sgt. Hastings murmured. "Relax."

It felt okay so far, but I realized I was jamming my left eye shut. This time close it easy and not press my glasses so hard on the sight.

Breathe out... hold it... squeeze... CRACK!

Through the sight it looked like the last two were dead center. I popped out the empty magazine and slid in a full one. I refocused on the far targets, concentrating...

Breathe out...hold it...squeeze... CRACK!

Breathe out...hold it...squeeze... CRACK!

Gunfire all around me, it sounded like I was in the middle of some battle. I worked my way through the magazine I guessed on about the same pace as the others, for when I stopped, after a few scattered shots the range fell silent. "Cease firing!" the P.A. ordered. "Lock and clear all weapons! Proceed to target area for down-range feedback."

I put my rifle on safe and got to my feet. "Let's see how you did."

I set my rifle in the rack beside my position and we walked through the wet grass to the target area. It seemed a lot closer on foot. Sgt. Hastings pulled my target off the pad and handed it to me. Aside from a few strays most of the holes were in the circle and several were dead center.

"Fine shooting, Bernard!" I was speechless. Sgt. Hastings and I made our way back to the firing line. "You've obviously done this before. But before you start congratulating yourself, let's wait and see how you handle moving targets." He turned to the next shooter.

We were directed to an area behind the range for a preliminary cleaning of our rifles, S.O.P. after every firing. Standing at the line of 55-gallon gasoline drums I had to laugh, we looked like chefs, at some kind of lethal barbecue. My nose and head were still filled with burnt gunpowder. Others were complaining about that too. Years after, just thinking about that firing range brings back that smell, strong as that first day.

Of the eleven Basic Rifle Marksmanship sessions, the first several would be devoted to rifle familiarization with stationery targets. We would practice firing from a standing position, over a wall, moving forward, from the hip, three-round bursts, automatic fire. The goal, my rifle and I a finely-tuned, disciplined team. I made progress – in fact, it was scary, I was shooting so well. Even guys who'd grown up with guns, had them around all their lives, were looking at me with new respect. A placard on the barracks wall put it like this:

THIS IS MY RIFLE.
THERE ARE MANY LIKE IT, BUT THIS ONE IS MINE.
MY RIFLE IS MY BEST FRIEND, IT IS MY LIFE.
I MUST MASTER IT AS I MUST MASTER MY LIFE.

I wouldn't go that far, but my fear of guns was fast disappearing. I was even enjoying the range. I'd always criticized others for their penchant for violence. Was the Army winning, I wondered, bringing out the worst in me?

ONE RAINY AFTERNOON we were standing at attention in the barracks in T-shirts and shorts, looking forward to an afternoon of disassembling, cleaning and reassembling, for building accuracy and speed. A few days before we started doing it with a kerchief over our eyes. Sgt. Baldwin moved down the line, inspecting our rifles, barking orders. When he came to me he put the same question to me as the others. "Your rifle has a name, soldier?"

"Yes, Drill Sergeant!"

I forgot to mention, early in our orientation Sgt. Baldwin told us to give our rifle a name. For me there was no question. "And what is your rifle's name?"

"My rifle's name is Fiona, Drill Sergeant!" I shouted.

"Fiona! You're shitting me! What kind of a name is that?"

"It's my mother's name, Drill Sergeant!"

I presented my rifle to him, he cracked it open and peered into the breech, then slammed it shut and gave it back to me. "You could do worse, soldier." I detected a flicker of a smile as he moved on to the next trainee.

We then set to work, sitting on our footlockers, parts spread on a clean white towel, repeating the process over and over, engraining it in our minds and hands. Halfway through I slipped on my kerchief. Sgt. Baldwin paced up and down the aisle, barking comments, ferreting out sloppiness, chewing out mistakes, riding Bobby Jenks hard, as usual. Rifle cleanliness is rifle godliness, he pounded at us. Anything less makes you dead. Jenks' marching had improved but the M-16 was giving him big trouble. Disassembly he did well enough, but he couldn't get the hang of putting it back together, especially blindfolded. It took him three times longer than anybody else. Jenks and I had settled into an uneasy truce. His bunk was three down from mine so we pretty well had to.

The week before Sgt. Baldwin had put us on notice, if Jenks didn't get his act together we'd all pay the price. Chickenshit as motivation – the buddy system – except for one hitch. Jenks had pissed off so many people nobody was inclined to help him. Sure enough, Jenks flunked his next test and there went our weekend free time down a rat hole. Latrine duty, KP, cutting grass, scrubbing and painting –

they piled it on. Suddenly Bobby Jenks' problem was everybody's problem. He was numero uno on our shit list. Sgt. Baldwin tied for first, but nothing we could do about him.

After today's exercise wrapped up I was looking forward to a free hour, thought I'd even pick up a book. I got along well with most everyone but I'll admit to a certain reserve, being older and not a participant in the sex and booze banter that was even thicker than college. The machismo was a turnoff, too. I pulled *Brothers* out of my locker and had just cracked it open when I was surprised to see Jenks standing beside my bunk.

"I wanna talk to you."

I lay *Brothers* on the bunk and gestured at my footlocker. "Be my guest."

"What's thet?" he asked.

"That's a book, Jenks."

"Ah know thet," he said, scowling. "Ah'm axin,' what's it about?"

"Three brothers and their father."

"Don't sound thet good." He sat down. "Ah was wonderin,'" he began, avoiding my eyes, "ah wanted to ax, could you give me a hand with this rahfle stuff?"

"All right," I said, startled. It must have taken a lot for him to ask. "When?"

He shrugged. "How 'bout now?"

An hour to dinner. What the hell, I said, looking at my book.

We sat on either end of his footlocker as he proceeded to take his rifle apart. Rather than have him reassemble it right away, I drilled him on the parts first. I had him lift each piece in turn and get familiar with its size and shape and heft, closing his eyes and trying to recognize them by feel, first randomly, then in order of reassembly. I also emphasized putting the parts in the same place on the towel every time. Routine, accuracy, speed. Guys passing by couldn't believe their eyes, the two of us together.

"What's this one?" I asked, handing him a long thin part.

"Bolt carrier," he replied, squinting.

"Keep your eyes shut. What about this?" handing him a part about the same size but thinner and with a handle on the end.

"Chargin' handle."

"And this."

"Fahrin' pin."

"Open your eyes."

He looked. "Fuckin' A. It's the retainin' pin."

"Right. Shut 'em again. This one."

"Chargin' handle."

"Nope."

He opened his eyes. "It's the fuckin' retainin' pin again. You tricked me!"

I shrugged. "The enemy'll do worse."

As our session went on Jenks kept screwing up. He simply couldn't get the hang of it with his eyes shut. After about ten minutes he stood up. "This is fuckin' IM-

POSSIBLE!" he screamed. He balled up the towel with all the parts in it and threw it on his bunk with a clatter. "AH QUIT!"

I shrugged. "Suit yourself," I said, with some sympathy but not a whole lot.

Well, Jenks didn't quit. I saw him sweating on his footlocker every afternoon but without much success. Sgt. Baldwin was all over him, all the time. The following week, one evening just before lights out, once again Jenks showed up at my bunk, this time practically in tears. "Sgt. Baldwin's gonna wash me out. Ah don' know what to do."

Now I did feel sorry for him, he really had been trying. I had an idea. "How about we sneak out tonight and give it a go, outside, in the dark."

"Outside? In the dark?"

"It'll be more realistic. After lights out we'll go over to the basketball court and give it a go." Moving around after hours could land us in trouble but I thought it was worth it.

He nodded. "Ah got nothin' to lose."

"Bring your rifle and poncho. Your cleaning kit, too."

About 2230 hours I slipped on my fatigues and stepped over to Jenks' bunk. He was sitting on the edge, ready. As we crept through the barracks I opened the screen door and looked around. There was usually a roving guard but I didn't see anything. Waited a couple more minutes... nothing. Skirting the streetlights I spied the basketball stanchions and crossed the playing surface to the court farthest from the road. Make or break time. He spread out his poncho on the asphalt and we sat down. He disassembled the rifle easily, then we patiently worked through the different parts. In the dim light he identified them without a hitch. "Ah've been workin' on this, ah want you to know."

"I've seen you. Now you've got the rifle apart, let's see you clean it."

He went through the cleaning and lubricating process, swabbing the bore of the barrel with silicone lubricant and pulling the long brush through, cleaning bolt carrier, lower receiver, ejector. Light sounds of metal scraping metal broke the silence of the still evening. An occasional car drove by. "Good job," I said, "now put it back together."

Jenks took a deep breath. "Heah goes." He began reassembling – slow, methodically, accurately. "Five and a half minutes," I said, tapping my watch after the last step, where together we installed the knurled hand guards around the barrel and secured them in place. "Fastest ah evah done it," he said, his eyes wide. "Ah could hardly see what ah was doin,' neither."

"Don't get too comfortable, we get you up to speed then the blindfold comes on."

"Yeah... thet has been mah problem."

"But you'll deal with it. You're halfway there already."

Jenks looked at me approvingly. "Thanks, teach."

"Anything to keep Badass off our back."

"Ah don't lahk thet, him an' evvybody on mah ass."

After a few more rounds I said, "we'll pick it up tomorrow – blindfolded."

BY NOW WE WERE IN WEEK FIVE. They upped the ante, an eight-mile run over a tough, hilly course. I sailed through the second physical fitness test, cutting my time for the mile to five fifty-seven. My weight was down to one seventy-two. Not an ounce of flab anywhere.

The obstacle course phase had us scaling barricades, wriggling through barbed wire and culverts, crawling on our hands and knees with field pack and rifle and, one memorable day after an overnight drenching rain, doing it through a sea of mud. Tough, demanding work. You go-go-go until you're ready to drop, then you go some more. We had forgotten the word quit. Physical toughness and mental toughness are inseparable. They support and build on each other. Or for the loser, they undermine each other and he ends up with neither.

One exercise was a team competition to figure a way across an area of simulated quicksand with one squad member lamed by a simulated broken ankle. Sgt. Baldwin faced us. "Five minutes for the plan, twenty to execute. The squad is no better than its slowest and weakest member. Communicate! Communicate! Communicate! Everybody's got to make it through! Selfless Service!"

For me "Victory Tower" was as much mental as physical, a thirty foot-high contraption of ladders, ropes, cables and nets. Climb to the top, then over and down, rappelling, pushing off, bouncing to the bottom. Thirty feet is a lot higher than it sounds, especially when you're balanced in mid-air, debating whether to throw that second leg over, knowing the rest of you will inevitably follow. Personal Courage. I was fast making up for all those trees I never climbed. Finishing right behind Murph who had to be coaxed over the top by an instructor, I nearly tripped over him, flat on his stomach, hugging the ground – thankyouthankyouthankyou. No time for a break. Next was "Sky Tower," six platforms stacked on top of one another in a metal frame thirty feet high. To the top then right back down, but this time no ropes, just you and your team. That night in my bunk I reflected on how Army training was forcing me to overcome my fears, igniting the spark of daring they said we each had inside. Maybe I did, too! A different Paul Bernard was emerging.

This week also began map and compass night maneuvers. A moon, if you lucked out, night vision goggles, faces camouflaged black, discreet flashlight, flares, noise discipline. Up, over and around obstacles, Sgt. Rice in the lead, the loudest sound your heavy breathing, your heart thumping. Under fire, getting used to the sound of automatic weapons, grenades, the whoosh of mortars, red and white tracer bullets overhead. That was a bitch at first, I'll tell you, for if you hadn't realized it before, you knew this stuff can kill you. We conditioned our eyes for low light, to I.D. objects before the untrained eye knows they are even there. No ammo. Last thing we needed was a freaked-out trainee running around with a loaded weapon. I smiled, recalling the night that idiot dog owner fired off a couple of rounds.

At one point Sgt. Baldwin ordered us to halt. "Bravo Company! You will now field strip and reassemble your rifles. You have ten minutes! GO!"

A cloudy night, we were in a thick grove of trees, close to total darkness. Spreading my poncho out, I did it fast. For me this was second nature. Nearby, Bobby Jenks was quietly swearing, then I heard a determined, "got you, you motherfucker!"

Sgt. Baldwin filed among us. He stopped beside Jenks and told him to stand and present his rifle. He cracked the rifle open, then shut it and returned it to Jenks. "Goddammit, Jenks! We may make a soldier out of you yet!"

The exercise culminated in a 10-mile night march to an objective and back, with us planning the whole thing, led by Fred McDaniel who had stepped forward as a strong and resourceful personality. "Owe it all to my mom," he said with a grin when I clapped him on the back, "her and the streets of Chicago."

As the end of Marksmanship training neared I continued to score at the top. For many, leading the laterally-moving target was a chore, but it came easily to me. I recalled my early weapons training at the French Carnival – Omer and Angelo and I blasting away with cork guns at the wooden ducks floating by. Despite my proficiency, one miserable day in a downpour I really lost it, couldn't hit a thing. "Forget it, Bernard," Sgt. Baldwin said, "we all have a bad day sometimes. That thin line between confident and cocky – looks like you found it today."

The hours of close order drilling were paying off. We were definitely looking sharp. Even Bobby Jenks had shaped up, to the point that the guys were talking to him again. He passed his rifle tests too, though it was close. Jenks had begun asking me for other advice, even bedmaking which I apparently had more experience with. It was better between us though we weren't exactly friends. We suffered a setback when he found out I'd spent time at Berkeley, a fighting word. He'd been raised in a foster home, I learned, his father leaving when he was born, then a couple of years later his mother died. I figured his poor, unlettered existence had a lot to do with his railing about the privileged class, which he insisted on including me in. Jenks had plenty of company in using the Army as a lifeline up, and he was man enough to admit I helped save it for him.

On Wednesday June twenty-sixth the old man of the Company turned twenty-six. The event passed unremarked except for mail call, a reward for our improving drilling. My booty was a card from my father and one from Catherine. Another coincidence, my Saint's Day is the feast of St. Paul. Not *the* St. Paul but one of a pair of fourth-century Roman brothers who left military service and gave away their belongings to follow Jesus. For their trouble they were martyred, a part of the story I didn't like to dwell on.

As combat training intensified I was gaining my "infantry eye." No longer were hills and streams and forests scenery – they were terrain and strategic positions. I could sense where an enemy was apt to hide. I was learning to spot ambush territory and how to avoid one, also how to spring a trap of our own. More hand-to-hand. We were introduced to martial arts techniques – judo and karate, throws, kicks, chops to the bridge of the nose and neck areas, lethal pressure points. Swift and silent dispatch with the garotte and the M-7 knife that doubled as our bayonet.

One day we were walking in a driving rain when Sgt. Baldwin shouted out with a big grin. "Love this shitty weather! Where you're going it rains all the time! Believe me, ladies, I been there, so get used to it!" Of course, this was the day he chose to practice fording a stream, swollen and swift from days of rain. Rock to rock, rifle over your head. Keep it dry, your ammo too, your pack. Feet? Forget about it. Pray for a warm sunny break. I'd heard stories of soldiers whose feet never dried out. I also recalled that Seeger song, with chagrin.

It builds confidence to know when your rifle gets mucked up which one day it surely will, you can field strip and clean it. Also deal with malfunctions, clearing a stoppage in under five seconds. I'd heard comments about the M-16 jamming in combat. In some quarters it had gained the name Mattel – you can guess why. I had fired an M-14, its predecessor, and in fact the M-16 did seem flimsy by comparison. Sgt. Baldwin said it was all a crock, so I chalked it up to grousing and complaining, hoping it wasn't true.

Through dry firing and live ammo drills, we trained on the range of weaponry. The M-60 machine gun, the M-79 grenade launcher called "the Thumper," mortars, the Claymore antipersonnel mine. A lot of time on grenades, the Infantryman's "personal artillery system." They started us out on fake grenades, then small charges. My first time throwing a real one was a nervous experience, knowing that a screw-up after the pin's pulled kills everybody in the vicinity including yourself. I'd heard about one guy who accidentally pulled the pin while trying to extract a grenade from his pocket. A mistake not to be repeated.

We spent time with gas masks, especially putting them on fast. They had outfitted a squat, thick-walled building as a poison gas chamber. After getting the routine down, we were herded into the building and ordered to don our masks as the gas hissed up around us. There we sat, watching the chamber fill with fumes, counting off the minutes then exploding out of the stockade and ripping our masks off, reaching deep for gulps of air. Guys were puking. I could taste the bile in my mouth but somehow kept it down.

We learned about the NVA and VC. As training progressed, snide remarks about the enemy became more frequent and I knew there was more to come. One steamy afternoon Sgt. Johansson started in on the dinks, slopes, zipperheads, slant-eyed godless sub-human Commie scum who're trying to take over this little country the U.S. has pledged to keep free. "The gook does not spare women. He does not spare children. He will torture and kill old people. What he does will revolt and disgust you. His women are known to insert razor blades in their tiny cunts, so a word to the wise there. It comes down to this," he said, pounding his fist on a table, "it's them or you. Let a VC slip away, next day he's back to kill you or your buddy. You will give no quarter! You will show no mercy!"

I looked around. Everybody was lapping it up, leaning forward, eyes gleaming. A trainee raised his hand. "How do you tell a VC sympathizer from somebody on our side?"

Sgt. Johansson's face twisted into a scowl. "On your feet, Shit-For-Brains! What is your name?"

"Private Parisi, Sir!" Tony Parisi, from Philadelphia. He had a reputation as a joker.

"Sometimes you can't tell the difference. How do you like that answer, Shitbird?"

"Sir! Private Parisi doesn't like that answer! Sir!"

Sgt. Johansson advanced toward him. "You're a troublemaker, Shitbird."

"Begging your pardon, Sir, but if you can't tell the enemy from a friend you've got a big problem! Sir!"

"Anybody say it'd be easy, Shitbird?"

"No, Sir! I'm just looking for information, Sir!"

A smile flickered across Sgt. Johansson's face. "What if I say it doesn't matter? What then?"

Parisi frowned. "Sir! Private Parisi does not understand that answer! Sir!"

"Well, Shitbird, lemme enlighten you. When you are in a hostile situation and you cannot tell if the gook is friend or foe, you will shoot first and ask questions later! Is there anything about *that* answer you do not understand?"

Pasisi nodded. "No Sir! Thank you Sir!"

There has to be a better answer, I thought. Hostile or not, these are human beings.

Now, having knocked the enemy down, Sgt. Johansson was obliged to rehabilitate him. "What I say next you're not gonna like, but listen up! The gook has no honor, no morality, but the fact is, he is perfectly capable of killing you. The NVA is a solid, disciplined fighting force. It is extremely well-equipped with Chinese and Russian equipment. As for Charlie, he knows every trick in the book. Guerilla tactics, infiltration, ambush, mines, sabotage, you name it. You will not enjoy being on the receiving end of being shot at, being shot at very well in fact, but let me tell you, it will happen. You will hate the gook but do not underestimate the little bastard. Do that, you get yourself wasted."

At the seventh week and we were tired to the bone, tired of Basic Training, fed up with each other. The close quarters had gotten to us – people from all walks of life, with unfamiliar, often offensive habits. Now I saw why Mark glommed onto my quiet little room. As we spent more time together, the dissonance, the bitching and moaning increased. The tension was especially thick around some of the black kids. Tyrone Brown from Newark was always talking about Huey and Bobby. I told Tyrone I'd seen Huey up close and more than once, too, but he didn't believe me. He never missed a chance to badmouth whitey and even my friend Fred McDaniel took his side when Tyrone painted Vietnam as a white man's war.

"Just look around," Tyrone would say, "rich white boys in college with their daddies' money. So who's out front getting killed? The brothers! They got no choice! You call that fair? You call that right?"

"What about Sgt. Baldwin?" I said, "that man's no Oreo. He's tough as nails."

Tyrone wouldn't give an inch. "The man work his way up, he do a good job. Shows how fucked-up the system is when the black man has to kiss white ass to get ahead."

Fred knew I had enlisted but he had to watch what he said in front of his buddies. "Who got the dough run the show," was his refrain. "Nuthin' new there."

There were compensations. We had absorbed a huge amount of information, pushed ourselves beyond our wildest limits. Endurance, the other side of the toughness coin. I was in the best shape of my life and the end was in sight. I soared past the last tests and got fitted for my Class A dress greens for graduation. And, wonder of wonders, *ti-Paul*, gun-shy until a few short weeks ago, qualified as Expert Rifleman in his final BRM test! 37 for 40 shots centered!

After several briefings on the NIC, Night Infiltration Course, one night Sgt. Baldwin told us to get our shit together on the double. At 2030 hours we assembled in full battle gear and climbed into a 'deuce and a half,' the ubiquitous five ton truck, for a ride to the remotest corner of camp, the far southern tip of the property. When we got there it was pitch black, a still, clammy, moonless night. Bravo Company was the first to go and I was right up front.

"Don't like the looks of this," Murph said as we lined up behind a waist-high wall, peering out at a large sand field. The eerie green lighting made the concertina wire look even more menacing. We would low-crawl on our stomachs the length of the field under barbed wire only a couple of feet off the ground. Only 150 meters long, they said, but it looked like miles. The whole time we'd be under live fire from the left and the right. You fervently hoped the gunners didn't stray from their calibrated height.

"Piece of cake," I said, meaning this one could really get you killed.

Sgt. Baldwin stood by, looking at his watch. Suddenly all hell broke loose. Red and white tracer bullets streaked across the pit. The heavy chatter of M-60s filled the night air. Mortar shells and flares lit the sky. "Bravo Company! Let's go! LET'S GO!"

Over the wall went Murph. I took a deep breath and followed, dropping to all fours, crawling, head down and rifle up. Crablike I advanced and I am talking centimeters under the wire and tracers. Explosions filled the air. The smoke from the mortars drifted down, settling about us. My heart pounded. I looked ahead...Murph was widening the gap. Better pick up it up or somebody's gonna run up my ass. Too busy to be scared, no idea how long I'd been out here, didn't matter, anyway. I was doing pretty well when all of a sudden I ran right into a roll of razor wire angled across my path. I followed Murph's feet to the right, hoping he knew where he was going. Sand up my nose, sand in my mouth, sand in my pockets. Push! I kept telling myself. Be tough! Don't quit! Left arm forward, right leg forward. Right arm, left leg. Push! PUSH!! After what seemed hours I eyeballed a bunch of people up ahead, standing. Had to be the end, otherwise they wouldn't be standing, they'd be dead. PUSH HARD! Finally the wire ended and I crawled out from under. The reptile ascends the beach. People were shouting and waving their arms.

"Way to go soldier!" "Good job!"

I jumped up. Murph cuffed me on the helmet. "We made it!" he yelled.

One by one they crept in, brushing off the sand, slapping each other. Sgt. Baldwin drove up in a jeep. First time I'd seen him smile like he really meant it.

One more ordeal, a bruising seven-day six-night field combat exercise that brought it all together. We were so close to the end I'm ashamed to admit I let my guard down, didn't steel myself well enough against the night forest, the sounds of small animals and nocturnal birds, the near impossibility of telling friend from foe, the screaming, shooting ambush they threw at us. I put myself back together, but the letdown taught me a lesson. Fear is a good thing. Fear means you're on alert, ready for anything. It's the other side of the survival coin. Tame it, control it, make it work, but whatever you do – don't lose it.

Remarkably, only two trainees from Bravo Company had been told to leave. Even Bobby Jenks made it. By now he was borderline amiable. That initial acting out, he must have been panicked he wouldn't make it through.

The night after the field exercise they threw a Rites of Passage bash with bonfires and speeches, hot dogs, burgers. Col. Banfield praised us for completing the transformation, civilian to warrior. I stood there, beer in hand, listening. Yes, I have finished the course, the Army has imparted warrior skills to me. The indoctrination has produced an unbelievably gung-ho spirit in some of my compatriots, but my warrior mindset comes with an on-off switch. I will do my part, my best, but I have never been a cog in a machine and I'm not about to start now. Distance and perspective, that'll keep the beast at bay.

Now we honed our close order drill to a keen edge. We were nothing like the weenies that straggled off those buses two months before. We were given personal time to write letters and get our heads together. Next would come thirteen weeks of intensive and specialized training, Advanced Individual Training. Then, orders to ship out. For AIT, those of us who chose Infantry would move down the block to a new barracks. The others, Artillery, Ordnance, Logistics, Quartermaster, they'd be boarding a bus or a plane. The young Lieutenant who counseled me made another push for OCS, saying I was great officer material, but my mind was made up.

For graduation, central New Jersey served up a brilliant warm day, Bravo Company's last day as a unit. We marched crisply onto the parade grounds following the Fort Dix Army Band, the Stars and Stripes and Bravo Company's red and gold. I sneaked a look at the grandstand but couldn't pick out my father or Jim. Along with Mark, Jim's six-year-old, they had come in the night before and stayed in a motel nearby. Catherine sent regrets but I'd catch her during my week furlough. On the plus side, her absence meant more room in Jim's new station wagon for the ride back to Providence.

We stood at attention facing the grandstand, all five Companies. When my name was read out for Bravo Company's Marksmanship Award I advanced to the front of our unit as Sgt. Baldwin pinned the medal on my chest. Smiling broadly he shook my hand. "Good work, Private Bernard. Good luck in AIT."

In his speech Base C.O. General Rainey said we were the newest soldiers in the greatest Army in the world, our nation's front line in the defense of freedom. Two months ago I would have been picking his words apart, but this morning I stood there and let them wash over me. Suddenly I noticed the drumming... was it getting louder? Hot and sweaty, I tugged at my shirt collar. Closer... louder... now it was I being played, not the drum. Of course. The drum, the band, the soldier. Mrs. D'Andrea's flag. I closed my eyes. When I opened them, same sea of green, Gen. Rainey droning on, but I understand. I am afloat on this sea of green, but after all this time, now I understand. Ordered to fall out, we are caught up in the shouting, the hugging, the farewells. People pour from the grandstand. We leave our comrades and make our way toward them. And the band plays on.

LIGHT COMING THROUGH THE CURTAINS woke me up. I laughed when I saw what I'd done to Jim's spare room. Duffel bag in the corner, dress uniform on a hook from the closet door, dress shoes beneath. Past and future in collision. The day before on the drive north, after a spasm of enthusiasm and catching up, we exhausted everything we had to say to each other, though my father kept trying. Circling Manhattan, he reached back to our New York trip. Jim and I looked at each other and grinned. Then he turned on the Sox game – they were in Oakland, the game just starting as we crossed into Connecticut. He reminisced about the good times driving to Fenway, the ham sandwiches, Fiona winning tickets in those contests, how we parked at the old Sears Building knowing we'd be caught in an awful traffic jam afterward. But it wasn't working. Memories, that's all it was. My next act would envelop us all, but nobody wanted to talk about it. Nor did I. I lacked the energy to invite them into my new life. The last few weeks had changed me, more than I had bargained for.

Walking in uniform to the local market I noticed stares, and I received some positively dirty looks visiting Catherine's apartment near Brown. Mild, I thought, compared with Telegraph Ave. It saddened me to see our turnaround lot was no more, two new houses jammed into it. I stopped to greet Omer's mother in her front yard. She said Omer was in the Army, himself. He'd been working in a print shop in North Providence when the draft caught him, was in his second Vietnam tour and thought he might make a career of it. She noted pointedly he was already a corporal, outranking me, and not just by one rank, either. Ironic, I thought, but so be it. Mrs. Arsenault had always been kind of emotional and when we got on Vietnam, she began crying. I told her I'd be there myself soon and she made me promise to look him up. I had no idea how to do that, but it made her happy to press the scrap of paper with his Army address into my hand.

Halfway through my furlough, I called Cambridge on the off-chance Meg might be around. Surprisingly she was, so next day I borrowed the Cadillac and set out. With her new degree from Yale Medical, residency at Mass General was next, but first a summer to relax, travel. Clyde – sorry, for me that name is still a fingernail on a blackboard – Clyde was visiting relatives in Florida. They still hadn't set a date. A Pat appearance was expected near the end of summer. After recovering from the shock of seeing me in uniform she stood back and inspected me, saying how good I looked.

"Best shape of my life," I said, offering her my bicep. "I'll match you guys on the mountain any day. Fifteen miles with a seventy-pound pack. How's that sound?"

"Thank you, no. I take it you're used to that sort of thing."

I nodded. I'd been concerned how she'd react to my being in the Army, and, her family such sophisticates, at not being an officer. Same sort of reluctance I felt about discussing my encyclopaedia summer – not the up-scale, neat thing to do. She expressed more concern for my welfare than my rank when I told her Vietnam was next. "It's so awful, what you see on television. I hope you'll take care of yourself."

"I've always had good survival instincts. Now I back them up better."

We talked back and forth, she probing for my reasons, I giving my sermon to the skeptical, for what, the thousandth time.

"I hear what you're saying, but this is not what I would have chosen for you."

"Fortunately it wasn't your decision," I said, not meaning to be testy but wanting to put the subject to rest. "Speaking of combat, was my friend your brother involved in the riots?" I'd heard that Pat's haunt, the Sorbonne, was in the middle of the action.

"He even got himself arrested! Next time you see him you'll notice something new."

She pulled out a picture of him holding a cobblestone like a quarterback back to pass. "This," she pointed to a long gash above his eye. "He was hit by a tear gas canister."

"If he was that close he deserved what he got."

"An inch lower, it would have put out his eye. He did get a dose of gas poisoning."

I shook my head. "Sorry, I have no sympathy for that form of expression. I had my fill of that in Berkeley. How're his studies coming, if I may ask?"

"Everything stopped, of course, they're just getting started again. He's doing his thesis on the Surrealists."

I smiled. Good old Pat, off-center as always. "I'll give you my service address, if you would pass it on," I handed the picture back, "though you're the one I want to hear from." I had been wondering, that is, hoping, that their long engagement might present a problem. That sort of thing did happen.

I didn't have the nerve to ask but I didn't have to, for she held out her hand, examining the ring on her finger. "It's confusing," she said, lowering her eyes, "next time you see me this may be a thing of the past," she spread her fingers then closed them. "Then again it may not."

I took her hand and covered the ring. "From my selfish point of view..." I felt my face getting warm, my embarrassment rising, "I... I don't know what to say."

"Just as well. As you said, it's not your decision."

"Whatever happens, I hope you'll write."

"I'm an emancipated woman," she replied. "Being married won't change that. You may expect the occasional letter from me to grace your mailbox."

"No mailboxes," I shook my head. "A sergeant from hell hands out the mail, makes a bunch of wise remarks, does everything but read your letters to everybody."

I was disappointed to hear *grand-maman* was away. Meg said she'd left the day before for a month on the Vineyard. She handed me an envelope. "She said give this to you."

I looked at the blue tinted envelope inscribed "For Paul" in tidy Gallic script. "I've never seen her handwriting before." I slit the envelope with my finger and opened her note.

Mon chèr Paul,

I am sorry we missed each other but wish to express my thoughts in this billet doux. I have always seen you as so reasonable a young man, I was surprised you have left your studies and joined the army. Doubtless you have your reasons, but it disappoints me that you lend your talents to this stupid mistake of Johnson.

My first husband was a military man, so I take a certain pride in what you do. Most of all, though, I have concern for your safety, as you will soon go to the war, to Vietnam that consumed so many French boys and now Americans. I pray for your safe return and look forward to a tête-à-tête to know why you are doing this. I have asked Meg to take a photo in your uniform for me. Know my thoughts and prayers are always with you.

Élodie.

I put the letter down. "Very nice. Very thoughtful."

"May I see it?" Meg asked. She read it and shook her head. "I've never seen *grand-maman* so upset. For some unaccountable reason she really likes you."

"Hard to believe, isn't it? Sorry to disappoint, but you do what you have to do."

"That's her point. Why are you doing it? I still don't understand."

"She got it right. We'll talk when I get back." I stood up. "Where's your camera?"

Her parting kiss gave me a glow I felt all the way back to Providence and then some. For my last day it was lunch at the Biltmore with my father. That splendid roast beef, but neither of us was hungry. Mid-afternoon we stood facing each other on the sidewalk in front of Union Station. "You'll be away a long time, longer than California."

I nodded. "How can you miss me if I never go away?"

By now we both had tears in our eyes. "Take care of yourself," he said, throwing his arms around me, letting go of his cane which fell to the ground.

"I will, and this time I know how."

"Yes you do," he said, "and this will help," he said, rubbing my marksmanship medal.

We shook hands. "You take care, too." I picked up his cane and opened the car door for him, going round to the other side and peering through the open window. "See you next year," I said, leaning in to shake his hand. Suddenly I took two steps back, stood at attention and saluted this man, my father. He nodded and started the engine. The Caddy pulled away from the curb. I picked up my duffel and walked to the train, not looking back.

32. DEAD CENTER

BACK AT THE HOTEL I take one look at what Dennis gave me and I call Jonathan. Get over here right away, I tell him. Here is what we read.

CONFIDENTIAL

TO: Lt. Gen. Dennis Riggs
FROM: Col. Bernard Syzmanski
DATE: 30 Sept 2003
RE: U.S. Army Investigation 03-1649

You requested me to look into the investigation of the 9 September 2003 attack in which reporter Paul Bernard and others were killed. Specifically, you asked me to determine why the investigation was terminated.

I believe the action to terminate was motivated by certain preliminary findings of the investigating officer, Capt. Roberto Martinez, which he reported confidentially to myself. I discussed this matter in strictest confidence with Capt. Martinez, who is angry and upset at being told to stand down.

Capt. Martinez was able to identify two individuals who took part in the attack plus certain additional detail. He confirms that a shoulder-fired RPG was employed, consistent with fragments in the roadway plus other evidence at the scene. The weapon is of Soviet manufacture and in common use by the Republican Guard.

The individuals so far identified are a Mohammad al-Safar and Ismail Husseini. Al-Safar was a General in the Republican Guard. He is from the Tikrit region. This individual has a past connection with the United States. During our support for Iraq in its war against Iran, Al-Safar was involved in procurement of weapons and materiel from American military personnel and spent some time in the U.S. He speaks fluent English. Nothing is known of Husseini other than his name.

Capt. Martinez believes it significant that Gen. al-Safar's nephew Abdullah al-Safar is employed by the civilian contractor Atlas which has responsibility for transportation and security for VIPs and certain other non-military personnel in and around Baghdad. Abdullah al-Safar was not cleared to see Atlas' Orders of the Day but would have had regular contact with those who were.

Several days ago the nephew was detained by Army personnel and is being held in an secure location near Baghdad for interrogation. Capt. Martinez was granted one meeting with Abdullah al-Safar and had a second scheduled when his investigation was terminated. In this interrogation Abdullah al-Safar admitted he was aware the reporter Bernard and his crew would travel in the subject motorcade. He also knew that for security reasons they had been switched to a Humvee from the Chevy Suburban which was S.O.P. He also admitted passing this information on to someone on the outside but refused to say who or answer further questions. That was to be the subject of the second interrogation which never occurred.

Capt. Martinez told me that he examined Abdullah al-Safar's Atlas personnel file and discovered that he had been recommended for his position by Nita Garrison, a civilian on the staff of L. Paul Bremer.

That is all for now.

Jonathan whistles. "How'd he ever get those names? Why is the Army so worried?"

"Dennis' business is finding things out." I have come to the conclusion he's doing a lot more than coordinating, whatever that means.

Jonathan is shaking his head, "Garrison, Garrison – why do I know that name?"

"Never heard of her. One of the many political appointments, I suppose. Experience no requirement, loyalty to George Bush is."

Jonathan snaps his fingers. "Len Garrison! Big oilman, wildcatter. West Texas. Thick as thieves with Bush One. I'll bet she's related to him. Beautiful! Now I've got something to run with."

I pick up the letter. "Read it over again. I promised Dennis we'd get rid of it."

"I'll just make a few notes."

"No notes. Use your memory, what's left after that gadget of yours."

"No problem. Give me a minute."

I go into the bathroom and wash my face. A moment later Jonathan comes in. We stand over the toilet as I touch a match to the letter and drop the paper in. As it steams I reach for the handle. The charred mess swirls in the bowl and disappears.

* * * * * * *

FORT DIX HAD NO TIGERLAND like Fort Polk so we made use of the mock Vietnamese village. How to enter a village, a "ville." How to search hut-to-hut, find the booby traps, figure out who's on your side and which guy (or woman! or girl!) would be the one to roll a grenade toward your feet. Despite Sgt. Johansson's facile answer we spent a lot of time on this. Some played the role of VC, others government loyalists, it was up to us to sort it out. An iffy proposition even for the instructors, though they tended to do better. Some techniques were common sense, others borderline criminal or worse. One day a Lieutenant just back took it upon himself to demonstrate some tricks with needles and fingernails, also how running a jumper cable from a field radio to Charlie's nuts was guaranteed to make him talk. Scream, yes, but talk? And useful talk? This one went in my file and forget drawer.

We fired M-16s in automatic burst-fire mode and semi-automatic three-round rapid fire, in a slow advance, running, upright and crouched low. From a high crawl, from a low crawl. From the shoulder, from the hip. Build accuracy, then speed. Suppressive fire into an area where the enemy is but you can't see him. Defensive fire. Surprise close-in targets, reflexive fire when there's no time to aim. Target discrimination, distinguishing threat from non-threat targets. Long range marksmanship, 300 to 500 meters.

One day after a long session on the range it occurs to me, a life with weapons is ruled by metal. I have thought about this since. Other materials do not threaten or dominate like metal. Wood is a baseball bat, it is pencils, tables, chairs, houses. Leather, my Marty Marion glove, shoes, my wallet. Paper and cardboard? Books – need I say more? Plastic, my ballpoint pen. Cloth is clothes. Glass and pottery are eyeglasses, water tumblers, cups, plates. But metal –metal is different. Metal and I are no strangers, of course – utensils, for one, my razor, my car, my father's shop, but this new relationship is worrisome. Here's the point. All these objects serve me, but as a weapon, metal puts me at its service, sweeps me up and carries me along, forcing me to do its bidding. The realization shocks me. Metal proclaims its power, thrusting me into situations where I am expected to act in ways I would never dream of, harsh, unforgiving ways. It hands me a destroyer's mask and says put it on. Perhaps, inchoately, I have known this all along. Is this is why I have never owned a gun? And what of my new acceptance of them... what of that?

Dix has plenty of swampy ground and we got to know it intimately. The summer was unusually wet, which added to the misery and realism. How about week-long maneuvers in the mud with mortars and artillery pounding all night so you're lucky if you get an hour's sleep? We trained as a squad – offensive maneuvers, defensive live-fire exercises, night live-fire exercises, simulated missions in the swamps and woods, cutting trail through the undergrowth with machetes, penetrating barbed wire, rolling down steep inclines keeping your rifle out of the dirt. Sound discipline, i.e. no talk. Radio clicks to communicate. Light discipline... even the glow from a cigarette can be fatal. Everybody smoked. I had still avoided the habit. I bummed one once in a while, that was all, so far.

We trained to exit a helicopter, shinnying down ropes and cables, from high platforms, then towers, then parachute drops like at big amusement parks. The real thing was a blast, choppers hovering fifty feet up, THWOCK-THWOCK-THWOCK of the rotors, spewing dust and pebbles, your face stinging as you descend the rope hand over hand with your rifle and a full pack, then drop into a crouching run. We were introduced to tank warfare, though they said you'd seldom encounter an NVA tank or heavy armed vehicle. For those rarities we trained on the new M-72 Light Antitank Weapon, the LAW.

Occasionally I caught sight of Sgt. Baldwin drilling a new batch of recruits. For AIT we had a different set of instructors, some right out of leadership school, others fresh from Vietnam. No question which was which. Most memorable was Captain B.J. Phelps, a worthy successor to Sgt. Johansson. Capt. Phelps didn't swear – he had once been a Sunday school teacher. Capt. Phelps didn't shout, he didn't have to. Medium height, wiry, with a deep tan, close-cropped graying hair and gleaming dark eyes in sore-looking circles, this was a man with more important things to do than sleep. A U of Kansas ROTC grad with three tours in Vietnam, he'd been Stateside a month. Capt. Phelps was a man obsessed – obsessed with exterminating VC. When he got wound up he could hardly contain his glee and didn't even try. He saw us as extensions of himself, acolytes in his mission.

"The VC is not human," he told us, speaking in a flat, uninflected tone that still gives me the willies. "Charlie is not human, the NVA gook is not human. Don't get suckered into thinking they are, for they are not. The VC and the NVA are God's mistakes. Let me tell you something, men, even God messes up sometimes and our job is to help Him rid the world of these mistakes. They are the enemy and they will kill you every chance they get, they will kill you and your buddies. You must take the gook out first. He is tough. It is you or him."

The instructors assumed we knew how to use our weapons. Their job was to insure we *would* use them, to eliminate any hesitancy to pull the trigger, toss the grenade, fire the M-60, set the Claymore. Every vestige of reticence had to be drummed out of us. When we were told to shoot, we would shoot. Lives depended on it. More training in close-range combat, rifle, bayonet and knife, hand-to-hand. Search, destroy, hunt, kill.

Capt. Phelps held up his M-16. "Your rifle is a tool, but only a tool. Why you will prevail is your cold, calm killer instinct. In combat you will have no time to think, you will have no time to weigh consequences." His eyes gleamed. "At that moment of truth if you hesitate, if you do not kill swiftly and gladly, you will die!"

To gladly end the life of another! To make a person grovel, dominate him in the most elemental way. What is the appeal? I'd heard of people aroused by battle. Maybe that's how Phelps gets his hard-ons. Fortunate indeed, B.J. Phelps – society provides you an outlet to indulge your need to kill. You are cast as a hero for doing what would otherwise land you in an institution or on Death Row.

I feel myself struggling toward an insight, something that had puzzled me a long time. Theater of war, war as theater. Now here, slapping me across the face is my answer. Reality Theater, Theater of Life, Theater of Death. I am on dangerous ground here. Have to keep my feelings hidden, play the role. But neither can I disregard Phelps, for warped as he is, he's here for my benefit. Pay attention, learn his recipe for staying alive and learn it well. Gus' disquisitions on violence are on my mind a lot these days. I have to believe all militaries have their share of psychopaths, but not all who kill are sick. Desensitized, yes – some of them – but not sick. Are not many simply skilled tradesmen, placed in a position where the tools of their trade and a deadly danger give them no choice?

A story about Capt. Phelps was making the rounds. One night his platoon was pinned down by VC fire. This was right after Pleiku in sixty-five. A guy in his unit had just taken a bullet between the eyes – he had foolishly removed his helmet, forgot to keep his head down. Phelps, then 2nd Lt. Phelps, lay the dead man down, prayed over him a moment, then told two of his men to get ready. Turning to his Sergeant he said, "give me ten minutes, then open up with everything you have." Then, the story went, he and his men crept out of their trench and flanked around the clearing until they were abeam the VC. The barrage began, and M-16s blazing and grenades flying, the three men took out the enemy position. Extreme bravery under fire, the commendation said. True as far as it went. Did it go far enough?

One night as I lay in bed, the worst day in my life flooded back. The bloody box, my rage at that coward who killed my dog. What would I have done, I remember thinking at the time – if I could have, what would I have done? Let's be honest. Back then if I had the tools and skills I have now, I would have shown no pity. A Gandhi I am not.

HALFWAY THROUGH AIT A BUNCH OF US used a weekend pass and caught a bus into town. Some of the guys, Murph and to my surprise Nathan, headed off to cruise but I was happy to linger over a few beers, an Italian dinner, just walk around. About seven-thirty we joined a crowd converging on what the little towns around Boston call the village green. We heard a band warming up and came upon a bandstand draped with a banner for the Saturday evening concert. High school girls and eight-year-olds parading about, showing off their summer dresses, hats, ribbons. Norman Rockwell all the way. We gave some women our chairs and sat atop the whitewashed low wall separating the green from the street. At eight o'clock the conductor turned and raised his baton for the National Anthem. We stood and saluted. Then Sousa. Show tunes, Carousel, South Pacific, Oklahoma, a pretty girl singing with an old coot in a cowboy hat old enough to be her father. *People Will Say We're In Love, Surrey With The Fringe On The Top...* who knows, maybe he *was* her father. She made me wish I was home, with Meg. Wallowing in my misery, I felt even worse.

Some guys had gotten a room in a motel, hoping for the best, but we bought ice cream and on the way to the bus stop decided for the hell of it to hitch. Right away this older guy and his wife in a black Chevy made a U-turn and stopped. The Base was out of their way, but they would give us a ride – the least they could do for "our boys." They thanked us profusely for everything we were doing. I was touched, and more than a little embarrassed.

Our longest AIT maneuver, seven days, would take us to a village suspected of harboring VC. We'd secure the area, establish a defensive perimeter, capture the chief, interrogate him and bring him back. Fred and I were given the job of devising the plan. We set the order of march, chose the point, who would bring up the rear, carry the M-60s, the mortar and grenade launcher, the ammo (still blanks), pack the radios. Where we'd bivouac, how we'd secure the village, our rally points, how to get back. I would be point – out front, totally exposed. Phelps and his men would be in the area and at the worst possible time, they'd spring a live-fire night tactical exercise on us. The return would be a fifteen-mile forced march. How we handled this exercise would make interesting reading, but I'd be rehashing the same ground when I tell you about 'Nam. Best wait for the real thing.

By the end of AIT our innocent optimism was gone. Some were so fired up they'd swung too far the other way. For me, the pretense of invincibility was sad, and dangerous. Fear wasn't pretty but at least it was honest. Some of us would not grow to manhood. I had to believe, in the quiet of each soul where machismo dares not tread, every one of us knew this.

33. FIRST BLOOD

THE NEXT MORNING Jonathan and I are back at it. "Some interesting correspondence here," I say, handing him a letter which, as it happens, is one of my own.

Oct. 16, 1968

Dear Paul,

A thousand apologies for not writing. It has been a madhouse here but what else is new? Are you through Basic Training? Unless something's changed Vietnam is next. When do you leave?

What a year this has been. Just when you think things can't get any worse, they do. At times it looked like everything was spiraling out of control. Must not despair, however, make positive energy, continue to seek the better outcome.

MLK, Bobby, so predictable, so sad. And Chicago, what a disaster, in the streets, and squandering our last best chance. We owe McCarthy a debt, though nobody knew what to make of him. And now more Nixon, that annoying and difficult man. In the misery-loves-company-department, for once Cal wasn't the only headliner. Columbia put us in the shade, and of course Europe was fascinating. The consequences may have more lasting effect there. Our skirmishing never seems to accomplish much. Enclosed are some Daily Cal clippings to catch you up.

Again we have a full house. Let us know how you are doing. Akiko sends greetings and joins me in wishing you safe passage. Stay well, we look forward to welcoming you home.

Gus

Jonathan looks up. "No clippings – does it matter?" I shake my head. "My parents talked a lot about 1968. A year to remember, they called it."

"More like a year to forget," I say, and hand him the second letter.

17 November 1968

Gus,

Your letter just caught up to me. At this moment I am six hundred miles north of you in the Pacific Northwest, the Fort Lewis Enlisted Men's Club to be exact, watching it rain. We wrapped up two weeks ago and I'm waiting to rotate to the Big Show, catching up on newspapers and reading, a real luxury. By the

> way, "wait" is the key word in this organization. You didn't warn me how much of that to expect. They say we ship out Wednesday, the day before Thanksgiving. Happy Turkey Day!
>
> Basic was awesome –I'll tell you about it some time. And if you can believe it, I'm the old man in every crowd! I have to admit I didn't appreciate my education until now, and I'm not talking about facts and figures. But you'll be happy to know the same person crawled out of the pipeline as crawled in. The early Christian all over again.
>
> I'm sending a picture of me in uniform that should be good for a laugh. My plans remain on track. Fall in behind our new Commander-in-Chief, do my part, get out. Can you believe it came up Nixon? I voted for Pat Paulsen.
>
> I look forward to seeing you and Akiko soon again. Have a great Christmas, say hello to everyone and when the ball falls, lift a cup for me. Know that I'll be raising a can of C-rations to you. Miss you all very much.
>
> Paul

"Picture's missing too but no big deal." He leafs through the rest of the folder and puts it back in the box. "And so we say farewell to Basic Training."

The first Vietnam carton is open on the conference table. I nod at the carton. "After you left yesterday I took a look and I have a suggestion. Vietnam is so crucial, why don't we let Paul tell it straight through, keep our comments til the end?"

Jonathan nods. "I was thinking along those lines too. Better if we see it as a whole."

* * * * * * *

AFTER BOOT CAMP Fort Lewis was a welcome break. Then, the day before our departure I called Meg and what she said knocked me for a loop. The engagement was off! Not only that, she sounded distraught when I said it'd be a whole year before I'd be back. I'd told her that before but I guess it hadn't registered. Sayonara, Clyde, I thought as we hung up, and once again it's hel-lo Paul. Unbelievable!

During my down time I worked on my Vietnamese, kind of wishing I had bought those tapes, but I figured, soon enough I'd be hearing plenty of the real thing. I moved ahead in *Brothers,* re-reading the Great Inquisitor. Amazing, disturbing. Bought a second notebook too, as I had filled a lot of the first with notes from Basic.

There was time to ponder the distasteful prospect that in less than two months Richard Milhous Nixon would be President. I had directed my absentee ballot to HHH but without enthusiasm. Right after the nomination he'd started backpedalling away from Vietnam. If that's the way he felt why didn't he say so sooner? I was still convinced of the cause, even if some of our leaders sold it short.

But Nixon's "peace with honor" worried me. No, I would not buy a used car from that man, or anything else for that matter.

I received a package from Gus with *Daily Cal* clips. 1968 was marked by a charade called "Vietnam Commencement." Egged on by radical faculty, hundreds of senior men pledged to refuse induction. Gus didn't say if he was part of it but I wouldn't have been surprised. The assassinations provoked malaise and soul-searching. By June, seeing nothing much happening, Berkeley's radicals fomented a riot *à la française* complete with burning barricades, shutting the city down for a few days. Everything considered, however, 1968 promised an upbeat finish with Apollo 8 and our first attempt to circle the moon.

One day in the rec room, I was making good headway in *Brothers*. Nathan was thumbing through an old *Sports Illustrated*. "You know, Paul," he confided, "I'll never forget that first night in the barracks. Nobody ever disrespected me like that Baldwin. I was so mortified, so angry. I really wanted to report him."

"At least nobody calls you O Henry any more."

He gritted his teeth. "They better not."

"Hey, he rode everybody. A lot of guys needed that to kick them into gear – look at Jenks."

"Jenks deserved it."

"It made him a better soldier. What about you?"

"Just the opposite. I was brought up to be responsible. Responsible was my middle name. We kept kosher, went to temple, I've always known what to do and I don't appreciate being treated like some idiot child."

"Me too, except the kosher part. I had a Jewish friend who's not very religious."

"We come in all shapes and sizes. Why'd you say 'had?'"

This stopped me. "I don't know. Maybe because he's from my former life. Maybe because who knows if I'll ever see him again."

"Come on, we'll make it through."

"But who can know? Nobody, that's who."

THE BIG JET BANKED STEEPLY then we rolled into an ear-popping descent. The stewardess came on to say we were on final approach to Cam Ranh Bay. Still dark but a glimmer of light on the horizon. An ordinary flight, I was thinking, until you look around and see everybody in green, everybody with the same haircut, the same apprehensive stare, the same nervous laughter. Jammed into the airplane, all 238 of us, last leg of a journey that began on a sleety Pacific Northwest afternoon. A stopover in Honolulu, then Wake to refuel. Somewhere over the ocean, turkey and stuffing, mashed potatoes, cranberry sauce on a drop-down tray. Oh, and pumpkin pie with whipped cream. Not enough but not bad.

Nathan had been in the seat beside me for the trip, Murph across the aisle. Very different, those two guys. Nathan of a serious mien, Murph more freewheeling. Bobby Jenks and my two black buddies from Chicago were on the plane, too. Spending time together waiting it out, Jenks had grown into a reasonable facsimile of a human being. Getting through Basic had given him a big boost. In fact, he fretted the war would be over before he got there and had a chance to bag himself some V.C. Good thing we had figured out how to get along – we could end up in the same unit.

With time to think on the long flight, I couldn't help dwelling on what I had gotten myself into. I was still convinced my decision was sound. Nagging doubts, but I figured you'll always have some. Best I could, I put them aside. Then there was Meg...

The landing gear dropped down and the engines went to high power. The plane's nose rose and I saw the flaps go as far as they could go. We were scooting along some moderately high hills and the distant outline of a higher range, *dãy núi.* Out the other side a foamy shoreline and beyond, the shining ocean, *đại dương,* we had just traversed. It looked a lot like the California coast, but I knew we were entering a strange and forbidding place. In the Fort Lewis library, I discovered Vietnam was about the same latitude as Central America and the Cape Verde Islands off Africa. Made me think of my old classmate Walt Gomes... maybe I'll run into him here – wouldn't that be something! Saigon's on a line with the island of Yap, along with Caracas, Conakry, Djibouti, Bangalore and a lot of empty ocean. If you stand in Saigon the hole you dig puts you some miles north of Lima, Peru. How far, how bizarre.

The plane touched down and rolled... and rolled... and rolled... My heart rose in my throat. Is something wrong? A preview, though I didn't yet know it, of the high anxiety that from now on would be SOP. Even if the answer is benign, there's rarely anyone around to tell you. After a long taxi we stopped in front of a complex screened by high rolls of razor wire. We stood and stretched, gathered our belongings, watching our duffels being offloaded onto the tarmac. Forty-five minutes later we made our way through a line at the air-conditioned processing center. Everybody spoke of Vietnam's oppressive heat and humidity – here it's only 0830 and our uniforms were soaked from the walk in from the plane.

Nathan, Murph and I found ourselves assigned to Company H, 4th Battalion, 25th Infantry Division, destined for Firebase Tango outside Tay Ninh, a city of forty thousand and the provincial capital. Bordered on three sides by Cambodia, Tay Ninh was a key location, astride a main infiltration route from the enemy's Cambodia sanctuary to Saigon. In sixty-seven, Tay Ninh Province had been the site of a large search and destroy operation called Junction City, with the 25th and others plus ARVN fighting to clear a large region of VC and NVA. They constructed airfields, landing zones and base camps including Fire Base Tango, but since the command chose not to leave enough men behind the enemy filtered back with ease. We'd see that again and again. It made no sense.

The 25th, nicknamed "Tropic Lightning" because of its good work in the Pacific War, had also seen action in Korea and was one of the largest infantry divisions in Vietnam. We received our shoulder patches, a lightning bolt over a red and yellow taro leaf in tribute to the unit's Hawaiian ties. It had been at Pearl Harbor on That Day.

Today we would finish our processing "in-country" and pick up equipment including the M-16s that would keep us company the next year. Fiona II, I christened mine. Come morning, we'd chopper out to our unit. As the Corporal who checked us in said, "Welcome to the 25th but don't make yourself too comfortable."

During the afternoon Bravo Company alumni compared notes. Fred and Wayne were also in the 25th, Bobby Jenks had been assigned to the 1st Infantry Division, "The Big Red One," and was headed for Highway Thirteen where the VC harassed supply convoys heading into the Central Highlands. "You're on your own," I observed. "You ready for that?"

"Man, ahm so ready ah cain't stand it."

Wayne nodded. "We always thought you was different, now we know for sure. Here we are, one day away from the shit and you still ain't scared?"

"Hell no. Ah aim to get me mah first Vee-Cee tomorrow, day after at the latest."

Wayne looked at me and rolled his eyes. "Somehow I can wait."

I nodded. "I see no need to rush things."

"A friend of mine clued me in about Tango," Fred told me as we walked to our barracks for the night. "They got a situation there."

"What kind of situation?"

"Oh, your typical race war. 'Couple of weeks ago a white dude was shot, one of the brothers, too. Had to send him home which is not all bad but that is a seriously wrong way to do it. They have a blacks-only clubhouse, no whites allowed, that kind of thing."

"You'll keep me out of trouble, right?"

Fred looked down at his feet. "I'll do what I can."

The next morning before dawn we grabbed our gear and clambered aboard a bus with windows covered by wire mesh for protection against grenades, flying glass. A lot of folks wanted us out of their country, better yet, dead. In the dim light I spied four huge twin-rotor CH-47 Chinooks, their drooped blades slowly rotating – our welcome to the Big Show. With Nathan and Murph close behind I climbed the ramp of the first chopper and we passed through its open maw into the narrow fuselage. Jonahs, I thought... hopefully we'll have better luck. We stowed our packs and gear beneath the canvas bucket seats, rifles at the vertical between our knees. As the slapping of the rotors grew louder, the ground tilted and fell away, the nose dipped and we moved ahead, gaining airspeed and altitude. Our destination was south of due west – 260 degrees, I estimated – a distance of 340 kilometers according to the pilot (call it 210 miles) and a flying time of about ninety minutes.

Soon we were over water. I thought of the shiny new Zippo in my pocket. No smoking here and thanks to Basic I was hooked enough to want one. Now entering an area of modest mountains, a wrinkled green carpet rose to greet us, the famed Central Highlands, then the earth flattened out again. I peered out at the morning sun's sheen on the paddies... there is much beauty in this place, enjoy it while you can. After a while my stomach began jumping around. The bumpy air... or was I kidding myself? From time to time I took comfort in rubbing the stock of my M-16. How far I had come, in so many ways. After a while, I caught sight of a large brown smudge in the distance. Has to be Saigon, I told myself, wondering how I could maneuver a visit with Father Trần. Maybe I could call him, at least, see how he was doing.

The chopper slowed and now we began a steep descent. Out the other window was a peak I later learned was called Black Lady Mountain, *Núi Bà Đen,* towering above the flatlands. With a burst of power we passed over the outer perimeter of Fire Base Tango, several belts of coiled concertina wire and a tall chain-link fence, then, pausing above the bare red clay, we settled to earth. The engines slowed to idle, we collected our gear, shuffled toward the open door and exited into the sultry morning.

UNDER THE COMMAND OF A COL. PORTER, Fire Base Tango was home to an Infantry Company comprised of a field artillery battery, two mortar sections, a signals platoon, a couple of infantry rifle platoons and two armed personnel carrier troops. Murph, Nathan and I found ourselves assigned to Rifle Squad Delta, a 12-man unit led by Staff Sgt. Rivers, a short, meaty New Hampshirite. The platoons were under the command of 1st Lt. Gibbs. Today was for getting acclimated, organized, stocking up on ammo, grenades, and the like. Show-time tomorrow – a three-day mission, out-and-back.

They sent us to a light pre-fab wooden building, sandbagged to the window sills, one of three bunkhouses for enlisted men. A fourth was for officers and NCOs. Twenty-four cots in ours, crammed together. I dropped my gear on an empty cot, propping my rifle barrel against the thin pillow. Nathan and Murph took the other vacant spots. Fred and Wayne, assigned to Rifle Squad Echo, were next door. A skinny dark-haired guy in a T-shirt and shorts sat on a bunk, working on his combat boots. Another sprawled on the bunk next to mine, intently studying a comic book, a cigarette dangling from his mouth. Music was coming from a tape player sticking out from under his bunk... *Ode to Billie Joe.* He looked up, dropping ash on his t-shirt that advised EAT SHIT AND DIE. "Wha's happenin?"

"Just got in," I replied. "Paul Bernard," I said, extending my hand.

He took a deep drag on his cigarette, glancing at the guy with the boots. "Christ, more goddamn cherries. S'all we need."

"What the fuck," the other muttered. "This fuckin' outfit is so fucked up."

"Paul, huh – well I'm John Wayne."

"Excuse me?" I replied.

"The real John Wayne, not the actor, not the can opener, but John Henry Wayne from Eudora, lower right-hand corner of Arkansas. Jes' before you cross ovah to Louisiana or Mississippi. Hell, thet asshole ain't even a Wayne, he's a Morrison, got some girl first name, too, Maryann or something."

"Then I'm pleased to meet you, John Wayne," I said, going over to his bunk.

"Evvabody calls me Shorty," he said, reaching up to shake my hand, "you'll see whah soon enough."

"And that's Murph... and Nathan." Nathan waved from the far end of the room.

"Tall, ain't he," Shorty said.

"Basketball'll do that to you."

I approached the guy with the boots, sticking out my hand. He didn't look up.

"If you say so," I observed.

"I do say so, dickhead," he replied in a low voice.

"Okay, take it easy." I returned to my cot and started emptying my duffel, looking for my Dopp kit. My mouth was big-time brown.

"Tha's Stoner," Shorty said, nodding at the other guy. "C.J. Stone, but everybody calls him Stoner. Mostly he's okay, other times, jes' leave him alone's the way to go."

Stoner was looking up, glowering. For some reason he'd singled me out for the evil eye. "Shut the fuck up. I don't like people talking about me."

"Stoner," Shorty said, "youah so interestin' sometimes we cain't help it."

"Fuck you." Stoner turned back to his boot. "You and those panty-ass college boys."

Early afternoon Lt. Gibbs assembled us in the tent that served as briefing room. Gibbs was young and tall, with a bony face and long, drooping ears that made him look like something from Easter Island. Another ROTC product, some small college in Oregon, the guys said he kept to himself and had a tendency to simplify things – not a bad trait in general, but for him it arose from a laziness that left the man innocent of the kind of details that could get you killed. He was not held in high regard.

In contrast, Sgt. Rivers, "Top" to everybody, a half-foot shorter, always a cigar in the corner of his mouth, a retread on his third tour. Top was very good at what he did and wasn't afraid to get his hands dirty. A no-bullshit guy, he had narrow, rounded shoulders, not a hunchback, exactly, but close enough to give you pause, and a very large head. One time later, he told me, "I got so many brains the Lord figured I needed something to put them in."

In his pressed green fatigues, the L-T was standing beside a large map on the tent wall. Those who got there early were sitting on folding chairs, the rest standing around the edges. As the stragglers filed in Lt. Gibbs gazed at the roof of the tent, tapping a pointer in his hand. Up front I could make out a red arrow marking our location, which was familiar from another chart I'd seen. The large scale of this map made it clear how close we were to the Cambodian border, a jagged purple line somebody said was only 20 kilometers away.

"Okay, let's get started." He jabbed his pointer at a green arrow north and east of Tango. "A few days ago a patrol encountered NVA regulars turning a ville into a supply depot. Tomorrow's mission will be outside the town of Loc Ninh which is right here." He tapped the green arrow. I was surprised how thin his voice was. "The terrain is wooded and hilly. It's some 80 kilometers northeast of Tango and snuggled right up against Cambodia. Delta, Echo and Foxtrot, everybody, we will chopper in there at 0830. Our objective will be to scope out what is going on then level the place. Our job is not to drive the enemy from the ville but make sure nothing is left of value to the NVA. Of course, the more of them we take out in the process the better – we're low on the kill board at HQ this month."

He talked about our tactical approach, the role of each squad including us new arrivals, whom he introduced by name. Cherries my buddies and I might be, but we were dialed in for a full share of the action. We'd carry our M-16s as well as extra ammo for the M-60 machine gun and the M-79 grenade launcher, our share of hand grenades and C-4. All of us were qualified on the more powerful weapons but they wouldn't be entrusted to us until we got used to the routine.

The L-T ended the briefing with the comment that this would be a tough mission but if everything broke right we'd have the drop on the enemy, "a good position to be in, for a change." He looked around at us. "You new men are part of a great outfit and tomorrow we are going to stick it to the enemy." His voice rose to a thin, reedy pitch. "You men are the baddest asses in the 'Nam!" He lifted his long, bony face, closing his eyes. "Yea, though we walk through the valley of the shadow of death we shall fear no evil! And why is that?" He put his hand to his ear.

"'Cause we're the meanest motherfuckers in the valley." A sing-song answer. I looked around, startled by the tepid response.

"That's right!" the L-T shouted, oblivious, "that is *right!*" He smiled broadly. "Well, good luck everybody. We'll see you in the morning!"

I walked out behind some of the old hands, Stoner, Shorty, others. Shorty was shaking his head. "Ah thought he'd finally cut out thet corn, ain't heerd it foah a long tahm."

"Tryin' to impress the new guys," somebody muttered.

"Tha's it." Shorty turned around to me, "How ole' you thank the L-T is?"

"I don't know," I replied. "Twenty-four, twenty-five?"

"Twenny-foah goin' on twelve," he laughed. "Thet man don' have a clue."

Going about our business, as the day wore on I learned two weeks ago somebody from Delta Squad had been killed in a firefight, Sam, a guy from Tulsa, Stoner's hometown. A bullet in the neck cut an artery and that was that. A second guy was medevac'd out with a hole the size of a fist in his chest. He died before reaching the hospital. It gave me the willies to know I was sleeping in a dead man's bunk.

That evening I broke down my new M-16, cleaned and oiled it, then did it again. My hands shook as I strung together the magazines, 400 rounds, 9 to a magazine, duct-taping them end-to-end. I tried to visualize what tomorrow might look like, but for all the simulations and prep work, I came up empty. I checked over my gear and carefully packed my ruck. I had got hold of a can of paint and my helmet now sported a gold circle with a slash through it. Why? Beats me. Better than skull and crossbones or a peace symbol.

I thought a lot about coming under fire the first time. Would I panic? Run and hide? I didn't think so, I'd be too ashamed. Would I be cool and calm? Perhaps, but I wouldn't put money on it. After the room settled down and everyone was asleep I crawled out of my bunk and got down on my knees. Please God, I said, give me the strength to do my job, do the right thing. Keep me safe, return me to my family, to Meg. Bless me... bless all of us.

Sometime during the night I was awakened by an explosion. I looked around in the dim light. A couple of people were sitting up, the rest hadn't stirred.

"What the hell's that?" Nathan asked.

"Fuckin' Charlie," Shorty mumbled. "Who else?"

"VC?"

I sat bolt upright.

"Tha's a rog, dummy. They live here too, you know."

There was a second explosion.

"Shouldn't we get our rifles?" Nathan again. Now I was wide awake, feeling around for my flashlight and helmet.

"Nah, they do this jes' to ruin oah sleep."

"But how can you tell if it's real or not?"

There was another blast, further off. I listened intently. No running around, shouting.

"You don' til it's ovah. Get some shut-eye, cherries, yoah gonna need it."

I pulled the pillow over my head. It took me a long time to get back to sleep.

THE LOC NINH LANDING ZONE WAS COLD. Skimming the hilltops, the terrain was a lot more rugged than it looked at altitude. The choppers touched down in a cloud of dust and, rifles at the ready, we hit the ground running. Lt. Gibbs led us toward a complex of low buildings as the first chopper lifted off and banked away. Several soldiers passed us, hustling a stretcher to the second chopper, a medic holding an I.V. bottle above the wounded man, his face swathed in bandages, only eyes and mouth visible. Close behind several others labored under long green plastic bags, sliding them in one by one. First time I'd seen body bags being used. Deep breath, say a prayer, whoever they are.

We collected around Sgt. Rivers, putting on our rucks, checking rifles and ammo. Nearby the other squads were assembling. I looked at Wayne who gave me a thumbs-up.

Lt. Gibbs was holding a map, glancing at the edge of the clearing where the forest began, then back again to the map. "Everybody ready?" Sgt. Rivers yelled above the racket of the chopper lifting off. "Move it out! Let's Go!!"

We crossed the clearing single file, Lt. Gibbs and Nick Kostopoulos, his platoon sergeant, leading the way. Tom Bates, a corporal, one of the old hands, was walking point. Bates was built like a truck, with black hair and a hawk nose, a full-blooded Arapahoe from Wyoming. People called him Tonto. I was in the first group to penetrate the woods. We found ourselves on a well-worn trail about four feet wide, heavy undergrowth and trees either side. I was in the middle of our column. Right behind Top was Frankie Rios, our RTO – radiotelephone operator – a short, skinny kid from Washington Heights in New York City. If they could manage it, a short RTO was SOP, for height made the radio antenna a target. And where the antenna was, an officer or a sergeant was close by. Another intense, voluble Yankee fan, Rios couldn't talk enough baseball.

"You watch," he predicted, "next couple years they'll be more Latinos in the bigs, a lot from the D.R. where my family's from."

Behind Frankie, Stoner carried the machine gun, then assistant gunner Billy Morse with the spare barrel and tripod and Pete Silvestri, one of Tango's two medical corpsmen. Shorty had the grenade launcher. Shorty was compact and well built. He kept a couple of weights under his cot and I watched him knock off a hundred lifts that first afternoon. Did it several times a day, he said, "to keep the ole bod in shape." Morse was a quiet kid from Kentucky and kind of a loner. He played the harmonica, to himself, mostly.

Corey Rogers was next, then me, lugging extra ammo for Stoner's M-60 as we all did. Rogers was a young black guy from Cleveland. Shorty, "a redneck and proud of it," went out of his way to warn me about Rogers, saying he's trouble, one of the militants. So far Rogers and I had exchanged only a few cursory words.

"'Thing is, tho'," Shorty added, "out here even yoah bad ass nigger gets in line. You put that bullshit behind you oah else."

Following me was Pham Văn, our "Kit Carson," a Montagnard of the Hmong tribe from the hill country in the far north. A tough little guy with a brown, creased face, he could have been thirty, he could have been fifty, no way to know. With passable English, Văn served as our interpreter and local guide. Some of the guys didn't trust him, said he used to be an NVA officer and how do we know he isn't still? Beyond that, they added, NVA or not, you can't trust a gook. Nathan and Murph brought up the rear.

Right away the trail steepened. The L-T told us it had rained hard for several days and the ground would be soaked through. I had no trouble keeping up, my legs and wind were fine, but I had to pick my way carefully over the wet roots and rocks. After an hour or so the trail leveled and widened and we made good time, but now we were in prime ambush territory. Eyes sharp for anything out of place, anything that could signal trouble on the trail – mines, booby traps, pungi sticks. We tried to keep the noise down but it's hard to make yourself small and silent when you're so weighted down. Our step was ponderous and the metallic clanging of our gear shouted that we were coming. Separation was at fifteen feet so if a burst came, hopefully it would take out only one of us.

Sorry, Dix, your toy jungle doesn't make it. Sliding into tangles of roots that will throw you and your heavy pack, the smell of rotting, fetid vegetation, branches and vines so thick you can't see the guy in front of you – this is real jungle. Hard to say where the jungle ends and you begin. Snakes? No doubt, though I hadn't seen one yet. After an hour of struggling we came to a clearing and Lt. Gibbs raised his hand to stop. Thank God. Since we started out my shoulder strap had been killing me – don't know why, it never gave me trouble before. I took the small towel from my ruck and folded it under the strap. This did the trick. A long swig of water from my canteen helped.

Gibbs and Rivers had their heads together, checking a map. Most of the patrol was strung out behind but being near the front I could hear their conversation. I caught a glimpse of sky through the tree canopy. Shafts of sunlight caught the still, humid air, brightening the foliage to a shimmering, iridescent green, a thousand shades of green, a sight that is fixed in my memory. My senses were on full alert, knowing any second a firestorm could erupt and shatter the tranquil scene. The other two sergeants came forward and joined the discussion. We were still some distance from the ville. Tonight we'd bivouac a distance away so their guards wouldn't spot us, but close enough to arrive at the ville just as dawn broke.

About three we came to a rocky outcropping where we made camp. Half a dozen men were assigned to guard the perimeter, staking out positions at the trailheads and in the jungle, one-hour watches. No lights, no fires, no smoke, no noise. At four-fifteen we'd break camp. As we were excavating the shallow depressions where we'd bed down, Sgt. Rivers pointed at Shorty and me and a couple of others, telling us to put down our entrenching tools and follow him.

Rivers got down on one knee and spread a map on the ground. "We're here," he said in a low voice, pointing at the map, "and the NVA is here." He stabbed his finger about two inches away, "about an hour away. We're gonna get back on the trail and proceed to the NVA position, scope it out, be back before dark."

"Jes' recon?" Shorty sounded disappointed. "No action?"

"If Charlie spots us we do what we have to do, but he better not or our cover's blown. What we're looking for – what kind of stuff they got there, where's it stored, where's their main force, how many of them there are." He tapped his watch. "Five minutes. Be ready."

I returned to my gear and gathered my rifle and bandolier, grenades. Leave the big pack. When I told Nathan what was going on he offered to finish digging my hole.

"Nathan, you're not half bad."

"Have a nice day," he replied without looking up.

We headed out on the trail, Tonto on point with Top next, Rios carrying the radio, then Shorty and Billy Morse. Stoner brought up the rear with the grenade launcher. It felt like the day's heat had been distilled into this one mid-afternoon hour. I was totally drenched. We were in another steep climb, every few minutes boosting ourselves up and over boulders. I had a headband under my helmet but it soaked through quickly and sweat was leaking from it. My eyes stung, my glasses were puddled with sweat.

After an hour of this, Rivers held up his hand and pointed to the side of the trail. Two boots were sticking out of the underbrush, which as I neared led to legs and a body. Our uniform. The dead man lay on his stomach. From the waist up his shirt was dark red, flies buzzed about his head which was turned sideways, cradled in long blond hair. Sand covered the side of his face. He couldn't have been more than eighteen.

My C-Rat lunch rose in my throat. Get a grip, I told myself, get a grip.

"Don't get close," Rivers said, "he could be booby-trapped. The little bastards like to do that."

There was a Big Red One patch on the sleeve. Shaking his head, Rivers noted the position. "Must be the guy they left. We can't bring him back now, do it tomorrow."

Rivers opened up his map and turned it around a couple of times, then pointed off the trail. "Go slow. In a combat zone you go slow. Always."

We entered the jungle in silence that for me was more about shock than discipline. Here the trees and undergrowth were so wet they tamped the noise down. With his machete Tonto hacked at vines that strangled our intended route. Again we climbed. In a half hour or so Rivers stopped. Through the thin edge of the trees I saw we had gained the top of a cliff overlooking a flat valley. A little stream ran down the center of it.

"Hold it up," he whispered hoarsely. "Take a look but stay out of sight."

One by one we moved up. A hundred meters away stood a number of thatched huts, the center of a ville, wispy smoke rising. Through my binoculars I saw beyond the huts half a dozen enclosures, stakes covered with black tarps, and farther still a collection of blocky sheds with bamboo siding and fresh roofs. Only sign of life, three women walking from the stream toward the huts, each shouldering a pole with baskets at both ends. A yellow dog trailed behind. Rivers pointed along the ridge path that topped the cliff.

"Shorty, Tonto, Stoner, get over there and take a look. The camp's got to be close. Keep your eyeballs peeled for sentries posted. Make it quick. Bernard, that notebook."

"Right here, Top." Before we left he'd handed me a blue 4x6 spiral notebook I tucked into my belt. I pulled it out along with the ballpoint I always carried.

"Okay, Rembrandt, get to it."

I started sketching, peering down into the ville. Don't know where he got the idea I could draw – maybe my glasses made me look competent or something.

"Sacks marked 'rice' next to that nearest enclosure." He's looking through his binoculars, "a bunch of it spilled, looks like. Make a note."

"Got it," I replied. "You read Vietnamese?"

"Enough to get by... hey, will you look at that." Rivers gave a low whistle.

From the side of the clearing several uniformed men appeared, pulling a two-wheeled cart loaded with something I couldn't make out. My heart was pounding. The first enemy I'd ever seen, and what are they doing? Moving stuff around. Same thing we do.

"Can you see what's on that cart?" I asked.

"Hold a minute... yeah, that's rifles, all right, all stacked nice and neat. Look like assault rifles, probably AK-47s."

The men stopped in front of the nearest storage shed. They opened the door and began hauling the load inside. "Yeah, those're AK-47s, all right. Make a note."

Several more soldiers appeared with a cart piled high with boxes. "That's the ammo."

I wrote "AK-47s & ammo" in a balloon with an arrow to the storage shed.

Several more soldiers, gesturing and talking. "Break's over," Rivers deadpanned. "Looks like I sent our guys in the right direction."

A few minutes later I was putting the finishing touches on my drawing. Top had me adding coordinates from the map when I heard our scouting party. Shorty's face was flushed with excitement.

"Found it!" he said.

"Keep it down," Rivers said, palming the air with his hand.

"A hundred meters thet way they's a clearing and another lookout like this. Twenty tents, couple of big ones. It's on a pond, some of them was swimming."

"How many altogether?"

"Hundred, maybe one twenty-five."

"Vehicles?"

"Coupl'a jeep types. Some roadwork goin' on, looks like they're improvin' a trail."

"Sentries?"

"One. We had to take him out. He was right on the trail."

Rivers frowned. "Trouble? Any noise?"

"By the book. Stoner took care of it. Helped he was asleep."

"Shit. They'll be missing him and they'll find him too, brush trampled down, broken branches." Rivers shook his head. "Don't worry about it, nothing you could do."

"This change anything?"

"Maybe. I dunno. Is there a way down from there?"

"Yeah, the cliff's not as steep at that end, they's a path runs along it."

"Paul, you done?"

"Yes, Sir."

"Come with me. You too, Shorty. Our artist needs to get a look."

Ninety minutes later after another sketch and a fast hike back to the bivouac, Lt. Gibbs was checking out my drawings. "Nice work, Private," he said, "just what we need."

After a meal of cold franks and beans we bedded down for the night. Several times I heard Gibbs on the radio. After he doused his flashlight it became very black. I lay on the poncho I was using for a groundcloth and looked up. Stars in abundance but the sky was confusing. Only familiar thing were the Dippers... one's where the other should be, and they're upside down! Not far enough south for the Southern Cross. Too bad, I was looking forward to seeing that, then I had this dumb thought. They say in the Southern Hemisphere when you flush, the water goes around the other way. We're about at the equator... does it go straight down or what? I need to check that out.

The night sounds kept me awake... lots of screeching. Monkeys? Birds? I pulled the mosquito net over my head and tried to sleep but something was bothering me. Those women we saw in the ville.

Next morning I cornered Top and told him I was worried about the women. "And where there's women there are bound to be kids."

"Shouldn't be there," he said, shaking his head.

"They have no choice."

"Probably not. All's I can say, we didn't put 'em there."

I grimaced and nodded.

"Look, I don't like it either," he said sternly, "but the job is number one, that and our men. Nice guys finish dead. Remember that."

Before daybreak we sat on the damp ground in front of Gibbs. A battery-powered lantern lit the area. Two sheets of butcher paper were tacked to a nearby tree. Nick K had made an enlarged reproduction of my sketches. "Yesterday's recon party located the ville," Gibbs began, "they found the enemy's supply depot and their camp." He pointed to the two drawings. "Sgt. Rivers is to be commended for his good work. There's a force of NVA regulars, we have to assume at least a hundred-fifty men and well armed. Their camp is right next door to the ville, so an attack on the depot will bring an immediate heavy response, no question. We'd have the element of surprise but I don't like those odds."

A groan went up from the group. Gibbs held up his hand. "Hold on one. We've ordered an airstrike for 0615 hours on the depot and the camp." His long, bony face broke into a smile. "That'll even the odds nicely. So our mission has changed. We'll be in a mopping-up capacity instead of surprising the enemy as per the original plan." He looked at his watch. "At 0445 we will head out so as to reach a staging area short of the depot just before the airstrike commences. We'll have a birds-eye view of the fun then we go to work. Sergeants will brief as to the role of each squad."

A soldier from Echo raised his hand. "What if the airstrike doesn't come off? If there's cloud cover or something?"

Gibbs shrugged. "That's an easy one. It's back to Plan A."

IN THE LEAD, Rivers wore an infrared sensor on his helmet so at least he knew where he was going. Gibbs was on his heels. Give him credit, I thought, he's right here with us. At this hour it was light enough only for shadowy outlines but I was surprised how familiar the trail was. A few minutes after six we arrived at the overlook. It would be a fine, clear day. Echo and Foxtrot headed for the side of the camp near the ville with the task of sealing it off to provide us cover in the depot. Each team would leave a spotter on the ridge in radio contact with the squad leaders. On a hunch Rivers ventured a quick side trip and returned with the news there was a path down from our side of the cliff as well, steep and rough but usable. Echo sent word that the NVA sentry's body was still where our guys left it, which meant the enemy hadn't discovered our presence. Or they had and were trying to deke us.

The ville was just coming alive, a few soldiers walking back and forth. We readied ourselves and waited. My mouth was dry and my heart pounded. Suddenly I began to shudder, a deep shaking inside, my stomach turning flipflops. Furious, I thought this can't be happening.

What's that? I looked at my watch. Exactly 0615. A high-pitched scream... it became a roar and two F-4s streaked right in front of us below the ridge, then climbed steeply away. Explosions in the ville courtyard! I counted four. The storage sheds were engulfed in flame. As we prepared to move out I got a good view up the valley. Another pair of jets closing fast, white-hot smoke erupts from their wings and a couple more sheds go up. Before climbing away they let their bombs loose, 500-pounders.

WHMMMMPPP! WHMMMMPPP!

One scored a direct hit on the main ammo shed. A huge explosion then seconds later the buildings on either side blew. Two more F-4s, firing rockets and dropping their ordnance just short of the ville, I figured they were aiming for the camp the other side of the treed area. Two more, this time canisters tumbling from their wings and a moment later an eruption of orange flame and dense oily smoke. Napalm!

"Man, will you look at that!"

"Don't you jes love them fast-movers," Shorty said.

My shuddering was gone, thank God. The air show must have done it. We moved out and picked our way down the steep path, watching the jets return twice more, finishing the strike with a long burst of 50mm cannon. After the first pass, antiaircraft fire had begun from several locations around the camp – SAMs and machine guns. A gunner opened up behind one of the huts in the ville. From what I could see none of our aircraft were hit but they sure stirred the hornets' nest for us.

We descended the exposed trail quickly, expecting a rude welcome from the enemy but somehow got to the valley floor before taking any fire. Zig-zagging, we ran, crouching, across an open stretch to behind the burning hulk of a storage shed where we paused to take stock. A couple of NVA were running toward the woods from the hut area. A machine gun sprayed fire in our direction.

Rivers was pointing. "Stoner, Shorty, Corey, Bernard! We're gonna circle behind the huts and take out that gunner! Rest of you guys slide over and cover us."

Running between the blazing buildings we followed Rivers, keeping an eye on the perimeter of the woods where there were plenty of NVA who saw us better than we could see them. The hut nearest the sheds was burning furiously and we went around behind it. We could hear a second machine gunner close by, but as the huts were in a semi-circle we couldn't see his location. We edged our way behind the second hut. "There they are!" Rivers pointed at two huts down a little rise. Several NVA had removed one machine gun from its mount and were frantically moving it forward for a direct line at us.

"Shorty! Stoner! You got a clear shot! We'll cover you."

Shorty loaded his grenade launcher. He and Stoner stepped out from behind the hut and the rest of us opened up. When Shorty nodded Stoner fired the M-60, spraying the enemy position. Then Shorty let fly. PUH! The hut went up in a massive explosion, guns and NVA sprawling, but through the smoke and dust I saw one of them pointing a rifle at us. Instantly I leveled my M16 at the waist and gave him a long burst. He dropped, screaming, before getting off his shot. My face felt hot. Wow! No time to stop. Let it sink in later.

Top nodded at me. "That's worth a beer. Maybe two."

Cautiously we advanced toward the smoldering, tangled mess. Blood and gore everywhere but no sign of life. My victim lay sprawled, a stain spreading across his chest.

Explosions and more shooting from the direction of the camp but Echo and Fox were on their own for now. Back toward the sheds, eyes stinging in the acrid smoke, we kept our distance from the inferno in case unexploded ordnance decided to go up. The USAF had done a hell of a job. Only two sheds were left unscathed. Top and I approached the first one, he opened the door and I did the honors, pulling the pin on a grenade and heaving it inside. We ducked and ran from the building as the grenade exploded. We looked at each other wondering if that'd be it, but a second later the shed went up with a thunderous roar.

As we ran toward the last shed I heard the whine of bullets and saw tracer smoke going in all directions from the shed we had just blown. Couldn't get the door open on the last one so Corey kicked it in and I repeated the procedure. Another huge explosion, more duck and run. Next, the tarp-covered enclosures, as we suspected from the day before empty except for bags of rice and what looked like other foodstuffs. A couple more grenades and the ville's food supply and storage were demolished.

The huts were next. We went one by one. Wood stoves still warm, sleeping mats, household items. "Let's torch them," Stoner said.

"Yeah," replied Rivers. "This ain't your peaceful ville no more. Go for it."

Stoner and Corey got out their Zippos and held them to the thatched roof. Nothing happened. "Goddamn straw's wet," Stoner said, pulling a grenade from his vest pocket. He pulled the pin and tossed it in, backing out quickly. We stood back and watched it go up in a maelstrom of straw that rained down on us. Down the line we went, peering into each hut, Stoner and Corey doing their thing. As we approached the last hut I heard a baby crying.

"Oh-oh," Shorty said.

Inside there was a woman, young and pretty, no more than a girl, really, clutching a squalling infant to her chest.

"No hurt me!" she cried, "no hurt me!"

"Jeez," Shorty said, "whadda we do now?"

"Take a look around," Rivers said.

Shorty went inside and poked around. The screaming became louder, baby and woman both. "Jes' normal stuff, looks like she lives heah."

"Five for six ain't bad," Rivers said. "So long, little lady. *Tạm biệt.*"

We moved away from the hut. Rivers was on the radio with the L-T who had gone to the camp with Echo and Fox. To this day I still don't know what made me look back but I did and there was the woman, standing in the doorway of the hut, holding the baby, a pistol in her other hand aimed directly at Top! I pointed my rifle at her head, and pulled the trigger.

NOTHING! OHMYGOD! IT JAMMED!

There was a burst of gunfire. The woman's hand jerked up and the pistol discharged in the air as she fell. Shorty ran to the woman who was lying on her side, twitching, clutching the baby. "Oh, Jeez!" he yelled. He poked at her with his rifle. Blood everywhere. "Jeez! It went right through the kid." I stared at the small bloody mass then turned away. But my eyes couldn't stay away. That's when I saw Stoner. No expression, his eyes vacant, nothing in them at all. He was blowing a wisp of smoke from his barrel.

"That one's for you, Sammy," he said in a low voice.

Rivers gave Stone a long look then turned to me. "This keeps up, I'm gonna owe you guys."

"We just leave 'em here?" Corey asked.

Rivers nodded. "We better beat it before they start coming out of the woods."

Top's radio came alive. "Rivers! What's going on?" It was the L-T.

He keyed the radio. "We're finished here."

"You taking fire?"

"Negative, but it won't be long."

"We're moving out. Any casualties?"

Rivers looked at Stoner. "Couple guys nicked, nothing too bad."

"We lost one guy, Palmer from Foxtrot. The rest is minor."

Top nodded. "See you at the trail. Can't chance the cliff, we'd be a sitting duck."

I turned back several times to look. "C'mon Paul," Shorty yelled. As I caught up to him he slapped me on the back. "Don't worry about it – not your fault your rifle jammed. You did good. We owe Stoner. That's what it's all about, pickin' each other up."

As we neared the trail junction I saw Corey bend down and stick something in the soft earth. What the hell is he doing?

On the way back we retrieved the 1st Division soldier, putting him in a body bag. We took turns carrying it... him... trading off the weight. I saw Foxtrot's bag. Grim faces there. When we cleared the ville Gibbs radioed for a lift from our bivouac area.

Corey was in high spirits, strutting down the trail jiving, saying "we're number one!" and throwing around high fives. When he sang out "piece of cake," Top finally had enough.

"Knock it off, Rogers, or I'll knock it off for you."

"Hey, all's I'm sayin', we did good."

"That's not what you're saying, Rogers, godammit! There's no bragging rights in this outfit! You start braggin' when you're at your DEROS and not a day sooner. A big head gets in the way of things. Stayin' alive, for one."

I didn't have a big head – how could I, weighed down by a bag with a dead guy inside that could be me. As we walked I tried to sort the welter of impressions. I wasn't a coward after all, though what to make of that shuddering? And that damned rifle! Jesus! And the baby. I tried to spare him and nearly got us killed. About then, the only thing I was sure of – I couldn't wait to down a couple of cold beers.

I had changed. No doubt I would change more.

34. WARS WITHIN WARS WITHIN WARS

LT. GIBBS PASSED AROUND the aerial recon photos. All that was left of the depot was one light-colored dot, that last hut. That night I awoke with another bout of shuddering. I sat on the edge of my bunk, sweat pouring off me. In my dream that wrecked baby had the face of my nephew Mikey. Mikey is allowed to live but not this little person. I went to Top.

"I don't want to hear about it, Bernard. That bitch was gonna drop us."

"That's not what I mean. The kid, I'm talking about the kid."

"You'll see plenty worse before you're through. Suck it up, forget about it."

"Stoner is crazy."

Rivers nodded. "Stoner is a warrior. Only reason we're alive today is because of him. You'd give that up for a gook kid?"

"I guess not," I said, thinking it wasn't that simple.

"Your first time out, you did good. Don't beat yourself up. But turn in that piece of shit and get a new rifle. They're much more reliable."

Now they tell me. What Top didn't know and I wasn't about to say, I was attempting a head shot, lowest percentage shot in the book, the exact wrong move when you're under fire. But I couldn't stop thinking I tried to do the right thing. Stoner, he's something else. Spring-loaded to kill. Fearless, resolute, ruthless. Lt. Phelps would have loved him. Quick to decide, quick to act, quick to forget. A clear conscience... or none at all. No question he was the better soldier.

"Anyway," Top was going on, "the L-T finally has some numbers for HQ. Think of it like this, Stoner made us higher by one and a half."

The next day Gibbs passed word that the Colonel and his boss the General were pleased at our taking out the depot and delighted at the exceptional kill ratio, some of which we would have to share with the USAF, of course, but that's teamwork for you.

Good result as far as it went, but the NVA could rebuild and resupply in a heartbeat. What kind of a victory is it if the enemy undoes our work and we don't even try to stop him? My buddies seemed to appreciate my efforts. If not yet exactly welcomed, I was less of a cherry. We got a couple of days to regroup, get our gear and heads in shape for the next patrol. Shorty clued me in. Every week or so Delta was assigned a long patrol, three days or more, otherwise it was out-and-backs in a day. How about that, I thought, a commuter war.

"Extra beer all around," Gibbs told us, strutting around the mess hall. "Get drunk, men, you earned it. Too bad I can't get you a piece of ass here, sorry about that."

But for that detail Fire Base Tango was well-equipped, one of dozens of American fortress islands spotted around the country. The mess I was already acquainted with, a large tent with ancient picnic tables full of splinters. The food line was outside under a canvas fly they rolled down when it rained. Lining up between rows of sandbags we shuffled forward to the pots, urns and plastic coffee jugs on planks laid end to end on packing crates. It was help yourself except for the occasional good stuff like roast beef or sausage which was doled out in miserly fashion. Often the cooks ran short and we made do with C-Rats.

Off-limits to grunts, the officers' club was a sturdy cinderblock building. Our hangout, a bamboo-sided, sandbagged shack called the EM, featured a dirt floor and a corrugated metal roof that made conversation impossible during a rain. A bar and stools, a few picnic tables, that was it for furniture, though the regulation-size pool table set on blocks was well used. A couple of ceiling fans hung from the roof but gave little relief against the heat. Did I mention, nothing at Tango was air-conditioned. Green-shaded lamps hanging off the walls provided the only light, except for a fake Tiffany at the end of the bar, the property of Staff Sgt. Alvin Burroughs, the proprietor and along with a Cpl. O'Doud, provisioner for the base. Burroughs had a small, sharp face and darting eyes that missed nothing, which accounted for his nickname, Gekko, though few called him that, as he could really mess you up if you got on his bad side. You knew he'd be leaving the Army with his wallet a lot thicker than when he started. The EM's street sign collection reflected some serious criminal ingenuity.

HAIGHT / ASHBURY TIMES SQUARE HOLLYWOOD & VINE

A couple behind the bar might have been funny, not any more.

JOIN THE ARMY, SEE THE WORLD, MEET INTERESTING
EXCITING PEOPLE AND KILL THEM

THE UNITED STATES ARMY
THE UNWILLING, LED BY THE INCOMPETENT
TO DO THE IMPOSSIBLE FOR THE UNGRATEFUL

And my favorite: FT. DIX → 8,485.2 MI

These were alcohol-powered facilities, no question. They said Miller was the preferred brew with the officers. The EM was partial to Bud, otherwise Jim Beam, Gordon's and free Marlboros, officially approved and the price was right. A scruffy black and brown mutt, a mournful little animal, made his home in the EM. He'd been brought back as a puppy from some long-ago mission. Terrier was the consensus. He answered to Kat-Sop after his real lineage, Heinz. Everyone fed Kat-Sop and he ate everything. People said, good thing for the tapeworm or he'd be a blimp.

At forty-two feet, the Finger, a wood-framed observation tower was the camp's tallest structure. Within Tango's perimeter was a helicopter landing zone and outside, a dirt strip for STOL aircraft like the Helio Courier. A number of tanks on low stilts were scattered around to catch rainwater and augment the meager supply from a nearby stream. Chinooks regularly resupplied the camp and hauled in water when we ran low, which was often.

The enlisted mens' showers were hose-on-a-poles outside the wash house. Our shitter was a four-hole plank laid across cut-down oil drums filled with lime powder. A wraparound metal shell and a tin roof completed the wretched business. You approached your daily routine hoping the digestion was ready to roll, for this was no place to linger. For me Vietnam will always be associated with the smell of shit, piss and lime. Everyone drew latrine duty which meant dragging the cans outside the perimeter fence to a long slit trench, pouring diesel oil in them then the cry of "burn the shitter!" The whole vile mess was then emptied into the pit. Occasionally they bulldozed the obscenity and scraped out a new one.

The picture I am trying to paint is a shantytown of sublimely mismatched structures and scrounged materials. The bunkhouses were on concrete slabs but everything else rested on the bare earth, so with the constant rain there was no escaping the muck, even "indoors." Mud covered everything and got into everything. Flies, mosquitoes, leeches and snakes made life uncomfortable and worse. Each of us dug and maintained a personal hole, rimmed by sandbags, for protection against mortar and rocket attacks except, of course, when we were occupied in fending off the VC. You don't want to know about my hole after a week of rain. On basically level ground, the whole camp had a tendency to become a lake.

A place of such extremes. After a couple of dry days the mud turned to a hard clay and with so many people and vehicles charging around the confined space, everything was coated with red dust that insinuated itself into your eyes, mouth and, you had to figure, your lungs. Dark clothes, black boots, they all turned red-brown. Wet or dry, Fire Base Tango was a miserable place to be, not even counting the danger that hung over it day and night.

On hot, dry days most of the enlisted men went naked from the waist up, especially for construction or digging holes, or filling sandbags for which there was a never-ending need. This gave torsos a chance to catch up with faces, necks and arms, deeply tanned from the tropical sun. I generally wore a cut-off T-shirt to soak up the sweat that was our constant companion. Waist down, fatigue pants only, no skivvies. Crotch rot. It was an aromatic place, but it beat the boonies where water for washing and paper for wiping were luxuries. With the extreme heat, flak jackets and helmets were rarely worn except when trouble was expected. A small-billed canvas cap, often worn backwards, was standard.

The old saw is absolutely correct – a soldier's life is a lurch from boredom to panic and back, not a lot in between. But aside for nighttime probes by the VC and the less frequent attack, base life was reasonably calm. Except, of course, for the anxiety you could never put down. But there were lighter moments. Many late afternoons, details done, guys would strip down to their shorts and dance on the sandbags outside the bunkhouse, their lithe, hardened bodies gyrating to somebody's tape player. What VC would dare interrupt this bizarre scene, that to them would have been incomprehensible? As long as I was there none ever did.

GOOOOODDDMORNINGGGGVIETNAMMMM! Around camp you couldn't go anywhere without Armed Forces Radio. Or the tapes. Beach Boys, Beatles, The Stones, Janis, Creedence, Jimi. Good stuff. In lieu of conversation, sometimes our home-grown artist, Billy Morse, would pull out his harmonica and sit in the corner of the EM, playing quietly. He was damned good, bending notes and all, but you could always count on somebody telling him to shut up as soon as he started. Stoner especially had a thing against music I never understood and didn't care to hear him explain, not that he would have.

We had little free time. Inside, calisthenics, repair and cleaning details and KP. Outside, perimeter patrol and into the treeline, ferreting out mortars or rocket launchers the enemy might have sited out there. Fire Base Tango mounted plenty of local search and destroy operations. From a reinforced underground bunker, the Fire Direction Center coordinated artillery support, up to an incredible 15,000 meters for the 155mm howitzers, less for the 105s embedded in hardstands. I already noted the industrial-strength chain link fence and razor wire, and should add that in this protective outer belt had been laid a field of trip flares, claymores and other greetings for VC sappers that periodically tested the defenses. A heavily sandbagged sentry post about six feet high was positioned in each quadrant and manned round the clock. A couple of timber towers shorter than the Finger held an array of radio antennae plus anti-personnel and mortar-locating radars.

I haven't yet mentioned the Black clubhouse, a tent maintained in defiance of regulations but allowed to stand as the lesser evil. The Sugar Shack was up a rise from the last EM bunkhouse. Loud music poured from it dawn to lights out when it was shut down after a sufficiently insolent interval. I asked Fred whether he would be hanging out there. "That's not my bag. Now Wayne, that boy he already be a charter member."

"What'd happen if I went over there?"

"Nothin'!" Fred laughed. "Not a damn thing! They won't let you in."

"What about you? You welcome there?"

"Not like Wayne but yeah, it's cool."

I asked Fred about Corey's strange behavior as we left the field the other day. He reached in his pocket and pulled out a business card. "'He was leaving one a' these."

POWER TO THE PEOPLE the card read. I turned it over... a black panther.

"Even out here?"

"You better believe even out here. Lotsa outfits got a death card, this is ours."

"I want to get inside that Sugar Shack," I said.

"Don' look at me."

"What about Wayne?"

"You'll hafta ask Wayne."

IN THE WEEKS AFTER THE DEPOT RAID we did a number of out-and-backs and a couple of three-day overnights. No serious action, but constant tension, then the deep relief as we dropped over the perimeter fence – it was enough to drive you nuts. My sobriety threshold was rising, though it would take a lot more time and beer to forget that destroyed baby. One afternoon after returning from a three-day patrol, we were hanging out at the EM. A lot of shouting, people letting off steam. This was the day for showing off girlfriend pictures. Nathan, Fred, Murph, even Shorty. I had one of Meg, actually the three of us, Pat included, in the lodge at Wildcat. After a couple of beers, I went to the bar for a refill and encountered Stoner sitting at the bar, hunched over a can of beer and a half-empty shot glass. Maybe it was the strangeness of the light coming through the tent fabric, but I'd never noticed what an old face he had, aged well beyond his years. Creased about the eyes, deep grooves either side of the mouth. Had he made his face, I wondered? Or had it made him?

"Some kind of day, today," I said, trying to draw him out.

He kind of nodded, then picked up his beer can and downed it in one long swallow. I was going to ask him if he had a picture of his girl but didn't dare. My impression was that Stoner's sole interest was getting drunk and staying drunk as long as possible. He banged his can on the bar and held it up.

"Stoner is a man of few words," Shorty observed as I returned to the table. "He really clammed up aftah Sammy bought it. Give it a rest. Mebbe aftah you been here a whahl."

"Known him long?"

"Went through basic together, Sammy too. 'Course they went way back, I don' expect he'll evah get over Sammy. You see thet watch he wears?"

I had, a fancy Rolex. "That must have set him back a few bucks."

Shorty shook his head. "Sammy's. Stoner helped hisself to it after Sammy got kilt."

I raised my eyebrows.

"No, it's cool. S'what Sammy would've wanted. Thet's how they was, those two."

"Does he have a girl?"

"Not that I know of."

"He always drink this much?"

Shorty nodded. "Evah since ah knowd him. Once in a whahl he'll break the place up but he nevah misses a roll call. Kahnd o' guy you lahk havin' on yoah side."

A few days later I told Wayne I wanted to pay a visit to the Sugar Shack. He frowned. "We be together since Dix, me and you, we get along okay, but the brothers, I show up with you they be all over my ass."

"Corey?"

Wayne nodded. "You got that right. Not just him, either."

"Tell 'em I'm friends with Huey and Bobby."

"You're jivin' me. You tol' me that once and I didn't believe you then neither."

"Seriously, I saw them lots of times, close up, too. That's more than he has."

"How you do that?"

"In Berkeley. Near Oakland where their HQ is."

He shook his head. "Still won't get you in."

"Come on, I'll make it worth your while. A pint of Jim Beam."

His face brightened. "Three pints."

"Two."

"Lemme think about it."

A few days later we were returning from a routine patrol. Plenty of traces of the enemy but no engagement. Sitting next to Wayne in the chopper, I said, "Sugar Shack tomorrow. You on?"

He stopped and thought for a moment. "Three pints. In advance."

I shrugged. "Three it is."

After a costly visit to Burroughs I handed over my bribe and we headed up the slope to the Sugar Shack. Three steps up, a platform tent large enough for maybe six cots. One side of the tent flap was tied back and I could hear music. Otis Redding. Corey and a PFC named Raymond Brown who'd been busted from corporal, a tough guy by reputation, were sitting on the steps, smoking... that musty, mellow smell.

"Hey bro," Corey called out, "wha' happen to yo shadow? S'lookin' mighty pale."

"Say Corey, say Raymond."

After an elaborate handshake, I counted five movements, Wayne said quietly, "Paul here wanted to pay a visit to your establishment."

Corey looked at me. "S'matter, boy, an educated honkie like you can't read?" He pointed at the hand-lettered sign sewn into the flap: SUGAR SHACK - CHUCKS KEEP OUT!!!

"Hey, Corey, how's it goin'?" I replied. I nodded at Brown whom I hadn't met.

They were wearing fatigue pants and combat boots, Corey a black t-shirt with a red graphic of an arm and fist brandishing a rifle. Shirtless, Brown was heavily muscled, with a wrestler's bull neck, his mahogany shoulders gleaming with perspiration. A pearl-handled switchblade with a red inlaid R.B. sat between them on the top step. Open.

Brown glared at me. "You heard the brother," he said in a throaty voice, "your kind ain't welcome here."

Wayne shot me his "good try, now let's get the hell out of here" look. Corey had lightened up some toward me since that first patrol. "Research," I told him, "for my journal." Since Ft. Lewis I had been jotting observations in a notebook, why, I don't know. It even contained a copy of my drawing of the ill-fated depot complete with text balloons.

"Hey, Ray," Corey said, "this dude's okay, he saved our ass the other day."

Wayne sensed an opening. "He even knows Huey and Bobby."

Brown took a drag on the joint and raised his eyebrows. "That I very much doubt."

I nodded. "I saw them a few times. Rallies, protests, that sort of thing. They were just getting started in Oakland."

"And what was your opinion?"

"Gut level, very impressive. Rhetoric's overblown but I understand why they do it."

"You understand? You un-der-STAND!" Brown frowned and raised himself up to full sitting height. "Whatever your name is, it is not within your POW-uh to understand! You see, to understand is to judge, and whitey has no right to judge the black man. The oppressor can never comprehend the black man, what he has been through, what he is destined to go through in his trial and ordeal of fire."

"Oh, I'm not so sure. My business is understanding people."

"PUH!" Brown waved his hand in the air, "you understand NOTH-ing! You do not even recognize slavery when it slaps you in the face! How many of us ask to come here? Ten thousand miles at the point of a gun, to die jus' so the white man can keep his heel on the brothers' neck. And by the way, boy, give that boot a lick while you're down there! It surprise you the brothers take up weapons and defend themselves? Man, you understand NOTH-ing! Don't even realize they're oppressing YOU, making you fight a fu-tile war! Where is your sense, man?"

Wayne was nervously shifting his weight from one foot to the other. He jerked his head to the side, toward the direction we came from.

Brown held up his thumb. "You see, here the black man has three wars to fight. We are at war with the white man, after four hundred years of slavery he remains the enemy." His forefinger. "Number two, we are at war with the friggin' U.S. Army, brought us here at the end of a gun and," the middle finger, "last and least, there is Uncle Charles."

"Seems to me you got your priorities backwards. You've noticed Charles has a nasty habit of shooting at us?"

Brown smiled and shook his head. "Take care of business back home, there be no occasion for him to shoot at us or us to shoot at him."

I edged closer. "How about I take a look around. I won't try to understand anything."

Brown glowered at me.

Corey shrugged. "Oh, what the fuck," he said, standing and waving me on. I stepped over the knife and maneuvered past Brown who didn't budge.

Inside, the tent reeked of pot, so thick I was nauseated. If I spent time in here, I thought, I'd be an addict even if I never picked up a joint. A folding table and a couple of chairs at the front of the tent, farther back, three cots. A guy in shorts was stretched out on one of them, a tube running from his mouth to a bong on the floor, a water pipe. He lifted his head from his pillow. I recognized him as Scooter, a guy from Echo Squad they said was into the hard stuff. A surprised look came over his face, then he smiled and closed his eyes.

A phonograph strung to a light socket hanging off the tent roof... Sonny Rollins on sax and Thelonious Monk. "Monk," I said, eyeing a couple more discs poised in position. "Brilliant Corners."

Corey nodded. "Points for that."

Points for Charlotte, I smiled.

Big sign across the back wall, NO VIETNAMESE EVER CALLED ME NIGGER.

Huey Newton as Napoleon in the wicker chair with the rifle and bandolier. Photo of the HAIGHT/ASHBURY street sign. On the table next to a stack of Panther calling cards I noticed a familiar little red book. "Whaddya know," I said, picking it up, "good old Chairman Mao. I left mine at home."

"You got one of these?" Corey looked surprised.

"You know the story behind them?" I asked.

"Of course. The Panthers sell 'em."

"No, how it started. Somebody bought a ton of them for, I don't know, a quarter apiece. Nobody knew what to do with them, then they had the idea maybe there's a market for this kind of thing in Berkeley – in Berkeley there's a market for anything. So they end up selling them for three bucks. Laughed all the way to the bank, or should I say the gun shop, and of course it pissed off the right wingers even more."

"Black capitalism at its best."

"You got it."

Corey gestured at the door. "Seen enough?"

"Guess so."

He preceded me out. Brown was still on the step and I ventured to sit down beside him. "Thanks for the hospitality," I said.

He nodded and took another drag.

I looked out over the camp. "Nice view," I said. No response. "You probably don't care," I went on, "but I'm here because I wanted to be. I wasn't drafted, I volunteered."

"What the hell you do that for?"

"I wanted to make our country better. For your people too, not just me. They drew the line here, so here I am."

Brown shook his head. "And I was thinking you seemed like a smart guy."

"It gets complicated sometimes, doesn't it?" I stood. "I'll be going now."

At the bottom of the steps I looked back. Brown was sullenly staring into space. No handshake offered. No joint, either. Just as well, one less thing to argue about.

Of course, the griping was endemic. Lousy rain, lousy sun, lousy heat, lousy bugs, lousy food, lousy Army. What the U.S. was or was not accomplishing was also hotly debated. It seemed the longer you'd been In Country, the farther our leaders' heads were up their ass. But it all came down to one thing – our return to The World, which meant any place that was not Vietnam. Number One on everybody's mind was time left In Country. Guys joked about the "good injury" that sent you home but didn't screw up your life too bad. Some of them, I couldn't tell if they were serious or not. There were plenty of stories about guys cutting off a finger or shooting themselves in the foot. Literally. I hadn't seen it happen yet.

Everybody counted time until DEROS, Date of Estimated Return from Overseas. Some constructed elaborate calendars. Playboy was preferred. It was a kick to see Miss Whatever's face wherever you turned, though who looked at the face? I used a simple 1968-1969 pocket type that counted down to my magic November 28. Some guys didn't get serious about this until 100 days out, but I started right away.

Superstition ruled. Not changing your underwear was a given, though this had obvious drawbacks and tended to be short-lived. Letting your jungle boots go native, the more scuffed and dirtier the better. For a cherry, black boots were a dead giveaway. Miraculous medals, enemy teeth especially gold, one guy had a shrunken skull. Whatever it took. My rosary would have qualified except from time to time I actually used it, though some would say that makes the point.

Christmas eve (338 days to go), we were getting our gear ready for an out-and-back. The brass must have figured the enemy wouldn't be expecting action on our sacred day. A little celebration was planned that we might or might not be back in time for. Al Burroughs contributed a scraggly plastic tree with gifts underneath, one for each of us. That night a bunch of us were sitting around, knocking back a few in honor of the occasion. I was keeping an eye on the small black and white TV behind the bar, because for me, tonight was a big deal, our first-ever orbit the moon. We hoped. Most of the others were comatose by the time the astronauts disappeared behind the dark side and radio contact was lost, but Nathan and I were on the edge of our seats. He'd been in science, remember. If all went well the spacecraft would enter lunar orbit. If not, well, we didn't want to think about that.

At the precise calculated moment the voice of Mission Control burst in. "We got it! We've got it! Apollo 8 is now in lunar orbit!"

"Houston, Houston, this is Apollo 8. Over."

"Apollo 8, this is Houston. Roger, 169.1 by 60.5. Good to hear your voice."

Nathan and I raised our beers. A cheer went up, as people latched onto what was happening. This round's on the house," Burroughs announced. Nobody believed him but cans of beer began appearing on the bar. Another first.

After several orbits we were thinking it's time to leave. The astronauts were describing what they were flying over, sending images so fuzzy you couldn't see what was going on. As I stood to leave something caught me up short. "In the beginning God created the heaven and the earth... and the earth was without form, and void; and darkness was upon the face of the deep..." It was Col. Frank Borman, Mission Commander.

I sat back down. "...and the Spirit of God moved upon the face of the waters. And God said, let there be light, and there was light. And God saw the light, that it was good. And God divided the light from the darkness..." He ended with "...from the crew of Apollo 8, we close with good night, good luck, a Merry Christmas, and God bless all of you, all of you on the good Earth."

"How about that," I said, nodding at Nathan, my eyes moist.

He nodded back. "Some of us on the good earth have a heavy day ahead."

CHRISTMAS IS ALL ABOUT SURPRISES and we got one, all right. Instead of the routine patrol we'd been briefed on, about three we were awakened and told to get our gear together, on the double. Another unit of the 25th on a night patrol near Bau Long, fifty kilometers due east of Tango, had been ambushed by a NVA unit and was pinned down, taking heavy fire. They couldn't hold out much longer. We were hustled onto choppers. The plan, Delta and Echo would land behind the enemy and attack from the rear, taking pressure off the trapped men. We'd make a low circling approach for maximum surprise, though it seemed to me if they landed us close enough to get there in time, the noise of the choppers would give us away. There I go, thinking again. But sure enough, that's what happened. As the pilot circled our dirt road LZ we immediately started taking fire from the bordering woods, tracers rising from the morning mist to greet us. The pilot juked violently up and down, sideways, trying to throw off the enemy's aim. If he'd broken off the approach I wouldn't have blamed him, but he was determined to insert us into the action.

If there's a worse feeling than being a sitting duck in a hot landing zone, I don't know what it is. Trapped in a slow-moving machine with little armor or defense, a lone machine gunner flat on his stomach pouring a stream of fire out the side door, you will yourself and your machine to be small, and hope for the best. In its hover the chopper is at its most vulnerable. Standing near the door I noticed a fresh line of holes in the side of the chopper exactly where I had been sitting. Jesus! A couple more seconds...! Being pushed toward the door I closed my eyes a moment... opened them, took a deep breath and jumped. Landed square and running, following Top and Shorty toward the trees bordering the road away from the firing. When you're out and moving you feel you have a chance, at least you're doing something. The chopper screamed over our heads in a steep bank and disappeared behind the trees. The second chopper followed, white smoke streaming from its engine compartment. Bad sign, bad omen.

After the choppers left, the enemy fire ceased and we regrouped. It didn't look like they were going to engage us here. Gibbs was in radio contact with the besieged unit's commander and told him we were on the ground and on our way. The plan was for us to cross the road, enter the woods on the other side then split our forces and circle the NVA, hammering them from both sides. Delta and Rivers would go one way, Gibbs the other with Echo. A lot could go wrong – heavy resistance in the woods, more NVA than anticipated, too big or too small a circle and the two squads end up firing at each other.

It was low-lying, swampy land. The first few men had to hack a way through tough trees and vines. We heard shooting not far off. We advanced deeper into the woods, rifles at the ready, but so far no opposition. Our welcoming party must have fallen back to their main group. They knew we were coming, just didn't know from exactly where. After a while we came to a trail with fresh prints. Gibbs held up a hand and conferred briefly with Top, who waved Tonto ahead to the point. Tonto had a nose like nobody else. A few more minutes on the trail and from the firing I could tell we were getting really close. The patrol halted again and I saw Tonto down on his haunches ahead.

"Trip wire," he said, pointing a few feet ahead.

At first I didn't see anything, then there it was, a slender strand about two inches above the ground running off the trail into the woods. Tonto traced the line with his finger. "Grenade or mortar, dunno which."

"We can't cut the wire, that could blow it and give us away." Gibbs looked around. He spotted Frankie Rios. "Rios. You stay back, guide the men over."

"What about the radio?" Top said, looking annoyed.

"Don't worry. He'll catch up before we need it."

"Fuck," Top said, looking at Wayne. "Frankie, take off the radio. Give it to Wayne."

Gibbs started to say something but turned away.

A couple of minutes later Wayne had the radio slung over his shoulder. I relieved him of his M-60 bandoliers, heavy, but nothing like the load he had picked up. Why didn't Gibbs just have one of us stay back, I was thinking. Should have left it to Top anyway, it was his call. It made no sense.

We moved ahead, Tonto still in the lead. When my turn came I made a high, careful step, clearing the wire with plenty to spare. Once again Gibbs put up his hand to stop. The woods were thinning and at the far edge of a clearing I saw men in NVA uniforms, backs to us, firing at what had to be the trapped men. "Rivers, take Delta around the woods to the left. I'll take Echo the other way, by the looks of things we should be able to surprise..."

Suddenly there was an explosion behind us.

"Jesus! What was that!"

We ducked back into the woods. A moment later Sgt. Crowley from Echo came running up. "Fucking Scooter! The goddamn pothead tripped the wire!"

"Christ! Is he..."

"Yeah. It got Rios too. Silvestri's working on him."

"Shit!" My Yankees pal. "Let me go back! I can help!"

"Get a grip, Bernard," Top shouted, turning back to the trail. "Move it out!"

Suddenly I heard automatic weapons fire coming our way. Goddamn Scooter! Why didn't he just give them one of his goddamn calling cards! Holding our fire, we veered off into the woods, trying to get out of sight. I was pushing through the tangle of vines and limbs, following Top and Shorty with the Thumper, Stoner and Billy Morse, Wayne with the radio. We soon outflanked their fire, Tonto keeping the NVA in view by dipping in and out of the woods. We began to hear more distant firing – that would be the trapped men.

Now we entered an area of larger trees, heavier trunks, where we had a good look at the enemy, this time from their left flank. Top signaled us to spread out and use the trunks for cover. I could see the enemy silhouetted in the dawn light, about a hundred meters away. Shorty and Max readied their heavy weapons. I took my rifle off my sling, put it on automatic. Standing beside Wayne, Top was on the radio to Gibbs.

Top turned to us. "Count of ten, give 'em everything we got."

He looked at his watch and lifted his right hand. "Seven... six..."

I put my rifle to my shoulder.

"...three... two... one..." He dropped his hand.

We opened up, pouring a sheet of metal at the NVA position. I fired short bursts. Targets of opportunity. Shorty let go with a grenade. WHOOSH! It exploded in the middle of the enemy position. I could hear screaming, people were running around, turning toward us, returning fire. I ducked behind my personal tree trunk, popped out, gave a burst, ducked back. Bullets were ripping through the leaves and limbs. Our rifles hammered away, Stoner's M-60, an incredible cacophony.

Disrupt, distract, draw fire. I slapped a fresh clip into my rifle, popped out, gave them another burst, ducked back. Stoner yelled for me and I crawled over to his position and left him a couple of ammo bandoliers. Smoke was rising from the NVA position. Shorty aimed.. WHOOSH! Special delivery number two! Pour it on, then pour it on some more. We wouldn't rush the enemy. That would bring us under fire, not only from the NVA but maybe with the geometry, from the trapped men and Echo as well. We could hear them doing their damage on the other flank. Top was on the radio, one hand to his ear, trying to hear over all the noise. "The L-T says our guys are pulling out! Time to really unload!"

We kept up the barrage for another ten, fifteen minutes. It looked like the enemy fire had tapered off. Were they were chasing our guys? Had we decimated them? I couldn't tell but they definitely weren't returning fire like before.

"They're on the choppers!" Top yelled. "Ours are on the way. Let's get outta here!"

I quickly helped Stoner and Billy pack up the M-60 and we backed deeper into the woods, the last of Delta giving a final barrage. Tonto picked up the point and we soon came to the area where the mortar exploded. It was a mortar. That side of the trail was totally blasted. There were dark red bloodstains on the trail and a body bag by the side I figured belonged to Echo. Only one, which meant Frankie might still be alive.

"Pete was able to move Rios back to our LZ," Top said. "Dustoff should be there about now."

"Will he make it?"

"Took shrapnel in his arm and shoulder but he's a tough kid."

"Thank God," I said.

"God and Pete and army medicine."

As we approached our landing zone I heard the whup-whup-whupping... a small chopper climbing away. Godspeed, Frankie. We took up defensive positions around the clearing facing the woods, though from all indications the LZ was cool. A couple of minutes later I heard a heavy rotor beat, same choppers that brought us in. Frankie was our only casualty, not counting the bag with Scooter, what they could find of him. Stupid, stupid Scooter.

I deliberately chose to sit at my same seat and showed off the bullet holes, but everybody was just staring past each other, totally spent. Where those bullets went I do not know. Enough to know where they didn't go.

Top finally broke the ice. "You guys did good, real good. I'm proud of you."

I looked at him and nodded.

"That other unit should appreciate what we did," he added.

"Tell 'em to send over a couple of cases," Shorty said.

Top lit a cigarette. "Guess I forgot to wish you a Merry Christmas."

"Same to you, Sarge," a couple of people replied.

"And Happy Holidays to you, Berg," Top added.

Nathan nodded. "Right. Thanks."

We got back about three. They flew a chaplain in for Christmas Mass which, needless to say didn't wait for me. Lying on my bunk I made a quiet space, thanking God for letting me survive another day. I visualized the infant Jesus and His family fleeing from the wrath of Herod. He made it through thirty-three years before they got him. As I lay there I began to shudder, lightly at first, then all over. It was hot and I was sweating but I wrapped myself in my blanket, didn't want anybody to see me. What the hell's going on? I do all right out there but when I get back I fall apart. What's to worry about? If I get it, I get it. Most guys don't even know what hits them. But I am not a coward, I told myself, pulling the blanket up over my head. I may not be a warrior but I'm not a coward.

I must have fallen asleep, for next thing I knew somebody was shaking me. I sat up with a start, wide awake. It was Nathan.

"You don't want to miss Christmas dinner."

"Yeah." I rubbed my eyes. "Thanks."

Looking around the mess hall it really hit me. These guys, most of them six, seven years younger than I, tomorrow any of us might not be here. I was really worried about Frankie... no word yet. A warm, protective feeling came over me, a new feeling. These are my brothers, I am coming to realize, the younger brothers I never had. Okay, none of them ever heard of Nietzsche and they don't know the Fifth Amendment from the Fiftieth, but so what? We give each other meaning, significance. Hanging together we keep ourselves alive. Except for these guys, nobody in this whole country gives a shit about me. With all my brilliance, nobody even knows I'm here. If I get nailed some other cog will be in my bunk before it gets cold, insulting my memory just like I did Stoner's friend.

That night in the EM I ran into Sgt. Rivers. Once in a while he stopped by to have a beer with us peons, that's the kind of guy he was. For some reason, this time he glommed onto me. "You're a Canuck, right?" he asked me over the noise and shouting.

"My dad was from the Gaspé. I'm second generation."

"Same here," he said, sipping the Bud I bought him.

"With a name like Rivers?"

"How about LaRivière? That do it for you?"

I nodded. "That works, all right. Why'd you change your name?"

"Not me, my father. All that French stuff he grew up with, he didn't want anything to do with it. It made him a second class citizen. Me, I can take it or leave it. He worked up to a good job, in an accounting office in Manchester." Top leaned back and laughed, his cigar bobbing up and down. "I'll never forget something he told me once. How he knew he really made it in the States was when he could afford steak for dinner every night."

"You must have had a lot of steak growing up."

He shook his head. "Franks and beans. Except on Friday, of course. He didn't eat steak that much, himself, that was more a figure of speech, what you educated guys call a..."

"A metaphor?"

"Yeah, one of those. I figured you'd know it." He downed the last of his beer.

"Let me get you another one," I said.

"Don't mind if you do."

"You have kids of your own?" I asked, returning with two fresh cans.

He reached for the watertight plastic pouch we kept our treasures in and pulled out a picture. Two girls and a boy, not yet teen-agers, him and his wife.

"Beautiful family."

"Yeah. My wife's a lot better with kids than me, but I miss them a lot."

"How many years you have in?"

"Eighteen. Two more and I'll be a free man. Get my pension, get a good job. They'll be in high school. I don't want to miss that. Say, something's troubling you."

"It's Stoner. I still have a problem with him."

"I thought we settled that."

"He's homicidal. You never know when he'll go off the deep end."

Rivers played with his can, swatting it from one hand to the other and back again. "Let me tell you something. Forget the hearts and minds crap, our job is to kill. That's what we're trained to do, that's why we're here. I kill but deep down I'm not a killer. You kill but you're not a killer. Stoner is a killer. You're right, he's weird, he's on the edge, but I am very happy to have him. I have a few extra rules for him, he knows I'm watching him. But when things get tough he's my go-to guy. Nothing personal, that's just the way it is."

I often thought about what Top said that night, glancing at Stoner's bunk. I didn't ask Top why Stoner had it in for me. I guessed that was for me to figure out.

Next day's mail call I really scored. Back in the bunkroom, I tore open the envelope from Meg, wouldn't think of profaning it with my bayonet, though that was S.O.P. with the guys. The scent... a touch of her across all the miles. Her residency at Childrens' Hospital goes well. Pat's home for the holidays, he says hello. Next week they'll all be in Conway, early snow this year. She wishes I were there to enjoy it with them. Then this: "From much too far away I embrace you and pray for your safe return. All my love, Meg."

I closed my eyes, remembering her face... her kiss.

After a while I turned to my father's letter. Steady handwriting, an amazing recovery. He feels pretty good though his hip is giving him trouble. Arthritis, that's all. He keeps busy and gets out every chance he can. Hasn't made any good friends, doesn't have much in common with the others – they act like old people! He likes Catherine's new boyfriend, much better than the bug man. Maybe this is the one. Little Mikey has the chicken pox and they're worried the other kids will catch it. Everyone's proud of you. Write when you can. Maybe when you get back we can take another trip together.

And one from Father Trần! Among the ton of letters I wrote at Ft. Lewis, one was to him. Hoping for the best, I had sent it to his last Saigon address. His reply was scribbled on a piece of paper torn from a notebook.

> Paul, I am still at St. Francis Xavier Church in Cholon. My private number is (84.8) 8 299 201. I look forward to our meeting but let me warn you, we must talk about the war and my disillusion with your country. You will have no difficulty finding the church but call first. For some time now I am being watched and it is not always possible to say ahead where I will be. Yours in Christ, Rev. Trần Văn Minh

I was disappointed at the tone but not altogether surprised. The longer I was here, the more I sensed the war was going poorly, though ironically, back in the States I knew a lot more of the details. Here we were in the dark, which was no accident. My job didn't call for me to see the big picture, any picture at all. The only view the Army wanted me to have was through my rifle sight.

Father Trần. Okay, I needed to find out how leave worked. I knew I got some but it wouldn't be for a while. When it happened getting to Saigon would be no problem. I'd heard stories about wild times in that wide-open city.

No letter from Gus. In a few days he and Akiko would gather for their annual New Year ritual, and I would be with them in spirit. I hoped they'd be in front of the television as they always were. And soon another Tet would roll around. I knew it was the Year of the Rooster, an animal which is said to be overconfident and prone to nonsensical plans. Didn't like the sound of that – too close to the bone. Coming up on a year since the 1968 disaster and, amazingly, here I am, where it all happened.

An uneasy silence hung over the camp. After the last mission they flew a minister in for a memorial service for Scooter and others who had fallen. I tried to give Scooter the benefit of the doubt. Maybe he wasn't stoned at the time, but the fact is, he put us all at risk. The thought occurred to me, why do guys who do dope bother me more than the boozers? A hangover is a hangover, however you come by it. A case of the devil you know, I guess. Not easy but I forced myself to say a prayer. Despite everything, Scooter, God rest.

WE GOT WORD FRANKIE WOULD MAKE IT. He'd stay in but his combat career was over. Now we could rag on him as a REMF – Rear Echelon Mother Fucker. This was the first dustoff operation I had seen, and I was mightily impressed. He would have bled to death. They got Scooter's bag out of there in a hurry, too. Looking around at the memorial service it all seemed so bizarre and incomplete. No coffin, no graveyard, nothing to remind us of the dead except words, a few photos and mementos. With all the good it did, dustoff really equals rushoff. Then again, every war has its own rules. A new guy showed up, another black kid, name of Jamal Roberts, from Detroit. Detroit's where they make cars, I didn't know much else about it. He said he was a follower of Malcolm X and a convert to Islam. He wore a tight black scarf over his head, knotted in back.

SOMETIMES YOU THINK YOU KNOW A GUY then something happens to surprise you. One day in the barracks Shorty pushed a piece of paper into my hand. "Ah'd lahk you to read this," he said.

"What is it?"

"A poem."

"A poem!" I said. I'd never even seen him with a book, a real book, that is.

"I been working on this awhile. It's about my girl. I said to myself, lemme give it a shot. If it's in my heart I can write it down."

I was floored. "That's terrific, Shorty. I didn't know you had it in you."

"After you read it, if you got an ideah where ah could send it to, you know, get it published and all. It would please her no end, seein' her name in a book. Oh, an' one other thing, don' let ennybody see it. They'd give me all kahnd of crap."

"My lips are sealed, Shorty. Trust me."

That evening after chow, I sat on my bunk and unfolded Shorty's paper. Single spaced, neatly typed... how'd he get hold of a typewriter, I wondered. There were a couple in the Colonel's office but off-limits to us. Anyway, in the interest of full disclosure and I don't know what else, here is Shorty's poem. You be the judge.

LAURIE ANN
by, John Henry Wayne
Laurie Ann she's good to me
Knows whose her man, that's plain to see
Run my fingers through her hair
Long and shiny, skin so fair
Feel her tits so round and fine
Like two melons on the vine
Gives me a hardon every time
Even in the grocery line
Thinking of them and
Her sweet honey
Make me come
Make me come
Make me come Laurie Ann
All night long
Make me come.

Jesus.

I folded the paper and set it down. Picked it up and read it again, shaking my head. The guy's not just guns and cars... miles ahead of me. But what am I going to do with it?

Next day he found me in the chow line. "Whadja thank?"

I took a deep breath. "Bring your tray over. Let's talk about it."

We found a space at the end of one of the picnic tables. "So whadja thank?"

"You've really got a way with words..." I began.

"Yeah," he smiled, "well, ah been workin' on it a long time. Off and on, a'course. Been thinking it maht go with music, you know, lahk a song."

I paused. "Don't often see this sort of thing written down, in my experience at least..."

His face fell. "Yoah sayin' you don' lahk it."

"No, that's not it at all, it's... you know, different."

"Oh well, different, thas' okay."

"Laurie Ann – you're sure she wouldn't mind seeing this in print. You know, everybody'd know her name..."

He shook his head vehemently. "She wants to be famous, she keep tellin' me thet."

"She just might get her wish. Tell you what. I've got leave coming up. I'll go to the library in Saigon and look up some names, maybe a certain type of magazine..."

A big smile came over his face. "Well now, that'd be raht whaht of you."

I handed the paper back to him.

"No, you keep it. Ah made two copies. Thet one's yours."

A couple of days later, when I opened the notebook I'd stuck it in, another piece of paper fell out.

Mosquito on my arm
casually looking around
drinking it all in

I couldn't help laugh... and here I'm giving Shorty grief?

The guys were salivating over a holiday visit from Bob Hope, that is, Ann-Margaret, but it didn't come off. Our area was too hot. Though we did get a couple of good films. I'd seen *2001* before but it was still terrific, especially with a real space exploit going on. And *Cool Hand Luke* with that all-time great line, Paul Newman just before they shoot him dead. "What we've got here is a failure to communicate." The mess tent went crazy. Surprised me they'd show this, all about nonconformity and beating the system, though on further reflection it was obvious why. In the end the system won.

About a week into the new year, one morning I was in the barracks cleaning my rifle when Nick K poked his head in. "Bernard, you got a call."

A call? Who in the world would call me here? Who *could* call me here?

"Came in on the base radio." He shrugged, "don't ask me how."

I followed him to the Colonel's tent. Lt. Gibbs was there. Seeing me, he gave me a funny look. They said Gibbs spent a lot of time with the brass. He knew how to make himself available, if not useful. Nick handed me a set of earphones with a boom mike like the chopper pilots I'd been seeing a lot of lately.

"Private Bernard."

"Paul, it's Gus!" The connection was poor, a lot of static but no question, it was Gus! "And Akiko too. I'm on the other phone."

"My God, how'd you find me?" I said, recovering. "How'd you ever get through?"

"I'm still pretty well connected," Gus laughed.

"I guess you are," I replied. "How are you guys, anyway?"

"We're fine but how are you? That's the question."

"Oh, we're getting along. Pretty busy here."

"You've seen some combat, I take it." He was cutting in and out.

"Roger that," I said, nodding. Leave it at that.

Akiko came on. "We thought of you New Years, we missed you."

"Same here," I replied, "it wasn't the same."

"I wanted to give you some advice about the new year," she went on.

"The Year of the Rooster," I said, showing off.

"Ah, very good, but this year is a special kind of Rooster, the Earth Rooster. This means you will find yourself with domineering, abrasive people who will test you severely."

"You just described the United States Army," I said, laughing. "Gus'll confirm that."

"That is so."

"Have you been able to see much of the country?" she went on. "Talk with the monks, see the shrines?"

"Unfortunately, no. They keep us busy on less interesting things. When I get leave I'll do some of that."

"I hope so. My advice, keep your perspective but most of all, your sense of humor."

We talked a couple more minutes when I noticed Nick tapping his watch.

"Gus, I gotta run," I said. "Your influence doesn't extend to unlimited phone service, not here, anyway."

"We want you to know we're thinking of you," Akiko said.

"I've got an envelope coming to you with a lot of *Daily Cals*. You'll hit the ground running when you get back."

"Absolutely. You guys take care of yourselves."

"You too," they said together. "Bye for now," Akiko added, "we'll see you soon."

We were on high alert for Tet, all kinds of rumors, but nothing much happened. As February went along, the command was thinking we'd escaped 1968's travails. One night, exhausted and aching from a three-day patrol, I was looking forward to a hot shower but the water ran out. Dirty and disappointed, I fell heavily onto my bunk. Nathan was already sawing wood. It looked like we were the first ones in, the others were still in the EM letting off steam. I must have fallen asleep. I was dreaming about explosions when there was a really loud BANG that made me sit up. Shorty and Stoner were putting their helmets on. "Get yoah ass in gear!" Shorty was shouting, "this ain't no drill!" By now the guard post siren was wailing. "Fuckin' VC sappers!" he yelled, bolting out the door.

I was pulling on my pants and boots, helmet and rifle and helmet at the ready. Suddenly, a whine I recognized as a mortar.

"INCOMMMING!!!"

There was another huge blast then a crash and the sound of metal falling as something close by came down in pieces. Heart pounding, I clapped on my helmet, stuffed extra clips and a couple of grenades in my pants pocket. Outside, a lot of running around and shouting and rifle fire. Delta's assigned post was at the perimeter fence facing the wooded area some hundred meters away. The first salvos had fallen outside the fence but they had us zeroed in now. Mortars and rockets were exploding in the central area of the base.

Our "Willy Peters," white phosphorous flares carried aloft by rockets, drifted down across no-man's land, turning the area into a ghostly daylight, making the ant-like figures advancing from the trees visible and creating eerie silhouettes of our men as they moved into position. The sentry post machine guns were working overtime, pouring out a stream of white tracers. An armored assault vehicle wheeled into position, machine guns blazing out across the clearing. WHUMP! WHUMP! WHUMP! Our 105mm howitzer firing deadly Beehive shells, exploding red-hot metal shards at the onrushing enemy. Some of the VC staggered and fell as they neared. I sure wouldn't want to be out there, I thought.

Taking up our position, we didn't have to wait long. Heavy fire began at the fenceline and several grenades lobbed over exploded near us. The VC had cut through the razor wire and fence and a couple were inside, spraying AK-47 fire around, shouting taunts.

"Goodbye Yankee!"

"Tonight you die!"

"OVER HERE!" Sgt. Rivers dropped to a knee and opened fire. I got down and leveled my rifle at a VC winding up with a grenade. My burst knocked him backward. In the smoke I saw Stoner leading a charge at the gaping fence hole, his M-16 blazing. I jumped up and followed, widening out a few feet to avoid hitting them. VC bodies were piling up where the fence had been breached and more were hung up in the concertina wire beyond. The hole was plugged for the moment but a sector back toward the ammo dump was in trouble. Rivers told Murph and me and a couple of others to stay put.

"Keep the fuckers out!" he yelled to us, loping along the fenceline. Intense fire and explosions were coming from where they were going, but in our sector the VC seemed to be losing their momentum. There was only an occasional burst of fire at the hole. We held our position, returning fire, adding to the body pile.

After the battle had been going a while, I recognizing the sound of an approaching aircraft as the much-feared "Puff the Magic Dragon," an old refitted C-47 that could deliver six thousand rounds a minute. It began circling and pouring down intense fire on no-man's land, every fourth round a red tracer, a spectacular sight. This really scattered the VC. In the distance I saw figures withdrawing into the jungle. It seemed the fighting had been going on for hours, though my watch said only forty-five minutes. Then, suddenly, an eerie quiet fell over the camp. Dust and smoke hung in the air. The place reeked of burnt gunpowder. The medics were attending to the wounded. Two of our men were hurt bad, one guy I knew, Ayers, the other I didn't at all, both from Foxtrot.

A while later somebody said Sgt. Rivers was looking for me. I found him with another officer directing a team repairing the fence and the sentry post that had been knocked out. When he saw me he broke it off and said follow him, he wanted help surveying the damage. I pulled out my little blue notebook. These days I carried it everywhere.

"The ammo stores came through okay," Rivers observed, peering into the reinforced underground bunker where our weapon and ammo were kept. "That, we'd have heard, for sure." Moving on, he shone his flashlight on the dumpster whose lid was caved in. "Have to bang that one out. Make a note."

"Think this was payback for our raid on the depot?"

"Dunno. Their intelligence is good enough to know where it came from. That's the price you pay for clean clothes."

"Clean clothes?"

"Those gook women that do our laundry – you seen 'em."

I nodded. They were ferried in every couple of weeks for a long day in the laundry room behind the officers' wash house.

"They hear things, they talk. We oughta do our own damn clothes."

I followed him around the camp, making notes. The mess hall was intact, barracks buildings seemed okay, we walked out to the fence where we saw the smoldering carcass of a chopper that had overnighted in the outside landing strip. A fire suppression team had poured on the chemicals but too late.

"Scratch one Huey," Top said, doubling back to the barracks area. "Well, whaddya know!" he said, stopping in his tracks. "Will you look at that!"

Behind the officers' barracks where the latrine once stood, pieces of metal and wood everywhere. All that remained were the four holes. Plus an unbelievably foul smell. Rivers laughed out loud. "One for the books." He looked at my notebook. "Give that one a star."

The Colonel called off the cleanup. In the morning we'd see the situation a lot better. It took a while to get back to sleep, lots of nervous talk going back and forth. But there was the one bright spot, aside from our having survived, that is. Lying in our bunks we could hear Shorty giggling. "The officers' shitter! Hot damn! Can you believe it, they got the officers' fuckin' shitter!"

"Something good came of the evening after all," Nathan noted.

"Yeah, but not for everybody."

"Whaddya mean?"

"The poor slobs that gotta to build them a new one, that's who."

The Sugar Shack survived, though at chow next morning Shorty observed that was too bad. "Shoudda blew it oahselfs," he said, "nobody'd a'been the wisah."

"Still can," Stoner said, "but wait'll it's full of niggers. Two birds with one stone."

"Mebbe moah," Shorty guffawed. "Black birds at thet!"

We shoveled the VC dead into a bulldozed trench some distance away from the fence. Sgt. Rivers led a team into the trees looking for clues to where the VC had gone, but we found nothing. Spooky. It was as if nothing had happened, no marauding force had traversed the forest last evening bent on destruction. Birds sang, the high limbs blew back and forth. Peace in our time.

Mid-afternoon Col. Porter called everybody together for a pep talk. He was proud, extremely proud of how we stood up to the enemy. They'll think twice before trying that again. So far so good, but when he got into what an important role units like Tango were playing to win the hearts and minds of the Vietnamese people, there was noticeable stirring and unease. He boasted about the strength of the Fire Bases, how merely defending ourselves made a helluva contribution to the body count. Every time the enemy tests us we really bloody their noses. I was thinking, next he'll be inviting attacks to push the numbers even higher. When he launched into how Gen. Westmoreland said he was seeing the light at the end of the tunnel, our eyes glazed over and I heard a couple of guys snicker.

Several nights running we remained on high alert, but some harmless scattered rocket fire was all. However, we learned this 1969 version of Tet had been much heavier elsewhere. At Cu Chi, not 20 miles northwest of Saigon, the headquarters of the 25th Infantry Division was overrun by sapper squads who did extensive damage on the airfield, destroying a number of Chinooks before being driven off. Long Binh Army Depot near Bien Hoa, just north of Saigon, saw heavy fighting and casualties. It was disheartening. No matter how well we beat off the VC and NVA, they could and did return at times of their choosing. To our American elephant, they were the wasp, a persistent, deadly enemy.

A FEW WEEKS LATER, ONE NIGHT we were in the EM after a tough out-and-back. Murph, Nathan and I were at our usual table next to the door. Shorty was with us and, unusual for them, a group of the blacks had slid two tables together and were partying. Laughing and joking, Raymond Brown presiding. They had commandeered the bar's boom box. Cat Stevens, Wilson Pickett, Junior Walker, James Brown, Little Richard, Jimi... always Jimi. As usual, Stoner was at the bar, tanked up, hunched over his beer and a bunch of empty shot glasses. Shorty and a guy a couple of tables over, Dave something from Foxtrot were shouting back and forth at them. Shorty was complaining about the nigger music, then he got going on how pothead Scooter fucked up and blew the mission's cover.

After this had gone on a while, Raymond Brown yelled over. "Hey, asshole! Shut your mouth or I'll shut it for you!"

"Fuck you, black boy!" Shorty shot back, giving him the finger.

Instantly Raymond was on his feet and at our table. "The man's dead, motherfucker!" he bellowed, towering over us, "let the dead rest in peace!"

Shorty was on his feet now, all five-seven of him. "What about Rios? Fuckin' Scooter nearly kilt him, he nearly kilt all of us! Can you believe steppin' on the fuckin' wire! Stoned, a'course. Nevah can count on you guys."

Corey was standing next to Raymond. "Scooter was not stoned!" he screamed.

Shorty laughed in his face. "Shee-it, man, that fucker was *always* stoned!"

"You got no cause to speak against a dead brother!" Corey shouted back.

At this point Raymond reached out and straightarmed Shorty to the head, knocking him back into his chair. Instantly Shorty rebounded and started going at Raymond with both fists. Like I said, for his size Shorty was very strong, and he caught Raymond off guard, driving him into a table which collapsed under his weight, drinks and cards flying all directions. Now everybody was on their feet and the melee was on. In the middle of it, I took an elbow to the side of the head and went down in a puddle of beer and broken glass. On my knees on the dirt floor, peering through the swarming feet and legs and with all the yelling and swearing, I rolled under the table and took my time getting up. This dumb, alcohol-fueled fight wasn't my fight. Nor, apparently, was it Kat-Sop's, who, whining softly, shared the safety of my space.

After a while I got out from under and made my way through the crowd, trying to clear my head, sucking on my hand which had suffered a nasty cut. By now a couple of MPs were at the door. Swinging their clubs, they waded into the crowd. Angry words continued flying back and forth as everybody backed off. Then, amid the rubble I saw somebody face down on the floor. Shorty!

One of the MPs went over to him. "Come on, buddy, on your feet! Time to sober up." He poked him with his billy club. "Jesus!" he cried.

As he turned Shorty over you could see the pool of blood. A red stain was soaking through his shirt. "Medic! Get a Medic!" the shout went up. The other MP was on his radio.

The first MP put his finger to Shorty's throat. "Pulse's weak. He's losin' blood."

Several more MPs had pushed into the room and taken up positions at the doors. "Don't nobody leave! This place is locked down."

Our other medic, Sanders, was already on his knees beside Shorty putting a towel to his stomach right under his ribs. "Somebody knifed the guy!" he cried.

Nathan came up to me. "You see what happened?"

"No," I said, rubbing my head. "I got pounded myself."

A few minutes later they rushed Shorty out on a stretcher, a medic holding a bag of plasma above his head. For the next hour the MPs took names, searched us one by one, told us go get back to our barracks, we'd hear from them later.

People filtered back into our bunkroom. The new guy, Jamal, was sitting on Frankie's bunk, totally closed in on himself, nobody saying a word to him. I wouldn't want to be him about now, I thought. I looked over at Shorty's bunk, shaking my head. Now they'll be needing to replace him, too.

Next morning Raymond Brown's knife was found in the bushes under a window. It had been wiped clean. As Brown was considered the instigator of the riot, he had been locked up overnight in the small brig behind the mess hall with a 24-hour guard posted until they figured out what to do with him.

Chow that morning was a subdued affair. The militant blacks always sat together but today they didn't show at all. Afterwards I walked out with Wayne. "The brothers, they really steamed," he said, looking depressed.

"Whaddya mean?"

"Why they pick on Raymond? Could of been anybody. Lotsa people had it in for Shorty – that man's mouth too big for his face."

"But it was Raymond's knife."

"Except he didn't have it on him."

"How do you know that?"

"Coupl'a days ago Corey told me it disappeared. Raymond was really pissed, said somebody stole it." Wayne looked at me sideways. "Some of the brothers talking about springing Raymond."

"That's insane. They'd never get away with it."

"I know. But they's talking anyway."

35. METAL IN MOTION

IT WAS SUPPOSED TO BE A ROUTINE PATROL. Our drop was outside the town of Hiep Hoa, a low-lying area of rice paddies situated between two rivers. Standing in the door next to the gunner I let my mind freewheel, mesmerized by the waves of reeds and grasses bowing to the downwash – light green, dark green, light green, dark green. Water buffalos grazed peacefully... the sight of them brought me back to reality. Shoot one by mistake, they dock your pay and give it to the owner. Farmers count on the placid beasts to till the soil, for company, for warmth on chilly nights. One shot could ruin a family's livelihood. Of course, one shot can also take out the breadwinner, but when it comes to VC sympathizers there were few restraints.

Perched on the landing skid, from a low hover we jumped into the knee-deep water and set out away from Hiep Hoa, gaining one of the levees that criss-crossed the acres of rice plantings. This mission would take us to a village some half-dozen kilometers distant that intelligence suspected was clandestine headquarters for a VC operative. We were to bring him back for questioning. Reconstituted, we were teamed with Echo and Foxtrot. We had two new guys along, Jamal of the head scarf, and Shorty's replacement, a gangly blond kid with large ears and an unruly cowlick, Herbert something, who showed up in the middle of the night.

Nathan and I were all of four months in-country and already senior to much of Delta. After we lost Shorty, I inherited his grenade launcher, a compliment of sorts, but I felt naked without my M-16. They said he was recovering in a Saigon hospital. Word was he'd be back but no time soon. Only good thing, it took me off the hook with that poem, for now.

After slogging across the open fields we came to a dirt road. Only mid-morning and my shirt was as wet as my pants. My left leg right above the boot itched and was burning like hell. I had to stop and deal with the leeches hitchhiking on me. I took off the boot and sock and Nathan lit a cigarette, burning off the leeches that were clinging to my leg, the ones I couldn't reach. Felt like a hundred but on a fast look all we could find was three.

We passed by settlements – thatched huts with smoke rising, chickens running around. You could hear pigs snuffling, rooting in the ground for whatever pigs root for. Barefoot kids approached us as they did everywhere, pleading for candy, gum, coins, cigarettes, any "numbah one." Outside one of the villes I spotted a small stone church with a caved-in roof. Wild grasses grew right up to it, although the graveyard next door, carefully tended, white markers, clipped grass, looked to be active. According to our briefing this area hadn't seen action recently, adding to the suspicion it was under the protection of the VC chieftain. Though what about that burned-out carcass of a school bus we just passed? That looked fresh. I asked Top if we weren't being too casual, sauntering along in the open like this. He shrugged and said the L-T wanted to make time and anyway we wouldn't be out here long.

Nathan and I smoked as we went along, nervously scanning both sides of the road. My insides were turning over, making gurgling sounds. "Lousy place to be," I said, tightening my intestinal muscles, trying to stave off disaster.

"We're asking for trouble out here," Nathan replied, flicking his cigarette aside.

The road widened and we came to an area of soft ground and ruts filled with muddy water, then a stretch of maybe ten minutes where we saw no signs of life at all. I lit another cigarette, trying to calm my nerves. Up ahead the road bent around a stand of trees that as we neared I saw were quite extensive, could be the woods we're supposed to penetrate for the last leg to our target ville. Top and Gibbs were conferring over a map and I thought maybe I could ask for a time out to take care of my leg issue but Gibbs was already waving us on, pointing toward an opening in the trees.

Suddenly all hell broke loose. Automatic fire poured from the woods. "Get off the road!" Top yelled, frantically waving his arm. "Get down! GET DOWN!"

We sprinted toward the marshy ground. Bullets cut the air as I made for cover. As I reached the road's edge about twenty feet in front of me the ground erupted and a plume of flame and dirt rose up and threw me back. I picked myself up and went on, tripping over something and nearly going down again. Temporarily blinded, I staggered through the dust and smoke, wiping my sleeve across my glasses. My eyes stung like a sonofabitch. Just as I gained the gully, from back on the road I heard, "I'm hit! Somebody help me! I'm hit!"

I crawled back up the slope. Through the smoke and dust there was a guy writhing on the ground. I grabbed hold of his ankles and dragged him into the gully. It was the new guy... that must have been what I tripped over. His face was contorted with pain, peppered with cuts. I put him down and bent over him. "My stomach!" he screamed, "oh, my stomach!"

I found a dry spot and turned him on his back. His shirt was all bloody. The firing from the woods was incessant. From our side of the road, our guys were spraying the trees with return fire. Pete crawled over to us. He cut open the shirt and ripped it apart. A grenade, probably fragments from a grenade, had opened a gaping wound in the guy's stomach and his intestines were hanging out. Sickened, I turned aside.

His pack off, Pete tore the paper off a morphine ampule and jabbed the needle into the wounded man's side. "Ohmygod," the new guy kept saying over and over, "ohmygod... ohmygod." The moaning became lower... then he let loose with this terrible sound.

"NNNNNNnnnnnhhh... NNNNNNNNNNNHHHHHH.

Oh boy. "What's the guy's name?" Pete whispered.

"H-H-Herbert." I had to force the word out.

"NNNNNNnnnnnhhh... NNNNNNnnnnnnnhhhhhhh"

"You'll make it, Herb," Pete said, using a big piece of gauze to stuff the guts back in. He covered the hole with a square plastic bandage and closed it over with tape, then reached over and squeezed the guy's hand. "We'll fix you up, Herb. You'll be good as new."

Now the guy was crying softly. "My mom, I want my mom. Where's my mom..."

Down the line we heard another scream. "I better get over there," Pete said, looking sadly at me. "Nothing I can do for this guy," he said under his breath.

I put my hand on Herbert's forehead. "Gotta go to work, buddy. I'll be back." I looked in the direction of the firing and spotted the M-16 and ruck he had dropped. Crawling out on my hands and knees I retrieved them. As I dove back into the ditch I saw dark-clad men advancing from the woods. Black shirts and pants, gray belts I knew held ammo.

The crest of the road was elevated so from the ditch we could see only the top parts of the trees. Which meant the VC couldn't see us, either, but they didn't need to, they knew exactly where we were. I checked over Herbert's rifle and extracted a couple of clips from his pack, then raising myself on my knees and elbows I joined the barrage we were laying down. Stoner's machine gun was hammering away. I saw a number of VC fall. I put the M-16 on automatic and swung it side to side, then ducked back down, letting it cool. Back up again, more VC charging us, falling under our fire. Rolling back on my side as I changed magazines, I had this dumb thought. They overrun us, we'll be dead in the water. Literally.

I sighted in on one particular VC who was rushing us, firing his AK-47. That misfire flashed into my mind but one squeeze and down he went. Thank you God, thank you rifle range. Another right behind, I pulled the trigger. He staggered forward a couple of steps and... exploded! He just blew up! I must have hit a grenade! Lucky shot. Took a couple of his friends with him. A couple of others were cut down by the fire on my left. I raised myself for a look-see. No more rushing us, best I could see.

Nathan crawled over to my position. "Top's hit! It's bad."

"Oh, no!" The picture of his family flashed into my mind. "God-DAMMIT! He's got a wife, kids."

"That's more'n we'll have unless we get out of this mess. Look!"

Nathan pointed at an opening in the woods. The VC were bringing a machine gun forward. White-hot, I reached for the grenade launcher and popped one into the breech. In an instant the machine gun and its operators were history. Direct hit, by the book.

"Score one for higher education," Nathan observed

The VC firing seemed to be waning, only an occasional burst. In a couple of minutes I heard Gibbs' command to cease fire. Crouching, I ran over to Pete who was ministering to Top. Gibbs was leaning over them. Pete looked up and shook his head. "He's gone."

Tears welled up in my eyes. I said a prayer for La Rivière. A good guy from a good place, he found himself in a bad place. Said one for his family, too.

"A great man," Gibbs was saying, his head bowed, "I could always count on him."

More than we can say for you, asshole. I turned away from his long, stupid face, couldn't stand looking at it any more.

As we gathered the dead and wounded, Gibbs detailed Sgt. Crowley and Echo to probe the other side of the road. Stoner came up to Gibbs and said something.

"I'm scrubbing the mission," Gibbs replied. "By now everybody in the province knows we're here." As if they didn't before, I thought to myself, parading along like a bunch of drunk Irishmen on St. Paddies' Day. A careless, dumb screw-up and look what happened.

"Nah, nah," Stoner was shaking his head, rubbing the barrel of his M-60, "we need payback." He pointed at Top laid out beside a bag, "I'm gonna get payback!"

"Knock it off!" Gibbs yelled in his shrilly voice. "That's the end of it!"

"That's what you think, asshole," Stoner said under his breath.

Echo Squad reported no VC in sight. Typical firefight. Short, crisp, enemy melts away. One of the Echo guys was showing off an AK-47. A little crowd was huddled around another one, Frazier, a crazy black kid from Cincinnati. He was waving something around. I went over to see... an ear! Frazier was laughing, this wild look in his eyes. "Hot damn, I got me a souvenir!" He held up the piece of bloody flesh.

"Don't let the L-T catch you with that," somebody said.

"Fuck the L-T!" Frazier said earnestly, stuffing the ear in his shirt pocket. ""Man's an idiot! Nobody gives a flying fuck what he say."

Foxtrot held back to guard the area around the road for the dustoff that was already inbound. Top and Herbert were dead, a guy from Foxtrot too, and there were casualties. A full load today. Delta Squad, what was left of it, would form up with Echo and return via the road, searching the villes we had passed earlier. Deal with any VC we found, there had to be some. How could they operate so close to the villes without friendlies?

As we neared the first ville we saw women sulking outside the huts, fear and suspicion in their eyes. Even the children, usually so lively, were withdrawn. They'd heard the shooting, saw our muddy, bloodied uniforms. Our grim, tense faces frightened them. Two and two add in any language. Unloved heroes, I thought, spreading freedom and democracy when all they want is to be left alone. Crowley went up to a shriveled old man in the doorway of a hut. He had one leg and was hopping around on a stick.

"You VC?" he yelled. The man looked at him blankly.

"Where the hell's Văn?"

"He went with Foxtrot," somebody said.

"That figures." He turned his attention back to the old man. "VC! You VC!"

The papa-san waved his stick in the air. "No VC! No VC! Boocoo love Americans!"

"Then we'll take a little look around." He pushed the man aside and stormed into the hut followed by two men. Others fanned out to the other huts. After a few minutes Crowley emerged with a packet of oilcloth maps. He shook it under the man's nose. "Found this in a hole under the bed! Why's a farmer need maps? For your other job? Your VC job?"

"Tôi không hiểu," the man mumbled. I don't understand.

"What else you got here?"

"Tôi không hiểu."

"I said, what else you got here!"

The man fell silent. Our men were emerging from the other huts. "Don't see nothin' else," Corey said. I peered into one and saw overturned cooking pots, ripped sleeping mats, clothing. Smashed pottery scattered everywhere. Rice, broken eggs, spilt water.

"You're coming with us, old man," Crowley said, dragging him to his feet.

"Why?" Stoner said. "Who gives a shit? Shoot him here."

"Maybe they can get something out of him. Tie his hands behind his back."

As Billy Morse approached him with a length of cord an old woman ran at him, screaming, pummeling him with both fists. He pushed her aside and she fell hard to the ground. A younger woman, perhaps a daughter, began yelling and cursing. The children we saw earlier cowered behind, bawling.

"Torch the hootches!" Stoner said, pulling out his Zippo.

"No!" Crowley was shaking his head. "Leave the hootches alone. Anybody needs a leak, that's where to do it," he said, pointing at a large jug that had been overturned, rice spilling out on the earth.

"Hey, when you gotta go you gotta go!" Corey laughed, unzipping his fly. Billy did the same and they began pissing on the pile of rice. Eyeing the young woman Corey began rubbing himself. Holding his dick in his hand he strutted over to her. "How about it, baby, wanna go boom-boom?" She turned away with a horrified look.

"Come on, let's get outta here," Crowley yelled.

Suddenly we heard shooting from back of the huts. Shooting and squealing. We ran around to the rear and there was Stoner, M-16 at his waist, firing at a huge pig. A tough bugger, the pig staggered around under the fusillade and finally went down in a heap next to another one writhing on the ground. A trail of blood led to a couple other pig corpses.

"WHY'D THE FUCK YOU DO THAT!"

Stoner had a big grin on his face. "Hell, I done 'em a favor! Now they got bacon to go with them eggs." He slung the rifle over his shoulder, pointing at the pigs. "That's for Top!" His old eyes were slits, his jaw jutted out. "I shoudda done them gook fuckers too. They're lucky I'm such a nice guy."

Assembling at the LZ the guys gave Gibbs the silent treatment. Same in the chopper. Everybody knew he had fucked up, marched us into an ambush and a better man than him paid for it. He knew it, too, first out the door when we landed and up the path to the officers barracks. The next week he made himself scarce which nobody minded, not at all.

BACK IN CAMP, THE FIRST TWO BACK, Nathan and I dropped our gear on the barracks floor, totally spent. I washed the red, swollen areas where the leeches had been and applied an ointment Pete gave me. I was embarrassed to bother him after everything he'd been through today. After we finished, lying on my bunk I heard Nathan flipping his Zippo open and shut, open and shut. Zippo was the only metallic sound around here that didn't make you jump.

"This is getting pretty old," he said. "Every time we go out we lose a guy."

"Yeah, but it sure beats the alternative."

"You mean..."

"Being that guy."

"Top didn't deserve it." I said

"Who does?"

I looked at the ceiling of the tent, studying the stains and dirt marks highlighted by the late afternoon sun. "The ghosts are adding up."

Nathan's smoke wafted over to my bunk. "That Stoner, he is really nuts," he said. "Why don't they do something about him, put him on report or something. Why didn't Crowley put him on report?"

Recalling Top's words, I said, "they love it, that's why. As long as he keeps his rifle pointed the right direction." I pulled out my pack and lit up.

"You're smoking more these days."

"Yeah." He was right, by now I was up to probably a pack a day. "They calm me down. It's not like they're the biggest thing we have to worry about these days."

I smoked silently for a while, reached for the little cooler under my bed and broke open a can of lukewarm beer and started sipping, feeling sorry for myself.

"You see the look Stoner gave the L-T?" Nathan asked.

"How could you miss it?"

"The L-T better start checking his backside."

"A fragging? Stoner?"

"Among others. Motive and means. A lot of that going around these days."

"Well said," I observed, "I'm impressed."

"I took a criminology course, liked it a lot. I've been thinking when I get back to the world maybe I'll get into that. You hear what happened to Raymond Brown?"

"No, what?"

"He got off. Not enough evidence. Nobody saw him do it, at least nobody'll say so. Transferred him to another outfit."

"Lucky them."

"Probably set the blacks off again," Nathan observed. "Ought to be happy their man got sprung but of course they won't."

Murph showed up, nodded at us and threw himself on his bunk. "What a day. What a miserable, miserable day."

"You got that right," I said, looking over at him. "You okay?"

"No, I'm not okay," he said. "How many years'd Top have in?"

"Eighteen, he told me."

"Jeez. And now he gets it." Murph sat up. "Paul, you can answer a philosophical question, right?"

"Depends."

"I've been thinking about this a lot. Every time we go out we roll the dice, right?"

"That's one way to put it."

"And we keep coming back."

"So far," said Nathan.

"That's my point! Am I on a roll? Or is the law of averages saying I'm about to get waxed? Tell me, Paul, I need to know."

I shrugged. "If I knew that I'd be a wealthy man." I shook out another cigarette and lit it from the glowing tip of the butt. "Everybody's scared, nobody wants to die. I'm not ashamed to admit that, are you?"

"I'm not." Murph lowered his head. "Fucking cocksucker of a place."

Guys wander in, grimy, exhausted, in a foul mood. Lying on my bunk I study my watch, visualizing the sliver of time that took a VC grenade from me and gave it to Herbert. Never even got to say hello, then it's the long goodbye... his guts hanging out. I took a long swallow of beer, squashed the can in my hand then reached for another.

A form darkened the entrance to the tent. Stoner. Passing my bunk he nodded. That's new, I thought, following him with my eyes. He put his pack down, stretched out on his bunk and pulled his boonie hat over his eyes. In a moment he was snoring loudly. Sleep of the blest? Or the damned? Unusual, showing his feelings. Stoner had no qualms about what he was doing, in fact he thoroughly enjoyed his work. Him and Phelps. And Johansson. What was it Gus said? The nineteen-year-old American boy is the most violent creature on earth. I laughed then – I'm not laughing now. Somebody told me Herbert's last name was Owsley... vaguely familiar, don't know why. With a name like that we could have been friends. Herbie, we hardly knew ye...

Don't remember going to the mess though I must have, because I woke in the middle of the night and puked what looked like meatloaf. I slept through breakfast. My clock said ten – couldn't believe it. Hungry as a bandit I scrounged some cold french toast, the older black guy in charge of the pots was cleaning up and doled me a huge portion. He nodded his head. "Hard night."

"No worse than the day."

"You're Delta. Sorry about Rivers. He was a good man. Exceptional."

"That he was." I raised my plate to him in a salute. "Thanks for the grub."

"No problem."

Mail call was tough. No more Top to holler at us, make wiseass remarks. Just a pile of paper on a table to sort. For once, I hit it big. Letter from Meg, one from my father, a package from Berkeley. Back in the barracks I opened my father's bulky envelope. Two hand-knit pairs of socks from Catherine dropped out, dry socks, thank you very much. My father said Héloise was in the hospital, liver problem of some sort. If I could find the time to write? Of course. Tante Héloise had always been a welcome placid presence in our unruly gatherings. Even my mother loved her. Catherine was still going out with the same guy.

I lifted Meg's letter from my pocket and held it up... that same perfume. Restraining myself I put it down and turned to Gus' package. The wrapper was dirty and ragged, and from what I could read of its many postmarks it had a three-month voyage. I slit the package and began pawing through the clippings. *Daily Cal, N.Y. Times, U.S. News & World Report,* much more. I must have opened the parcel upside down, for at the bottom, that is the top, I found a creased piece of yellow paper. "We hope this news from home finds you in good health and good spirits. Akiko and I count on your safe return. I even put a word in with the Big Guy, which is not easy for me but you're one of the few people worth the effort."

For such an organized person, Gus was a slob. There was no discernible order to the pile. Articles about the imminent handoff in the White House, which by now was ancient history. Speculation Nixon would turn the war over to the Vietnamese. There continued to be talk of that over here too, units might be pulled out and men sent home. Wishful thinking, but they even had a word for it – Vietnamization.

The *Daily Cal* clippings included pictures of Moses Hall trashed by the militants last October. Lots of arrests, personally led by that same Edwin Meese III. The University's discrimination against people of color was the big issue, this time not only Blacks, but as the Latinos were now styling themselves, Chicanos. Asian students were also pushing their agendas. I also found the Political Science Department pages from the course catalog with a scribble to the effect that I'd enjoy seeing some semblance of normalcy remained.

Halfway through the pile I couldn't stand it any more and pulled out Meg's letter. Miss you... think of you often... wish you were here with me... oh, man, I found myself getting hard... all my love. Something else, a picture, and what a picture! Lying on her bed in this sheer nightgown, a wish-you-were-here-right-now look on her face. I took off my glasses and studied it. On the other side, "For Paul... come home soon." All right by me, I said to myself, then I had this ridiculous thought. Who the hell took the picture? Who saw her like that? Then I remembered, that camera of hers had a self-timer. Yeah, that had to be it. I opened my pocket calendar then shut it immediately. April 6. 235 days to go. Sixty-four percent left. How depressing.

That afternoon I fired off two letters, one to Tante Héloise, one to Meg. The one to Tante Héloise I won't elaborate on. Meg, I told her how beautiful she was, best thing ever happened to me. It is very difficult, here in the field... back off that, don't want to alarm her. The thought of you keeps me going. "I have leave soon, maybe we could meet in Hawaii. Counting the days until I see you, my darling."

Never before had I called anyone that but before I knew it, there it was on the page. Leave it. Here's her letter, after all, her profession of love, that picture...

We were so short of men, they decided to combine us with Foxtrot. A rumor went around we might be moved but nothing came of it. Tango was too important. There was talk of bombing Cambodia. No announcements, though I noticed a marked increase in B-52 vapor trails headed that way. Tet 1969 had tested the new President and his reply was to pound the hell out of bases and supply networks inside Cambodia. Good for him. Fewer bullets with my name on them.

On one of our patrols we were fired on by an ARVN unit which mistook us for the enemy. In dense fog we were picking our way through trees and brush when suddenly machine guns started hammering us close in. Dropping to the deck we began returning fire when I heard Gibbs screaming into his radio. As suddenly as it had started the firing stopped.

"Jesus Christ! What the hell is that?"

Sgt. Crowley got to his feet. "Fucking ARVN. Can't find their ass with both hands."

This wasn't the first time our so-called allies had fucked up. For the most part ARVN troops came across as unreliable and gun-shy, except when we were defending a village where they had ties. Then they fought with courage and conviction.

"Search and destroy?" said a livid Sgt. Crowley after another particularly bad experience. "More like search and avoid."

It's painful to say this, but the enemy was a lot more motivated than our ARVN ally, more than we were, for damn sure. Don't get me wrong, within our sphere we did well. We fought hard and for the most part effectively, but often, as soon as we took an objective we were ordered to pull back, leaving it wide open for the enemy. From what you heard, this was S.O.P. all over. It made no sense. Grand strategy? A blindfolded guy moving chessmen around, no idea what he's doing. I don't need to tell you who the pawns were. My doubts grew darker. Self-preservation was Numero Uno. We heard about the fat cat REMFs in Saigon and the Pentagon. No wonder most grunts didn't give a shit. Made you appreciate those of rank who were got down and dirty with you. Sgt. Rivers of happy memory. Sgt. Crowley, he wasn't bad. Gibbs too, though otherwise he was a kiss-up and stupid.

They say give it time, you'll get used to the dismembered bodies, the limbs strewn around, the corpses with bloody stumps for necks. Not so. Nor the stench, a fetid mixture of urine and feces and blood and dirt and decay. My first time, we were returning from a patrol in the hills outside the town of Bu Na, just this side of the Central Highlands, when we came upon the site of a recent, fierce battle, VC and ARVN. From what the uniforms looked like, it was hand-to-hand at the end before they broke it off, leaving their dead. We shooed away the scavenging dogs but you knew they'd be back as soon as we left. Like the VC. Like the tide. What really got me, though, a mass of vines at the side of the trail with pieces of flesh tangled in it and a clean, perfect hand. A right hand, I remember, severed at the wrist and hanging on for dear life... dear death. Satan's Christmas tree.

We had some of that ourselves. One time Floyd McNeece, a black guy from Foxtrot, a solid citizen, he's in front of me by a couple dozen paces and he steps on a mine. The worst duty you can imagine, you and your entrenching tool and your sodden eyes, scraping up pieces of what used to be a guy you shared laughs and beers with, shoveling them into a body bag. At least we were able to identify McNeece and get him back to his family. Sometimes the best you could do was tag it "Body Parts - Unknown."

Get used to it? I didn't puke that much any more but I still had to fight to keep it down. McNeece. The shattered baby.

That Bu Na night we were stretched out on our ponchos, for a change somebody else had guard duty. A cool, gorgeous night to close a grim and revolting day. "Paul," Murph says to me, "you're still a good Catholic."

"I think so," I reply. "I hope so."

"Those stars up there. What do they say to you?"

I look up, my head resting on my ruck. "That there's a God. That He created the universe and put us in it."

"And our bodies shall rise from the dead, reunite with our souls and we'll be happy with him forever and ever, amen. If we don't screw up too bad, that is. You know, I was taught there's something special about the human body even when it's dead. Great-uncle Frank in his best suit, hands folded, rosary, candles, the whole bit. But this?" He raises himself up on his elbow. "What don't I get? Bodies without heads, heads without bodies, it's a fucking jigsaw puzzle! And those dogs! I don't get it. Even for God it'd be a stretch to sort it all out. Paul, tell me, when you see this, how can you believe the soul is immortal?" He paused for breath. I didn't know what to say. "If people come back lookin' like that? You wanna look like that for eternity?"

I thought a moment. "Lord," I replied, "I believe. Help my unbelief."

"There you go again! You and your goddamned riddles."

"It's the gospel story of the possessed boy, that's the boy's father talking. If I remember, just before he cures the boy, Jesus says 'all things are possible to him who believes.'"

"You're going around in circles. How can God let his Number One creatures do this to themselves?" Murph fell quiet. After a while he said softly, "I don't know. All those sisters, all those priests. I guess deep down I never believed any of it. I envy you."

"Murph, I don't know why God lets us mess up so bad. Here we are in this beautiful place trying to help these people and what do they give us for tools? Guns and mortars and grenades. Why not books and shovels and music? Who decided this is the way to go? Is anybody deciding? Then once it gets going it takes on a life of its own. It makes no sense, but for me enough else does. I accept the bad with the good. Not sure what else to do."

"Sort of like kill for peace."

"I guess."

"How about 'fuck for virginity?'" He guffawed.

"That's more like it."

"Hey, you guys, knock it off." Sgt. Crowley's growl finished our evening.

Later that night, I finally heard it. About 0300 I was awakened to Vietnamese music, strange strings, flutes, drums, gongs, accompanied by the purr of engines. Another old DC-3, this one part of Operation Wandering Soul, probably circling Bu Na several valleys away, broadcasting voices from the grave. The sad-voiced girl singing of her far-off lover, fallen in the futile service of the North. Surrender... come home... come home to me.

Sent chills through me. I rolled up in my poncho... never did get back to sleep.

EARLY MAY AND I'D BEEN IN COUNTRY five-plus months. I was about to turn the page on 200 days, but until you reach thirty you aren't considered "short." The short-timer enjoyed a special status, the butt of razzing, of course, but he also became a sort of pariah. Some commanders steered him away from the most dangerous assignments, because so close to the end something was bound to happen to screw him up – an ambush, a friendly fire fuckup – and that'd fall back on everybody else.

I HAD A WEEK'S WORTH OF LEAVE COMING. I should have heard back from Meg by now, but no letter, so I decided to spend it in Saigon, look up Father Trần. I hitched a ride on a chopper headed for Tan Son Nhut airbase in the west outskirts of Saigon. As I cruised along in a freshly-laundered and pressed dress uniform, duffle at my feet, I thought this is my first chopper ride ever where I was heading away from danger. Late afternoon I checked into an cheap hotel GIs frequented and after luxuriating on my first real bed in a long, long time, made a call. To my surprise Father Trần picked up the phone, and we set a plan to show up at his eight o'clock Mass next morning. This left me a free evening in what people called one of the wildest cities in the world.

But first things first. I would treat myself to Saigon's best steak and damn the expense, so on expert advice I headed for the Hôtel Continental, a shrine to French colonial good life. Passing through the faded but still elegant lobby I was shown to a shaded outdoor veranda. I felt somewhat out of place in uniform, and the only enlisted man at that, though there were plenty of them in the streets outside. A group of Marine officers sat at one table, several others occupied by men in suits. I was the only one dining alone.

Checking my rusty French against the menu, I ordered *un steak-frites, haricots verts et salade mixte.* To start, *un martini très sec,* a first for me, then a Bordeaux the waiter said was of a suitable vintage. Happily, what arrived looked like what I thought I ordered. At one point the waiter, a gray-haired gentlemen with a thin moustache, noted, *"Vous parlez très bien le français, mais vous êtes américain, n'est-çe pas?"*

"Bien sûr," I replied, gratified, *"et merçi pour le compliment."*

He eyed me over his moustache, shaking his head. *"Ah, dommage! Pour un vrai français, la vérité n'est jamais un compliment, il est simplement la vérité."*

Oh, well. *Brothers* stayed on the chair beside me as I soaked up the scene. After a few sips I was thinking my first martini could very well be my last, then I lit a cigarette and, glancing about, proceeded to feel more cosmopolitan than I had any right to feel. I pulled out a little note pad I had stuck inside *Brothers* and jotted several observations which, in fact, I am using to jog my memory as I write this many years later.

The waiter arrived with my *biftek,* poured a glass of wine, then a second, and I grew mellow and comfortable, the wine compensating for the errant martini. For dessert I chose a *plât fromage,* thinking I would pass on the *pâtisserie.* But, cheese and wine running out simultaneously, I thought, why not? and requested a second viewing of the dessert tray, choosing a decadent cream-filled Josephine.

"Café? Cognac? Un cigar?"

"In a moment, perhaps. *Merçi."*

I was just finishing the pastry when the waiter reappeared. "The gentlemen over there ask if you would join them," he said, nodding at a nearby table. "They would like to buy you a drink." I had noticed the two casually-attired men, at times slouching, at times bent forward talking animatedly. Surprised, I nodded at the men. The waiter eased my chair out and I rose with as much dignity as I had left. Nearly forgetting *Brothers* I reached back for it and crossed to their table. One of the men stood to greet me. He was very tall, looked to be in his late forties, with a ruddy face and thinning, slicked-back hair. He stuck out his hand.

"Frank Gillespie, Associated Press." He had a broad Aussie drawl and an impressive grip.

"Paul Bernard. U.S. Army."

"We noticed," he said, gesturing at the other who didn't stand. "That's Ed Reynolds, he's with a little family rag you may know, *The New York Gazette."*

I reached down and shook Reynolds' hand. I knew the name. Edwin Reynolds was the *Gazette's* lead correspondent in Vietnam, one of the superstars, right up there with Halberstam and Sheehan. He was a good deal younger than the Australian, dark shaggy hair and thick horn-rimmed glasses. He came across as serious, even scholarly. "Have a seat," he said, "what's your poison?"

I looked at the waiter. "I was about to order a brandy..."

He nodded at the waiter. "François, a Rémy Martin XO Spécial for the Private and a refill for us. What're you reading?" I handed over my book. "Where are the cartoons?"

"The war'll be over before I get through it."

"You must be an extremely slow reader. How long have you been here?"

"A hundred eighty days, One eighty-five to go. Almost halfway there."

He nodded. "Everybody knows his number. Kind of an odd way to fight a war."

"I'm here because I chose to be," I replied. His eyebrows rose. "Though I doubt I'll overstay my welcome."

"I didn't mean you guys," Reynolds said, "I'm talking about Washington. The grand design, if you will." By now the waiter had brought our drinks and I lifted my glass to them.

"I've seen your byline," I commented. "You're not afraid to take on the powers-that-be." I was surprised to hear myself saying this. Courage in a bottle.

"Another way of saying that – Edwin is on everybody's shit list," Gillespie observed.

"Somebody's got to tell the home folks what their money's buying. Or not."

We talked back and forth. "Unusual," Gillespie noted, "an enlisted man in a place like this. I've got it! You are the black sheep scion of a rich and famous family, frequently pictured in the society pages." Gillespie nodded at Reynolds, "debutant balls, charity events, that sort of thing."

"Sorry. Haven't been seen there for some time."

I told them about college, my newspaper experiences, but they were most interested in Berkeley. "Good preparation for combat," I told them with a laugh, "everything but bullets, and at times it seemed we weren't far from that."

"I get the impression those radicals have a lot of hidden agendas," Gillespie noted.

I shook my head. "The agendas are pretty much out in the open. What's not well known is who funding it, keeping it going."

"You're talking Communist influence?"

"Sure. Russia. To some extent Cuba. China. If you knew where these people travelled the last few years, if you could track the money, that'd tell the story. Some of them even brag about it, though not for publication."

"I daresay your government keeps tabs on that."

"No doubt. You know, Mr. Gillespie, I have no problem with people having a different point of view," I was really getting into it now, "what pisses me off is when they try to bring our country down. Some of them, their ideology tells them it's beyond hope, needs to be destroyed. That bothers me a lot."

"Call me Frank. It bothered you so much you volunteered to come here?"

"Exactly. And when I go back I'll continue trying to make it better. Not sure exactly how but that's what I intend to do."

"I don't suppose you can talk about where you're stationed, what kind of action you've seen," Reynolds ventured.

"You're right. That's off limits."

"What's your impression about how the war's going?" Reynolds asked.

"This is not for attribution. Right? The people I work for wouldn't appreciate seeing me quoted in the *Gazette,* or anywhere else for that matter."

"Totally off the record, very deep background."

I thought a moment. "My perspective is limited, but as I see it, we're going around in circles. Before I came here some people told me we didn't have a good plan. I didn't believe them. I do now."

"Such as."

"Such as how you fight your ass off to take a ville, a hill, next day you're out of there and the VC or NVA are back in. Meantime you've lost a few more friends. Such as how we're demolishing the country and making enemies of the people we're supposed to be helping. How they push us to get the body count up as if that'll do the trick. I'm waiting for it to make sense but I have to say that is slow in coming."

"You know, Frank, it'd be interesting for Paul to sit in on the five o'clock follies. We can get you a press pass," he said, turning back to me. "Take off your uniform for a day, listen to your generals and colonels. As a former reporter it'd be instructive to hear how they explain what you know better than they do. How long you going to be here?"

"Saigon, just a couple of days. I have a good idea what they say, I saw a lot of your reporting before I came here. No more – the day job keeps getting in the way."

We talked back and forth over another round and I gave them my impressions, some stories, whatever I felt free to share. Reynolds observed that as a "trained reporter" – I liked the sound of that – I had an unique insider's perspective on the war, a perspective that was denied them no matter how close they managed to get. Finally I looked at my watch and saw it was way after ten. I drained the last of my cognac and motioned the waiter over for my bill. As the waiter laid it on the table Reynolds covered it with his hand.

"This is on us. We don't spend enough time with you guys who're doing the hard work. I wish you continued good health."

Reynolds pulled a worn business card out of his wallet and gave it to me. "Stay in touch. Give me a call when you get back to Saigon. Or New York. I won't be here forever, I hope."

Stepping from the hotel's front door onto the hot pavement of the Saigon evening, I debated whether to check out the neon light district, then I thought, Murph and Nathan'll be here tomorrow, that's all they've been talking about for a month. Do it tomorrow. A good sleep's what I really need. As I fell heavily into bed, I thought how interesting it was, meeting those guys. It also occurred to me that I have something of a taste for the good life.

SAIGON'S MAIN CHINESE DISTRICT and home to its Chinatown, Cholon is three kilometers from the city center. I made a note to ask Father Trần about the problems he had mentioned, but on this cool June morning Cholon looked fine to me. My taxi skirted the sprawling outdoor market already bustling at this early hour and deposited me in front of St. Francis Xavier Church in a quiet neighborhood off a busy street. Early for Mass, I paused a moment across the street at a shaded grotto where a statue of the Blessed Virgin stood. Ave Maria. The whitewashed facade and green trim bespoke its church's colonial origins and was a reminder, not that I needed one, that this was the tropics.

Walking in, I immediately felt at home. It could have been any Catholic church, anywhere. Walls painted white, columns, arches and ceiling also, the altar a half-dozen steps above the congregation, the same dark wood pews you find everywhere. Good crowd for a weekday morning – mostly older women, same as everywhere. I chose a seat near the rear. Long time since I've been in a real church, I thought, a while since I'd been to Mass at all.

At precisely 0800, a bell sounded and a priest in green vestments appeared on the altar, preceded by a single server, a boy nearly as tall, garbed in the traditional black cassock and white surplice. I looked carefully... Father Trần.

Father Trần said the Mass in Vietnamese. When I walked up the center aisle for communion he greeted me with a nod and a smile. I returned to my seat, thanking God for His protection, asking Him to bless me with Meg's love and bring us together soon. Mass ended, I made my way to the front of the church. The sacristy door was ajar, I knocked and went in.

"Paul!" Father Trần embraced me then we stood back and looked at each other. "You look different!" he said. "The uniform, and you've really filled out!"

"And you, you look good," I said, though I had to force the words. In just a few years my friend had aged tremendously. His face was sallow and wrinkled. It looked like he hadn't slept in months. He was still in his alb, the long white Mass garment. The server was folding vestments and putting them away in a drawer.

He shook his head. "Thank you, but your kind words will get you in trouble with the Eighth Commandment."

"You've had a rough time of it. I'm sorry."

"Yes, yes, though not as difficult as you, I'm sure. Here, let me finish," he said, untying the string at the neck of the garment and slipping it over his head. He handed it to the server, a boy of about twelve. "Dũng is one of our most faithful servers. Dũng, this is my old friend Paul."

"I am happy to meet you," the boy said in perfect English.

Seeing the boy staring at my uniform, Father Trần observed, "We don't see many servicemen in church, not since the French soldiers left, I am told. I have lived in Saigon for some time but I am new to Cholon. My family is originally from Hué, the old capital. Come, let us have breakfast. You are hungry, I trust. We will go next door to the rectory. The fare is simple, though for special occasions our cook does well."

"Anything will be fine. A whole lot better than I'm used to, these days." I wasn't about to mention my feast of the previous evening.

"Yes, of course. You are in the field, somewhere you cannot tell me about. I'm sure it is not as pleasant as some of the higher officers have in what they call the rear."

"We have a name for them, I won't repeat it in front of you."

"I believe the expression is REMF?"

I laughed. "You know the American slang."

"We keep up," he said with a nod. "Do you get to Mass often?"

I shook my head. "They fly a chaplain in maybe once a month but I'm usually on one of my business trips, so to speak. I pray a lot, though, that comes with the territory."

I followed the priest into a corridor. At the door to the outside he paused, his hand on the knob. "Do you know the story of this church?"

I shook my head.

"You're not in a hurry, I hope."

"Not this week."

He turned and led me down a flight of stairs. I followed him into a long basement room with tables and folding chairs stacked against the far wall. "This room is used for social functions," he said. Reaching a heavy door he took a key ring from his pocket, inserted a key and turned the knob, reaching for a wall switch. "Please. Come in." It was a small room, furnished with a table, two wood chairs and a sofa. Wires dangled from a telephone box but there was no phone. "This used to be an office but it has not been used for years." Father Trần's face darkened. "This is where President Diem and his brother were betrayed."

I remembered they had been captured in a church. And here I was, in the very room. "The coup leaders promised them safe passage, but of course they lied. Nor were the soldiers who killed them acting on their own, though that is how it was explained."

"It happened in a truck."

"They were put in a military vehicle and as they drove they were shot to death and their bodies mutilated. Sanctuary is supposed to be sacred, above politics." He fell silent a moment. "Of course the Communists rejoice to see us destroying ourselves."

"You're bitter," I said.

"Should I not be? Diem and Nhu were cousins of my mother. Ironic, is it not, being assigned to this church with such a personal history."

We made our way back upstairs and across the courtyard to the rectory. He led me to a small dining room on the shady side of the building where two places had been set. A white china bowl with intricate blue floral designs for each of us, ceramic spoons, chopsticks, a large, steaming bowl of broth with noodles and rice, bean sprouts and some sort of green leaves. I wondered about the knives and forks. In a moment a woman with gray hair done up in a bun appeared and set two bowls of what looked like hot cereal in front of us.

"Trầng Dao, our housekeeper and cook," he said, "we could not live without her." She set the bowls beside each of us, smiled, bowed, and withdrew silently. Father Trần seated himself and gestured for me to do the same. He took the serving spoon beside the communal soup bowl and ladled out a portion for each of us.

"This is *phở gà,* our national dish." He smiled, "not once did I see *phở gà* in Kimball Hall." He brought the bowl to his mouth and began to eat with his chopsticks. "I thought they might have done that, perhaps just once. Please," he said, "begin." After a moment he sampled the second dish. "And this is *cháo,* a rice porridge. You will like it also, I'm sure."

The soup was delicious, the porridge less so. After a few minutes Father Trần put down his spoon and lay his chopsticks in the bowl, nodding at me. I did the same, leaving some uneaten. Polite practice, I had discovered.

"That was excellent," I said.

"Thank you. And now Trầng Dao has prepared a special treat." At the mention of her name Trầng Dao appeared again and set down a pie plate filled with a colorful custard. Father Trần cut a large wedge for me, a smaller one for himself. "From our French heritage, a quiche, but with a Vietnamese twist. See if you can guess what it is."

I took a forkful. "There's something fishy about it."

"Yes! Instead of the customary ham, Trằng Dao has used diced prawns, not to mention our famous fish sauce, *nước mắm*. Trằng Dao is truly a genius. *Bon appetit!*"

I finished my portion and accepted a second. Warm croissants appeared, covered with a cloth napkin. During the meal Father Trần asked me about myself, my family, my last years at Holy Cross, about Berkeley. He was critical of our radicals. "Anarchy will lead to no good." He told me about teaching science at the local high school. I showed him a picture of Meg, a yearbook-type photo I carried around.

"Ah, I see. This is the girl." I beamed as he held the picture up. "Yes, yes, she is very beautiful. I wish you well, both of you. Perhaps you will ask me to officiate at your wedding," he said with a wink.

As we finished the last of the papaya and lemon, Trằng Dao began clearing the plates. "Thank you," I said, "that was wonderful."

"You will take coffee?" she asked in halting English.

"Of course," I said. *"Cà phê."*

"Ah, you know some Vietnamese," Father Trần remarked.

"A few phrases. Just enough to get into trouble."

Father Trần nodded. "I hope you learn more of our language. It is very beautiful, like our country. As for the *cà phê,* I warn you Vietnamese coffee is extremely powerful."

"I'll do my best."

He invited me to join him in his office a few rooms away, where Trằng Dao was already filling two cups. She left the ceramic pot on a hutch. I took a sip... very hot. Then another. Father Trần was not exaggerating, even with milk this was the strongest, sweetest coffee I'd ever tasted.

"This'll have me bouncing off the walls the rest of the day."

"That is normal." He put his cup down. "Paul, it is indeed good to see you, to see you doing well, but I would be less than honest if I do not express what is on my mind."

"Go ahead."

"When I was in your country there was a saying, 'with friends like you, who needs enemies.' Pardon me if this sounds like a joke. I don't mean it as a joke, I am very serious."

"I don't follow you."

"Don't take personally what I am about to say. I know you are a good man and a uniform does not change that. The trouble is, you Americans, your enterprise here has been a disaster, a monstrous failure for us and it seems your country as well. At the beginning, yes, we welcomed your military strength – we had such confidence in America, I might even call it blind trust. We felt there was nothing you could not do if you put your mind to it. But it has become clear you cannot help us."

My neck was warming up fast. "What are you saying? You asked us to help you get rid of the Communists, didn't you?"

"Yes, and that remains our goal, but your country is here for a different reason. I know this now, and that is the key to your failure. The game America really cares about is with Russia, with China. Vietnam is the pawn. You dare not go all-out against the North for fear of rousing the sleeping giants. You wanted everything but you wanted it without the political risk. As a result you will leave with nothing."

"You can't expect us to start World War Three over your problem," I shot back. "That's what we're trying to prevent!"

"Over the problem of some third-rate country, that is what you mean. We expected you to engage our common enemy effectively. You led us to believe that." A sad expression came over his face. "There is more. The damage done by your bombing, the damage to our cities, our countryside and crops, we may never recover from. Do you recall the comment of one of your officers about Hué, my native city, you have heard it, of course. He said in order to save Hué you had to destroy it. Candor is a virtue, Paul, insanity is not!"

My host hit the table with the flat of his hand. "Your vast needs, your money that flows so freely, the black market you have nourished. Your countrymen's casual ways have corrupted many of our young people as well, our young women in particular."

"Now wait a minute, that's going too far..."

"You have spent how many nights in Saigon?"

"One. Though I didn't see that much of it."

"Well, look at it tonight. Walk down Pham Ngu Lao Street. Observe the strip joints, the massage parlors, and you will know what I am saying. I am no pollyanna, Paul, nor am I a prude, but it is much worse than with the French, and I am sure they were normal young men with normal urges."

"I'm sorry you feel that way."

"No more than I." He shrugged. "I am sorry to be so direct, but you see, soon you Americans will leave and for those of us who remain what will be left? Communist control. Precisely what we asked you to help us avoid. And without the shadow of a doubt that is coming, for you and we are losing this struggle. Of that I have become convinced."

Now I was really hot. "Had your government done half the job it should have," I said, my voice rising, "we wouldn't be here at all. A tenth, and the war would be over. You talk about candor, Father, I'd like some from you. The Communists want to win this war a lot more than your people do. They're smarter about it, too. They know how to reach the little people and from what I've seen, it isn't all threats and force. Even I can see that!"

I paused to catch my breath. Father Trần was silent. He sighed deeply. "That is so. That is so. Much of what I say is out of dismay at my own people. We have lost touch with who we are, who we should be."

"And what is that? Who you should be?"

"To answer that is not easy. But it is not to be a little America. It is not to adopt your ways, though sadly, that is exactly what we are doing. We Vietnamese have our own culture and history. It is not true that inside every Vietnamese there is an American trying to get out."

"But what about democracy? Your uncle Diem was no fan of democracy. Rigged elections, squelching the Buddhists, corruption, death squads. How much worse would a communist government be?"

Father Trần held up a finger. "The right to choose our government, that we will be denied. The right to own property, to be secure in our homes, to practice our religion. Those rights will be denied. We want a government that provides these rights to its people..."

"That's what I'm saying! Diem didn't give you that!"

"Perhaps I should say, a government that aspires to provide these rights. Too often, yes, there was a gap between Diem's actions and his words, but clumsy as Diem was, his heart was in the right place. Diem's mistake was he didn't trust God well enough. He tried to do everything himself, control everything. Remember this, Paul, without God the possibility of goodness, the possibility of civic virtue is lost. That is what the Communists will deny us – the possibility of a good society."

We went on a while longer, then seemingly by mutual agreement we realized there was nothing left to say. "I think it best you not come again," Father Trần said. He stood and held out his hand. "We were honest with each other. All too rare, these days."

We walked to the door together and I opened it against the bright late morning sun. "Well, goodbye," I said. *"Tạm biệt."*

He smiled sadly. "God be with you, Paul. *Tạm biệt.*"

I walked back through the open air market, along back streets, thinking maybe it wasn't a great idea to be walking around here in uniform alone. I looked at everything but saw nothing. I was overcome by Father Trần's bitterness, his disillusion with America, with why I was here. It startled me, thinking back on my words. I meant to defend America but ending up praising the Communists, the enemy. A thought kept coming back, why should we be spilling our blood for a government that won't help itself? In a strange way we were becoming like our reluctant ally, the government of the South. Just as they had no convincing story to rally their people, the reason why we were here was coming apart.

EARLY AFTERNOON I SETTLED DOWN, went souvenir shopping. I was tempted by an orange *ao dai,* thinking of Meg, how terrific it would look on her but I didn't know her size and it gave no room for error. Late afternoon I was back in the hotel, lying on the bed in my shorts, half-asleep in the steamy heat, a ceiling fan lazily rotating, when there was a banging on the door. I jumped up instantly. Zero to sixty in a tenth of a second.

Another loud knock.

"Who is it?" I said through the door.

"Ho Chi Minh!"

"And Chairman Mao!"

I opened the door.

"Guys, that's not funny."

Immediately Murph flopped on the bed. Nathan commandeered the soft chair. "Nice," Murph said, "verrry nice!"

"What's the matter, no bed in your room?"

"Yeah, but this one's better. How'd you rate a single?"

"Just lucky, I guess. Where'd they put you guys?"

"Second floor," replied Nathan, now at the window, "the low-rent district.

Look, Murph, he's even got a view."

"At heart he's a French colonial. Wanna walk around?"

"Too early," Nathan said. "Let's hit the pool."

In a couple of hours we'd had enough pool time and got clean, put on fresh uniforms and headed out. We went Chinese, ending up at a greasy spoon bigger on decor than food. Then, like iron filings to a magnet, we found ourselves heading for the club district. We walked along Pham Ngu Lao Street, my memories of those New York neon nights surging back.

"I can still taste the chow mein," Murph said, belching.

Nathan nodded. "It's going to be with us a while. Kind of sticks to your ribs."

"Among other things. So, Paul, how'd you do last night?"

"What do you mean?"

"Last night. You got laid, right? That's why we're here, after all."

"Had a good dinner, hit the sack, that kind of thing."

"What is wrong with this picture? Well, you're up for it tonight, right?"

I shook my head. "I'm taken, if you remember."

"Speak for yourself," he replied. "Nathan and me, we are ready!"

"More than ready," Nathan said, "but I've got to find myself a nice Jewish girl."

"Good luck. You know what they say, when in Rome go with the slope."

"Exactly."

We sauntered along, fending off the little kids, the hustlers, the barkers, joining the throngs jamming the street, dodging pedicabs and scooters that blocked traffic and strayed onto the sidewalks, the whole time swimming in fumes, smoke and Saigon heat. We and what seemed like a battalion of U.S. military personnel. Father Trần was right. VOLCANO CLUB. BOURBON STREET MASSAGE. PUSSYCAT LOUNGE – TOTAL NAKED LADIES. MANHATTAN GO-GO. M-G-M. Loud music spilled from dark entranceways. We ducked into a couple, but Murph, our cultural leader, kept shaking his head, moving us along. Several times we were accosted by drug dealers. One urchin handed us cards to an opium parlor. I took one to say I did. Murph did me one better, shelling out $200 for a deck of fifty OJs – thin marijuana cigarettes soaked in an opium solution.

"Why the hell're you wasting your money on that?" I asked.

"I'll keep a few but the rest I can resell on the base. Triple my money, easy."

I shook my head but said nothing. I would content myself with a couple of quarts of Jim Beam from the PX. That'd be good hospitality for Tango. As the entertainment district began to thin out we stopped to regroup. Murph thought for a moment. "What's the name of that place, the one with the bikinis out front?"

"Ranch House," Nathan said.

"That didn't look too bad."

"It's not supposed to be bad," I observed.

"But it is, right?" He nudged Nathan, "the resident Catholic talking."

"That's a joke. Catholic's got nothing to do with it."

"Don't shit me. Been there, done that. All right! Ranch House it is!"

We turned and started back. The sidewalks were now so packed we had to edge through servicemen at every entrance. Most of them were standing around, beers in hand, looking for a sign from those straggling out, some of them with silly grins on their faces.

"There it is! That's the one!" Nathan pointed at a squat bamboo-sided building ahead. Their neon, a blue shack surrounded by a red lariat.

♥ RANCH HOUSE ♥ WE LOVE G.I. ♥

As we crossed the street a couple of girls in bikinis and high heels waved at us.

"Hey soldier! In here!"

"This best place! We show you good time!"

One of them already had her arm around Murph's waist. "So what's inside?" he said.

"What you want, we got. Drink, music, girls," she said, leaning against him.

"You got A.C.?" Nathan asked the second girl who had glommed onto him.

"Lotsa A.C. You have hot time in cool place," she laughed. She was very pretty, taller than most Vietnamese women, slim and shapely.

Murph led the way through the door, his escort hanging on him, the other one right behind. I brought up the rear, engulfed in a cloud of cheap perfume.

Times Square all over, I tell you, except I was down front in the action. On the raised stage above a long bar, two girls in bikini bottoms and white go-go boots were twisting and gyrating. *Mustang Sally. These Boots Are Made for Walking.* Well, I thought, it is the Ranch House, after all. From time to time a girl and a uniform would climb the stairway on the back wall, a while later he'd reappear. Murph and Nathan were seated at a table in the middle of the room, new friends on their laps, draped all over them. I don't know how much they were shelling out for drinks but standing at the bar, just one can of Bud set me back five bucks. I was sticking with something I could open myself. I'd heard stories of drinks watered-down, even drugged, guys ending up in an alley sans wallet and I.D., beat up or worse.

I had plenty of offers but tonight I would take in the scene, enjoy the life, the music, and I kid you not, the breathtaking beauty of some of these women. You're probably tired of hearing me say this wasn't the time for me, so I won't. After a while they stopped asking. I let myself fantasize about Meg. A great dancer, she was, knew all the moves. I pictured how she'd look up there in a bikini bottom or less. Hopefully I'd soon find out.

But after downing my third Bud and watching my friends ascend the staircase, I have to admit I was feeling sad. Recently a troubling thought had been kicking around my mind. I could get killed over here, there was a very good chance I could get killed before ever making love with a girl. How dumb would that be? Depressed, I stared at my can of beer, when I heard the sound of a rock organ. *California Sun.* A new girl had taken the stage, long shiny hair flying about her head. Gorgeous, really gorgeous. She shed her brassiere and tossed it to the crowd... it sailed over my head and the scramble was on. I couldn't take my eyes off her. After a couple of songs she disappeared through a door at the side of the stage. I wondered how strong my resolve would be if she reappeared.

I ordered another beer, sipping it slowly. Another dancer took her place... no comparison. I looked at my watch, wondering what was taking Murph and Nathan so long, when a Zen thought came to my rescue... or maybe it was a Catholic thought. Maybe both. If death is meant to precede love, if that's the way things go, I told myself, so be it. Amen. I loved Meg enough to save myself for her. What a fitting coda for the evening! I felt clean again, strong, in charge of myself.

I'd spent enough time waiting for my friends... I'd had enough. "To hell with this," I said to myself, dropping a couple of bills on the bar. "I'm outta here."

The next days were more of the same plus sightseeing. A waterfall, a pagoda. The Cao Dai Great Temple Akiko told me I had to see. A mixed bag of a building, she said, like the odd religion it celebrated. More souvenir shops. I thought about calling Father Trần but I didn't. Somehow I would patch things up, after the war. I didn't blame him feeling like he did – trouble is, he shook up how I felt. Why *were* we here? Why was *I* here? Now that I could see what was really going on, did I think I was accomplishing anything?

I picked up an *International Herald Tribune* at a newsstand and found an article about Nixon's supposed Vietnamization policy. Sounded like a done deal. He had even met with Vietnam's President Thieu the month before, was talking about withdrawing twenty-five thousand troops for starters. First time I heard about this it sounded good, then I realized it meant less support for those of us left. Not good. Despite morale troubles at the bottom and bumbling at the top, our men knew what they were doing a lot more than ARVN. More to the point, these are your buddies and you can count on them when the chips are down.

After that first night I declined my friends' offer to join their partying. For me Neon Saigon was a spectator sport and I had lost interest. To fill out the rest of our leave, we decided to check out the coast and the beaches. A couple of hours' bus ride brought us to Long Hai and a beachfront complex specializing in R&R for U.S. servicemen. The salt water was tonic for my aching body and the USO facility just what I needed, a friendly haven away from the field, from Saigon. Unfortunately, three days is all we had, then back to Saigon and the boonies, the jungle, the action.

One more piece of business to take care of. Saturday afternoon when I got back from Long Hai, I found Omer. After leaving my stuff at the hotel I went back to the central area and dropped into an Army office. At the counter I found a very nice young Vietnamese woman, a civilian employee, and after telling her about my good friend from back home I hadn't seen for a long time and wanted to know how he was doing, I handed over the piece of paper with his mother's handwriting. "Corporal Omer S. Arsenault, Americal Division, 11th Light Infantry Brigade, 1st Battalion, Charlie Company." The girl said she'd see what she could do. As I waited I thought, he's in the field, there's no way we'll be able to get together. Though if she could get me his contact information I'd try to reach him and pass on his mother's greetings.

"Private Bernard?"

I went back to the counter. "I checked on Corporal Arsenault. I'm sorry to tell you but he was killed in action. February 16th this year."

"Oh, no..."

"He was buried with full military honors in... Providence, Rhode Island, it says here." She gave me a long look. "He was your friend... I'm so sorry."

Tears in my eyes, I left the building and stepped out into the glare. I was flashing back to that hot summer day at the turnaround. North Africa: Maurice. Italy: Cosmo. Now Vietnam: Omer. A flag for Mrs. Arsenault, a gold-lettered thank you.

The first friend of my life... how many others had Vietnam claimed? I found a bench under a banyan tree and sat there as a wave of shuddering swept over me. On and on it went. Frightened, I tried to move but my legs wouldn't respond. Finally I pushed myself up and stood there, but my two pitiable stalks were rooted to the earth. After a while some life seeped back and I found my way back to the hotel. The next morning we headed for the airport. Show up at the office, punch in. As I gazed out the window of the chopper I felt a foreboding like I never had before.

36. METAL AT REST

WHAT A BUMMER. The briefest taste of life, now here we go again. And poor Omer, who lost his bet. I lay on my bunk listening to rain on the roof. Nearly halfway to my DEROS, Meg was on my mind constantly. Six months, eighty-seven hundred miles. I ached to be with her, now that I'd come to my senses, now she'd opened up to me. Bittersweet... enough to make a guy weep.

Next day before dawn we headed out on a three-day patrol back down toward Long Xuyen in the Mekong Delta. Search and destroy. We searched but didn't find much – few traces of the enemy and not all that recent. Times like this you wondered whether military intelligence is an oxymoron. Or some other kind of moron. I found it really hard to concentrate, my mind wandering when it should have been focused. Not like me at all. I'd better step things up a notch.

There were rumors of a longer mission in a couple of weeks, near the Cambodian border where the NVA had an ammunition depot for ops in the Song Be region north and west of Tay Ninh. Our success in cutting the Ho Chi Minh Trail supply link was spotty at best, so here we would sit back, let the enemy do the hard work of hauling, then blast the hell out of what they'd done. Kind of a repeat of that first mission. Our platoon would combine with another unit from the 25th and several ARVN units.

In my worm's-eye view, the more coordination a job took, the better chance it had of getting fucked up, and sure enough, that's what happened. Tango was one of three pincers of this night attack which would converge from different directions. Night missions were confusing enough, unseen and unknown shading into the unreal, working your imagination and fears overtime. By the time we were finished, the depot was in shambles all right, but even before engaging the enemy, once again ARVN and we nearly wiped each other out. This time we lucked out. Minor wounds only, though our other platoon lost a man and ARVN four. Next patrol, we weren't so fortunate.

We were working across an open field under cover of reeds and high grass and had just paused at the edge of a wood. Up a path lay a village, today's objective. Sounds like a broken record, but once again we were detailed to ferret out and suppress any VC followers. Anti-aircraft fire had been reported in the vicinity the past few days. As we proceeded along the path, I heard a scream ahead. Sgt. Crowley held up his hand. Word came back, somebody had impaled himself on a pungi stick. As I passed the guy stretched out on the side of the trail I recognized Marty Miller, from Foxtrot. The stick was so sharp it had penetrated the heavy sole of his boot. Marty's face was contorted with pain. Pete had extracted the stick and was working the boot off. "It's a dirty one," I heard him say. The stick was lying beside him, brown and bloody at the tip. Looked like it had been dipped in shit, one of Charlie's tricks. Miller was in line for big-time infection unless he was real lucky.

Crowley and Tonto were up front. Crowley circled back to us. "Go slow, keep a sharp eye. Pile of leaves, anything looks funny we call a halt, check it out."

We proceeded another ten, fifteen minutes. "Should be at that ville soon," Murph said. Again the word to hold it up. "Fuckin A," Stoner complained, "what the fuck's goin' on?" We'd been standing around a few minutes when word came back that Tonto had come upon a series of trip wires across the trail. He was disconnecting them from the grenades they were attached to, hanging waist-high in the bushes.

"Nice welcome," I observed.

"Real hospitable, ain't they," Murph replied.

About fifteen minutes later we came upon the ville. We entered slowly, fanning out, rifles at the ready. It looked ordinary, half a dozen huts, people standing around, chickens and dogs scattering. Gibbs had started the day in a foul mood anyway, now it turned really ugly. A man down, and but for a sharp eye and luck a bunch more could have been wiped out. An elderly man, the first Vietnamese male he saw, Gibbs slammed to the ground. Standing over him with his rifle he yelled, "You're VC here, the whole bunch of you!"

He prodded the elderly man with the tip of his rifle barrel.

"Talk, you bastard. Talk!"

Pham Văn stood by but Gibbs' meaning was clear. The man lay squirming on the ground. "No VC! No VC!" he shouted.

A woman came running up to us, screaming. A couple of little kids were peering from the doorway of the hootch, huge eyes taking everything in. Gradually a crowd of women and children gathered. "Where are your men?" Gibbs demanded.

A gabble of dialog. "They out working the fields, they say," Văn replied.

"The hell they are," Gibbs said under his breath. "Mining the trails is more like it. Crowley!" he yelled, "go hut to hut! I want this fucking place turned inside out!"

In a half hour we had amassed a pile of radio equipment, wires, grenades, sharpened bamboo reeds, several boxes of ammo. No SAMs, though, no rifles. That's where their fucking men are," Gibbs said, kicking an ammo box, "out there using this shit against us."

But not all of them, for in the rearmost hootch cowering in a pit under a ragged piece of carpet we found three men hiding. Nathan, Wayne and I stood over them as they climbed out of the pit, naked except for shorts and sandals.

"What's that in there?" I asked, spotting something dark.

"Lemme take a look." Wayne lowered himself into the pit. "Take a look at this!" he said, emerging from the hole. He held a balled up wad of black cloth. VC pajamas!

"Rather careless on their part," I observed as we marched them hands aloft up to the pile of weapons and equipment.

"Well, well," Gibbs said, glaring at the men, "what have we here?" He held up the uniforms. "Funny outfit for a farmer. Tie 'em up!"

I held my rifle on the prisoners as Nathan and Wayne secured their hands behind their backs. The older man was on his feet now, his hands also bound. Hate and rage filled the faces of the two younger men but the elder obeyed stoically. The villagers were standing around. Gibbs beckoned to Crowley and Stoner. "Work 'em over. I want to know everything. Name of outfit. Size. Where's the rest of 'em. Who do they report to. Everything!"

Under the glare of the mid-day sun they interrogated the unhappy prisoners. We herded the women and children together and watched them while keeping a careful eye on the perimeter. Stoner was in his element. He took a particular interest in one of the younger men, whacking him repeatedly with his .45 across the side of the head which was now covered with welts and oozing blood. At one point he had the barrel in the man's mouth and made a display of cocking it as Văn screamed at the guy in Vietnamese. After about an hour of this the three men were slumped on the ground, semi-comatose. Văn went over to Gibbs. "It no use. They not talk."

Gibbs' face became rigid. "They not talk. They not talk. They know I got a soldier with a pungi stick through the foot? They know I do not appreciate them trying to kill my men with their fucking booby traps?"

"I tell them already. They say they not do it," Pham Văn shook his head. "They know nothin' about no outfit, nothin' about ammo, grenades, no idea." His voice tailed off.

Gibbs stared at Crowley. "This is very unfortunate," he said softly. "You know,

Crowley, the book says we take these bastards back and leave them to the experts but I have a lot of confidence in you. I'd say you're as good an expert as anybody. Don't you agree?"

"If you say so." Crowley didn't look very happy.

"Since they don't know anything, what's the point us going to all that trouble? Especially if we can teach the others a lesson at the same time, so here's what we're gonna do. Untie the gooks. Give 'em each an entrenching tool and have 'em dig a hole. Right there." He pointed to a spot in the middle of the clearing. "Six by six. Four feet deep. When they're done have 'em shovel everything in," he said, pointing to the pile of equipment. "And get the men to torch the hootches."

In about an hour the hole was completed, the captured equipment in the bottom of it. Gibbs went up to the edge and leaned over. "Nice job, fellas," he said to the three men who lay on the ground, exhausted. "Tell 'em that, Văn."

Văn spoke to them in Vietnamese.

"Now tell 'em get in the hole."

"In the hole?" Văn replied, "with the grenades?"

"You hard of hearing? Whaddya think I said!"

Văn barked at them again. They looked at Gibbs, alarm in their eyes.

"I'm running out of patience, Văn. TELL THEM GET IN THE HOLE!" The L-T gestured to Stoner. "Corporal, how about applying a little persuasion."

Smiling, Stoner went up to the older man. He pointed his rifle at him, then gestured at the hole. "Get in the hole! Goddammit, get in the hole!"

The man looked at Stoner and shook his head.

Stoner aimed his M-16 toward the man's foot and squeezed off a round. A puff of dust erupted behind his heel. The man leapt out of the way, but toward the hole. Stoner fired again. He moved closer. Stoner raised the rifle and pointed it at the old man's head.

"Một..." Now he was at the edge of the hole.

"Hai..." The man got down and put one foot in, teetering on the edge.

"BA!" He landed hard in the hole and stood there defiantly.

"Good man," Stoner said, "smart fella." Max pointed his rifle at the next man, a slim young fellow with a scarred face. "Your turn. Move!"

He glared at Stoner then stepped over to the hole and climbed in next to the old man. Stoner turned to the third man who was already moving. He dropped in beside the others. Stoner pointed his rifle at the three, gesturing for them to lie down on top of the junk.

"Crowley!" Gibbs yelled. "Torch the hootches!"

Six hootches, ten, twelve, who knows how many Zippos. In a few minutes the straw huts were burning furiously. I was standing with Murph on the side of the clearing nearest the trail. The women and children stood by, frantically moaning and screaming.

"Tell them women to get the hell away!" Gibbs yelled, a wild look in his eyes. "Pull our men back! NOW!!!"

We moved quickly toward the trail, some fifty meters from the conflagration. I lingered and looked back at the hellish, unreal scene. The women went the other way, herded by several of our men who then circled back along the edge of the woods.

The Gibbs looked at Stoner. "NOW! GO FOR IT!!!"

Stoner had fashioned a rag on the end of a bamboo pole and set it ablaze. He walked up to the pit. The faces of the three Vietnamese were peering over the edge. Stoner tossed the flaming ball into the pit, backing away several feet. One of the men threw it back. Stoner stepped back toward the pit and tossed it in again, squeezing off a single round as he did. Only two heads now. Again he backed away. A second man stood up and Stoner fired a burst at his chest, toppling him as a grenade exploded. Faster Stoner backed away, then he turned and sprinted for the trail. A second grenade went up then a third then all of them in a massive explosion. As we fled into the woods you could hear bullets going off in all directions, like some infernal popcorn machine. Stoner and Gibbs were slapping hands with each other. I prepared to be sick to my stomach.

In the chopper on the way back I was pulverized. "Murph," I said, "that was way out of line, that was just plain wrong. I got half a mind to report him."

"Look. Gibbs screws up and gets Top killed, today he makes up for it. What're you gonna do, go to the Colonel? Your ass'd be in a sling before you could say boo. And hey, he pumped up the body count, that's what matters."

"But that was murder!"

Murph rolled his eyes. "You're on your own, man. You won't get any help from this crowd," he said, looking around the chopper. "Everybody's tired and fed up. 'Far as they're concerned anything goes if it gets us out of this miserable place."

"That the way you feel about it?"

"No, but I mean, who's to blame? Gibbs or the people who sent us here?" He was quiet a moment. "Thing is, Paul, shoot at the king you damn well better get him, and I got news for you, there's no way they'll give you a clean shot."

The next few days the execution scene was all I could think about. Somebody had to do something about it. Evil triumphs if good men to do nothing. Burke said that and he was right. I tried to put it out of my mind but it kept coming back. Going back and forth, I argued Gibbs' side, making excuses for him. A). These were VC, or so close it didn't matter. B). Kill VC in a firefight, kill them in a hole – what's the difference? C). What's fair play got to do with it? The war is not a gentlemen's pastime. Pungi sticks, tripwire grenades – what chance do they give our men? In the field you have to cut a guy some slack. It's not easy dealing with prisoners, go by the book and you can get killed. Shit like this happens all the time, this was just an extreme example. What it came down to, what disgusted me the most was Gibbs' glee, his and Stoner's. Cheapen the Vietnamese, turn them into vermin and civilized restraints fall away, become laughable, even. Murph was right. To justify themselves the people who sent Gibbs here should give him a medal. Phelps. Johansson. Now Gibbs.

So there was my answer, my weak, cringing answer. What devastated me, even with all the justifications the god of battle supplies, I knew *thou shalt not kill* admits no exception for people who are smaller than you, have a different skin color and eye shape, happen to speak a different language. What Gibbs and Stoner did was terrible and wrong and my heart ached even more, for I knew I wouldn't do a damned thing about it. I didn't have to wonder what Father Ronan would say. My only solace in the whole sordid mess was knowing I had something pure and fine waiting for me at the end of it.

The month of June unfolded with Miss June Playmate spread in all her glory across the barracks walls. As far as our missions, as Nathan was fond of saying, same old, same old. Psyching myself up to board that chopper or that deuce-and-a-half was an ordeal I had to fight through every time, much harder than it had been and it never was that easy.

Faithfully I struck off the days, looking ahead to a nice round number to end the month, 150. Milestones were one of the mind games you invent, casting about for solace, for meaning. Trouble was, each day you went out, you had the same chance as any other to come back in a bag. Fate is no respecter of calendars. Fate shits on wishful thinking.

One day Sgt. Crowley pulled me aside and said he had recommended me for promotion to PFC, Murph too. Should come through sometime in July. He told me I was a fine soldier, would be an asset to the Army if I made it a career, so how's about it? I appreciate that, I said, not letting on this was the last thing I would ever do. I wondered why Nathan wasn't on his list, he'd done everything I had and more. I didn't mention the news to him, didn't want to make him feel bad.

RUMORS WERE FLYING about another action, a really big one some distance away. The rumors proved out, as the last week of June began a series of briefings about Operation Jackhammer, or as everyone below the rank of Sergeant called it, Jackass.

Near the northern terminus of the Da Lak Highland, over the Ya Lop River and close to the Cambodian border lies Hill 874, a small mountain actually, that the NVA had held forever. Though geologically associated with the Da Lak range, Hill 874 stands alone, a massif rising from the grassy plains. Pleiku is the nearest city, some 75 kilometers to the northeast. From our perspective, level Hill 874's strategic significance appeared to be nil. It menaced no Fire Bases, there were no airfields within miles, no supply depots. Granted, it directed the occasional SAM at our aircraft and choppers passing within range but that didn't seem reason enough for an all-out assault. But then, what did we know? It couldn't possibly be as simple or as dumb as our command wants it because the enemy holds it. Or could it?

At any event, commencing on the Fourth of July (!) we would take Hill 874 and clear the area around it, thus denying same to the NVA and VC. At least until the brass decided to move us elsewhere. This was no three-day out and back. As long as it took, that's how long we'd be there. "We" was Tango plus personnel from three other Fire Bases, also a battalion from the 25th and an ARVN Infantry Battalion. On the plus side, they had dialed in close air support – fast-movers, Cobra gunships and guest appearances by Puff the Magic Dragon.

THE LETTER TOOK NO TIME TO REACH ME. Postmarked June 28th, Meg had the decency not to send it from the Bahamas. The Bahamas, where she and Clyde were spending their honeymoon. "I'm really sorry to tell you this, Paul, but Clyde and I are going to be married Saturday." I sat down. It got worse. "I believe it's all for the best, as I finally know Clyde and I truly love each other. It was wrong, what I said. I must have been temporarily out of my mind." So that's what it takes to love me... thanks for letting me know. "...I hope and pray for your safe return. Meg." Hey Meg, why bother?

I reread the letter with sighs that shook the barracks. Murph came over. "Paul, you look like shit. Wha'sa matter?"

I held up the letter. "Got a Dear John," I mumbled.

"What'd you say?"

"Are you DEAF! I GOT A FUCKING DEAR JOHN!" I crumpled the letter into a ball and heaved it at the open window. It hit the screen and bounced back.

"Sorry about that." He sat down on the bunk and put his hand on my shoulder. "Good shot, anyway."

I glared at him.

"No, I mean listen, that's gotta be tough. These things take time to get over..."

"How about forever."

He shook his head. "All you need's another girl."

By now Nathan had joined the festivities. "What's happening?" he said.

"What time is it?" I asked nobody in particular.

Nathan tapped his watch. "Fifteen hundred hours."

"The sun is over the yardarm."

Murph squinted. "Yeah, it is. Actually it always is. "

"Let's get drunk," I said fervently.

"Sounds like a plan," Nathan replied.

Since Fourth of July we'd be occupied elsewhere, we celebrated the eve by getting shitfaced at the EM. The beer flowed freely and Al Burroughs had gotten hold of some Sousa march tapes. At one point we had a conga line going, waving little paper flags I noticed were made in Taiwan but what the hell, they're an ally.

Closing in on lights-out we were sitting around, putting off tomorrow as long as we could, when Billy Morse started in on his harmonica. He was sitting alone in the far corner as usual, but this evening we were resigned and mellow and after working through the usual insults we listened. From Kentucky, Billy was, so you know what came first. Then Dixie, then Old Black Joe. I glanced over at the blacks' table. Tonight they were cool, Corey nodding in time to the music, even mouthing the words. No Raymond, though... I kind of missed the big guy and his bluster. It was getting late... a couple more, then...

Da dumm di di daa daa, da dum di di da...

Jesus, what is that? It's so familiar...

Da dumm di di daa daa, da dum di di daaa...

I stared into my beer...scraps coming back... Of course! *The Patriot Game!* My mother used to sing it, sang it the last time I was home, the last time I saw her. Tears came to my eyes. She's somebody a guy could count on... not like that bitch Meg. How does a guy find a girl like her? I reached down and felt the rosary in my pocket. Please, God, bring me through this. And give me a reason to go home.

I stood unsteadily and looked at the paper flags strewn all over the floor. Patriotism. we never speak of it. Nor of buddies maimed and killed. Danger, we talk about that. Fear, too, sometimes. Resentment and grievances, a really tough mission tomorrow. It comes down to this – we are in it together, we will get through together. Glory? That saccharine thought would never occur to us. Survival. That's more like it.

Anesthetized, I fell onto my bunk. My last thought was of Meg – embarrassing, disappointing Meg. For a lot of reasons I had to get her off my mind, not least of them Operation Jackass.

Next morning they choppered us through a driving rain into a secure field outside the town of Plei Bai, then we piled into deuce-and-a-halfs for the trip over rugged terrain to the plain north and east of Hill 874. This would take a couple of hours give or take. We'd complete the journey on foot so as not to attract attention. No more attention, that is, than eight hundred men in full battle gear had already attracted. As I mentioned, this was an infantry operation – rifles, machine guns, mortars, rockets – which meant we were basically limited to whatever we could carry. Resupply as able.

Hill 874 was 874 meters high, of all things, and shaped like a pear, except picture a pear sliced in half and lying on its flat side. At approximately the 650-meter level on the gradual slopes of the west, south and east quadrants, dense foliage gave way to grasses and stalks higher than your head, then bare dirt and rock. The steep north incline was almost all rock and dirt, the whole thing topped off by a rocky horned peak. From the briefings we knew the rock above treeline harbored a complex network of NVA bunkers and tunnels that'd be an absolute bitch to dislodge, but those were our orders. A diversionary force would probe from the west and east but the main force would attack up the north face since the defenders would least expect this, and for good reason – the degree of difficulty on a scale of one to ten, maybe a hundred. Need I mention what part of the force we were detailed to?

It added to our discomfort to learn the 101st Airborne found itself in a similar predicament shortly before, a lengthy and brutal battle for an objective called Hamburger Hill, up north in the Ashau Valley west of Danang, so named because the NVA ground up a large number of our men before we finally prevailed. We crossed our fingers that Hill 874 wouldn't be a repeat of what the grapevine was calling a first-class disaster.

I was nervous as hell the night before the assault, kept waking up, pissed off one moment, sad the next. How, with one sheet of paper inscribed with ink scratches, could a woman turn a life around so completely? One day, I was a man with something fine to live for. Now, angry and embarrassed, I didn't give a shit about anything. I awoke with a splitting headache.

WE'D BEEN TWO DAYS IN THE SLOP. Five meters up, ten back. Ten meters up, twenty back, sliding on our backsides, banging into rocks that sliced through your poncho and raised ugly welts on your arms and legs. Sisyphus. That's my role in this production, Sisyphus, with mud. Nuts, the whole thing, absolutely nuts. The rain has been constant and I was fantasizing about dry season right around the corner. Supposedly. With my luck, this year it'll skip us. All monsoon, all the time.

As we fought our way up the hill, low clouds scudded past on sheets of rain. Give our big guns credit, they did a number on the dug-in NVA. The first day after making our way to treeline we came upon a redoubt blasted by our artillery, abandoned by the NVA. Dozens of corpses left behind. Under cover of darkness Delta/Echo/Foxtrot moved higher. Then a halt was called and we settled down for the night. Cold C-Rats, followed by a few winks, then as dawn comes we find where good old Gibbs camped us – on a grassy slope with no vegetation, not even a tall bush. Sitting ducks we were. Just dumb luck we weren't blown away during the night.

Rock to rock was all we could do now. Our friend the fog and mist made it harder for the NVA to find us, but low visibility meant no air support. Don't want fast-movers smashing into Hill 874, don't need them firing on us by mistake which wouldn't be the first time. Until the crud lifted we'd count on the more nimble Cobras to give us a hand.

About noon we started coming under heavy fire. You could see how close the bullets were hitting from the splats of mud. Now Gibbs decides we should traverse up the hill, zig-zagging instead of straight up which the slippery terrain made impossible. We worked our way around to the shallower southwest slope and found ourselves staring up at a cliff, when all hell breaks loose. We had emerged right under an NVA machine gun emplacement and they welcomed us in grand style. We were spread out among the boulders and rocks and after a few minutes Sgt. Crowley gathered together the old Delta/Foxtrot combo, Murph, me, Nathan, Corey, Stoner, Wayne, Fred, a couple others. Squatting behind a rock formation he told us we're gonna split off to the east and flank around the NVA gunners, scramble up to their level and catch them while their focus is downhill on the main body of our force. We got down and started crawling, under the brow of a footpath gouged into the mountain. After an hour of this, mud in every orifice, we came upon a grove of bushes and low trees. We could still hear shooting but it was around the corner and fainter.

"We're flying blind here," Crowley said. "We top that rock face," he points at an impressive hunk of granite, "come out above them, maybe thirty meters to the side. On the other hand, I can't promise we won't run right into them."

"Hey Sarge, we won't hold it against you." Fred and Crowley had become unlikely comrades, the Sergeant from tidy, whitey Bridgeport, Mayor Daley's neighborhood, the black kid from a distinctly different part of town.

"Okay, let's move it out. Heads up... take it slow."

At the rock wall I boosted myself into a narrow crevass... reminded me of Yosemite. My thoughts strayed to mountains in general then Meg's face floated by, Meg and goddamned Clyde on some beach in the goddamned Bahamas and here am I in this goddamned muddy hell. I shook my head. Get rid of that shit! Concentrate! After a half-hour of really tough scrambling we gained the top of the rock. Standing there panting, I was exhausted, but exhilarated.

By now the clouds were lifting and I scattered patches of blue were starting to appear. We lucked out. No NVA, and a big thicket of bushes between us and where we thought they were. Crowley pointed at Stoner.

"You and me let's check this out. The rest of you stay put."

They disappeared into the bushes. A minute later they're back. "Beautiful!" Crowley whispers, "they're down there on a ledge, shootin' their little hearts out." He pointed at the bushes, an opening and a path I had missed earlier. "We go single file through there then spread out. Ten meters and over a rise you'll see them. On my command give 'em hell."

All right. Love it. 'Bout time. Lots of muttering from our group.

"Stay low. Don't want our guys mistaking us for the gooks."

It was, as my hunting friends would say, a turkey shoot. There were maybe a dozen NVA and before they know what hit them there weren't any. With M16s on automatic and grenade launchers, they had no chance. Little return fire, nothing close to the mark. Nor were there any other NVA in the vicinity, at least none that cared to engage us.

"We cleaned their clock." Crowley on the radio to Gibbs downhill.

"So we saw. Much appreciated."

The rest of the day, more of the same. In the face of stubborn resistance we made progress. Gibbs was mulling whether to regroup and try a different tack up the hill but those of us who had invested our sweat in this particular slope didn't want to hear this. We bivouacked in a semi-protected area, swilled our C-Rats and slept in shifts.

The next morning we wake to a beautiful sunrise. CAVU. Gibbs orders us to regroup. Grousing and complaining, we form up with an ARVN platoon, but at least Gibbs doesn't give away a lot of the altitude we worked so hard to gain. We maneuver around to a gentler slope on the southwest face where the brass who are directing all this from observation choppers and a base camp below think we might make better gains. We start out okay but by late morning have stalled out, coming under heavy fire from another NVA dugout uphill. That's the nature of the mission – they are up, we are down trying to get up.

Problem is, this crowd has a grenade launch operator who is damned good, almost as good as me. He soon has us zeroed in, and the ground around us erupts in earth fountains – mud and metal flying every direction. Two, maybe three machine gunners up there, too. I am not feeling good about this. Nathan and I have been working side by side but at one point we get separated. Darting out from behind a big rock, Murph and I and a couple others return fire when I see a blast maybe twenty meters away and hear a scream. Nathan! Was that Nathan? Jesus! Don't let it be Nathan!

I start crawling toward the explosion but the battle rages and I have to back off. A few minutes later, dodging from rock to rock Stoner comes running up. "They're gonna take out that nest to get the dustoff in."

"Was that Nathan?"

"Dunno. There's a couple guys down."

"Aw shit," I said, my stomach sinking.

"They called in a Cobra. When we hear him we lay down a field of fire to divert the gooks. Then we mop up."

"How long?"

"S'on the way."

In three minutes, no more, I hear the THWOCK-THWOCK-THWOCK of the Cobra. We raise ourselves, peering over the rim of our rock and start firing. All of a sudden out of the corner of my eye I see a streak of light disappear into the NVA nest, then an explosion. Then another, and another. Its rockets spent, the Cobra fires a parting cannon salvo then banks steeply and breaks away. By now the NVA position is a mass of smoke and dust.

"LET'S GO!" Stoner shouts.

I slam another cartridge into my M-16 and hold the trigger down as we charge from behind the boulder, trying to gain traction on the hill. A few winks of light and I hear a solitary rifle but as we get closer Stoner tosses a grenade into the dugout and that is it for the rifle. We clamber up the last part of the hill and cautiously look into the blown hole. Charred bodies everywhere, an arm without a body, a head with its top sliced off, the guy's brains spilling out all over the place. Fresh blood everywhere. I take a deep breath, then another. We did it.

"So much for them gooks," Stoner says, firing a burst into one of the corpses for kicks. The enemy soldier looks like Clyde! Wouldn't mind doing that to him, the asshole...

We start down the hill. I see a chopper approaching, Nathan's Dustoff. I look around... he can't land! It's too steep! Then I think, of course – he'll hover. They'll lower a pallet. Slipping and sliding I rub my sleeve across my glasses, smearing them even worse. Up ahead a huddle of people, two men stretched out, one of them long and lanky. I run faster. My heart's in my throat, pounding. Plasma bag, medic's holding it up... tourniquets, bandages... my friend. Must get to him... wha... something in front of me... rolling... gotta stop... too fast too fast go around... can't go can't stop... can't

37. OMELETS AND EGGSHELLS

WHEN PAUL'S FATHER CALLED, right away I said I'd go. Of course. For him a long trip was out of the question. Akiko and I had been mulling over a visit, her parents up in years, and we were overdue. I had planned a quiet summer, nothing my R.A. couldn't handle. Within twenty-four hours we were on a plane for Tokyo.

Early evening we landed at Haneda in a hot, driving rain. Paul had been in the coma six days. I figured better Akiko go direct to Kyoto than hang around the hospital. I would stay here. I put her on the train and pointed the rental car toward Zama. I'd learned Paul was in such bad shape they had to overfly the field hospital and take him straight to Saigon. They kept him there long enough to amputate the leg, what was left of it, the other one they saved, thank God, and they got most of the shrapnel out. The pieces that caught him in the head, they backed one out of the brain, too risky to do more. He carried a fair amount of metal around the rest of his life. After a few days they figured he'd do better in an Army hospital so he ended up in intensive care at Camp Zama, southwest of Tokyo. Lucky those splinters were the only head injury, aside from the concussion, that is, the most severe kind. A miracle his stomach wasn't torn apart like usually happens in these cases.

I had been here many times. Before the Army took it over it was the old Imperial Japanese Academy. Even in darkness the grounds looked familiar, but I could see they'd done a lot of adding on. Paul was on the fourth floor in a large, airy room with a couple dozen beds, all hooked up to monitors. They had him flat on his back, his head covered with bandages though you could see most of his face. He looked serene. He also looked about twelve, just a baby. His chest was wrapped, both legs elevated with a cord and pully contraption. I choked when I saw the short one. They'd taken it a couple of inches above the knee, the doctor said. With the danger of gangrene the Saigon surgeon couldn't risk leaving more.

I pulled a chair up next to the bed. As I said, he seemed peaceful, his chest rising and falling, and though I didn't know what I was looking at, the graphs on the screen seemed regular enough. At times his mouth twitched as if he were trying to swallow. A good sign, I wanted to think. Often I took his hand, telling him Gus and Akiko are here, you're going to be fine, hang in there, everybody's pulling for you. Your father says hello. Before you know it you'll be home.

At 9:30 they kicked me out. I went to the pay phone to call Akiko. No need to rush back, I said, this is going to take a while. A few hours jetlagged sleep in a motel, then back for the morning visiting hours, the afternoon visiting hours, the evening visiting hours. Same thing next day, the day after, the day after that. In a couple of days they upgraded him from critical to serious but stable. He looked calm but I could imagine the fight he was putting up.

* * * * * * *

...MY HEAD... MY HEAD... MY HEAD... it hurts so bad. Does that mean I'm alive? It wouldn't hurt unless I'm alive would it? Mouth's hot, eyes are hot, everything so bright... am I outside? It looks like sunlight. Sometimes we get a breeze at night... will we have a breeze tonight I wonder... we always hope for a cooling breeze and sleep... blessed sleep...

Trying to remember... remembering's a good sign too... if I was dead I wouldn't be trying to remember. I fell... from a great height I fell then what? Everything went black... black and red. It's so hard. Tired... tired... put it down... leave it alone. I hear a voice... harsh and rasping, it makes my head hurt. Somebody says the name Ivan. The voice goes on... the poor, the weak, millions of the poor and weak are not capable of your freedom... peace and bread is all they want. Makes no sense. They don't care about the freedom you bring, Paul. Paul. He said my name... why did he say my name? So why are you here Paul... why do you persist... Leave them alone, these little people... let them be...

I want to turn the voice off but it goes on. It is the powerful who value freedom. The voice is a hammer, every word a nail. We are strong enough to endure freedom. These people want nothing from you. Now I see the speaker... he wears a monk's robes, his face nearly hidden by the cowl... a worn face, burning coals for eyes. Go Paul, he says, go. You and your companions... take your gifts and your guns and go.

A second man appears, younger, in a white robe soiled at the hem, dusty sandals. The monk turns to him. You were wrong, he says. Had you turned those stones to bread, the multitudes could have been saved... but you spurned the Great Spirit. It was your pride, pretending to be God. The one I call the Great Spirit you call Devil. Yes your arrogance drove you too far... you asked so much of man you would have destroyed him, but we have remedied your error... after your lamentable start we have got it right.

The man in white stands facing the old monk, a smile about his lips, his face radiant. The face, the robe make me dizzy. I turn away. Yes you are godlike and powerful but those who came later were not... that was your error. The people do not seek God, it is miracles they crave... your arrogance led them to false prophets, to chaos and rebellion, wicked masters who promise glory but set brother on brother. And all the while peace and bread was all they needed. Sadly, history proves your foolishness... you must have known you were asking too much of them, far too much. Why did you do it? Why?

I'm tired. I want to sleep but still the old man harangues the other. Hear me when I say we have finally have got it right. Today the Church says yes. YES! His shout stabs me. YES! we have joined with the great spirit and YES! the multitudes find respite in our arms YES! these children are no longer burdened by your free will YES! we offer the allure of heaven in this life and they are happy. It is their only life after all... beyond the grave there is death and nothing more. The man in white shakes his head. Placing his hand on the shoulder of the monk the two turn and stare at me, then fade away. It is quiet... blessed quiet.

I hear a noise... a banging, thudding. What is it? Thud...thud...thud, above my head three four five six now they sounds are softer and again it is quiet. That was Jesus! I MET JESUS! But something's terribly wrong... He didn't invite me to live with him! But neither did He say depart from me, accursed one. He's supposed to say one or the other! WHY DIDN'T HE SAY ONE OR THE OTHER! Is there nothing more! IS THERE NOTHING MORE!

"Take it easy, Paul, take it easy." A woman's voice. A shape towers over me. I feel something behind my back, propping me up. I'm sitting. I am sitting!

"We can't have you jumping around, you'll rip out the stitches."

Everything's blurry but I can tell she's nice looking. Pretty. I remember what that is. "I'm alive," I say, my mouth thick and dry.

"You are alive and lucky too. Let me congratulate you on surviving Vietnam."

"Vietnam. What happened? What's going on?"

She eases me down on the bed, shaking her head. "Shhh. I'll get the doctor, he'll want to know you're with us again."

I try to raise my head but I... can't move. Out of the corner of my eye I see bandages and tubes... my head feels like it's wrapped up. Jesus... I must have done a number on myself. Was I in an accident? I close and open my eyes... everything is fuzzy. "My glasses! Where are my glasses!"

"You must have lost them. Things were rather confused over there."

"But I need them!"

"You had a spare?"

"Back in..." I drew a blank. "Back in... I don't remember."

"Do you have a picture of it in your mind?"

I close my eyes again. "A bunkhouse. I remember a bunkhouse. My footlocker, all my stuff's in it. That's it! The Army! I'm in the Army. I'm in Vietnam!"

"You had a bad concussion... still do, they take time to heal." She lifted a clipboard from the end of the bed and flipped through some papers. "Let's see... you're in the 25th. Fire Base Tango. That ring a bell?"

"Tango. Delta Squad... Delta, Echo, Foxtrot."

"See, it comes back. Generally takes a week or so for your things to catch up. We'll find some glasses for you."

"I had a notebook too. At Tango."

"That'll be in the package too, most likely."

Something more... "This friend of mine... tall, skinny kid with a blotchy face. I have this friend, he was hit... he was hurt bad. We were on a hill. Nathan! I was running down a hill!" I tried to lift my head again. My eyes filled with tears.

The nurse put her hand on my forehead and eased me back on the pillow. "All in good time. Lie back. Rest. You've been through a lot."

"But I need to know what happened to Nathan."

"We'll find out but your job is to get well. Oh, by the way, you must rate, you have a visitor. He's been here every day. Came a long way to see you, too."

"Who's that?"

She shook her head. "Says he wants to surprise you. He shows up every day, stays the whole day." She looked at her watch. "I'll tell him you're awake but you're in no condition to see anybody yet. Let me get Doctor Abrams."

The doctor was young, dark haired with black horn-rimmed glasses, at least as far as I could tell. I was feeling slightly more together. "Welcome back to the land of the living, Private. How're you feeling?"

"Okay, I guess."

"How's your head?"

"Feel like I'm hung over."

"In a way you are. We've been pumping you full of medicine."

"How long was I out?"

"How about eleven days?"

"That's hard to believe."

"Not really. When bad things happen the body shuts down certain functions so others can operate better. They come back, little by little, sometimes all at once. Looks like you're an all-at-once type of guy."

"Bad things? What bad things?"

He looked down at the clipboard. "You got pretty banged up. Listen, first get used to the idea of being alive. Be thankful for that. We'll discuss your condition later."

"Another thing, I've got this itching, my leg, down low. It sort of aches, too."

He looked up. "Which one?"

"The left."

"We'll be giving you a complete exam, we'll go over everything then."

The nurse reappeared and the two of them conferred briefly. The doctor moved on to another bed and she came over with a couple of pillows. "Would you like me to raise the bed?" she asked.

"That would be good," I said. "I'm really dry."

"How about some apple juice? Doctor Abrams cleared you for liquids."

"Wouldn't happen to have a Bud, would you?"

"My, aren't we the frisky one. Ah! The first smile. That's good to see."

"What's your name?" Even in my myopic condition she was pretty. Short blondish hair, a turned-up nose, a red smear for a mouth, nice-looking red smear.

"Lieutenant Dutton, but everyone calls me Bobbie. Three Bs plus an i-e, that is."

"Bobbie Dutton... famous name."

"You're thinking of Betty Hutton. People say I look like her."

I took a deep breath. "I have some things to sort out, don't I?"

Her face turned serious. Why was that, I wondered. "People aren't here unless they have things to sort out. But you will, and you have all the time in the world to do it."

"Where am I?"

"An Army hospital near Tokyo. You're in the Intensive Care Unit."

"Japan, huh. They're not going to send me back, are they?"

She smiled. "Not hardly."

I relaxed. "Find out about Nathan. Please. I need to know."

I remember her holding the apple juice... I drank it through one of those bent straws. My arms were bandaged and my hands were ponderous and hard to move. Then I must have fallen asleep again. When I woke she showed up again to take my temperature and blood pressure. "We're doing better this afternoon."

"Yeah."

The rest of the day was like that... in and out, mostly out. Still nagging at me that hard, raspy voice and the other man, the one in white... I needed to get to the bottom of that...

As I lay there, I kept hearing this shuffling and rustling and hushed voices. Somebody was always talking... nurses, doctors... other patients. One time a priest came through. I closed my eyes and made like I was asleep. He stopped at the bed next to mine. After a while I heard this low conversation then some mumbling.

Next morning I woke up more refreshed. Had my first food, mushy oatmealish glop. For some reason that P&T night came to mind, passing out. Man, I thought, I made so much of that but it was nothing compared to this.

I must have drifted off again for next thing I knew this familiar face was looking down at me. I figured I was dreaming but when the mouth opened I heard good morning. It was Gus! "I don't believe it. How'd you get here?"

"I swam. Damned long swim, too!" He reached down and put his hand on my bandaged paw. "The question is, how are you?"

I nodded, best I could with all those bandages. "They say I'm doing better. You've been here the whole time."

He smiled. "Your father called me. Akiko and I were in the neighborhood so we thought we'd drop by."

"Akiko? You guys are too much. Where is she? Is she here?"

"With her folks but she'll be here today."

"I had some strange dreams. At first I thought you were one."

"A nightmare, perhaps? I've been called that."

"They say a grenade got me."

He nodded. "They also say you're fortunate to be here. A helicopter was there right when you needed it. Talk about service!"

"A friend of mine got hurt. I need to know what happened to him."

"What's his name?"

"Nathan Berg. We're in the same unit. Fire Base Tango."

"I'll see what I can find out."

"That's why I was in such a hurry."

"Hurrying. That's usually a mistake."

"Yeah. I guess I was asking for it."

Gus looked hard at me for a moment then turned away. Seeing my empty glass on the stand next to the bed he asked if I'd like more of whatever it was.

"It's thirsty in here. Apple juice."

He returned in a minute with a refill and held it while I drank. "Good man. You'll be out ordering pizza before you know it."

"Pizza. I haven't thought about pizza for a long time."

"You have some catching up to do."

"Say would you mind reaching under the covers and give my foot a scratch. That itch is really killing me."

"Which one?" Gus asked.

"The left one."

He sighed deeply, saying something under his breath.

"What'd you say?"

"Nothing. I was just feeling sorry for myself."

"Why? I'm the one's messed up."

"Because..." Now he had this really sad expression. "They haven't told you..."

"Told me what?" Suddenly my face felt very hot.

"I can't scratch your foot, Paul."

"Whaddya mean you can't scratch my foot? Of course you can scratch my foot!"

"They took your leg, Paul. They had to take your leg."

ohmygod... ohmygod... ohmygod... they... took... my... leg...

"It was that or lose you altogether. It was that close."

I stared at him. "You always had a rotten sense of humor..." I squeezed my eyes shut and pressed my head back on the pillow... could feel tears welling up. I opened them expecting to see a big grin, but there was no grin. "It's not a joke."

He shook his head. "I only wish it were."

"How much of it... um... do I still have?"

"They took it just above the knee. There's plenty to work with, they do marvelous things these days with prosthetics."

"An artificial leg, you mean."

"Yes."

"Jesus. What else didn't they tell me?"

"The concussion you know about. A piece of shrapnel got you in the head, a sliver penetrated your brain and caused some bleeding but it's nothing long-term. They dug out a lot of other metal. Your other leg got peppered but everything else is functional. No paralysis, no organ damage. All in all I'd say you were lucky."

"Lucky." I stared at his indistinct face... I guess that's when I lost it. "You've got a nerve calling me LUCKY!" I remember I started crying. "GET OUT OF HERE! GODDAMMIT, GET OUT OF HERE!"

He stood, a confused, sad look on his face. "Blaming the messenger's a bit unfair. I am truly sorry to be the one to tell you."

"UNFAIR! SORRY! What about me! WHAT ABOUT ME!"

He started to leave, then turned back. "One thing I do know. You're not a quitter and neither am I. I'll be back."

"FUCK YOU! I NEVER WANT TO SEE YOU AGAIN!"

Bobbie appeared. "What's that shouting?" she asked. The guys in the other beds were looking at me.

"You said I'm okay! I AM NOT OKAY! THEY FUCKING CUT MY LEG OFF!"

"Ah. Your friend told you."

"WHAT THE FUCK DO YOU THINK! IT'S MORE THAN YOU DID! YOU AND THAT SONOFABITCH DOCTOR!"

"I'm sorry. We figured it might be best to hear it from your friend."

"Great thinking! Really great."

She looked down at me and shook her head. "Take heart," she said gently, "You're going to be okay... just different. Guys adapt, they live normal lives. And you'll have all the help you need."

My heart was pounding like crazy and my head was killing me. She looked up at the monitors above the bed and frowned. "I'm going to give you something to settle you down. You've been doing very well up til now and I don't want you to..."

"Up til now... damn! DAMN! WHY ME! WHY'D THIS HAPPEN TO ME?"

She left the room for a moment then returned with a small paper cup.

"Open up," she said, placing the pill on my tongue. "Now drink this."

Christ, I thought, that's all I need, a female priest. I took a suck through the straw... ice cold. I could feel it slide down into my stomach. At least my stomach's still there. I don't trust her. I don't trust anybody.

"I am sorry, Paul," she said again, "but believe me when I say you are one of the lucky ones. You're alive. You have a life to live."

She had me lean forward and fluffed up my pillow and... that was it. What she gave me knocked me out. I had a dream, I dreamt of running and jumping, baseball and basketball, my St. Teresa's uniform, muddy football fields, boot camp, running, jumping... running no more...

WHEN I WOKE THERE SHE WAS with her thermometer and the blood pressure thing. "Looking better," she said, reaching over to wipe my eyes with a Kleenex. "A little watery, aren't we?" She handed me another glass of juice.

"What happened?"

"You made a scene... not something we encourage. You were really angry."

"A scene... what kind of scene?"

"Would you like to make a phone call? To family, some special friend?"

"There is no special friend."

"The offer stands. Just let me know."

Now it was coming back. I had screamed at her. First Gus, then her. I felt bad... she was only trying to help. "Sorry, I didn't mean to bite your head off."

"Don't worry, the tooth marks don't last."

"It's not your fault I'm here."

"That is true. Now what about that call?"

I thought a moment. "My father. I could call my father. I should do that."

"Do you know the number?"

"No. My address book is with my stuff."

"Give me a name and an address. We'll find it."

"Julien Bernard. He's at Graylag Manor, Chepachet Rhode Island. That's all I know."

"Small town, that should be easy enough."

"How do you know it's small?"

"I'm from Vermont. I know something about Rhode Island."

"Ah. That's why you talk so funny."

"Ay-uhp," she laughed.

We determined it was seven in the evening of the previous day where my Dad was. Bobbie cranked the bed up and nestled the phone between my shoulder and the pillow. I still couldn't bend my arms. I got right through. "Boy am I glad to hear from you," he said.

"You heard what happened."

"It was a grenade, they said."

"No, I mean what they did to me."

"Yes. I'm sorry. But it's for the best." There was a silence on the phone. "I guess you'll be putting your baseball career on hold for a while."

"That supposed to be funny?" I snapped.

After a long pause he said, "I didn't mean to make light of it."

"I know. That's okay. There'll be two gimps in the family now."

"Speak for yourself. I get around fine."

"How is everybody?"

"They want to be remembered to you. Actually Héloise isn't so well."

"Sorry. Lot of bad news going around these days."

"Catherine has set a date. September 14th. We hope you'll be back."

"I haven't even thought about that, getting out, that is. So she's finally going to do it."

"That leaves only you."

"As Richard M. Nixon would say, 'I don't have any current plans.'"

"What a disaster, that guy."

"I thought you liked him," I said, surprised.

"Hell no. ...I don't trust him any farther than I can throw him." He was quiet for a moment. "They treating you okay?"

"I'm kind of woozy and I have this headache all the time. They haven't let me get up yet. Outside of that I'm great. Gus is here. He said you called him."

"What a good friend, coming all that way. He left me a message that you woke up."

We talked back and forth then he asked how my spirits were. "Scale of one to ten, maybe a two."

"I figured you for a six. That'll take time, I guess."

"I guess."

"Just remember one thing. Some very good people come back in a pine box or not at all. And for something wasn't their fault either. Look at Maurice."

"And Omer. Omer Arsenault."

"I heard. That's too bad. You and he were great pals. Well, keep your chin up. You'll get over this... a lot of people are rooting for you."

"I appreciate that. I will."

Dinner was whipped potatoes and pureed carrots. Fucking baby food! Bobbie brought me a pair of eyeglasses, standard issue green frames like my old ones but too weak. Tried to read a sign on the wall but I couldn't make it out. Frustrating. On the other hand, I was practicing looking on the bright side – til then I couldn't even tell it was a sign. What's that song... country song... keep on the sunny side, always on the sunny side...

"They're not strong enough but thanks anyway."

"Your things'll be showing up soon."

TRUE TO HIS WORD, that evening Gus returned with Akiko. Seeing her helped, as did Bobbie's unrelenting cheeriness. I apologized, said that was a shitty way to treat him. He shrugged it off. Radiant as ever, Akiko brought me a gift of flowers – several tall thin plants in a dish filled with black dirt and decorative stones. "The art of Ikebena," she said, setting it on a stand a nurse wheeled in. "This is from my father's garden, made especially for you. He is a master of floral arrangement. He is eighty-seven years, going on thirty."

"What kind of flowers?" I asked, trying to be cheerful. They looked familiar but I didn't know why.

"Hollyhocks. The plants represent man, earth, heaven. The tallest one is heaven, the white flower, naturally."

"And man's the little one."

"Actually man is the middle plant, for he resides between heaven and earth. Earth is purple. Man is white with purple tinges since he is of both."

"I came pretty close to joining those tall ones."

Gus nodded. "We're grateful you are still with us." I noticed his eyes were moist. Then he started in with news of my family. I cut him short, said I talked with my father. "Well, then, that's even better."

"We hear your sister is getting married," Akiko said brightly.

"It's about time," I said, "she's been going with the guy for years."

"I don't blame her," Akiko said. "Marriage is too important to rush."

"Or do at all," I replied.

I stared down at the covers, at the mounds which were my legs. The one for my right foot was where it should be, but the other... I had to look away. From time to time during the day a doctor would peel back the sheet but they hadn't yet shown it to me. My heart caught in my throat whenever I thought of it. Part of me had died, what good was the rest? A partial man, a fraction of a man. I was thinking I should ask Gus to bring me a pint of scotch or something to squirrel under the covers for the unveiling.

Another nurse, not Bobbie, stopped to check me, jotting the results on her clipboard. "You're doing better. Keep this up, we'll be kicking you out of ICU." When she finished fussing I shifted my weight to face Gus. I was moving around better in the bed. With what small steps do we measure progress.

"Gus," I said, "I'm sorry I yelled but I'm not letting you off the hook. I really am pissed at you."

"Of course. When did we ever agree on anything?"

"No, I mean it. You see, I was out there in that jungle six-plus months, more than enough to see what a fucked-up..." I caught myself. "Sorry, Akiko."

"I'd be surprised if you hadn't picked up some new expressions."

"I mean what a mess this war is. You try hard, you do good work, then it's back to the base and leave the winnings to the enemy. We had this one program, WHAM – win their hearts and minds. No way. People just want us the heck out of there."

"Hell," Akiko said.

"So far we have no disagreement," Gus interjected.

"I'm getting to that. My point, here my buddies and I are humping, trying to win the war, whatever that means, and you're back in Berkeley pulling the rug out from under us."

"That's not true, Paul, though I was, am, and will continue trying to bring this sordid business to an end. Even if you're President, *especially* if you're President, if you make a mistake like LBJ did, like JFK did before him, like Nixon is doing now, the only responsible thing to do is admit it and change course."

"But what you were doing made it less likely we could win the war under any conditions. That's what bothers me."

"Sorry, but the way we approached it, it was doomed from the start."

"Meaning?"

"Meaning we tried to be too cute. Weren't willing to go all out, take out the North's infrastructure like we did Germany. And Japan, as Akiko saw to her sorrow. But no, that would have incurred the wrath of Russia and China."

Sounds like Father Trần, I thought... Father Trần!

"No," he was going on, "if you mean to go to war, you do it right. Have the courage to level with the people, get them behind you, then go in with everything you've got. I never advocated this war, mind you, it wasn't worth it in any event, but it breaks my heart to see a half-hearted effort like this."

Akiko broke in. "'Half-assed' is what you usually say, Gus."

"Right," he replied, frowning. "Paul, the problem isn't the protests or the protesters. It's not even the so-called patriots who support the war, least of all is it you guys on the ground. The explanation is much simpler. A profound failure of leadership. Our leaders lack wisdom and they lack character. They put pride and personal interest ahead of their country. Getting re-elected, keeping their jobs, for them that is number one. And they didn't trust the people, an unforgivable error.

Those who were supposed to be our stewards let us down, not to mention what they put you guys through."

Suddenly I felt very tired. My head throbbed. "I'm done arguing. Let's just leave it I have a big problem with you."

He reddened. "I hope you're not saying I'm responsible for your..." He glanced at the foot of the bed.

"Of course not. I was the one threw the dice. I may get over this, but believe me, I will never forgive you and your radical friends for keeping us from doing our job."

The next afternoon Bobbie came in, all smiles, waving an envelope. "Is this is what I think it is?" It was a letter on Army-issue letter paper, return address... what? Pfc. N. Berg! Postmarked July 13th, just a few days ago! What the hell is going on?

"It's from your friend?"

"Apparently so."

"Sorry we didn't get a line on him but there you go."

"Hello, Paul," the letter began, in a cramped script. It occurred to me I had never seen his handwriting before.

> Sorry to hear you got hit and everything. Everybody says hello and wishes you a speedy recovery. You're the kind of guy who comes through for everybody else, you'll do fine, I am sure. Stoner said you thought I got hit but it must have been some other tall guy. I am writing this as soon as I can. We spent nearly two miserable weeks on that hill. We got to the top and planted a flag. Nothing like Iwo Jima, I'll tell you. The brass has reduced the guys there to a skeleton crew but what else is new. The day we got back I got promoted to PFC. Murph said you did too.
>
> Take care of yourself and let me know where you end up. At least you're out of this shitful place and will go home. Sorry how it ended but you'll do okay. Murph sends greetings, also Wayne and Fred. Stoner is crazier than ever.
>
> See you in New York. We'll go to a Mets game. Maybe Murph can sneak us into the Stadium when your Sox are in town.
>
> Your friend, Nathan

I let the letter fall to the floor. Unbelievable. Fucking unbelievable! I try to help my friend, I run into a fucking grenade and for what? FOR NOTHING! How could God fuck up my life like this for a mistake! FOR A GODDAMNED FUCKING MISTAKE!

THAT NIGHT I WAS FEELING VERY SORRY FOR MYSELF. Bummed out, ashamed, embarrassed, so caught up in my troubles I couldn't bring myself to rejoice that my friend was alive. I had enough sense to know I was letting him down now, myself too, in a spiritual way. It took me some time to realize that my good intentions, however misplaced, maybe they counted for something. Finally I said the hell with it and started to play with my pecker under the covers but with the bandages I couldn't really get hold of it. I figured it'd been so long that wouldn't matter and tried to rub it with the back of my paw but nothing. Nothing. Suddenly I had this horrible thought. They said I caught some shrapnel around my groin... maybe it cut a nerve or something and they're afraid to tell me. My sex life, over before it even started! Panicked, I tossed and turned a long time before dozing off.

Don't know what time it was I woke up but when I pushed the call button I was surprised to see Bobbie there. "Why are you awake?" she asked.

I rolled onto my side to see her better. "Can't sleep. What're you doing here?"

"I traded. You want something to drink? Something to help you sleep?"

"Yeah, a drink."

She looked at me in the dim light. "Something's bothering you. What is it?"

"It's not the kind of thing I can talk about."

She laughed. "There is no such thing. What is it?"

"You really want to know?"

"I *need* to know. It's my job."

"Well, if you insist." So I told her.

She broke out laughing. "What a worrywart. You are just fine. You have some superficial cuts but there's nothing to be concerned about, nothing at all."

"How can you tell? I tried to check it out but nothing happened. I'll never have a family. I've heard what happens when you get hit there."

She was quiet for a moment, then sat down on the edge of the bed. Pushing my blanket aside, she reached down under the sheet and put her hand on me. "What are you doing!" I whispered.

"Shhhh... be quiet."

She took my thing in her hand and started rubbing and squeezing it, gentle at first, then harder. "Jesus, what if you get caught?"

"You are a world-class worrier, aren't you? You'll make a fine lawyer. Go to law school when you get out."

"I don't think so... oh, that's nice..." She really was doing it... I was getting hard. "I feel like I should be... doing something."

"Just sit back and enjoy the ride," she said, reaching her other hand in with a kleenex. "Tell me when you're almost there."

"This is the weirdest thing..."

"We aim to please, if you hadn't noticed."

Suddenly I felt myself coming... "Now!" I whispered loudly, "now!"

She put the Kleenex under me and started rubbing me up and down, up and down... then...! "Oh my God," I said, lying back and breathing heavily. "Oh my God."

She deftly wiped up the mess and withdrew her hand with the wad of tissue. "See, what'd I say," she said brightly. "You're just fine. Now go back to sleep. Somebody'll clean you up tomorrow."

"I think I'm in love with you," I said.

"With my right hand, maybe. Do I need to tell you this is strictly between us?"

"Of course."

She bent down and kissed me lightly on the cheek. "You're very nice, but don't get any ideas. A one-shot deal, all in a day's work."

"Or a night's."

"Or a night's."

I had the best sleep I can ever remember. No worries, no guilt either. Something in me had changed for the better. Maybe I'll be a man after all.

Gus and Akiko came in every day for about a week. I guess I wasn't as gracious as I should have been, though I was over shouting. The two of them wheeled me all over the hospital and one beautiful, crisp July day about the grounds, first time I had been outside since my injury. I had decided to call what happened "my injury."

One day Gus brought in a copy of the June 27 issue of *Life*. He'd put it aside for me as soon as he heard about me. "Keep this to yourself. I imagine the folks running this place wouldn't want it getting around. Far as I'm concerned, it's something to reflect on."

The date won't mean anything to you, but that was the issue with pictures of the 242 U.S. servicemen killed in one week in Vietnam. Just one week, May 28 to June 3. Gus said it caused a furor, a lot of people damning *Life* for running it, others praising their courage to report the truth in a dramatic way. I could imagine Nixon and his crowd going crazy. Not an image his fellow Americans would be comfortable with. Gus' point – maybe it'd help me think twice before feeling sorry for myself. True, I replied, though easier said than done. In my mind I pasted Omer in one of the little squares, Maurice in another.

LITTLE BY LITTLE THE BANDAGES DISAPPEARED. Punctures were cleaned and rebandaged, gauze pads and adhesive tape introduced for those healing the best, stitches came out. Your body'll have a lot of scarring, they said, and that cut on your face will take some getting used to, but the biggest relief was my arms and hands. I was moving them freely again. They said I was down to one fifty-two from my normal one-eighty. Some of that was probably from being in the field, the dysentery on the Hill I didn't tell you about, but most of it had to be the leg. What a way to lose weight. I don't recommend it.

About a week after I came to they showed me the stump. I didn't go nuts or anything, probably because I'd already been cruising along at a moderate level of depression. After the shock I felt removed, like somebody else's feelings were running through me. Maybe the magazine did help. I almost felt worse when I looked in the mirror at the red slash running from my forehead to down under my ear. By now the bandage was off and there it was in all its glory for everybody to see. They said it would lighten up in time but I didn't believe them.

The first night they unhooked my stump from the pulley cord, I managed to pull a chair over to the bed and carefully maneuver myself down on the floor. I had been thinking about this... I wanted to kneel and pray and grieve and give thanks, everything. Problem is, I couldn't bend my other leg, it was so stiff and sore, and even if I could have, I was scared to put weight on anything. So I just lay on my side in as close to a kneeling position as I could manage. After a while I was feeling the cold of the floor through my hospital gown so I tried to raise myself up and get back in bed but couldn't make it. Not the most brilliant stunt I've ever pulled, I told myself. After a while a nurse making her rounds noticed me. Startled, she asked how I got on the floor. I pointed to the chair. "Why'd you do a thing like that?"

"I felt like some exercise."

"Well, don't ever do it again. You're sure you didn't fall?" she said as she started for help to get me back in bed. I paused a moment, considering my response as she disappeared around the corner.

"Yeah," I said softly, "I fell."

The stump was red. It looked like the end of a sausage, though it was knitted together with thick black twine and knots. The thigh above was red and blotchy, though they said that would lighten as scar tissue developed. There would be salves to help it heal and exercises to toughen it, build it up, for that's where my new... my new leg would be attached. And don't forget the other leg, they said, it'll hurt some but you need to exercise it, pay attention to it. They were right, it throbbed much of the time and I had to take painkillers that made me feel like I was floating.

Keep on the sunny side, I kept singing it over and over, that simple little tune. KOTSS. Carter family, I remembered. In the spirit of things I named my foreshortened limb Mr. Stumpy and thought of asking people to autograph the bandage. I mean, break a leg and people write on your cast so why not? Or would this be too grim, too scary? As you can see, I was trying. I had two options, try or cry. And there was this real oddity. In the face of incontestable proof, I still had this itching and soreness that for the life of me was coming from my missing foot. This was normal, I was told, and they even had a name for it – phantom pain. They said I was lucky to be in that coma after the surgeries. I was spared the excruciating pain that is visited on people who lose a limb.

What I liked best about the hospital, nobody was shooting at me, nobody was shouting at me. I wasn't tense and scared all the time. It was mostly quiet though if somebody dropped a bedpan I jumped out of my skin. Noise = Danger. A direct electrical connection from my ears to my nerves, totally bypassing the brain. The shrink who came by "for a chat" said that would take time to get over, some people never did, years later still diving under tables and desks. Then there were the dreams, nightmares I guess they were. I hadn't seen the monk and prisoner again, but every few nights I woke up in a sweat, thinking I was falling from a great height. The devastated baby was a frequent visitor. I wasn't coming unhinged or anything like that, more like locked into a sadness where everything was hard. Sisyphus in spades. The shrink said considering what I'd been through a certain amount of mental clutter is normal. Also, for some guys the worst doesn't show up until much later. Bolt out of the blue kind of thing. Cheery guy, that doc. I was ready to take him on about what's normal but I figured, he's right. Vietnam does that to you.

By now I was a master wheelchair pilot, careening through the corridors, traveling to the rec room where I regained my nicotine habit, in the gardens, trying to recall details of Akiko's Zen garden back in Berkeley. So uncertain about what was next for me, waking up to cigarette throat provided an oddly comforting reference point. I spent a lot of time talking with the staff, the cleaning people and janitors, the bed-wheeling orderlies. They were some of the best people. There was only one female doctor in the place as far as I could tell. Short, stout and middle-aged, looked nothing like Meg but the fact she was a she made me angry. I didn't know what I'd do about that shipwrecked part of my life. If I never saw Meg again that would be soon enough.

I poked into the different wards, finding especially compelling the psycho ward where often you heard guys crying and screaming. I had no trouble imagining what they were seeing, what they were hearing. Whatever they had, I figured I probably had a case of it too, though thankfully not as bad. One day two grim-faced orderlies rushed past me, chasing a guy down the corridor, strait-jacketed and with this fearless, crazy expression on his face.

As seemed to be my way these days, I didn't go out of my way to try and make new friends. I was content to miss my old ones, Nathan, Murph, even Stoner. And how's this for perversity – sometimes I even wished I was back with them.

Citing remarkable progress, they moved me to the Orthopedic Ward. I liked the change, though I missed Bobbie. She came by from time to time. "Good morning, Lieutenant Dutton," I greeted her, honoring her for going the extra mile or, more like it, inches.

"Good morning, Private Bernard," she'd respond. For me she'd always be special, the one who was there when I came back from wherever I was those ten days.

One evening a nurse came around asking who would like to get up early to see the moon landing the following morning about 5:15 Tokyo time. I signed up and was one of the many patients and staff who packed the rec room, looking up at the beautiful big-screen Sony they'd brought in for the event. "Houston, Tranquility Base here. The Eagle has landed."

A great cheer went up. For a moment we put down our troubles and were proud to be Americans. It brought me back to Apollo 8 and the earthrise. So much had happened in that short time. Later on, Gus and Akiko came in and we watched Neil Armstrong's historic descent from the lunar module. "That's one small step for a man, one giant leap for mankind." Armstrong's stiff-legged walk made me wonder how I would do when my time came to try. KOTSS.

It was Gus and Akiko's last day before heading down to Kyoto for a final visit. They'd fly out the following day. I'd be sad to see her go, him too, in spite of everything. A couple of times I caught her staring at my cut. She quickly looked away but she knew I knew what she was thinking. But she was cool. "When will we see you in Berkeley?" she asked. So far I'd steered our conversations away from my future.

"For sure I'll visit," I said. "I don't know if I'll be coming back to Cal."

"You don't want to waste all those years of study," he said, shaking his head.

"Didn't you once tell me, nothing is wasted, it's a matter of how you use it?"

"I may have. I say a lot of things."

"But if not that, what will you do?" Akiko asked, her brow furrowed.

"I don't know. That's something I have to figure out."

"Would you live in California at least, the Bay Area?"

"I don't even know about that. I'll just have to see."

We parted on good terms, though much was weighing on me. One thing for sure, my life would never be the same. The other thing, I didn't want it to be. The afternoon they left, the nurse came in to tell me my belongings had arrived, if I'd like her to wheel me into the rec room she'd help me sort through them. I was especially relieved to find my diary slash notebook. As I mentioned, this has been invaluable, though telling a tale like this was the last thing on my mind back then. In my backlogged mail I found an official letter confirming my promotion to Private First Class, which I greeted without enthusiasm. Also my copy of *Brothers,* none the worse for its travels halfway across the world. I had already figured out the dream, of course, but I needed to visit the Grand Inquisitor again.

I met with the orthopedic team over my new leg, what was involved in fitting it, when I'd receive it, how to get ready, but first things first, they took me through the procedures and tricks for crutches, about a week away. I thought of my father. If he could do it, damn it, I could too. A physical therapist outlined the program for getting used to my new leg, putting it on, taking it off, standing, sitting, walking. I asked her about kneeling. That is a problem, she said, and though a lockable hinge provides some flex, ninety degrees is beyond the current technology. I figured God would cut me some slack on that one.

YOU MAY HAVE NOTICED, I haven't said much about God since I got hurt. When I woke up, the first few days I was confused and bitter. Frightened. How could He do this to me, I kept thinking, how could this be happening to me? My whole life, it seemed whenever I needed something I looked up and my lucky star, that is God, showed me the way. Where was it now? Would it reappear?

As I grew stronger, I figured some things out. One thought that helped – why should I be different from anybody else? Bad things happen to people. And it isn't your looks or education or luck that separates you from the pack, it's how you deal with the setbacks. Seeing the lemonade in the lemon, so to speak. Then it occurred to me, maybe there's a way I can turn this to my advantage. I couldn't bring myself to thank God for what happened, but at least I didn't blame Him any longer. Not as much.

Many days I wheeled myself into Zama's chapel for Mass, sometimes remaining behind as everybody cleared out. One day I meditated on the Grand Inquisitor – I had reread it the night before. Since we have free will, God must want us to have free will. Obviously. That's the easy part. But why give us this power to make bad decisions? Why let us do the horrible things we do? Terminate with extreme prejudice, indeed. Phelps. Johansson. Gibbs. Stoner. Bernard. Bullets, grenades – I'd done it all. A hypothesis: He is testing us, to see what kinds of choices we make. Good choices get you points, bad choices, you lose points. And this choice business must be supremely important to God's scheme because it is so risky. When you join choice to frail human nature, you see He has conscripted us for a very dangerous game. As I wheeled myself out of the chapel I thought, why waste time condemning God for setting the bar so high? Better to realize we have an intractable problem and do the best we can with it.

A team of doctors and nurses and specialists worked with me daily. I came to view it as a game, the game of getting back on my feet. I should say foot. KOTSS. I also had a session with a counselor about mustering out and what to do with my life. He was a lot better with the first issue than the second.

As I was no longer much use to the Army, they would "separate" me from them and return me to the States. The date was already set, October 15. Until then I would continue to draw Army pay, then once disability kicked in I'd be receiving it indefinitely, plus of course, medical care. The rehab would be in two phases. First, a couple of months in Letterman in San Francisco where I'd get my leg and learn how to use it. Then a VA Hospital to close out the treatment. I gave some thought to the Providence VA I had driven past as a kid, but decided on Boston, down the road from Pat's Museum of Fine Arts, overlooking the Jamaicaway my father and I traveled for ball games. It would be like coming home, except I no longer had a home. The word no longer made sense. My next home I would have to build from scratch, myself.

38. IN MY DELICATE CONDITION

"JONATHAN HAS BEEN OUT A FEW DAYS, but he should be back today. Truthfully, the break was welcome. That last batch of remembering has been terribly difficult. Not only that, my Plaza bill is a disaster. Jonathan said he'd try to get the magazine to cover it but I can't count on that. We really need to pick up the pace. That dream of Paul's I found really interesting. I've flagged that to go back to and spend more time with.

As for my Tokyo visit, when it was clear Paul would survive, a great sadness came over me. His outburst was a shock, though I should have seen it coming. Then when he arrived at Letterman I made a point of visiting every few days. He was there only six weeks before transferring to Boston. Just as well. Given Berkeley's sour mood, even in civvies the leg would have been no protection against insults or worse. Another Pandora's box that goddamned war opened – the disrespect for our men who served and sacrificed. Appalling. I spoke out on the campus but not to much effect.

In a week he was getting around reasonably well and we took walks beside the Golden Gate. As his spirits improved we talked of many things. "No more library stacks for me," he said one day. "That would drive me up the wall."

"I tell you to have some adventure and look what happens."

"I made the mistake of listening to you," he laughed.

I had been toying with an idea and thought I'd spring it on him. "Have you thought of rehab work? I should think that'd be a natural."

He pointed back at the hospital buildings. "I want to put all this far, far behind me. Same with the military." At this point, I distinctly remember, Paul reached out and put his hand on my shoulder. "We have our differences, you and I, but we always come back to the center. One thing I know, whatever I do I've got to stay involved. I have Berkeley to thank for that, and you." He was quiet a while. "I've been thinking I might give newspaper work a try," he said softly. "I liked it, though I never thought I'd end up there. What do you think?"

"You could do worse. It's an honorable profession, and it would bring your academic work into play. Somebody once called newspapers 'history in the raw,' which is a fair assessment, for the best ones at any rate. I can put a word in at the *Chronicle.*"

I shook my head. "It's got to be east coast. Anyway, you've had enough of me."

He smiled. "That's true. It's Akiko who'll really miss you."

Next time we got together I had something to add. "Let me play devil's advocate. I'm not so sure you're suited for journalism. You're too nice a guy to be a good reporter."

"What do you mean by that?" he asked, surprised.

"To be effective a reporter's got to be a real pain in the ass. Aggressive, pushy, willing to turn people out of bed at three a.m. to get his story."

At first Paul looked surprised, then he put his head back and roared.

"No," I said, "I mean it. And there's a question of mental toughness too. You can't believe something just because somebody says it's so. Whatever I think about our Jesuits, they taught us how to ask good questions. You've got to question everything, all the time. Are you up to that?"

Paul stared at me. "Outsmarting people who're trying to kill you, that does wonders for your *cojones.*" He stuck out his leg and rubbed it with his hand. "Let me introduce you to my mealticket. I'm going to play this little beauty for all it's worth." I nodded. "I'm trying to convince myself of that, at least," he added with a wan smile.

Those visits were the last I saw of Paul for some time. We stayed in touch, but it wasn't until I moved back east myself that we spent time together again.

Jonathan shows up around eleven. Over a sandwich in the conference room I fill him in on Tokyo. Right away he gets excited. "Pushy! A pain in the ass! That's what you think of me?"

"Do you disagree?"

"No, you're right. As for Paul's leg, I have a friend, all he could see was light and dark but he made himself into a top student – Columbia, NYU Law. He used his handicap shamelessly. Figured he'd been cheated, so he grabbed everything he could. These days he's a big deal, doesn't need the sympathy card any more. Paul's saying the same thing. I say, good for him." Jonathan sat back in his chair. "By the way, I see no need to parse Vietnam line-by-line. I'm more interested in how the experience affected him. He supports the war, he volunteers, he comes out fractured and disillusioned but with a plan. What do you think?"

"I agree, let's look forward. One thing he discovered, the only way to understand things is see them for yourself. That was my point, credulity versus skepticism. What do you learn as you're being marched over a cliff? He learned a valuable lesson from that."

"You know, Gus, I am trying but I still don't get a lot about his Catholic thing. How many years was he immersed in their teaching about killing, yet there he was, rifle and grenade, big as life."

"That's what I'm saying – experience matters, and he didn't have enough until it was too late. Whenever you realize you're being fed lofty words, that's the time to be on your guard. Remember that dog of his? A hard lesson but he needed more. It took Vietnam, unfortunately."

While I was waiting for Jonathan I had pulled the carton labeled "Gazette #1" to our end of the conference table. "Before we start on this," I say, "anything new on the investigation?"

"I meant to tell you," Jonathan breaks out in a big smile, "Hersh is off the story. Apparently he's on to something else – it involves torture at some Iraq prison. The kind of story reporters dream about, is what they're saying."

"Which Hersh has a way of turning up."

"No question the man's good, but I heard he wasn't getting anywhere on Paul."

"Does this mean you'll pick the investigation up again?"

"Knock on wood. My editor says it's looking good. One other thing, I asked Susan to open a door at ETVN – I've met with them too. They say they're interested in collaborating on the investigation but I said I need to talk to you first."

"Why would they want our help? Why would they help us?"

"They think we have something to offer. I'd rather they're with us than against us."

"We don't want our work turning up in some half-baked docudrama."

"Susan says their Iraq team is very good."

I shake my head. "If we can do the whole thing ourselves I'd rather go that route."

"I need to get back to them but I'll be careful."

"Up to you," I say, going to the credenza across the room. I pulled out a key and unlocked it. "Take a look at our new toy." I reached in and pulled out a compact black device about the size of a toolbox. "Present from Dennis. To make our calls secure."

"I'm impressed," Jonathan says.

"I won't take the time to show you now but we've checked it out, it works fine."

"How about that," Jonathan says, running his hand over the smooth matte surface. "Our very own black box. I've always wanted one. We should give it a name."

"It already has a name – Enigma Junior."

"How about that." He nodded. "Let's hope it's half as good as its predecessor."

* * * * * * *

I DO APOLOGIZE, GUS, for my fuzzy recollections. What I gave you is the best I can, plus observations I began scribbling in my notebook when I got it back. One thing I notice, even after so many years, a lot of those Grand Inquisitor questions remain. Anyway, too many holes in this, but maybe I can plug some as we go along. Others, way it goes. On a phone call my first day at Letterman my father said something you know innately but it was good to get out in the open: "who ever said life's supposed to be fair?" I also pondered Father Ronan's "Let's get on with it!" I thought of him often, those days.

The big event was my new leg. I had down days but that means I was having up days too. KOTSS. I was intent on making the damned peg work, putting myself back in the game. The surgical cuts had healed and the stiches came out shortly before leaving Japan. My face, that would take time. Mr. Stumpy looked raw but, anxious to do his part, he was toughened and ready for action. They made a plaster cast impression and in a couple of days I was looking my new leg, a dull black titanium shaft, at the top a socket custom-built from the cast of my stump. The other end, a plastic foot something like a shoe tree. Later on I would get a cosmetic upgrade, a lifelike plastic molding over the metal shaft that looked for all the world like a real leg, hair included. No tattoo, though, not my style. Besides it disturbed me that for the Army tattoos are off-limits but mutilation and amputation, they're okay. One's in the game plan, one is not.

The first time I slid my stump into the socket, a hole, really. It seemed kind of loose, but the doctor said not to worry, they never fit perfectly the first time. They'd monitor it closely, adjustments are to be expected. The sock I had taken to wearing over the stump now had another use, to help cushion the rubbing and tighten the fit. Sometimes I needed a second sock. I practiced with a walker and graduated to crutches, then as my balance and confidence improved, a cane. The first few days my foreshortened leg was pretty sore, also my back and stomach muscles, so long unused, so they temporarily upped the pain medication I was being weaned away from.

It felt good to be moving around on my own. It looked like they got the length right so I was again able to greet the world from my six-one. The knee was the problem. Since they cut me so high, transfemoral they call it, my leg needed an mechanical knee. It was hinged so it flexed in walking mode, with a spring and lock device that allowed it to bend for sitting.

Each day twice a day we assembled for physical therapy. Pushups, pullups, leg lifts with both legs, weights on pulleys, on your back, on your stomach, on your sides. I'd never been much of a swimmer but it surprised me how much I enjoyed the pool. The buoyancy almost made me forget my troubles. Kicking with only one leg was tricky because I tended to wobble off course, but they showed me tricks – mainly work my left arm overtime to compensate. I increased to two lengths of the twenty-five meter pool, a far cry from those miserable after-school sessions at the Olneyville Y where I was awarded my minnow certificate only because nobody ever failed. Now I was looking forward to building my endurance at the Boston VA in a few weeks, the beginning of September.

You take so much for granted. Getting in and out of bed I mastered quickly. Taking a leak, no problem. Shitting, more complex in the getting down and up, making sure your clothes are out of the way. Bath and shower were tricky. I was in love with handrails. Getting dressed, particularly pants, took serious coordination. The good leg came first, pulling the pants over, then socks and shoes. Only then was the peg ready to attach using the strap and belt device that secured it around my waist. And of course, everything takes ten times longer than it used to. Frustrating as hell. Learn to manage your expectations, they said, or as Murph used to say, "aim low, you're rarely disappointed."

I wondered how Murph was doing, couldn't wait to see him and Nathan. I thought about all my friends, but my Vietnam buddies were present to me with exceptional clarity. I couldn't wait for them to come home, their DEROS only a couple of months off. I would meet them in New York, I had it all worked out. A Yankees game, sightseeing, good restaurants. I made some acquaintances at

Letterman but didn't try too hard. And I had a steady stream of visitors, Gus of course, often with Akiko.

One afternoon a Berkeley flashback – out of nowhere Benny and Gideon appeared! It was pouring that day so they found me in the solarium (is there an equivalent rain name?) that looked out on the grounds. We were having an okay though kind of awkward visit as they updated me on their academics for which I had little patience. Benny was nearly finished his degree, Gideon had stalled out and was trying to regain traction. About a half hour along, who should show up but my old roommate Mark. Mark was a cool guy, but he and Benny got into a shouting match about the war, Benny offering me as Exhibit One for why the war was a disaster and Nixon a war criminal. Mark would have none of it. He touted the war as a success. He looked down his nose at Benny.

"It's thanks to guys like Paul you have the freedom to badmouth our government. What have you done for us lately?"

"We need to fix our own problems," Benny shouted. "This society is sick through and through." I could see gray heads in wheelchairs turn our direction.

Gideon's response was more measured. "You've got to pick and choose your fights. No country, no matter how wealthy, can police the world."

I never got into the conversation. My condition seemed to inhibit them from asking about my views. And when I thought about it, what I had to say would be more personal than political and probably not of that much interest. The political I was still sorting out.

Benny and Gideon left but Mark stayed on. We chatted about Vietnam, the sights and sounds, the fears, the hilarity. Being with him was easier than with my academic friends. I almost used an expression I'd been toying with, "the new me," but held back. Mark mentioned RAND which he couldn't say anything about except he'd been back to Vietnam a couple of times. After he left I stared out the windows at the rain pondering everything, realizing it was indeed a new Paul Bernard I inhabited.

I made a list of people who might be able to help me find a job when I got back to Boston. Father Ronan – I needed to talk with him about a lot of things. My father's friend Dave LaPointe. Then a long shot, my Saigon dinner. Ed Reynolds would be surprised to hear from me, shocked even. On one of his visits Gus threw me for a loop. I told him about my idea of newspaper work and he said I was too nice a guy to be a good reporter. A reporter has to be a pain in the ass, his exact words. Question everything, take nothing for granted. Don't guess, don't assume.

"What makes you think I can't do that?" I said.

"So far I haven't seen it."

This offended me. I wasn't such an easy mark. I'd always made my presence felt, at the Cross where it was all too easy to go along with the official program. At Berkeley, who else stood up to the protesters and put his money where his mouth was? But I thought, take his comment for what it's worth, if anything. The new Paul Bernard, gearing up for his new role. The prospect actually excited me. One other time Gus tried to cheer me up but I told him don't bother. I'm not going to let my so-called disability get me down. I didn't ask to be a disabled Vietnam Vet but it's part of me now, something to play for all it's worth.

As my Letterman stay ended I was getting around so well they trusted me with a commercial flight. It took a beer in the lounge and a couple more on the plane to settle me down, from the stares, I mean. Partly the uniform, it was San Francisco after all, but the scar, raw and fierce, was what did it. Adults stared or averted their eyes and one little girl I'll never forget, she took one look, drew her breath in and clamped her hand over her eyes before diving into her mother's skirts. Did I look that horrible? Kids don't lie. I hated how I looked, I hated how I walked. By now you know I am a very private person. I don't like broadcasting myself. If somebody's interested, he or she will find out soon enough. If I like them I'll even help. But here is my face, my walk, announcing to the world – hey everybody, step right up, see the war freak, fresh off the boat. Will I be stuck with this my whole life, I wondered, ringing the call button for another beer.

CATHERINE AND STAN MET ME at the airport and after a weepy reunion and a stop in the North End for lunch, they drove me to the hospital. They were cool about my appearance, which I appreciated after a maudlin five hours in the air. Stan was a musician, a violinist in the semi-professional R.I. Philharmonic, in real life commuting to a research job in Norwood off Route 1. Catherine seemed to have a thing for scientists. They had taken a larger apartment in her building on the East Side, she was still at Classical. I liked Stan immediately – tall, skinny, with an open face and a real sense of humor. In what was left of his waking hours he was finishing a master's in math at UMass extension. Impressive. Catherine caught me up on family doings and said as soon as I was settled she was throwing a big party. I protested, but privately appreciated her thought. They saw me to my new quarters, helping me in with my one bag. This was the pattern these days, wherever I went I beat my things there. After they left I went through the intake procedure and was officially admitted to the VA Medical Center - Boston, on South Huntington Avenue.

My stay figured to be six weeks to three months, depending. The wounds were mostly healed except a couple of deep gouges on the inner thigh and calf of my good leg and these were down to a daily cleaning and dressing change. They discovered a couple of metal pieces near my heart but decided to leave those alone. The only lingering effect of the concussion, sometimes a headache would hit without warning and hang around a long time. Also, by the end of the day I was pretty fatigued.

Something I had wondered about, one of the docs set me straight. I was tremendously lucky, he said. Our body armor was skimpy, a nylon shell that left a lot of the vitals exposed. Most of the guys who got hit low didn't pull through. Great gaping wounds in the abdomen and chest did them in. And here I am, still able to gripe and complain.

The goal of this stay was to build my endurance but mostly make me comfortable with the new leg. Endless sessions in the whirlpool, massages, exercise routines several times a day, counseling for my re-entry to the real world. I spent time in the limb and brace shop where they fine-tuned Mr. Stumpy and his fit. They told me about special limbs you can get for skiing and other sports, even one with a swim fin! I was a specimen, picked over by specialists, well-meaning but often tiresome. I had also turned into a gym rat, spending long hours with the weights and on the treadmill. The pool was a great pleasure and after a couple of weeks I was up to ten laps nonstop.

A psychologist, Dr. DeSantis, came by regularly, probing for depression, anxiety, lingering effects, what came to be called Post Traumatic Stress Disorder. He claimed to find some but it wasn't the big deal he tried to make of it. Nightmares woke me occasionally. I already mentioned my reaction to sudden noises. I hadn't dived under a table yet but I could see it happening. Often my mind would drift off, chasing a thought or an image, always suffused with green. The baby we killed was with me a lot, and I often found myself putting faces to victims I never really saw. I think it helped that I was aware of what was happening to me and why. Was I tougher than others, or less sensitive? I didn't know, but at least I wasn't waking up screaming or going berserk like some did. This guy in a bed near me had it right. One day an aide forgot to secure the stopper of his piss bag and it came loose and sprayed everything with urine. He blew up, cursed the aide in language I hadn't heard in months, finally security had to be called. A doctor gave him a tongue-lashing and an injection, and as the sedative took hold the guy looked up.

"Fuck you," he said softly, this triumphant smile on his face, "fuck you all. There is nothing you can do to me that hasn't been done already."

I told Dr. DeSantis, sorry, but I am not nuts. He warned me that symptoms can appear years later. I said don't sit by the phone.

What really got me down, the terrible waste of lives. The quadruple amputees, the guy with nothing but scar for a face, others with one ear, no nose. What did they think when they looked in the mirror? Sometimes in my quiet moments a terrific anger welled up inside me and I railed against life, but all I had to do was look around. I'm ashamed to say I used those sad cases to help my own head. I can walk, I told myself, I can piss and shit without one of those ghastly bags, but mostly I thanked God my time of being shot at was over. Then I'd head for the exercise room.

The other downer was seeing the older vets, guys "warehoused" from World War Two and Korea. I was shocked that nurses talked about them like that. The oldest oldtimer had been gassed at the Marne, a bag of bones for whom every breath was a struggle. He'd been like that for fifty years. Just hanging out, these guys, nothing happening, no plan, no future. The thought of getting out terrified them. Wasted lives. That really got me down.

One thing they did for me, though. One day my favorite nurse, Kim, saw me without glasses and observed what great-looking eyes I have. "It's a shame to hide behind those glasses," she told me.

"What are you saying?"

"I'm saying give contact lenses a try. They're a lot better than they used to be, lighter, not as scratchy, you'll see a thousand times better." I had never thought about that but why not? "Your insurance'll cover them. Besides, a change will be good for you."

That day I visited the opthalmologist. My contacts arrived the next week. At first it was an ordeal putting them in and taking them out, particularly the left one, for some reason, but I got the hang of it. Kim was right, and what a change! Facing the world without those coke-bottle bottoms! I liked what I saw in the mirror, too, and it made me feel good to recognize the person in my old photos, the little kid with the huge, dark eyes.

One afternoon soon after I arrived I had a teary visit with my father who drove up with Jim and the kids. Jim took me aside and said Dad had been on edge ever since I went overseas and my injury really hit him hard. He had slowed, stopping often to regain his balance as we walked around the grounds.

"Why don't I get tickets for the Red Sox?" I said, trying to cheer him up.

"Those stairs, I don't know if I can manage them."

"If I can, you can. It'll be like old times." The sixty-nine Sox were decent but the Orioles blew everybody away, everybody but the Miracle Mets who won the first Series they ever played in. The Sox finished twenty-two out. We never made it to a game.

"Save September 14th," Jim said. "There's a big party. You can stay with us."

"Great," I said, but I didn't need more fawning, much less from a swarm of relatives.

A couple of days later I was in the weight room when a nurse came by to tell me I had a visitor. Toweling off and pulling on a sweatshirt I went out to reception. It was Pat!

"How're you doing, old man?" he said, throwing his arms around me.

"Great to see you. You finally back?"

"No way. I've found my true home. Say, you don't look so bad," he said, stepping back and giving me the once-over. "Where's your glasses?"

"Long gone. Wish I'd done it years ago."

I looked closely at my old friend. He'd always been slender but his face was rail-thin now, accentuated by a Ché Guevara-style moustache-beard and an inch-long scar over his left eye, souvenir of the Paris riots. Thinning on top, his hair was pulled back in a ponytail. His skin looked sallow, unhealthy, made me wonder if there was something wrong. "You doing all right?" I asked. "Not sick or anything."

"Nah, I'm okay. Haven't been sleeping well recently, that's all."

He put his hand to my face and felt my scar. "I thought mine was good but yours puts me to shame. Much more gallant."

"If you say so. How're your studies?"

"Less than a year to go on my dissertation."

"What's it on again?"

"Avant-garde Paris in the early part of the century. I'm focusing on Satie."

"Who?"

"Erik Satie, the composer – very big at the time. He influenced Debussy, Ravel, a bunch of others. His circle was the precursor for the Dadaists and Surrealists but you almost have to be a specialist to know him these days."

"Your degree's in Art. How do you qualify for music?"

Pat grinned. "What I don't know I can fake. Anyway I'm studying the confluence of music, art and literature. It was an amazing time, everybody knew everybody, everybody collaborated. Picabia was a friend, Braque, Cocteau, Apollinaire. Diaghilev's ballet *Parade,* Satie wrote the music, Cocteau did the libretto, Picasso designed the sets."

"But why this period, these people?"

"Their spirit of play, that's one of my themes. Somebody said Satie wrote music a one-year-old could enjoy, simple, childlike, full of jokes. Rousseau was another so-called primitive. Remember my tiger staring out of the jungle?"

"Of course. He woke me up every morning."

"They made fun of everything but they knew exactly what they were doing."

"Sounds like you."

"And they hung out in Montmartre. Incidentally they were nuts, most of them."

"There you go."

"Back then everybody was nuts. Consider that the War to End All Wars happened on their watch. Will you go back to Berkeley?"

"No more academia but I have a plan. Let's go outside, get some air."

We sauntered around the grounds. "Let's see, we can rule out Olympic sprinter."

"You still have a way with words."

"Sorry, I had to take my shot. I know! The law!" He looked at me and shook his head, "no, not the law." He snapped his fingers. "Pulitzer Prize-winning reporter!"

"Aw shit! How'd you guess?"

"It makes sense," he said, brightening.

"I'm getting up my courage to make some calls."

"When should I look for your byline in the *Times?* Six months? A year?"

"Give it two," I laughed.

We sat down on a bench under a large tree. The shade felt good, it was a hot day. He looked at me carefully. "I bring greetings from my esteemed sister. She says hello and hopes you are on the mend."

I forced a smile. "She does well, I trust."

"As far as anybody can tell. She's finishing her residency. She and Clyde are living in Jamaica Plain. You're practically neighbors."

"Don't expect me to pay a visit. She really screwed me up... I was so pissed."

"What do you mean?"

"What do you mean? You don't know?"

"Know what?"

"She and I... after she broke her engagement off we, well, we were getting it on. All phone and letter, of course, but still..."

He shook his head. "Leave it to her..."

"I don't follow you."

"They never broke anything off. They had a big fight but they patched it up."

I could feel my face getting red. "Now I'm really confused."

"Join the club," Pat said. "She comes across so solid and dependable but dear twin is one of the most fickle people you'll ever meet. I mean, she liked you a lot, but you and her an item? No way. Anyway, you've got too much sense to get involved with our Meghan."

I was silent a moment. "This comes as a shock..."

"Don't let it. You have better things to do with your life."

We talked a while longer then I steered him back to the cafeteria where I bought us coffees. "How long're you going to be here?" I asked

"I fly back tomorrow." He was quiet a moment. "I just found out you were here and had to drop in. When you get on your feet you'll have to come by to see us."

"I'd like to... what's this us business?"

He looked at me smiled. "I have a friend I'm serious about."

"What's her name?"

"Michel."

"Michelle. What's she look like?"

He shook his head. "Michel. He's an artist, a terrific talent, not a pretender like me. We've known each other a couple of years. I moved in with him beginning of the summer."

"Unbelievable. You son of a gun, I would never have guessed."

"Well, that was no accident, I mean keeping it quiet. There were signs, you must have missed them."

"What about your parents?"

"I haven't told them. Michel was here for a visit – let me put it this way. Paterfamilias suspects. He was barely civil. As usual Mother is clueless, but *Grand-maman,* now there's a real woman! She loves Michel, said she'll work on the parents when the time's right."

"Amazing," I said. "Will wonders never cease."

"The day they do will be a sad day. Come to Paris, we'll paint the town red."

"How about pink? Wouldn't that be more like it?"

"Pink indeed! That's the spirit! Incidentally, *grand-maman* wants to see you."

"I will when I can."

After Pat left it took me a while to collect myself. I knew I had some blind spots, but this! And Meg! The letters, the calls, that picture... she was using me! What an idiot! How could I be so far off? Forget her, I told myself. Pat had it right, I have better things to do.

BEFORE THE PARTY I VISITED Tante Héloise. She didn't recognize me but I tried to cheer her up anyway. My dad gave me a ride and explained his car's hand controls. We took a tour past the old house, he said let's stop and get out, but I said just slow down. I didn't want to run into Omer's mother. I needed to visit her but not yet. As we drove by, a splash of white and purple along the fence caught my eye... hollyhocks! Of course! I grew up abusing hollyhocks, listening to the sound they made when I popped the buds. Recalling the loving attentions Akiko's father paid them, I felt ashamed.

I asked my father to invite Dave LaPointe to the party. He had just retired from the *Journal-Bulletin* and was eager to talk about the trade. It doesn't pay much at the start, he said, and it doesn't pay much later, either. That didn't worry me, though. I'd be cashing Uncle Sam's check every month the rest of my life, and I still had that Nu-Gem stock I didn't know what to do with. The other downside was the long hours, Dave said, but seeing your work in print is worth it, in his case, a picture that smacked people across the face. He'd be happy to put me in touch. When I told him I was more interested in Boston, he said he knew people up there too.

As to Jim, our role reversal was complete. With his sedentary lifestyle he had put on a weight, though he was doing well otherwise – partner in a plumbing business, a nice family. These days I was the hero. Kind of wistful, he kept trying to draw me out.

"What's it like, people shooting at you and all?"

"It gets your attention in a hurry."

"What they say about the VC using women and children for cover, is that for real?"

I closed my eyes. "Let's leave that one alone."

"Sorry... maybe after you've been back longer."

"I don't think so."

As I became stronger my time at the hospital grew short and I realized I'd better find somewhere to live. I had always liked Beacon Hill and discovered a furnished one-bedroom could be had for fourteen hundred a month, a townhouse on Mt. Vernon just above Charles. No handicap amenities, but I was learning to get along without them. Snow, stone steps and brick sidewalks would be a challenge but I told myself, go for it. I wondered if the neighborhood would remind me too much of Meg, but my answer was the hell with that – here is where I want to live. I signed a year's lease, put down deposits and called Gus with my new address. I offered to pay the freight on my things but he wouldn't hear of it.

My other call was to Father Ronan. My news hadn't reached Worcester and it hit him hard. He offered to come to Boston but I said I'm working at acting normal. I already had a special Mass. driver's license, passing the road test in a specially-equipped car a local dealership makes available to the VA. A couple of days before my trip Dad volunteered the Caddy and checked me out on the controls. Over lunch, at the Biltmore, of course, memories of our last parting flooded back. Much had happened since.

Walking up Mt. Saint James was a real workout. I arrived at Beaven somewhat fatigued and found a bench to rest and collect myself. Fall semester was well along, crowds of young men looking more like high schoolers crossing the campus. A few of them stared at me as I walked along stiffly, in civvies, of course, but with hair shorter than the norm. Third floor, same door, a welcome fixed point in my uncertain universe. The door was ajar and I knocked and looked in. "Father Ronan?"

He took a long look and put his hands on my shoulders. "You've come home," he said, his eyes moist, "thank God." He ushered me into his tiny office. I saw him glance away as I maneuvered myself and my leg into the deep soft chair. "We've lost several graduates," he said, shaking his head. "You remember Phil Grady."

I nodded. He was on the basketball varsity, a year ahead. I didn't know him well.

"Shot down. Ah, well," he sighed. "Coffee?"

"Only if it's instant," I said, trying to break the mood.

"That is on the menu," he smiled. "Now, last time you were here..."

"Christmas 'sixty-seven."

"Yes. You were just deciding between your degree program and the service."

"Did I ever decide." I pointed to my leg. "If you'd like proof."

"I'll take your word for it. You're getting around well, your spirits seem high."

"Compared with a lot of guys I have it easy."

He set two mugs on the table, swiveling his desk chair around. "Well," he said, raising his mug, "cheers! And welcome back."

I raised mine in reply.

"I understand the medical profession has made tremendous strides. They routinely save men who not long ago would have died."

I pointed to myself. "You're looking at Exhibit One. They got me to a field hospital within the hour, two weeks later I wake up in Japan."

"Too bad our genius doesn't extend to avoiding this sort of thing in the first place."

"You'd be talking about something better than human beings."

"Perhaps you could find room for this issue in your Ph.D. dissertation."

I shook my head. "Sorry. No dissertation. No Ph.D."

Father Ronan looked surprised. "I'm disappointed. You were on to something important. Government and citizen in times of crisis. Very topical, in fact all too topical."

"That's what I want to talk with you about. I've decided to try my hand at newspaper work. I wondered whether you might open some doors for me."

He put his cup down. "Interesting, very interesting. You're certainly qualified for it. You recall I was on the *Globe* a couple of years before I got in this line of work..." He waved his hand around the room – the familiar texts, the crucifix on the wall. In fact my old friend Charlie Atwood is Managing Editor, we began as reporters the same day. We did well, in our different ways," he smiled. "I'll give Charlie a call."

"That'd be great."

"I don't know anyone on the *Herald* these days. You're limiting yourself to Boston?"

"I'd better be, I've just taken an apartment there. How long were you on the *Globe*?"

"A year and a half. I liked it fine, but I found there was a better direction for me."

"And so here you are."

"And so here I am. How about New York? Would New York interest you?"

"I don't know, I've moved around so much. Though if something really good came up... In fact, in Vietnam I developed a contact at the *Gazette*..." I related the story of my dinner. He knew of Edwin Reynolds though not Gillespie. "I should get in touch with Ed."

"God works in mysterious ways. Offhand I can't think of anything in New York but I'll poke around. How does one reach you these days?"

I gave him my new address. "I'm still at the VA but they'll get a message to me."

"And how is our mutual friend? Are you still in touch?"

"In touch?" I laughed. "He and his wife came to Japan to see me. Her family lives there but still, that was a big deal for them."

"I'm not surprised. Beneath that rough exterior there's..."

"A rough interior."

"Well said," he laughed.

"He was disappointed I'm not going back to Cal. We saw each other in San Francisco, gave us a chance to renew our argument about the war."

"Remind me."

"He's always been opposed. My position, well, you know what it was or I wouldn't have been over there. I've been thinking about this a lot – the difference between Gus and me comes down to trust. When our government said the country was in danger he didn't believe them. I was willing to give them the benefit of the doubt."

"How do you feel about that now?"

I tapped my leg. "This won't change my position but seeing so many guys hurt and maimed or psycho or dead puts a heavy weight on his side of the scale."

"And if you remove credibility, not much left on the other side." The priest leaned forward. "We talked about this before. As I recall you weren't satisfied with our discussion."

"You recall correctly."

"My point wasn't just about the need for the war, but the alarming lack of candor about what it would take to prevail. What I found most disturbing, we went in there with no good plan, yet the leaders and the generals still won't admit that."

"They can't," I responded. "We look to them to get it right. How can they admit they were just making it up as they went along?"

"It sounds like your views have changed."

"In some ways. But I had to see for myself, didn't I?" I shook my head. "What I found, just like you said, it all came down to body count. Our job was to kill so many VC they'd eventually run out. We counted bodies going out, we counted the same ones coming back – women, kids, animals, whatever it took to satisfy the brass. Some of us wanted to make a difference – that's why I went there, for God's sake – but did we get inside those people's heads? Did we change anybody's minds? Not at all. We even turned our friends against us. Whenever we'd do something right, something'd happen to mess it up. An airstrike in the wrong place, a ville torched, more corpses, more body parts..."

"That was my fear, that killing would envelop the goal, make them one and the same."

"You mentioned credibility. For me that's what it came down to. Telling the truth would have been so much better. Tell the truth and let the chips fall."

The priest sat back. "You know, Paul, there's another aspect to this. Whenever man uncorks the war bottle he creates an unmanageable situation – guaranteed unmanageable. The genie takes over. Errors are inevitable, and as you say, they so often lead to disaster."

"It's so crazy, Father, you have no idea. In the end it was all about surviving. Stay alive and get out. Nothing else mattered. Why we were there? Totally beside the point. And it's not just mistakes, the killing itself does it, and the training for the killing. That mindset – good little robots, human sensibilities gone, the reluctance to kill gone. Brutality, it's like a wildfire spreading from one person to another. I saw that happen, and more than once too." I thought of Gibbs and Stoner executing those prisoners. "Sometimes you'd find yourself laughing for no good reason, no reason at all."

"Trying to hang onto that shred of human sympathy must take its toll. After all, for the civilized man, killing his own kind is most unnatural. You mentioned laughter. Another way to cope with it is to abuse the language. The euphemism of war, some call it. Body count. Friendly fire."

"'We had to destroy the village to save it.' How about that one?" The last of my coffee drained, I put my mug down, hard. "Sorry," I said, startling myself with the noise, "that one got away from me. You know, what I have to live with – I wasn't forced to go. It was my decision. I had to see for myself."

"You followed your conscience, your immature conscience. The Lord won't fault you for that, but heaven help those who intentionally deceived so many. Such unnecessary suffering, and for all Nixon's platitudes it's far from over. Those who bring their psychic wounds home, for those damaged souls it will never be over."

I thought of letting him know about the nightmares, the cold sweats... but I didn't. We fell silent a long time. "Did you ever know a Father Trần?" I finally asked, "he was here about my time."

"The Vietnamese priest? I've often wondered what happened to him."

"He's at a parish in Saigon, teaches science in the local high school. I looked him up when I was there. He's very down on the U.S., thinks we didn't give it our best shot. Basically thinks we used Vietnam as a pawn in the Big Power game. Or a domino."

"There's something to that. Vietnam was always a hard sell, why we were there, what we meant to accomplish. As I see it, when you're in the realm of morals, and war is the moral issue *par excellence,* complexity is a warning flag. When a person strays from simplicity he is asking for trouble. Same for a nation. I'm not saying take the easy way out. I mean give us an explanation it doesn't take a genius to understand. The more facts and figures and arguments you have to pile on, something is wrong."

"I don't follow you."

"Take this war, take any war. What's the moral principle? Thou Shalt Not Kill, of course. If somebody is beating you over the head or trying to rape your sister, obviously you react. But the more convoluted your justification, the more complex your motives, that is a sign you may be going down the wrong road. God must love ordinary people, Paul, he made so many of them. Not everyone is intellectual or learned, but everyone is expected to do the right thing. The multitudes must be capable of figuring out what that is. God does not impose moral burdens without giving the means to bear them."

"Is there still such a thing as just war?" I asked.

Father Ronan thought a moment. "I want to say yes. Clearly, self-defense can be justified, but modern weapons are so powerful, so indiscriminate, the means overwhelm what would otherwise be legitimate goals. What we were saying about killing, a small, weak country may have more latitude when it comes to warmaking than a Great Power – a Mouse that Roared syndrome, if you will. Though I'm not happy with that answer either."

"I take it you're no fan of Cardinal Spellman."

Father Ronan rolled his eyes. "The classic fearmonger. He did our country a great disservice, our Church too. Those anti-Communist crusades of his were so convenient, so self-serving. We have to have confidence in our fellow Americans, our fellow Christians. If a churchman refuses to inspire that confidence, who will?"

"His rationalizations were too complicated."

"Exactly."

"Where is the Holy Spirit when we need him?"

Father Ronan nodded. "One might hope for a bit more visibility."

"The Bishops haven't been much help."

"They're getting there, but I agree, it is maddeningly slow."

"I hope some day I'll be in a position to do something about such things, say something at least. That's partly why I'm thinking about newspaper work."

"I'm sure you will. And considering what you've been through, people will listen. Your special burden will be to justify that trust." Father Ronan smiled. "So, what news of friend Padraic? Have you heard from him?"

"Funny you should ask, I saw him just a few days ago. He came by the hospital on his way back to Paris."

"He's still over there, then."

"It looks permanent. He's almost finished his degree, in fact, concentrating on the Dada movement, whatever that is. He's totally wrapped up in it."

"A rather eccentric group of people, as I recall, always railing against something." Father Ronan shook his head. "For friends, you and Pat couldn't be less alike."

You don't know the half of it, I thought to myself. "How do you mean?"

"Well, there he is, in one of the world's most exciting cities, living the good life, following an enjoyable career path. Don't get me wrong, art is a gift from God – it's how he gets there. He appears content to avoid the serious issues while you, on the other hand you've experienced total immersion and here you are about to do it again. If I had to put labels on the two of you," he went on, "yours would read, serious, public-minded. Would it be unfair to label Pat frivolous? The Dadas, for God's sake! Some say they had a point, they were condemning those who led us into the First War, but look how they went about it! Acting crazy, having themselves a roaring good time, just as I suspect Pat is doing. Talk about having your cake and eating it too!"

"From time to time I would like a little cake," I said, fielding a wave of self-pity. "I've been such a damned straight arrow my whole life it's depressing."

Father Ronan put his head back and laughed. "Cheer up! I'm sure you'll have your share. What I'm saying, your focus will be on important things. More truth and justice than beauty, if I can put it that way. Am I wrong?"

"I probably won't be spending much time in museums, if that's what you mean."

We talked a while longer. Father Ronan looked at his watch and reached for his clerical collar. "Fifteen minutes to senior Ethics. Thank you for the pre-game warmup."

We left it that he'd let me know what his efforts turned up. I'd keep him posted as well. "And stand by to write some letters," I added, my hand on the door.

"For you, my recommendation comes with a clear conscience."

ON THE WAY BACK I decided to take care of something that had been on my mind. I glanced at the car clock. Plenty of time. Heading down Route 146, at North Providence I cut down Fruit Hill Avenue, down Manton Avenue, a quick backtrack to see how my old house was faring. Not well. Trees gone, junker car on blocks in the driveway. Past St. Teresa's... Spanish signs around, Puerto Ricans, Mexicans moving in, I'd heard, corner stores, *bodegas*. A couple in Vietnamese too, and why not? Hopefully they'll honor the neighborhood like we new arrivals once did. My father's old buildings seemed in good repair, big NU-GEM sign silhouetted against the sky. As I approached Olneyville I felt anxious that where I was going wouldn't be there anymore but... there it is! I pulled up in front of QUALITY RADIO SALES AND SERVICE – ALL WORK GUARANTEED. No broken radios, no parts strewn around, no insect corpses, the front window was filled with shiny new twenty-seven inch RCAs and Sylvanias. As I opened the door a familiar chime sounded and a young man looked up from a repair. "I'd like to see Mister Lemieux. Is he still around these days?"

He nodded. "You're in luck – half an hour you would have missed him."

"Tell him Paul Bernard's here. Julien's son."

A moment later, Mr. Lemieux appeared from the back room, wiping his hands on a towel. He looked much the same, after what, it had to be twenty years. Slightly stooped, his face more creased, but it was him all right.

"Paul! Ça va, mon jeune ami!" He stuck his left hand out and I grasped it. *"Mon dieu,* aren't you the spitting image of your Dad! And how is the old goat? He don't come around much these days. Tell him I'm not speaking to him any more."

"He's well. Recovering from a stroke, you probably heard."

"Yes, I saw him after that. So! This is a grand occasion! Let me offer you something. Come on back," he said, motioning me into the historic back room. It also was clean and tidy, new televisions on shelves, but it pleased me to sense that things were still not totally under control. Mr. Lemieux motioned me toward a folding chair and I took a seat as he rummaged through a cabinet, pulling out a bottle and two shot glasses. "Never too early for hospitality, that's what I say."

I found myself fixating on his right arm and hand. He had traded in the old hook for a modern prosthesis. Realistic. Very impressive.

He noticed my stare. "Wonderful what they do these days, isn't it." He reached down to pick up one of the glasses, fitting his fingers around the rim and setting it on a small table. The bottle stuck under his arm, with his good hand he unscrewed the cap and deftly poured a shot for me and one for himself.

"Bienvenue, Paul! Santé!"

"Santé!"

"À nôtre ami Julien. À son santé!"

I tilted my head back and downed the shot. The whiskey roared down my throat. I hadn't done this for a long time.

"Excéllent!" He wiped his lips with his sleeve. "Let's see if we can't improve on that." He poured two more, we touched glasses and another inch of amber fire disappeared. I was thinking about how to raise the subject but all of a sudden he beat me to it. "I read about you in the papers," he said. "I called your dad and he told me it was touch and go for a while, but it looks like you're managing well. I'm happy to see that."

I bent over and pulled up my pants leg. "Have a look."

He inspected Mr. Stumpy, the steel rod. I pulled the pants leg higher... the attachment, the straps, the pads, the whole deal. "Mind if I see what it feels like?"

"Be my guest."

He touched the shiny metal, gave it a light rap with his knuckles. "Amazing. Just amazing. I bet you walk fast."

"I can run too, though it's kind of hard on the stump."

He nodded, then unbuttoned his shirt and slid it off his right shoulder. Stump, same as mine though it looked like polished wood compared to my pink butt end.

"When I was little I wondered what was in there but was afraid to ask."

He smiled and nodded. "You kids were all alike – nobody had the guts to ask. You've learned the hard way, sorry to say, but there's no mystery, is there." He pulled his shirt back on. "The only mystery is why we keep doing these things to ourselves." I lit a cigarette, offered him one but he shook his head, sliding an ash tray over.

"I've had a lot of time to think," I said. "I understand we men fight. What I don't understand is why we keep getting ourselves into situations where we have to fight."

"Come again."

"I enlisted. I did it because I thought our country was in trouble, needed to take a stand. But how did we get maneuvered into that position in the first place?"

"I was no hero," Mr. Lemieux said evenly, "I got drafted. So I end up leaving part of me over there. I figured if that's the price for keeping my country out of Hitler's hands, so be it. The Japs too, though I had nothing to do with them. I have never been happy about this," he said, gesturing with his arm, "but I'm at peace. I feel like what I did was worthwhile even though I had no choice. Can you understand that?"

I pulled my pants leg over Mr. Stumpy. "I envy you, Mr. Lemieux."

"How's that?"

"I'm not sure what I did was necessary. Or useful. Or even right."

"Don't second-guess yourself. It'll drive you nuts."

"What I'm saying, I'm not sure I bought us anything worthwhile. A lot of guys, they gave everything."

"What I said, that didn't come to me right away." Mr. Lemieux refilled the glasses. "For a long time I wished I'd left the rest of me there, but my family was here and my friends, your father's always been great to me, I finally come around. It'll happen for you. Just wait. It'll happen for you."

My father was already asleep when I dropped the car off. Just as well. I had a hard day... and a whiskey headache.

HOPING FOR THE BEST, I sent my letters. The *Globe* and *Herald American* I coveted. I wrote to the *Journal-Bulletin* without enthusiasm. The paper would have been fine, but I didn't want to go back to Providence. I dug out Ed Reynolds' card and wrote him care of the *Gazette* in New York, hoping he would get it soon enough to do me some good. Oh, I also spent a stamp on the *Times* too, though without expectations. In each case I referred to my injury and impending discharge, assuring them I was fully functional and ready to go.

As I waited for the replies, first week in October I was formally discharged from the hospital and the Army, same day. Honorable, for medical conditions. The staff had a little party for me in the ward, as much to encourage the other guys as bid me farewell. I hadn't gotten to know any of them well but was happy to be made an example.

Strictly speaking, you don't need a car to get around Boston, but I envisioned trips to the White Mountains, New York and points beyond, so my Dad and I went shopping. He steered me to the Pawtucket dealership where he got his Caddy. I settled for something less imposing, a two-year-old blue Beetle outfitted with hand controls that would set me back fifteen hundred over three years. That is, if my father hadn't been there to push a check at the salesman. "Gas and oil, upkeep, insurance, those're on you," he said, "but I'm not going to let you start in the hole." I resisted, but not much. As I said, my attitude had changed. If others wanted to lend a hand, I was not about to turn it down.

The replies dribbled in. The *Herald* had nothing, though stay in touch and by the way, good luck. The *Journal-Bulletin* gave me an interview and I decided to go through with it for practice. If they made an offer and I had nothing better going I could always commute. Then the *Globe* surfaced. My first interview was with a personnel lady in their new Dorchester complex. I left a folder of my articles, columns and photos. Two days later I had a meeting with an Assistant Editor. He took me to lunch at their cafeteria and offered me a starting reporter job, subject to my references checking out.

On the phone to my father I could hardly contain my excitement. Seven thousand a year! And my number one choice! That night I bought a bottle of wine to celebrate and invited the girls from the second floor for Chinese takeout. Only problem, I hadn't heard from Ed Reynolds, and the *Globe* was expecting an answer. The following morning as I was heading out the door my phone rang. "Paul Bernard, please."

"Speaking."

"Paul, Ed Reynolds here."

"Mr. Reynolds!" I practically shouted into the phone.

"The very same. Sounds like you've had some adventures since we met."

I pulled the phone over. "That is true. This is a good connection. Where are you?"

"Apple City USA. They pull us in every few months to read us the riot act. So, I understand you're interested in our esteemed rag. Could you be here day after tomorrow? I'd like to see you before I head out, have you meet some colleagues. How would noon be?"

I decided to take the train, which gave me time to ask myself, why am I running off to New York? I like Boston, I have a great offer, a nice place with a year's lease. Is this another case of be careful what you wish for?

The Gazette Building was a blocky eight-story structure with a mustard-colored brick facade, a stone-sculpted The New York Gazette positioned on a pedestal at the front entrance, a torch with a powerful electric lamp at each end and massive concrete urns astride the front steps. The north side of the building was bordered by a broad alley filled with delivery trucks and beyond it, a parking lot. On the other side, a towering apartment building with a street-level grocery, fruit and vegetable displays in front. On the way I had detoured to West 43rd Street to eyeball the *Times*. I had pretty much given up on them, though if I had a chance later I might drop by and try to embarrass somebody into talking with me.

At the fifth floor the receptionist led me through a large, noisy room filled with people bent over desks, typing, reading, talking on phones. Somebody bellowed over a PA system and I watched two people about my age – reporters, I figured – leap to their feet and disappear into an office on the far wall. Reynolds was on the phone, his chair tipped back at a risky angle, feet on his desk, glasses over his forehead, a cigarette dangling from his mouth. He waved me at a chair beside his desk.

"Yeah, yeah, that's so dumb... the oldest excuse in the book. No, no, talk to Prentiss, he's the only one has a clue." Reynolds rolled his eyes at me. "Twelve's too late, you know I gotta have it by ten. Right. Call me back. Bye." He hung up, shaking his head. "Hard to get good help these days." I stood and shook his hand as he swung his desk forward. "Well, how's it feel to be a free man?" he asked, dragging on his cigarette and motioning me to sit.

"Damn good," I said. "You mind?" I pulled the pack of Marlboros from my jacket pocket. My best suit, gray with a thin stripe. I'd salvaged it by having the pant leg widened so I could pull it on over Mr. Stumpy. A white shirt and maroon striped tie completed my presentation.

"A Zippo, the real deal."

I broke the lighter open and lit up, snapping it shut with a satisfying clack. "Souvenir of the ball game," I said. "Goes with my other one."

"Sorry about that. Not the sort of thing you wish for."

I nodded. "You know the odds but you never figure it'll happen to you."

"You get around okay on that thing?"

"Oh sure, haven't lost a step."

"I was just on the phone with Saigon. It's..." he looked at his watch, "it's the middle of the night there now but a deadline's a deadline."

"I heard the *Gazette* was once an afternoon paper."

"Around the turn of the century. They were going head to head with the *Times* and the *Trib* and losing, so they changed. Everybody hated it, even the publisher thought it made them a second-class citizen so a few years later they switched back."

"How much time do you spend in New York?"

"Enough to make me happy to leave. Sometimes this place makes Vietnam look good." He stubbed out his cigarette. "Let's talk about you. What do you have for me?"

I reached for my briefcase, a gift from my father upon graduating from college, drawing out two manila folders, handing them over. He started right in.

"Not bad... not bad at all. I like the JFK interview, how'd you ever get that? These your photos too?"

"I've done a lot of photography though not much recently."

"It's good eye training. If you can translate it into words you're halfway home... well, what do you know!"

"Which one's that?" I asked.

"'Little Rock - A Personal Opinion.' I was there too. One of my first assignments."

"What a way to break in. I caught flak for that column."

"That makes two of us." He read the rest, then lit another cigarette. "Be better if you had more but you've been busy recently."

"I could send you some of my academic stuff – seminar papers, that kind of thing."

"Nah, no need. Your resumé said you were working on a doctorate in, what..."

"Political Science. At Berkeley."

"That must have been a trip. You plan on finishing?"

"No. But I figure it won't be wasted, the insights and so on."

He laughed. "What we'll have you doing here, you won't need insights. Years ago some managing editor decided reporters need to break in on the police beat. He figured all news is crime news, one way or the other. Nobody's ever changed the policy."

"Guess I'll put my insights in reserve."

"That's the ticket." He closed the folder. "Okay, this looks fine. I'll pass it on. Sid Greenwald, he's the City Editor, in fact..." he picked up the phone, "...if he's free I'll pass you on to him. He's way the hell over there," he said, nodding at the opposite corner of the newsroom. Give this to him," he handed me the folder. "Sid has the last word on new-hires. I need to spend time on that thing I was on the phone about, if it ever shows up that is. Doing a piece about PXs and the black market, you saw some of that, no doubt. Come back at two, we'll grab a sandwich. When can you start?"

My heart leapt, then it sank. I thought of my complex, hard-earned Boston web. "How about tomorrow," I laughed. I figured I should tell him something about the *Globe*. "One more thing, there's an offer on the table I need to deal with."

"Whatever it is, believe me there is no comparison," he said seriously, "none at all. You will not regret coming here. And don't worry about finding a place. When properly motivated our personnel people are moderately helpful."

I spent an hour with Sid Greenwald. Greenwald was middle-aged, overweight, with a large, fleshy face. He looked flabby and soft, but by reputation was anything but. A Bronx native, he had headed the Metro desk for twenty years and also had the job of monitoring pool reporters – new hires before they're assigned to foreign, business, sports, and old-timers who never stuck anywhere. Even in this first meeting he complained about his management duties, though not too seriously. He spoke with affection of the *Gazette's* heritage, told me it's the best place in the world for a young reporter. "You get to handle big stories right away – well, as soon as we know you can be trusted." I'd hear from him in a few days.

Ed escorted me down the elevator and to the market next door, Gristede's, "an old New York chain. The food's almost edible. Forget the dog food upstairs," he said, referring to the *Gazette's* second floor cafeteria. "Not for nothing do we call it The Last Resort."

I had a pastrami on rye, he ordered something called a knish he said you couldn't get in Vietnam so he was making up for lost time, then it was back to his desk. As the late afternoon came on the pace picked up and I watched it build toward the evening deadline, the PA blaring out names and orders, reporters streaking to hassles with copy editors. "You need to see this. It's a fucking miracle we ever put out a paper but we do it, day after day."

"It is amazing."

"What's amazing, every day you start from scratch." He waved his hand around the room. When I'm in the field I really miss this. In my less lucid moments I even enjoy it when I'm here."

Back in Boston the clock was ticking on the *Globe's* offer as I waited nervously for the *Gazette*. I spent time at the Boston Y I had just joined, causing a sensation when I took off my leg and stowed it in my locker, Mr. Stumpy and I hopping to the pool.

A week to the day from my visit, I got a call from Sid offering me the job. "Sixty-five hundred to start. Six months, you're in line for an increase if you work out. Letter's in the mail, keep one copy, sign the other and send it back. As far as where to live, get hold of Frankie" – Frances Nagy, the personnel lady I had spoken with – "she'll give you some leads."

To Sid my acceptance was a given. To me it wasn't that simple, but long story short, I accepted. Less money to start, in what everybody said was a much more expensive city, abandoning familiar surroundings, going somewhere I knew next to nothing about and had few friends, a job probation which if I messed up would leave me high and dry, turning down an offer to die for, cancelling out on a terrific apartment, losing my deposits and moving at my own expense. Again I was going for it. Berkeley, Vietnam, New York. Exciting, yes. Crazy? Absolutely.

Thus it was, mid-afternoon on the Saturday three weeks hence, Beetle and I wheeled down the Henry Hudson Parkway and through the maze of the West Village to my new home, a studio half the size and twice the rent of Boston. When I told Frankie about Beacon Hill, she steered me to an agent in this leafy brownstone and brick neighborhood. Only thing missing was a hill. A guy reading a book on the steps next door saw me struggling with my cartons and offered a hand. That cost a sixpack from the corner store, but well worth it. My new neighbor, Arnie, observed I must live under a lucky star, finding a parking space right in front of my place when I needed it the most.

"And a friendly neighbor," I added.

"There's more of that than people give us credit for."

And so, a second heroic move behind me and with great uncertainty ahead, but too dumb or too green to be properly terrified, my lucky star and I stretched out on my new bed, second one in less than a month, and promptly fell asleep.

PART FOUR

STRIVINGS

39. BREAKING IN

ABOUT NOON JONATHAN BURSTS INTO THE ROOM. "I'm back on the investigation! And the magazine's getting me credentialed!"

I am not thrilled. "You know it won't be easy over there."

"It's not like I'd be starting from scratch. They'll make their contacts available, I just have to figure out how to get there. They're not interested in paying for a trip, they think I can cover it as well from here. Well, there's always ETVN. I met with them last night."

"Have you told your editor about ETVN?"

"I'll tell them eventually. My lawyer says I'm on solid ground. They have print rights but not television."

"In the interest of good relationships wouldn't it be better to tell them now?"

Jonathan wags his finger at me. "Did they give a rat's ass about relationships? They want the story, everything revolves around that."

"It makes me nervous your going off by yourself like this, and don't stick your finger in my face. That's not good for *our* relationship."

"Sorry," he says. "It's been hard keeping it all together. I apologize."

"Accepted. Now let's get back to work."

"Incidentally," he added, "my ETVN contact told me something interesting. Nita Garrison from the Martinez memo – Anita – she is indeed Len Garrison's daughter. Twenty-seven years old, a Wellesley grad. She was a researcher at AEI then quit to work on W's campaign. Next a job in Commerce, congressional liaison."

"Then Iraq."

He nodded. "One of the first people they sent there. She's on Bremer's staff, a big job working with the contractors."

"How's her Arabic?" I ask, preparing to snicker.

"Believe it or not she's fluent."

"How about that. But what does all this do for us?"

"ETVN gave me a list of Iraqis she works with. Abdullah al-Safar is on it."

"Why do I know that name?"

"He's in Martinez's memo. He's an interpreter for Atlas, the security contractor for that area. ETVN's working on an expose on the contractors, how the administration gives their cronies work the military's always done, but they don't know about his uncle, much less his involvement in the attack. I really need to get hold of Bernie, take it the next step."

"What next step? What are you saying?"

"I'm saying Nina Garrison is a spear carrier for the Bushies, a trusted member of the fraternity, the inner circle."

"So?"

"Let me spell it out. Paul Bernard was on their enemies list, right at the top. Two, people like them stop at nothing if they feel threatened which they did. Three. We're going to connect them up with the bandits that killed Paul. What does that make Four?"

"It makes us part company." I shake my head. "It's a pipe dream, Jonathan, face it."

"What if we find evidence?"

"What? Cash receipts? Taped confessions in Arabic? Come on, you're watching too many crime shows."

He leans over the table. "This is big, Gus! Really big!"

"Sit down," I say. He sits. "My friend, I wasn't born yesterday. Of course nothing's beyond the powers-that-be. That's how they get there in the first place." I notice I am wagging my finger at him. "If you're going to play this game, you need more a lot more horsepower than we have. And while you're at it, how about hiring us a food taster?"

* * * * * * *

I FELT DIZZY, HAD TO STOP. Deep breaths, I told myself. Focus. I let my eye follow the trail of blood from the candy rack past the glass case back to the cash register. The till was open, a few bills on the counter, some scattered around the shopkeeper's body on the floor. He had been shot once in the chest, once in the neck.

The cop's badge said O'Malley, NYPD, Fifth Precinct. His partner, a burly Chinese, was Officer Yoo. A young paramedic knelt in the tight space, open cigarette cartons dangling from the shelves above him. "He's gone."

I shut my eyes, then opened them. The stocky, grey-haired Korean woman had her hands to her mouth. Her sob rose to a wail, an all-too-familiar keening. The younger woman put her arms around her, speaking softly. Sophie Park, a daughter, I would learn, her eyes were filled with tears. I looked up from my notebook. Red and blue lights of the ambulance and police cruisers bounced about the interior of the little neighborhood market. My partner, veteran *Gazette* photographer Lennie Markoff, was clicking away.

O'Malley shook his head. "For a few bucks some asshole takes it upon himself to smoke a guy. Another night on the Lower East Side, another family ruined." A radio crackled to life. The cop put it to his mouth. "O'Malley."

"Al here. We've apprehended a Puerto Rican dude. Bloodstains on his pants, a bunch of bills in his pocket. 153 East Third. No weapon but we'll find one."

"Piece of cake, all's you got's four blocks to look." Looking at the older woman he spoke to Yoo. "We better take her down to ID the bastard. Where the hell are our guys?" He took off his hat and wiped his face with a handkerchief.

Just then the investigators showed up. After a fast briefing O'Malley let out a long breath. He reached for his wallet and pulled out a card. "Listen," he said, turning to me, "you'll be using our names so you want to get them right. I wrote out Officer Yoo, Raymond Yoo. The arresting officer is Officer Alfredo Gonsalves, that's G-O-N-S-A-L-V-E-S. You'll want to talk to him, too."

"Thanks," I said, taking the card. I wondered how many rookie reporters he'd trained.

I had started my first night as a reporter holed up in the Cave, a basement apartment in a decrepit building on The Bowery and East Third owned by the *Gazette*. Other papers shared a similar facility, the Shack, behind Police Headquarters, but the Cave was our own. Same uptown, a Shack on East 51st Street, a Cave two blocks over. Other reporters swapped information about the crime or fire *du jour* before filing so nobody screwed up, missed some important fact or got it wrong, but not us. We were on our own. That first night we were hanging around monitoring the scanner, Lennie and I and some other recent hires, when about eight-thirty something broke. Marty Rossi, my Assistant City Editor had me up first so Lennie and I piled into his Falcon and raced to the scene.

My first assignment... I must have forgotten something. I got the interior and exterior cold, the neighborhood, names, ages, descriptions, detail about the killer extracted between Mrs. Park's sobs, that was no fun, I'll tell you, more from an eyewitness who'd come in for a quart of milk. The arrest I would mention, tomorrow's arraignment, the D.A.'s details when he put them out. Who, what, when, where, why, how. Check. As Lennie and I hit the sidewalk we ran into a couple of guys approaching the store. "Whaddya say, Sammie?" Lennie nodded at one of them with a couple of cameras around his neck.

"Catch you on the newsstand," the other guy said with a wave.

Lennie slid behind the wheel. "*Daily News*. We got an hour on them but they hit the street same time as us."

I sat at my gray metal relic of a desk. Tucked into a distant corner of the vast room with several other reporters, one grizzled veteran with an unlit cigar set permanently between his teeth, several other newcomers, I pecked away as fast as I could on my IBM Selectric, one finger on each hand, wishing I had taken that typing class. There'd usually be no time for a second draft, this first one was an exception. Around eleven I handed my roughed-out story to Marty. Sleeves rolled up, his hair disheveled, two cigarettes going in his ashtray, I should have known better than to expect immediate attention. He tossed my work into the DEADLINE tray. "I'll call you."

When a reporter got through probation he delivered his story to a copy reader for review, but Marty kept close tabs on the rookies. The building's PA system gave us a longer leash but there was no escaping it, even in the restrooms. I was ordering a coffee and danish in the cafeteria when I ran into Lennie. "How's it coming out?" he asked.

"I'm waiting for Rossi."

"C'mere, show you what I got."

We took the elevator to the third floor. I followed him to the back of the building where I scented hypo. I'd already told Lennie of my interest in photography, about Dave LaPointe. Lennie picked the top photo off a stack of glossy 8 1/2 x 11s just run through the ironing machine. The paper was still warm. "This is the one, though with our beloved Photo Editor it's always a crap shoot."

The print showed the proprietor from above, lying in a pool of blood, sandwiched between the cigarette cartons and the front counter. The cash register was open, money strewn about. "Lot of information in that shot," I said, "good composition, too. Weegee couldn't have done it better." Weegee, Arthur Fellig, was New York's pre-eminent crime photographer until his recent demise.

"I knew Arthur well. It's weird not having him around."

I flipped through the others, one of the two cops, one of the widow and her daughter. An exterior with the Golden Flower Market sign, the flower and vegetable stands...

"Paul Bernard!"

Oops...the P.A. "Paul Bernard, report to Marty Rossi."

"Gotta go."

"Good luck," Len said, "you'll need it."

As I approached Rossi's desk he motioned me to a chair. I saw red marks all over my copy, line-outs, marginal scribbles. "I've improved it," he said wearily, "nothing personal, but my approach is the one that counts. Your grammar needs improvement. Here," he tapped the paper with his pencil, one of those half-red, half-blue types, "we don't use contractions. It's 'they are' or 'they were,' not 'they're.' Only exception, when you're quoting somebody. Another one. The paramedic team, 'it was working feverishly,' not 'they were working feverishly.' We're not a British rag. The nuns beat this into me, good writing starts with good structure. Remember diagramming sentences? I loved diagramming sentences. If you don't think clear, you don't write clear."

After twenty minutes and a ton of slashes we were done. A lot of them picky, but he was the boss. He showed me how to "slug" a story, the two-line block in the upper left corner with your name and in two words or less what the story's about. "The lead paragraph, very critical. It tells the reader what happened so if a story gets cut we don't lose the guts. Your length is good." Rossi went on, "Wednesday we go with the arraignment. Did you get a style manual from Personnel?" I shook my head. He frowned. "Idiots." He reached into his desk for a wrinkled sheaf of papers stapled to an orange cover. "Seeing as you didn't have this, I'd say you did very well. Look it over," he said, handing it to me, "but the best thing is just read the paper. What's in there is the *Gazette* style or it wouldn't be in there."

I ripped through Rossi's fixes and half an hour later tore the last sheet out of my typewriter. Revisions complete, hand it in. Vibrating with excitement I got back to my place about two, thinking if these are normal hours I'd hate to see what overtime looks like. Eight-thirty a.m. I'd hit the arraignment, say seven-thirty at the precinct station, see what happened overnight. When I fell into bed my mind flirted with images of Vietnam. What luxury this is! Who needs sleep, I said to myself as I dropped off.

A couple of hours later, I picked an early edition off a news stand rack. There it was...on the front page!

EAST VILLAGE MARKET ROBBED
OWNER KILLED - TEEN HELD

Front page! *Gazette* photo by Leonard Markoff. No byline for me, not til you pass probation. I scanned the front page, turned to page 7 and read on. Word for word, not a thing changed! Did Rossi just run out of time? There was my Sgt. O'Malley quote, the references to Officers Yoo and Gonsalves, all spelled correctly. About seven-fifteen I arrived at the police station and asked for the night's booking sheet. I ran into Sgt. O'Malley in the ready room, reading the *Daily News*. "Bernard, right? From last night."

"You got it. Any details on the suspect? Anything happen overnight?"

"Let's go where we can talk. C'mon, I'll buy you a coffee."

I followed him to a coffee shop down the block where a woman with purple-rinse hair greeted him. "Where you been, Tommy? You better come around more or I'll forget how you like it... one sugar, right?" she said with a straight face.

"C'mon Maggie, you know it's two."

"See?" She slid the mug across the counter, spoon in. "What about your friend?"

"Black's good," I replied.

"A truck driver, this one," she said with a wink.

O'Malley appropriated a *Gazette* from a nearby booth. "That was a good story, me and the other officers, we appreciate that. I keep a scrapbook at home, you know, something for the grandkids. Twenty-seven years on the force, it's pretty thick by now." He eyeballed a plate of donuts the waitress brought over. "Help yourself," he said. I reached for a jelly stick, smudge at one end. "I checked you out with Brannigan," the cop said, referring to an old-timer I met the night before in the Cave. "He says you're okay."

"Good to hear." Apparently the system was working.

"What we know, the kid's named Sanchez, Roberto Sanchez. All of fifteen years old and can you believe, he lives two blocks away. Here's the address, I wrote it out for you. You'd think he'd be smarter than knock over a store right in his own back yard."

"Did he have an accomplice?"

"Looks like he acted alone. I see you got the booking sheet. He'll be arraigned this morning, you better sit in on that. Eight-thirty next door."

"Right."

"A capital case like this, racial angles and all, they'll fast-track it." O'Malley shook his head. "All the hopheads, too many ordinary people get hurt. I been doin' this a long time but you never get used to it."

"Were drugs the motive?"

"Don't quote me, but of course, it's always drugs. They found pot, needles, syringes, whatever, in his flat. Lives with his stepmother and a brother, that'll come out at the arraignment." He blew on his coffee. "You new? I haven't seen you around before."

"Yesterday was my first day."

"Nice way to start. By the way, I noticed last night, you walk with a limp. For a reporter that's kind of unusual. If you don't mind, what's that about?"

I usually deflected such questions but this was different. "I left a leg in Vietnam."

He raised his eyes. "Everybody's got a piece of that one. I lost a nephew, my brother's only son. Marines."

"I'm sorry."

"It's a bad business but you do what you have to do. You're not from around here."

"Boston. Rhode Island originally. I just moved here."

"Lot of Yankee fans in Rhode Island, I hear."

"That's true but I'm not Italian."

He laughed. "Then you're a..." I nodded. "Why am I helping you, for chrissakes? Say, Maggie," he shouted, "gimme these in a cup to go. And bag the donuts – my friend here has to get to court." The cop put a dollar bill on the counter and raised the waitress' hand to his lips. "Take care, Maggie." He pointed to the newspaper, "that's his story on page one."

"What's your name?"

"Paul Bernard. See you again."

"It will be my pleasure," the woman said with a warm smile.

Later that morning I would write up the wild scene at the arraignment, Roberto Sanchez held without bail, his friends and relatives screaming you got the wrong guy, getting themselves thrown out.

SOMETHING ELSE HAPPENED THAT DAY. Outside the courthouse I spotted a newspaper rack... later edition, different headline. I dropped a dime in and pulled one out.

VIETNAM ATROCITY
KILLINGS AT MY LAI

Rooted to the sidewalk, I raced through the article. Americal, the 23rd Division... March sixty-eight right after Tet... beserk... unarmed women gunned down, children, babies... hundreds killed. Captain Ernest Medina... Second Lieutenant William Calley. Army coverup. Westmoreland.

"You gonna stand there all day?" I looked up... woman with a baby carriage.

"Sorry," I mumbled, stepping aside. As I looked at the photos inside my own terrible day came roaring back... Gibbs, Stoner. I sleepwalked through the morning, wrote up the arraignment, handed it in to Rossi. Thank God he passed it almost unchanged. Old news, tomorrow's page twenty-seven. Two more Lennies,

Sanchez in manacles, crowd yelling on the courthouse steps. A couple of reporters congratulated me on making page one. Rossi even clapped me on the shoulder. "Good job," he said. "Figure this one's your story, give me a heads-up before you file something."

Leaving the building I decided to head back to my place, collect myself, maybe get a couple of winks before The Cave. I poured myself a stiff drink, then a second, sitting on the chrome chair that came with the kitchen. The newsreel of my mind looped back... it always ended the same, with me, the gutless wonder. I was exhausted but sleep was out of the question. I tuned in WINS and inside a couple of minutes heard an account of the story and an interview with the reporter who broke it, a guy named Seymour Hersh.

Suddenly I knew what I had to do. I picked up the phone and after fumbling in my address book for the number, dialed Worcester. After several rings Father Ronan picked up. He asked how I was faring, seemed a bit disappointed I hadn't walked through the door he'd opened for me at the *Globe*. When I told him about my first story, though, the front page treatment, he got excited. I told him about The Cave, the blood on the floor, the anguish. "Have you seen the papers today?" I said.

"Ah, yes," he said, "now I know why you're calling."

"It wasn't so unusual. That sort of thing happened. My own company was involved in some of it."

"Not you personally."

"One time they executed a bunch of prisoners... you couldn't tell a civilian from a VC, you have to understand. Our lieutenant didn't want to take them in... he was out of control, and this other guy, homicidal is the only way to describe him. I just stood there, didn't do a thing, didn't say a thing. I should have turned them in but I didn't do that either."

"Don't be too hard on yourself. You did what you could."

"You start out in control..." I pictured a hot LZ, my buddies and me exiting the chopper, running across a field, dodging bullets, "you're clear-headed then something happens, it doesn't have to be much, any little hitch'll do it. The LZ wasn't supposed to be hot but it was. Or you look around, no water buffaloes, no farmers. Things begin to pile up. You miss a landmark, take a wrong turn, now it's raining, visibility goes to hell, the map says there's a bridge but where is it? You're worried, you're scared, at night you're always scared. Somebody hears a noise and starts shooting. Everybody panics. It's contagious. The little kid wants its mama but he's got his rifle. And you use it, do you ever. At that moment that rifle is the most important thing in your life. It is all that stands between you and oblivion. You know what I mean, Father? Am I making sense?"

There was silence on the line. "I'll pray for you, Paul," Father Ronan said after a moment, "that's the best I can do right now. Try to see somebody."

"Yeah," I said, "you do that. Keep the faith."

Fall turned to winter and I covered dozens of stories. A jogger bludgeoned in Tompkins Square Park, bank holdups, drug busts, murder-suicide of two tourists in an Alphabet City flophouse. By now, nothing can faze me, I am thinking. Familiar with the routine, I wrote and filed my copy. Invariably my work was buried in the City section, which made me realize how rare that first-day front page was. Not everything I did made it in, and much of what did, Rossi mangled. Over time, though, Rossi intervened less, maybe he was growing comfortable with me or more likely, I was learning the *Gazette* way.

I did a painful follow-up on the Park family, then for a second installment dug into the suspect's background. This was totally out of character for the young man, an okay student with a part-time job, he'd even been an altar boy. The older brother Carlos, though, according to Father Ruggerio at Old Saint Patrick's, that kid was trouble. Petty theft conviction at sixteen, up for aggravated assault the next year though charges were dropped. Not Roberto, the priest told me, no way Roberto could have done it. I was granted an interview with Roberto who continued to deny his involvement. I could imagine what he was going through. A nice-looking kid, his bright eyes tinged with sadness. The D.A. was pushing for a trial date even though the gun still hadn't been found. I wrote all this in a second follow-up, though not the part about the older brother.

IT'S TIME TO TELL YOU SOMETHING about the *New York Gazette.* It took a while to find out, myself. The world knows the *Gazette* as one of the world's great newspapers, published continuously over a hundred years, its three thousand employees providing national coverage and foreign reporting, a stellar bureau in Washington, others in Chicago, San Francisco, London, Paris, Moscow, Tokyo, Sidney, Johannesburg, more recently Saigon. Business news, sports, arts and culture second to none, household names for columnists, left of center editorially on social and economic issues, politics more middle-of-the-road. All this greatness, yet always in the shade of the *Times.* Aside from getting scooped or the occasional goof, two things drove Managing Editor Tom O'Connor wild. The *Gazette's* reputation as New York's "second paper," and the *Times'* refusal to admit the *Gazette* existed. Not even the *Gazette's* lead over the *Daily News* and *Post,* which occupied different turf satisfied O'Connor. Every major decision he made was measured against the *Times,* what it was doing, not doing, or expected to do. I was with him. Of the papers I contacted they were the only one to snub me.

Ferociously protective of its news reporting, the *Gazette's* management also prided themselves on putting out a more entertaining product than the stuffy Gray Lady. Lively layouts, extensive use of photographs, modern typefaces were part of it. Through the years the *Gazette* had sponsored contests and stunts for boosting circulation. Perhaps the most notorious was the Great Martini incident, where an imposter later found to be an out-of-work Chicago actor named Reilly plunged to his death from a tightwire strung to the building across the street, crashing through the safety net to the pavement below. Numbers games results in a cleverly-disguised cartoon (think "how many animals can you find in this tree?") was a big draw until shuttered under pressure from City Hall.

The *Gazette* was founded in 1861 by one Peter McNeeley, a well-traveled Irishman who hit it big in the Gold Rush then meandered east looking for opportunity. Newspapers were in McNeeley's blood, his family publishing a Dublin broadside for many years. The *Gazette* distinguished itself during the Civil War, opposing slavery and backing Lincoln. It was one of the first to assign reporters to the front lines, and through an arrangement with *Harper's Magazine,* twice a month the *Gazette's* front page featured a Winslow Homer sketch of a battlefield scene. Circulation soared, but by the turn of the century McNeeley's unsteady heirs caused the paper to falter. To this day stories of that painful period surface during the hard times that periodically revisit the paper. By 1900 the *Gazette's* circulation was as low as its reputation. Forced to bring in a partner, the family sold out within the year.

Aided by a big loan, Sam and Martin Astell, publishers of an upstate New York daily, began making investments in the *Gazette.* They remodeled the West 44th Street building the year before the *Times* built theirs on 43rd, installing high-speed presses and enticing from competitors the cadre of talent on whom the *Gazette's* worldwide reputation was founded. In the Twenties the *Gazette* established a pipeline to Columbia's School of Journalism. During the turbulent first half of the century, through foreign adventures, two world wars and a depression, the Astells built the *Gazette* and nursed it toward financial health. Since 1956, Franklin Astell II, grandson of Martin, has been the *Gazette's* publisher, with Franklin III being groomed to take over. Walter Shoenweis, the Executive Editor, top management's contact with the "real" editors and the worker bees, was a shadowy figure you rarely saw around. He was the hatchet man, Astell's bad cop. I had never met him one-on-one.

Dating back to McNeely's time, the *Gazette's* passion for the underdog made it the favorite of immigrant Irish and Italians, less so with the Jewish population. It had an uneasy relationship with the Tammany machine, applauding its support of newcomers and the semblance of order in the streets while decrying its graft and corruption. The paper was pro-union, in fact it maintained a closed shop, but in the Thirties it suffered a catastrophic strike, the newly-installed printers' union bringing production to a halt for six weeks and erasing the modest profits from years of effort. Since that time the editorial page has taken a pragmatic stance on labor issues, evaluating each dispute on its merits.

In the heart of Hell's Kitchen, the *Gazette's* building had been erected by the Kugel Company in the eighteen-seventies as a leather goods factory before relocating to Astoria in Queens. The leatherworking machinery had been housed on the lower floors, heavy pillars interrupting the large open bays, but the enormous weight of the huge high-speed presses presented a problem. The Astells' solution, excavate to four stories below street level, one section at a time, and lay in reinforced concrete, iron bars and rods and all. One of the most thrilling parts of the job was hearing "Roll the Presses!" and seeing those monsters rumble into action. From the remove of my fourth-floor desk the vibration in my feet was the tipoff.

I know all this from the *Gazette's* half-day "training program" with optional building tour. How much training can you do in one afternoon? I also devoured the official *Gazette* history authored in 1958 by Miles Entwhistle, a former Executive Editor then at Columbia. As we new hires toured the basement, the press run for the early edition was in full swing. I understood why the men down there wore earplugs. With the water table only inches below the basement floor, heavy pumps added to the cacophony, running constantly, fans trained on the walls to fend off mother nature.

Giant conveyor belts fed the stream of bundled *Gazettes* through a ceiling cut-out, to freight elevators and on to delivery trucks at the alley loading docks, waiting to speed the *Gazette* to the New York Metro region, to Port Authority, to Penn Station, to LaGuardia and Kennedy Airports for the country, Europe and beyond. Once a week huge rolls of virgin paper came rumbling down an ingenious system of zigzagged ramps into the basement, pausing only briefly before being impressed with the news.

ADAPTING TO THE *GAZETTE'S* RHYTHM, I developed my own routine, centered on The Cave, its smoky room, ratty carpet, malfunctioning toilet, the dice and card games, the laconic jargon of the police scanner, the racing sheets, the resident bookie, a wizened gentleman in a scruffy sport coat with slips of paper sticking out of the pockets. I showed up around four. With furtive glances and wise remarks we neophytes goaded each other, then it was race to the breaking stories, write them up, hand them in, sit down with the editor. Rookies were forbidden to phone a story in, though if a deadline left no choice you did it. I rarely made my way back to the apartment before midnight. No regular days off, though I was usually excused Wednesdays and Thursdays. We worked weekends, a big time for crime. Several crime reporters rotated through, hanging around to show us how to get along with the cops, accompany us on stories, generally explain the ropes, and on rare occasions, share sources. Tell the truth, I found Lennie and the other photographers just as helpful as reporters and a lot less temperamental.

With all its griping and slanders and fish stories, the Cave is where I got my real initiation to reporting. The Cave is where I learned to tolerate cigar smoke, it was either that or move my chair to the sidewalk. One old-timer was always pecking away at a banjo, a dirty instrument with what sounded like wooden strings, humming through a cigarette. Guys sucked on beers or sipped whiskey while they played cards. When a promising call came through they'd slide the half-pint into a coat pocket, stand, stretch, and head out. All the old-timers wore hats, fedoras of various shapes and colors which we disdained. One time I tried one on, wondering what was so funny until I went into the restroom and looked in the mirror.

I was coming to know the East Village aka the Lower East Side. Squeezed between Little Italy and Chinatown, it was home to watering holes, restaurants and greasy spoons, stores and shops and industrial blocks, lighting fixture stores, restaurant supply outlets, leather goods shops, used book stores, colorful gardens that suddenly rose before you and put a glow in your day, parks. The other side of the coin, dilapidated tenements, squatters, derelicts in doorways asleep or dead, couldn't always tell which, stripped cars, broken glass in the gutters and streets, drug dealers, prostitutes and pimps. I learned how in the Fifties real estate interests began championing the term "East Village," but despite pockets of gentility it had a long way to go.

I mentioned the training program, but the most valuable tip of all came from Rossi. One night he asked me how I planned to keep track of my contacts, my sources. "I've got a folder, pieces of paper, notes."

He frowned. "Not good enough. You gotta get organized." He reached into a desk drawer and pulled out a thick spiral notebook, its cover dirty and creased, the pages swollen from years of abuse. "I been using this thirty years," he said, handing it over. I thumbed through the notebook. Page upon page of addresses and phone numbers. "Could be better organized but I know it so well that'd only mess me up. Get yourself one."

The next morning in a stationery store I purchased what would become my friend, companion and bible for the rest of my career. A notebook, loose-leaf, five by seven with tabbed dividers. After debating a moment I splurged on red leather. Government contacts, business, reporters print and TV... well-placed friends and acquaintances, debits and credits, favors I've done them, they've done me... names of wives, husbands, children, even food and drink preferences... where I saw them last, talked with them last. Meet my little red book.

The overall framework of my work was set but little else. New, unpredictable, every night a different night, waiting to be discovered. But with all the excitement, I was beginning to chafe at crime, feeling I was ready for bigger things, though exactly what these were remained to be seen. I knew sooner or later I would write about Vietnam, following the war avidly, and events at home. One day the *Gazette* ran a brief item about a Lincoln's Birthday march by a group of Vietnam Vets protesting the war. I brought the paper over to Rossi open to the story I had circled in red magic marker. "Marty," I said, tapping the page, "I want in."

He looked up. "That's Foley's beat," he said in a tone that said end of discussion. Ed Foley was an old-timer, a bird dog on a story and an alcoholic, on or off it. I'd said hello to him a couple of times, that was about it. I pulled my pants leg up and stuck my leg out. "See this, Marty? I have something extra to bring to this one."

Rossi looked at me for a long minute then nodded. "Maybe you do, maybe you do. How long you been on the crime beat, anyway?

"Three months."

He nodded. "That's long enough. Matter of fact, it'd do you good to spend time with Foley. I'll talk to Sid, lemme see what I can do." Later in the day Rossi called me over. "Congratulations," he said, shaking my hand, "you are officially off Crime and on the City beat. Foley's on board, and as for that probation of yours, let's just say you made it through."

"You won't regret this, Marty."

"I don't expect to."

THE MORNING OF THE EVENT was low and threatening, snow forecast by noon. A couple of days before, Foley interviewed the organizers who were led by a former Army corporal named Phil Johnson. Johnson had served in the 25th, though our paths had never crossed. On the F train from Washington Square, I fingered the flyer.

STOP THE WAR!
LINCOLN'S BIRTHDAY MARCH
JOIN US! FEB 12 - 10 AM BRYANT PARK
VIETNAM VETS AGAINST THE WAR

I found Foley at the corner of Sixth and 42nd, hands in his pockets, his breath standing out in frosty plumes. Ollie Newton, who'd been on a couple of my stories, was with Foley, three cameras hanging around his neck. I was in my new ski parka with a pulled-down knit hat. Gloves would be pocketed when my notebook and I swung into action. My leg was tolerating the cold well enough. Long johns didn't add much, though Mr. Stumpy liked them. I wasn't looking forward to the icy sidewalks.

"Johnson's the tall guy over there," Foley said, nodding at a young man in a small group nearby. Bare-headed with longish dark hair, he was wearing a fatigue jacket with stripes and service ribbons. Several TV crews were on hand, one interviewing a police official, another staked out across the street. Down the block toward 41st, the direction of the march, a large number of police, some on motorcycles, on horseback. The goal was an Army recruiting office just below Madison Square Park. "C'mon," Foley said, "I'll introduce you." He walked up to Johnson and his group. "Ed Foley, *New York Gazette*," he began, "we talked the other day."

"Right," Johnson replied, "good to see the press here."

"Wouldn't miss it for the world. Meet Paul Bernard, one of our reporters. Paul was in Vietnam," Foley added.

"What outfit?" Johnson asked.

"Twenty-fifth," I replied. "Fire Base Tango in Tay Ninh Province."

"I was in Saigon most of the time, just lucky, I guess. When were you there?"

"Fall of sixty-eight until I caught some grief at Hill 874."

"Yeah, I heard about that one, a bad scene. At least you came out of it okay."

"More or less." I glanced at Foley. We had scripted our parts. "Listen," I said, "I'll be doing interviews along the route. Like to spend some time with you at the end."

"Yeah, that'd be good. Maybe we could interest you in our organization."

"I already am."

One of Johnson's lieutenants had a hand on his arm. "Duty calls. See you later."

My job today was to capture reactions, Foley's to convey the larger scene and the expected opposition. How the police handled the situation could be an issue, marches in other cities had resulted in scuffles and arrests. Getting to know Foley the last couple of days, I wondered if Marty included me for balance. He might think he knew where I stood, though I was still figuring it out myself. A decorated World War Two veteran, Foley was VFW and American Legion all the way. In as many words Foley told me this rag-tag outfit should be taken out and shot, though from what I'd seen of his stuff he hid his antagonism. Or that could have been the Copy Editor's doing, or Rossi's.

I began interviewing participants milling about in the street as the marshals tried to form them up into some kind of order. Looked like a hundred at the most, it was my job to make a count. By ten-fifteen everybody was pointed the same direction and behind a VIETNAM VETS AGAINST THE WAR banner flanked by two American flags, the first rows stepped out.

Not a single Vietcong flag, I thought, pleased. Though, breaking with solemnity, a couple of signs promoted the joy of pot. And four young women marched under WOMEN FOR PEACE - MAKE LOVE NOT WAR. Over her jeans one of them wore a large leather belt that looped down across her groin area. SEX OR BOMBS - IT'S UP TO YOU read her sign. Ollie burned some film on her. After the first element came the band, trombone, two trumpets, a young woman on clarinet, tuba, kettle drum, bass drum loaner from Fordham Prep, the ram's head taking a pounding. Even with my leg I kept up easily, walking alongside, chatting, making notes. I felt comfortable here and my limp certainly opened guys up. I made more notes for possible use.

AGENT ORANGE
I DIED IN VIETNAM AND NEVER KNEW IT

WAR IS ~~GOOD~~ GREAT FOR BUSINE$$

THE VIETNAM VET
SOMETIMES A SUCKER, NEVER A COWARD

BEING SPIT ON ISN'T THE WORST THING

VIETNAM VETS TO AMERICA: YOU'RE WELCOME

How bitter, some of these guys! Why wasn't I? What was I missing?

After finishing an interview I drifted back and picked up with someone else. One was a long-haired guy with a ponytail and a First Division patch on his fatigue jacket sleeve. "Paul Bernard, I'm a *Gazette* reporter. What's your name, soldier? Why're you here today?"

"What are you, fuckin' stupid?" he shouted over the band, He pointed to his hand-lettered placard: OUT OF VIETNAM - NOW!!

"I get the picture," I said. "What turned you off the war?"

"Nothin' fuckin' turned me off. Lost my deferment, got nailed, end of story."

"At least you got back in one piece."

He sneered. "I haven't had three hours sleep in two years. Anyway what gives you the right to ask me questions?"

"One, it's my job. Two, I was there myself."

"Just 'cause you ask doesn't mean I need to answer."

He turned away and began talking to the guy next to him. I was nearing the rear when I came upon a short, mustachioed black guy hopping along on crutches, both pants legs flapping behind. He wore a fatigue jacket with Marine insignia and a peace pin. A red headband lifted his Afro into an impressive tower. "Paul Bernard, *Gazette*. What's your name, Marine? Where're you from?"

"Cyrus Thomas," he replied, a puzzled look on his face as I walked stiffly alongside. "You one of us? What happened to you?"

"A grenade," I said. "Hill 874. How about you?"

"A dumb mine. Never saw it coming."

"Same here." I waved my free arm at the marchers. "What do you think of all this?"

"It's a crock, same as 'Nam. None of us should've been there. But we got to tell people where it's at."

"A Marine, huh." I pointed at his lance corporal chevron. "You made your choice."

"That I did. The Marines made me a man. 'Nam took it away."

"You working?"

"I give away shit nobody wants. Flyers for a tailor, strip joints, magazines that don' cost nothin.'" He laughed severely. "Just look at me. Can't be a cop, can't be a fireman, can't even collect fuckin' garbage. How'd you get a job anyway?"

"Lucky. I had experience. Where'd you say you were from?"

"South Bronx." He looked me over, "not your type neighborhood."

"Try me sometime." I pulled out a card and stuck it in his jacket pocket. "Give me a call if you ever want to talk."

He brightened. "Thanks, bro. Hey, any chance me gettin' on with the Gazette?"

"I don't have that kind of pull. Buy you a beer sometime, though."

"Sounds like a deal," he said as he walked on.

The march moved along, chanting, singing, some applause from the sidewalks, some shouting and catcalls, lots of American flags. Foley had stopped to talk with a group of older guys in VFW caps. By now I had worked my way back to the Army jeep that was bringing up the rear. I had wondered how they managed to get hold of it. As it drew closer I saw it was a homemade paint job. In the back seat was Johnson and a silver-haired, jut-jawed man who looked familiar. Some retired general, I figured, with the sense to wear civvies and not screw up his pension. I made a note to find him when the parade stopped.

As we approached Madison Square it started to snow. The recruiting office was at sidewalk level on West 23rd Street across the street from the park. The organizers had wanted to engage with the recruiters, but Foley told me their permit confined them to the park. Cross 23rd Street, they'd be arrested. As the marchers filtered into the park I made my count, eighty-seven in all. They assembled in front of a platform and as the speeches began, more people attached themselves to the fringes. For the next hour I worked the crowd, keeping one ear on the speeches, underlining a couple of names for later interviews. Turned out the jeep occupant wasn't a general but a bird colonel, Edwin Parkham by name, who I did recognize now, an early and severe critic of the war and, not surprisingly, an early retiree from the Army.

After the speeches wrapped up, Phil Johnson made his concluding up remarks, expressing disappointment that the city had prevented them getting into the recruiting office but proclaiming the march a great success. "So now let us return to our homes and places of work to continue the struggle against the war."

As he stepped down a bearded guy wearing a red bandanna and carrying an army helmet took the platform and started yelling into the mike. "Are we gonna let cops and politicians tell us what to do?"

A few people in the crowd looked up, I heard a few shouts. "Hell no!"

Johnson was looking at the interloper but was in no hurry to intervene. "We came here to talk to those recruiters," he was going on, "and we're gonna talk to those recruiters!"

Now he had the crowd's attention. A cheer went up. "SO LET'S DO IT!!"

He jumped from the platform and strode toward the street. Several others in red kerchiefs followed, waving the crowd on. The crowd began to move with them. "We want the Army!" they chanted, "we want the Army!" "Come out, come out wherever you are!" somebody yelled and the crowd picked up the cadence.

Across the street, the police in riot gear, visored helmets, metal shields, had already taken up positions on the far sidewalk. Tapping their billy clubs in the palms of their hands they stood two deep and the width of several storefronts either side of the Army office. As the crowd reached the sidewalk I watched the police stiffen. They lowered their visors and raised their shields. The crowd paused as a florid-faced Captain gave a warning on a bullhorn. "Disperse! Do not attempt to cross the street. If you attempt to cross the street you will be arrested. Disperse now!"

Now the leader and his cadre had their helmets on. Slowly they began crossing the street. Part of the crowd followed but most stayed on the sidewalk or in the park, waving their signs in the air and shouting. From somewhere a trumpet sounded. I was in the street with Ollie, who was snapping furiously. He changed to the camera with the long lens. Now the spearhead was halfway across, no more than twenty feet from the police line. At this point the police began to advance, deliberate, disciplined, the second row of cops moving in behind. A third line occupied the sidewalk, filling in from the sides. Behind us, more police at the Sixth Avenue end of the street. Ahead, I saw they had Madison Avenue sealed off too. Blue sawhorses everywhere. The crowd was trapped. So were Ollie and I.

The bullhorn barked. "I order you to halt! Go any farther you will be arrested." A rock flew toward the police, then several bottles.

"Here we go!" Ollie shouted. Suddenly the police charged.

Clubs flying, they waded into the crowd. People scattered, fighting back, on the ground, cops standing over them, clubbing them. With the action spilling in my direction I cut my note-taking short and made sure my press badge on the chain was outside my jacket. The scene was getting more confused by the second, shouting, yelling, pulling, shoving. A girl screamed. From the park, a second police phalanx had reached the sidewalk. They split in two, half of them facing the park, the rest turning and advancing on the street, squeezing the protesters in their vise. Several protesters broke through the police and started throwing rocks at the recruiting office. Other rocks rained down on the street, thrown from farther back. I could hear glass breaking, saw the front window of the recruiting office smashed in, the laundromat next door too. Now the police were strapping on gas masks.

"Oh, oh. Time to split," I yelled.

"I believe you're right."

We moved quickly toward Sixth Avenue. The first tear gas canister exploded in a cloud of smoke, quickly followed by two others. I'll have to find out what kind they're using, I thought, as the familiar odor wafted toward me. At the barricades I showed my press pass to a cop who waved us through. "Paul! Over here!" Ollie was shouting. He'd found a concrete planter and was trying for a foothold on the rim. "Steady me! I need some crowd shots!" I reached up and grabbed him around the waist. Clouds of gas were rising from the battle scene. I could hear Ollie's camera going.

Sirens blared and several paddy wagons drew up to the barricades. With the bodies in the street contained, the police were now thinning out the crowd, handcuffing people, frog-walking them, stuffing them in the wagons. As one left another immediately took its place. Good planning. A breeze had picked up and was blowing the tear gas toward the East River, away from us. The scene was beginning to taper off, a few still being hustled away but most everybody just standing around. We talked our way back through the barricades and I began looking for people to interview.

A comment from the Captain, unsuitable for a family paper. Back in the park I found Phil Johnson, as usual surrounded by a group. When he noticed me he broke loose. "Bernard, make sure you write Vietnam Vets did not authorize this action."

"Didn't try very hard to stop it," I replied.

"Those people were not part of our group. That kind of bullshit only hurts our cause."

"How come you didn't get on the mike and say that?"

"Somebody cut the power. Had to be those assholes."

"Who were those people?

"Some idiot offshoot of SDS. They've caused trouble other places."

"Did any of your group follow them into the street?"

"Only a couple. Essentially nobody."

"Seemed like more than that, but I guess the arrest reports'll tell the story. What's your comment on the police action?"

"What can I say? This wouldn't have happened if they'd let us talk with the recruiters. That gave those jerks the opening they wanted."

I wanted a comment from that Colonel but couldn't see him around. "See Col. Parkham anywhere?" I asked Johnson.

"He cut out after the parade."

"Thanks for the quotes, I may give you a call when I'm writing it up." I hoped Foley had nabbed the Colonel before he disappeared.

Walking back out to Sixth Avenue I spotted a familiar face. "Sgt. O'Malley, as I live and breathe!" I said.

"Top of the mornin' to you, Bernard. Lovely day for a riot, is it not?"

"Couldn't be better. I score it cops twenty, protesters two. What do you say?"

"I say what two?" he laughed.

"I figure a couple of your guys probably got dinged."

"We took some casualties. Say Paul, can I call you Paul? I've got something for you on that robbery-homicide. You in tomorrow?"

"Sure. I don't get days off."

Back at my desk I wrote up the story, gave it to Foley for a look as Marty said. It was a thoughtful piece, weaving interviews of the vets through my narration, balancing their criticism with my observations about their personal situations. A couple of hours later I went over to Marty's desk to go over what I had written. "I expected it to be more one-sided," he said, "pro vets, I mean."

"I wrote it straight. That riot at the end had a life of its own."

"You're improving," he said, handing my work back. He had chopped it to pieces, folding what was left of it into Foley's report. Red marks all over mine, almost nothing on his. Foley's account of the riot dominated the piece. Marty noticed the dismay on my face. "Hey, don't feel bad," he said, "all part of the learning experience. You're doin' fine."

Next day, first page of Metro,

VIOLENCE AT VETS' MARCH - DOZENS HURT

Two bylines this time, Ed Foley and Paul Bernard, and Ollie's fantastic picture from the planter, police, milling crowd, swirling clouds of gas. Inside they ran a shot of the leader of the breakaway group Foley had identified as "Vets for Justice Now" being dragged away, another of a cop being treated for a broken arm. After absorbing it I sauntered by Marty's desk. "You changed the emphasis," I complained. "Have a little march with your riot."

"Hey, you give the people what they want, within limits, of course." He smiled. "Listen, what you wrote was very good. Fair, interesting, we just didn't have room for it all. You kept a copy, right?"

"Yeah," I said, nodding glumly.

"Hold onto it. Maybe we'll use it for a backgrounder."

"Well anyway, I learned one lesson today."

"What's that?"

"What it takes to sell papers."

About eleven my phone rang. It was O'Malley. "We're off the record, right?"

"Right," I replied. Another thing I was learning, sometimes you have to gentle a source, kind of creep up on him sideways.

"I hate to tell you this," he said in a low voice, "but we got the wrong guy. I don't know if you're still following the case..."

"I am."

"The D.A.'s going to dismiss the charges tomorrow."

I recalled my interview with the priest, others who had only good things to say about Roberto Sanchez, my talk with the kid. "Can't say I'm totally surprised. What happened?"

"We found the murder weapon. There was a bunch of prints but none from him. Thing is, our case was falling apart anyway. The bloodstains on his pants, they didn't match up with the victim, we've known that for some time and now our witness is backpedalling."

"The guy with the milk?"

"We put him through another lineup, now he can't swear to it being him."

"What about Carlos, the older brother? The two of them look a lot alike." The stepmother had shown me pictures of the two.

"We are on top of that."

"You happen to find his prints on the weapon?"

"I'm not at liberty to say but don't bet against it."

"Assuming he's the guy, when's it coming down?"

"We're taking it slow. The D.A.'s got enough egg on his face already."

I could understand that. District Attorney Hanratty's crime-busting, candidate-ready mug had been all over TV those heady first few days of the story, in all the papers. One of the first things I learned, the *Gazette's* editorial approach was pro-police, tough on crime. Cops do their job, sometimes mistakes are made. You close ranks and move on.

"Egg salad... that's one way to pitch the story but it's not our way."

"It's tough enough out here without the papers crucifying you when you mess up. Call me Wednesday, I'll give you a head start."

And so it was I wrote yet another story. Two families, two tragedies. The good kid in the wrong place at the wrong time, covering up for a brother who didn't deserve it. The immigrant family whose hard work ran afoul of the city's ugly side. No winners in this one.

Marty and Sid packaged my set of stories and the paper submitted them for a Polk Award. Fantastic, I thought. Things are going well. Oh, I got an honorable mention for local reporting.

40. IMMERSED AGAIN

"THE DEED IS DONE!" Jonathan breezes into the conference room. "They agreed to everything. Tomorrow I meet Sharif, their Iraq lead. He's back for a week."

"The one you see on TV all the time? Dark hair, glasses?"

"Waguih Sharif. He's important – he knew Paul well." Jonathan takes a seat across from me, peering over the Gazette #2 carton. "And I managed to track Bernie down – he's in the Pentagon phone book, if you can believe it. He says they knew about Len Garrison which ticks me off. I also told him we need Martinez, but no luck there."

"Only a matter of time. And now we know the story of the famous little red book." We had found it in one of the cartons.

"Mine's black. Works just as well."

We turn to the carton *du jour*. At one point Jonathan mentions My Lai. "That hit Paul hard."

"I have to believe Paul's errors were of omission. Not speaking up when he had the chance. But when it comes to war no person, no country is immune from savagery. In Vietnam, the North was as brutal as any."

"The situation in Hué after Tet, what was it, several thousand massacred?"

"At least. That should have opened the eyes of our radicals but of course it didn't. What didn't fit their world view was not to be believed. Ah, the comforts of tunnel vision."

About four o'clock I was losing my focus. It didn't help that I could practically taste that first scotch. I don't know why, but on the road hard liquor appeals to me. At home I never touch the stuff.

The phone rings, Jonathan picks it up. "For you. Reception."

It's Carol, a young black woman, the rare person whose smile lifts your spirits. Somebody's in the lobby, she says, a messenger of some sort. Curious, I walk out there, stiff from too much sitting. It is a scruffy-looking guy with a bike helmet. "Augustus Flynn?"

"The very same."

He reaches into his canvas pouch, pulls out a large envelope and hands it to me. "Have a good day." He turns to leave.

"Hey, wait a minute! What's this all about?"

As the elevator door opens he looks back. "It's all in the package."

I turn the envelope over. It smells of lawyer – Rosenberg, Something & Something. I slit the envelope with my finger and pull out a sheaf of papers. Oh boy, I say to myself, here we go.

: IN THE SUPERIOR COURT FOR THE STATE OF NEW YORK :
: LATIMER BROADCASTING NETWORK, INC. :
: vs. :
: INTERNATIONAL NEWS NETWORK CORPORATION :

plus a bunch of others and right before John and Jane Doe there I am, they even got the F.X. It is an

APPLICATION FOR MANDAMUS IN RE: RESTORATION OF PERSONAL PROPERTY WRONGFULLY TAKEN AND RESULTING DAMAGES

There are also Interrogatories with my name on them. Papers in hand, I proceed down the corridor, shouting at Jonathan as I go by. I see Steve Samuels through his open door. "The shit has hit the fan," I say, handing the papers to him.

He nods. "I just got off the phone with ETVN's attorney. His client has had a similar happy event. Let's take a look," he says, flipping through the papers. "Standard Andy Rosenberg," he says, "he's LTN's outhouse counsel."

"Good for him," I say or words to that effect. "I better let Cahill know."

"Tell him we'll fax it to him. Huh, twenty pages of Interrogatories – that's a bit much, even for Andy."

Jonathan pokes his head in. "I'm not in there, am I?"

"Not by name, but I'll lay odds you qualify as a Doe."

"How'd they know to find me here?" I ask.

Samuels smiles. "Nothing stops a good litigator. Except a better litigator."

Well, this kills our day. I feel like clearing my head, so after a short reprise Jonathan and I part company. I set out along Broadway then cut over to Fifth Avenue and proceed uptown. I always commune with the stone lions. I should go in, it's been years since I spent any time there. It is a long walk to the Plaza, forty-plus blocks, though being such a fine evening I'm thinking I may make it the whole way on foot.

Speaking of the Plaza, I'll be leaving there. A couple of weeks ago Susan Leone discovered another stash of papers in a storage room, from the television years. Thank God, for nobody knew if they even existed, but it sentences me to another month, plus the holiday rates are about to kick in. I've located a month-to-month efficiency off Gramercy Park, not far from Steve's office.

I do need to get back up to Maine. Around Columbus Day Joseph buttoned the place up – storm windows, outside faucets, that sort of thing. In a recent letter he said there is water in the basement and I have a cracked water pipe. Plus, I miss my home. New York is well and good but nothing compares with the salt air and the quiet. So I will celebrate Thanksgiving there. Walking up Fifth Avenue I get an eyeful of what passes for Christmas spirit these days. Ah, don't be a Scrooge, I tell myself – the windows are colorful, full of life, but by now I am in a foul mood. That damned lawsuit. Steve and Cahill say I have nothing to worry about, but the prospect of dealing with the legal bullshit is enough to depress a person.

* * * * * * *

MY NEW ASSIGNMENT FORGED AN INTIMATE BOND with the NYC transit system. Beetle was racking up the miles as well. Sprung from my life of crime, the whole city lay open, whatever came to Sid Greenwald's fertile mind. Midtown for an exhibition of war photography back to Matthew Brady. The section on Vietnam brought me up short. My Lai. Malcolm Browne's famous monk immolation. In my review I hazarded a personal note, saying "this reporter, then in uniform," had stood on the very spot some years later. To Chelsea for the opening of a disco club. That one needed a second look, maybe a third. I discovered the outer boroughs. Another anti-war protest, this time at the Brooklyn Navy Yard. The World's Fair site falling into disrepair. Flag-draped caskets at Kennedy Airport. A march and rally at Queens College. Nathan should be out by now, Murph too. With all the changes in my life I needed to let them know where I was.

The day the Queens College story appeared Sid said to stop by and see him. I knocked on his door, one of the string of editors' offices along the 44th Street wall. "Come in. Have a seat. You doing okay? The work agrees with you?"

"I'm having a blast."

"Good, good," he replied mechanically, briefly looking up. "How long you been with us now? Lemme guess, coupl'a months?"

"Four," I said with a laugh.

"How about that. Time flies, whatever." He closed the folder he was working on. "Irene!" he yelled out the door. "C'mere!"

Sid's diminutive secretary popped into the room. "Get this to Harry and tell him I need it by six." Harry Combs was a senior rewrite man. "You know Paul, right?"

"Of course," Irene said, giving me a wink as she exited. One of the people who made the place go, she and I weren't yet buddies but we were getting there.

"Make it five-thirty," he yelled after her. "No excuses!"

He turned back to me. "Don't let this go to your head, but I want to say we like your work. Upstairs has even noticed it," he said, referring, I figured, to Tom O'Connor, "which is unusual, especially for a new kid. Mostly what I hear about is the screwups." He sat back in his chair and lit a cigarette. "How would you feel about running the anti-war beat? That's plus everything else you're doing, of course."

What a kick that'd be, I thought, but don't act too eager. "It'd be familiar ground, that's for sure," I replied.

"You saw a lot of that at Berkeley, right?"

"Good training, as it turns out."

"You'll have to learn the territory, get with Ed's sources, develop your own. There's a lot of responsibility too – you got to be thinking with these people, know what's coming down. So, how about it?"

"I'll do it," I replied. I was doing most of the work already.

"Great, great. Our coverage's been too loose, we've missed out on some things. Get with Ed, pick his brain, have him introduce you to everybody. We're shifting him to City Hall. Between us he's stale, he needs a change." Sid stood and reached across his desk. "Congratulations," he said, shaking my hand, "this could be the start of something big."

"Seems to me it's already plenty big."

"It's only going to heat up, too. Incidentally, the fact you're a veteran is excellent, you've got a unique perspective. Your... experience may come in handy."

"You mean this," I said, tapping Mr. Stumpy.

"Yes, yes, that's what I mean. It's good you're not reluctant to talk about it."

I nodded. "It got me down at first, but I see it as a down payment on something, and as long as I do the job, what the hell, maybe it'll even help." That was my standard line. I didn't tell him about the waves of anxiety, trying to remember what was bothering me, going letter by letter through the alphabet. Hearing stuff like, "earth to Paul, earth to Paul," worrying they didn't level with me about that splinter in my head.

"Kid, that is one terrific attitude," Sid said, "and there's something else I should tell you. We haven't figured out exactly how to do this but we're thinking of running something that'll feature you as a person."

"As a person?"

"Yeah. Remember your backgrounder on the vets' march? How about picking some interesting angle, develop it into an extended piece, maybe we run it as a feature in *G!* We'd work in some bio, couple of pictures, something along those lines."

G! was our Sunday Magazine. This would be a really big deal... "I'd have no problem with that. Just tell me what you need."

"Good, good." He again took my hand. "I should tell you Foley's bummed out but he'll get over it. He gives you any shit, let me know. Let's figure later in the week the three of us sit down. Marty too, then we'll cut it over."

At the end of the day I floated out of the building. Amazing, I thought, as I tossed my briefcase on the bed, flipped through my mail and headed out for a couple of beers with some new friends. Truly amazing.

YOU KNOW, GUS, LOOKING OVER THIS LAST SECTION it strikes me I haven't said much about my personal life – what there was of it, that is – since the *Gazette* claimed all my waking hours and not a few of the others. So here goes. First, the neighborhood. It was everything I hoped. Bank Street, mid-block between Bleecker and West 4th. Tree-lined, as most streets in the area were, buds mid-March, shady in season, convenient to everything, close by a little park filled with mothers and children. I knew of Greenwich Village's bohemian spirit, of course, its beatniks and coffee houses, the folk and jazz scene, but I didn't realize how many writers and artists also had called it home.

The first weekend I discovered two watering holes that became regulars. Chumley's, number 86 Bedford Street, was easy to miss. The front door was unmarked and there was no sign. What Chumley's did have was a bar manned by off-duty firefighters and walls plastered with author photos and jackets of books they worked on while they sipped and smoked. People like e.e. cummings and Ernest Hemingway – big dose of salt for this one. Supposedly also once a speakeasy. I found myself spending more time at the other establishment, the White Horse Tavern. Here Dylan Thomas took his last drink before falling ill in the Chelsea Hotel and expiring the next day. Though I occasionally had a bite in these two establishments, there wasn't a lot of cash after the essentials so I tended to load up in our cafeteria midday or failing that, open a can of something when I got home.

Now on a more regular schedule, I especially enjoyed coffee of a Saturday morning, finding a bench in Abington Square Park to pore over the *Gazette* and the *Times.* Though I had come to know the East Village and admired its creative dysfunctionality, the contrast with my Village was stark. Sure, we had muggings and the occasional murder, but the streets were mostly clean and the buildings well tended. I had lucked onto a cloister of sanity where you could actually hear yourself think. Shutting my front door on the day made me appreciate the calm and sanity I had regained after leaving the Army. Come morning, my brain was in gear again and I was ready to go. Coffee, cigarette, subway, *Gazette,* excitement.

Most Sundays I made the trek up and across to a Jesuit church on West Sixteenth Street between Sixth and Fifth. A couple of others were closer but I cast my lot with St. Francis Xavier, as much as anything for the occasional mind-stretching sermon that brought me back to my college days. For me, on my bad days God's design was perverse, merely inscrutable on others, but I couldn't put my Faith down. The more vulnerable I felt, the more chinks in the Church's facade, the stronger its hold. Only a dolt would scuttle that spiritual life raft. Even a modicum of solace and hope was welcome in these times.

Speaking of college, I was startled to hear of a problem at my alma mater. During the fall SDS had protested defense company recruitment and a crowd blocked students from interviews. Black student leaders contended the disproportionate number of blacks cited for rules violations was a clear case of racism – they were simply easier to recognize in the mostly white crowd. The college's black students including future Supreme Court Justice Clarence Thomas came together behind the four accused. If they were not granted amnesty, the rest would leave the school. High stakes. Graduation and career versus upset and uncertainty, and looming behind it all, Vietnam.

When the decision to suspend the four along with the others was announced, hundreds turned out in their support. The college President, Raymond Swords, whom I knew as a decent and caring man, had the prospect of a general strike on his hands. I called Father Ronan who said, in his mind, rules to protect normal functioning must give way to fundamental fairness. After excruciating deliberations, Father Swords announced his decision, saying the identification procedures were so flawed it was wrong to single out only some. If any were charged, all should have been charged. This defused the situation and it gave me new respect for my old school. Maybe there's hope after all, if people can do the right thing in such a confusing, charged situation.

The last week of December I took time and drove to Providence to spend Christmas with the family. After a couple of days of Jim and Sheila's scene I'd had enough. All their kids were in school and the oldest, Mark, was a real handful. That acorn didn't fall far from the tree. My father was in reasonably good spirits, but I thought how odd it was to see him age while, frozen in time, my mother remained forever young. We talked some about disabilities, tricks he'd learned for getting around.

The biggest family news was Catherine's pregnancy. Due date early summer, she was already showing. Totally in love with the idea of motherhood, she had already amassed the maternity clothes, the baby clothes, the stroller, the bassinet, you get the picture. I was happy for her, just had to give her a hard time. After returning from this visit, mingling with the female of the species at my hangouts, at parties, at work, after work, I sometimes found myself thinking of my sister, proud of her but jealous too. I couldn't rid myself of my ridiculous and I surmised unique approach to dating – that if I couldn't see being serious about somebody I didn't want to waste time on her.

Most memorable was my visit to Omer's mother. I'd been putting this off, worried about her reaction. I decided to drop in unannounced. If she wasn't there, I'd leave a note. Going round back, I walked up the stairs and knocked on her door. Something different... no stale cabbage odor. I knocked again and was fishing in my pocket for a piece of paper to write a note when I heard a rustling at the door. "Allo. Who is it, please?"

"It's Paul Bernard, Mrs. Arsenault. I came by to see you."

The door opened a crack and a face peered out, then it shut and I heard the chain slide. The door opened. A short woman, she had always been bulky but her faded floral housedress made it plain she wasn't taking care of herself. I felt as if I were being scrutinized. Why are you here and my son is not? After a moment, however, she smiled and threw her arms around my neck. "Paul, Paul," she said, backing off, tears in her eyes, "how good it is to see you. How good you are looking."

"You're not half bad yourself, Mrs. A." That had been my name for the mother of my first and best friend.

"You'll have coffee, of course? I was just brewing a pot."

"Of course." I smiled. She'd forgotten I used to refuse it.

"Come in, sit down. We'll sit in the kitchen, the rest of the house is too much a mess"

"My favorite room," I replied.

"You haven't changed," she said, "still have your good appetite, I'm sure. Have some bread and jam. I baked yesterday."

"Every Tuesday, right?"

"Monday is washing, Tuesday is baking..." her eyes disappeared in a vacant stare. "...I'm trying to remember something – your father, his name..."

"Julien."

"Julien! Of course. And your mother would be Fiona, then. They are well?"

"My mother passed away a while back," I answered. I distinctly remembered Mrs. Arsenault at the wake and funeral, the whole neighborhood in fact.

"Of course. That accident, so sad. Your father, he is still with us?"

"He's in a home in Chepachet. He had a couple of strokes but he's doing okay."

The electric coffeemaker fell silent. "I always make extra," she said, pouring two cups, "people often come by." She sat down and pointed at the milk bottle and sugar bowl on the table.

I shook my head. "I like it just this way," I said, taking a sip, then a second. Terribly weak.

"Your father was always so kind. After Mr. Arsenault died I could always count on him. One time they raised the rent and I thought I'd have to move. I offered to pay him back but he wouldn't take a penny, your father, keep it for the next rainy day, he said." I'd never heard that before. Chalk one up for my father. "He's in a nursing home, you say?"

"More a retirement home," I replied.

She looked around the kitchen. "I'll never move from here," she said with a little sigh. As far as I could tell it hadn't changed a bit. The coffeemaker was new, but the same round-shouldered fridge in the corner, same gas stove with the iron feet, same wallpaper, blue bells and roses, same ceramic blue and white skating scene over the exhaust vent, same portrait of the Sacred Heart, mournful, effeminate, bony finger pointing to the glowing organ, same sink under the same window, same curtains blowing in the breeze, laundry on the old line I had noticed on the way in, towels, housedresses shapeless as their owner.

"I'll be here when my time comes. Can't afford to move so it will have to do."

I had already spotted a photograph of Omer on the far wall next to a calendar of Our Lady of Lourdes Church, big ad for Arpin Funeral Home under the month December 1969. We went on about everything but Omer – I didn't want to be the first to mention him. She asked what I was doing, asked if I had any clippings which I did not but promised to send. Jim and Catherine too, though she had forgotten their names. Omer was her only child, nothing else on her side of the ledger. Finally I figured I'd better say something.

"Mrs. Arsenault, I want you to know how bad I felt when I heard about Omer." I reached over and put my hand on hers. She was silent a moment, collecting her thoughts.

"Thank you," she said in a small voice. "You raise a child, you put all your love into him, you expect him to be your refuge and strength, and look what happens. You have no idea what I'm talking about, wait til you have children of your own."

"It's not fair, but he served his country honorably, I'm sure." I actually knew nothing about how he died, how he lived, for that matter, though I had tried to find out.

"Country, pah! This country isn't worth the nail on my son's finger. His sacrifice was for nothing. Every day more boys dying and for what? A bunch of Orientals or whatever they are. If they can't defend themselves shame on them! Why stick our nose where we're not wanted, and Nixon! What an awful man!"

"I can't disagree with you there." I looked at my watch.

"You don't have to leave already, do you?"

"I'm afraid I do. I'll stop in the next time I'm here." I noticed her watching me, stiff getting up... we'd been sitting a long time.

"I heard you lost your leg..."

"You manage, you do what you can..."

"At least you're alive, that's more than my Omer is. They tried to talk me out of it but I did it anyway."

"Did what?"

"After Omer's funeral, two soldiers came to the door. The Army had found his medals, somehow they were misplaced. One was a Purple Heart, and oh, a bronze star, one of those in the box, too." Her eyes glistened and her mouth quivered. "A pretty little box, blue velvet inside. I took one look at them and I said, no thank you."

"No thank you?"

"I don't want them, I said, they won't bring my Omer back. But you've got to take them, they said." She smiled, "those boys, just trying to do their job. I don't have to do anything, I said, not after what they did to my Omer. Well they just got in that car and drove away. Next week a package arrives. Please accept these in honor of your son's memory, it said. Well, I sent it right back. That was the last I heard. They thought they could buy me with a few pieces of metal. Honor, you say. I gave them my son and they even couldn't keep him safe. What kind of honor is that, I ask you?"

She began to cry. I went over to her and put my arm around her shoulder. She looked up. "Don't mind me. Most of the time I'm all right."

I sat with Mrs. Arsenault until she had composed herself, then bowed out as gracefully as I could. As I drove past my old house, I thought about another handful of metal, silver, by the story, returned in guilt and despair. I recalled a remark an Army doctor made to me in Japan. He'd been in the operating room I don't know how many hours straight. You see so many die, he said, why anguish over a single individual? I couldn't believe he meant that, I guess in that job you have to harden yourself or go crazy. For the answer to that question, though, look no further than Mrs. Arsenault. In the presence of such love, reasons are beside the point, as they are when the sparrow falls to earth.

WORK PERMITTING, two, three times a week I dropped into the Carmine Street Rec Center, working out and swimming in their indoor pool. I was getting better at staying in line. I found a trainer who worked with amputees and took me on when he saw I was serious about getting in shape. Weights, rowing machine, exercise bike, stretching, some running though I gave that up when Mr. Stumpy complained. The regimen had a big effect on my chest and shoulders. After a few months I had to replace my dress shirts with 17 1/2 necks, up a size and a half, and my t-shirts grew to XXL.

I was relieved to get through my first winter. Oh, I slipped several times and hit the deck once, right in front of my apartment building, of all places. Our one big storm, shoveling the Beetle out was a major balancing act. Home away from home was the White Horse. Some liked the noisy front room with the TV sports but they could have it. The middle room window wall freaked me out, so I gravitated to the dark, quiet back room where it turned out the habitués, of which I had become one, hung out. Did I tell you – first thing I do on entering a restaurant is determine where the nearest exit is. I never sit with my back to a window, always taking a corner seat with a view. If there's none available, I leave. I saw Norman Mailer in the Horse a few times and would have dearly loved to meet Jack Kerouac who lived in the neighborhood some years back, but he'd moved to Florida and died last October. Age 47, too young. Another former regular, Jane Jacobs, was much discussed. I became familiar with her battle to keep lower Manhattan from Robert Moses blight. She was living in Toronto and I never got to meet her, either.

One rainy Saturday as I sat over a beer with my friends, I couldn't help thinking how Gus would fit in here. For all I knew he'd been here – I'd have to ask him. The back room crowd had a strong left-radical tilt, union officials, socialists, members of the Catholic Worker organization who pressed me to come to meetings and, of course, anti-war organizers. Political bent determined hairstyle, though that would change as middle-America grew hip, or at least hirsute. Most males wore their hair long, with mustaches, beards, sideburns. I have to admit my hair was longer than it had ever been, my sideburns too, though I drew the line at moustache and beard.

I learned that standing a couple of particular denizens of the Horse to a few beers got me good tips on the protest scene. Berkeley all over again, I found myself taking the other side of any argument just to stir things up, or to balance the level of passion which after a while got old. I'd been wary of unions ever since the summer I worked for my father, and exposés about fat-cat bosses had confirmed they were every bit as bad as their tycoon antagonists. Now, ironically, I was a member of the Newspaper Guild myself. No card, no job.

When people discovered what happened to me they couldn't fathom why I didn't speak out against America, but I argued it was wrong to trash a system that did a decent, if imperfect job, including, I noted, protecting our right to meet in the White Horse Tavern and trash LBJ, Nixon and everybody else. Try that in Hanoi. Improve, yes, undermine, no.

I came to know Sam Meriweather well, a C.O. who had spent eighteen months in federal prison for refusing induction. Sam was active in the Catholic Worker movement and contributed articles and essays to its newspaper. He knew David Miller, the original draft card burner, and offered to introduce me. Sam credited me with influence at the *Gazette* I didn't have, telling me I should be moving the paper's editorial policy leftward.

Sam and a couple of others shared my affinity for music, and we frequently ended up at jazz clubs – Blue Note and Village Vanguard, particularly. We applauded folk musicians too – Sonny Terry and Brownie McGee, Lightnin' Hopkins, Ramblin' Jack Elliot, Bob Dylan. Also lesser lights, Monday being open mike night. Any mild evening or Sunday afternoon you'd come upon hootenannies in Washington Square Park. Once in a while the Clancy Brothers entertained at the Horse, and there was word of a Dylan sighting, though I'd never seen him. My attitude on *Masters of War* had matured since that first hearing. Weekends, there were more parties than there was time for, music and dancing, the Beatles and their changing personas still dominant.

Drugs were abundant. Pot of course, heroin, cocaine and LSD as well. One night I smoked a couple of joints at a party at a pad near The Cave, but aside from dizziness and a splitting headache, it did nothing for me. I felt my life was plenty vivid without jacking it up artificially. As for drinking, if there had been designated drivers those days I would have been in demand. A couple of beers, wine with dinner, a mellow glow, that I liked, but there I drew the line. I'd seen too many guys wasted on drugs and booze. Smoking? Thanks to the Army I was hooked. I was at a pack a day, Marlboros. My Zippo never failed to provoke conversation. So except for tobacco I guess you'd say I played it pretty much down the middle, avoiding excess and extremes.

Another source of sociability revolved around the *Gazette*. At the intersection of West 44th and Ninth two bars stand caddy-corner to each other. After work, editors and older reporters who liked reporting the news more than managing it, hung out at The Golden Spike, "the Spike." The other establishment, Kells, attracted those still in the striving game. A couple of blocks south, similar facilities existed for *Times* personnel though I'd never been there. Most evenings I repaired to the White Horse but a couple of times a week I made a point of stopping by Kells.

On the sports beat, Frank Flaherty had been with the *Gazette* several years – baseball and hockey. He'd had quite a run this year with the Mets and their first World Series title which delayed his turning to the Rangers. I bemoaned the fact that the upstart Mets, once baseball's doormat, could win it all while my Red Sox – well, enough said. Of course I was shouted down at Kells and everywhere else. Frank and I had Vietnam in common but we didn't agree on that, either. He'd been a Marine Sergeant and wasn't shy about his opinions. He had no sympathy for the vets group I was covering, calling them a bunch of whiners and losers looking for attention.

"Anybody needs a parade that bad's got his head up his ass," Frank would say. "Get a job, get married, you'll have no time for that shit." I told him it wasn't that simple. Frank respected me personally and I went up a couple of notches when he joined me in a workout at Carmine Street and observed my forty laps in an hour, him a big high school athlete in Westchester. He'd been a lineman and a catcher, he told me, so heavily muscled he'd never been much of a swimmer. His excuse was he sank.

Ed Fiore was newer to the *Gazette* than I was. He wrote for the Business Section, a neat fit with the Johns Hopkins doctorate in Economics that got him excused from Cave duty. He told me he nearly abandoned his Ph.D. program too, but hung in long enough to get past the draft, then it seemed a waste not to finish. He'd gone to Jesuit Canisius in Buffalo, was surprised to hear I still attended Mass. He said Vatican Two had really turned him off.

Pam Snyder had a degree in fine arts from, of all places, Rhode Island School of Design, and had studied fashion at Parson's. She readily admitted the *Gazette's* fashion pages weren't on a par with the *Times,* "though we're catching up." I invited her to a movie and since then we'd gone out every couple of weeks. Not your classic beauty, she was a bit heavyset, but always with a smile, relaxing to be around. One thing I appreciated, she wasn't fazed by my leg, or my scar for that matter, from time to time reaching up to caress it as if to say you look just fine. Actually it was fading pretty well.

It was magic, what she could do with a pencil. More than once I'd watched her turn a napkin into a fabulous caricature. I said she should apply for the editorial cartoonist job, as our Pulitzer Prize winner, Ray Archibald, was getting up in years. After she'd had a couple she would sometimes go on about how lonely it was not having more women reporters around and the ones who were, were given the "soft" assignments – fashion, society news, cooking. First time I heard this I made a point of walking around the newsroom to check it out. She was right. Damned few black faces, too. The only ones I knew well, Rory Peters, a Kells habitué, covered football and basketball, and Chuck MacKinnon the uptown beat. I had a standing invitation to explore Harlem with Chuck – the jazz clubs, the Apollo.

I was also taking out a girl I had met at a party, a pretty blonde named Diane Archer who worked at Goldman Sachs. My social life was looking up, except for one problem, and it was a big one. On top of the reticence my male friends saw as odd, I worried how women could ever find me attractive? It had taken me a long time to get used to Mr. Stumpy – what would *they* think? Odd, for he and I went everywhere with aplomb, and as far as I taken things with Pam and Diane, it seemed not a problem. In my more maudlin moments I thought maybe this was just another excuse for not getting involved.

Kells turned out to be more than just a drinking place. Meeting colleagues from all over the paper gave me new perspectives. We second-guessed everything, shredded each other – with good-humor, mostly – yet our competition for the big scoop, the front page story, the promotion, was very real and always just below the surface. Our main preoccupation, though, was the lousy management. For Arthur Graves, the Science Editor and Ron DiPino, an Assistant City Editor, some spent hours plotting torture, murder and worse. Especially graphic was a long-running account of Graves' impending vivisection by Andy Pappas, a medical school dropout who worked for him. I told Andy to write it up – there's a horror flick in there somewhere. Andy had his degree in journalism from Columbia and our talks about approach and technique always offered me something new, as I was all intuition and OJT. But whenever he tried to snow me with buzzwords and arcanity I replied – give me content over style every time.

MY NEW ASSIGNMENT meant more time in the field, which was what I wanted, but the newsroom never ceased to amaze and fascinate. I've waited until now to paint it for you – it took time to sort it all out. The *Gazette's* newsroom occupied a good two-thirds of the fourth floor, with pillars here and there but almost devoid of partitions, a room so vast that several times a day a certain editor would climb on a chair with his binoculars to see who he could grab for an assignment. Fluorescent ballasts hung from the tiled ceiling, casting a flat, shadowless light which hurt your eyes after a few minutes of close work. But what really got you was the noise. Typewriters everywhere, teletype machines, phones ringing, radios, pagers, talking, shouting, moving around, the infernal PA, the exercise bike screeching next to the rowing machine, for some unaccountable reason the two of them named Harold and Maude. The only semblance of quiet – three TVs on pillars in the Assistant Editors' area, tuned to the major channels but muted until somebody noticed a breaking story or got bored and turned one up all the way for the hell of it. Next to combat, this was the most intense situation I'd ever been in – impossible deadlines and insufferable din propelling everyone into a frenzy. Late night was the only time you got to hear yourself think, and even then you knew when the presses were starting from the rumble under your feet.

October through March, no matter the outside temp, tall silvered radiators around the edge of the room poured out steam heat, making the room unbearable. Mid-winter, they had the fans and air conditioners running full blast. What a waste, I thought, then I discovered this condition is endemic to all Manhattan buildings, though I never heard a good reason why. Even for a smoker the air was stale enough to make you ill. Fresh air might have had a chance via the window wall running the length of the far side, but Editors' offices blocked that possibility. I didn't venture into them often, but when I did I enjoyed the memorabilia, the signed celebrity photos, the framed front page stories. Most of these guys had a couch they used for the not-infrequent all-nighter. Assistant Editors sat at desks clustered in a rectangular area called the Bullpen, within shouting distance of "Editors' Row."

A large, round desk with a center cut-out stood at the far end of Editors' Row. Marty Rossi's rank entitled him to an office, but as City Editor he needed to be in the middle of the action. Marty was responsible for reporters, photographers, columnists, cartoonists, rewrite men and headline writers, as well the topical departments. The corner office belonged to Managing Editor Tom O'Connor, who decided what did or did not get into the paper. With a staff of talented writers he also laid out the editorial page and generated the *Gazette's* editorials. Shoehorned into Editors' Row was a conference room from which shouting often could be heard. O'Connor managed the production side of the paper too, the trades, printers, composing room, photo-engravers and mapmakers, as well as the teams of receptionists, secretaries, telephone operators, cafeteria and medical personnel.

An ingenious system of department store-type pneumatic tubes sped memos, galleys, papers and other small objects around the building. I always smiled when I heard the whoosh of an incoming container and saw it drop out onto somebody's desk.

The pillars I mentioned served as boundary markers, with signs. City, where I had my desk, Sports, Foreign, Business, Science, Real Estate, Music & Dance, Drama, Society, Health, and so on, and of course Obituaries aka the Irish Sports Pages. A world apart, the paper's moneymakers, Advertising and its profitable stepchild, Classifieds, had their own partitioned area – "The Great Wall," per the placard – in the northeast corner. Affixed to the pillars was a wide variety of posters, a couple from old MOMA exhibits, Peter Max concert psychedelia, Yankee 1956 Championship, a few serious art prints.

The location of your desk was crucial. With pool reporters, it didn't matter so much, jacks-of-all trades covering stories whose context they might or might not understand. Fast on their feet, these guys operated in the no-man's land between fact and fabrication. Other departments, the closer you sat to your Assistant Editor the better, at least in theory. My first day I mistakenly occupied an empty desk, but the stares told me I'd screwed up. Finally somebody clued me in – this was a desk awaiting assignment. Somebody was moving up and it wasn't me. "You're back there," my informant said, pointing at the furthest-most desk next to the pillar marking the line between City and Music & Dance. Give me a break, I mumbled, stuffing my things in my briefcase and retreating to the City limits.

Desks were identical, gray government issue. Chairs had castors, which encouraged short-range visiting. For every desk a crookneck lamp, and aluminum cylinders for pencils and ballpoints. A week or so after I was in my actual desk, a package wrapped in newsprint arrived. I was enormously pleased to find a nameplate, black plastic with "Bernard" in white letters on a wooden block with green felt dots on the bottom. Some desks sported colorful child art, ceramic pencil holders being big. No surface was without a taped handwritten note. A tall rack of pigeonholes, mail boxes, was propped against a partition at the City limits, next to bulletin boards with notices and messages. Under every desk an overflowing wastebasket, spent carbons and wadded paper on the floor, pink and green mixed in with your basic white from the multiple copies of our typed stories. Some desk areas were carpeted, that is a rug swatch that served no function except to immobilize the occupant's chair. I had no framed pictures, though I did have a mason jar part-filled with chunks of metal. You can guess where that was all about.

Having escaped Marty's oversight, after I finished typing I'd yell for a copyboy who, if not chasing a sandwich for a reporter or an editor's theater tickets, rushed my copy to a copy editor to pencil in his changes, cut paragraphs apart and reassemble them on a clean sheet of paper with sweet-smelling paste and brush. Shades of Buzz Sawyer and Terry. The unwanted snippets he would impale on a brass spike on his desk. Sometimes an entire story ended up "spiked." Often, as deadline loomed I was still in the field so I'd phone one of our rewrite men, geniuses with nimble minds and fingers who added their experienced sidebars to our babblings, molding the thing into a polished product.

Next the edited story was rushed to the composing room by a copyboy who clambered down the circular iron staircase, disappearing through a hole in the floor then passing through a semi-soundproof door. Amid overpowering din, linotype operators keyed in text which appeared miraculously in lines of type formed by hot lead. Thus the name. Next, the galley or proof was sped up the circular stairs to the copy editor for one last workover. The linotype operators, old-timers all, wore earplugs which I didn't think twice about it until I noticed them communicating in sign language. *Gazette* hiring policy, I learned, probably made worse by the job.

Most nights I left after working my story over with a copy editor, but sometimes I returned later to breathe in the atmosphere. For those whose home life was non-existent or worse, for those who didn't feature Kells or the Spike, most nights when the last edition was put to bed, a bottle party was hosted by Ed Saunders, a well-liked old timer on the City Hall beat. Told years ago he was unpromotable – i.e. we don't fire family, but you're never going anywhere – Ed maintained a wheeled cooler with ice, beer, mixers and a bottle of Jim Beam never less than half full. From time to time even some of the higher-ups dropped by. Only rule, bring your own glass. The first night I ventured by, Tom O'Connor was there in shirtsleeves, his feet on a desk, swapping stories with the peons.

After hours, the animals who lived in the building came out – the four-footed variety, that is. Every floor had a cat that showed up for handouts and companionship. Ours was a huge tabby named Slicker, black but for a white front foot and a star, also white, on its forehead. Slicker lived in a cubbyhole behind the men's room. He (she?) accepted largesse from all and foraged endlessly for mice and rats. Eight was also home to a mangy mutt called Milhous, living openly and notoriously, as we on the crime beat liked to say. The Nature Editor kept a brace of birds, some sort of parakeet I think, in his office. There were gerbils and geckos, though I never saw them. No doubt other wildlife prowled the *Gazette,* but these stand out in my memory.

41. DIANE

"HOW'D IT GO?" It is shortly before noon and Jonathan has just returned from his meeting with ETVN.

"I'm disappointed. They don't know half as much as we do."

"Unless they weren't letting on. What about that inside source of theirs?"

"He didn't open up on that either, though we did discuss them paying my way."

"Even if they did, how would you find the time?" I ask, pointing at the newly-discovered cartons against the back wall. He rolls his eyes.

Earlier today I had a long talk with Cahill. People like him and Steve have it figured out. If the litigation pot gets cold they're out of a job so they've got to keep the flame under it. Our "Answer" is due in twenty days. I have to start drafting responses to those questions. They also want to see and copy everything, but to that one Cahill says no way.

* * * * * * *

A WEEK INTO MY NEW ASSIGNMENT and Ed Foley was giving me trouble. Chagrined at the demotion, he was telling his sources not to cooperate. I was about to complain to Sid when a series of events intervened and altered the dynamic for the better. The previous fall an SDS splinter group called the Weathermen after the Dylan song, debuted with a riot at the Chicago Eight trial. They then issued a Declaration of a State of War against the U.S. government and burrowed in for what would be a series of bombings. March of this year, in the basement of a townhouse only blocks from my apartment, a blast first attributed to a faulty gas main killed three of them as they assembled a bomb. I volunteered for the follow-up, interviewing residents, gathering comments about the three killed and the two who went missing. A series of bomb threats the next week caused evacuation of several office buildings, and shortly thereafter I did a story about two more blowing themselves up in another Lower Manhattan bomb-making factory. I began to think these people should find another line of work.

Then, Richard Nixon's carefully orchestrated peace with honor force reduction came unglued. In a televised address, he announced U.S. and South Vietnamese troops had invaded Cambodia for the purpose of destroying North Vietnam's supply caches. I knew something of Cambodia, those high-altitude B-52 contrails had been pretty obvious, and I crossed the border with my unit, sometimes in error, sometimes by design, though that was peanuts compared with this. Finding and destroying an elusive and possibly non-existent North Vietnamese Army headquarters was a primary goal. But the real theater of war was at home.

To the opposition, Nixon was talking out of both sides of his mouth, bragging about peace while widening the war. Protests spread quickly, involving millions of students on more than four hundred campuses. Scattered violence only, but it was spectacular, with ROTC buildings destroyed and the National Guard mobilized. On short notice a hundred thousand protesters assembled in Washington, same in San Francisco. Congress initiated steps which culminated in a prohibition against U.S. ground action in Cambodia and Laos, and in a belated nod to history, rescinded the Gulf of Tonkin Resolution.

Monday afternoon May 4, my phone rang. "Sid here. I need you right away." Two hours later I was on an American Airlines flight to Cleveland. That morning, the Ohio Guard had shot and killed four students at nearby Kent State University.

The *Gazette* had a Kent stringer, a part-timer for tips and local stories. A grad student in Journalism, Stan Phipps had been doing the job for a couple of years. He'd filed a couple of stories on the protests though none of it had run. But this was a huge story and I was pleased Sid sent me, for a mature perspective, he said, and to back up Phipps. In a peculiar twist, one of my radical contacts told me the officially unidentified third townhouse victim was from Kent State, leader of an earlier student rebellion there and a Weatherman founder. On the plane I was thinking, while I was at Berkeley nobody had ever been killed, though I heard someone was shot later on a rooftop during a street riot.

I found Stan in the lobby. The day after Nixon's speech there'd been a demonstration, he told me, followed by an alcohol-fueled disturbance downtown, store windows smashed, trash barrels set afire, prompting the mayor to declare a state of emergency. For the next two days large crowds gathered on the campus, an abandoned ROTC building was burned and the Guard called out. Facing re-election later in the year, Ohio's Governor Rhodes called the protestors brown shirts and Communists, claiming they were the strongest militant revolutionary group ever assembled in America.

Our press passes got us through for a fast tour, then we repaired to my room to work over the story. They were holding the space and a byline for me and I told Sid be sure Stan gets one as well. I reread our work in the bar and phoned in a rewrite punching up the lead paragraph. Stan mentioned that a friend of his had a stunner of a picture, a young girl screaming, kneeling over a victim. The photo ran next day across three columns of our front page and probably every other paper in the world. Stan and I shared the byline, my first front page credit, though I didn't tell him that.

We did a follow-up piece discussing the mystery of who gave the order to fire and if, as most said, there was no order, what the hell happened. I sensitized Stan, who had no military experience, to the importance of command discipline and told him to try and find out why it apparently broke down here. Then I flew back to New York. That weekend more than a hundred thousand students massed in Washington against the war, turning the White House into an armed camp. These protests fed the President's paranoia as Agnew, his V.P., mounted sarcastic attacks on the nation's young people.

Back in the city, a source called to tell me some union guys were going to disrupt a memorial planned in lower Manhattan for the Kent State victims. That morning a group of anti-war protesters, most of them high schoolers and college students, gathered at Broad and Wall. By late morning over a thousand, they moved to the steps of Federal Hall. Ollie and I mingled, photographing and interviewing. Just before noon I looked up the street and saw a mass of people coming our way. Men in hard hats, red, white, blue, yellow, waving small American flags, parading behind a huge American flag spread out like a sheet, sidewalk to sidewalk. More hardhats appeared from side streets, swelling the crowd, which continued to advance. Ollie's camera was smoking. I was jotting observations, notably how vulnerable the students were, only a thin line of police between them and the hard hats.

"This doesn't look good," I said to Ollie.

"Whenever I go on a story with you I get in trouble. Why is that?"

The hard hats halted right in front of the police. I thought that would be it, but they began pushing, testing the police line. Suddenly they broke through, attacking the students, chasing them as they scattered in all directions. Now we were in the middle of a mob scene, people rolling on the ground, trying to cover up, tumbling down the steps. Some guys in suits appeared from nearby office buildings and tried to aid the students but the hard hats turned on them too. I told Ollie get a picture of the cops standing by, not raising a finger.

I noticed a smaller group of hard hats heading north and decided to follow them. Ollie stayed behind to cover the aftermath of the riot which was beginning to tail off. The splinter group assembled on the steps of City Hall. In a moment a guy appeared on the roof, raising the American flag to full mast. The other day we had carried a picture of it at half mast, the city's tribute to Kent State. Heading back I saw hard hats attacking other buildings, chasing students, attacking them with clubs and crowbars, breaking windows. Mayor Lindsay criticized the police for their inaction, drawing sharp fire from police and union leaders. Wasn't it interesting, I wrote – long hair, then drug abuse, now Joe Sixpack's playing the street game. What next?

In the days following, the unions kept up the pressure with rallies blasting the mayor, culminating two weeks later in a parade of some hundred thousand unionists through lower Manhattan under streamers of ticker tape. New York union leaders including Peter Brennan, the local boss, were invited to the White House and presented Nixon his very own hard hat. Nixon's political advisors elevated union support on their agenda. Funny thing, Peter Brennan was later named Secretary of Labor. That outpouring of support for the hard hats, the police letting it happen, reminded me of the brutish German streets not so many years ago. How to account for New York crowds cheering these people on to assault and pillage? Had Nixon tapped into the real soul of America?

Ten days after Kent State, city and state police fired hundreds of shots at close range at an unruly crowd on the campus of Mississippi's Jackson State College, killing a black college student and a high schooler and wounding twelve others.

The dearth of media coverage compared with Kent, was stunning. Do black kids count for less? And why so much ink spilled over the four at Kent while Vietnam's daily deaths merit only a statistic on some inside page? I was tempted to insert these questions into a story, but they wouldn't have survived the edit.

Despite the bullyboy backing, anti-war sentiment was wearing heavily on the administration. By the end of June, Nixon had withdrawn all U.S. troops from Cambodia, claiming a resounding victory, of course. As to military morale, particularly Army, more reports of fraggings, desertions, AWOLs, sometimes entire units refusing orders to fight. Our government's moral authority was in tatters and getting worse.

My run of exposure apparently had its effect on Ed Foley, who one day presented me with his entire list of contacts. "Imagine that – just found them in my desk!" I was pleased the rift was mended. For all his bluster, his experience would be a plus.

DIANE ARCHER AND I WERE SPENDING A LOT OF TIME TOGETHER. In fact, by the fall she had supplanted Pam and everyone else on my list. What was Diane like? Five-seven, a little shorter than Meg – why is Meg still the standard? Strong face, straight nose upturned at the end, green-gray eyes and shoulder-length hair, a brilliant smile and, really interesting – at repose the corners of her mouth rose like a cat's. What makeup she wore she disguised well. Clothes expensive, on the conservative side but at times revealing enough to make me want to see more. A quick mind, well read. Her sense of humor was ironic, as if she viewed things best at an angle. She was a good athlete, had played tennis at Smith, shared my interest in swimming, and grew up sailing. She detested practical jokes and the first one I tried on her, she didn't speak to me for a week. Last souvenir stand T-shirt I ever gave her. She was very loyal and seemed to have a particularly close relationship with her father.

The family owned an estate in Oyster Bay on Long Island's exclusive north shore called Hyades (correct spelling) after the daughters – or sisters, depending on the version – of Hyas, tragic archer of Greek mythology. Diane had her MBA from Harvard Business School, and as I mentioned, was an analyst for Goldman Sachs in corporate bonds. For her, thinking in money terms was second nature, her father being a senior officer at Chase Manhattan. What was it about me and girls with banker fathers, I wondered.

She lived alone in a townhouse off Washington Square about fifteen minutes from my place, a gift from her father on joining Goldman. There I often ran into her sister Penny, a junior at Bryn Mawr. Except for two years at a Swiss boarding school Diane spent her early years at an exclusive girls' school on the Upper East Side. Knowing the City intimately, she delighted in playing tour guide. It would have taken me a long time to discover the Whitney or the Palisades or Montauk Point, or the Amato Opera or any number of ethnic restaurants I could almost afford or see the Yankees crush my Sox from a box at the Stadium. Ugly, that one. As summer melted into fall and winter came on, I was beginning to think maybe she's the one, except for one little problem. She wasn't a Catholic. But then, fat lot of good that did me with Meg.

One snowy Friday, after dinner and a movie, M*A*S*H, I distinctly recall, we returned to her place and were listening to music, drinking wine and making out. At one point she went into the bedroom and I stepped over to the window, pulling the curtains aside and looking out. Surprising me, she came up behind me and put her arms around my waist. "Rotten night," she said.

I turned and kissed her. "It's slick out there. Maybe I should just stay the night."

"I wouldn't want you to slip."

One thing led to another and next thing you know, we were in bed under the covers, our clothes all over the floor. Next afternoon back in my place I sorted through the haze. What I did was wrong but I couldn't help thinking, I've paid my dues, maybe I have some credits piled up. Do I love Diane? Does she love me? As they used to say in Boston, if it looks like love and sounds like love and acts like love... All I knew for sure, last night was fantastic. And Mr. Stumpy had no complaints. As I knelt at Mass Sunday I pondered my situation. Maybe I should talk to one of the priests. I sat in the bench as others went to communion. Give it a pass today... I need to figure things out, don't want to make the problem worse, if it is a problem, that is.

A couple of evenings later I asked Diane to dinner. We were in the bar of the Washington Square Hotel, quiet and intimate, when the conversation turned to our relationship. I knew Diane was a modern woman, and here, over our third glass of wine, it comes out she's on the pill. Frankly, I'd been a little concerned, it came on so suddenly with us and, no surprise, I was totally unprepared. My first reaction was relief, then I hemmed and hawed and she acknowledged that yes, she'd had other partners though not that many, and it was always a steady.

"A steady? What's that mean?"

"Someone you like a lot and he likes you. You know, an exclusive. I'm surprised you have to ask."

I fell silent. I was disappointed and angry. But why? She was an adult. She saw the concern on my face. "You're not my father, you know."

I nodded. "Whatever else I am I'm not that."

"I have to be really attached to a person. I don't just sleep around."

"I never said you did." Yes, it was her life but now, for the first time, it's possible we could be talking about *our* life. Suddenly it came to me, something I'd been wanting to say anyway. "Seems to me like we're going steady. If not, how about it?"

She smiled and took my hand. "I thought you'd never ask."

We ended up at her place again. Next morning, for the first time in my career I called in sick. That was the day I first saw the Cloisters in the snow. Before the Unicorn tapestry, I presented her the friendship ring I had bought a few weeks before, hoping I'd have the chance to use it. An opal, for her birth month, October. Green, like her eyes.

As spring went on we were inseparable. I was on top of the world, though there was occasional static. We ran into a guy I surmised was one of her former "steadies" and I was perturbed. Not that she did anything inappropriate, but I didn't need reminding what an attractive target she was, plus I was having this gigantic guilt trip about our making love. Not in the moment, when the whole world came down to just the two of us, but afterward it seemed hollow and incomplete. Instead of giving ourselves, it was like a short-term loan with strings and conditions. I went to confession but stumbled over the part about amending my life. Far from repentant, I wanted to fall, and eagerly looked forward to the next time. Diane sensed something was wrong, though I didn't demean her by letting on what a problem she was for me. But there was a solution. If we were going to act like we were married, we should get married. So, out of moral fatigue as much as anything else, after a few more months I asked her and she said yes.

The parents. Mother Eleanor was a Lowell, a *grande dame,* her people loyalists back when that mattered. Relative newcomers to our shores (eighteenth century), the father's line was Scottish. The Archers' speech, their bearing, their home, everything about them oozed entitlement, quiet assurance, old school tie. For J. Peter Archer it was Yale, Skull & Bones, which I asked about but never got a good answer, and Harvard Business. Her mother was in the family line of Smith women that Diane continued, though not her sister Penny, who often acted the rebel. A display in the sitting room included pictures of Diane's coming out, as young women of good breeding did, but no similar picture for Penny.

I knew little about diamonds but Sid Greenwald steered me to a friend on West 47th Street in the Diamond District. I left a month's wages on the counter and departed with a payment book, the proprietor's *mazel tov* and a large diamond I gave to Diane that Saturday night over dinner. I steered us to one of my favorites, a quirky little Irish pub restaurant on Sixth called McBell's, not far from her place. She had little feeling for things Irish, which was understandable considering her heritage, but seemed willing to learn. She knew even less about French-Canadians. Though her parents were friendly enough, I suspected there'd been sharp conversations after I broke the news to her father. I wondered whether they would have been as welcoming if my name didn't appear from time to time on the front page of a major New York newspaper. Though even that was a mixed blessing, for they identified with the *Wall Street Journal* and were partial to the *Times.*

My family was thrilled I had found someone, or someone had found me. The week before Christmas good old Sheila threw an engagement party at their house, and in excellent form my father insisted on hosting the two of us the next day at an elegant lunch, at the Biltmore, of course. He was utterly captivated by Diane, but Catherine's reaction was quite different. "What are you doing marrying a non-Catholic?" she whispered when she got me aside. "You of all people!" I wasn't sure whether she was joking, she acted so serious.

"You of all people," I said, "what's that supposed to mean?"

"The priest in the family marrying an Episcopalian! I am shocked! Utterly shocked!"

"A married priest! Isn't that a problem right there?"

She shook her head. "I might give you an exemption on that one."

With a date the following May, it was shaping up to be a very big deal. I insisted that we be married in the Church. Diane agreed though it took some persuading. "This Catholic thing isn't easy for me," she said, as we started through the hoops and hurdles, the paperwork, the counseling. I wanted children. Diane wasn't opposed, as long as they didn't foul up her career. Child care, I said, day care, whatever it takes – with two incomes we'll manage. Surprisingly she was okay that they be raised Catholic

Until I got to know her well, I assumed Diane was into materialism, raised as she was in comfort and surrounded by expensive things, but oddly, her upbringing seemed to have relaxed her acquisitive tendencies. I had a feeling, however, that since her needs and desires had always been gratified, she assumed the future would be no different. I also discovered the intensity over her career was mostly about getting ahead, making her mark as a woman. Financial instruments, arrangements, deal making, for her it was a game, though one she was very good at. Diane's indifference about churchgoing actually helped our religion issue. Nor were her parents serious about religion, or put it this way, spirituality was not high on the list. For them the social aspect is what mattered, an attitude I had always disparaged. Beneath the smiles and civility, how my future in-laws felt about the impending union, my disability, how they actually felt about me, I could only guess.

A few weeks later my father gave us another scare. It looked like a stroke, the doctors saying he couldn't take too much more of that, but it was a false alarm and he was out of the hospital before I made it to Providence. Dad said the doctors had gotten through to him about his smoking, and I believed him, sort of. I made it a point of abstaining around him, which was a push, because these days I wouldn't think of sitting down at the typewriter or having a cup of coffee without a cigarette. Diane was after me to quit too, at least cut back, but it was out of the question.

Driving me back to the airport, Catherine picked up where she had left off the last time. "Don't be angry with me, okay?"

"I reserve the right to be angry. Why should I be angry?"

"What I'm about to say..." she paused, searching for words, "let me say it straight. I don't think Diane's right for you."

"Oh, the religion thing again."

"No, I'm over that, anyway I was half joking. I can't put my finger on it but I just don't see the two of you together for the long haul. She's too, what, too self-contained. Chilly, even. You know what I mean?"

I shook my head. "Once you get to know her, she's a very warm person."

"You're not confusing sex with love.?"

I flushed. "I'm aware of the difference."

"I should hope so. You were in the Army, you must have learned a few tricks there."

Catherine made the turn to the airport and a moment later pulled up in front of the terminal. She turned to me. "Sorry I'm not explaining myself well. I like Diane and all that, I can understand why you're attracted to her but she strikes me as being all about Diane. Me first, if anything's left over, fine. That's not you. You're generous and open, everything she's not."

"Are you finished?"

"Sorry if I hurt your feelings but I don't want you to make a mistake, not on something this important."

Biting my lip I reached in the back for my bag. Standing on the sidewalk, I looked through her half-open window. "Your interest in my welfare is appreciated. Check back in a year, see what you think then. You couldn't be more off base."

ONE OF THE GREAT PLEASURES of my work was getting to know Alan Mauro. Alan was one of the city's most revered reporters and best known men-about-town, for the last twenty-two years author of the twice-weekly column *ETC*. Of the *Gazette's* many columns, *ETC* was by far the most popular. He ranged the city, vacuuming up dirt and nuggets. Nothing was too trivial or too shocking. Every Tuesday and Thursday, readers turned to the left column on page one of the City Section. Politics, theater, sports, restaurants, education, society, shopping, the ethics and practice of journalism, raking the *Times* and the *Trib* and yes, even the *Gazette* over the coals, he missed nothing, opined on everything. He used a beat-up old Rollei to put faces to his interviews. I first met Alan when he came by my desk to take issue over my hard hat story, my chiding the cops for taking the construction workers' side. Alan was pro-police all the way, but as we talked he began to nod. He went out and did some digging and wrote a follow-up expressing sympathy, if not support, for my position.

Short, chunky, balding, always in a white shirt, soup tie and rumpled sports jacket, a voluble, funny dees-and-doser with a command of profanity in several languages, an encyclopedic memory and a steel-trap mind, Alan was on a first-name basis with every notable and politico. But his best work came roaming the streets, spending shoe leather in the service of ordinary people, their dreams and woes, the little guy against the stacked deck. His columns had championed the neighborhoods in their battle to save lower Manhattan from Robert Moses and he loved to regale us with tales of Jane Jacobs and her Goliath.

For some reason I never fully understood, Alan took me under his wing. He hated phonies, so I took this as a compliment. From time to time I'd get a call to accompany him on his way to a City Councilman's office. Or drop in on the owner of a Chinatown eatery struggling to reopen after a fire. Or commiserate with the Lutheran pastor in Yorktown about his declining German congregation. Or visit a ballet school for blind kids on the Upper West Side. Or cadge a slice of pizza and a soda from a Red Hook deli while interviewing a laid-off longshoreman. Or interview the City's Chief Building Inspector about the mammoth World Trade Center project. Now, that was an interesting one.

Of course I had seen the behemoths reaching for the sky, but until Alan clued me in I knew nothing of the battles behind the scenes. Alan was looking into a possible conflict of interest, curious how any developer could be left in charge of its own safety compliance, in this case the bi-state Port Authority, exempt from the city's codes and inspection services. On the way back to the office I reached back for some perspectives from my political science studies. This surprised him, he hadn't known that about me.

A benefit of the job I hadn't expected, reporters have a lot of power and respect, even those relatively new to the trade. At social gatherings people often responded with an "aha" or "oh, really" when I told them what I did. That it was the *Gazette* added cachet. Our competitors the next street down referred to themselves as Timesmen but we had no such affectation. What we did share was an almost physical bond I could feel deepen as the months went on and I became part of the club. One night I had just filed a complex story I had to babysit to the end, don't even remember about what. The early edition was on the presses and I was preparing to leave when I ran into Alan at the elevator.

"Heading to the Spike?" he asked.

"If you invite me," I laughed. "Kells is more my speed."

"Let's do it." I was reaching for the DOWN button but he leaned across and pressed UP. "But first I gotta show you something." We exited on the eighth floor, space hallowed by the Publisher and Executive Editor. "Ever been here?" I shook my head. "I'm gonna give you the tour."

We walked through the dimly lit area. Friday night, it looked like everyone had fled for the weekend. Treading across the carpet, a couple of turns and we found ourselves in front of a pair of heavy unmarked doors. Alan turned the shiny brass knob but the door was locked. He reached into his jacket pocket and extracted a huge key ring – there must have been thirty keys on it, all shapes and sizes. "In your spare time you must be the super."

"Second job kind of thing. Helps in a high wind, too." The key turned easily. "It's always locked but we have our ways." He pushed the door open and reached around for the light switch. "The inner inner inner sanctum," he said, bowing and doffing an imaginary hat, "the Board Room of the mighty *New York Gazette.*"

The walls were a deep blue, lined with portraits and photographs, plush carpet blue but with a gold fleck. Rows of canisters with recessed spotlights were inset into the flocked white ceiling. Alan turned a knob and brought the lights to high. The largest conference table I'd ever seen, surrounded by upholstered swivel chairs, twenty by a quick count. At each place, a pad of paper and two black wooden pencils with a *Gazette* logo.

"The Board meets here first Monday of every month, but that's not why this is interesting." He walked down the table to the end with a larger, taller chair than the others and pointed at the wall. "Recognize this guy?"

Two large oil paintings, a rough-looking man with a handlebar moustache, a bag slung over his back, astride a small stream, hills behind him. Next to it the same man, older, in a business suit with high starched celluloid collar, holding up a

Gazette in the original typeface. "The honorable Peter McNeeley, to whom we owe all this," he said, sweeping his hand around the room. "That picture shows how he made his money, this one how he lost it."

He sidled down the line of portraits, pointing to an even larger paintings of two ruddy-faced men, one with a full beard, the other with a moustache and mutton chops. "Sam and Marty, the Astell boys. The paper was going down for the count when they stepped in. If it wasn't for them we'd be working for the *Times.*"

"Speak for yourself," I said wryly.

"Yeah, I wouldn't want to work for them either."

"That's not exactly what I meant."

We worked our way around the room, stopping to admire others in the line of Publishers, Editors and Executive Editors, Pulitzer Prize winners. At the far end of the room we came to a gallery of reporters, pamphleteers, cartoonists, photographers and broadcasters who had added luster to our profession. Tom Paine, William Lloyd Garrison, Lippmann, Murrow, Shirer, Sevareid, Lowell Thomas, W. Eugene Smith, Bourke-White, Mauldin, Herblock. On the near wall a display of *Gazette* executives mingling with those they helped make famous or even more famous. Morgan, Rockefeller, Teddy Roosevelt, Taft, Wilson, Hoover, FDR, MacArthur, George Marshall, Truman, Eisenhower, Kennedy, LBJ, Nixon. Queen Victoria, King George, Churchill, DeGaulle, Queen Elizabeth II and Prince Philip, Fidel Castro on his 1960 visit to the U.N. Jimmy Walker, Robert Wagner, John Lindsay. John J. McGraw, Christy Mathewson, Ty Cobb, Ruth and Gehrig, DiMaggio and Rizzuto, Casey Stengel, Hank Greenberg, Mickey Mantle, Roger Maris, Tom Seaver, Ted Williams (another foreign leader, I thought with a smile). Whirlaway, Man o' War, Secretariat. Some early prints legended in white ink reminded me of my first photo album. Signed best wishes from all who could, florid hands and scrawls. One hoof print, Secretariat's.

Circuit complete, we stood before three portraits. Tall, white-haired, crew-cut Tom O'Connor whom I encountered nearly every day. Executive Editor Walter Shoenweis of stern visage and low visibility. Franklin Astell III, Publisher and Chairman of the Board, the family resemblance obvious even when adjusted for his lack of facial hair. "Quite a show. It's amazing."

Alan ushered me toward the exit. I stopped to look at a display case next to the door. "The Homers, courtesy of *Harper's*. You know the story?"

"I do," I said, giving them a fast scan.

"You know, all of us, we get so wrapped up chasing this story or that story, we forget we're part of something very special."

"As the new kid on the block it's good to be here."

Alan pulled the door shut and turned to look at me. "What happens, you work here for a while, then one day you wake up and you realize there's nothing else in the world you'd rather do. In fact, you'd do this job for nothing if it came to that – don't tell Tom I said that. I come up here sometimes, to stay in touch, charge the batteries."

"Thank you," I said, pushing the DOWN button. "You're right, I'm hooked."

"I wasn't at first." Six... seven... eight. The light dinged on. "Something happened to kick my ass into gear, I'll tell you about it sometime. Speaking of that we better get ours over to the Spike. We're playing catchup tonight."

AS THE YEAR DRAWS TO A CLOSE everyone steps back and takes stock. Twelve months into "the Seventies," I had a fabulous job in the most interesting city in the world and was getting married to a great girl. Even my moral anxiety wasn't getting me down too much. I rationalized it as the down payment on a good life.

The *Gazette* published its annual year-end retrospective. Vietnam topped the list. Even as Nixon drew down troop levels, the numbers of U.S. dead and wounded continued to mount, climbing past 44,000, though more slowly than before. I saw that my old unit, the 25th, was pulled out in December. The fighting continued, seemingly no end in sight. Talks between Nixon's emissary, Henry Kissinger, and the North Vietnamese, were at an impasse, and for good reason. Our country was beset by division and rancor, insubordination and drug use in the military. Well aware of this, the North was prepared to "negotiate" forever, confident they would outlast us. Meantime, on a happier note, work continued on efforts to put the nuclear weapon genie back in its bottle. The Strategic Arms Limitation Talks showed signs of progress, and earlier in the year a Non-Proliferation Treaty came into force.

Diane and I took in a great film, Catch-22, and I picked up a copy of that amazing book and read it for the first time. I'd been warily watching but as far as I knew, no novels or films about Vietnam. The wounds were too fresh, I figured, too painful.

Continuing on the anti-war beat I was getting to know some of the veterans active in the movement. The one-legged Marine I met in that first vets march, Cyrus Thomas, was a source and becoming a friend. Running into him at another march we set a date to tour his neighborhood. As I drove us around the Grand Concourse section of the Bronx I noticed him wistfully watching me maneuver the Beetle in and out of traffic.

"You could do this, too, you know," I said, "all you need's a special license."

"Get real, man, I ain't got no car and I ain't about to get one. It's hard enough chasin' down my next meal."

I felt like reaching into my pocket but caught myself. I did promise myself to see what I could do about finding him a job. The *Gazette* was off limits, but maybe somebody else would take a chance on a decent guy down on his luck. Maybe a city job? I'd ask Alan for his advice. As we drove, Cyrus pointed out where he lived, a public housing project in the lee of the towering Cross-Bronx Expressway, a Robert Moses King Car project rammed through a community not as savvy as the Village.

"This ain't no place for a white boy," he said, as we drove down a block of abandoned buildings, their windows smashed, few boarded up, "a black boy, neither. An' you sure don' wanna be around here at night. Think I like livin' here, well think again."

"Where are the cops?"

"That's my point. Where are the cops? They smart, they don' wanna be here neither."

Something had been nagging at me, something I'd been meaning to talk with him about. "Cyrus, let me ask you something, how come you never got yourself fitted with legs?"

"I get along okay, man – don' worry 'bout me."

"But you'd get along a lot better if you could walk. Why not check in with the VA, you've probably still got benefits."

Cyrus shook his head angrily. "I tol' you don' bother 'bout me!" He paused. "Oh, shee-it, if you gotta know, I had legs one time, man. I sold 'em."

"Sold them!"

"Yeah. Kept me high a coupl'a months. Too late, man, too late. Ain't never gonna get no better for me."

DURING THE YEAR, social ferment drew me into other stories. Womens' lib, where Diane and Penny gave me useful perspective. Also what was being called the gay rights movement that kicked off the previous year, literally, with a Rockettes-style chorus line during the Stonewall Rebellion, several nights of rioting following a police raid on a Village gay bar. But the issue I identified with most was the environment. The first Earth Day, April 22, occurred before I took the assignment but I was looking forward to covering the next year's events at the U.N.

And, five years since Vatican II, I made an effort to catch up. My inner turmoil over Diane had led me back to reading and thinking about religion. The new liturgy was bitterly opposed by many old-timers, convinced the Church had lost its way and abandoning its special, distinctive character. At Mass, I could testify personally, sociability and mostly boring guitar music had replaced dignity and silence, some said holiness as well. Ironically, Paul VI's *Humanae Vitae* had affirmed the one traditional position many including his own advisers thought should have been scrapped – the ban on contraception. I agreed with them, while wondering whether these days my judgment was suspect. Formerly unheard of, scores of men were leaving the priesthood, and there were signs religious women would follow suit. New faces began appearing in the pews – immigrants from Mexico, Haiti, the first refugees from Southeast Asia, adding diversity and challenges.

As the Church turned to outreach and acceptability, Catholics were assimilating into American society faster than ever. The first Catholic President had largely dispelled fears about Rome, but everywhere the American Church was in turmoil. Wealthier, more successful in business and the professions, educated increasingly in non-Catholic institutions, many Catholics no longer viewed religion as central to their lives, but as a Sunday tangent, if that. No longer "in it but not of it," they had stopped casting their ancient, critical eye on the world around them, instead wholeheartedly pursuing its benefits.

As I still considered myself a good Catholic, mostly, I felt these tensions keenly. I hoped Diane would accommodate my religious needs, but I couldn't see her as a helpmate in this vital part of my life. Attending Mass in my semi-estranged state, from time to time I wondered whether Catherine might not be right after all. I felt powerless to change course but the truth is, I really didn't want to.

42. TWO INTO ONE

I'M BACK FROM MY TRIP TO MAINE. Faithful Volvo fired right up after sitting three months. The Swedes certainly can build a car. I was apprehensive about the house but I needn't have been. Joseph got the leak fixed and before a hard freeze, too. Good man. If he'd been born a car he'd have been a Volvo. They had to dig up fifteen feet of lawn to find the leak so I said what the hell, why not ruin the rest. Now I have new plastic pipes all the way to the city hookup. Come spring we're looking at a big landscaping job but it had to be done.

Thanksgiving eve we had neighbors over for drinks, and the young couple next door were nice enough to invite Joseph and me for dinner the day of. I finished my interrogatories, sent them off to Cahill. Never get involved in a lawsuit. To think some people, lawyers that is, do this day in and day out. Of course they're paid well, some of them. Cahill is decent about his fees. Takes his pound of flesh somewhere else, I expect.

When I get back Sunday night I have a message from Jonathan. Out of the blue our Captain Martinez has surfaced and Jonathan is heading to D.C. Friday to meet him. "What's going on?" I ask when we get together Monday morning.

"I don't know, but he sounded agitated."

"Maybe they're ready to open up." I am thinking I should be there too, but I'd rather stay here, plus I'm travel-weary. I'll trust Jonathan, though I remind him how sensitive Dennis is about Martinez. "Be careful. I know you will. And not a word to ETVN."

"My lips are sealed."

I am not totally comfortable but I'll have to live with it. Maybe I'll call Dennis to be sure he knows of the meeting, that it's okay with him.

* * * * * * *

I GOT THROUGH THE HOLIDAYS though it was a stretch – time in Providence, homage in Oyster Bay. When Catherine asked me how things were shaping up my mind must have strayed too close to the problem side of things because she shot me a funny look before changing the subject. First day back, it was about eight and I had just arrived home after a long and frustrating Monday. One of my sources stood me up and I had to scramble on a story about a vets rally. I winced as the phone rang.

"Paul! How the hell are you?"

"Who's this?" I asked.

"Murph, who else?"

"Murph! I didn't recognize your voice. How are you? Where are you?"

"Would you believe in a bar."

"I believe that. Where?"

I heard rustling on the line. "Where are we, Nathan?"

"Nathan! He's there too!"

"Prince Street, some joint called Fanelli's. Nathan says hello."

"Hello to him. That's not far from where I am. I'll be right over."

I splurged on a cab and fifteen minutes later I was sitting at a red-and-white checkered table in a crowded, lively room hoisting a beer with my old friends. They were in uniform, both sporting sergeants' stripes.

"How long has it been?" Nathan asked.

"That date is engraved in my head," I replied. "Eight July nineteen sixty-nine. Hill 874."

"Operation Jackass. How quickly they forget."

I patted Mr. Stumpy. "Want to see?"

"Some other time."

Murph counted off on his fingers. "A year and a half, that makes it."

"All that time, don't tell me you haven't been back. You never called."

"We didn't know how to get hold of you," Murph complained.

I looked at Nathan. "I gave your parents my number, told them to forward it to you." "Never got it."

"Let's drink to the Post Office!" Murph shouted.

"The United States Postal Service! Long may it wave!"

"To the United States Army mail service!"

"To the United States fucking Army."

"To civilian life," Nathan offered.

"Civilian life! What's that?"

Did you know I'm working for the *Gazette?"*

"A rifleman?"

"A reporter," I laughed, "same thing."

Murph made a face and threw a limp wrist at me. "A reporter, my how fancy."

"I started out on the crime beat, now I get to cover the anti-war stuff. So you guys made it through okay. Congratulations!"

"Let's drink to making it through!"

"To making it period!"

"Here's to getting laid!" Murph shouted.

A couple of guys nearby overheard him. "To getting laid!" they yelled.

I sat back in my chair. "Catch me up on the old crowd. Stoner, what about him?"

Nathan nodded. "He re-upped again. Haven't heard from him since we left 'Nam which doesn't bother me at all. He was certifiable, that guy."

"They try to get you to re-up?"

"Of course. More pay, soft job in Saigon, but I had it with that place."

"Same here," Nathan added. "They shipped us to Japan. We're in a retraining unit. We train guys on the new weapons."

"Did they ever fix the M-16?"

"Made some changes. Trouble is, you never know what you're gonna get." He drained the last of his beer and signaled for another pitcher. "What you hear is right, my friend, morale is in the toilet. Things ain't what they used to be."

Nathan shook his head. "They never were. So Paul, looks like you're doing all right. You had us worried. You get my letter?"

"I got it all right, you asshole."

"Whaddya mean? You should feel honored. I don't write, that's what my parents tell me."

"I thought you'd bought it. That's why I was running down that fucking hill."

"Don't blame me."

"That's the problem. There's nobody to blame but myself."

"You're doing okay now, that's what counts. You get over that Dear John?"

I reached for my wallet and pulled out a picture of Diane. Diane and me on her father's sailboat. His thirty-two foot sailboat. "This is Diane."

"Nice... very nice," Murph said, holding the picture up.

"We're getting married in June. Play your cards right, you might get an invitation."

"I meant the yacht. Diane, yeah, she's all right too. She put out for you?"

I reddened. "Let me say we have a good time."

Murph clapped me on the shoulder. "Way to go, man! Way to go!"

"Paul always said he was waiting for the right girl. This must be her."

We spent the next couple of hours shooting the shit. They filled me in on the other guys. Fate evened the score with Lt. Gibbs, indications were he'd been fragged but nothing ever came of it. Sgt. Crowley was now Lt. Crowley, transferred to another unit when they pulled the Twenty-Fifth out. "Crowley was okay."

"But not too smart. Should have got out when he had the chance."

"Did Shorty ever make it back?"

"Yeah, then he got hurt again – this time the enemy got him. Good enough to send him home. I lost track of him after that."

"I never did anything about that poem of his..."

"Poem? What are you talking about?"

I smiled. "That was between him and me. Remember my buddy Jenks from Basic? He went with the Big Red One. What ever happened to him?"

Murph shook his head. "Don't have the foggiest."

"So what's in store for you guys?" I asked, chewing on a bite of pizza. "Your three years'll be up in May, right?"

"Can't hardly wait," Murph said. "I dunno, probably go back to school."

"Same here," Nathan added, "I went over to my college yesterday to get the paperwork started. Got a lot of funny looks, I'll tell you."

"You in uniform?"

"Yeah. The kids don't know what end's up, but this professor starts giving me shit and I walked out on him. Better than bust him in the chops, the asshole."

When Nathan got up to go to the bathroom, Murph leaned over the table toward me. "Paul, you really doin' okay? Tell me the truth."

"Oh sure. You get used to things."

"I don't mean just that, a lot of guys go bonkers. I know a couple."

"I have dreams. Sometimes I don't sleep. That's about it. You?"

"I'm too dumb for anything to bother me but you, you got sensitivity. That kind of guy it affects the most."

I rapped on the table. "So far, so good."

"If I can ever be of help, let me know. I mean that."

"Thanks, I will."

"Still go to church?"

"Yeah. Why do you ask?"

"Those long talks we had." He shook his head. "I don't understand how anybody could live through that and still go to church." He took a deep drag on his cigarette. "Anyway, whatever works."

Nathan was back. "Let me try something out on you," I said, "I'm covering a rally tomorrow, you guys interested in coming along?"

"What kind of rally?"

"Vets Against the War. You'll spend a couple of fascinating hours in Union Square."

"I'll pass," Murph answered. "We got people coming over to see the war hero."

Nathan nodded at me. "Sure, why not?"

The rally was uneventful. Three inches on an inside page. Speeches and signs but no march, the group denied a permit. Though some hotheads blocked cars and jammed traffic anyway. More interesting was the encounter between Nathan and Phil Johnson. If I gave you the idea I was not enamored of Johnson, you got that right. The more time I spent with him the more weasely he seemed, a guy who lets other people do his dirty work and splits when things go south. When he heard Nathan was getting out soon, he put an all-court press on for him to join. "We need people just back from 'Nam, fresh blood. Tell it like it is."

"I mean to keep my blood, thank you. That's what the last three years were all about."

"We've got some terrific events coming up. D.C.'s going to be big. We're even working it out for some of our guys to testify in Congress."

"You assume I agree with you. What gives you that idea?"

"Why else would you be here?"

"People go to the zoo. That make them giraffes and zebras?"

"I fail to see your point..."

"My point is, I've done my country a great service and I don't like people shitting on it. What unit were you with, anyway? Were you there at all?"

Johnson drew himself up to full command height. "Sergeant, you're in for a rude surprise. After you've been back a couple of months come talk to me. You'll find there's no welcome mat, nobody to thank you except a bunch of geriatrics whose idea of fun is dressing up for World War One. Nobody wanted this war, and there is nobody – I repeat, no-body – going to reward you for fighting in it. Nobody gives a rat's ass about you." He waved his hand at the dispersing crowd, many of them long-hairs and beards in fatigues and combat boots, guys wheeling themselves or hobbling around. "Believe me, we are on your side. We're the only ones that are."

I could see Nathan starting to lose it then he caught himself. "What I did was honorable and it was right. I don't need your thanks. I don't want it."

Johnson turned on his heel and rejoined his lieutenants who were looking on from a distance. "Asshole," Nathan threw after him.

During the rally I'd been looking around for Cyrus and I finally spotted him. "Hey! Cyrus!"

Cyrus flashed me a big smile and waved.

"Somebody I want you to meet." We walked across the street and I went up to Cyrus balancing on his crutches and gave him a hug. "Cyrus, meet Sergeant Berg, Nathan to his friends. Nathan, Cyrus Thomas. Nathan and I were in the same outfit."

"Howyadoin' Nathan," he said, extending a hand. He looked at Nathan's stripes. "I never made it past Corporal but I still outrank you."

"How's that?"

Cyrus tapped his Marine insignia. "Marines, man, the Marines."

"You must have been one tough dude, I'll give you that."

"You got that right. But as you see my situation has been somewhat diminished."

"Nathan's Brooklyn but I have another friend from the Bronx."

"Whereabouts?"

I turned to Nathan. "Where's Murph from?"

"Riverdale."

"Them's the wealthy folks. Night'n day, man, night'n day."

"He's an okay guy, you'd like him."

"You still there?" Cyrus asked Nathan.

Nathan shook his head. "I did my year. I'm in a training unit in Japan."

"You lucky man, not sheddin' parts like me'n Paul. How much longer you got?"

"My three's up in May."

"Whaddya think of all this shit?" He nodded at the thinning crowd.

Nathan nodded at Phil Johnson who was expounding for a TV camera crew. "The leadership doesn't get any better when it retires."

"You mean John-san?" Cyrus said, "John-san is a piece of work. Say, can I bum a smoke from one of you guys?"

I reached for my pack and shook out a cigarette. "Take a few," I said, "more where this comes from."

"Thank you, my man, don' mind if I do."

I held up my Zippo and he lit up, inhaling deeply.

Nathan took one, too. "Three on a match, that's not good."

Cyrus shook his head. "Don' believe that, not for a minute. You gotta stay positive."

"That's the right attitude," Nathan observed.

I was happy Cyrus was having one of his up days. He suffered from wild mood swings and the shift could come on suddenly, without warning.

"I tell you... Nathan, is it? My att-ti-tude used to be, if it warn't for bad luck I'd have no luck at all. That's how I used to think, but no more. I'm out there humpin', lookin' for a job. Paul's gave me some leads, things're definitely lookin' up for this cat. You know, Paul, I think maybe you got a wrong impression of our organization here. Sure there's assholes, but that's everywhere. Some of the guys're red hots – against everything, against the war, against the military, against the U.S. That ain't most of us. We're here to pick up our friends, help 'em through a rough time."

"Nothing wrong with that," Nathan added. "Just 'cause the politicians and generals got their head up their ass doesn't mean the rest of us do."

Cyrus nodded. "Even after what they did to me, I love my country, man. I wouldn't want to live anywhere else. Not London, not Tokyo, not Paris..."

"You sure about Paris?" Nathan laughed. "They say it's full of hot ladies."

"Yeah, I dig them mad-dem-why-selles. Okay, I'm cool with that but irregardless, the States is the place to be, man, no question. This is where it's at."

The following evening I got together with Nathan and Murph again and we made a pact to hang out when they got back. I promised to bring Diane by. It'll be good to have my friends around, I thought.

ON TO WASHINGTON. When the shuttle landed, at the gate to greet me was the *Gazette's* number two man in Washington, Assistant Bureau Chief Tom Massey. Short of stature and quick of temper, I had met him at a social function a while back. Backtracking to the Capitol Hilton to check in, he updated me on the VVAW's week-long "Dewey Canyon III" event. I was here to cover the marches, the speeches, the Mall encampment that was going ahead despite an injunction, their appearance at hearings on the Hill. I would have felt honored at the welcome, except I knew the main reason Massey was there to make sure Bernard understands who's in charge down here.

This would be my first time working with the *Gazette's* Washington Bureau. Marty Rossi clued me in on the rivalry with the New York editors which sometimes flared into open warfare. Massey's boss, Charlie Stebbins, had built Washington into a world-class team of reporters, taking pains to establish his independence from New York, which in turn tried and failed to rein him. Nominally Stebbins reported to Tom O'Connor, though the line was considerably less than dotted, Charlie being a personal favorite of Frank Astell. Not insignificantly, Stebbins was married to Astell's niece. As well as running the Washington Bureau, Stebbins was a keen observer of federal and national issues, his column syndicated in over fifty papers around the world. Admired and envied, respected and feared, Stebbins' position at the *Gazette* was unique.

I checked for messages then beat it to the lobby where Massey was waiting. We headed over to the Mall where he dropped me off and I set to work, exploring tent city, interviewing. Scruffiness was the order of the day – long hair and headbands, sideburns, old military garb you could tell had been earned. I had changed into my

Army green field jacket, sporting my press badge, of course, and hiking boots for the mud. Massey told me they had three reporters and a photographer detailed and made a point of saying Charlie Stebbins was bummed out. Tom O'Connor had insisted I file my stories direct and not through Stebbins, the usual practice. I picked up a briefing packet and a schedule of events at the press tent and found the area abuzz with word that an appeals court had lifted the injunction order.

Tomorrow – Monday – the action would begin. I hung around until late afternoon, observing, interviewing, making notes, had a beer with the New Yorkers, then split to write my story. I had made a point of seeking out one of the *Gazette* photographers who coincidentally also turned out to be from the Twenty-Fifth, and he agreed to link up with me and get me some pictures. Had my old Leica around my neck too, with a couple of new lenses. Though I wouldn't be filing pictures, as a matter of fact to this point I never had, I'd be looking for shots that might serve for a later feature.

Next morning I walked alongside the marchers, over a thousand, led by Gold Star Mothers. Crossing Memorial Bridge we were shocked to find ourselves locked out of Arlington National Cemetery. Leaving their wreaths at the gate, disappointed and angry, the marchers reformed and headed back across the bridge, down the Mall and up to Capitol Hill. I got some quotes from Congressman Pete McCloskey as we walked along, more as other officials addressed the crowd from the Capitol steps. That evening I returned to a party thrown by a couple of Senators including Rhode Island's Claiborne Pell. I spent some time with him and reminisced about Senator Pastore helping me get that summer job. He told me he knew my father slightly, said our paths would certainly cross again and wished me well. During the function word came that the Supreme Court had reinstated the injunction. That plus the insult to the Gold Star Mothers was too much. The vets vowed to continue the encampment even if it meant getting arrested.

Next day more than fifty vets attempted to surrender as war criminals at the Pentagon but found no takers. Meantime, showing true common sense, Park Police refused to make arrests on the Mall. On Thursday, I was in the audience as former Navy lieutenant John Kerry testified at length against the "criminal hypocrisy" of the war. "How do you ask a man to be the last man to die in Vietnam, the last man to die for a mistake?" A lot of what he said made sense, but something about the guy turned me off. Not insincerity, exactly – more like his ambition was so blatant. A politician in the making, I thought to myself – already on the make.

The week's last event, hundreds of veterans tossed their ribbons, medals, war mementos onto the Capitol steps, some with measured remarks, others openly angry. Brought to mind the parable of the bad tree and the bad fruit which, of course, I couldn't use. Another comment I read once – to the military a bright button is weightier than four volumes of Schopenhauer. Doubtful these guys were voting for Schopenhauer but it was clear what they were against. I didn't use that either.

I never saw Charlie Stebbins that week, but he needn't have worried. The week-long series came together beautifully – what his staff wrote, my contributions. The photography was a telling mix of pathos and humor. New York loved it. There was talk of submitting it for an award.

PREPARATIONS FOR THE GREAT DAY were well along. When Diane and I went over the arrangements I was surprised so much had been accomplished. We had selected St. Albert the Great, which would have been the Archers' parish church had they been Catholics, and were involved in familiarization sessions – indoctrinations she called them. I thought of asking Father Ronan to officiate, but in the end I didn't call him, I'm not sure why. Nor did I contact Father Trần. I felt bad how things ended between us.

The guest list was settled and invitations mailed. Aside from an uncle of Diane's from Australia, my California contingent would take the honor for distance travelled – Gus and Akiko, also Mark Hightower. I hadn't heard from Benny whose invitation I sent care of his father. Gideon's came back "addressee unknown." Unlikely Pat would show. The reception would be at the Midlothian Yacht Club where Mr. Archer was a Commodore. "The Club has a wonderful kitchen," Mrs. Archer assured me importantly, "very choice."

The plan was I'd move to Diane's place and I had no problem with that – I practically lived there on weekends anyway – but the idea of giving up my friendly little pad was distressing. The honeymoon also presented some angst. My father suggested the Mt. Washington Hotel where he and my mother had spent theirs. I liked that idea, thought it would be a nice tribute, but Diane had something more glamorous in mind.

"There's a resort in Bermuda I loved as a child. Swimming, biking, a real British flavor, and less than two hours from JFK."

"I guess," I said, not wanting to make a big deal about it, but reluctant to begin married life saddled with debt.

Seeing me hesitate, Diane played her trump card. "Daddy wants to take care of it, it'll be his wedding present to us. Can you imagine, two whole weeks, just the two of us?"

I didn't want to start off indebted to my in-laws either, but it would be unseemly not to accept. "Tell him thank you," I said, reaching over and stroking her hand. "If it makes you happy that's what counts."

"You'll love it. It's a wonderful place."

I would love to see the bill for this, I thought – it'll dwarf the GNP of that small South American country that sells the band uniforms. A few days later when I learned the Archers had honeymooned at Waterloo House I felt doubly sad, as if I'd sold my father out.

As it turned out, Nathan and Murph were being mustered out in mid-May and would be back in time to serve as ushers and, more important, as Murph said, put the bachelor party together. The thought crossed my mind to invite Cyrus, but picturing him and Mrs. Archer together, however briefly, I scotched the idea. The bachelor party would normally be Jim's job as best man, but it made sense for the natives to take it on. This all-male event would commence after the rehearsal dinner my father hosted after the walk-through at the church, at a fine North Shore restaurant of Mrs. Archer's selection. Nathan had the brilliant idea of commandeering one of the limos to ferry our group of merrimakers to Manhattan. A good thing too, for the way things were going none of us would be in any condition to drive. Even Jim stepped off the wagon and had a few beers... truth be known, more than a few.

It was a very long day. The rehearsal I found bizarre. First of all, I had never been inside the church and the scene was quiet to the point of creepy. Many on Diane's side I had just met and I sensed were silently accepting of "Paul's Catholic thing." I have to give Diane credit – once her father rolled his eyes at the priest's comments and I saw her kick him in the ankle. The other time she whispered loudly for him to knock it off. Not many could get away with that.

A few words about the bachelor party. Jim, Nathan and Murph were along, of course, another usher, Fred, a cousin of Diane's, plus a neighbor, Doug. As a courtesy we invited my father and Diane's but, sensibly, they declined. After traversing the Queens-Midtown tunnel the limo took a route directly through Times Square. Jim gave me a wink and a cuff on the shoulder. "Some time we had back then, Paul, me and you – remember that?"

"Sure do, Jimbo," I said, whacking him back.

Plunging deeper into Hell's Kitchen we crossed Tenth and turned on West 39th. Halfway down the block the driver pulled to the curb. Above a dingy doorway a flickering red neon sign marked the WEST SIDE BOYS & GIRLS CLUB. "Never saw a Boys and Girls Club like this," Doug guffawed. "How'd they get away with using the name?"

"Maybe they give kids a discount," Murph answered.

"Whadda they have inside? Ping pong? Basketball?"

"Something like that."

A tall, burly guy blocked the doorway. "ID's," he growled, looking us over. We flashed our wallets in his direction. He opened the front door. "Go in," he said as an afterthought.

Inside, we were greeted by the odor of stale beer. The place smelled like it hadn't had been scrubbed down in years. Loud music was coming from a juke box in the front, the other side was a bar and at the rear a slender black woman was hanging listlessly on a pole on a small, elevated stage. A server sauntered past us with a tray of drinks for some guys at a nearby table. Another nodded at Murph who was motioning to put two tables together. As my eyes adapted to the dark, I saw the place was practically empty.

"So, what'll it be?" The server stood there, hand on hip.

Murph looked at us. "Buds all around?"

"We're okay with that. Buds in cans." The server disappeared with the order. Murph nodded, "place like this, never order anything you can't open yourself."

In a few minutes our beers arrived, and with them two scantily clad ladies who emerged from a far corner of the room. "Hi, guys, wanna party?"

"That's why we're here."

One of them took the empty chair and sat down. "Why's this called the Boys' and Girls' Club?" Doug asked.

The other lounged behind, a tall Chinese-looking woman who was already massaging Doug's shoulders. Glossy red lips, eyes heavily made up, shiny black hair, a high-necked dress with a zipper down the front and a very short mini. "You don't know?"

"No. I mean, that's why I asked."

"Give it time. You see."

I looked over at Nathan who was laughing behind his hand at Murph. Murph pointed at me. "Our friend here's getting married tomorrow." I knew the asshole would say that.

"Getting married?" the Chinese woman said, turning toward me. "Good for you," she purred in a voice that sounded like too many cigarettes, "you last night of freedom."

"I don't see it exactly that way."

"My name May Lee, what yours?"

"Paul," Nathan said.

"Want some company you last night of freedom?" she asked, plunking herself down on my lap. "My God, what's that?" she said with a start.

She had sat on Mr. Stumpy. "I have only half a leg."

"Ah, that too bad. How about you buy me drink? Champagne twenty dollar. Whole bottle fifty, we go to party room, just me and you."

"Think I'll pass," I said.

The other woman looked around our group. "Anybody?" she asked sullenly.

"Maybe later," Murph said. "Check back later."

Sensing defeat the two women left, dissolving into the far corner.

We sat around, finishing our beers, ordered a second round. Murph was slouching in his chair, looked like the day was getting to him. After a while I felt someone behind me. It was the Chinese woman. She wasn't exactly attractive but there was something... intriguing about her. "You last night of freedom, I make special deal. Lap dance only ten dollar."

"No thanks," I said, "I'm doing fine."

She was quiet for a moment, pouting. Suddenly she sat down on my lap. "Oh, fuck it. I give you something, when you get tired of the missus you come back." She unbuttoned my shirt, started rubbing my chest. "You bored of her, remember May Lee, okay?"

The other guys were looking on, laughing. I played along with it, going with the flow, when she took my finger and hooked it onto the gold loop at the top of her zipper and guided it down to her waist, throwing open the front of her dress, shoulders, a filmy bra, the whole works. After fixating a moment I said to myself this is enough, when suddenly she grabbed my hand again and put it on her crotch.

"Jesus!" I yelled, standing straight up.

With a loud crash the woman slid to the floor. The table teetered to one side then rocked back, knocking the drinks over.

In confusion and consternation, I looked down. "You not nice, Paul," she said sternly, picking herself up. On her feet again, she lifted her skirt and displayed the unmistakable bulge in her panties. "You not nice at all."

"What's going on here?" It was the bouncer.

She pointed at me. "That asshole threw me on the floor," May Lee announced in a suddenly deep voice.

The bouncer hitched up his pants. "You guys gotta choice. Leave or get thrown out."

"Yeah?" Jim shouted, "You an' who else?"

"Me and the NYPD, that's who." The bartender and the other dancers were now massing behind the bouncer. The dancers looked more formidable than before.

"Calm down," Nathan had his hand on Jim's shoulder, "we've had enough of here."

"They haven't paid their tab," the server said.

"How much?" the bouncer said.

"Thirty eight."

Murph pulled out two twenties and tossed them onto the beer-soaked tabletop. "Don't spend it all in one place."

We backed out of the room, keeping an eye on the bouncer and his retinue. The limo was standing at the curb, motor running. The bouncer followed us out, giving us the finger then slammed the door shut and went inside. We piled in the car, all but Jim, that is. Now back at the front door Jim had dropped his pants and was urinating on the sidewalk. After an interminable time he pulled them up, zipped his fly, and with a big grin slid in beside me. As we pulled away the door opened and I saw the bouncer step outside for a look around. Then he looked down. He was standing in Jim's puddle. As we turned the corner the last we saw of him he was waving his arms wildly.

"Christ!" Doug said, "how'd you find a place like that?"

"Hey, you live in New York, you know things."

"I live in New York and I never seen anything like that."

"Where do you live?"

"Manhasset."

"That ain't New York."

I felt foolish being had but I figured so what. "I got one too few legs," I said, "May Lee's got one too many. On the average everybody's doing fine. Thanks, a lot, Murph," I cuffed him on the shoulder, "now my life is complete."

"Nah, you still got a ways to go."

"What I wanna know, how'd they do that?" Doug asked.

"It's a wig, idiot!"

"I don't mean that."

"They take stuff, you know, chemicals."

"Nah, pads. It's all pads."

"C'mon, seriously, how'd they do that?"

"You don't want to know. Believe me."

My contingent was staying in a motel the next town over from the church. They told me the day dawned brilliantly but the first inkling I had was a banging on my door. "Rise and shine, soldier! It's nine a.m.!" It was Nathan.

"Shit!" I said, looking at the clock. I had to hustle, we were on at noon. I looked in the mirror. Matted hair, sleepy eyes, dark stubble. Not to mention a splitting headache.

Twenty minutes and a couple of aspirins later I had showered and caught up to the guys, those who were stirring, in the motel coffee shop. After a quick bite, Nathan, Murph and I drove into town looking for a barber shop for the groom's traditional shave and haircut.

"I appreciate all the trouble you went to," I told Murph. "I figure it was your doing."

"Nathan was a party to the crime," Murph grinned. "Hope you enjoyed it."

"The perfect end to the perfect day."

Under a hot towel in Leon's Hair Cuttery, I began to revive, feeling almost human. Then back to the motel to wrestle with the tuxes. Jim assured me he was ready to roll with the rings. Murph mentioned he had a fifth of vodka if I was interested. "Bloody Mary, Screwdriver, you name it." I declined.

As the morning went on there was a lot of kidding around but I didn't hear most of it. I was taking deep breaths, trying to avoid reflecting on what I was doing, what I was getting into. I had made my decision. I was happy with my decision. It was a good decision. Nothing left but show up and let it happen.

The ceremony went better than I expected. All discord was skillfully submerged. Having been to so many Latin rite weddings I was surprised how moving the simple vernacular was, the prayers, the readings. Diane looked gorgeous, white satin showing her figure to great advantage. At the end when she lifted her veil and we kissed, all doubts, all fears fell away.

At the reception my father was in his element, turning on the Julien Bernard charm. He and Mr. Archer seemed to do okay, though Dad told me later he found it hard to talk to him. By now he and Gus were best friends. Sid and Marty showed up, also Alan Mauro and several of the reporter rat pack, even Pam Snyder who seemed to be over any hard feelings, though I don't know if she was all that devastated. Once during the day I had a strong sense my mother was there, looking on, dancing, flirting with my friends. It was sad to think she and Diane never got to know each other, though how she and Mrs. Archer would have got along, that might have been a different story.

We ate and we danced, I was feeling very confident out there though I didn't push Mr. Stumpy too hard. It was a wonderful night. Guilt behind me, I was in love, fulfilled, relieved, and very, very happy.

43. DOUBLE EXPOSURE

DENNIS CONFIRMS HE AUTHORIZED Capt. Martinez to call, in fact he is so fed up he *told* him to call. "It's a sham, Gus," he tells me – I am on the secure phone – "but I didn't expect anything better. You trust this assistant of yours?"

"He is very discreet."

"Remember, it's my ass on the line. Take good care of it."

"Not to worry, Dennis," I say, though I do, some.

Jonathan calls as soon as he gets back, says meet him early at Samuels' office. Next morning I haul myself out of bed and plunge into the cold, sacrificing my Saturday morning lounge. I sign in and take the elevator to twenty-seven where a young woman I have seen around lets me in. I grab a coffee on the way. Jonathan is already in our workroom.

"How'd it go?" I say.

"We're finally getting somewhere." He folds his copy of the *Times* and puts it down. "You say your friend Riggs is pissed, Martinez makes two. Guess how many times that Board's met?" Jonathan holds up one finger. "One lousy meeting in three months. Apparently the new investigators found the same things Martinez did. Far as the brass is concerned it's all about keeping it quiet."

"Where has the press been all this time? And Congress?"

"Martinez expects something to break soon, about the investigation or lack of one. There are a bunch of FOIA requests in, ETVN included."

"Should you do one?"

"My editor's working on it."

"What can be so interesting it has everybody tied up in knots?"

"Roberto called me last night. Abdullah – you know, the nephew they were holding – he's dead. Happened last week, at Abu Ghraib."

"The poor lad, he must have come down with a fever."

"No doubt. But here's the interesting part. Martinez told me when that guy passed the information about Paul to his uncle, he wasn't acting on his own. Somebody had said things would go well for him if he did it, somebody on our side."

"That wasn't in Bernie's memo."

"They didn't want him to put it in writing. Martinez told Dennis personally."

I let out a long whistle. "Let me get this straight. Some unnamed American tells this guy to give sensitive security information to the enemy."

Jonathan shakes his head. "Oh, we know who he is." He looks down at his notes. "Felix Langer. And guess who Felix Langer works for."

"Would her initials be N.G.?"

"You got it, and there's more. According to Martinez' sources, the General has gone bonkers. The Americans disband his Army, put him and his men on the street, now they kill his favorite nephew. He wants to talk. It might as well be me he talks to."

"Oh, come on! We're writing an article, for God's sake, not a detective story! Anyway, none of this makes any sense. How would telling his story avenge the nephew?"

Jonathan leans toward me. "A Bush loyalist colluding with the enemy? Passing along secret information to rub out reporter enemy number one. Can you think of anything more damaging?"

"Who's to say the dead guy was telling the truth? The uncle, you say he's nuts. Even if you could find him who'd believe him?"

"You're missing the point. Why is the Army stonewalling? It's clear, they got orders from way up the line. That's why your guy is so pissed." Jonathan sits back, a smile on his face. "You laughed at me. You said we couldn't tie Paul's death to that gang in Washington. Well, here's the evidence, damnit! We're not there yet, but we are getting close."

I throw up my hands. "You have one world-class imagination."

"Don't sell me short, Gus." Jonathan fixes me in his stare. "I'm going to get to General al-Safar. I will blow this thing open and Roberto Martinez is going to help me do it."

* * * * * * *

UNLIKE MY NEW WIFE, I wasn't born to the water, but events had made me a decent swimmer. Every day I spent a couple of hours peering at fish darting about the coral, doing laps with one eye on the pink sand beach. When Diane challenged me to race for a distant rock I made it easily, a respectable second. Exhausted, we lay laughing in each other's arms on a tiny sand beach.

The flagstone patio off our bedroom had a majestic view of Hamilton Harbor and the marina. "They say England's out there," I observed one morning, as we lingered over breakfast. "Let's make that our next trip."

"I'll never turn London down."

"With a side trip to Paris to see Pat."

"Pat who didn't show up for the wedding."

"That's his style," I said. Though his telegram did draw a lot of laughs when Jim read it out. Diane knew except for that one big trip my travel experience was extremely limited, but she didn't flaunt hers. She'd been all over Europe and South America, spent that time in Switzerland and her college junior year in Edinburgh. In fact once she accompanied her father to Moscow and Leningrad on some State Department boondoggle.

Our first week was all serendipity. In our green MG we stopped for lunch in out-of-the-way places, overnighting in a bed and breakfast at Horseshoe Bay and, Bermuda being about bikes, we biked. My therapist had helped me get comfortable on a bike and I rode my three-speed Raleigh on weekends. We walked everywhere, climbing Town Hill, the island's highest point, visiting old forts, taking in concerts and a Shaw play, coming upon great jazz in a club, trying out a Sailfish. I sampled cricket but found it too glacial for my taste.

I summoned the courage to get on a horse, which I'd never done before. A patient instructor helped, though I needed a hand getting on and off. Diane was cool about my condition, even with the stares, particularly from some older guests at the pool. Out of consideration for her I toned down my Mr. Stumpy act. Several times she remarked what drive I must have to try and lead not just a normal life but an exceptional life. One time she let her guard down about her work. "I'm a money person," she said with a faint smile, "I guess it's genetic. Good thing we're not in the same line."

I soon discovered how much I had underestimated the demands of day-to-day intimacy. So far, most of her little surprises were good, though I'm sure not everything I brought to the party was appreciated or admired. With luck, though, I thought, we will survive this initial voyage of discovery.

Instead of climbing the walls, in a few days Bermuda had unwound me and I was feeling on top of things for the first time I could remember. We celebrated our one-week anniversary with dinner and a surfeit of Bordeaux at the French restaurant in our hotel. Wednesday we would hop a cruise ship for a three-night excursion then it was back to New York. That night I distinctly remember seeing two thirty through the haze as I got up to answer the phone. "Paul, this is Sid. Sorry to bother you but we got a problem."

"Mrrmmmhh," I answered, something like that.

"I'm looking at the *Times* early edition. The bastards just scooped the world."

"World... scooped?"

"They're publishing a bunch of classified documents about Vietnam, something McNamara started way back. How we got into it, who lied to who, that kind of thing. Some guy got hold of it and he's feeding it to Neil Sheehan. Pentagon Papers, they're calling it."

I looked over at Diane, who was stirring. "Hold on, lemme take it in the other room."

I went into the sitting room, closed the door and picked up the phone "Go ahead."

"We are behind the eight ball on this one, I mean way behind. I just talked with Charlie. Apparently there's been rumors for a while but everybody figured, it's classified, deal with it when and if. Now here it is."

"What're we doing about it?"

"I just got off the phone with Ed Reynolds – he's flying back. Charlie's on his way here now. I wanted to give you the chance to get involved, if you want to, that is. I know it's a bad time so feel free to say no. We can get somebody else."

"No, no... let me talk with Diane. I'll work it out."

"Thing is, we need to field our best team for this one. Can't count on getting access to the documents. Man, I'd like to know who those *Times* sons-of-bitches paid off. What it means, we fall back to analysis mode. What does this stuff show we didn't know before? What's it mean? What's it do to Nixon, the war, the protest shit, which is where you come in, we need an angle, something we can do better than anybody else."

"I'll get right back to you."

"Good man. We're counting on you."

When I returned to the bedroom Diane's bedside light was on and she was sitting up. "You were on the phone."

"Sorry. That was Sid."

"What's happening?"

"The *Times* just broke a story. They got hold of some secret documents about Vietnam. It's all over their front page. We've got to react."

"And Sid wants you part of it."

I nodded.

"Can't it wait?"

"If I don't do it they'll get somebody else."

Diane was quiet for a moment. "You'll be working with the big guns. It's a great opportunity – of course you have to do it. If you don't it'll make both of us miserable." She shrugged. "That's the way it goes sometimes. If my boss called I know what I'd do."

I sat down on the bed and put my arm around her. "Don't think I'm not disappointed."

She turned her face away. "I'd better call the airline."

She got up and threw on her bathrobe, knotting the cord with a vigorous pull. "You owe me, Paul Bernard. Boy, do you owe me."

LATE SUNDAY WE WERE SITTING AROUND Tom O'Connor's table – Tom, Sid, Marty, Charlie Stebbins, Tom Massey, Ed Reynolds and me. Sid's secretary was there, notebook in hand. Tomorrow's front page would put our ball in play with a report about publication of – official title – *United States - Vietnam Relations, 1945-1967: A Study Prepared by the Department of Defense.* To this were joined a backgrounder and initial congressional and White House reaction. Nixon was predictably livid.

Barring a miracle, we would have to wait for each day's *Times* to find out what we had to write about, an uncomfortable position to be in. Our initial attack would flesh out the circumstances, explain the documents – why McNamara commissioned them, who put them together, stuff the *Times* might or might not reveal early in the game. Stebbins' Washington staff was combing the District. Our real problem, although Tom kept referring to it as an opportunity, was to find some fresh peg to hang a *Gazette* exclusive.

I read the *Times'* first selection on our flight back. In fact I bought two papers, asking Diane for her insights. "This is awful," she said, putting down the paper. "I always thought we were drawn into this, but we go as far back as the French. We were financing them all along. You'd think we might have taken their experience to heart."

"We are Americans and we can do anything we put our minds to."

"Somehow I'd forgotten that."

"So did some others."

Normally Diane's views were far more conservative than mine, though compared with her father she was a flaming liberal. The family wealth gave her a major stake in the system, making my Nu-Gem stock look piddling by comparison. Her financial smarts and training gave her a nose for the money trail. Of a deal she would ask, who stands to gain? In this we were alike, for I had learned that when money talks, politicians listen, as do the people who call themselves statesmen. Here, however, she shared my chagrin at being misled.

What came into focus as I read was the duplicity – no, let's call it by its real name, the lying by high government officials. It brought me back to my old research project. Gus always insisted on a causal link between dishonest leaders and bad policy. These documents showed exactly that. And here, those entrusted with checking the executive, Congress particularly, were denied essential information. The seeds of an article were growing but I forced myself back to the role I'd been assigned, the anti-war movement's response. My solution – work twice as hard and give them both.

About nine-thirty the meeting broke and I went back to my desk to make phone calls. When I got home Diane was still up. Home was now her townhouse, though I still had a lot of stuff to move from my pad of happy memory. The next few days I chased around the city building a story, with Thursday targeted for the first installment. There would be rallies and forums and speeches, but so far nothing mammoth scheduled. These revelations would be used to fuel the cynicism already there. The basic reaction, "I told you so." I was surprised to see the origins of our involvement went as far back as Truman, Mao, and the onset of Korea. Eisenhower was in with both feet, JFK also duped by the anticommunist zealots.

The *Times* series ripped away any doubt about LBJ's double-dealing. Getting himself elected on a platform of no wider war and no American blood while scheming to do just that. Ordering a draft of what became the Tonkin Gulf Resolution months before the alleged incident. And much, much more. I was less surprised than dismayed. I recalled the Berkeley criticisms, how I had chalked them up to the anti-American axe they were grinding. Now it turned out the nay-sayers were right. What did that say about my supposed powers of discernment? I vowed never again to discount comments just because they came with a warning label. Get humping and check it out for yourself.

Attorney General Mitchell was now demanding that the *Times* cease publishing the documents and return them forthwith. Temporarily enjoined, the *Times* printed the telegram on its front page. Eventually the Supreme Court ruled in its favor, and when the dust settled, friends over there told me about the excruciating pressure on their publisher and editors, their fear of criminal prosecution, the fact they sat on the documents several months before going ahead. Showing remarkable spirit, even as the *Times* stayed its hand because of the injunction, the *Washington Post* began publishing the documents, other papers followed suit and even we got into the act. Thankfully the Supreme Court went the way it did or some of my new heroes would have spent time in the slammer. It made me proud to play a part.

My first piece ran in Friday's *Gazette,* the second ten days later, but my real coup was the editorial. I'd given Sid a longish article to use as he saw fit – it didn't belong in a news story – and figured that would be the end of it. But after the *Times* finished its series, O'Connor published an editorial that took up half the page and was co-signed by Franklin Astell II, condemning "this sordid affair whose only merit was to showcase American journalism at its finest." The last paragraphs were mine, with a nod to Jacques Maritain.

> Thus the ordinary citizen finds himself in an untenable position. Not knowing what his leaders are up to, he cannot hold them to account, which is, of course, just what they want. It is a sorry state of affairs when even the Congress is duped by executive secrecy, when winning elections is bigger than candor on the vital issues of the day.
>
> Classified material, official secrets, security requirements – important in limited circumstances, but their misuse undermines our democracy. Consider what confronts Americans today. Insecure leaders, hiding behind military bluster. Timid leaders, afraid to face the people. Dishonest leaders, trapped in a web of lies. Imperious leaders, their agendas hidden from debate. Un-American? You bet it is.

Whatever else this exercise taught me, I knew I had found a profession that mattered, that could shed light where it was needed. Oh, and I heard this from several people who read my first draft, next time tone down the purple prose.

THIS BROUGHT BACK MEMORIES of my tilts with Benny. I needed in the worst way to talk with him again. I called his old home number and his father picked up the phone! As it turned out, Benny was teaching right here in New York, at Queens College! Nathan's old school! He'd been in Israel for a year. I got his number in the Park Slope section of Brooklyn and left a message. He called right back. Until his father told him, he had no idea what happened to me and he was devastated. I said I'm doing fine, and after I told him about my work at the *Gazette,* particularly the exciting last few weeks, his old feistiness started coming around. "I hate to say 'I told you so,' but..."

"You're too late with that one," I said. "It seems you got your Ph.D. in good style."

"I did. Gideon too, he's living in Israel."

"Are you and Leah still together?"

"Together! We're married! Benjamin Junior's a year and a half. By the way, let me wish you *mazel tov.*"

"No thanks to you."

"How about we make it up to you and your bride. Come for dinner."

Two weeks later Diane and I showed up on their doorstep, a run-down brownstone in a neighborhood that must once have been magnificent. "Benny!"

"Paul!"

"This is Diane."

"I feel as if I know you already," she said. "Paul says you two go way back."

"He's about my oldest friend," I said. "You know Omer got killed."

"My God, no. I am really sorry."

Suddenly something rushed up and grabbed around the knees. "Hi, Unca Paul!"

"Benny Junior, I do believe." I reached down and lofted him into the air.

"Benjie, we call him." Leah appeared in the doorway, wiping her hands on an apron. "He's not at all shy, as you can see." She put her arm around me and gave me a big kiss, greeting Diane warmly.

"I was actually at your campus not long ago," I told Benny. "I would have called you if I'd known. By the way, I need to sign you up as an official source. "You're still doing the anti-war thing?"

"Of course. Sure, we can always use the publicity."

"It doesn't work exactly that way, but I'll try. I'll even quote you if you say something intelligent."

"There is always that chance. You know, we're starting to see something really interesting – more veterans on campus all the time. Some of them just want to be left alone but others bring a great perspective from what they went through."

"Not all oppose the war."

"That's true, but plenty do or they're so disillusioned it amounts to the same thing."

"I have a name for you. Nathan Berg."

"A good name."

"One of my best friends from Vietnam. He'll probably show up in one of your classes soon. He did a year there before he got drafted."

"Have him come by and say hello."

"Did you see that big editorial in the *Gazette?* The Pentagon Papers wrap-up. 'Shame and Hope,' it was called."

"Yeah, I remember that."

"I had a hand in writing it."

"That was strong stuff." Benny looked at Leah. "You know, maybe he has changed."

"I was sorry to hear about your injury," Leah said. Benjie was sitting on the arm of the chair, fussing with her hair. "But you seem to have adapted."

"I have, but that's not what changed my position. Read the editorial again. I'll send you a copy. That sums it up well."

Leah picked Benjie up and he started squalling and wiggling. "I'd better put this guy to bed and see about dinner."

"What can I do to help?" Diane asked, getting up from the sofa.

"Maybe you can hold Benjie down while I change him." Diane wrinkled her nose. "Sure, why not?"

Later, lying in bed back at our place, I said how good it was to see my old friends, how happy they seemed, what a great little kid they had.

"You'd like one of those, wouldn't you?" Diane said.

"I guess so. Yeah, actually that'd be really nice."

"Our lives would never be the same."

"We could handle it. Together we can handle anything."

"Brave words, Mr. Bernard. What if I hold you to them?"

"Try me."

"Well then, let's see what we can do about it," she said, turning toward me and running her fingers through my hair. "Maybe it wouldn't be so terrible."

A FEW WEEKS LATER Sid Greenwald called me into his office. Marty was there as well. Sid motioned me into a chair. "It should come as no surprise but we're very pleased with your work, so in your next paycheck there'll be something extra. And your next check will reflect your increase to eighteen thou a year. I'm sure you can use it, newly married and all."

"I don't know what to say, but thanks."

We stood to shake hands. "You've put a charge into our reporting and what you filed on that Pentagon Papers business was outstanding. Oh, and one more thing."

What could top this, I wondered. He had the answer.

"That *G!* piece we talked about, we're starting to put together something featuring our Vietnam team – Ed Reynolds, Charlie Stebbins, Tom Massey plus yourself. A little self-promotion never hurts and you guys have done well on a tough assignment."

"We're targeting Fourth of July weekend," Marty added, "our annual patriotic issue."

"A full spread, pictures, the whole bit."

Diane was really excited. "Do you think they'll mention wives?"

I was a little surprised, but then I thought, if I deserve exposure why shouldn't she? "My guess is it'll be heavy on our reporting with a sprinkling of personal, but I'll find out. How about a photo while I'm at it," I laughed.

"I'll need a new outfit, have to get my hair done too."

"Hey, do that anyway. Nothing but the best for the Bernards." I smiled at my father's old words. I polish my apple, but it's his tree I'm sitting under.

Soon after I got the word on *G!* the phone rang and Diane picked it up. After a couple of minutes she handed it over. "Gus," she whispered.

"Doctor Flynn, I presume."

"Just calling to see how you guys are getting along. I told Diane a wedding present's on the way. I think you'll like it, Akiko's good at that sort of thing."

"I'm sure we will. Thank you."

"I meant to call when I saw that editorial. It looked like your work."

"It was, the last part of it. By the way, I owe you an apology."

"What for?"

"Vietnam. You had it pegged."

"No need to apologize. When you've been around as long as me you get it right once in a while. This one had con job written all it."

"You know who I just saw? Benny Kaplan."

"Benny! How is he?"

"Married with wife and child. He's teaching history at Queens College."

"A very good place. Underrated. Same girl? What was her name?"

"Leah, Gideon's sister. And he's living in Israel."

"Doesn't surprise me. While we're on this, you know who I just got a letter from? Hamid Rashid!"

"Of all things! What's he up to?"

"He's in London, finishing a book of short stories."

"I always liked him, but I found him hard to fathom. Send me his address."

"Sure. Maybe the stories'll shed some light. I won't keep you, but stay in touch. Let me know when the present arrives, if you don't like it the Salvation Army will."

"Not a chance. Oh, keep an eye out for the *Gazette's* magazine, Fourth of July weekend. It'll be worth a look."

After dinner that night the conversation came around to Gus. "He makes me uncomfortable," Diane commented. "I don't understand what you see in him."

"He's been known to rub people the wrong way, but he's a very solid citizen."

"Solid? His opinions were outrageous. I don't know whether you noticed but he and daddy really got into it. Daddy said he's a Socialist, maybe even a Communist."

"Hardly," I laughed, "but he does believe people who've been held down should have some extra help. That's a reasonable position to take."

She shook her head. "That's not how this country works. If you've got what it takes, you do well. If not, too bad."

"Goddamn it, Diane, Gus is as loyal as anybody. He was in the war, he was in Tokyo with MacArthur. He thinks enough of this country not to let it go down the tubes."

"That's not about to happen, and don't swear at me!"

"A lot of people would disagree with you – they think we've got big problems."

"That doesn't make them right and me wrong." She lowered her voice. "Anyway, I don't think he liked me either."

"Where'd you ever get that idea?"

"You can tell that about a person. I felt he didn't respect my opinions."

"Understand one thing about Gus. He knows how to spot the weakness in an argument and he's not afraid to go after it."

"So you think I'm stupid too, just like he does."

Things were in danger of flying out of control. "No, but nobody's right all the time."

"With two exceptions!" she shouted. "Gus Flynn and Paul Bernard!" With that she stalked from the room and slammed the bedroom door.

I spent the night on the couch, a first. To the list of surprises I added one I'd only glimpsed before, a fabulous temper. Plus, I noticed for the first time, a touch of paranoia.

WHAT THEY DID WITH *G!* FLOORED ME. Who was there but yours truly on the cover! With Ed Reynolds and Charlie Stebbins on the steps of the *Gazette* Building. Inside, more photos, though none of Diane. What did show was a black and white shot of me at Firebase Tango, rifle, fatigues and all, a cigarette in my mouth, "photo courtesy of Nathan Berg." There was one of me wrapped in bandages, my short leg in the sling, one of me and my new leg on the Stairmaster. Pictures of Ed at his desk in Saigon, in the field with General Westmoreland and one of our cameramen, one of Charlie with Senator Goodell and Representative Cellar. Charlie and Tom Massey on the Capitol steps.

What the article said was accurate, but embarrassing, some of it. They really laid on the war hero bit, cited a number of stories including my Korean grocery "portrait of two families." Since I was still reporting on the protests it wasn't my place to be offering opinions about the war, so I didn't. But there was an awful quote from Sid. "Sidney Greenwald, the *Gazette's* City Editor, commented, 'we've got something special in Paul Bernard. We're lucky to have him, so are our readers." I had to close the paper when I read that. Before the day was out my co-workers had dubbed me "Mr. Lucky." It didn't last, no nickname ever did, but the attention was a heady experience.

Diane seemed genuinely pleased. Her disappointment was salved since no other wives made it in either. She and I patched things up, and I resigned myself to weathering the occasional storm. I would sleep on the couch, the sun would rise again.

One of the plusses of my assignment was getting closer to Charlie Stebbins. I heard he liked my Vets' Week work and he was pleased I wasn't just another overbearing New Yorker out to yank his chain. In fact when he took our whole interview group out to lunch, I found in him a dedicated journalist, and a lifelong Republican who couldn't wait for the Nixon era to end. "I hope and pray he's a one-termer," Stebbins told me afterward. "There is nothing to admire in that man except survival instincts and that's not enough."

"We've had a failed haberdasher, alcoholics and crooks, now a guy who wouldn't make it as a used-car salesman."

"To the world's sorrow Germany had an unsuccessful art student. How would you like to have been the admissions officer who turned him down?" Stebbins leaned back and lit up a cigar. "So tell me, Paul, you've been with the *Gazette* how long?"

"Two years November."

"You'd fit well in Washington. What would you think about joining us?"

I caught a whiff of Potomac fever the week I was there but I was having such a good time in New York, plus my new life, it wasn't in the cards for now. Anyway, my flights of fancy touched down in London, Paris, Moscow. Shirer, Murrow,

Sevareid, Collingsworth. "At some point I'd like to," I said, "but I think I need more seasoning."

"We'll be the judge of that."

"How about a rain check?"

"It's yours, but call me before you make a move." He stretched out his hand. "Deal?"

"Deal."

From time to time I saw Alan Mauro. One morning in mid-July he called, saying drop what I was doing, he had something better. We caught the A line a couple of blocks from the office and rode it downtown to Chambers Street, emerging in a light rain. As we headed down West Broadway I sighted the hulk of the World Trade Center North Tower rising into the mist. "The South Tower's where it's at today," he said, "the topping off ceremony."

"Never been to one of those."

"You won't today either but we'll get close as we can." Standing at the corner of Vesey and Church we looked straight up into the mist. "Just have to use our imagination."

A stand was set up for officials and I could hear voices coming over a P.A. but couldn't make out the words. "Stan Barry's in there covering it," Alan said as he saw me straining to hear, "I just want to soak up the color."

"What happened to your story about building codes?"

"A dead end. Turned out the Port Authority told their architects to follow the city's code – a meet or exceed kind of thing. I couldn't get anybody on the record about oversight. That's a story but it isn't my story. I'm no engineer, just a political hack."

We hung around a while waiting for a glimpse of the tree and the flag at the top but no luck. Finally Alan complained about being hungry. "C'mon, I'll buy you lunch."

In a pub a couple of blocks away Alan congratulated me on the magazine spread, observed I was on the *Gazette's* fast track – work hard, don't screw it up. Waiting for our sandwiches he chugged down his drink, a double Manhattan straight up, I recall. He asked me how I was taking my celebrity. I said I didn't think of it that way, I just liked what I was doing. "'Course," he went on, "if the *Times* called I expect you'd pick up the phone."

"I suppose, but what more could they do for me?"

"In the ideal world, you're right, but this ain't that. You've heard the rumors?"

"About our financial situation? Everybody's going through hard times, what with the economy and all. Is there more to it than that?"

He sat back and signaled the waiter for another round. I was nowhere near finishing my beer. "A little history. From time to time the *Gazette* gets its ass in a sling and loses a ton of money. This time the economy's what's killing us."

"How serious is it?"

"We're running out of cash. We've been talking merger, God forbid it'd be a takeover. Maybe they'll find an investor, that'd be a better way to go."

"I didn't realize we were in such bad shape."

"We even got the distributors mad at us now. I don't know how much you're aware of the business side of the paper."

"Not enough, apparently."

"We've always credited distributors for papers they don't sell, we send 'em out to be pulped, but apparently no more. Lotta hard feelings. Next time you talk to the guy on the newsstand I wouldn't mention where you work." The waiter set our drinks down. "Way I see it, the only thing to do is keep on writing. Make more people want to buy the *Gazette*. Somehow, life goes on. Life will go on for Mauro, life will go on for Bernard."

Alan's last remark was reassuring, but not enough to compensate for his gloomy message. I debated whether to tell Diane, but decided not yet. Nobody really knew where this was going. Recently she had been ultra-friendly, cooking nice dinners, swamping me with home improvement ideas, some of which I even liked. Our time in bed was outstanding. The evening of my Alan visit we were watching the news when the screen filled with clouds. "Hey, I was there today!"

"How come?"

"Alan Mauro invited me to tag along. He's one of the best people around."

Diane was quiet a long time. I looked over, she reached out her hand and I took it. She smiled. "I'm pregnant. I went to the doctor yesterday, they called with the results."

I squeezed her hand, leaned over and hugged her. "Happy?"

"I wasn't sure how I'd react but I feel good about it. My parents will go crazy."

"I should call my family."

"Give it a some time, make sure everything's okay."

"There not a problem, is there?"

"No, but I have a checkup in two weeks. I told Penny but swore her to secrecy."

"Whatever you say... it being your department."

"For now, darling," she smiled. "Soon enough it'll be *our* department."

44. AFTERSHOCKS AND OTHER SEISMIC EVENTS

WE'VE BEEN FOCUSING SO MUCH on your hobby we're neglecting the reason we're here. This is an important time for Paul – a lot is happening."

"Okay," he says, looking pained, "where do you want to start?"

"Well, we got Paul married and her with child. I hope you're satisfied."

"I am. You've made harsh comments about his bride. I see the feeling was mutual."

"I didn't know she was so explicit. Guess I bring out the best in people. The two of them together, like the sister said, it just didn't add up."

"She didn't seem to have much sense of humor."

"You're right, and that bothered me. Being so serious himself, Paul needed somebody with a lighter touch."

Jonathan nods. "Odd that he hooked up with a financial type, though I don't know, it could be simpler than that. Maybe it just came down to the sex."

"Given his less than stellar record with women, when he found someone who responded he might have figured grab while the grabbing's good."

"Now if he'd just played around more he wouldn't have married the first girl he jumped in the sack with. They sure didn't waste any time, did they – having a kid, I mean."

"No," I said. "He loved the idea. With her, I'm not so sure it wasn't tactical."

"Could be. Do you know the White Horse Tavern?"

"Somebody took me there once. It was okay, not great."

"Let's go there. I want to visit his old haunts, see what's become of them."

"You're on. What's your take on Paul the rookie reporter?"

"What he describes is painfully familiar. But what's most impressive, how he finds people to mentor him. I was never very good at that. And that magazine! It was in the carton, did you see it?"

"Very impressive."

"The *Post* never did anything like that for me."

"You didn't lose a leg in the service of your country."

Jonathan nods. "He used the *Gazette,* they used him. To answer your question – the newsroom, the editors, the chaos, it all rings true. I wonder if he's enjoying it as much as he says. For me the first few years were a chore – the deadlines, the pressure. When I went over to features it was a lot better."

"Did you start out on the crime beat?"

"Absolutely. I spent a lot of hours in that Shack. And it's true, the *Gazette* guys were a breed apart. Though one-on-one some of them were all right."

* * * * * * *

AFTER ALAN'S ALARMIST TALK I did some snooping around. None of the old timers seemed too concerned. Rumors crop up from time to time, they said, nothing ever comes of them. Fred Mueller, our Business Editor, lived on my old block and we often visited in the newsroom. Fred blamed the economy. A costly war without the means to pay for it brought on inflation – my Berkeley expert's scenario. And as production slowed, higher prices were pinching everybody. "If your choice is food on the table or the *Gazette* on your doorstep, that's a no-brainer. Circulation's down, advertising revenues too, the old double-whammy. People're fed up. Nixon has to do something and with him it's always an adventure."

By August the seed was asserting itself and Diane had switched to a loose-fitting wardrobe. She was beset by morning sickness but bearing up bravely. "They tell me it doesn't last more than a couple of months," she said from her bed one morning as I brought her toast and tea. Penny would be over shortly. She was great about helping, and really into the idea of aunthood.

"We'll take it easy from now on," I said, putting the tray on the bed. "That trip took it out of you." We had arrived back late the night before from a fast weekend in Providence, our first visit since her news. During the train ride I watched her growing greener as we proceeded southward and packed her off to bed as soon as we got in. She was up several times in the night, retching. We saw everyone, spending time with my father who was thrilled, his sixth grandchild, "but who's counting." It made me sad to see him, his face so gaunt, and he tired easily. When I asked, Catherine shook her head. "Nothing specific, the doctor says, but it doesn't look good." He was sixty-five years old. We talked about arrangements. Catherine had taken things into her hands, forcing him to meet with his accountant and lawyer, insuring he make his wishes known.

With this dose of reality and the *Gazette's* uncertainties, I decided to look into my own finances, which came down to Nu-Gem. That string had played itself out – the three of us had in hand all the stock my father set up to be distributed. I didn't know but I figured we all got the same, thirty-five hundred shares. Mine was squirreled away in a metal box in the back of my closet along with Tante Jeannette's watch and other treasures. Checking the financial pages I found NUG at 47 3/8. I was worth over a hundred sixty-thousand!

That was it for my side of the ledger. I knew no details but Diane and Penny had trusts which kicked in at some point. So far we hadn't been able to save anything out of our combined incomes. New York is expensive, even in a two-bedroom somebody else paid for, and with our family about to expand, we were talking about, as Diane put it, the need for a larger place.

WELL INTO WHAT THE SEVENTIES, from time to time I pondered what sort of world my child would be born into. For one thing, he or she would vote at age eighteen. Elementary fairness, long overdue. If you're old enough to be sent to war, you're old enough to choose who will send you. Overlaying Nixon's peace with honor was the reality of a dead end. Some comfort, at least the South Vietnamese now were bearing the brunt of the fighting. From my semi-insider position I heard the peace negotiations were still stalemated. We wanted mutual withdrawal, a non-starter with the North. It was insisting that Thieu go.

Weariness pervaded public life. The view ahead was so disheartening many preferred to look back and, no surprise, a nostalgia craze was sweeping the country. "Old is In," declared *Life Magazine.* My friend Pam Snyder and her counterparts reported on ankle-length skirts, steel-rimmed granny glasses and the Rita Hayworth (!) look. Swing music was in, with Glenn Miller, Harry James and Benny Goodman commanding radio time, and sound-alikes headlining in concert and dance halls. Rock continued to draw and "soft rock" made its debut – Elton John, The Eagles, John Denver, James Taylor. I already had tickets to *Jesus Christ Superstar* opening on Broadway in the fall. Sadly, my son or daughter would never see Jimi or Janis but could look forward to *Hair* which seemed destined to run forever. Some relative would make a gift of a Mickey or Minnie Mouse watch, and he or she would thumb through reissued comics – Dick Tracy, the Hulk, Little Orphan Annie. I hoped my nephews were taking good care of my old Hardy Boys collection. Original retro was commanding high prices, besides I wanted them for my kids-to-come. As the Seventies dawned, Charles Reich's *The Greening of America* put a philosophical footing under the counterculture, promoting personal freedom and inner consciousness. It proved prelude to a wider narcissism endemic to the Seventies, but more on that later.

So far seventy-one had been a quiet year on the campuses, but I pictured Gus and his colleagues holding their breaths. The vets scene continued apace but I found my attention drawn increasingly to other city news. Tall, urbane John V. Lindsay was our mayor, elected as a Republican, then when his party turned against him, on the Liberal ticket. He had the distinction of defeating William F. Buckley in his first mayoral race. Though controversial, Lindsay was seen as presidential caliber, but the unions proved his undoing. On his very first day as mayor they shut down the subways and bus lines. He resisted, then caved. In years following, he battled the teachers' union, the sanitation workers, the police and white collar workers. The city's economic and fiscal problems would worsen, crime increase and companies flee to the suburbs. Many were calling New York ungovernable.

There was a growing belief that Richard Nixon was vulnerable. The vituperative attacks by his Vice President were counterpoint to news of Nixon's reprisals against his enemies. Some had thought we'd left the old Nixon behind. Wrong.

As I dug into city issues, I often found myself in the Morgue, our repository of back issues and clip files, my favorite room at the *Gazette.* Organized by topic, it shared the third floor with the photographers and the compositing room. To explore files you petitioned Marian Wheeler – Marian the Librarian, of course – who ran the show. Marian was the longest-serving *Gazette* employee, having joined the paper in Harding's time. She kept up with things, though, and these days was shepherding the *Gazette's* microfilm project set for completion in 1973, "if I live that long." This massive effort invariably produced holes in your research in exactly the wrong place. Marian and I were buddies. I always brought a blueberry muffin for her to enjoy in her office – NO EATING OR DRINKING permitted in the main room. Periodically somebody would tape an addendum to the sign, it was always the same – BUT FEEL FREE TO SPIT. I remember those afternoons fondly, poring through back issues at the long wooden table, the smell of old newsprint enveloping me, squinting in the glare of the green-shade lamps, stubby yellow pencils in leather-sided cups, little stacks of 4x6 notepaper. As the Morgue was a one-trick pony, however, I regularly removed myself to the Public Library at 42nd and Fifth. A rather decent backup.

As we turned the corner to Thanksgiving Diane was nearly six months along. She was over her morning sickness and eating like a horse or, she corrected me, two horses. She cajoled me into classes on childbirth and infant care. She would have the baby at St. Vincent's, in our neighborhood. Her mother pushed for the North Shore but in a show of independence I applauded, she said we live here, we'll do it here.

On quiet evenings Diane would sometimes raise her shirt and place my hand on her stomach so I could feel the baby move. Unbelievable! Our love life continued apace, though at first I felt somewhat squeamish about it, but she said no problem, it's the most natural thing in the world. As far as daily living was concerned, we were still getting used to each other. People told me this is a life-long process. From time to time I endured her temper, usually a quickly passing storm, thankfully not your tepid drizzle that hangs on for days. While unpacking my books I had come across an old mythology tome. Diana, goddess of the hunt, associated with fertility and quick to anger.

We celebrated Christmas at our place, hosting her parents and Penny, plus Catherine and Stan who came down to show two-year old Tracy the windows and the tree. Catherine hadn't said anything negative recently – I don't know whether the baby changed her mind or what, though she never missed a chance to say how much she liked Penny. Maybe that was her way of digging Diane.

The vets gave me my best present. During Christmas dinner, Tony Hart, a VVAW official, called to offer a tip, provided I keep it confidential and hold the story "until the deed is done." I agreed. "Tomorrow we're going to occupy the Statue of Liberty, about fifteen of us. Stay til New Years' Eve, raise the flag, put out a statement."

"Why this? Why now?"

"We've got to get the war back on the front page. People forget guys are still dying over there. Five o'clock tomorrow, the visitors leave, we stay. You know Jim Murphy, right? Ed Hayes? They're in charge. We're counting on you. Give us a good write-up."

Early afternoon I told Ollie Newton we had a story to cover, I'd tell him what later. I had already alerted Marty Rossi to hold space. He pushed me but I said I promised to keep it under wraps until tonight. As our ferry approached Miss Liberty I showed Ollie Tony's statement the vets would issue that evening. "We, as a new generation of men who have survived Vietnam, are taking this symbolic action at the Statue of Liberty in an effort to show support for any person who refuses to kill."

We installed ourselves near the ferry landing. Mid-afternoon a couple of guys I recognized got off the ferry, sauntered up to the statue and went inside. The next ferry, about ten more, one of them flashing me a victory sign. All wore backpacks, with provisions for their stay, most had long hair and beards, some in fatigues, combat boots. We exchanged brief greetings with teams from the *Times* and the *Daily News*. They knew why I was here, I knew why they were here.

As darkness fell I was glad for my parka and hiking boots. I grew impatient in the cold waiting for the action, facing a ten-thirty deadline. Eyeballing a stand of phone booths I would need to beat the others to, I patted my jacket pocket for my stash of dimes – always carried a pocketful. About seven I heard shouting and a man in a Park Service uniform emerged from the base of the statue and got on a radio. I approached him, he said he was the night watchman and had just been ejected from the building. "Bunch of hippies in there. They think it's a fucking hotel."

From inside I heard scraping and banging. I learned later they were dragging construction beams around, barricading the doors. Next a light came on in the upper level of the base and Ollie squeezed off some frames of the occupiers through the windows. The torch in the arm of Miss Liberty, normally dark at night, flashed on and Ollie caught them planting a flag on the crown, upside down for distress. The event launched, I called Marty to let him know I was on the story. The newsroom had just taken a call from the vets and he'd been frantically looking for me. Relieved to hear I had the inside track, he was pissed I hadn't let him in on it. "We better have a little chat. See me tomorrow."

As I hung up I heard a shout. "Hey, Paul!" It was Ed Hayes. He was peering through the barricaded front door which they had let open a couple of inches. "C'mere."

As I walked over the *Times* and the *Daily News* moved along with me. "Hey, man, good to see you," Ed said, reaching his hand through the crack. Ollie got a shot of him peering out the door.

"You guys okay in there?" I asked.

"We got food, running water, a coffeemaker, all the comforts of home. You get our statement?" I nodded. The *Times* reporter held his up but the *Daily News* guy said he needed one. Hayes slipped it through the crack in the door. "I expect the Park Police and the NYPD will show up anytime now." Ed turned to go.

The *Daily News* reporter looked at Ed. "Gimme a break, here we are freezin' our ass off, you got to give us something."

"Look at the statement. There's fourteen of us plus a guy from WBAI."

"You on the air with this thing?"

"He's taping. We spent the last couple of days in Valley Forge, a camp-out against the war. A couple more actions're coming down – all I can tell you, one's in Philadelphia, one's in California."

"You're a big help," the *News* reporter complained. "What's with the torch?"

"We're gonna keep it on all night."

"What's your name? Where're you from?"

"Albany. No names for now. Paul, you cool with that?"

"Not a problem."

"Let me make the point that we will leave this place just as we found it. No damage, no confrontations, no violence. Write that down. If they arrest us, we go peacefully."

"This thing have a name?"

"Operation Peace on Earth. Get it?"

"You got something against Hanukkah?"

"That works too."

One by one other protesters took Ed's place at the door. We talked back and forth a while when I heard the sound of a boat approaching. Walking out to the docking area I saw two tugs had just berthed. One of them was unloading a couple dozen NYPD and Park Police. I sought out the Park Police lieutenant and learned the National Park Service was asking NYPD to stand by while they mustered their own team who'd be here tomorrow. He said they'd agreed to let the vets stay overnight but tomorrow all bets were off.

It looked like everything had happened that was going to happen, so I called in the story. Rewrite said they had some good quotes from the Park Service they'd splice in. Plus some filler, like the statue stands 305 feet, Liberty Island has 12 acres, on an average day 12,000 visitors, gift of France for our centennial though ten years late. I told him to hold space for pictures, that we'd bust our butt to get back with them. Ollie and I caught a ride back on one of the tugs then hopped a cab, were there by nine-thirty. The article was a smash and even the pictures made the early edition, a three-column shot on the front page with Liberty's crown and the upside-down flag, a smaller one inside had the vets waving from their temporary sanctuary.

Marty and I talked, but Tom O'Connor's delight at our insider take on the drama overrode his irritation. "Next time I'd appreciate a heads-up," was all he said.

As the days went on I wrote about the irritated tourists, the show cause order obtained by the Park Service. At one point the vets handed out a typewritten statement calling on President Nixon to end the war: "You set the date. We'll evacuate."

He didn't, but they did. On Tuesday the 29th, proclaiming victory the fifteen vets left peacefully, heading for a feast in midtown where I joined them for color and detail to wrap the story. I particularly liked what the vets did as they tidied up the space. Ollie got a shot of the message they posted in the employee lunchroom. "Brothers and sisters, thank you for the sugar and coffee and food." Next to it was an envelope with five dollars in it.

THE PREGNANCY CONTINUED UNEVENTFULLY until April first when the first labor pains hit, a false alarm, of course. Three days later another set, considerably stronger, and I hustled Diane to the ob-gyn who nodded cheerfully but said she wasn't nearly there. The false alarms were getting her down, and she was weary and not sleeping well. I finally opted for a sure-fire remedy somebody told me about. Driving to a remote part of Queens I treated Diane to an hour-long tooth-rattling ride over washboard roads. That night, sure enough, I hustled Diane and her bag to the doctor who made a couple of measurements and said get right over to St. Vincent's. At eleven-seventeen on April 9, Peter Julien Bernard bade the world hello.

I can't describe my feelings that night as I held my son for the first time. I was very, very fond of my nephews and nieces, but this was altogether different. I kissed Diane and patted her face with a cool cloth. While carrying the baby she had looked especially radiant – I'd heard that happens with some women and it certainly did with her. She couldn't contain her relief and happiness. "I did good, didn't I?"

"Great. Unbelievably great," I said, passing the little bundle back.

Penny had sat with me while we waited and now, auntie pride in full flower, she kept Diane company as I made calls. Next day I handed out cigars. Everybody already knew, even his name – there are no secrets in a newsroom. It thrilled me that the wrappers were blue. Deep down I knew Diane was hoping for a girl and I was tempted to say we'll try again, but after what she'd been through I held my tongue.

In the last few months I watched our place shrink as the equipment piled up. Bassinet, changing table, diapers, bottles, bottle warmer, formula, bibs, clothing, carriage, stroller, high chair, furniture and play equipment, stuffed animals, balls, toys, books for the future, ditto for the potty – all this meant less room and no privacy. Peter's crying, which people said was standard, made the place even smaller. I took my turn on the night shift, enduring colleagues' comments about bloodshot eyes and falling asleep at my desk. Looking in the mirror, though, I did wonder if the bags were here to stay, and those stray hairs, were they really gray? Just shy of my thirtieth birthday, I was a father. Dethroned, yet deeply in love with my son – a complex set of emotions. So tiny and fragile, I feared in my ham-handed way I might inadvertently harm him. I hoped I'd feel more comfortable when he got bigger. It took me a while to realize how sturdy these little people are. I had to admit Diane was right, and found myself saying, let's get hold of a realtor and see what's out there.

I was dead set against leaving the city. The White Horse seminars had confirmed my intuitive antipathy for suburbs, how they siphon off brainpower, vitality, jobs and revenue vital to the cities, leaving these essential organs of our society to rot from within. Sure, city life had downsides but cities bring enormous benefits and in my view, their problems are solvable. When an old friend needs you, you don't up and quit on him. I read somewhere, maybe Jane Jacobs, to live in a suburb is to express a preference for the private over the public. I agreed with that, and I didn't like it. Clean air, trees, a backyard, that I could see, but for enough money we could get that in the Village. I had to believe Diane's being a child of the suburbs was part of her motivation, and I couldn't help wonder if she just wanted to be closer to her parents, though she wouldn't admit that.

Leaving the city would complicate my life tremendously. Was I being selfish, as Diane told me straight out one day? The commute would be an immense pain, hours every day in a car or on a train, in fact, depending on where we lived, several trains. Ditto for her when she returned to work, though she downplayed that. We decided to put off the decision a bit, though she took every opportunity to needle me about the city's perils and the advantages of living in, as I had taken to calling it, Panaceaville. She didn't think that was funny.

The next couple of months, we settled into the new routine. And we visited. Her parents often, of course, and Penny was a frequent guest. We traveled to Providence, which reminds me, add to the list a travel bed for Peter and a car seat, gifts of Penny. My father continued to surprise, alert and getting around much better. One of the proudest moments of my life was handing his grandson, my son, to him. Seeing the little guy seemed to turn his clock back years, though I knew that was wishful thinking. Jim and Sheila and their brood came down for the baptism and acted as godparents. Diane was cooperating with my Catholic needs – not a bad word, not even a hint. She kept her end of the deal so well it made me realize I couldn't hold out forever against her desire to live farther out.

RICHARD NIXON'S STANDING WAS LOW and getting lower. His razor-thin margin in sixty-eight was one burden, the harassment of a Democratic Congress another. But the comeback kid rallied, posting a number of impressive primary wins which bolstered his chances of re-election. When an insane gunman took George Wallace out of contention, Nixon's nomination was assured. But first came the trip to China – yes, Mao's China – confounding Republican hard-liners and throwing the Taiwan government into despair. In the sports analogies he favored, Nixon was not above changing his game plan, nor reluctant to go deep. One priority of the China visit was to worry the North Vietnamese. Seeing their Chinese supporters make nice with the imperialist enemy, maybe they'd take the peace talks more seriously. It was a delicate matter to finesse his China visit with the Russians, whom we had finally noticed didn't love the Chinese any more than we did. The Cold War theorem that all Communist societies are alike was by now totally discredited. On the domestic front, Nixon boldly unhooked the U.S. dollar from the gold standard and imposed a wage and price freeze to counter rampaging inflation. The month before the election he even signed a bill massively increasing funding for Social Security.

But Vietnam kept hanging around. In May, peace talks resumed after a six-month hiatus and the NVA marked the event with a major offensive, routing the South's Army and overrunning the DMZ. After several days Nixon appeared on television to inform the country he was initiating an air and sea blockade of the North's ports. Bombing of communications and military targets would commence, including Hanoi and Haiphong. To face down the North and restore leverage in the negotiations Nixon was risking his summit meeting with Brezhnev two weeks hence.

Editorials condemned Nixon. Democratic contender George McGovern accused him of flirting with World War Three. The campuses erupted, demonstrators flooded the streets, I covered marches and rallies. It was during "Operation Linebacker" that we saw the Pulitzer Prize-winning photo showing the little Vietnamese girl running naked down a road, screaming from her dousing with napalm.

In the end Nixon was the one standing. Two weeks later he met with Brezhnev in Moscow. Compared with the largely ceremonial and symbolic China visit, this summit achieved substantive gains. Meantime at the *Gazette* we picked up a report that the Soviets were actively urging their Vietnamese client to settle. Our actions had blunted the North's offensive. They gained little of strategic importance and lost thousands. From the depths, Nixon's standing with the American people was on the rise. His timing couldn't be better.

But by mid-year, static re-appeared. On June 18 the *Washington Post,* the *Times* and the *Gazette* reported a break-in at Democratic National Committee headquarters in the Watergate office complex. Five burglars were nabbed in what seemed a minor police matter, but one of them turned out to be in the paid employ of the Committee to Re-Elect the President, CREEP. John Mitchell, formerly Nixon's Attorney General, now his campaign manager, expressed dismay and denied White House involvement. However the *Post,* spearheaded by two young reporters, Bob Woodward and Carl Bernstein, along with the *Times* and ourselves and later in the game, CBS, continued to pursue the story of espionage, dirty tricks, harassment and cover-ups that became known collectively as Watergate. The public was somewhat disquieted but, for the most part oblivious.

On October 26, Henry Kissinger announced a breakthrough in Paris. "Peace is at hand," he proclaimed, though to cynical observers his timing seemed all too convenient, less than two weeks before Election Day. The prospect that Vietnam might soon be behind us propelled Nixon to a landslide victory with sixty percent of the popular vote, forty-nine states, the largest number ever, and the second-largest electoral college score in history, 520 to 17. Their only negative, the Republicans would remain a minority in the new Congress.

Kissinger's peace soon leaked away in the face of intransigence of North and South. As Christmas neared, Nixon, frustrated and furious, sent his B-52s aloft in the most massive bombing raids of the war. Areas of Hanoi were reduced to rubble. Civilian casualties ran high since many targets were within city limits. Nixon was vilified and even old supporters were saying they'd had enough, but Moscow and Peking's surprisingly tepid reaction must have weighed heavily on the North Vietnamese, for on December 30 the bombing was halted and within ten days the Paris talks were on again.

With the news of war and peace, the election, the widening Watergate morass, I thought often of Charlie Stebbins' proposal. In my fantasies it was only a matter of time before I made some kind of change, but married, now with a child, and considering Diane's roots, it would be difficult. Burrow in, I told myself, build your networks, hone your craft. There was one nagging thought. If the war did wind down, and I sincerely hoped it would, my anti-war beat would go away. One way or the other, I'd have to make sort of move.

Life Magazine gave the world an early Christmas present – Apollo 17's view of earth from the Mediterranean to Antarctica, the famous Big Blue Marble photo, and a reminder to me of Nathan and I at Firebase Tango hanging on Apollo 8's narrative of the earthrise. How beautiful our home is, I thought. My second reaction, how simple things seem from a distance, led me to formulate Bernard's Law of Geopolitics – The complexity of human affairs is in inverse proportion to the distance you are from them. Vietnam, a dot you couldn't even make out. Nor Watts, Detroit or Roxbury. Somehow we have to hang together, I concluded, else we'll hang separately. And by the way, be kind to your Mother.

CONSIDERING HOW NEW I WAS TO THIS BABY STUFF I thought I was doing well. One night when Peter was a couple of months old, I had him nestled in the crook of my arm, he was sucking on his bottle. Peter Julien Bernard, I repeated softly, savoring the words. As he looked up I recalled the awesome power I felt when I named my dog, in a way gave him his identity for life. Same thing here. Peter Julien Bernard. So contented, so trusting.

It was a warm night and I stood by the living room window in t-shirt and shorts, looking through the blinds and the security grille at the street below. Normal sounds, car horns, police sirens, trucks racing up Sixth Avenue, clack-clack-clack of Manhattan heels on the sidewalk. Then some arguing and yelling broke out under my window and I heard what sounded like shots. A car sped away. Instinctively I ducked away from the window and backed across to the inside wall. Breathing heavily, I shielded Peter with my body. The bottle shook so hard I yanked the nipple out of Peter's mouth. Confused, he looked up but... it wasn't my son, it was that shattered baby. Images raced through my mind – dead children, maimed children... everything going a thousand miles an hour. I shuddered. The gruesome sight of a young Vietnamese came back to me. I thought I had forgotten him. Eleven? Twelve at the most. Stoner nailed him point blank then sliced off his cock then pried his jaw open and stuffed it in. Jesus! Even a Vietcong was once two months old, two years old. I saw a tall, gaunt white woman with a boy hiding in the folds of her skirts... Stoner! Hiding as that Vietnamese boy had hidden.

Self-defense! a voice shouts. I shake my head. Forget Stoner, forget his games. Freedom, democracy, such fine words, immunizing us for what we're told to do. The training, so thorough, so clever, drilling out the last semblance of empathy. A perfect fit, young men and violence. The state welcomes you. Without you it cannot survive. Thrill to the danger, boys, thrill to the hunt. Boys' games with grown-up toys. Terminate. Deadly. Force. I knew everything about original sin but nothing of evil. How stupid! Had I listened to Machiavelli, Hobbes, Dante, had I known the history of my race I would not have been shocked. Faith and innocence are found only in little children and they disappear before the young man has down on his cheeks. More faces flash by... the newsreel roars ahead. Insane, all of it – insane!

By now I was shuddering uncontrollably, my back to the wall. Slowly I slid to the floor, protecting my little bundle. I hit the floor heavily and he began to scream, his face all red and twisted. I was crying, too. My other hand still held his bottle... I stuck it back in his mouth. The bedroom door opened... Diane standing there in her robe. She rushed down the stairs. "What's happening! What are you doing! Peter! Poor little thing! What are you doing on the floor!" She picked Peter up, now-now-now-ing him, cuddling him. I reached out and offered her the bottle. "Are you crazy! It's been on the floor!"

I shook my head. "It hasn't been on the floor," I said evenly.

She disappeared into the kitchen and I heard the refrigerator door. A few minutes later she returned. Peter was sucking contentedly. I was still on the floor. "Are you all right? You don't look well."

"Had a relapse or something."

"You should see the doctor. I haven't said anything but you've been talking in your sleep. You yell too, you know that?"

"I have dreams. Yelling I don't know about. Yeah, I'll look into it."

But I didn't. My last visit to that VA quack he really pissed me off, leaning on me to come around more often. You're lucky to be alive, he said, don't complain if you have to see me once a month. I nodded, thinking the whole time I'll handle this alone and with a lot less grief.

The next day I checked the sidewalk under our window, the street around. I pored through the *Gazette* and *Times*. I made a trip to the neighborhood precinct house, asking for the crime report. Nothing. Nothing anywhere. Diane took over the night feedings. I needed my rest, she said, but what she was really saying – she didn't trust me. I didn't fight her, not that I agreed with her because I didn't – I would never hurt my child. The whole time I was in total control though distracted. An expression from boot camp came back to me, "successful completion of the maneuver was never seriously in doubt." Exactly.

That evening, the gunshots or whatever they were, the pressure of being a father, they marked my descent into a period of introspection and brooding. I was already feeling put out, no time to myself, little of Diane's left for me. My only private moments came at Mass. I felt sad that the person I shared my life with was absent from something so important to me. Whenever our conversation turned to religion she invariably snuffed it out with a comment like "how can you still believe that stuff?"

Actually, I have to admit I had backslid in my churchgoing, wasn't as faithful as I always had been. I had developed into a world-class rationalizer, never lacking for an excuse. My insomnia was back big time too. After filing my last story I took long walks down Eighth Avenue, skirting Port Authority and Times Square, stepping around the broken bottles and broken people, foolishly giving personal safety no thought. I didn't carry a gun, didn't own a gun, didn't want a gun. The thought had crossed my mind – with a family to protect, should I keep one in the house, but it was always the same answer. My life has been too much about guns. If we ever have a problem I'll deal with it a different way.

I did wonder about these people in the dark doorways, their stories. Some of them had to be my comrades – a lot of those on the street, more all the time. I should stop, talk with them, maybe do an article, draw attention. Generally I crossed over on Twenty-third, past the Chelsea Hotel, took a right on Sixth, down past the landscape and garden stores, the antique and clothing shops, always glanced down Sixteenth for St. Francis, locked at this hour, churches never used to be locked, slowed at the Village Vanguard, should drop in there some night, past Sheridan Square's bars and clubs. The apartment was usually quiet but sometimes Diane was up with Peter. Where have I been, she'd ask, what was I doing? Was I okay? If she only knew, I thought – I'm wondering the same thing.

My troubles had opened a space between us. It was not possible for me to tell her what I had seen, what I had been through, that it was still with me. The time I needed her help the most, I couldn't bring myself to ask for it. Why? To this day I do not know.

So much of the news was ugly. The attack on Israel's athletes. I called Benny, though the call was more for me than him. Things were boiling over in Northern Ireland too, an attack in Dublin, then what they were calling Belfast's Bloody Friday. To whom should I turn for that? In Vietnam the long-awaited pullout happened but I knew our impatient nation's support of our ally was bound to weaken. It was only a matter of time before the South sank into chaos and savagery and Father Trần's fear became reality.

Even at Mass, Vietnam was present to me. What of my Church, I asked, how had it acquitted itself? There were heroes, but not enough of them. And as always, Communism the foil, the convenient refuge. Send forth the lambs, the organization comes first, at all costs the organization. Though I don't claim that as an excuse – I needed no help to make my mistakes. I was the one who looked at a rifle and saw a cross. For all his bluster Gus was right. With his careful balancing Father Ronan was right.

Evil has washed over me, dissolved my castles, my summas. I think of God's Dumb Ox, his great plan of existence, the Great Planner. So sublime, so simple, so sure. For a moment let me think the unthinkable. What if Aquinas was wrong? I know now, reason is not in charge, nor goodness. He got that wrong, for sure. Gibbs, Phelps, Stoner... if they are also reflections of the Divine, was the Inquisitor right? Is God evil? Impotent? Second only to angels, is man the failed experiment? And endless winter our fate?

When all is said and done, I was a cog and a killer, just like the others. I was there for my country, all right, then I discover it was for a lie. The lie of men who preen and puff out their chests but beneath the tunics and ribbons there is nothing. Hollow men who cheapen our country, sully our patriotism. Criminals. Criminals! At times I felt like unhooking my leg and throwing it in the river, letting it drift wherever it would. I was sorry for myself, for the folly that made me a fraction of a man. I wanted to hate those who abused my innocence, but I could muster only weariness and disappointment. They say you make your own face. These days I dared not look in the mirror.

45. NEW HORIZONS

I WILL BE HERE OVER CHRISTMAS, need to push ahead. Jonathan is still trying to persuade ETVN to send him to Iraq on their nickel. He had another meeting with Captain Martinez and it appears Roberto – everybody calls him that – is willing to put him together with that General. What I don't understand – that guy is an enemy, a wanted criminal. They've got a duty to bring him in. Or maybe I just don't understand the game Dennis is playing.

It is eleven and Jonathan has just shown up. "I didn't expect that gunshot episode," he says. "I thought he'd put that behind him."

"Not I. I was surprised it took so long to surface. Psychological scars – the slightest thing can reopen the wound, just when it's least expected. He called me right after it happened. I told him to get help, but he was stubborn."

"It also surprised me he opened up like that, on the political thing."

"The bloom is off the rose-colored glasses, so to speak."

"So to speak. I'm starting to see your point about Diane, too. That move is going to be trouble. Somebody's going to be odd man out and it won't be her."

Deep in December, nine months into the Iraq morass, Saddam Hussein has been captured. Acting on a tip, our troops found him, disheveled and defiant, hiding in a hole near his home town of Tikrit. Of course before you can say boo, W is on TV crowing. Come together, Iraqis, reject violence and build a new country. Fat chance. The violence continues. Whoever dares to help us risks everything. When we cannot protect those who would be our friends, that is a formula for defeat.

* * * * * * *

I WANT TO SET THE RECORD STRAIGHT. What I was saying – don't get the wrong idea. I was clear-headed, totally in control. Sure, I got gloomy from time to time but who doesn't? As I mentioned, my anti-war beat was fast disappearing and that was a concern. By early 1973 most Americans had put Vietnam behind them. Not too cynical to say that when the draft went away, so did the protesters. The all-volunteer military was coming. The heat was off young American men.

On January 27 a peace treaty was signed which we called a toothless farce. It was concerning to the South, for within sixty days the U.S. would pull out and VC and NVA remain, even the political cadres. An international force would keep the peace until the country was reunited "by peaceful means." Well, nobody believed that would happen. Beyond irony, the only warring party to withdraw was the United States. Sixty thousand men killed, three hundred thousand wounded, billions of taxpayer dollars gone, and the best we can do is cut and run. Father Trần's angry words stung.

In a signed editorial Tom O'Connor congratulated our political leaders for finally being right about something, noting that the American people would never have backed the war if they'd been told the truth. In a letter a retired Colonel blasted us for Monday morning quarterbacking, and an MIT political scientist argued that in time of war presidential decisions are entitled to deference, that's how our system works. Tom fired back. Monday morning quarterbacking's better than none at all, he said. He advised his antagonists to read the Pentagon Papers. By their deceptions, he went on, successive administrations had forfeited the public's support, and it wasn't just Democrats either. Eisenhower's fingerprints were all over it, and Watergate made anything the current President said or did suspect.

In March of seventy-three the last of our military that had reached 536,000 left the country. Dismantling of U.S. bases was underway. Congress soon moved to prohibit U.S. military operations in or over Indochina. Military aid to the South would continue but how long before that funding was cut off too?

About this time I asked for a meeting with Sid Greenwald. When I pointed out my beat was about to disappear he sympathized. "Unfortunately we've never been much for career development, but let's see what we can't come up with."

The next week he called me in and said I was officially off anti-war and back on the City Desk, which I had never actually left. He went on to discourse about how in New York and nationally, politics was splitting into factions. Interest politics, identity politics, single-issue politics. "It's an old approach – the unions built their empires on it, these days everybody's doing it. The blacks, of course, then you have the Latins, the Orientals, the feminazis, the fags, the farmers, the disabled. Even old folks are buying into it. People figure if they gang up on an issue they'll do better and they're probably right. It's big now and it's only going to get bigger."

I told Sid I had recently been exposed to the feminist aspect. Penny had invited Diane and me to a "consciousness-raising" event, a fund-raiser at an Upper East Side penthouse where I met some of the lights including Gloria Steinem and Bella Abzug. "Are they good contacts?" he asked. "Can you go back to them?"

"Those people are always looking for press exposure."

"Terri Abrams is our gal on that beat but I'd like to add a male perspective."

A few days later Sid called again. "How're your contacts in the gay community?"

"I know a few people, that's about it."

"Get with Jonny Rollins. He can use some help, says there's a lot going down soon."

I knew Rollins fairly well. I had first seen this flamboyant character at the White Horse and was surprised to learn he was a colleague. Speaking of the Horse, I made a note to check back there again soon. Family duties were crimping my old bachelor style and I had to do better. My talk with Sid made me think about Pat – I wondered how he was getting on. But back to Rollins. First of all, his designer wardrobe set him apart from most reporters for whom style was an afterthought.

He was proof that one person, at least, was paying attention to those far-out men's fashions Pam pictured in her pages. One day Rollins showed up in the newsroom wearing a kilt, at least I think it was – it was plaid. That thing better be a kilt somebody yelled at him. He also was known for elegant prose most of which didn't survive the copy editors. He lived in Gramercy Square with an older man said to be heir to a liquor distributorship fortune.

"You saw Rollins' piece on that guy who exposes gay celebrities." Sid grinned, "I mean outs them. Those people make for good copy and you can always count on the NYPD for the occasional gay-bashing. That market's going to be huge when it gets going. We've made a decision to focus more advertising there, so we need them buying the paper which means give them stories they want to read. That's where you come in, you and Jonny."

As I burrowed in, I found the anger so evident in the black movement was flowing through these other groups as well. We're different but we want the same rights as everybody else. Kind of a stretch but hey, what's logic got to do with it? As for women, their history of political action meant they were much farther along. The Equal Rights Amendment had passed both Houses of Congress and ratification was being heavily promoted in the states.

In January, the week before I talked with Sid, the Supreme Court had handed down Roe v. Wade. I had followed the case in the news, and had strong opinions about it. When I sat down at Terri Abrams' desk to discuss working together she started in on me right away. "A great day for women," she said, a big smile on her face. "Out of the alleys and into the light. It's been a long time coming."

I shook my head. "What it means is killing on a massive scale, killing of the most vulnerable among us. All in the name of a women's so-called right to choose."

Her face dropped. "Surely you don't disagree that women should be able to control their own bodies."

"Of course they should. How about controlling it so you don't need an abortion in the first place?"

"Meaning?"

"Meaning contraception, meaning wait until a child is more convenient – there are plenty of ways that don't involve ending a human life."

"Boy, are you out of touch. That's not how things work these days."

"You're right and it's only going to get worse. It's a dark day when people don't stand up for the powerless."

"You admit no exceptions?"

"I didn't say that. If the mother's life is at risk, that can be a reason to do something you otherwise wouldn't do."

"What about rape? Incest?"

I shook my head. "Life is tough but that's no excuse for ending somebody else's. Have the baby, get counseling, get on with your life. There are adoption clinics, you know."

Terri looked at me severely. "You were in Vietnam. How do you square that with this holier-than-thou attitude?"

That brought me up short. "How many babies did I kill? Is that what you're asking?"

"Something like that. And while you're at it how many adults?"

"You know, Terri, that is a really low blow."

"What's the difference? Killing is killing, right?"

I tried to compose myself. "I didn't kill anybody who wasn't trying to kill me first. Never did I kill someone for my convenience or to cover up a mistake I made in bed."

She flushed. "The Catholic party line. I'm not surprised."

I shook my head. "It's not about Catholic, it's about conscience. Something as wrong as this is wrong whether you're a Buddhist or a Catholic. Or a Jew."

She rolled her eyes. "Oh, vey. Working with you is gonna be a barrel of laughs."

"Yeah. I can't hardly wait."

The rocky start didn't sink our relationship but it made us wary. How we managed – Terri didn't ask for help on abortion stories and I didn't volunteer any. But there was plenty else, and as we got going I became aware what a professional she was, how scrupulous at keeping her opinions out of her work. She had a wide network of women's righters and was on a first-name basis with everybody. After working with her on a couple of stories I was able to drop names that impressed even Penny.

Working with the larger-than-life Jonny Rollins was something else. Incidentally, that is how he spelled it. Walking beside him on any Village street was to run a gauntlet of handshakes, hand-slaps and air kisses (him only). In addition to gay issues he had taken on the fringes of the music scene our jazz and rock expert Clay Eggert was reluctant to cover. I contributed some insights from my Lower East Side time and helped on the not-infrequent police actions at the clubs. At first I thought I might assist on the music aspects too, but I found I had no affinity for that brand of music or the performers either. The wannabee crowd was a real turn-off too – the nose rings and lip-piercings, the green spiked hair and tattoos. If that's the kind of show the Dadas put on, Pat could have it.

I did willingly accompany Jonny to David Bowie, Iggy Pop, and some others he reviewed for Arts & Performance. I assayed interviews of patrons and sat in as he rapped in the stars' dressing rooms. Some of his work showed up free-lance in Andy Warhol's *Interview* magazine. When I asked how that set with our employer he just laughed, saying his notoriety gave the *Gazette* a cachet it didn't deserve. Jonny was also a film buff and steered me to some greats I might have passed on – *Taxi Driver, Joe, Tall Blond Man With One Black Shoe, The Last Picture Show.*

He was interested in my Vietnam experience and explained how the drug culture was spreading to blue-collar America. When I said I saw little or no instances of homosexual behavior in the military he said I didn't know what to look for, which was likely true. I was happy to be off the anti-war beat, but feminists and gays weren't my cup of tea either. Not until seventy-three did I find what I was looking for, more on that later. From time to time Ed Foley asked me to sub for him and I was surprised how much more I enjoyed my old beat – what was left of it, that is.

As seventy-three opened, Watergate continued to bubble along. The burglars were convicted, given draconian sentences, and Richard Nixon's world started coming unglued. John Dean sang, Nixon's trusted Haldeman and Ehrlichman were implicated, and Nixon forced to can them. Next, he appointed Elliot Richardson as Attorney General replacing Richard Kleindienst who himself had resigned. In turn, Richardson named Harvard Law professor Archibald Cox independent special counsel for the congressional inquiry which was just starting its televised hearings. Stay with me, it gets worse.

During the hearings our TV monitors were on nonstop. I wasn't the only one to comment on Cox' uncanny resemblance to Tom O'Connor. In mid-July Alexander Butterfield, a former aide to Haldeman serving as FAA Administrator, revealed during routine questioning, almost inadvertently, that Nixon had installed a recording system in the White House. Every Oval Office conversation had been taped! Apparently Nixon, mindful of his legacy, had been recording and illegally wiretapping, friends and foes alike. Within days Cox issued a subpoena for the tapes. Nixon refused and ordered Cox to drop the subpoena, which he declined to do, asking John Sirica, the federal judge handling the burglary trial, to compel the President to show cause why he shouldn't be held in contempt.

The widening scandal filled the papers. Suffering through gay pride parades and women's lib rallies, as I read Charlie Stebbins' accounts I fantasized about being in the nation's capital reporting on this constitutional crisis in the making. I needed a change, though to what I didn't know. I wasn't looking forward to broaching the issue of a disruption with Diane, considering how much we had going on already.

IN JUNE DIANE ANNOUNCED we were going to be parents again. "I knew you wanted another one," she said, "but this time it had better be a girl."

I threw my arms around her and whirled her around the living room. "Boy, girl, this is great! Does Peter know?"

"He was the first to know. He was with me in the doctor's office. The sitter cancelled."

Peter was a solid fourteen months, walking and talking a storm, if toddling and babbling count, which of course they do. People said Peter looked like me, though I thought that depended on the viewing angle and his mood. His smile, which he practiced a lot, was definitely mine, the solid build, too, as well as the dark hair and skin. He had her nose.

We'd talked about a second, so the news was no great surprise, but it would complicate Diane's return to work. For the last few months she'd been commuting to the city to keep her hand in, bringing bond documents home, massive piles of paper that make the financial world go. But she missed the give and take of client contact and butting heads with the rating agencies, lawyers, underwriters, her Goldman Sachs team, which led directly to the attitude – let's get this childbearing thing over with. Her revelation stripped me of all defense against moving, though we were still at odds over where. One evening after a long and testy conversation, I agreed to tour the North Shore with her and an agent friend, if she'd do the same in the Village.

I had a bad feeling about this from the start. The animation in Diane's face as we drove the tree-lined streets past one mansion after another, confirmed what I already knew. I had to admit, once away from the thruways there was a certain charm, an appealing orderliness, but it was with a heavy heart I returned from these scouting trips, seeing my city life and liveliness slip away. After several months of looking, she, that is we, settled on an older home in Glen Cove, several towns over from her parents. We would close on the deal and move after Labor Day, well before the baby arrived.

Diane wasn't zealot enough to deny my commute would be a burden. The real killer would be when I finished late. Our compromise – we'll hold onto the condo for now, use it as a *pied-à-terre*. Realtor friends told us this would be smart and Fred opined that Manhattan home prices are bound to soar if the city ever gets a handle on things. You might ask how could we afford the luxury of two places in one of the world's most expensive urban areas. I certainly did. The answer, once again, Diane's father. For first daughter and his treasured grandson all things were possible including a second down payment. And, as he offered over drinks one night, a Midlothian Yacht Club membership, now that we lived so close, pointing out their excellent programs for the little ones. I demurred, content at being invited from time to time, but when he wouldn't take no for an answer, I insisted on kicking in five thousand from my savings toward our new home. To raise the funds I sold some of my Nu-Gem shares which, incidentally, had doubled in value even with a 3:1 split.

And so it was, on a steamy, overcast August day we signed papers and became the owners of a five-bedroom, three bath, split-level on an acre-and-a-half at the end of a cul-de-sac, which looked a lot like what we called a dead end in my old neighborhood. Child-friendly, shopping, good schools, a walk to the LIRR, and a long, long, long way from West 44th and Ninth. The following Saturday the movers arrived and we buckled Peter and our other valuables into Diane's BMW and headed out, my Beetle following, leaving enough clothes and kitchen equipment behind for in-town evenings and the occasional weekend.

Mid-afternoon, tired of choring, I left the cartons and crumpled paper to Diane and Penny and went outside to clear my head. Prowling the grounds, I decided there was something to say for what we had just done. First time I had owned anything of consequence, and this little patch did feel like country, topping even Gus' Berkeley place for the greenery, the feeling of remove. I caressed the trunk of my tallest evergreen, surveyed my little pond – with some work I could see Peter skating on it – and climbed to my overlook which in a few months promised a glimpse of Hempstead Harbor, the famous "partial winter view."

THESE WERE THE HEADY FIRST DAYS of the "small is beautiful" movement. I found Schumacher's book confirmed many of my prejudices. But buying a big house and spending hours each day commuting – that was neither small nor beautiful. It sure wasn't simple. Though I had to admit my grassy little acre gave me a certain contact with nature, however imperfect. The nursery and Peter's room were the first to be refinished. Peter's crib matched the sky-blue walls Diane had arranged to have painted. She had plans for the whole house but I pleaded for time to digest what we'd already bitten off.

We had just arrived home from dinner with Penny when I looked into my new study. The answering machine light was blinking. It was Catherine. From her tone I knew something was terribly wrong. Dad's dead, she said, a heart attack earlier in the evening. I sat down heavily, letting her words wash over me. My eyes filled with tears, I said a prayer and left the room, heading toward the voices. Diane and Penny and the sitter were in the living room. Diane looked at my forlorn expression. "Paul, what's wrong?"

"My father's dead. He had a heart attack. That was Catherine."

"I'm so sorry." Diane put her arms around me, her head on my shoulder. We leaned on each other for a long time. Blinking hard, I looked around our new living room, suddenly resenting everything about it. "Can I do anything?"

"I'd better go up there tomorrow, see what I can do to help."

"Just tell me what I can do."

"Be yourself," I said, releasing her. "That's what I need."

I don't know anyone who likes cemeteries but Vietnam had turned my mild aversion into borderline dread. What a poor, sad substitute for life and love is the engraved tablet, but since it's the best we can do, we do it. The wake, the funeral Mass – in French I was pleased to see, at Our Lady of Lourdes – then a get-together hosted by Jim and Sheila. The day before, touring Diane around my old neighborhood, I was ashamed to see it looking so shabby, our house needing paint, the fence nearly falling down. Even more Spanish and Vietnamese signs on the little stores. Diane said all the right things, but I was chagrined.

This was Diane's first exposure to the extended family. I was surprised to see she had chosen a dress that clearly signaled her pregnancy. She modeled it for me in our room at the Biltmore. Three months along, she barely showed, but I saw it as her way of expressing solidarity with these people, my people. I have to say it was a real time-warp, turning the calendar of faces ahead ten, fifteen years. Afterward my relatives probably compared notes about me, too, the famous war hero, the cripple. As I hoped, Albert and Geneviève showed up, Tante Jeanette also, Pièrre and Céline and their oldest, Anne, a quiet young woman, pretty and dark-haired. But no *Pépère*. "Eighty-six he'll be, his next birthday," Albert explained, the pneumonia last winter nearly did him in. We have to sit on him not to do too much."

"He sends his thoughts and prayers," Geneviève added.

Aunt Moira was there, cheerful as the occasion allowed, with her daughters and their husbands I hadn't met before, one in insurance, Catherine told me, the other an accountant. Uncle Antoine was sticking close to Aunt Roseanne who appeared pale and shaky. Lung cancer, an operation several months ago and uncertain prospects. Mary Elizabeth Finnegan, Uncle Paddy, Steve and Terry, now thirtyish, balding and overweight. I noticed Steve and Pierre laughing together, probably reminiscing about the Great Ham War. Tante Héloise had been gone several years, as had Grandmother Kelley, and Uncle Eddie who finally succumbed to the grape.

Gus and Akiko didn't show, that would have been beyond the call, but what they sent blew me away. Next to the casket in the funeral parlor, standing apart from the lilies and roses, three thin hollyhock stems, purple and white, in a simple dish of black dirt and stones. It sobered me to think how close I came to claiming that white flower.

My emotions were running high. Last bag in the Beetle, I tipped the doorman and reminisced about farewells in this place, portal to important chapters of my life. On my own, lonely and frightened, I looked across at the person I had chosen to share my life. I wanted her to be everything to me, wanted things to be right, but we were very much, as they say, a work in progress. But then, so was the life my parents fashioned, as far as a small boy could grasp such things, as the man he became viewed them through the filter of time.

In the wider world, it was one shock after another. Chile's Marxist President Allende was overthrown by the country's military in an action that had CIA written all over it. Barely three weeks later, on Yom Kippur, a surprise joint attack by Egypt and Syria across the sixty-seven cease-fire lines overwhelmed Israel's forces in the occupied territories. Counterattacking in the Golan, however, after three days of fighting the Israeli Army was within striking distance of Damascus. But in the Sinai, they were in desperate straits, many aircraft and tanks destroyed with sophisticated Soviet weaponry and fast running out of ammunition. A massive USSR resupply effort for Cairo and Damascus was already underway. How would the United States respond?

As these events were developing, the U.S. Attorney in Baltimore formally charged Spiro Agnew, the administration's alliterative attack animal, with bribe-taking while governor of Maryland. Agnew was allowed to plead *nolo* to a single charge of tax evasion on condition that he resign the vice presidency. Another new low.

For Richard Nixon, Friday October 12 was the day from hell. A. The appeals court ordered him to turn over the Watergate tapes. B. In an awkward ceremony he presented his choice to succeed the disgraced Agnew – House Minority Leader Gerald Ford. C. He and Kissinger pondered their dilemma – aid Israel and risk war with the USSR, or abandon our ally in her time of peril. As to C, Nixon rolled the dice, the C-5s took off, and an epic airlift was on. Spirits lifted, stores replenished, the Israelis retook the Golan Heights and poured across the Suez into Egypt, cutting off the Egyptian Army just as a U.N. ceasefire came into effect.

When the attacks began I called Benny but didn't hear back for a few days. His first words, "Golda knew it was coming, days ahead she knew. The generals wanted to go for a pre-emptive strike but she turned them down. A good thing, too."

"A good thing? Why?"

"The airlift is saving their ass, that's why. Gideon told me Kissinger said if she attacked first the U.S. would stand aside. They would have been totally on their own."

"She is one gutsy lady. I thought you were a peacenik, Benny."

"Depends on the war – you ought to know that by now. But I have to tell you, we just dug ourselves a big hole. Those territories we took, they're going to cause us a lot more trouble than they're worth. Except the Golan, that's important from a defensive standpoint."

"I think you're right. Is Gideon still teaching in Tel-Aviv?"

"Among other things." He paused. "What can I say? Gideon is Gideon."

As the conflict played out, U.S. pressure dissuaded Israel from destroying Egypt's trapped Third Army. Egypt and Israel would disengage militarily. It would take Kissinger's shuttle diplomacy to persuade Syria and Israel to do the same.

Meantime, the next Watergate shoe. Daringly successful on the international scene, dumb and dumber at home, Richard Nixon tried to fire Archibald Cox. He said he'd release summaries of the tapes but nothing more. Again Nixon ordered Cox to back off, again Cox refused. Our banner headline captured it nicely –

NIXON OFFERS SUMMARY
COX SAYS NO DEAL, DEMANDS TAPES

– and the Saturday Night Massacre was on. Attorney General Richardson refused the President's order to fire Cox and resigned. Richardson's deputy refused, then *he* resigned. Nearly out of options, the President's men persuaded Justice's number three, the later-famous Robert Bork, to do the deed. With mounting calls for his impeachment, Nixon was forced to name a new special prosecutor, Leon Jaworski, who would press on with the investigation.

I WAS BUSIER THAN EVER with protests over the incredible Potomac sideshow, but halfway across the world events were occurring which would profoundly affect my career and life. The Organization of Arab Petroleum Exporting States had been around for a decade, a vehicle for oil-producing nations to exert some control over their lifeblood resource, and now it took a step that rocked the world. Reacting to the U.S. resupply of Israel, OPEC declared an oil embargo against the U.S. and the Netherlands, also a traditional friend of Israel. At the same time, members raised prices and cut production, affecting everyone, completing the revolution the Saudi oil minister, Yamani, had envisioned for years. Joined with a nearly twenty percent price increase, the cut in production had a devastating impact on the western economies and Japan. In December OPEC pushed through a second price hike, bringing the increase to nearly two hundred percent. By 1974 the price of oil would quadruple to nearly US$12 a barrel. Frantic bidding would push it above $16.

The producing states soon realized the new high prices meant they could reduce production and still increase revenue. But as the months went on, policing the cuts became difficult, and Anwar Sadat, whose bold military stroke had precipitated the crisis, decided that the embargo, a spectacular success, should be ended. Over the objection of Syria and Libya, on March 18 the OPEC ministers agreed. The industrialized nations had been taught a lesson, and now saw themselves in a condition, perhaps permanent, of oil shortages and huge transfers of wealth into Middle East treasuries. From here on out, uncertainty would be the name of the game. Nothing spooks the markets like uncertainty and, led by the United States, global GNP numbers declined and unemployment shot up. Not until 1976 would signs of growth be seen again.

When I heard of the OPEC action my immediate thought was, now we're really in for it. My second thought was personal – might this be the assignment I'd had been looking for? I was no Middle East expert but had closely observed that part of the world. It troubled me to see our country squandering its resources. I was appalled at the waste and inefficiency I saw in Vietnam. And now, for once, we were the have-nots. Dependent on the volatile Middle East? Beholden to people who hate us? A bleak prospect, indeed. Were there alternatives? As for me, I had reinvented myself before, I could do it again. Why not get on board with what was shaping up as the story of the century? I sounded Fred out. He said let's go somewhere we can talk. We met in the cafeteria.

"What do you think?" I asked, "Is this hair-brained or am I on to something?"

"It's a great idea. You'd bring a helluva lot to it, but you'd have to get up to speed. Let's think about that." Fred offered me a cigarette. He took a deep drag, closing his eyes, then rocked forward in his chair. "Did you do any work on oil at Berkeley?"

"In an International Econ seminar. That's about it."

"Languages?"

"Fluent in French, passable German. The rest's not worth mentioning."

He was silent several minutes, smoking, thinking. "Okay," he finally said, "here's the plan. We'll find you a course, NYU or Columbia – either'd be good. A few months won't make you the world's foremost expert but it's a start. The other thing, we've got to get you speaking and writing Arabic."

"Arabic." I looked him straight in the eyes. "You're not kidding."

"Not at all. You'll be more effective if you speak the language, particularly in that region. Most Americans don't have a clue."

"Plenty of times I wished I spoke Vietnamese. Arabic, huh. How do we get at that?"

"A tutor. I'll have my secretary research that one. And we need to find you somebody to talk with on a regular basis, informally. We've got an Arab guy here, one of our computer experts, I'll introduce you." He thought for a moment then snapped his fingers. "Of course! Ed Said! He's a young prof, a Palestinian, teaches at Columbia. Literature or something – he's very good. You'll learn about the region and he has strong opinions. I know him slightly."

"You're really making a project out of this."

"Hell, I'm doing my employer a favor. And speaking of that, we'll have to get Sid and the others on board. If you hadn't noticed, the Gazette does not do sabbaticals unless you're writing a book, but we need to free up some time for you."

"I was wondering about that."

"Meantime let's get you switched to a beat that's got something to do with oil. I can use you some on business stories. Right away you'll help with local color – the lines at the pumps, the public outcry, that sort of thing."

"Can't seem to escape the protest scene, can I?"

"Not the way this country's heading. Do you know Hal Kenny?"

Harlan Kenny was the foreign news editor, a legendary figure at the *Gazette*. Charlie Stebbins and he were thick as thieves. "I've met him socially, that's all."

"I'll arrange a lunch. If he'll pick up the rest of your time that'd be perfect – between business and international you'd be set. By the way, I hope Diane's an understanding sort."

I paused. "She's good."

"Get her on board fast. This is going to soak up some serious time."

I winced, thinking of my three hours a day commuting. "I'll do what I can."

Sid grumbled and needed some handholding but he came around. He warned me about Professor Said. "Take that one with a grain of salt, if I were you, a whole sack full when it comes to Israel."

Kenny was older, tall, with waved silver-gray hair, impeccably dressed, right out of Saville Row. He looked like the diplomat I figured he needed to be in his line. "I've seen your work," he said, "very impressive, and I understand you've done graduate work in Political Science, that's all to the good. Much in International Relations?"

"That was one of my concentrations. International Econ too."

"But the Middle East will be new to you."

"I've followed events there closely, as a matter of interest."

He turned to his colleague. "So Fred, when can we have him?"

"I need Tom to sign off. I thought we might approach him together."

And so, on the first of November I set one foot in the *Gazette's* Business Department and the other on its Foreign Desk. Word spread quickly and the calls poured in. Ed Reynolds congratulated me on becoming a foreign correspondent, sort of. I even had a call from Charlie Stebbins, who professed disappointment tongue-in-cheek.

Most of the business stories Fred assigned closed by six, so on nights I wasn't meeting my Arabic tutor I got home earlier. On the other hand, I was chasing Middle East sources and they were seven hours ahead. Diane was enthusiastic about the change, even her father seemed to warm to me. However when she realized how time-consuming the training would be she became sulky, complaining I wouldn't be around to share the load. I reminded her the commute she orchestrated was a big part of the problem. I didn't have the heart to detail the traveling that before long would be part of the routine.

My first assignment was interviewing motorists in gas lines, where I found equanimity and good humor coexisting with frustration and anger. People didn't seem to mind wasting gas idling, or driving to distant stations to save pennies. Many comments I jotted were unprintable for a family paper. Drivers with license plates ending in odd digits bought gas on odd-numbered days, even digits, even days. A 55 mph speed limit was imposed. In January, Daylight Saving Time became a year-round phenomenon. I spent pre-dawn hours at school bus stops talking with parents and kids waiting in the dark.

As we suffered, others prospered. Oil exporters were awash in cash, and not just in the Middle East but the Soviet Union, Brazil with its innovative mixing of ethanol with gasoline, Alberta in Canada. U.S. companies couldn't increase domestic production fast enough. A constant even after the Standard Oil breakup early in the century, suspicion and distrust of the big oil companies deepened as record profits were reported. I worked on features exploring this fundamental challenge to the American car culture and our self-esteem. Our long post-war winning streak had spoiled us. We didn't want to hear about the deprivations suffered by our parents and grandparents.

I called Benny to let him know of my new assignment, and the Saturday before the holidays we put together a dad's day out, taking our little guys to the Metropolitan Museum. Ever since Diane turned me on to the museum experience I enjoyed the occasional visit, and this season was especially festive. We took in the Christmas tree and crèche, Peter and Benjie in their strollers oohing and aahing. Of course Benny rolled his eyes and said for a myth it's a very nice myth. During a child-fractured lunch in the cafeteria Benny advised against Edward Said, whom I hadn't yet met. He misrepresents, Benny said, which is too bad – you don't have to lie to make the Palestinian case.

To our surprise, about a week later, on New Years' Day, Diane gave birth to Paul Maurice Bernard, Jr. Premature by a few weeks, he had difficulty breathing and spent time in an incubator. We didn't take him home until mid-January. Fortunately, he soon started eating, drinking that is, and gaining weight. There was never anything wrong with his vocal cords. We'd been told about "second-baby syndrome" but his shaky start blew all that away – he had more attention than he probably needed. We hired a live-in helper, a Norwegian girl in nurse training, who turned out to be a godsend. While Peter Julien's name celebrated the older generation, Paul Jr. was my special trophy. Talking through names as her time grew near, it was Diane who suggested this one. I was pleasantly surprised. Peter and Paul – believe it or not, I didn't make the connection until after we'd brought him home.

Sometimes I wondered whether Diane's willingness to expand our family was her way of buying my cooperation in all the changes she wanted, but I did the math and loved it. For me, one plus one was a whole lot more fun than two. Not so for Peter. Even at his tender age, he knew his world had changed and not entirely for the better. At once pleased and scared, he sometimes smiled as he held the baby but often frowned. We put away our book of names, though I had the feeling Diane had left a marker at the page where girls' names began.

46. I ~~HAVE~~ HAD THIS TO SAY ABOUT THAT

"PAUL'S GOT ANOTHER PRESSURE COOKER GOING," Jonathan said, shaking his head. "Arabs, Israel, oil – there's a recipe for disaster."

"Or great journalism," I observe. While paging through yesterday's material, I remember something I've been meaning to ask my young friend. "By the way, what's your position on the West Bank and Gaza? I don't believe you've ever shared that with me."

"I disagree with Benny. It is worth the trouble. As part of the Jews' ancestral home, that alone would justify holding on, but I'm also pragmatic. Its greatest value may be as trade bait. I say hold on, keep turning up the pressure."

"You're talking about the new settlements?"

"The more of them there are, the more in return when the time is right."

"Those settlers won't ever leave," I say.

"The government has to show its chutzpah. They could make it a real-estate swap, if nothing else. On the personal side, Paul seems to be coping with the loss of his father."

"The two little ones help a lot."

"That is so. By the way, I talked with Roberto last night. He's working on getting us together with the General."

"I still don't understand why Dennis doesn't report that guy."

"After they pump him maybe they will. By the way, I think I've got ETVN going my way too. Should know in a couple of days."

* * * * * * *

NEEDING MORE CAR SPACE, one Saturday in June I wheeled a shiny red Volvo wagon into our driveway. I could have hung onto my little blue friend but the idea of three cars offended the Schumacher in me, so it was left behind as a trade-in. A neighbor took our picture with the newest member of the family. Peter, a sturdy two, sat on my shoulders, Diane held Paul Junior, now six months. Got a nice note back from Gus.

Diane was pregnant again. Even with the help we had, she was often worn out when I arrived home, and now this. I sensed she was taking a last shot at a girl. I should also mention, we had a dog now, a Golden Retriever mix. I'd been feeling down about my Beetle and one visit to the animal shelter is all it took. I figured Max – that was already his name – I figured he'd be a nice surprise, telling myself he was really for Peter. After all, every boy needs a dog. Diane told me to take him back. I said I couldn't and I wouldn't. Give it time, I said, you'll get used to him.

What sold her was Penny. If we didn't want him she'd take him in a heartbeat. The deal was sealed when Diane realized I was serious about dealing with puppy mess.

Most days found me in my regular seat on the LIRR in a congenial enough crowd – they left you alone if you wanted to work. I read for my Columbia course and listened to Arabic with my new earphones and tape player. The first semester of the Columbia course was nearing an end – "Geopolitics of the Near East," taught by a Lebanese woman. In scramble mode, I had missed lectures about the Palestinian mandate, the birth of Israel, the Arab League attack, the threat even back then to curtail oil exports. The second half would be filled with oil diplomacy or, more often, stalemate. I learned about the origin of the passions that continue to sweep the region. The Iran discussion brought me back to Gus's kitchen table debates. The course continued into Nasser's seizure of the Suez Canal and the abortive British-French invasion, then events I remembered well, notably the Six-Day War. Finding my limited return to *academe* great fun, I was finishing a paper, optional for an auditor but a useful topic – Great Power promises and expectations over Palestine.

Arabic was a different matter. The language was extraordinarily difficult – the pronunciation, the vocabulary, everything. For the longest time even the letters were indecipherable. My tutor, Fouad Habbal, was a middle-aged Egyptian engineer who got sideways with Farouk, came to the U.S. and never returned. It wasn't his fault that I was a slow learner. He and Shadia, his wife, had Diane and me to dinner at their place in Washington Square near his NYU office where we met three evenings a week. A friend of Edward Said, Fouad had good things to say about him. I still hadn't met the man.

AS WE TURNED THE CORNER INTO 1974, unable to convince OPEC to lift the oil embargo the U.S. convened a "World Energy Conference" in Washington, to try and repair the western alliance and discourage bilateral dealings between producer and user nations. Also, to begin looking seriously at alternative energy sources. Fred told me to get my feet wet there, so off I went to Washington for three days. Covering it for Charlie Stebbins was Ray d'Agostino, about my age but with considerably more experience. I had seen his byline often on oil stories.

The oil-producing countries did not show, and the all-western meeting was rife with discord. France opposed abandoning the Europeans' favored position. I filed a story on this internal dynamic and how fear of being whipsawed by the producers won out. Thanks to an embassy staffer I had befriended, I was able to gain an exclusive interview with France's delegate, its Foreign Minister Michel Jobert – in French, I'll have you know – and gave voice in the *Gazette* to his dissent. Though the newly-formed International Energy Agency would be sited in Paris, France declined to join. I spent some time burnishing my relationship with Charlie Stebbins who told me the door was still open, complimenting me on the Jobert story.

With the approach of spring, Watergate continued to dominate the news. Mired in judicial appeals the content of the tapes was still a mystery, but on March 1 seven former close Nixon aides were indicted, among them Haldeman,

Ehrlichman, Mitchell and Colson. John Dean and Nixon's personal attorney, Herbert Kalmbach, had already pled guilty and rumor had it the President himself was named an unindicted co-conspirator by the grand jury.

Late April, Nixon went on television to announce that he was releasing some of the tapes – "all portions that relate to the question of what I knew about Watergate or the cover-up and what I did about it." These partial transcripts were an amazing insight into the man's rough and profane character. We and the *Times* published everything so far released, all thirteen-hundred pages. Even the heartland was now calling for Nixon's resignation. Wednesday July 24 was the fateful day. In the morning the Supreme Court issued its historic ruling that the President was obliged to turn over the tapes. That evening the House Judiciary Committee began formal proceedings and by Saturday three articles of impeachment had been voted. Now only action by the House and Senate stood between Richard Nixon and removal. As what was on the tapes seeped through the capital even his staunchest allies made themselves scarce. The most damning conversation came a few days after the break-in where the President and Haldeman schemed to block the FBI investigation by having the CIA falsely claim national security was involved. This revelation destroyed the President. For two years he had lied to everyone, as an incensed Barry Goldwater said, even his family.

On August 8th, Nixon announced his resignation. Gerald Ford would succeed him, the first-ever appointed President of the United States. Among his first acts, Ford would nominate Nelson Rockefeller, former New York Governor, to succeed him as V.P. Soon thereafter Ford granted Richard Nixon a full pardon, stirring suspicions of a backroom deal.

As a neophyte, I found most impressive the dogged professionalism of reporters Woodward and Bernstein and the *Post's* perseverance in the face of invective, threats and recriminations. I was immensely proud of my profession. Gerald Ford proclaimed "our long national nightmare," but by now my faith in position and power was shaken. Lying is the attractive alternative, the easy way out, and as Watergate proved, if not for a free press can be all too effective. The *Gazette* front page the day after Nixon's resignation blew me away. The centerpiece, Tom O'Connor's Pentagon Papers editorial, my words:

> Consider what Americans have overcome today. Insecure leaders, hiding behind military bluster. Timid leaders, afraid to face the people. Dishonest leaders, trapped in a web of lies. Imperious leaders, their agendas hidden from debate. Un-American? You bet it was.

I was so pumped. If anyone on the train that night had asked what business I was in, I would have answered simply, truth. I'm in the business of truth.

I FINALLY GOT AROUND TO WRITING HAMID. By return mail he said he'd be in New York soon and would love to reconnect. I'd been meaning to pick up a copy of his short stories that came out the year before, so I worked a visit to the Strand into my day, finding the slim volume on a table at the back of the store, a favorite New York haunt. The cover was a startling photomontage, a mosque under a dark sky with a crescent moon and not a minaret, but an oil derrick towering above it. I smiled at the small black-and-white photo on the inside back cover. Same Hamid, though fuller of face and sporting a splendid moustache. That evening on the train I read the first story, "Blood In the Sand," also the name of the volume. Turning to the front pages for the translator I found none. So Hamid is writing in English. Impressive, I thought, but no surprise, recalling what a linguist he was.

We met at an Indian restaurant on the East Side. He was in New York to talk with his editor about the novel he was working on. "The short story is a sharp, fierce sprint, but the novel is a marathon." We toasted each other, I with red wine, he with pomegranate juice.

"How did it do financially?" I remembered the *Gazette* reviewer praised it but the *Times* was lukewarm.

"For the most part the reviews were gratifying, but it has not been a financial success. However one of the stories has been optioned, possibly something will come of that."

"Your letter said you are teaching."

"At my old school, Eton. Literature, also creative writing. It pays the rent, as they say. Have you seen Gus recently? Or Benny?"

"I see Benny from time to time. Gus and Akiko were back for the wedding three years ago. We stay in touch." I brought out my wallet and showed him my family pictures.

"Very nice. I have not yet been as fortunate. Tell me about your newspaper job."

"I've just begun covering the Middle East, with a special emphasis on oil."

"Have you been there yet?"

"I hope to soon."

"Remind me to give you some names in Tehran."

"You are still welcome back there?"

"Oh, yes, though after my novel is published I'm not so sure. My family is still there, they will be happy to show you around."

"I remember Gus calling your father a survivor."

"Gus did not appreciate that in my country many accomplished people do not survive. The Shah is arbitrary – today you are up, tomorrow you are down or worse. By the way, I was sorry to hear of your injury, though you appear to get around well. Gus told me in a letter some time ago. I should have written."

"Don't give it a second thought. Do you still climb?"

He nodded. "I've spent time in the French Alps the past couple of years and a month last winter in New Zealand which was fabulous. Are you able to do much, yourself?"

"I've become a good swimmer. I swim two, three times a week."

The waiter appeared with our dinners. After tasting everything and exchanging comments, we ate for a while in silence. "Do you mind if I ask about "Blood In the Sand?" I asked. "It's not often I get to interview an author."

"As long as you say nice things, go right ahead."

"Off the record, of course," I laughed. "In that first story you're critical of modernization, of the disparity of wealth. I don't recall that when we were at Berkeley."

"It takes time to develop one's philosophy, if I can use that term."

"But still you accept the benefits of modernization, value them, even."

"That contradiction is endemic to my country for it lacks an effective system to distribute the benefits. I love my father and I honor him," Hamid said, sipping the last of his juice, "but what he has done to get ahead always troubled me."

"You're not a fundamentalist, are you? I never detected that in you."

"In religious terms, no, but I revere tradition. I would say my approach is closer to Sufism than anything else. I do not like forcing women to wear the *burqa* or shut themselves away. I respect their right to an education and a life beyond the family. I also think music and art and, of course, literature, is important for a full life."

"What is your position on the recent hostilities?"

"I have no patience with arrogance, Egyptian or Syrian, but I start with the millions of people wrongfully dispossessed in Palestine for the Zionist state. Those people must be given back their land. If I knew how to do it I wouldn't be writing stories, but until it happens, whoever takes up the cause of those people, I support."

"The enemy of my enemy is my friend. That's a dangerous road to travel – you associate yourself with terrorists, hijackers, killers of the innocent. What about Tel Aviv airport? Munich? Don't tell me you support that!"

"No, but hear me out. Who is completely innocent? Symbolism is important and symbols have a way of becoming targets. The enemy of my enemy, yes, that can lead one down a dangerous path, but until a better one appears..."

"I'm surprised you and Benny remain friends."

"Why should we not? One hopes passions do not become so inflamed no room exists for friendship. Though I have few illusions, that could certainly happen."

Hamid insisted on placing our after-dinner order. Coffee that makes a spoon stand in the cup – I envisioned seeing two o'clock this night, three o'clock, four o'clock. A sweet pudding topped by tangerine slices and coconut shavings with a plate of sesame and honey cookies. We reminisced about the Berkeley house, people we had known. After a while he looked at his watch and stood. "For every New York visit you must promise me one in London. And I am pleased at your interest in my part of the world."

"You don't know the half of it," I said. *"Ma'a saalama. Araka fi ma ba'd."*

Hamid looked shocked, then a big smile spread across his face. *"Araka fi ma ba'd,* indeed! Until we meet again." He put his arms around my shoulders and kissed me on one cheek, then the other. "Good luck, do wonderful things. *As-salaamu alaikum."*

"As-salaamu alaikum. Peace upon you too."

PEACE WAS IN SHORT SUPPLY, not only in the Middle East but much closer to home. Earlier in the year a federal judge had ordered the Boston School

Committee which for years had been dragging its feet, to fix the schools' racial imbalance and do it now. Massive city-wide busing was the mandated remedy. Few were pleased with the result which meant turning children out of their neighborhood schools and criss-crossing the city, black kids to white neighborhoods, white kids to black. As the first day of school neared, the *Gazette* sent a colleague of mine, Roger Bailey, to augment our stringer network.

On September 12 the buses rolled. In white neighborhoods, rock-throwing, jeering crowds met the buses carrying black students. The busing plan had paired South Boston High with Roxbury, one of the city's poorest and, as outsiders saw it, most menacing black neighborhoods. Racist graffiti appeared on school walls, and as black students ran the all-too-familiar gauntlet, shouts, epithets, rocks, bricks, eggs rained down on them. Even the neighborhood cops gamely trying to keep order came under attack. It was page one in the *Gazette* with a two-page photo spread inside. Roger slid in a personal comment about his close encounter with a brick. Mayor Kevin White banned street gatherings in the troubled sections. Somehow, the city got through the first couple of weeks. The feared major explosion, a riot in "Southie," Gus' old neighborhood, failed to materialize.

The country's media gloated. Arrogant Boston, no better than anybody else. In Roger's interviews, leaders and ordinary people, students, even some cops vented their feelings. People resented the imposition by the feds and the suburban outsiders. Black parents were upset too, and not only at the treatment their children were coming in for. "We want to improve our schools," one told Roger, "give us the tools to do it."

I pulled my old high school paper from a file cabinet. What an irony. Little Rock to Boston, 1957 to 1974 in one short step. My friend Terry Grimes had been so furious, calling our local racism worse than the South. Now, reading Roger's stories, watching the news, I saw what he meant. I wondered about the white kids in South Boston High. How many of them were standing tall? Right about now my rhetoric looked pretty thin. Not wrong, but in the face of home-grown reality, naive. As the year went on, the unrest settled, people papered over the tensions, politicians retreated. A running tragedy, a festering sore, but the vigils, the occasional eruption fell from the national spotlight.

By now my little family was no longer so little. Peter, nearly two and a half, weighed 34 pounds. He was one of those kids who takes over every room he enters. He literally ran before he walked – I saw it happen. Nine months old, my namesake was crawling and pulling himself up on everything. Diane's due date was March 15. She seemed more mellow, as if she knew this time her hard work would be properly rewarded.

A year into our new house, we had settled well into the neighborhood. During the first month we'd been invited to a couple of neighbor houses, but I felt we weren't meeting people fast enough, so we decided to host a housewarming party. From that point living in the suburbs became congenial, a lot better than I expected. I enjoyed pretending I was master of the endless forest when I walked out onto my wooded patch. I could envision a tree house too, fondly remembering what Benny's father had done for us. Even had the tree selected, a massive oak, five feet up in the crotch of three sturdy limbs.

I missed my Saturday morning amble to the corner store for bagels and newspapers, but had little time to reminisce. Too much going on, with the boys clamoring for attention, and property upkeep which would become a full-time job if I let it. I got my city fix five times a week, six and seven when we had something hot. Though we used the condo infrequently together, I overnighted several times a month.

I MENTIONED THE NEED for re-establishing my ties to the White Horse and Kells, and now I began using my in-town nights to visit the old haunts. Many familiar faces, though this one had moved away, that one passed away. I spent more time in Kells, as it was easier to reach on late nights, plus it was my fraternity. I recall the first time I walked in after the long absence, something seemed amiss. Welcomed to my old regular booth, I kept staring at the bar, to the point that Ed Fiore finally asked what I was looking at. "That," I said, pointing at a thick book in a display case above the bar. "That book. It's new, right?"

"Hell no," Ed said, "it's been there forever. It's you that hasn't been here."

I slipped out of the booth and crossed to the bar. The bartendress, Patty, smiled her usual excellent smile. I asked to step in, something I needed to check out. "Be my guest. You haven't been around lately. Where you been? It's Paul, right?"

I nodded. "Too busy to have fun, if that makes sense."

"Makes no sense at all."

I treaded across the puddled rubber mat and up to the display case. Inside was a thick book, maybe a foot by ten inches, its dark brown cover filled with colorful swirls, gold, red, blue, and rectangular labyrinthine designs. Looking closer I noticed people and animals in the leafy branches surrounding the ornate capital letters X and P which I recognized from my science days as Greek letters Chi and Rho. "What in the world is this?"

Patsy looked over her shoulder from the Guinness tap. "The Book of Kells. A genuine replica." Of course! Now I remembered, sort of. "Illuminated manuscript," she went on, "Celtic monks, around 800 AD. The original's at Trinity College in Dublin."

I noticed the glass door had a lock. "Do you have a key? Can I take a look?"

"To answer your first question, yes, but nobody knows where it is. Second answer's obvious but there's nothing to see anyway. It's hollow inside. Somebody gave it to the owner as a joke. He decided to raise him one, thus the display case."

I laughed. "Thanks for the history lesson. And the drink," I said, toasting her with the Guinness she slid across with a wink.

"It's on me. Nice to see you again, don't be such a stranger."

As I rejoined my friends, who should stroll in but Frank Flaherty and Pam Snyder. "My God, look what the cat dragged in!" Flaherty gave me a thump on the shoulder.

"We thought you'd outgrown us," Pam said. "How long's it been? Two years? Three? Life on the elegant North Shore must agree with you."

I moved over to make room and gave her a friendly kiss. "You may not believe this," I said, "but I really miss this place."

She shook her head. "Not good enough."

I hung my head. "Sorry. I plead guilty."

"You are hereby sentenced to spend the next month in this booth, every night until last call. Only then will we believe you."

"Can't promise that but it's great to be here with you guys."

"How'd the game come out?" Ed asked Flaherty.

"Rangers. Four-three over the Boston Bashers, I am happy to report," he crowed.

"Oh, well," I said, "can't win 'em all."

On another Kells foray I learned about a function the *Gazette* crowd was planning the week before Christmas. "Bring that wife of yours," Frank Flaherty added, "we want to see what she has we don't."

On the appointed evening, Kells' dark interior was festooned with colorful Christmas lights. Same hard-working band as before – fiddle, guitar, accordion, bodhran, the hand-held drum, flute, carols along with the jigs, reels and bawdy songs. I made a special point of introducing Tom to Diane early in the evening and he seemed taken with her. I was proud to show Diane around, spectacularly pregnant in a long green silk dress, a red scarf at her throat. All my cronies were there, some with spouse, some without. Ed Fiore, Frank Flaherty, Rory Peters, the whole bunch. Diane and Pam had met a couple of times but not until I saw the eye daggers did I realize how they felt about each other. I guess I was flattered.

The high point of the evening, Sam Purcell, an Assistant City Editor, a Spike mainstay but popular with the younger reporters, had promised to demonstrate how he lettered in crew at Princeton. He arrived doffing a glittery red and green derby, bowing to all. As the evening wore on, his pump primed, Sam finagled an empty beer carton and a couple of mailing tubes, lowered himself in and took to the course between bar and booths, propelling himself along with his legs, keeping flawless cadence. The floor being as well-waxed as Sam, he glided effortlessly. At the far end a neat pivot and turn, then back to the finish line, the crowd madly cheering from the banks.

Late in the evening a bunch of us were relaxing in my regular booth. I looked around the room at my friends and had to laugh. How modish we were – long hair, sideburns, a lot of little moustaches, though so far I had avoided that. Dress code tonight a cut above the office norm, and no tight jeans or bellbottoms. A bit in her cups, Pam leaned across and let her head flop on my shoulder. Instinctively I touched my head to hers and closed my eyes a moment. Suddenly I felt a kick under the table. Pained – literally – I looked up. Diane had a severe expression I had never seen before.

On the way home she let me have it. I had flirted, and not only flirted but right in front of my friends. People who mattered.

"My God," I said, "it was nothing."

"Nothing!" she yelled. "I can imagine what you do the nights I'm not around."

I was stunned. "Forget it!" I shouted. "You're so far off base it's pathetic!"

"So I'm pathetic, am I! A fine thing to call your wife!"

"That's not what I meant!" I looked over. She was crying. "Aw, come on. I didn't mean it like that. It was nothing, nothing at all." I reached over and put my hand on hers.

She yanked hers away. "You're not talking your way out of this, mister star reporter."

I turned back to my driving, dismayed. "Sorry."

Needless to say I spent the night on the couch. As I tossed and turned, I had an odd thought. What Diane said – maybe she had a point. Alcohol, high spirits, people thrown together, glances, arms on shoulders, around waists, friendly kisses sometimes crossing the line – it's normal, the most natural thing in the world. And I really had enjoyed Pam's attentions. Nor was she the only one in the room with that certain gleam. All of a sudden I'm thinking, maybe monogamy isn't everything it's cracked up to be. Why not add some variety, a bit of spice? I chewed on this for a while before turning over on my pallet. Oh, well, get some sleep. Tomorrow's another day.

ED REYNOLDS WAS BACK FOR THANKSGIVING and we squeezed in a cafeteria event to talk things over. He told me he took full credit for my success. About Vietnam, his sources were saying something big's coming up, so big and chaotic that after briefing Tom O'Connor, Tom asked if he wanted out. "I was insulted, til I realized it was a joke. Cover it from Tokyo?" Ed shook his head, "that's for weenies. Where the action is, I am."

"That has a certain ring," I observed.

Ed promised he'd tip me off when it was about to break. "I know you have a personal investment in that place." Mid-December he called. "It's on. You saw what I filed yesterday. They're gunning for Phouc Long."

A mountainous region I knew well, about sixty miles north of Saigon.

"That piece of paper they signed ain't worth shit. The North doesn't even give it lip-service. There's a big debate, some of the generals want to play it safe, prepare the ground for a general uprising, what didn't happen with Tet."

On January 6, Phouc Binh, the provincial capital, fell. The U.S. non-reaction deepened Saigon's gloom. Reading the same tea leaves, an emboldened Hanoi took the town of Banmethuot in the Central Highlands. Thieu ordered his troops to abandon the northern provinces and fall back. Accompanying Ed's stories were the familiar heart-rending photos of refugees on the roads, sure sign a government has lost control. Hué fell, then Danang came under rocket attack, many locals attempting to flee by sea. We watched in horror as people clinging to the rear stairs of a World Airways jet fell to their death as the overburdened aircraft struggled away from Danang airport.

In mid-April Ed called and left a message. "Saigon before the rains. Curtains." On April 21 Thieu resigned and left the country, calling the U.S. a feckless, ruinous ally. By the twenty-ninth, NVA forward columns were inside the city limits and the massive helicopter evacuation of our embassy was on. To many the fall of Saigon was merely an irritating reminder of a page already turned. To me, enemy tanks in the streets, NVA regulars strolling familiar landmarks, evacuees clawing up rope ladders – it was enough to turn my stomach. But I held tough, didn't let the awful events get to me. I wondered what fate had befallen Father Trần. Would I ever see him again, have the chance to set things right?

The second-guessers were in full cry, but the end was terribly sad – all our good work for naught. We who fought were still blamed for the war, and all Americans were dishonored by the callous abandonment of our ally. Our weakened leader and his Metternich couldn't postpone the inevitable, nor could his successor. Some early observers had it right when they saw in the United States' sulky response to the Geneva Accords a foreshadowing of the lies and deceit of the next twenty years. Good tree, good fruit? Not necessarily. Bad tree, bad fruit? Absolutely.

47. THINGS COME TOGETHER, THINGS FLY APART

"I REMEMBER THIS WELL," I say. We're watching old videotape, the final hunched-shoulder salute then into the helicopter with the man and he is gone. It's impossible not to smile, though it's no funnier now than it was then.

"Tricky Dick's finally down for the count," Jonathan observes.

I have been thinking about historical parallels. "It amazes me how often Nixon was right about foreign policy, at times even brilliant."

"What about Vietnam? The man diddles, then he cuts and runs. He got nothing he couldn't have had four years earlier. Not exactly brilliant, if you ask me."

"I doubt anyone could have done any better with the mess he was handed."

"Reading Paul's notes on Watergate, he has you always waiting for the other shoe. He would have given anything to cover that story."

"It made him feel good about his choice of a career."

Jonathan has a far-off look. "I'm not a romantic, Gus – for me it's a job. Once in a while you stumble across something big but not that often."

I know what's on his mind. After some difficulty I manage to retrieve my thought. Recently I have been pondering Watergate. "Not even the guy at the top can be above the law," I say, "and to see this crook and his gang trampling on our most sacred myths."

"Myths? Sacred? Explain, please."

How to put this? "Our great common beliefs, Jonathan, our principles. It's not too much to say the President has a priestly duty to celebrate these beliefs, show they still have life, validity. Give proof through the night that our flag is still there – that's what I'm talking about. Unfortunately that petty man wasn't up to the job. Oh, we survived, but it took decades for the presidency to recover – now we've got another bad apple doing his worst."

"I knew you'd draw a parallel."

"Nixon was right about many things but wrong about one big thing. But as they say in baseball, Bush has drawn the collar. He and that insolent crowd of his have been wrong about everything. That's what Paul said. That's why they hated him."

"If I'm right, Paul Bernard will be counted as one of George Bush's mistakes."

"That is your horse, Jonathan, I'm not getting on it."

"We'll see about that, Professor. You'll be along for the ride."

* * * * * * *

JUST AS I HAD HOPED, oil was the key to a fascinating new world. Over the next year I wore out my passport, covering OPEC meetings in Vienna, Venezuela, London, and a trip to the Middle East. No Paris yet, though. The travel was exhilarating, though it was a serious disappointment to see Diane withdraw into a funk whenever I pulled the suitcase out for another trip.

Slowly my Arabic was gaining traction. Fouad was relentless. He drilled me hard, building comprehension and speed. Later we would turn to the language of business and oil. Still later, we would circle back to reading and writing. I was still uncomfortable with the language except around people I knew well, then about the ninth month I found myself attempting more, and from that point a certain momentum built. I practiced several times a week with Tommy Aziz. An bonus extra, I learned more about the emerging world of computers, though we conversed mostly in English on that complex topic.

I was not a natural linguist. French had been relatively simple, German harder but attainable, I did some Russian on my own, tricky stuff, but Arabic was really pushing the envelope. It reminded me of my so-called athletic career, desire outstripping ability, though getting along in three going on four languages isn't all that bad. My language project was a standing joke in the newsroom. One day my colleagues presented me with a red and white checked *keffiyeh,* the traditional Arab headdress, that Tommy picked out and showed me how to fold and wear.

I finally met Ed Said one afternoon in his office at Columbia. He greeted me amicably, inquired about Fred Mueller and, as it was a fine early spring day, asked if I'd like to stroll about the campus. He lifted a checked sport jacket from a coat rack and pulled it on. He had thick black eyebrows under a mass of dark hair. Early on I confessed I was a neophyte as far as the Middle East was concerned, but eager to learn.

"Good on both counts," he replied. "The enthusiasm speaks for itself, and it's to your advantage you haven't read too much. Most of the literature is so biased it's not worth the paper it's written on. You are a product of the West so whatever impressions you have are incorrect, though you probably don't even realize it."

"In what way incorrect?"

"Let's sit here." He gestured toward a bench down from Low Library. A stream of students crossed in front of us, some sunbathed on the library steps, two boys and a girl sailed a frisbee on the lawn. "For one, your conception of the people of the Middle East, or as we prefer to call it, the Near East. As I am a professor, I am obliged to give you a test. What's the first thing that comes to mind when I say "Near East?"

"The desert."

"What else?"

"Oil. Sand... I said that. Lawrence of Arabia. The Arabian Nights. Cairo, Casablanca, Jerusalem. Israel. My Iranian friend..."

"What about terrorism? Hijackings?"

"I was coming to that."

His dark eyes flashed. "Other than your friend about whom I cannot comment, your bias is clear. Why did you not say astronomy or mathematics or medicine, or Averroes or Avicenna, or the Koran, or the Prophet Mohammad? Instead you choose caricatures, cardboard cutouts."

"I said I wasn't yet well-versed."

"That answer is unacceptable. If you are serious you must empty your mind of preconceived notions. Be aware, however, this will be difficult, for you don't even know what your biases are. All right, let's try a different tack. When Fred called and said he would like me to meet you I asked him for your resumé which I read with interest. I note you attended Holy Cross College. Their sports teams are called Crusaders, if I'm correct."

"They are."

"And what is your opinion of crusades and crusaders? Does thinking of them give you a warm feeling?"

"The more I learned the less I admired them, though some involved had wholesome intentions."

"Few and far between. When you were eighteen you were all for the crusades?"

"As far as I thought about them at all, but that's not why I chose to go to college there."

"Of course not. But in your mind or the mind of your family, you didn't object to associating yourself with slaughter and rape and pillage. That wasn't enough to prevent you from attending that school."

"Obviously, and I'd do it again. But I'd hope to have a more balanced view than I did at the time."

"You mentioned Israel and not Palestine. Why is that?"

"I don't know. I could have mentioned Palestine."

"But you didn't." Said picked up a frisbee and tossed it toward the players. "Why do you want to speak with me? What is your interest in the Near East?"

"Professional reasons. It's home to great issues which are only going to get more important. Israel, the Palestinians, oil. I want to report on them knowledgeably, let people know what is going on and why."

He nodded. "Most of what passes for reporting is infected with erroneous attitudes. If you can attain a more enlightened point of view, that is potentially useful, but I suspect oil is your real interest. You spend what part of your time on oil stories?"

"Half. Maybe sixty percent."

He nodded. "You see us through the lens of western self-interest. That's what I am saying – to get it right you will need a new pair of spectacles that allow you to see in three dimensions – see the people, the literature, the music, the art, the science, the religion..."

"Don't forget the oil. That's a major reason for the region's troubles."

"I don't disagree." He looked at his watch. "Paul, I am happy to meet with you from time to time, but let me be frank. I have my doubts. You are obviously intelligent, but I fear your assumptions are so entrenched you will end up no better than others who pretend to report on the Near East. But we shall see. I will keep my word to my friend Fred. Give me a call after you've made some progress on your perspectives."

I met with Said every month or so. His comments about the dispossessed Palestinians mirrored Benny's critique, though he added a provocative dimension. "How can the West continue to align itself with Israel," he asked. "How can you call it a plucky, democratic country when it vents racism on the 'others' within its borders?" His comments about the Holocaust remain with me to this day. "A people to whom such evil has been done turns around and perpetrates such evil? Disgraceful! It's not that the Jews are unaware. They exploit this tragic episode in their history for political gain, then they don the oppressor's cloak when it suits them. There is a word for that. Cynical."

ON FEBRUARY 2, 1975, Emma Lowell Bernard, a blue-eyed, red-haired charmer, joined our family. I'd never seen Diane happier, giving me hope this great event might make her more content. Proposing the name Emma, she explained it was a strong name, she liked its sound and texture. The Jane Austen character she found intriguing though not altogether admirable. Fair enough. Chunky, pouty lips, blue eyes, the temper of a redhead, from Day One our daughter took over the household. The red hair gene was Fiona's, for sure. I was touched to think Emma and Fiona would have had much more in common, if the first hints of willfulness proved out. Of course Diane's parents were thrilled, and as she handed Emma to her father I was convinced she had met a challenge she'd set long ago. From his daughter the gift of... *her* daughter! The boys were crazy about her. She wouldn't want for protection, that was for sure, though I suspected in time she'd take care of herself quite well.

I mentioned Diane was not pleased at my travel, sometimes a week or two at a time. I didn't blame her. Even with our child care network, keeping track of these demanding little creatures was a chore. But when she bragged to family or friends, showing off my bylines from Riyadh or Caracas, I was torn between being gratified or irritated. I never called it hypocrisy, but the thought crossed my mind.

Getting to Sunday Mass when I was home was an adventure. Once there, though, the accolades came thick and fast. "Such a fine Catholic family, you don't see three so close in age these days, and is the mother under the weather?" I smiled and thanked them. Diane showed up for the big holidays, if that. Making the best of the situation, I counted Sunday mornings as my gift to her. I appreciated her staying in the background, though when time came to choose a school I expected a struggle.

ONE OF MY MOST MEMORABLE REPORTER MOMENTS happened at my first OPEC meeting. I was assigned to trail the Saudi Oil Minister, Sheikh Ahmed Zaki Yamani, record his public comments, get an interview. Linda Dobbins was also in Vienna. A New York staffer, she'd cover the personal angles while I handled the business and politics. Her take – a dashing young man rises from modest origins to power and fame, spearheads the dramatic power grab that ties the West in knots. Yamani had been chronicled before but an update was due, following the recent assassination of his patron, King Faisal, by a nephew, which occurred in his presence. Speculation was that Yamani might be out of a job. Mike d'Agostino was covering from our Washington bureau, and how the three-cornered quilt would be stitched together remained to be seen.

I had nurtured an acquaintance with a Saudi press spokesman, Sami Adjani, since a briefing at the U.N. where I quoted him extensively, and he said he'd try to put me together with Yamani for an impromptu one-on-one. I was standing in the middle of a crowd in the Intercontinental Hotel lobby when Yamani and the Kuwaiti representative emerged from a conference room. I saw Adjani waving and pointing toward an alcove off the lobby. I looked around for Linda but she was nowhere to be seen. She'd be really put out to miss this, but I had no choice except go for it myself.

"Sheikh, I would like you to spend a moment with Paul Bernard of the New York *Gazette*. He presents our views fairly and accurately."

"Can't ask for more than that," Yamani responded, shaking my hand and gesturing toward a cluster of plush chairs. "I know the *Gazette* well. In fact when I was a student in the States I read your paper extensively, that and the *Times*."

"Pleased to hear that, Your Excellency." Following university in Cairo he had been a law student at NYU, then at Harvard, earning two masters' degrees. I was struck by his unwavering gaze and the little Van Dyke beard that gave him an exotic air even apart from the flowing robes that were *de rigueur* in formal settings. "I appreciate your giving me a few minutes of your time."

"Not at all. Without the press our story would not get out. What can I do for you?"

I thought I'd give it a try, right out of the box. "We've heard rumors that the new King may appoint a new Oil Minister. Is there any truth to that?"

He leaned back and folded his hands across his chest. "I am the last person to ask," he answered, smiling. "Indeed, if that comes to pass I will probably be the last to hear. The fact is, I expect to serve the Kingdom for many years to come, but any announcement would have to come from the Palace, of course."

"Of course," I replied. "Thought I'd give it a try."

He shrugged. "Nothing ventured, nothing gained."

I consulted my notebook. One of the biggest issues revolving around this meeting was the prospect of another oil price increase – the buzz had it as high as ten percent – though certain members were said to be against it at this time. "Can you tell me whether OPEC will take the decision this week to raise the price of crude?"

He smiled again as he began his answer. I leaned forward. His reputation for speaking softly was well-founded. "...of course this is a very important issue but we must await the action of the ministers. Any announcement will come through the normal channels," he said, nodding at his press spokesman.

"Does Saudi Arabia favor a price increase at this time?"

"I can tell you we are not yet fairly compensated for our vital national resource. There is still much distance to go."

"Will you get there this week? At least part of the way?"

"I wouldn't be surprised."

"How much of an increase?"

"That I cannot say."

Scribbling hard, I copied everything Yamani said, word for word, using a shorthand of my own devising. Another few minutes back and forth and I noticed Adjani and Yamani exchanging glances. Yamani stood, smoothed his robes and extended his hand. I accepted it with a slight bow, expressing my sympathy for his recent unfortunate loss.

"It is kind of you to remember."

"As-salaamu alaikum," I said.

He raised his eyebrows. *"As-salaamu alaikum,"* he replied. And with that, the Saudi party swept away. I shook hands with Adjani, thanking him for the courtesy of the interview.

Under the headline SAUDI: OIL HIKE LIKELY our next day's front page carried my account of the interview along with my interpretation that, led by the influential Saudi delegation, a general price increase could well be in the offing. The headline writer stretched the point but I had no control over that. The wire services carried the story and, as usual, television and radio news seized on it and fed it back. The first sign of trouble was the call to Tom O'Connor. The caller, some Assistant Secretary of State, said the Saudi ambassador had read them the riot act. The Saudi delegation, even the King, was furious at the suggestion Yamani had ever said such a thing. A retraction and apology were demanded. "What are your people smoking over there?" the State official asked Tom.

"Same thing you smoke in Washington," Tom replied.

And so I found myself on a TWA night flight to New York. I couldn't sleep, I was so worried I had screwed up. I read and reread my notes which by now I knew by heart. "We are not yet to the point of being fairly compensated... still much distance to go... this week... I wouldn't be surprised." But even if I got it right, it was my word against theirs. I should have had Linda there, but had I waited I'd have blown the chance altogether. Truth or no truth, somebody might want a head to roll and I knew one that was all-too-handy.

Shaving in the lavatory, throwing cold water on my face, I put on the clean shirt I was saving for my last day in Vienna. At JFK I grabbed a cab and headed directly to the office. Racing to forty-four I checked in with Fred. He had this funny look on his face, half serious, half bemused. "I want to know just one thing. Did Yamani say what you said he said?"

"Damn right he did."

"You're absolutely sure."

"Absolutely sure," I said, pulling my notebook out of my pocket.

"Put that away. C'mon, let's go see Tom."

O'Connor was on the phone but waved us in. "Okay... okay.. I hear you. Later."

He hung up and swiveled around in his chair to face us, standing in front of his desk. "Well, young man, you've achieved something extraordinary. In the span of twenty-four hours the *Gazette* has managed to piss off both the Kingdom of Saudi Arabia and the United States government. Congratulations. That is no mean feat."

I nodded. Couldn't think of anything to say.

Fred jumped in. "Paul says he got Yamani down right and I believe him..."

"Anybody else hear him?" O'Connor asked, looking at me.

"A roomful of Saudis, nobody else."

"That a big help. We're you on the record?"

"Absolutely. No restrictions asked, none given."

"Yamani hasn't complained directly, in fact he hasn't been heard from at all which is unusual," Fred said. "The story was a straight piece of reporting, Tom. If anything it was the headline went overboard."

O'Connor frowned. "That may be, but however you parse it the *Gazette's* on the hook. The guy at State's pushing us to retract the story."

"What's Kenny got to say about it?"

"That's who I was on the phone with. Brother Kenny is in Barbados, which is exactly where I'd like to be about now. He says we should fall on our sword." O'Connor let out a deep sigh then was quiet a moment, steepling his chin on his fingers. "Okay, here's what we're gonna do." He stood up and came around the desk. "I'll put out a statement this afternoon. If anybody picks it up, fine, if they don't, fine. We'll run on page one. It will consist of one sentence. "As to the interview with Oil Minister Yamani in Wednesday's paper, the *Gazette* stands by its story."

"Good show," Fred said, smiling.

O'Connor looked at me. "I'm not doing this for you, Paul. You have a bright future but at any given time a given reporter's skin is expendable. The paper's reputation is what counts. We'll admit when we're wrong, but backing down when we're right," he shook his head, "that's not the kind of message we send."

He put his hand on my shoulder and looked me straight in the eyes. "Next time you're involved in an important interview, make goddamn sure you have somebody else with you. Or get it on tape. Or call the guy back to confirm. Or all of the above." He nodded, "It's not easy when things are moving fast, but that's how mistakes happen." He took his hand off. "Okay, enough of this crap, let's get back to work."

My legs felt wobbly as I followed Fred out the door into the newsroom. As we parted, I looked around the newsroom, relieved I was still part of this chaotic, fabulous scene. And proud to be working for people like Tom and Fred.

The OPEC meeting adjourned with no announcement of a price increase. But curiously, two weeks later OPEC issued a statement that its member nations, most of them, Saudi Arabia included, were increasing the price of crude effective immediately. I felt gratified, sort of. Then the following week an envelope bearing the crest of the Kingdom of Saudi Arabia arrived at my desk. Inside, this hand-written note –

My Dear Mr. Bernard,

I regret that our conversation caused such difficulties for you. You got it right. By the way, this time we are off the record.

With kindest regards. *As-salaamu alaikum.*

Zaki Yamani

I showed the note to Fred, who grabbed me by the arm and marched me into O'Connor's office. Tom read it at one glance. "I love it!" he said, breaking into a broad grin and pumping my hand. "Get this framed."

When I showed the note to Alan Mauro he said it reminded him of a situation he got himself in as a young reporter with less happy results. "You probably don't know I started with the *Trib,* but one time I engineered something that got my ass booted out of there. No, no, I deserved it. I made up a story about a secret society that meets every Halloween in Central Park. The fact it was our April One edition didn't cut any ice with my editor. I'll never forget his parting words. 'As a reporter you write good fiction.' I guess he was right. My column kind of splits the difference, wouldn't you say?"

"I say all's well that ends."

"That's for damn sure."

Although the United States was gone, the misery in Southeast Asia wasn't. Ed Reynolds reported on the North's consolidation of power, its "education programs" and resettlement camps for former sympathizers, the disappearances, but also the absence, so far, of the major bloodbath everyone had predicted. Where the going was really tough was Cambodia. About the time Saigon fell, communist Khymer Rouge forces backed by the Chinese captured Phnom Penh. Commanded by a French-educated communist, Pol Pot, within days they put their form of Maoist insanity into practice, forcibly evicting parasitic city-dwellers from their homes and "transferring" them to the countryside to work the fields. The lucky ones, that is, who weren't murdered straightaway. Within weeks, millions had been uprooted in a replay of Mao's failed plan for a nationwide agricultural co-op ruled by the peasantry. Temporarily in Bangkok, Ed covered the early months of the genocide but the real workhorse was the *Times'* Sydney Schanberg, whose story and that of his Cambodian photographer Dith Pran was told in *The Killing Fields.* Speaking of films, as I write this I recall thinking back then, nobody was rushing to make a film about Vietnam. For me never would be soon enough.

In what turned out to be the last battle of our Vietnam War, several weeks after the fall of Phnom Penh, U.S. air and sea forces boarded the *SS Mayaguez,* a cargo ship that had been commandeered by the Khymer Rouge. After a fierce fight the crew was found safe. Eighteen U.S. servicemen were killed and forty-one wounded in the attack. Then, in a stunning development, in 1977 Vietnam would react to Khymer incursions into its territory by invading Cambodia, now calling itself Kampuchea, and prevail after several years of struggle. While Hanoi had maintained its close ties to Russia, the Khymer Rouge government was a Chinese client. Once again, the myth of monolithic Communism was exploded. The enemy of my enemy proved the stronger dynamic.

IN APRIL I TRAVELED TO LONDON for interviews with officials from BP and the British Foreign Office about their tug-of-war with the Government of Kuwait. In March, Kuwait had announced it was going to take over the last forty percent of the Kuwait Oil Company it didn't already own. On my truncated Vienna trip I had spent time with the Kuwaiti Oil Minister and had a good understanding of his views. It came down to sovereignty and, not incidentally, money, a great deal of money. He said they were moving ahead with or without an agreement. BP was privately resigned to the event, though they continued to resist. Later in the year a one-sided deal would be struck – the colonialist had been well paid for its efforts, no further thanks needed. These new realities would resonate for years, emboldening other oil-producing states to grab for the gold, the black gold.

I didn't get to see Hamid on that trip. He was visiting family in Tehran. But I had time to read the local press and speak with people about the "troubles" in Northern Ireland, which had spilled over into England itself, the IRA bombing pubs in Guildford, Woolrich and Birmingham with extensive loss of life. I wondered what Fiona would have thought.

My second stop, Paris for an IEA conference, was personally more successful. I made a side trip to the *Gazette's* Paris bureau officed on the *très chic* Champs-Élysées midway between Place de la Concorde and the Arc de Triomphe. The Bureau Chief, Didier Lemaire, was complimentary about my work and after showing me around the office treated me to lunch at a bistrot next door. Over *croque monsieur et salad mixte,* he commiserated with me about *l'affair* Yamani. Everybody knew about it, he said, a *cause célèbre* within the organization. Of course Yamani's message had to remain confidential – we couldn't hang him out to dry. I left with a good feeling and my interest piqued by his suggestion that perhaps I might like to work with them. We got along easily in French though at one point he felt obliged to comment on my accent. "It is *americain?* Or more *canadien?"* he asked.

"Je sais pas. À mi-chemin, peut-être."

"Ah," he said with a smile, *"le deux marchent."*

I stayed the weekend to visit Pat. Incidentally, we spoke French the whole time, though I won't burden you with that here. I figured Michel for a flamboyant, cosmopolitan character out of the Jazz Age, but no, he was a very normal-looking guy. It was Pat who still featured the beard and beret and a foolish cape that made him look like a *flic* in a second-rate French film. At least he looked healthier. Maybe this odd arrangement was good for him. I slept on the couch in their *appartement* in Montmartre on Rue Lepic, just downhill from the white massif of *Sacre Coeur.*

Pat had finished his doctorate and was shopping his thesis around. A few nibbles, so far no bites. Meantime he taught art in a *lycée* across the city uphill from the Sorbonne, near the Place de la Contrescarp, near the building with a plaque certifying Ernest Hemingway once lived there. Next time he'd show me all that.

His father had put two and two together and confronted Pat the last time he was back for a visit. "For him there is the moral issue but his real worry is about continuing the line. One of these days he'll be cutting me off."

Michel maintained a gallery in a storefront on the first floor of the building he owned. There he exhibited his paintings which in all candor, though I didn't tell him, I thought were awful. Spectacular color, but all slash and swirl and gobs of paint. I kept looking for faces and clouds and ponies but Pat said – wrong. Look at it as a whole and let yourself go, bypass the brain. I had the impression Michel's pieces didn't move very fast, though at his prices it wouldn't take many to keep him going. Turned out Michel was more realistic than his art. A licensed electrician, he maintained enough clients to keep bread and wine on the table.

Saturday morning Pat tried to cajole me into visiting the Louvre but it was a nice day and I'd been cooped up all week. "Let's do something outdoors," I said.

"I know just the thing. It's a little unusual but you'll love it. A surprise."

He propelled me down the hill toward his neighborhood Metro station, *Abbesses.* Eschewing the elevator we plunged into a long spiral staircase for the subway platform. One change of train, *une correspondence,* and forty-five minutes later we emerged into the bright sunlight in front of a... cemetery! "Not just any cemetery, *mon ami,* this is *Père-Lachaise!* One of the most fabulous spots in Paris. After we walk around you'll understand why."

We strolled the shaded lanes of *le Cimetière du Père-Lachaise,* climbed its hills, poked around the gravesites and stones. He was right. Captivating stuff – Chopin, Bizet. Proust, Oscar Wilde. Gertrude Stein and Alice. Edith Piaf. Jim Morrison! *La famille* Hugo.

"Where's Victor?"

"In the Pantheon, of course, among the Immortals. The crypt there creeps me out, but between there and here you'll see everybody who was ever anybody." Pat pointed out a greened bronze sculpture of a man on his back, a green top hat at his side. "Victor Noir. Shot dead by Napoleon's cousin. A shame, only twenty-two years old. Notice anything odd?"

I looked more carefully. Yes... in one area the green had given way to the statue's natural bronze, of all places right at the groin. "There," I said, pointing to the shiny spot, "the oxide's been rubbed off."

"Only a scientist would think of that. What else?"

"It looks like he's got a hard-on," I said, pointing to the bulge.

"Proof that dueling is exciting. Monsieur Noir is a big attraction, people come from all over to see him, kind of an erotic Lourdes. It's said touching him there makes a woman fertile, a man more virile. Go ahead, give him a rub. Everybody does."

"No thanks," I laughed, "that's your department." I'd been wondering whether to try and broach the subject of two guys living together or just leave it alone.

"That is true," he replied, unfazed.

I noticed a sign nearby, translating – INDECENT RUBBING IS *INTERDIT.* "Does that mean what I think it means?"

"Up to a year in jail or *six mille* francs."

"For once law and morality on the same side."

"Oh, come on. It's not so terrible – get used to it."

Back on the Metro, I thanked him for showing me around. "That is one amazing place," I said. After a light bistrot lunch and a tour of Nôtre Dame which made me eager to re-read Hugo we strolled along the Seine, browsing in the book stalls. When you're not looking, that's when you get lucky. I picked up several paperbacks including *A Moveable Feast* in French translation. Pat said Hemingway wrote it in that building near his school. I bought a copy of *L'Étranger* and, recalling that Camus was Algerian, in a fit of confidence, a French-Arabic dictionary.

But the day couldn't pass without a downer. Atop a stack of unsold papers at a newsstand, I came across an old *International Herald Tribune* with a front-page story about the World Series. I had watched it on TV, of course, Carlton Fisk's sixth-game miracle, then that colossal let-down. Three failures in a row, all in seven games. Snake-bit, that's us.

By late afternoon Michel had joined us and we were ensconced in a sidewalk cafe on the Champs-Élysées. Pat laid on the table a copy of the day's *Gazette* whose front page featured a replica of the *Daily News* headline the previous day:

FORD TO CITY: DROP DEAD
VOWS HE'LL VETO ANY BAIL-OUT

"I see your adopted city is still having troubles."

"By all accounts it's close to bankruptcy." I pointed to the headline. "Politics as usual, but Ford'll come around." And he did, within weeks offering a package of loans and guarantees that helped resolve the crisis. though that took a whole lot longer.

Pat looked around. "We're expecting a fourth, a friend I want you to meet. *Ah! Lucie! Tu es ici! Bienvenue!*"

A pert, fresh-faced young woman was standing at our table. *"Bonjour tous."*

Pat and Michel embraced her, planting a kiss on each cheek. "Lucie Devereaux, meet Paul Bernard. Paul, Lucie."

I stood up and reached across to take her hand. *"Enchanté faire votre connaissance."*

She was very pretty, with dark eyes, bright red lips and short black hair, the *gamin* style familiar from French films. Medium height, about a head shorter than me. Against the chill breeze she wore a shaggy pullover, a knitted hat and scarf and blue jeans. Pat poured the last of our bottle into Lucie's glass and signaled for another. He nodded at me. "When I told Lucie about my friend the famous journalist she expressed an overwhelming desire to meet you."

"That is not what I said," she replied, blushing. "Patrice exaggerates everything." She reached into her purse for a pack of cigarettes and shook one out. I was reaching for my lighter but Pat beat me to it. "An uncle of mine is with *Le Monde* and I always thought he leads the most interesting life."

"Plus it gets you around to see your friends," I lifted my glass to Pat, then to her, "and meet new ones."

"Lucie is a curator at the Louvre," Pat said. "She's a neighbor of ours, a couple of streets over. I tried to get Paul into the Louvre today but he insisted on visiting a cemetery so we ended up at *Père-Lachaise.*"

"The second-most interesting place in Paris," Lucie laughed. She spoke in the high lilt common to French women. "Next you must see the Louvre. Did you visit Abélard et Héloïse? They were original residents, so they say."

"I missed them."

A dreamy look came over her. "That is the most romantic story."

"Bien sûr, and tragic." I remembered some details. Famous teacher seduces girl. There is a child. Teacher hides girl and child in convent. Vengeful uncle castrates teacher. Teacher becomes monk. Girl becomes nun. Famous correspondence ensues. "And what kind of curating do you do?"

"My specialty, it is medieval art. I am interested in the tension between the sacred and the profane as expressed in art, particularly sculpture and *les belles heures,* you know, the illustrated prayer books."

I nodded, wondering what kind of young woman would immerse herself in such a musty topic, but her comment also rang a bell. "I also specialize in tension," I said, "tension between governments and the governed."

"That is a much broader topic, and I daresay more important."

"Lucie is one of the foremost authorities in her field," Pat interjected.

She smiled. "Hardly. Perhaps some day."

"Possibly we can compare ideas about how tensions are resolved or not resolved. In your field is there much left to discover?" I asked, "or is everything known by now."

Lucie shook her head. "Things come to light all the time, pieces are found, writings discovered, connections scholars had overlooked."

"You'd better stick to oil, Paul," Pat commented. Turning to Lucie he said, "I'm sorry to say but Paul has an aversion to art."

I frowned and shook my head. "That's not true."

"Well then, to museums."

I sighed. "I would like to know more but I haven't the time to do it properly. So much to do, so little time."

"Many things I also should learn more about," Lucie said, "but if you like art, it is best to jump in. Curiosity is enough. If you await the perfect time you will miss much enjoyment. The next time you're in Paris I'll give you my first-class docent tour. I guarantee you will want to come back."

"I already do." I lifted my glass to Pat, to the table. "Thank you for including me in your *çercle des amis.*"

"And the next time you're here," Pat said, "I'll give you my 1968 tour, show you where we manned the barricades, the square outside the Sorbonne where I got my trophy..." he pointed to the scar over his eye.

Warmed by wine and food and conversation and overhead heaters as the temperature sank, we saw the sun set and the city lights wink on. On the road ten days I'd been looking forward to going home, in fact, this morning had examined my plane ticket, my family photos, the teddy bears for the boys, a *Babar à New York* for Emma and the Hermès scarf for Diane. But these perfect last hours of my first visit to Paris, with this intriguing new acquaintance, thoughts of home and hearth were far away.

I reached for the bill. "I'll take care of this. The least I can do for your hospitality."

"Paul always does the least possible." He winked at Lucie, "of course I exaggerate."

She winked at me, co-conspirator in a new friendship.

The year ended with a shocker. Just before Christmas, a gang of Arab and German terrorists stormed an OPEC meeting in Vienna, killing three and taking the oil ministers and their aides hostage. Coercing Austrian radio into reading a "communique" condemning Israel and promoting the Palestinian cause, they were given a jet which flew them and their prisoners to Algiers, then Tripoli, then back to Algiers. The terrorists singled out two hostages for execution, the Iranian Oil Minister and Yamani. After payment of a large sum of money some said was pocketed by their leader, Carlos the Jackal, the hostages were released unharmed. My note to Yamani expressed relief that he came through this harrowing episode safely and I looked forward to seeing him again soon. His reply thanked me for my kind thoughts and warned me to expect security next time like I'd never seen before.

When I first heard about the attack I was disappointed to miss such a great story. At the last minute I had cancelled, as nothing newsworthy was up for discussion and, travel-weary, I decided to take a few days at home. I phoned in a backgrounder but it wasn't the same. Perverse solace, knowing the oil beat would present plenty more opportunities for my crime reporting skills.

48. WITH LIBERTY AND JUSTICE FOR SOME

JONATHAN BURSTS INTO THE ROOM. "I did it! I'm going!"

"I take it ETVN came across," I reply calmly. "How much did you tell them about the General? When is the great event?"

"Three weeks from now. Roberto's arranging it all at that end and no, I didn't tell them anything about the General."

"Who are you representing, may I may ask?"

"ETVN, of course. *The New Yorker* doesn't know I'm going. I could have told them but that would have complicated things."

"This is one hell of a balancing act you have going."

"When I get back we'll need a full-court press to finish this thing. My editor's getting nervous."

"And he doesn't know the half of it. Well, I too am looking forward to finishing. I love New York, but I never wanted to live here." Something has been gnawing at me and I decide this is a good time to bring it up. "You've never let me see your draft. This would be an excellent time for me to take a look, don't you think?"

"Good idea. It's just, my writing process isn't as straightforward as some people's."

"Apparently not. But how would I know?"

* * * * * * *

THE YEAR NINETEEN HUNDRED SEVENTY-SIX meant a big birthday for the U.S. and a presidential election which – was it too much to hope? – might actually help heal the nation. Grand festivities were planned everywhere, and though the nostalgia craze had crested, books, articles, television and school curricula were fixated on American history and Americana. Leavened by reality, pride was once again in vogue.

Occasionally accounts of the Boston busing appeared, puncturing the good feelings. Though time and weariness had calmed things, the root problem was no closer to solution. The federal judge, Garrity, continued to draw fire for his overcontrolling attitude, then a phenomenal *Herald American* photo blasted into the national psyche. We ran it on page one above the fold, under this banner –

SAD DAY IN "CRADLE OF LIBERTY"

Taken in front of Boston City Hall, the photo shows a young, long-haired white male lunging with an American flag at a black man being grabbed from behind so the assailant can get a better shot at him. The black man under attack by the white establishment? A patriotic white man defending his maligned community? People saw what they wanted to see. Before escaping the black man suffered a broken nose and contusions and had his glasses broken. Then the back story began to emerge. A Boston attorney, Ted Landsmark had grown up in East Harlem public housing, attended New York's prestigious Stuyvestant High, St. Paul's, Yale and Yale Law. That day he was headed to a meeting concerning minority hiring in construction. The flag-wielder, Joseph Rakes, a school drop-out with a part-time job, was with a group which rallied against busing, encouraged by certain officials and politicians. Before encountering Landsmark, the marchers had a brief altercation with a passing group of black school children. When I saw the photo I immediately went to see Ollie Newton.

"Helluva shot, ain't it?" he said. "Photographer's the same guy got the lady and kid falling off the fire escape."

"I remember that. What do you make of this one?"

Ollie put his glasses back on. "As a photograph it's fantastic. Composition, the action, the faces, the emotional tone, you can't beat it. As a piece of journalism, it stinks."

"Somebody said the kid with the flag wasn't trying to spear the black guy at all."

"That's my point. My friend at the *Globe,* he told me the kid was waving it back and forth. See the guy holding the black dude? Looks like he's trying to pin him, right? Fact is, he was helping him up." Ollie reached in his desk and pulled out the *Herald American.* He pointed to a second picture below the flag shot, showing another white youth kicking the black man who was down on all fours. "This was taken *before* the flag picture. Not after."

"The sequence makes it look just the opposite. That is really misleading."

"Yeah it is, but it makes a better story. Or maybe they were just leading with the most dramatic shot. We didn't run the second picture at all."

Later in the day I stopped by Alan Mauro's desk. He also had a copy. "It's asking too much for a picture to provide its own context. Photographs lie, and when they're on the front page they shout. Our headline didn't help at all. A paper's gotta tell the reader up front if there's more to the story. There was here, for sure."

Back at my desk, I tried to sort things out. I recalled conversations with Gus about growing up in white Southie, me in white Providence. Clannishness, xenophobia, neighborhood pride gone bad – is that what we had here? Some think laws change hearts and minds. Do they? Can we wait that long? A partial answer came next day when the AP wire carried an account of a mob of black teenagers stoning a white man's car, dragging him out and crushing his skull with paving stones. When the Boston police arrived the crowd was chanting, "Let him die! Let him die!" Not surprisingly, he died.

AS THE FOURTH CAME ON, so much was happening I was volunteered to cover the city scene. I revisited some of my old protest crowd and duly reported their remarks, but this day dissent remained on the fringe. This party was too massive, too necessary, too much fun to be spoiled. The relief was palpable – you could feel the nation exhale.

I spent the day in the streets, then mid-afternoon met Diane and the kids in Battery Park for a look at the tall ships, boarding one of them. Then we repaired to the World Trade Center South Tower where a Goldman client was hosting a party with a view. Sailing ships, fireboats, helicopters, an amazing panorama. About nine we retrieved the kids from the day care to watch the fireworks. We had turned down an invitation to join her father in the yachting flotilla. Incidentally, our family were now full members of the Midlothian Yacht Club with all rights and privileges attendant thereto. The Club did us the great service of occupying the kids on weekends, freeing Diane and me to have something of a life. Emma's arrival had put a damper on Diane's return to work, though after the first few months, she was again spending one day a week in the city.

Violence and instability continued to furnish proof, if any were needed, that our involvement in the Middle East was a chancy and costly proposition. In July the newly-appointed U.S. Ambassador to Lebanon was shot and killed before he could even present his credentials. Chalk another one up for the Popular Front for the Liberation of Palestine. Lebanon's civil war raged on, ravaging what was once a garden spot of culture and civility.

The PLF again joined with German terrorists, hijacking an Air France flight from Tel Aviv. After diverting to Entebbe, Uganda, the hijackers released non-Jewish passengers but held over a hundred Jews and Israelis. Encouraged by Uganda's notorious Idi Amin they pressed Israel to release Palestinian prisoners, threatening the hostages. Stalling for time, Israel put together a daring plan and sprang it a week later, landing commandos who freed the hostages from the airport terminal building. Ugandan troops resisting the attack suffered casualties and the Israeli commander was killed. Incredibly, Amin asked the Security Council to condemn Israel for violating Uganda's sovereignty. Equally incredibly, the U.N. refused to condemn Uganda for supporting the hijackers.

In the Far East, an earthquake claimed over two hundred thousand lives in China, and that country suffered a different sort of tremor with the deaths of Mao and Chou En-lai. Vietnam began another era began as well, unifying under the Communist government of the North. Saigon was renamed Ho Chi Minh City, though the old name wouldn't easily go away. Then the U.S. vetoed the unified Vietnam's admission to the United Nations. Though the predicted bloodbath did not occur, reeducation, resettlement, torture, imprisonments without charge and widespread poverty caused hundreds of thousands to flee. Many perished in frail watercraft on the open seas. The survivors were hard-pressed to find welcome. Ed Reynolds picked up a Pulitzer for his heart-rending dispatches. The U.S. provided financial aid, but little of it reached the refugees, crowded into camps in neighboring countries. In 1975, over a hundred thousand Vietnamese refugees were transferred to the U.S. and settled in communities across the country. In 1977 a second wave of immigration would commence.

I WAS SENSITIVE ABOUT THE BURDEN my traveling meant for Diane. In late 1977 the Concorde would enter service and cut my Europe travel time, but the cost meant I used it only sparingly. When at home I did what I could to make it up to her. Pitching in around the house was not a problem, not after all that travel. I liked our little patch of land, and seeing the boys, now four and two, roam and romp. Max had grown into a beautiful animal, more than a little flaky but that's the nature of Goldens, we learned. I even looked forward to my twice-a-day train, time to read and think. And the simplicity of our town was a nice change of pace from the city's frenetic ways.

Sometimes on Friday nights Diane and I would meet for an early dinner and a film, then stay over. I didn't move a muscle during *All the President's Men,* returning to see it alone a couple of weeks later. A big Faye Dunaway fan, Diane insisted on taking in *Network* the day it came out. That one really got me thinking. Maybe I'd stay with newspapers all my life, but maybe not. Down the road what about television news? Might that be a logical next step?

With the daughter she'd set her heart on and her professional life restarted, Diane was in better spirits. Knock wood, it looked like she might be coming around. But before long the outbursts, the blame game resumed. It was disheartening. From time to time I fantasized about other women, how easy it would be, but I did nothing. The old sad scenes still weighed heavily – Julien's wandering, how it hurt my mother, our family. He set such a lousy example that, perversely, he turned out a good example. I'd been a straight arrow all my life, though no one knew how foreign that posture had become.

I had assumed Diane was used to her father being away, but I soon learned Mr. Archer was no globe-trotter but the bank's inside man, the glue of the organization. Of course he was no stranger to the company plane or a Pan Am first class seat, but most nights he was home for his two daughters. As I've said, her father could do no wrong, and in a leap of faulty logic Diane took my road time for ineffectiveness and lack of devotion.

As an experiment, Goldman had acquired a number of "personal computers," a sample of what was just coming on the market. She was test-driving something called the Apple II their tekkies had installed at home. She liked it, said she could do more work faster, calculations, spreadsheets, reports. I was impressed, but when I mentioned it to Marty he shook his head. "It'll be a cold day in hell before the *Gazette* forks out for those gadgets. Get used to it – the typewriter's here to stay."

With Diane in front of a computer screen much of the time, it was natural that Peter should insist on his turn, and once he saw the games on her machine he was hooked. That came to a halt the day she found him tapping away and her day's work ruined. Next evening I came home with a carton under my arm. Now Peter had his own fixation, PONG.

Weekends I took immense pleasure from our games of catch, though with Paul Junior it was more like roll the ball. Julien, Jim and Paul all over again. Big in the neighborhood, though new to me, was soccer, and we often kicked a ball around.

It took some doing at first but Mr. Stumpy managed tolerably. Five days a week, Peter attended the local Montessori. Next year would be real school. I was dreading the process of choosing one.

While Diane got busier, family duties were growing. In my short experience, it's exponential. Two kids, a fourfold increase, Emma made that at least nine. After months of debate we finally hired a live-in nanny, Kristin, a dark-haired Swedish woman something north of forty. The children loved her, but to me she had no personality. That's all right, I thought, let her save whatever she has for the kids, that's why she's here.

AFTER THE BIG BIRTHDAY BASH, the presidential campaign took center stage. The incumbent was carrying a lot of baggage – his unapologetic pardon of his predecessor, the fall of Vietnam on his watch, the Panama Canal issue, the worst economy since the Depression. A few stumbles, literally and figuratively, made him the butt of jokes about walking, chewing gum, and forgetting to wear his college football helmet. Old nemesis Reagan brought stiff opposition from the conservative wing but his political persona had not gelled, and Ford narrowly beat him out for the nomination.

On the Democratic side, a relative unknown, former Georgia governor James Earl "Jimmy" Carter vaulted into an early lead with wins in Iowa and New Hampshire. Carter was a complex individual – an Annapolis graduate, nuclear power expert, owner of a successful farm business and a committed Christian. He plowed methodically through a crowded field to gain the nomination. He and running mate Walter Mondale, a Minnesota liberal in the tradition of HHH, prevailed in the general election, 297 electoral votes to Ford's and Rockefeller's 240, while garnering only a slim majority of the popular vote.

Carter had run as a Washington outsider, a reformer pledged to restoring competency and compassion to government. Like the man – informal, almost austere – his presidency would be down-to-earth, rooted in common sense and moral sensibility. He soon crossed swords with Congress, however – his candor ("I will never lie to you") at odds with Washington's cronyism and special-interest politics. The result, some of his major initiatives were blocked or so altered as to be unrecognizable. For years James Schlesinger, Carter's energy guru, had preached energy conservation and self-sufficiency. The new President was also of that mind, but once the gas lines disappeared people blithely forgot about the problem. Combining with our Washington bureau, I reported on Carter's pledge to bring order to this key aspect of our national life. Now we did a series of follow-ups as Carter rolled out his program. Wind, solar, nuclear power and synthetic fuels would be the targets.

On his first day in office Carter issued an unconditional pardon to Vietnam draft avoiders, a step that angered veterans groups and many politicians. I was asked to author an opinion piece, which would be a first for me. Three days after Carter's decision, my article appeared on the *Gazette's* editorial page. Many said Carter set a terrible precedent which would encourage young men to refuse service.

My view – a war conceived and fought on false pretenses did not deserve to stand for anything, let alone fester as an open sore. I went even further, stating even deserters should be welcomed back if they showed a credible religious or moral basis for their decision. I became a target, receiving scores of stinging letters. Even some of my VVAW crowd cried foul, though many backed my position.

Carter's other big priority was energy's evil twin, inflation, which would continue to rise, reaching 20% by 1980. Productivity growth was puny, at times negative, and unemployment high. It wasn't just oil shocks, either – our national debt from Vietnam was a huge drag. The bill for the years of poor leadership had come due.

In another initiative, Carter embraced the effort begun by Nixon to deregulate transportation. The goal was to strike at inflation by lowering prices for the American consumer. Ironic that a Democratic President and Congress made these first cracks in the New Deal's regulatory framework. Energy deregulation was Carter's own initiative, though Nixon had set some useful precedents there. Carter's successors, notably Reagan, would open the floodgates, notably in communication and banking. More on that later.

EARLY IN SEVENTY-SEVEN, Marty and I laid out a pair of stories about the oil industry effort to tap new sources. The first would send me north to Alaska, where the 800 mile-long Alyeska pipeline was slated for completion in June. The huge North Slope oil field had been eyed for years, but only lately had the project escaped the snarl of environmental fears, politics and litigation. To avoid the expense of a photographer, Marty told me to bring a camera. To go with my old Leica for black and white, I requisitioned the paper's big Nikon with its great lenses and shot a dozen rolls of color. The series was slated for the daily but when Tom O'Connor saw my photo gallery he shifted it to *G!* It ran in a big spread the first Sunday of April.

What did I capture he liked so well? A caribou and her calf alongside the pipeline in the Brooks Range. Another stretch where it crosses the tundra on stilts to protect the permafrost. Construction workers at a pumping station, their plumed breath in the forty-below air, one joker sticking his tongue on a cold-soaked wrench. A backlit Alaska Airlines 737 de-icing for an early-morning flight. A herd of moose fleeing my helicopter. My favorite, with a borrowed tripod, two bell-clear shots of the Aurora Borealis – brilliant reds, blues, greens. Ollie and his friends rode me mercilessly, accusing me of fuzzy focus here, awkward composition there. I pointed to *G!* and rested my case.

Bookended was a visit to the North Sea. People warned me the North Atlantic can bite any time of year, and I have to say our landing on an oil-drilling platform in gale winds and fifty-foot seas was as heart-stopping as anything Vietnam ever served up. Good thing I had a camera along, otherwise my colleagues wouldn't have believed how wretched it was on that tiny floating city. Fast shutter speeds on that trip.

When I told Diane's father flight schedules gave me a night in Glasgow he asked me to look up a distant cousin. Turned out the cousin was a lot more distant than he thought – he had died the previous month. But the try earned me points. My land legs regained, next came interviews in London and another trip to BP's headquarters. A senior BP official had taken offense at some observations I'd made about their Alaska operation and I took this as a chance to unruffle feathers or, as it turned out, cause a few more to fly.

The timing worked out for dinner with Hamid. His first novel, *The One-Eyed King,* had just appeared – in fact it was the featured review in our book supplement the previous Sunday, authored by Book Editor Ben Pickering himself, no less. The *Times* also had it on their page one. Both reviewers praised it. "Thrilling. Lofty, yet down to earth." "Characters that come alive." Set in Tehran, it told the story of a young man from a well-to-do Arab-Muslim family whose promise propels him into a first-class education abroad. A functionary in the oil ministry, the father periodically falls out of favor but the powers-that-be keep bringing him back. For his experience, yes, but he also knows where the bodies are buried – in some instances literally. I started it on the plane back, got about a hundred pages into it.

"If it sounds somewhat familiar, it is," Hamid said. He had chosen a Persian restaurant in Soho for us. "The character isn't me, but some of the situations resonate. I'm going to attempt something in Arabic next, a novella perhaps, or stories, something shorter in any case. I'm tired, I need a break."

"Why Arabic? Your English style is so good."

"If I don't stay in touch with my origins I will lose them. I owe it to my readers, too, now that I have some. I want the people back home to be aware of me, be proud of me."

"Your character is critical of the Shah. He joins organizations, makes speeches."

"Can you blame him? That man is driving our country into the ground. He thinks he's the second coming of the Persian Empire. Your President Carter is not doing us any favors, cozying up to him like he does."

"It's all about the oil. And our position over there, though that's about the oil, too."

"Of course. But at least Carter has taken him to task on the human rights issue. I wish him well but don't hold your breath. You've heard of Khomeini? Have you got to that part in the book?"

"The dissident cleric? The one with the beard?"

Hamid laughed. "They all have beards. But keep an eye on this one in particular. He is intelligent, resourceful, and totally committed to bringing the Shah down. I have him appear about halfway through the story. He's been in exile for years but works hard to build his support within Iran. He now lives in a holy city in Iraq. A few months ago his son was murdered and there is talk that our beloved secret police, the SAVAK, did it.

"Why I bring this up," Hamid went on, "the Shah is not going to change, and as time goes by, people will abandon him. It is inevitable. As a tree rots from within, one day a high wind comes along and topples it."

"Do you support Khomeini?"

"Far from it. I am not advocating, I am predicting. I fear that man very much. The Shah's western ways, if anything he absorbed them too well, but Khomeini would send Iran back to the seventh century. Art and culture will suffer, women will suffer, education will be controlled by the mullahs, it will be a theocracy of the most severe kind. No, I am very worried about what comes after the Shah."

"Your book is a form of politics, isn't it? In the guise of art but still political."

"Some may see it that way."

"I haven't got that far but I understand the father disappears and that helps the suspense. What does your father think about that part of the book?"

"I almost took it out but it's so important to the story I had to keep it. When I told him he laughed, told me to go ahead. Said he's not afraid of the SAVAK."

"I hope he's right."

"So do I."

As the evening went on I remembered Hamid's Columbia connection and told him I'd met Edward Said a number of times. "Ed was my thesis advisor," Hamid said, surprised. "How do you happen to know him?"

"He was part of my crash course on the Middle East. People said he was someone I needed to know, hear his perspectives on the issues, Palestine, Israel. We still get together from time to time, though the last year he's been in California working on a book."

"At Stanford, which of course we have a problem with. Tell him that for me the next time you see him."

"I already gave him grief."

"Ed is thoughtful and controversial, but fair warning – if you are seen as an acolyte, expect to be criticized. That's the nature of New York with its influential Jewish community."

I laughed. "I gave that up acolyting years ago. In any case, I don't find him totally persuasive, though I agree with him on some of Israel's policies."

"What I'm saying, if your paper's readership is sympathetic to the Zionist cause, you'll find letters to the editor addressed to you or worse."

"I'm not being paid for my opinions in that difficult area. Not yet, anyway."

"You know Ed has a book coming out next year."

"His big book, he calls it. *Orientalism* is the title, says he's working like a dog to complete it, get it to his editor."

"I'm familiar with his argument, he's been making it for years."

"He'll be pleased to see you write something in Arabic."

"No doubt. You realize, Paul, I'm not one of those good little Arabs he talks about, schooled in the western tradition and returning homage to the colonial power. I want my people to stand on their own feet."

"Nothing wrong with that – just don't forget who your friends are."

The next morning, a Saturday, Hamid picked me up at the hotel with my bags. After breakfast he would drop me at the airport for a flight that would put me in New York early enough to get reacquainted with the family. Threading the streets we saw signs for the M4 Motorway and Heathrow. "Next visit, make time for a hiking trip," he said, then I noticed him glancing down at my leg. "Sorry, I didn't mean..."

"I'll keep up with you, my friend," I said brightly. "Anything but rock climbing."

"That's good to hear." He turned on the wipers against the rain which was falling lightly. "North of here there is wonderful country, the Cotswolds. Did you know modern mountaineering was invented by the British? In fact some even claim they invented skiing."

"I never heard that."

"But of course that's not true, skiing was invented in Iran, around 2000 BC."

"Never heard that either."

"Don't listen to those Norwegians, they'll tell you anything." He laughed, "I really don't care. As long as we can get out and enjoy it, that's what matters. Plan on it."

I finished *The One-Eyed King* and dropped a note to Hamid congratulating him on a great piece of work. It helped me understand his part of the world, but not nearly enough, I said, we definitely needed to resume our discussion.

Several months later Hamid called. I had never heard him so excited. *The One-Eyed King* had been short-listed for the Booker Prize, impressive for a first novel. I was so proud I marched into Ben Pickering's office and told him any time he wanted an interview with the author I'd arrange it. The fact he didn't win was no comment on my friend's coup or the success it augured. It went to Iris Murdoch – pretty good company.

JULY 13, A NIGHT TO REMEMBER. I was in the City Room when a little after nine-thirty the lights went out. I was vaguely aware they had dimmed and flickered, but was so busy I didn't pay attention. Looking out, it seemed the whole city had gone dark. By now our emergency generator had kicked in and a skeleton bank of lights was back on. In a few minutes the TVs began reporting we were in the midst of a city-wide blackout. A swelteringly hot day and evening followed by thunderstorms and lightning strikes had disabled key transmission lines. I made a quick call to Diane. She'd heard the subways weren't running and said just stay the night in the condo.

I finished and filed my story in the semi-dark when my phone rang. It was Marty.

"Can I talk you into putting your crime hat on for a few hours?"

"Might as well, I can't get home anyway."

"We lucked out in 'sixty-five but this smells different. I just talked to the Police Commissioner – they're calling in off-duty cops, the whole bit. I want you and Ollie to link up with Frank DiNardo in the Bronx, find out what's going on."

The police scanner said the action was heavy in the Grand Concourse area where we'd meet Frank, our Bronx expert. I thought of Cyrus who I realized I hadn't talked to in a while. I hoped he wasn't caught up in the mess. We picked up

Frank on a street corner. Up ahead we could see an orange glow. "That's where we're going," Frank said, "a building on fire, looks like."

We passed people running the other way, carrying boxes filled with other peoples' stuff. A few blocks from the action police barricades blocked us so we parked and made our way on foot. Not a pretty picture – cop cars with sirens blaring, gunshots, the smell of smoke, tear gas. Fascinated, I watched three young men secure one end of a rope to an store security grate, the other to their car. In a minute they were clambering through the window, piling stereos and speakers into the car. Furniture stores, drug stores, food stores, liquor stores, coffee shops, beauty salons, their fronts staved in, glass all over the sidewalks, sparkling in the streets. In the light of bonfires cops chased guys carting TVs, people ran in all directions with shopping carts full of booze, diapers, chickens, roast beefs.

Frank introduced me to a police captain who said he'd never seen anything like it. "I got no reinforcements. This shit's happening all over the city."

"The inmates are running the asylum," another told me, showing me his hand wrapped in a blood-soaked bandage. "Plate glass window," he gestured, "the window won. I know you guys got a job to do but stay the hell out of the way."

We stopped for a brief word with a Channel 2 camera crew. "Great visuals," the young cameraman said excitedly, "it's like a war zone."

"Whoopie," I replied.

After a while we had everything we needed. Frank said let's pay a visit to a hospital emergency room – that'll be good for color. "The nearest one's Bronx Lebanon," Frank said, "their ER's down from Yankee Stadium, where, incidentally, they're playing Game Two of the World Series as if nothing's happening." We got back in the car and drove the dozen or so blocks, overtaken once by an ambulance with lights flashing and siren screeching. "Just follow him."

Ollie pulled into a no-parking zone outside the hospital, stood his PRESS placard on the dash and we edged through a line of people strung out the door, gathering a few dirty looks and comments, then into a reception area so bright it made me blink. A heavy-set nurse with an armful of plasma bags dangling cords, shook her head at DiNardo. "I love you, Frank, but not tonight."

"Just need to talk to a coupl'a people. Is Vince around? A minute's all I need."

She gestured with her head. Frank led us through a set of swinging doors and down a dimly-lit corridor. Through an open door I saw a white-jacketed man on the phone. "I need it yesterday, understand?" He slammed the phone down and reached across to shake Frank's hand, "don't let this fool you," he said to me, "I am not my hospitable self tonight."

"Not a problem." Frank nodded, "Vince Rubin – Paul Bernard, Ollie Newton."

"That was the Red Cross. We're running out of blood." The doctor picked a piece of paper off his desk. "Statistics. You guys like statistics. It's what, one-fifteen?" he said, looking at his watch. "As of eleven, twenty-six patients treated for wounds, six gunshots, eighteen cut and stabs. Two cardiac arrests. Some thugs broke into an old guy's store, he's resting comfortably, his wife didn't even make it to here. Forget the kids with sore throats and broken arms. Triple that, you'd be close."

"How are your brother hospitals coping?" Frank asked.

"It's scattered, big where you'd expect – Harlem, Crown Heights, Bed-Stuy. Everybody's running full speed, trying to keep up."

We spent a couple more minutes, then the doctor said he had to kick us out. "Come back in a couple of days I'll debrief you, but I gotta keep things moving."

Looting continued through the next day. Mid-afternoon I left a message for Cyrus, he got back to me and I went back up there a couple of days later. He toured me around the blighted areas. "I was inside the whole time, man, I wasn't goin' no-where!"

Sixteen hundred stores looted and damaged, over a thousand fires responded to, over five hundred police officers injured and three thousand seven hundred and seventy-six people arrested, the largest mass arrest in city history. We keep breaking records. An early estimate put the damage at $300 million. When a Con Ed spokesman called the power failure an "act of God," Mayor Beame differed in most colorful terms. Restoring public confidence would take a long time. What everyone remembered – Howard Cosell's comment as ABC cut away from the ballgame game to a helicopter view of a large fire blazing. "Ladies and gentlemen," Cosell observed, "the Bronx is burning."

PETER WAS NEARLY FIVE and we were searching for a school. As I expected, Diane bucked me on the parish school. Though indifferent to my personal religion, with Peter and next year Paul in their Sunday Tots program she was beginning to worry about their young minds. There was a private boarding alternative in Manhattan in the five figures, but by all accounts the local elementary school was quite good. We ended going with the public school plus Sunday CCD classes I would be responsible for.

Diane was now commuting to the city three, four days a week. Days I didn't have to be there at dawn we rode in together. She was able to keep most Fridays for herself and the children, though even then, much of the day was spent working at home. Let me say up front, Kristin was a lifesaver. I had revised my first impression. She definitely had a personality, she just didn't like men much. It took a while for her to warm to me, and me to her, but after she realized I didn't have designs on her we got along fine.

In the spring Mr. Archer hired a contractor to erect a world-class playground at Hyades – swings, slides, a jungle gym. He even showed me plans for a tree house but I asked him to put that off to let the boys' climbing skills catch up. Plus I had a tree on our property already picked out. Neighbors and I spent a strenuous weekend building a play area in back of the house, a pale shadow of Mr. Archer's but well-used by children, mothers and nannies for blocks around.

As summer neared an end I thought about this time as a golden moment. The children were healthy and beautiful, our home fitted us perfectly, I no longer pined for the city. Diane and I were going through a better stretch, the arguments less frequent and less wrenching. She seemed more accepting of my traveling. My work was interesting and recognition continued, hers was fulfilling without being too burdensome. With two incomes plus our other sources and her support system, we didn't worry about money, though as a child of insecurity I made sure I always knew where we stood financially and guarded the family purse strings closely.

OFTEN MY TRIPS OFFERED THE CHANCE to spend some extra time in an interesting place. I routinely asked Diane to come along but she routinely declined. In fact I think she enjoyed the space when I left, which sort of bothered me but not a lot. However, earlier that year she did opt for Paris. Created after the OPEC embargo, the "Conference on International Economic Cooperation" had been sputtering along with little to show. There were signs it might soon come to an end, if not a conclusion, and I needed to be there. Seven hours of Air France comfort and we poured ourselves into a taxi and headed for downtown Paris. Our accountants' largesse ended at business class, but when I mentioned to Fred that Diane was accompanying me, next day he stopped by to say the paper would host us in first class as a thank you. I'd already decided to upgrade on our nickel but kept that to myself.

The conference ended with an ambiguous statement that claimed failure in as many words. Developing countries made clear their disappointment that the rich countries had not made changes to the world economic order nor acted on other pressing problems. I was able to ferret out other information including a planned billion-dollar program to help meet the needs of certain poor nations, plus off-the-record comments that it would never happen.

Diane had never met Pat but we remedied that our last evening with a fine dinner at *la Tour d'Argent.* He and Michel had given us the tour of the Sorbonne, the Pantheon, the Mouffetard area, Hemingway's house, and though Diane was reasonably familiar with the city, he opened new vistas even to her. We ended up club-hopping in the Marais where we ran into Lucie and a friend of hers. Good thing the evening out happened on our last day or it could have soured the whole trip. As it was, our flight back was conducted in icy silence.

"I cannot believe you countenance the... the relationship between those two," Diane said as we waited in the boarding area. "Did you see them holding hands, and the way they were dancing, for God's sake! At least they had the decency not to kiss in front of us."

"Maybe next time," I said sourly. "Listen, Diane, if I had to approve the lifestyle of everybody I know, I wouldn't have any friends left. Besides, who am I to pass judgment?"

"It's not a question of passing judgment," she said, lighting a cigarette, "it's a question of who you choose to associate with."

I turned back to my newspaper. "We're just going around in circles. Let it drop."

"And that woman, what was her name, Lucie? What do you see in her?"

"What do I see? I don't know, an interesting person."

"But she's so critical, as if the French can do no wrong, and that little high-pitched voice of hers."

"Most women in Paris talk that way."

"I didn't realize you know most women in Paris."

I let out a breath. "The ones I do, many of them have high voices."

"That's different."

"What she does, she does well, and she's certainly attractive enough."

"There you go, you've got a thing for her, I can tell."

"Oh please. Leave it alone, we have a long flight to get through."

"I think I'll see if they have a seat in economy," she said, starting to get up.

"You do that and you're going back alone." Now I was really pissed. "Drop it. I won't inflict my friends on you again."

"Don't worry, you won't get the chance."

I remember waking up the first night back and, unable to get back to sleep, wandering the house. It seemed every time Diane saw me acting agreeably in the company of an attractive woman, she pulled out the green glasses. If Diane's that negative about Lucie, I thought to myself, maybe next time I should take a closer look.

THE U.S.-IRAN AXIS continued to spin. In November His Imperial Majesty, King of Kings, Light of the Aryans, paid a visit to the humble peanut farmer who happened to be the most powerful man in the world. Fred thought I should be there and Charlie Stebbins provided me a press pass, my first time on the White House grounds. Also my first taste of tear gas since Berkeley, used generously by the District Police to disperse anti- and pro-Shah demonstrators on the Ellipse upwind of the South Lawn. I watched the fumes waft toward us and soon everyone, principals included, was choking and blinking. I sent Gus and Hamid a picture of me wiping my eyes. An embarrassment for Carter and a humiliation for the Shah who was featured on Iranian television in this most un-royal situation.

One of the year's most noteworthy events was the visit to Israel and its Prime Mister Menachem Begin, by Anwar Sadat, a first for an Arab leader, and an implicit Egyptian recognition of the state of Israel. Thus was initiated a dialog that would prove fruitful for both countries. Except for Jordan's history of practical accommodation, no other Arab head of state would dream of taking such an step. Sadat was heavily criticized. Both men's courage would be put to the test.

At year's end the Shah hosted Carter in a Tehran stopover during a trip through Europe and India. Carter thanked the Shah for his moderation on the price of oil and his efforts in human rights, trying to undo the damage from the tear-gas incident. In televised remarks at an impromptu banquet Carter offered an effusive toast to the Shah, averring how beloved he was by his people. This enraged leftist and Islamic elements in the country. Several Iranians I called said the King of Kings was in deep trouble. Khomeini's tidal wave was moving and headed directly for the Shah. It was only a matter of time.

49. KING OIL

JONATHAN WAS IN WASHINGTON YESTERDAY finalizing his trip. He'll be in briefly today, then he is gone for as much as three weeks. I must make good use of this time.

Reading about Boston really got me down. Of course I sided with the judge. Only by shaking things up is progress even remotely possible. But the violence, those sick reactions, they are terribly troublesome. My old neighborhood tearing itself apart. Rabble rousers like Hicks aside, plenty of people, blacks and whites both, didn't want their kids subjected to busing. I sympathize with this. It's one thing for adults to protest, quite another to send a seven-year-old into the front lines. It makes me reflect on Berkeley – our kids were older. Old enough? I always thought so, but this does give me pause.

As for Carter's pardon, I also am of two minds. Yes, the war was wrong and misconceived, and yes it was wrong to criminalize those who followed their conscience, but how do you tell the moral individual from somebody gaming the system? You can't leave that call to the knee-jerk jingoists on those draft boards. I'm not worried we'll run out of men (and women!) to serve. If our country is really threatened they'll be there – and that's the only kind of war we should ever send them into anyway. Anything less, as far as I'm concerned, let our so-called leadership volunteer themselves, and their own children.

Tomorrow's a lost cause, a meeting with the lawyers. Cahill is coming down. We are going to file something and I have sent him what I wrote up. A most miserable business. About three, Jonathan sticks his head in. He is on his way to the airport.

"Wish me luck, Gus. This could be very big." I look at him sideways. "Aw, come on," he says, "I want you with me on this."

"I am with you, Jonathan, I just worry about doing our job right."

"Two months, we'll be done, my editor's happy and we've solved the mystery."

"And I have a fine bridge to sell you, too."

"Hey," he laughs, "that's my line. By the way, Roberto laid this weird comment on me. He's picked up a report that the Mossad was nosing around Paul. Apparently the Israelis were disturbed by what he'd been saying. Been going on a year or so."

"He's not saying they're responsible for the attack, is he? That would shoot your Bush theory out of the water."

Jonathan shrugs and raises his eyebrows. "Hopefully I'll find out more soon." He fishes in his briefcase and hands me a computer disk. "Something to remember me by."

"Don't you have a paper copy?"

"Man, are you old fashioned – read it on the computer like everybody else. Or print it out, whatever. I even set it up so you can edit it, it shows up red with underlines. Saves time on the back end." He looks around the room. "Well, I'm off. I'll miss this place."

"I doubt that."

"You got that right. See you."

I shake his hand. "Good luck. I really do mean that."

"I know. With you it's all bark and bite."

"Not the first time I've been told that."

* * * * * * *

SIMPLE QUESTIONS, TOUGH ANSWERS. The price of oil rises and falls, yet either way the oil companies win. How can that be? When crude goes up, drivers pay through the nose, when it falls we still pay through the nose. How can *that* be? The experts I talked with hemmed and hawed and never gave me a straight answer. Since the nineteenth-century, populist sentiment has viewed the big oil companies as bad guys. And now we have foreigners, worse yet rich foreigners, worst of all rich Arab foreigners, messing with our God-given right to drive.

One Saturday in January as Peter and I shoveled snow, I fumed about shelling out a buck-fifty a gallon at the pump the week before. It bugged me, knowing so much about the industry, its politics and economics, but still having no answers. That evening I told Diane about an idea I had been mulling over. "A report laying it all out for the ordinary reader. Do a quality job and package it right, it could be a real plus for the paper."

"And for you."

"That did cross my mind. I see Fred, Linda Dobbins, Mike d'Agostino, a couple of junior people for legwork, Alan Mauro for man-in-the-street. If we come up with some answers, great. At least we can explain what's behind all this mystery."

"Well then, go for it!"

Fred asked me for a proposal. It took a day to pull it together. I sat there as he read my page and a half, unsure what to expect. He finally looked up. "I like it. I take it you have the answers?"

I laughed, relieved. "This will mean some serious digging."

"And it may be we never get there. I've never seen a good answer, myself."

"I was thinking, we should have an economist, a name, somebody to give us direction, check us as we go along."

Fred nodded. "Agreed. I think there's a chance here for a real story. I'll send it on to Tom with my recommendation." The next afternoon I was sitting at my desk when Fred called. "We're on. Five minutes in Tom's office." When I walked in Fred was already there, also Alan Mauro.

"Charlie Stebbins on the speaker."

"Greetings everyone," I said. "Hello Charlie."

"Is that Paul? Greetings to you as well."

O'Connor held up my paper, shaking his head. "Anger at the pump, can't afford to heat the house, that's what you've got here. So the first day we sell a bunch of papers, then you bring in your economic theory and say good-bye to the average Joe."

Fred laughed. "Hey, two days' worth of papers isn't bad."

"This has got to grab you the whole five days." O'Connor frowned. "Bottom line, what the hell's it about? What's the point?"

I reddened. "We pull in the readers, show what's at stake in a way they can understand. For that I see a bunch of Alan's man-in-the streets. Now you've got everybody shaking their heads – how can things be this bad? Then a dose of history, some theory, again in understandable language. We show how the oil companies put the little guy down – no matter what, they make out, he gets screwed. We show how the government could ease the pain but won't because they're in bed with Big Oil."

Charlie Stebbins came on. "A lot of Carter's energy legislation has been sidetracked. We have reams of material on why – the oil lobby, Congressmen in their pocket. It's dynamite and it's there for the telling."

I picked it up again. "For the why and how we'll need some graphs and charts but not too many. Our economist will keep us from embarrassing ourselves. Not original research but sifting through what's already there, for the nuggets."

"The answers," Tom said, his lips pursed. "Do we know what we're talking about? Does anybody? There's even talk of the government decontrolling the price of oil. What the hell would that do?"

I glanced at Fred who had a half-smile on his face. "Forget definitive answers," Fred said. "But we can shed light and do it in an entertaining way. We're not an evening paper, this is not bedtime reading."

Tom shook his head. "I'm not about to promise our readers something we can't deliver."

"We'll make that point right up front – in fact, we'll tell them we're on a quest for answers and they're right there with us."

"I still worry about holding people the whole week."

Fred nodded. "I believe we'll find some explanations are simpler than we think. The oil companies, the oil-exporting countries – it serves their interests to complicate things. In fact, that's an important piece of the story, how they keep everybody in the dark. If the little guy knew how much money those people make off him he'd be even more pissed, especially if we can show it doesn't have to be this way."

"Hear, hear," Charlie Stebbins said.

"This gets back to our hook," Fred continued. "People are frustrated because they don't know what's going on. Stick with us, we'll tell them, by the end of the week you'll know a lot more and you won't like one little bit."

"Who's going to pull this together?"

I looked at Fred again. "I'm ready to take it on."

"While still keeping up with your other work."

"Of course."

Tom tapped my paper. "In here you say six months. I did some snooping around and 'far as I can tell, the *Times* hasn't got anything like this in the works, but you never know. What if I said I want it in three?"

I swallowed hard. "Cut us a little slack. Four."

O'Connor went over to his wall calendar, leaning forward, glasses on his forehead. "Today's January fifteen. We'll slot it for Monday May One. May Day! The Peoples' Paper scores again! Preview Sunday, start Monday, wrap Friday."

O'Connor looked around the room. "Questions?" He turned to Fred. "Give me a budget by the end of the day. I'll want a report every Friday, what you're coming up with, and I am reserving final say on that economist. There's some guys out there I wouldn't touch with a ten-foot pole. And need I say we've got to keep this quiet."

As we broke O'Connor put his arm around my shoulder. "Paul, if you can pull this off we'll really have something to crow about. We can use a win. It's been a while."

"We won't disappoint you."

"Good luck. You'll need it – there's a reason nobody's done this before."

IT WAS THE WORST SNOWSTORM anybody had ever seen, the great blizzard of seventy-eight. Peeking around the shade at six a.m., it was already coming down heavily. Normally that wouldn't faze me – I'd be in and out of the shower, jumping into my clothes and charging out the door. But this morning I woke with a headache and a scratchy throat. I mumbled something to Diane, turned over and went back to sleep. Around noon when I came to, our front hall was filled with wet boots and jackets. Diane had already retrieved the kids from their shortened day. By mid-afternoon everything was shutting down, people leaving work early. The plows weren't keeping up. Even public transport was laboring.

I tried to cancel a couple of appointments but nobody was answering the phone. Luckily, over the weekend I finished my last big piece of work before starting the oil series and had called it in. I found Fred in the process of packing up for the thirty-block walk to the Village. Marty and a skeleton staff were about to pull an all-nighter for lack of a way to get home or, the way it was looking, return the next day. Reporters were mushing here and there to cover the storm story. The microwave on two would be well-used tonight, along with sleeping bags squirreled under everybody's desks.

After a late lunch of chicken noodle soup I felt well enough to enjoy the rare weekday at home. Watching Peter, bright, quick, into everything – nearly six and on the verge of what we used to call the age of reason, eager for life. His favorite word, hands-down, was "why?" So far his school had served well. He was bringing home real work – letters and numbers, stories, poems, maps, drawings, watercolors. The first-grade teacher remarked on his reading, no surprise for he'd had his nose in a book since he could hold one. I was touched whenever he picked out my byline and proceeded in his fashion to read the article aloud. The maps in his geography text took on an added fun dimension after I returned from a trip.

Stranded at home, I began laying out the big report. The longer I sat at the computer the more I realized what an audacious idea this was. I made a round of calls to colleagues I could reach and talked with Fred about the economist. I told him I'd be in tomorrow, which I was, spending the whole day writing. I told Diane I'd be staying in for a few nights.

Alan had already begun scoping out his interviews and we discussed what kind of people to include. Charlie Stebbins had a lawyer on staff who'd report on the regulatory framework. Mike d'Agostino would take the political side. Fred and I ran our short list of experts by Tom and chose an MIT emeritus, Benjamin Skinner by name, a noted oil economist and former member of Nixon's Council of Economic Advisers. He was more of an industry cheerleader than I wanted, but his perspective would keep our critiques honest. He gave me a copy of his text, the gold standard, he called it. Two days later a mound of articles eight-and-a-half inches thick landed on my desk. Much of it was too theoretical to use, the rest I began wading through, about an inch a day. I started interviewing oil company executives, pushing them hard, careful to step around the piles of B.S. they left.

After a couple of days I was nervous, after a week I was worried. Fred steered me into O'Connor's office. "You're telling me we can't prove what you said we'd prove?" Tom shouted.

"Not exactly, but there's no consensus out there. I'm sorry, but facts are facts."

"Then get some other facts!"

"There aren't any. I've looked."

"So I have to tell our readers when they're pissed at the oil companies they're wrong? They're stupid? I have half a mind to kill the whole thing!"

Fred and I looked at each other. When I looked back Tom had a big grin on his face. "C'mon guys, I'm pulling your leg. I told you this'd happen."

By the end of week two I circulated a draft. The prof's copy was back by return mail, covered with red slashes, worse than grad school. After calming down I read his comments more closely and saw what he was getting at, not that I agreed with all of it. The next week we had him down for a meeting with Fred and Linda Dobbins. After two hours at the whiteboard it was clear the amount of detail he was pushing on us would indeed lose us ordinary Joe – O'Connor's nightmare. Skinner did confirm here is no easy explanation why oil companies always do well. Many factors are in play, and, as he reminded us, the industry is cyclical.

We had set April 7, three weeks out, as the internal deadline. That left a couple of weeks for edits and layout. As the editing proceeded I held my breath. How would the brass react? The last week in April I had my answer. Tom O'Connor called Fred and me in. His table was covered with paste-ups. He had personally done the final editing and markup of the first two segments. The rest we were frantically trying to finish.

"Not bad," he said. "If the rest is this good we'll be okay." I let out a deep breath.

"Don't think I've done too much damage but take a look."

"Editing the editor," Fred grinned. "I never heard before."

O'Connor nodded. "Don't get used to it."

Somehow we made our deadline, and there it was, in a box on Sunday's front page above the fold, the teaser –

STACKED DECK – WHY THE
OIL COMPANIES ALWAYS WIN

It's the best of times, it's the worst of times. Well, which is it? The answer depends on who you're talking to.

The folks at the gas pump – hey, that's us! – lately, not a whole lot to cheer about. Vacations in the family car, hauling the kids to soccer practice, a drive-in movie with your girl – goodbye to all that if the price of gas keeps climbing.

Nobody knows what to expect, with one exception. Year in and year out, the big oil companies rake in the cash. But how can this be? How can they report fabulous earnings even in bad times?

To answer this, the *Gazette* sent a team of reporters into the field. We interviewed experts, oil executives, government officials, foreign leaders, and you, our readers. Starting tomorrow and for an entire week, you'll see what we came up with. It's a fascinating story, with twists and turns that would have 007 scratching his head. We invite you to be with us as we try to answer the billion-dollar question: why do the oil companies make out like bandits while the little guy keeps getting screwed?

So pick up tomorrow's *Gazette*, buckle up – always a good idea! – and come along for the ride!

Tom O'Connor, Managing Editor

The initial feedback was good. We had the beginning of a buzz. Luckily no train wreck or celebrity murder to bump us from Monday's front page, top and center.

OIL COMPANY EXPOSÉ – YOU DRIVE A CAR
AND YOU WANT ANSWERS

- Are big oil companies out to screw the consumer – or does it just look that way?
- How can the big oil companies be profitable year after year?
- How can they make money when the price of crude oil goes up?
- Where are *our* savings when the price of oil goes down?

FOR ANSWERS TURN TO PAGE FOUR

We debated how to start the series – it came down to Alan Mauro and our readers. We invented the questions, but Alan said he'd heard them from many of his interviewees. So there it was, top of page 4, Alan's signature logo –

ETC Special Report – THE OIL COMPANIES AND YOU

Right below, photos of six New Yorkers – make that five, one was from Jersey. "I'm mad as hell and I'm not going to take it any more," complained Harold Browne of Mamaroneck. Alan asked if Mr. Browne had seen any good movies lately. "No, why do you ask," he replied. Sasha Rivkin of Tudor City keeps her car in the garage. "I'm thinking of selling it – I need a car, I'll call Hertz." Rose Sabatini of Carroll Gardens is of two minds. "Better this than they go out of business and nobody's got any gas."

Beneath Alan's piece, an essay on pages 4 and 5, sketching the course of the crisis since OPEC. High prices, shortages, lines, uncertainties. We then stepped back to an industry survey authored by Fred and some terrific images from the morgue. Young John D. Rockefeller at his first refinery outside Cleveland. Spindletop, the first Texas gusher. Pretty girl at the wheel of a Model T, a filling station attendant washing her windshield. We ran a photo of Ida Tarbell, the enterprising journalist who exposed the muscular tactics of Rockefeller's mighty Standard Oil. With a strong effort from Charlie's staff we detailed Standard's anticompetitive practices – the price gouging, rebates, interlocking ownerships, the huge profits. I related the mistrust and bad feelings that in 1911 led the Supreme Court to explode its cartel, precursors of attitudes prevailing to this day.

At the end of the article appeared the names of all the contributors. Space was being reserved in the last issue for a picture and bio. Each day my name led the page one byline, followed by "Charlie Stebbins, Fred Mueller, Alan Mauro and the *Gazette* reporting team." Professor Skinner asked that he not be mentioned, calling us anti-industry, one of numerous issues we disagreed on.

Our Tuesday headline: WHAT GOT US INTO THIS MESS? Now for the guts of the story. Some of it I had written in other contexts so I relied heavily on my clips file.

> We're in big trouble because every one of our energy sources is in big trouble. Oil, gas, coal – declining assets all, and a blight on the planet. Nuclear – expensive, and to many, frightening. Alternative power – immature, and powerful interests don't want it to grow up. Conservation – irksome, some even call it un-American.
>
> How did we get into this mess? Increasing use, the price of success. Declining domestic production, dependence on foreign regimes, that range from indifferent to hostile. Complex government policies, beset by politics and special interests. And at the heart of it all, the big oil companies.

Up front we identified our focus as the firms that control product from well to pump – the "Seven Sisters." Exxon, Royal Dutch Shell, Texaco, Mobil, Gulf, BP and Chevron. Though some independents explore and extract, they mostly focus on the downstream functions – refining, transportation, marketing, petrochemicals. ARCO, Occidental, Phillips, Sinclair, Sunoco are the most important of these.

Then of course, the myriad of support and service businesses, drilling companies, refiners, and so on. But, we went on,

> whipsawed by oil-producing states the big oil companies are no longer masters of their own fate, if they ever were. Opening their pockets to exploration and development, much of it unsuccessful, they extract and send oil into worldwide markets created through their ingenuity and labor. Refiners move the product through distribution systems to end-users – auto gas, diesel, aviation fuel, lubricants, heating oil, petrochemicals. They have seen their immensely profitable ownership - partnership stake reduced to tenancy. These days they are hired hands bending to meddling, irascible, unpredictable heads of state.

Professor Skinner got us permission to use an elegant chart juxtaposing our growing use of foreign oil against declining domestic production. He provided data he had developed on the increasing cost of finding and extracting oil, which our graphics people arrayed in tables and charts. We ran stock pictures of the key oil execs, several of whom agreed to be interviewed. Also a lengthy Q&A I had with energy czar Schlesinger.

The *Times,* the *Post,* the *Daily News,* as far as we knew none of them had ever done anything of this depth. Monday evening local TV picked it up, Channel Two showing a picture of our front page. Tuesday night, NBC network news featured the series, with shorter segments on ABC and CBS Wednesday. They saw our story as a news event in its own right, and I appreciated NBC detailing what we were saying at some length.

We had originally seen Wednesday as the heart of the story – in Fred's shorthand, "Prices and Profits," with the government section to follow. But when we saw what Charlie was sending, we flipped the two. Thus, Wednesday:

WE'RE FROM THE GOVERNMENT
AND WE'RE HERE TO HELP

We began with Charlie Stebbins' dictum that government is why we're in this fix.

> Federal policy is the key determinant of profitability, as well as your price at the pump. The global price of oil matters greatly, so do supply and demand, but they are ingredients. Washington stirs and seasons the unsavory stew.

The tangle of laws, regulations and policies governing the oil business was a logical follow-on, but Tom O'Connor fretted that we'd already gotten too theoretical, so he decided we'd lead with profiles of the players. Congressmen, Secretaries and Assistant Secretaries, agency heads, millionaire oilmen, and the cadre of lobbyists, consultants and influence peddlers. Mike and Ellen put together a Who's Who in Oil Policy since the Thirties. Not surprisingly, Texans led the list.

Included among the donors to politicians and campaigns are oil company executives, of course, and companies skirting the law with a variety of subterfuges. Tom and Charlie had a shouting match over this section. Tom got nervous when he saw what Charlie had dug up, and it didn't help that the *Gazette's* lawyers were warning of libel. In the end, with support from our general counsel, Andy Lipton, and Fred Astell's strong backing, disclosure won out. The price, and a good idea anyway – one more round of fact- and source-checking, this by the attorneys. The result, a forty-six line table with three columns:

Donor | Contribution | Recipient

As the Table made clear, it's mostly about the money but not altogether. Foreign junkets, island trips, golf outings, overpaid speeches, fundraisers, refurbished homes, farms, vacation retreats are also part of the mix. In a few instances, Charlie's staff was able to associate legislative or agency action with contributions from people and companies standing to gain, some of this already on the record. But our hope of a fourth column, "At Stake" it was tentatively called, didn't materialize. We did note the most flagrant abuses, along with resignations and indictments, footnoted, all. These folks were in good company, Charlie observed. After all, Teapot Dome, the great scandal of the Twenties was about oil.

Next, for our dive into the regulatory and legal thicket.

> Texas Railroad Commission limitations on production in the Thirties, struck down by the courts. FDR's unsuccessful try to legislate domestic oil production. Eisenhower's foreign oil import quotas, and of course his Interstate Highway System that guarantees high levels of consumption indefinitely. Domestic price controls, supply limits and allocations from frantic post-OPEC maneuvering. The place of honor, however, goes to tax policy and legislation.
>
> It is no secret how Big Oil gets off paying less income tax than most industries. A "depletion allowance" permits deduction of nearly thirty percent of a well's first million in gross income every year for its first ten years. That is right – *gross income!* Other industries deduct their *costs*. In seventy-five this loophole was closed but a compromise lets them deduct most set-up costs the year they are incurred, the rest over five years, best in the tax code. There is also a credit for pursuit of difficult and costly reserves.

Trying to be even-handed, I cited the rationales my company contacts pressed on me, the main one being to encourage exploration. But, I went on, the tax breaks don't stop here.

> Oil companies enjoy benefits available to all taxpayers, the foreign tax credit for one, offshore tax havens for another. They enjoy at no cost a vast infrastructure supporting use of their products, financed by state and local governments and users – roads and bridges, airports, the air traffic control system, to name a few.

By now we figured the reader would be wondering, who's standing up for the little guy? So we presented a list of those who have sponsored measures to rein in consumption, cap prices and limit environment damage, notably through auto emission and mileage requirements. This brought us to Jimmy Carter, but we deferred him until our Friday look-ahead. Our assumption was that even though Carter was having rough sledding, his vision was bound to be the vision of the future. If not, we were in far worse trouble than even the pessimists thought. We sounded a cautionary note about deregulation.

> Transportation was first, the airlines, then trucking and the railroads. Fanning the flames, now candidate Reagan is touting his "hands off business" approach as the panacea to our economic ills. If freed from government's restraining hand, how will the oil companies react? Not so far-fetched, for even now we are hearing calls for price decontrol of domestic crude. The answer is obvious – of course they will increase prices, as much as they can get away with.

Thursday was our big day.

OIL COMPANY PROFITS
THEY WIN, YOU LOSE - THE HOW AND THE WHY

The most technical and difficult segment to write, to me this was also the most important. If we did a good job here, we succeeded. If not, it didn't matter how great the rest was. I spent many hours waiting for the light bulb to illuminate issues even experts disagreed on. I also had to fight our headline writers on this one. Until I talked them out of it they were going with MYSTERY SOLVED or some such inanity. My conclusion – it comes down to an array of factors which, aligned right, create immense profitability. Nor did I have to turn in my press card to add "and this is not all bad."

> Industry spokesmen take pains to explain that profits bankroll exploration and R&D, as well as the halting first steps at mitigating environmental damage. Nor do investors, pension funds or widows complain about profits – historically Big Oil pays out in dividends about half its earnings. At the other end, another complex array of factors serves to infuriate drivers, though when are drivers ever content? The price at the pump is the sum of costs plus a markup for market power. And, as we pointed out yesterday, the impact of tax policy is immense.
>
> Most small or independent companies purchase crude on contracts with "equity producers," the big integrated companies. They pay the fixed contract price for each barrel. Since the equity producer takes the risk, when the global price of crude increases, inventories gain in value and drive up his net worth. When prices fall, the reverse happens.
>
> Refining converts crude into a range of end-products – gasoline, diesel, heating oil, aviation gas. Petrochemicals, once a stepchild, are a huge moneymaker in their own right. Environmental costs are growing, as consuming nations involve themselves more heavily in the downstream phase of production. Natural gas, once merely a by-product, has developed into a huge industry with a wholly different scheme of government regulation, worth a series of its own.

A word on vertical integration. Controlling the process from start to finish gives the producer management control, quality control, a shot at cost control, and the tools for squeezing the competing specialist. Also, the chance to play accounting games when goods or services are exchanged between internal units.

Fred offered us a primer on calculating profits and a glossary of terms, though I pressed to keep it simple. Average Joe again. He also gave a rundown on financial statements and annual reports, saying there are so many ways to obscure the facts, it's next to impossible for the layman to grasp the "true" financial picture.

For the other side of the equation, the income or revenue side, we showed the money rolling in – from purchasers of crude oil and refined products, from owned or captive gas stations, from heating oil suppliers and other retailers. Warming to the task, we reviewed the factors contributing to the price of gas.

It's a given that price should cover cost, and usually the price at the pump does that, plus some. But the biggest factors are supply, demand, and market power. When the price of gas rises, some people who can limit their driving will do so, though many in our dispersed society cannot. If the price keeps going up, more people find ways to cut back. Over time, lifestyle factors can be altered – where people live, where they work. How much and how quickly are tied into a phenomenon called "price elasticity of demand."

On the macro scale, demand for gas and other end-products tracks global economic cycles, which in turn affect the demand for crude oil itself. The second key factor, market power, is the ability to set and maintain the price of its product, whatever its relation to cost. Think "markup," you'll get the idea. Many factors are involved. Competitive climate, product distinctiveness, the "relevant market," the possibility of collusion (say it isn't so!). When factors combine to make demand for his product strong, the seller has power to impose a higher price.

Friday, and the finish line is in sight.

THAT'S ALL, FOLKS – OR IS IT?

Now we were ready to deal with those "simple" questions that opened the series. Here's what we came up with.

- Oil companies aren't out to screw you, the consumer, though it can happen. They are out to screw the competition, whenever and wherever possible.
- Not every big oil company is profitable every year, but they are smart, diversified, and sometimes lucky. A lot of ordinary people count on them making a profit.
- When the price of crude goes up, oil inventories are worth more. And as long as people continue to drive, they'll keep the price of gas high.

- When the price of crude goes down, we do see lower prices, though not all the decrease is passed on – and what is, we don't see right away.

We created a special section for the forward-thinking Jimmy Carter. In yet another table we listed his policy initiatives – enacted, defeated and pending – what each was meant to accomplish, who supported and who opposed, and if enacted, the likely effects of each. The narrative accompanying the table discussed what he had accomplished not quite halfway through his term, and where he had fallen short.

Finally, to preview the road ahead.

> Almost all experts agree we have reached the top of the supply curve. We are past the point of "Peak Oil" and are on the downslope, where each barrel extracted costs more. Some believe world supply is also on the back side of that curve. With U.S. energy consumption increasingly dependent on foreign sources, stability in the Middle East is crucial, but the signs aren't encouraging. Iran for one. If Iranian oil is denied us, that would knock out nearly ten percent of the world's supply.
>
> Conservation and reducing hydrocarbon emissions, fuel-efficient vehicles, mass transportation, alternative energy sources, cleaning up toxic waste sites – it seems inevitable we must set sail in those directions. But so far, the attempts have been tentative and inconclusive. As some suggest, the only way to wean us off our petroleum habit may be to make it so expensive we have no choice but cut back and look elsewhere for our energy fix.
>
> Do not expect the oil companies to be out front on this one. Their *raison d'être* is creating products to make money, not championing the environment. Saddled with the bad hat for over a century, at times deservedly, the oil companies are simply doing what they are designed to do, and for the most part doing it well enough. It can be counterproductive to ask them to assume other responsibilities. For example, when we let them shape and conduct the nation's foreign policy through their commercial dealings, the results have sometimes been disastrous.

And our wrap-up:

> Whatever good Big Oil does will always be viewed as outweighed by the bad. That's just how it is, and no amount of Masterpiece Theaters or Metropolitan Operas will ever be enough. P.R. missteps erase claims about the common good, exploration, clean-burning fuels, environmental safeguards. Mobil's diversification into Montgomery Ward for one, Gulf's bid for Ringling Brothers another. What may be a sensible business move looks cynical when an oil company does it.
>
> Can anyone prove whether Big Oil impacts our lives for better? Or for worse? We have tried to add to our readers' understanding, but as far as the public is

concerned, facts are really beside the point – except one, that is. Like it or not, the oil industry is here to stay, and so is the bad hat it is fated to wear.

This segment included photos and bios of our reporting team, with yours truly credited as the series' principal author. Looked good, felt good.

Sunday's editorial page led with Frank Astell's recap and a challenge to our leaders: put rancor and partisanship aside and face up to the nation's problems. As to deregulation, handle with extreme care. Oil companies cannot be left to their own devices. "I hope the *Gazette* has moved the discussion to a higher level," Frank wrote, "for no less than the American way of life is at stake. Whatever happens, count on the *Gazette* to report faithfully and fully, and contribute the occasional helpful insight."

Alongside, Ray Archibald outdid himself. In full costume – mask, cape, an "H" emblazoned on his chest – one of Ray's stock characters, Hydrocarbon Man, straddled a gridlocked Times Square, brandishing an auto plucked from the streets below.

Reactions? Let's say we weren't universally praised. Several commentators blasted us. We ran a scathing counterattack by Exxon's Chairman denouncing our one-sided, unfair portrayal. The letters were also mixed. Several academics criticized our shallow analysis and specious reasoning. That was okay, we weren't writing a scholarly tome. But Average Joe got it. Newsstand sales were up sharply for the week, and though they fell back, they leveled off higher than they had been.

I got some ribbing, but I detected in my colleagues a certain... I hesitate to say respect, but it sure looked like that. A couple of networks spun the story their way. The *Washington Post* reviewed our Washington segment, adding some excellent reporting of their own. The *Wall Street Journal* did a lengthy op-ed piece dissecting our analysis and finding it basically sound. Not a peep from the *Times*, but a month later a long article appeared in their Sunday Magazine covering the same ground in condensed form. Barney Abel, their oil reporter, whom I knew well, called me to say it was coming. It was a nice piece of work but didn't add much to what we had done first and, I have to say, better.

The brass was pleased. Frederick Astell set up a lunch at Sardi's. For a man laboring under the burden of a failing business, he certainly knew how to enjoy himself. After a couple of liquid hours with a decorous amount of food thrown in, Astell stood and tapped his water glass. "Gentlemen," he said, beaming, "I'm delighted to tell you we've decided to put our oil series in for a Pulitzer. The reaction has been tremendous. It gave our circulation a nice bump, but most of all, you fellows did a bang-up job of reporting. I even had a call from President Carter the other day telling us what a great job we did – a vital public service is how he put it. Of course, when politicians praise you, you'd better watch your backside, but I would say from that man, on this subject, it's a compliment."

Astell looked around the table. "And now, for the newest member of our team, Paul Bernard. I'm told the project was Paul's idea – he laid it out, defended it against my senior staff's doubts and forebodings," this with a big grin, "which, incidentally, is why I pay them so much. Prudent criticism, I call it. And I haven't even mentioned the long hours something like this takes. So thank you, Paul. We look forward to more of your excellent work. I'm sure our readers do as well."

"Hear, hear," Stebbins responded. Everybody lifted his glass.

I said a few words, nothing I need trouble you with here. Fred later remarked that words without actions are like music without notes, something like that. "Take a look in next week's paycheck," he told me, "a more tangible thank you, if you will."

"Milk for the baby, shoes for the kids, thank you one and all."

"You'll find this is something more than that."

And so it was. Fifteen thousand dollars! Diane was impressed, and thrilled at the idea of a Pulitzer. It'd take months to hear, but word we were up for it spread quickly.

I began receiving invitations. The first big one, *Meet the Press,* made me nervous but I got through it. Despite a cheery call with Diane in the airport, though, on the plane I was gloomy, thinking of points I should have made, where I might have gone on the offensive but didn't. Staring out the window I asked myself, what is this adventure about, this life of mine? Take Vietnam. What good did I do my country? And look at what it did to me. Though the truth is, I learned more there than all my classrooms put together. I hope I'm the wiser for it, a better man, but who knows? And what's next for me? Who, what, when, where, why? And how?

My boast to Pat came roaring back, and I thought – what possible difference can I make, in a world far more complex, more intractable than I ever dreamt? A world which, when you push, pushes back, sometimes brutally, trying to make you its own.

Made in the USA
Charleston, SC
13 September 2012